PATTERN BLACK

SEAN PLATT

JOHNNY B. TRUANT

STERLING & STONE

To YOU, the reader.
Thank you for your support.
Thank you for the wonderful emails.
Thank you for the thoughtful reviews.
Thank you for reading and loving our stories.

PATTERN BLACK

ONE

Obey

ABOVE WAS a lightbulb in a milky shell, its glass rubbed matte as if scratched by steel wool, its glow the yellow of jaundiced skin. Ten filament stalks poked from what looked like candle wax in its center, each resembling a match with a burning head. Mason, rubbing his eyes to fight the fog, had an unusual thought.

How can it work if none of the wires touch?

Across from him, Cruz snapped his fingers. "Shaw. You paying attention?"

"Yeah."

"You sure?"

Irritation swelled. *"Yes,* I'm goddamn sure."

Watt, on his right, chimed in. "You look like shit."

He was one to talk. Had breath like a slaughterhouse and shoulder-length rat-trap hair. At least, *most* of it was shoulder-length. Like many things about him, his hairstyle seemed accidental. It looked like he'd cut it himself without a mirror. And his *teeth* — like an addict who ate his meals out of an exhaust pipe.

"I have a headache."

"Why?"

"Fuck you, *why.*"

1

"He's hungover."

"I'm not hungover."

From the corner near the big van's cab, Buster said, "That'd be a first."

She snickered, begging Mason to punch her. Too bad she was twice his size and he'd break a fist if he tried. He focused on the job instead. Couldn't remember the details of how it was all supposed to go, but of course, he couldn't go home — well … *"home"* — until he found out.

Cruz, still eyeing Mason, continued. "Watch the corners once we're inside. Buster, you go left. Shaw, you handle the guards to our right. Two of them, just like we said, standing by either side of the poster."

"'By the poster'? You think you know exactly where they'll be once it starts?"

Cruz ignored Mason and turned to Sasha near the rear doors. "You handle the manager. Thin woman, by the fat man. She can still trigger a hard-wired alarm until the jammer is set. Got it?"

After Sasha nodded, Cruz turned to his right. Opened his mouth to address the giant man with gold hoop earrings and a gleaming white head. The guy who'd been staring directly at Mason for as long as he could remember. A minute at least. But instead of talking, Cruz's eyebrows drew together, and he stared at Baldy. It almost looked like he didn't know who the man was, despite sitting right beside him.

"Preacher," the man clarified, his voice gruff and bothered.

"Thought you were D'Abo," Cruz said, his brow still furrowed.

"I ain't."

Mason blinked. Behind his eyelids was a field of pure white blighted by a tiny speck of black — a distant tunnel seen from inside a void. When he opened his eyes again, the bald man, Preacher, was still waiting to hear his role.

"You watch the doors," Cruz finally said.

"See if I does," Preacher replied.

"We got a problem?"

Instead of looking at Cruz, Preacher stared back at Mason. "I don't. But maybe you do."

The van hit a curb, and most of them braced against the bench seats. Except Mason, who spilled to the metal floor like an asshat then scrambled back to his perch.

Cruz turned to Watt. "You handle the old lady."

"What old lady?" Mason asked.

"Just do your part, and everything will be fine."

Mason's fingers strolled the oiled metal of the weapon in his lap. He'd forgotten about that. An unusual thing, like nothing on the force or SWAT — or, as far as he knew, the military. Like a MAC-10 with a triple-wide magazine, lighter than it looked. He'd had the briefing, knew where the safety was and how it kicked.

Had that been yesterday? He pressed his eyes again. This fucking headache.

"We have six minutes." Cruz made eye contact with the five other passengers. "Six minutes *exactly*. It's plenty of time. In, pin the guards, watch the customers — and Sasha, you go for the vault. The manager has a key. But she'll tell you she doesn't."

"Maybe I just shoot her and *take* the key."

Cruz shrugged at Sasha. "Your choice."

Mason raised a hand. "Now wait a sec, Hopalong."

"She makes *her* decisions, wiseass. You make yours." Cruz shot him a finger. "And I know nobody's going to tell Watt how to do *his* job."

The odd answer shut his mouth. That seemed to make sense. There was only so much you could plan in something like this. It came down to people. Nervous people and their nervous decisions. Not that Mason knew a damn thing from this side of the gun.

"Masks on," said Cruz.

Buster reached behind her back, pulled out a ski mask, then dragged it over her head. Watt pulled his on. Sasha followed. Cruz watched them before doing the same.

Mason finally took the hint. He reached into his waistband for the hot black sock. Pulled it over his hair, down to his throat. It was like being vacuum-packed and strangled. Must be a hundred degrees outside, but at least the lobby would have AC. Good for all the running and rushing this would require. Good enough to staunch the adrenaline, he hoped. He glanced at Preacher, who hadn't put on his mask and was still staring at him. "Planning on letting the cameras see you, Mr. Clean?"

"Dunno. Ain't that what worked for your Daddy?"

"What did you say?"

Preacher shrugged. "Not a problem for Daddy no more, though."

Mason tensed. He was about to leap when the van hit a second curb then stopped. His gaze stayed on Preacher, who smiled and dragged the ski mask over his head.

With everyone suited, the van's occupants looked less like bandits, more like torsos topped with expressive raisins.

The rear opened like a pair of kitchen doors. The bank was right there like they'd pulled up for a delivery.

Cruz grabbed Mason's arm as the others spilled to the sidewalk, guns raised.

"You sure you're okay, Shaw?"

"I'm fine."

"You're not fine. You're preoccupied."

True. Mason *was* preoccupied, but his headache was making it impossible to explain why or how. Part of it was family and another part duty. Most of it was the mission.

Calliope.

Where was Calliope? Time was running out, the five-year clock long past ticking.

Not now. Not here.

"It's not a problem," Mason told Cruz.

"You can choose to stay. You won't get——"

Mason blinked. The white space. The black dot. For reasons unknown, it felt like doom.

"I said I'm fine."

He nodded at Cruz but didn't wait to see his response. Mason leaped from the van, blinked against the brightness of the nuclear sun. Masks, long clothing, the conspicuous lack of body armor.

Cruz had said they couldn't get armor, but Watt had said something else — *What's the fun if there aren't any stakes?*

Mason was reaching for the bank's front door when the shooting began.

"Fucking Buster. *Every goddamn time.*" Cruz rushed past him.

The glass door flicked through panes of transparency and glare like a picture show. Mason grabbed, yanked, then followed.

The lobby was already chaos. A grenade of human beings.

Buster's gun was up and swinging, its barrel smoking. The floor was littered with customers and employees, flat like Pick-Up Sticks. Most of them had hands over heads or over family, parents atop children as human shields. One woman by Mason's foot looked up, eyes pleading, a hundred-thousand strands of her tiny girl's hair spilled beneath her. He could hear the child crying — more a whimper, insulated by her mother's body. His knees bent reflexively, kneeling to help. But instead of showing comfort, the woman's face was a horror show. The girl beneath her peeked up, eyes wet.

No, he told himself. *Don't try.*

It'd be kinder to ignore their cries than to tell them it would all be okay when he was part of the problem.

He looked over and saw Cruz staring at him. Instead of issuing a reprimand, the man only waited, touching fingers to his concealed earpiece. Mason straightened.

Cruz lost interest. He raised his hand and shouted, "This is a robbery! Stay where you are and nobody gets hurt!"

But it was as if Buster didn't speak English and hadn't understood a word. Another cough of rounds spat from her MAC-10, or whatever it was.

Glass shattered. Screams like daggers pierced Mason's ears.

Cruz shouted at her, then at Preacher, who, instead of doing his job, just stood near the door like a bemused spectator.

Movement caught Mason's attention. He scanned the ground. Nobody was dead. Yet. But seconds were sands in an hourglass, and according to the big clock on the wall, two minutes were already gone.

"SHAW!"

Mason blinked, triggered by Cruz's shout. Instinct kicked in. He remembered what he'd been so carefully taught, both before Revival and since. He'd been in these situations before, though never quite like this.

The guards. I'm supposed to watch the guards.

He swung to the side and raised his weapon.

A pair of uniformed security guards flanked a framed poster — a stylized illustration reminiscent of old Soviet propaganda. Black, white, and red. Hard lines and too many edges. Image of a cop, eyes hidden behind sunglasses, shotgun raised. Both barrels aimed at the viewer, muzzle bores the size of oranges. One hand unseen on the trigger, the other stretched toward the viewer, palm forward. A black bar beneath it held a single-word caption in bold white letters — OBEY.

The guards hadn't reached the floor and were either too untrained or too stupid to have gone for their sidearms. Nobody had addressed them yet. That was Mason's job.

Something clicked. He rushed forward, old habits donning uniforms. Mason hadn't always been a criminal. Nothing new here. The same-old, same-old, no matter whether he was aiming at cops or robbers.

Shoot through them. Find the contact.

A strange thought, not quite native. Like a whisper in his ear.

"Hands where I can see them!" he shouted.

The guard on the poster's left raised his hands so fast, Mason half-expected a hallelujah. The other was either brave or stupid. Mason saw precursors of disobedience — inflexible face, determined eyes, subtle muscles poised to reach for the gun instead of the ceiling tiles. Mason, weapon already aimed, had a full-second lead, maybe as much as two seconds. His finger tapped the trigger, its pressure insufficient. No. He'd put the man down with his elbow, not a bullet. He had time for that.

Then the guard's head tried to make a break for it, bone and brain dashing for the wall through the rear exit behind him. The rip of gunfire was almost an afterthought. The guard's body slumped, leaking fluids. Mason spun to find Sasha's firearm near enough to feel the heat.

"What the fuck?"

"He's faster than you'd think. He always is."

"Who is?"

Buster shouted before Sasha could answer. Mason didn't see what she was yelling about, but he did see Watt unload a few shells in three concussive bursts, two through furniture and one over Cruz's shoulder to give the window a glittering starburst. It was chaos-fire — Watt panicking at Buster's shout compounded by his own lack of composure.

Yelling followed immediately. Groans. By craning his neck, Mason could see Watt hadn't fired randomly after all. He'd pegged three do-gooder customers who'd pow-wowed and found improvised weapons, dying to be heroes. Now, they were just dying.

How had Watt known where to shoot? How had Buster?

"Three-thirty," said Cruz, looking at his watch. "Two-point-five minutes remaining."

Until what? Mason felt like he'd dozed off, missed part of orientation. His brain's pattern-recognition centers were registering something not-quite-right — or, perhaps, a bit too much for comfort. What he'd taken for random action wasn't arbitrary at all. Cruz was conducting, and the band was playing the perfect tune.

Sasha and Buster, both bigger and stronger than all the men but Preacher, were scoping the scene with purpose, not firing knee-jerk at random. But, so far as Mason could see, they weren't following Cruz's laid-out plan. That'd been about in/out timing, numbers of opposing guns, and layout of the target. The women were doing something a level above that, tracking the customers' and employees' movements as if they were choreographed.

And Watt hadn't truly *responded* to Buster's shout. To Mason's eye, he'd seemed more *reminded*.

Now Cruz was skulking around, kicking upturned debris with his boot, searching with purpose. Only Preacher wasn't doing some version of duty, now at the entrance with his arms crossed. He sat in a rolling chair and put his feet on a bullet-riddled desk while Mason watched.

I thought you were D'Abo?

I ain't.

You watch the doors.

See if I does.

Preacher gave Mason an ivory grin. Then, impossibly, he raised both hands and made finger guns. His lips moved, and Mason could have sworn he silently mouthed, *You can run, but your ass can't hide.*

"*SHAW!*"

Cruz again. Dammit, nobody was supposed to use names.

He hadn't finished the thought when the sluggish, sky-reaching guard grew some balls and grabbed for Mason's aimed weapon.

Mason grappled back, slamming an elbow into the man's throat. The MAC-30 sputtered fire, puncturing a teller window as if connecting the dots. Several someones screamed. The guard's eyes, close and frightened, ticked toward the door. Something happening there. But it was fine. Preacher, *D'Abo*, had eyes on it already.

See if I does.

That voice. That tone. Why did it rattle his skull?

With fair fighting now moot, Mason kicked the guard in his jimmies. He went down.

Then Mason spun to Preacher as the big bald man watched a family of three sprint into the sunlight outside, waving wildly as they went.

"*GOD DAMMIT,*" said Sasha, firing at the escapees and missing.

Preacher laughed, his attention still on Mason.

Sasha was supposed to be handling the manager. With two minutes left on the clock, the manager mattered most. She was where Cruz had predicted — prone, hands on her head, as instructed.

The fat man Cruz had mentioned wasn't by her side. In the confusion over the guards and doors, he'd made a break for the desk and the hard-wired alarm. And he'd made it. Tiny white lights were strobing, suggesting an alarm was braying somewhere.

Another gun coughed. The man spattered red flesh, his chest turned to burger.

Eyes wide, Buster turned to Cruz. "Abort?"

"If you'd like," he said.

"What the fuck do you mean, '*If I'd like*'?"

Gazes circled the room.

"Go," said Watt.

"Go," Sasha repeated.

Preacher said, "I wanna see how much he can take."

Staring at the man, Mason saw the white space press against his awareness. The tiny black dot.

Behind Mason, Watt yelped with recall and gave a little *Oh-Shit* hop. Remembering something dire, he'd turned and was rushing like hell for … for …

Mason wanted to rub his eyes.

… for a small elderly woman behind a walker. Watt barreled headlong, rushing for her as if she were a live grenade. He stopped short, weapon inches from her face. She hadn't gotten down. From where Mason stood, that seemed to be the problem. But it shouldn't matter. The woman was frail, couldn't swat a fly.

"GET DOWN!" Watt screeched.

After Mason made sure his remaining guard hadn't moved, he turned. "Easy," he told Watt.

"I SAID GET DOWN!"

"And *I* said *EASY!*"

Watt's gun shook in his hand. His eyes were large as if he'd remembered some terrible truth. His body language bellowed terror, or frustration, maybe indignant fury. As if the little old lady had wronged him, or threatened him, or was the linchpin about to end them all.

Watt turned the gun around, hit her in the back. Granny buckled and screeched but didn't go down. Tough old bird clung to the walker like the grim reaper's knuckles on his scythe.

Mason rushed forward, but Cruz put out an arm to stop him. "His job. His call."

But that went against Mason's code. He tried to move around, but now Cruz, who'd only observed and led so far, finally raised his weapon … and used it to stab him in the breastbone.

"It falls apart if you fight it," Cruz said. "Come on. You of all people know that."

"Yeah," Preacher agreed. "You of all people, bitch."

Mason shoved Cruz aside, but Watt had turned to defend himself, leaving the old lady to wobble. His face twisted as he came at Mason, battle on his mind.

But Watt didn't make it to Mason.

Granny pulled a tiny pearl-handled pistol from the bag hanging from her walker and used it to blow a miniature hole in his spine.

Buster shouted. Sasha shredded the woman like a cat shredding drapes.

Watt went to his knees. Cruz watched it happen, refusing the dying man's hands as he reached out for him. Then he pressed his earpiece, neither pleased nor surprised, and said, "We're done here."

Mason stared at him. "What do you mean, 'We're done here'?"

"Watt's down. Call for extraction."

"Are you talking to me?"

"Clock is at plus one-oh-six."

"We can still do this!"

But Cruz had checked out. He was somewhere else.

Mason turned to Sasha. She was holding the vault key. There was still time.

"Call it," said Cruz.

"We've got a full minute left!"

"Call it," Cruz repeated. "*Now*."

Mason groaned and sprinted toward Sasha and the key. He remembered the briefing, knew where the vault was. Shockingly easy to access, according to intel.

Sasha wasn't moving, but Mason would. He hadn't ruined his life for nothing.

They'd do this. Or die trying.

But as Mason took his first step, the entire front wall of the bank blew inward, turning glass into rain. Cuts peppered his neck and hands, the shockwave of what must be artillery blowing him to the floor.

Then the gas. A thick white fog so obscuring, it was almost otherworldly.

His eyes sagged. Closed. Opened.

Mason saw the white room. The black dot. A grid of geometric spirals looming somewhere, maybe real or maybe imagined.

It's beautiful, he thought.

But then his eyes closed for good, and Mason thought nothing at all.

TWO

Old Hope and New Agony

THE INTERVIEW ROOM WAS A CLICHÉ.

Officer Friendly was in his forties, white and balding, with an athletic body gone to seed. He wore a long-sleeved dress shirt that probably cost fifteen bucks off the rack at Old Navy, rolled up at the elbows to reveal shoddy stitching and forearms like a pair of mourning hams. His name seemed to be Clifton, judging by the calls Mason had heard as they'd led him through the station. He looked like a Ralph, or maybe a Moochie.

The man was a statue against the wall. Mason kept trying to engage him, but it was like trying to initiate a conversation with the guards at Buckingham Palace. He tried the comparison on for size, found it giddily hilarious, and desperately wanted to dance in front of Moochie's face to see if he could make the officer flinch.

"Aren't you gonna read me my rights?"

Clifton's composure barely broke. "They read your rights on the scene."

"I don't remember. Prove it."

Clifton looked away, showing Mason a profile that looked even more like a Moochie than his front. Now would be the perfect time to try the Buckingham routine, but that clearly wasn't about to happen.

"Tell you what," Mason said. "Read my rights again, just to be sure."

But … nothing.

Mason crossed his legs. From the outside, it couldn't possibly look as casual as he wanted. His chair was behind a table, both metal, both bolted to the floor. It looked like a mortician's slab with a lot of wear and tear, too many dents in the surface. He knew the kind well.

"What's your name?"

"Officer Clifton." He shot Mason a loathing look.

"No way! I fucked Officer Clifton's mom!"

With a sigh, Clifton pounded a fist into his palm. He stepped away from the wall, finally ready to give Mason what he wanted. He did it with grim duty, his body language saying, *I don't want to hurt you, but I guess I have no choice.*

Clifton was two feet away. Mason was bracing for impact when the door opened. There was a small hook above the wire-mesh window, and someone had hung their dry cleaning on it, still in the clear plastic bag. The interrogation rooms were all surveilled in theory, but to Mason, the dry cleaning said something different. Like at his own station, a few of the dirtier rooms were probably missing their cameras. Nobody bothered to block the room's only window unless there was no other way to see inside.

A second cop entered — a black-haired woman with high, severe eyebrows and a clipboard tucked under one arm. She stopped when she saw the pair of them, the big cop's shoulders coiled to strike.

Clifton backed off.

Mason said, "Oh, good. My noodles are here."

The woman must have known what she was going into, but a blocked window buried the truth. Her face fell when she saw it. "*Jesus Christ.* Is this really how it's going to be?"

"I just really want noodles."

She approached the metal table. "I'm not talking about your

mouth. I'm talking about how hard you keep making it to give you the benefit of the doubt."

"Well. That's up to you, Dakota."

She shook her head and looked at Clifton. "Take off his cuffs."

"He resisted arrest."

"He's a twice-decorated officer, Carl. Show some respect."

Clifton puffed up. "Pfeffer said the same thing. You know, before dickless here broke his nose."

"I told you," Mason said. "That was an accident."

"How was it an accident?"

"His face got in the way of my fist."

"I should beat the shit out of you, you know that?"

"Because I fucked your mom? She was begging me for it. Right there in the supermarket, she dropped her pants and grabbed her ankles."

"Why, you little—!"

"That's enough!"

They both stopped. Clifton looked assaulted — but Mason, seeing himself saved, smiled and blew the other man a kiss.

"Take off the cuffs. *Now.*"

Grumbling, Clifton bent to unlock the handcuffs, keeping Mason's hands behind his back. He was following his superior's orders, but Mason noted how he kept one hand behind his hip. He wasn't wearing a piece, so that hidden hand was probably a balled-up fist, ready for any excuse.

Flinch, his eyes said, *and I'll knock your teeth out.*

Mason understood. He'd been in ol' Moochie's shoes before, restrained by the law in ways the subject never was. But then his understanding departed, and the fat fuck was plain old Moochie again — an example of everything Mason had spent his career making sure he wasn't.

He knew how close he'd come to a beating. Maybe he should've kept his mouth shut, but he couldn't resist a jab. "You're cute when you're angry."

But Clifton did him one better, his voice barely above a whisper. *"I know all about your son, you know."*

Mason would have laughed, but he didn't want the punch. He'd gotten a vasectomy at twenty-five and still applied condoms like layers of paint. You didn't bring kids into a world like this. That right there had been his father's mistake.

"I don't have a son."

If his face had been a television, Moochie's expression would have been the black between channels. He reset as if catching a dumb mistake. "Your father, then. We worked together. *Before* he lost his fucking mind."

Clifton's face stayed close, daring Mason to try something. He smiled then straightened, knowing who'd won. And by how much.

"Give us the room," said the woman.

"Sahar told me to stay."

"I'm telling you otherwise."

"—to stay *especially* if Lieutenant Ward said otherwise."

She waited.

Ward had transferred to Union City, adjunct to Internal Affairs. The way Mason heard it, she should be dead. Four masked assailants had cornered her on her walk home. Lord knew Union Station had lost its share of women walking alone. But Ward had broken three legs, two on the same man. An officer who sat ten feet from her at USPD had called in sick the next day, saying he'd fallen down the stairs and shattered both tibias. Another had been on crutches and gave Officer Ward a wide berth.

"Noticed a new Tesla Prime in the parking lot," she told Clifton in the silence. "Funny thing. It was in your spot."

"I got an inheritance."

"Unrelated, I heard all charges against Leonard Demonza were dropped. Someone lost the evidence. Isn't that funny?"

"You inferring something, Ward?"

"I'm actually implying. Maybe *you* could tell me what you 'infer' from it all."

Clifton seemed to be considering a rebuttal. After ten seconds, he turned and walked out. Before going, he grabbed the hanging bag covering the window. So it was his dry cleaning. Mason should have known. The slacks were ghastly.

With the door closed, Ward sat.

Mason rubbed his wrists. He hadn't worn cuffs since the academy when they'd also tried pepper spray and stun guns. *Best to know what you're inflicting on others.* That was before Revival and the HROs, before the only crime had been crime itself. If he had a nostalgic bone in his body, Mason might've felt sad.

He nodded at the closed door. "Thanks."

"Don't thank me. Don't say anything to me but 'Yes, sir.'"

"Isn't that a bit sexist?"

"Is this a joke to you, Carter?"

Mason waited to see if she'd correct herself.

"*Mason.* Sorry."

"Should I be threatened that my father's on your mind?"

She answered seriously, dodging the sarcasm. "I'm just a bit preoccupied with his bullshit. Carter made quite a mess for IA. Not just the break-in. He didn't go quietly when they caught him in Blake's office. You know Vincent? Broke his face."

"Bad week for Vincent," Mason said.

His light tone missed its mark. Ward was still a friend, but her patience seemed tissue-thin.

"This is my day off, you know. Internal Affairs is important, but it's not supposed to be urgent. Dirty can always wait until Monday."

"That's cute. Got it on a plaque up on the fifth floor?"

"All except for the Shaws," Ward went on. "The Shaw family is somehow a constant bundle of *right-fucking-now.* First Carter's break-down, followed by his break-*in*, then——"

"That wasn't a breakdown."

"Well, was it a break-*in*? Both on Saturdays. You know what I like to do on Saturdays? I take a nice, long bath. Toke up and let Calgon take me the fuck away. Twice, Sahar pinged me right in the middle of my goddamn bath. I had to get out and get sober just so I could come here and deal with your father's bullshit. What day is it today, Mason?"

"Christmas."

"It's fucking *Saturday*, that's what. And I was in the tub. That's three. *Three fucking times,* I had to drag ass to this shithole on a Saturday with red eyes and cottonmouth, all because of your family."

"Fun fact," Mason said. "The accident? *Also* on Saturday. I know because I was watching cartoons with my nephew when we found out his daddy was dead."

Low blow. Dakota was furious with him — partly because of his father and partly because of Mason — and his no-big-deal mention of the Logan thing was his way of punching back. In truth, her fury was justified. Mason was an asshole to use his brother's death as a reason to unseat her. But courtesy, which had always been part of his character, was now the least of his concerns. In here, that kind of softness could kill you.

Ward sagged. "I know you've been through a lot."

"Logan was an asshole. We both know it."

She sighed, refusing to meet his gaze. Logan had been the *president* of assholes, but he'd still been Mason's brother. Plus, there had been a passenger in the car that day — one Ward knew about perfectly well, but one even Mason wouldn't use as a joke or as leverage.

"I don't know what to do with you, Mason."

"Do whatever. Who fucking cares what you do with me?"

"*You* should. What *happened* to you? The Carter Shaw I met six years ago was a good man. Now you're—"

"Seriously going to keep calling me 'Carter,' huh?"

Dakota closed her eyes and took a pair of slow breaths. In those beats, Mason could feel the world reset. Then she opened them, present in a way she hadn't been before.

"I guess I can't believe this is happening to both of you. That you both went bad. Don't you remember how you used to be, Mason? You saw your father's illness in the most mature way a son possibly could. You helped IA without ever betraying him. You did the right things without being disloyal."

"And look where that got us."

"I didn't know how far Carter would go any more than you. I

mean ... when Reeves disappeared, and he started talking foul play ..."

"I'm going to prison here, Dakota. Maybe while we're on my dime, we don't talk about Elisabeth Reeves?"

"Point is, I thought we were friends."

"You're right. We really haven't hung out enough recently. Wanna go back to your place? Light up a blunt and make some bubbles?"

Dakota dropped her clipboard on the table. Most of the department used tablets, but IA still did most things on paper. Ironically, in the digital age, it was the more secure medium — the only one you could burn. She flipped over a sheaf of pages then tucked them behind the thing's wooden back.

Her finger touched a page halfway in. She looked up, her eyes no longer angry. In the mess his life had become after his father's fall, and after things with Logan and his mother, Mason's relationship with IA had perversely become the most stable one in his life. No matter how Dakota wanted to sugarcoat it, Mason's testimony had stuck a knife in Carter's back. So, what had Mason done to assuage his guilt at betraying his father? He'd made buddies, of course — because God knew nobody else on the force would talk to him.

It was all her fault. Dakota said she'd never take the gig with Internal Affairs. She was a street detective forever. After she'd fired that bullet and eluded the reprimand, she'd very nearly ended up in an even worse spot. But then IA called, and apparently, the prospect of prosecuting cops had struck her as slightly better than going through the grinder.

"They say you resisted arrest."

"That's what you do with things you'd rather not be part of. You resist them."

"And we already know you broke Vincent Pfeffer's nose."

"I was aiming for his dick. That nose is just so damn huge, and his dick is so small."

"Were you drunk?"

"I'm drunk right now."

Dakota folded her hands on the clipboard and met his gaze. "This is serious."

"Then why do I hear carnival music in my head?"

"They want to send you into HRO 22. Did you know that?"

"Oh, cool. Dad's old stomping grounds."

"I can't save you if you won't help me."

His character broke. It was no fun being a smartass when nobody else was playing along. "Oh, *whatever*, Dakota. It was no big deal. You've gotten into worse."

"Worse!"

"So, I had a bad week. Got into something I maybe shouldn't have."

"*Something you—*" She stopped, tried for composure, then resumed as if speaking to a mental defective. "All jokes aside, you know what this means, don't you? You're not getting a slap on the wrist. It doesn't matter how many medals they gave you or how many sheets wrote you up, or how many bad cops you helped put away in the past. *You are going to prison.* Do you understand me? In this state, that means a Human Restoration Outpost, and based on jurisdiction, you're headed into 22. Didn't Carter tell you enough about 22 to get through your thick skull just how bad it is in there?"

Mason crossed his arms. He'd visited his father once. *Once.* Carter had been as good as dead after that.

"It's bad. But I can pull favors. I can't promise anything, but if you'll just wake up and stop being an asshole, you have my word I'll try my best."

"I don't need your charity," Mason told her.

"Really? Because from where I'm standing, you most definitely do. If you're lucky, you'll spend the rest of your idiot life inside a city populated by thieves and murderers. And that life isn't likely to be a long one. You'll probably be dead inside a week."

A chill ran across his scalp like spreading fingers, gone as soon as it came. A moment later, Mason felt nothing. "One more dead Shaw. It's almost poetic."

She flipped pages again. Mason recognized the new form. He'd gotten the same one in the mail, also paper. Social services was the only state organization more antiquated than the police.

"Have you considered what will happen to Hunter if you go away?" Dakota asked.

"Logan wasn't much of a father even when he was alive. Hunter will do like any kid in his situation. He'll stay with his mother and learn to hate his old man like the rest of us."

She half-flinched at Mason's words but seeing it only made him want to dig deeper. He knew what she thought — he was using his anger as a shield against mourning. But he felt differently. He'd long ago dismissed Logan as futile. When Dakota was his partner, she'd urged him to reconcile. But making nice with Logan Shaw was like licking a scorpion. It made you look stupid, and no matter how careful you were, the sting was coming.

Dakota shuffled papers. "We'll see. Would you like to *ask* his mother about that? She's next door. Two of the downtown guys picked her up around the same time they got you. Drugs *and* prostitution. Not just fucking. *Dealing.*"

"Good for her. She's moving up the chain. Living life as her own boss."

"Raylene is on two strikes. You're more optimistic than me if you think she'll steer clear of a third. We've talked about this, Mason."

"Hunter isn't my kid. There was a reason I didn't have kids — and even if I wanted them, my girlfriend wasn't interested in commitment." He leaned forward and stared into her eyes.

Dakota was beautiful if you could see through the mask her job demanded. "Raylene goes away, and your nephew becomes a ward of the state. That's not how I read your brother's last wishes."

Mason forced a laugh he didn't feel — not at all. "You're an only child. You think those 'last wishes' mean Logan trusts me, but really it's his final fuck-you. *He* dropped the ball. Why is it my responsibility to pick it up and—"

"Mason."

Anger simmered at Logan for dying, at Carter for starting this, at Dakota for telling the truth.

He crossed his arms and looked at the wall. At the window. Maybe if he picked a fight, they'd drag him off to HRO 22 right now and spare him this moment of emotion.

"Mason."

He forced himself to look into her hazel eyes. Something he hadn't done since she'd made her decision.

"Logan didn't leave you a dog or an old, musty record collection. Hunter is your *nephew*. I used to watch you guys play. You were like father and son — dare I say, more like father and son than he and Logan. Remember that?"

Mason sharpened his gaze. "Sure. I remember. You watched us 'play' from the couch. But then you left one morning and never came back. Wouldn't even talk about it. Remember *that?*"

Touché. Dakota took her hands off the table, leaned back in her chair, and sighed.

He could almost hear her brain switch tracks. The current conversational door closed, and another one opened. She flipped more pages.

"Will you let me cop a plea for you?"

"Don't I have to do that myself?"

Hazel-eyed stare, boring through his skull.

Even with his question unanswered, Mason spoke next. "Would it work?"

"Maybe, if you show remorse and kiss the appropriate asses. If we flaunt your decorations and rewards and you let me paint you as a Scout. Shouldn't be hard. You used to be so straight-laced, you barely ate candy."

"Nauseating, right?"

"It worked for me. Hard to find good cops in this city. Harder still to find good *men*. The world's going to shit, Mason. You were one of the few who gave me hope. You don't realize how special that was."

Was.

It hurt more than he'd admit. He shrugged and looked away.

"What happened to you, Mason?"

"*Life* happened to me. *The world* happened to me. You said it yourself. I was always the outlier. Now I fit in."

"Was it your mother? Was she the last straw?"

He didn't want to answer that.

"I used to hear about Mason Shaw all the time. Mason Shaw always stood up for the little guy. Mason Shaw was tough with the bad guys and kind with the good guys. Mason Shaw was the one cop in this city you could hold up as a prime example of—"

"And what does that tell you if I was the only one playing by the rules?"

"But now I hear about you for the opposite reasons. You show up late. Or not at all. You're obsessed by things that should be left alone."

"My father was obsessed. For *years.*"

Dakota continued as if she hadn't heard him. "You snap at everyone. You shout and hit things when you can't get your way. You're drunk half the time and belligerent the rest."

"I'm working on that. If I beat the rap, I'll be drunk *all* the time."

Dakota sighed then took a moment. Mason knew this routine. He'd seen it when they'd fought when she'd regretted her temper and tried to make nice. Even now, even with the millennium's turn so far behind them, only a hard woman earned the respect of the adrenaline jockeys at USPD — especially a woman just coming out of Internal Affairs, set to take command of Union Station's HRO away from a legendary misogynist.

Coming down from that — first to baseline, then to overt tenderness — took time. It wasn't flipping a switch but rather allowing boiling water to cool. She had a routine for empathy and compassion, and this moment, this sighing and resetting of limbs and voice, was how it began.

Mason let it happen without interruption, unsure why he held his tongue, now of all times. Maybe he still cared for Dakota. Or maybe it was because, despite all that had happened, he subconsciously understood his last chance was coming. A fork in the road, with old hope on one side and new agony on the other.

"I know you're going through some really bad shit, Mason. I wanted to attend the funerals, but I thought my being there might make things worse for you. I also heard about Carter going Pattern Black. And I know you signed the release, not that it makes a difference. I'm sorry."

"Don't be."

"But maybe there's a chance you can see it as light at the end of the tunnel. Your father isn't coming back. You've known that for months." She flipped more pages on her clipboard until she found a number on a sheet topped with Carter Shaw's unsmiling photo — his *USPD badge* photo, adding insult to injury. "I show twenty-three days until they let him zero out. Then you can bury him. One more month, then it'll all be over."

"Is that how it works? One last body in the ground and *abracadabra*, the evil spell is broken?"

She gave a longer, and surely final, sigh. "I can't save you if you won't save yourself."

Mason considered for the briefest of seconds, a flood of conflicting emotion tearing through him like the flash of a train speeding by.

Then he said, "What's the point?"

THREE

In a Body Bag

Two hours later, after a routine AI trial that felt more like DMV processing than an assessment of justice, Mason sat inside a sealed room at HRO 22's intake facility. A uniformed woman put a strange hat on his head. It seemed to be half scalp massager and half spider. The face-sucker from *Alien*, but a dumb one attached to the wrong side of his head. It had long fingers with tiny brass balls on the ends. Every time Mason moved, the balls pressed his skin, clinging to it. He raised a hand to scratch.

"Don't touch it," said the woman.

He scratched anyway. A sound like ripping paper came from a speaker on a wheeled cart, as if the spider thing had a microphone. It seemed to be listening to his hair, maybe to see if it had a secret life. *How are things back in the cowlick?* one strand might ask. To which those at the front might reply, *At least we're not receding.*

"I said, don't touch it."

"It itches."

The tech sighed. "I was asked to leave you uncuffed, but there's a guard right outside if you won't cooperate."

Mason's hands went back to his lap. "Maybe you put it on wrong."

"You're feeling an itch because there's a small electrical current running through your scalp."

"Because you want my hair looking its best when they toss me inside?"

"Through your scalp and into your brain."

Mason stopped. That wasn't as funny for some reason.

"If you don't let me get a baseline, the drones will kill you," she explained.

"Kill me for doing what?"

"For existing."

"If that's the way it is, why don't you just shoot me?"

The tech considered him. Mason was pretty sure most new inmates went through all of this with a decidedly different vibe. Punchier, less accommodating. A file was clearly following him as he made his way through the intake process like food through a monster's intestine. He knew that much because people kept reading his vitals aloud in the same order. Officer's status had earned him gold-star treatment so far ... by prison standards, at least. That might change.

Dakota, on the cusp of a promotion, had one foot in IA and the other in her new position as Director of Intake for Human Restoration Outpost #22. On the HRO side, Mason was a distinguished prisoner. But once they put him back in the hands of cops he'd worked with, finked on, then gotten busted by, he would be considered scum instead of a VIP.

"What?" Mason asked as the tech regarded him.

"Is it true you were given the Union Station Award of Valor?"

"More or less."

He saw her make a decision. She'd typically rush a regular prisoner through, but this hero cop apparently deserved the courtesy of some answers.

"Nobody's explained the drones to you?"

"Drones enforce the rules."

Everyone knew that, same as everyone knew about Chamber Therapy. Revival's privatized prison system had become a curious breed of social celebrity. Prison cities once offered no hope of escape. Now, the public saw them as halfway houses.

Mason knew from his father's stats — the ones he'd actually believed, from back when he'd been working quietly with Reeves — that only around one percent of prisoners were ever released. Still, the idea of "curing crime" made headlines, even if almost everyone still got a life sentence, anyway. Mason had seen Nathaniel Blake profiled in *People* and even *In Style*. The latter had asked the scientist about his skincare routine. He had a Labrador and three kids pictured in a two-page spread even as a killer drone sat behind him on the counter of a sun-drenched kitchen. It was all so charming.

"HRO drones don't enforce autonomously anymore. Not since the PHTP started protesting."

"Is that pronounced *'phppt'?*"

"The drones are now primarily a means of surveillance. Docent guards have been taken entirely off-duty for now, but stay inside long enough, and I'll bet the union gets them back on the job."

"Fascinating."

"Drones only engage when authorized by human operators, and even then, only after they're informed by verifiable insider intel."

"You mean the drones are only allowed to act after a snitch rats out one of their fellow prisoners?" That hadn't been covered in *People*. The "snitch economy" was officially sanctioned and encouraged since prisoners form underground economies anyway, and this was the HRO's idea to control it. Still, they kept all mention of snitch chits and informant kiosks mostly quiet, ideally white-washed if not officially denied. If not for his father's obsession, Mason wouldn't have known about it, either.

But the operator didn't flinch, either unsurprised that Mason knew or hardly caring.

"If you like. There are only two reasons for drones to act autonomously in the new system. The first is for curfew violations. Rack time starts sharply at 9:00 p.m. Pacific time and ends at 6:00 a.m. the following morning. Be inside your assigned crib during those hours. Nine means nine sharp, not 9:01. Curfew is vital to the

HRO's operation, so enforcement is straightforward. And strict. Drones don't require authorization before acting."

"*Acting* how?"

"Missing curfew is the easiest way to get out of prison." She paused, then added, "In a body bag."

Mason swallowed. Drones could vaporize, not just kill. It was cleaner that way. He wouldn't leave in a bag so much as a dustbin.

"What's the other time the drones are authorized to 'enforce' on their own?"

"When they don't recognize you." She nodded to the face-sucker hat. "Hence the need for a baseline reading, so the drones know who you are."

"So, I should let you finish," Mason said.

"That would be my suggestion."

The thing buzzed. His scalp itched. Again he raised his hand.

"Don't touch it," said the tech.

This time, Mason obeyed.

Another Layer of Control

Mason and maybe thirty fellow scumbags sat in a room that felt like the strange offspring of a theater, an old-fashioned classroom, and a gymnasium built by an inebriated architect. Bleachers faced a screen and covered the entire floor rather than limiting their expanse to opposite walls. Cheap aluminum alloy was bolted to the deck, pierced at five-foot intervals with sturdy grapefruit-sized hoops. The chain connecting Mason's cuffs had been strung through the steel hoops, his arms dangling between his legs like a penitent.

They had seen two short orientation films so far — *Human Resource Outpost Incarceration: What You Need to Know* and a production bluntly named *Snitch and Get Rich*. The first looked like it had been made by the folks behind the Duck and Cover campaign for school kids in the 1950s. The second had been faux-animated with illustrated jump-cuts.

"What're you in for?" asked the man on his left. His hair would have made the 1980s proud.

Mason didn't answer.

"You hear me?"

"I heard you."

"So, what're you in for?"

"Does it matter?"

"I'm just trying to be friendly." But he looked like a predator. Knowledge was power inside, so Mason hesitated to open his mouth and give the man any information he didn't already have.

Carter had told him about the need to speak carefully in prison, after his arrest but before going into Chamber Therapy.

"I don't need any friends."

"Tough guy, huh?" The man huffed. It smelled like he'd been giving oral to a toilet. "Guess I can respect that."

A woman on the long bench ahead turned to look at them. Mason assumed it was because RATT-hair was the only one in the room talking, but then he saw her eyes. The HRO swallowed everyone, from mass-murderers to rapists to guys who stole groceries. This woman — really just a girl — looked like she belonged at a part-time gig at Mickey D's or having game night with her family.

Mason tried to give her a nonverbal message. *It'll be okay.*

But then she turned back, afraid or offended rather than mollified, and the room fell into silence.

Tone-deaf to the mood, Mr. Mullet opened his mouth again. "They tell you about Immunity?"

"Yeah." Mason already wished he'd stayed mum. The prison resistance was another thing Carter had told him about, but his father had been so paranoid before the Revival break-in, he might as well have claimed the moon landing was staged. Admitting he knew about Immunity either made him a plant with more knowledge than he should have or just as nuts as his father. Neither was good.

"You hear they blew up a building in the Inner Circle?" Then the man lowered his voice and added, "People say Calliope was behind it."

Now *there* was an unwelcome name. The last time Mason had heard Carter say it, his father was in cuffs the next day.

"Calliope's a myth," Mason said.

"Uh-huh. *A myth.*"

From what Mason had been able to tell back when the issue had felt pressing instead of moot, "Calliope" was an *I-am-Spartacus* situation. No solo hacker had the keys to everything. There was a *community* of mouth-breathing basement-dwellers pooling their talents under a lone moniker. Pretending Calliope could be one person was half delusional and half savior-seeking. With no one to save their world, the powerless invented a God of Vigilantes to soothe their existential souls.

"My cousin told me about it."

"Your cousin's in prison, too?" Mason raised his eyebrows. "I'm shocked."

"He said all sorts of shit happens inside that nobody talks about. Like the no-fly zone. Not supposed to be drones near the Inner Circle, right? He saw them all the time. Only they're not like the normal drones. These are hacked."

Mason grunted.

"Because of Calliope," his new friend added.

He turned his head to roll his eyes. Calliope was like an old-world legend that existed to scare children into behaving. The disenfranchised loved singing his praises, but Mason suspected it was just another layer of control, sanctioned to provide hope where there was none.

As if any significant chaos inside the prison would be allowed, Carter once told Mason, at his most paranoid. *You know what Elisabeth told me?*

What? Sigh. *What did Elisabeth tell you, Dad?*

The AIs running the HROs have a low tolerance for things that don't go according to plan. You ever heard of an HRO just kind of ... self-destructing?

No, Dad. No, I haven't.

Well, then. I guess nothing's bad enough to force their hand yet.

Mason drank heavily that night. It was the first time he'd truly seen the writing on his father's wall.

"I got the scoop," Longhair continued. "You want to be on the inside track, you stick with me. Name's Frank. I heard them call you Shaw. That right?"

Mason's eyes darted. He'd personally put enough people into HRO 22 to populate a sports bar. He nodded curtly — just enough movement to answer Frank so he'd shut up.

"My cousin had this place in the palm of his hand. Reggie built himself a little mafia underground. Every time I came to visit, he had this secret language of taps and gestures. He'd say, 'Frank, you go do this or do that.' I was his hands on the outside, and you know what? Got a peek once at the balance in the account Reg had me making deposits into. Like sixty mil in there. Getting thrown in the joint was the best thing for business."

The slight man on Mason's other side was craning to listen, but he snapped back to center once Mason started eyeing him.

"You wanna know how I got busted?"

Mason shrugged. He could give less than a fractional shit.

"Reg finked on me. Ran right to one of those snitch kiosks they showed in that one video and told the man his cousin on the outside was laundering money. I hear the very next day they gave him one of those big roll-up TVs and a box full of the best bukake porn. But I got his ass back. You know where Reggie is now?"

Another shrug. Frank was a failure at taking a hint.

"He's worm food. You know why? They asked me when I was comin' in if I wanted to earn some of them snitch chits. So, sure, fuck that guy. I wanted all the chits I could get if I was going inside, so I told 'em all about Reggie and where he hung his shirts. They watched him with drones then sent Docents inside. Course Reggie didn't go quiet, so I had to say good fuckin' riddance."

Mason wondered at Frank's profile, curious whether he knew this was an abysmal recruitment speech. *Join me and end up in a shallow grave.*

The screen flickered as one film ended and another queued. Frank seemed finished, but then his greasy hair swung in Mason's peripheral vision as his ceaseless mouth opened again. "Hey. You wanna hear a joke?"

"Not really."

"Why did the HRO inmate cross the road?"

"The movie's starting."

"Come on. Why did he cross the road?"

"I don't care."

Frank gave him a fucker's laugh. "Because he was having a flashback, and there were three fags chasing him with their dicks out!"

As jokes went, Mason had heard better.

FIVE

A Humanitarian Alternative

Now linked like a chain gang, Mason was starting to wonder if maybe there was no prison city. Maybe the Hell-on-Earth he'd been sentenced to wasn't the HRO itself. Maybe his sentence was standing in line and watching orientation films with Frank stinking the air beside him instead.

They were in a long hallway with a stripe down the middle. The building itself had, from the start, struck Mason as a place that belonged in a Japanese horror film — the kind with backward stop-motion wherein pale-faced ghouls turned out to have been hiding behind the hero all along. Everything was splinters or threadbare. Green lighting was making Mason sick and giving him the creeps.

"Listen up!" barked a man with military cadence and a head like a dropped grapefruit, dented large enough on one side to have been punched by a giant. "You have been injected with your blood dongles. They will be in your veins for the rest of your lives. Removing them would require a transfusion — and believe me, tagged blood will hang on tight if you're trading it for untagged blood. The results won't be pretty or pleasant."

Mason caught the eye of the woman from earlier. She'd been looking at him but quickly flinched away.

"You have now completed orientation. In case any of you are slow learners, do not forget curfew. You must be in your assigned crib between twenty-one hundred hours and six hundred hours each day — 9:00 p.m. to 6:00 a.m. just so there's no confusion. You will find yourself unable to argue with a drone, should you arrive late to your assigned crib or decide to depart early, and enforcement is strict. I strongly suggest you find your crib *early*. Nightfall comes around seven, and cribs are marked by sky-pointing spotlights you should have no trouble seeing. You'll have two hours to find your place if you start looking when the sun goes down, so don't wait until the last minute or you will be sorry. Cribs are denoted by color. This group will be in the *red* crib. You will recognize your assigned location by its bright red spotlight. Are any of you colorblind? If so, it's important you tell me now."

One woman raised a reluctant hand. Dent-Head nodded at a bland-faced guard, who escorted her away. Might be showing her a map so she wouldn't need color to recognize the spotlight. Or maybe she was getting thrown into a chipper.

He watched her go then returned his attention to the line of shackled prisoners. "You have already been convicted and sentenced for your crimes. You have been given the opportunity to provide incriminating information on your fellow inmates or on people you know outside the prison to mitigate or possibly forgive your sentence, earn chits to spend on the inside—"

A hand went up. Frank's, no surprise.

"So, the people who were with us a while ago but ain't here now. Did those fine folks 'get their sentence forgiven'?"

"This is your intake group," said Dent-Head, not answering.

"But it's smaller now. So, the folks who ain't here no more … they snitched to get out? Like snitched on some of *us*?" Seemed like Frank was worried about his loose lips. Some eavesdropper might have told a guard what he said about his cousin's operation and how some of it may have migrated into his private account.

Dent-Head looked at a tablet, back at the guards, then continued as if Frank hadn't spoken. He looked at Mason because he and Frank were besties now.

"The Revival Corporation, in conjunction with the state of California, has ruled that life inside a human restoration outpost may, for some of you, be unacceptably cruel. I do not agree. But regardless, it is our policy to offer a 'humanitarian alternative.'"

Frank looked to Mason, but his eyes were on their leader. The way he said those last words made it clear just how ridiculous he found them.

"The doors we just passed" — Dent-Head gestured, indicating a row of ten wooden doors with maybe four feet between them — "lead into small cubicles with a second door that opens into the main intake hallway. You will each enter a cubicle, one at a time. Whether you come out on the other side is up to you. Inside, you will be offered a small black pill by the trade name Remulin. Here at Union Station, we call it 'Fly and Die.' Accept this pill, and a third door will open to a short slide that will shuttle you to a room underneath us. In that room, under the kind hand of Fly and Die and in more comfort than this officer feels you deserve, sixty minutes of euphoria will precede a painless death."

"Why do we have to go into a closet to take a pill?" asked a balding man down the line.

"Are you religious?"

The man didn't seem to know what to make of the question. "N-no."

"Then no reason. But for those of you who are so inclined, there is a single button on the wall. Press it, and a door will open to an adjacent cubicle where a member of the nondenominational clergy will discuss your choice, should you desire. Ignore the button and walk out the door on the backside if you wish to start serving your sentence, or accept the pill and make your way downstairs without council. There is a strict limit of five minutes with the clergy. Anything that happens inside the cubicles is confidential. You are not to discuss your time or ask others about theirs. Anonymity will be strictly enforced. Do you understand?"

He saw a wave of nods, though this was the first Mason was hearing about a suicide pill — and, for that matter, a last-ditch chance for clergy. One more dirty side to the already controversial HRO system Revival had managed to mostly silence.

The balding man spoke again. "What about Chamber Therapy?"

Dent-Head stared at him, apparently unused to fielding Q&A. But most of the room must have been wondering the same thing. "What about it?"

"Well, we won't be inside for our entire lives if we go through Chamber Therapy, right? We could, you know, be rehabbed or whatever."

Dent-Head nodded. "That is the case, but as you saw in the orientation video, this facility's population is large, and its capacity for Chamber Therapy is limited. Whether you decide to play the odds is up to you."

"Can we hang onto the … the black pill and see if we need it later?"

"Negative. But rest assured, once in, killing yourself will be easy enough, should you choose to do so after entering the prison. It will, however, be significantly more painful." He waved. "Form a single line, then enter the first available door, indicated by the green light mounted on the wall above."

The line shuffled toward a second guard. Mason's restraints tugged as they tightened in front of the doors, then they relaxed. The new guard began unlocking chains, starting with the woman in front. She entered the leftmost door, followed by the others at the front until they were full.

"Fun times," Frank called back, now a dozen inmates in front of Mason.

Mason, who felt his stability tipping, wasn't so sure.

SIX

Perception is a Choice

MASON TURNED THE DOORKNOB.

It was loose in the socket and rattled with the jangle of screws.

He entered what looked like an ad-hoc confessional. The door closed of its own accord, and once inside, Mason — not Catholic or used to the cramp of God's tiny spaces — felt a surge of claustrophobia. There was a padded kneeler on the floor to his left and a utilitarian sliding panel, now closed, above it. The button mentioned by Dent-Head was beside the panel. There was a Dixie cup at its bottom edge with a single black pill inside. The cup was on a tiny conveyor, with an even smaller panel on the sidewall behind it. Presumably, the booth cycled empty cups and new pills between supplicants.

Mason looked at the pill, picked up the cup, then shook it into his palm without knowing why. The pill was coated, like candy.

It could all be over.

But no. He had a job to do.

Mason regarded the pill a final time before dropping it into a slot marked *trash*.

The door was locked, so he tried again. Turned, but still nothing.

So Mason faced the entrance, figuring he'd give them a surprise by coming back the wrong way. But that door was locked as well.

The wall panel rose. A silhouette sat behind a loosely woven square of lattice in the adjacent cubicle, sideways to Mason.

"So," said the priest. "What' choo wanna talk about?"

"I didn't press the button."

"You did."

"Sorry. I don't need to talk. I'm ready to go, but the door's locked."

"Is it? Now that ain't right."

The man's tone was wrong. And … familiar. Mason tried to make him out, but the adjoining cubicle was dark and barely lit. He could see the shape of the other man's big bald head.

"Can you let me out?"

"Sure I can't."

"I'm not taking the pill."

"Why not? Too scared? You'd be doin' yourself a favor. Lord knows what's waitin' for you inside."

Mason squinted. The man was wearing earrings — big, dangly hoops — but he still couldn't make out any of his features.

"Nice pep talk."

"I ain't here to coddle you."

Mason was still squinting. Listening. Turning on all those fine-tuned cop senses. "Do I know you?"

"Dunno. Do you?"

"Are you a priest?"

"If I was, maybe I give you last rights. 'Woe to those who call evil good and good evil, who put darkness for light and light for darkness, who put bitter for sweet and sweet for bitter.'"

"What the hell are you talking about?"

"Means you's fucked up, *Mista Shaw.* Means when God comes before you to bargain, you ain't seein' *shit* of it."

Mason tried the handle again. "Let me out of here."

"I ain't heard your confession."

"I'm not offering one. I didn't even touch the goddamn button."

The man's basso voice swelled in volume, suddenly stern. *"Do not use the name of the Lord in vain! This is the house of God!"*

"Yeah. Okay." Mason, feeling agitation he couldn't name or explain, turned from the silhouette and toward the door. He wrenched the knob, heaving into it with his shoulder.

But of course, the construction only *looked* fragile and antique. It was still a prison door, reinforced accordingly. Inside the ancient moldings were hardened deadbolts on solenoids, operated electronically like cellblock doors.

"Tell me about your mother. What about her makes you wanna die?"

"Let me out."

"First, you tell me about your motherfuckin' mama."

Mason banged on the door. Then shouted when nobody came.

"Funny thing. I'll bet if she'd been goin' for groceries alone, that other car wouldn'ta T-boned her ass. Logan drivin', Mama dyin'.' Course, I guess Logan got it, too." His tone fell in faux sympathy. "How'd that make your ass *feel*?"

"Who the fuck are you?"

"You don't know?"

Mason turned his assault from the door to the mesh. He slammed his face and hands against it, but the wicker look was only for show. It was plenty sturdy, wood ornaments probably cored with steel. So, he tried to peer in.

The man laughed and moved toward the corner, his silhouette now more visible. He was large, and very bald.

"Open up, and we'll talk like men."

"Now tell me about your daddy," he said, ignoring Mason.

"Fuck you."

"Fuck me? Fuck *your daddy!*" Another laugh, more gleeful. "What did you think when he went after Kindly Old Mr. Blake?"

Mason rattled the mesh, making a racket, finding it impossible to believe nobody heard or came running. The chambers might be soundproof. Made sense if they were built for confession.

Unfazed, the priest-man spoke again. "Did you know his little break-in was comin'? Were you surprised when they sentenced him here, and he didn't even fight it? Did you testify? Or did you figure fuck the old man, let 'im rot?"

Mason banged his fist against the mesh.

"You ever wonder how it was for yer daddy? How long he lasted' fore karma caught up wit him?"

"Come over where I can see you."

The big man went on as if Mason hadn't spoken. "If only there was a way for you to see what he saw, so's you know what he knew. 'Course, what will *she* think when she finds out you here?"

"Who?"

"Who you think?"

Mason kicked the door. He shouted, but the priest-man only laughed.

"You know what happens next, Mason Shaw? You remember?"

"What the fuck are you talking about?"

"So, you *don't* remember." He made a *tsk tsk* sound as if Mason were naughty. "What about Calliope?"

"What about him?"

"When Calliope ring, you gonna have no choice but to answer. But no matter what bitches say, Calliope don't know everything. Gonna want it from you, and you gonna wanna give it, but you ain't really got what you gonna be asked for — and what you *ain't* asked for, you best learn not to give. You not the right man, Mason Shaw. You think you is, but there's one big thing you ain't figured out just yet. You dig?"

Mason didn't *dig* one iota, but he wasn't about to be bested that easily. He squared his shoulders and barked at the man like a cop would if the officer were still in charge.

"*What* does Calliope want?"

The big man finally leaned forward, displaying a sideways grin — the kind that laughed *at* Mason rather than with him. Now that he could see, the man was still only vaguely familiar. Any memory Mason had was buried in fog. Muscular, but not lean. Broad-shouldered, a bit like a genie, or maybe Mr. Clean.

He tapped his bald head. "It's in here. And to say it, you ain't even gotta open your mouth."

Mason stared, unsure what else to do. Nobody could hear his shouts. Nobody could feel his pounding or kicking. Wasn't his time in the cubicle up by now? Shouldn't they come in and get him?

"Problem is you can't trust yer eyes, or yer ears. I seen the scans they done on you. Sometimes, you can't even trust yer *mind*. Yer head's in the clouds, Mason Shaw. You think you down with yer feet flat like all the others, but you and yer daddy're both flyin' high."

"My father is dead."

"But he ain't use ta be."

Mason lowered his tone, maybe starting to understand. He was seeing the situation wrong, not approaching this strange interloper in the proper way.

"Did you know him? When he was here, did you talk to him? Did the two of you … have an *arrangement?*"

"Tell you what," said the big man, still leaning forward. "'Stead of givin' it to Calliope, maybe you give it to me."

"Give *what* to you?"

"You *angry*, Mason Shaw?"

"I'm not playing this game with you anymore." Mason banged the door again, but this time a buzzer sounded, and the red numerals of a digital clock appeared above the panel door. Sixty seconds remaining.

"Time's almost up," said the big man.

Mason grabbed the partition harder, agitated for reasons he could barely understand. Parasites tunneled inside his mind, inside his body. They seized and squeezed his heart. Crushed it. Something had pulled all his triggers. He didn't understand this reaction, and it didn't feel like his own. Instead, it felt somehow handed down from above, tweaking nerves and synapses into frightening new configurations.

Panic came. Mason's fingers were through the mesh, pulling and rattling, trying to bring it down.

"That's it. Make a scene. Get it all out now, so you cain't serve it up later."

Fear turned into anger. Nobody riled Mason Shaw. Never. "Come out of there, and we can talk about this face to face."

"It ain't time for that yet. I ain't got my shit in order."

Face to the wicker, Mason panted for breath. Bringing down the partition and shutting the mouth of his strangely familiar abuser was suddenly essential.

The man in the shadows leaped forward. He grabbed at Mason's fingers, where they came through the mesh. A knuckle popped. Then another. Mason wanted to shout in pain but refused to give him satisfaction.

"You *see things*, Mason Shaw?"

"What the fuck do you want from me?"

"You *hear* things?"

Mason wrenched back, trying to free his fingers.

But the other man held tight, bending them in ways they weren't meant to go. "You *believe* things, Detective?"

Mason used the only implement at his disposal and slammed his head into the mesh, aiming for the spot where the priest man's head was touching it.

Blinding pain, blurred vision, and a chuckle from the other side were his instant rewards.

"Because that's the funny thing I've found. What you want to see? That's what you see — whether it's what you'd ever *think* you'd want or not."

"What are you talking about?"

"You pick up what someone else lays down, but in the end, perception is a choice."

"Let go of—"

But the cubicle was gone.

And so was the other man.

The world was white all around him.

No walls, ceiling, or door.

Even the floor had gone missing.

In this void, there was but one imperfection — a tiny black dot, far in the distance.

Mason blinked, then the white was gone.

He was back in the cubicle. His hands were no longer through the mesh, and he was now slumped and paralyzed in the closet's corner. The partition was still raised but without a man behind it.

And … a noise. A buzzer.

Time's up, baby.

The door opened.

Mason had been sideways against it. His limp form flopped to the deck. He rolled onto his back. People gathered above him. The balding man who'd asked questions — Frank. Other inmates, already through, none knocked flat by what they found inside.

He scoped their eyes, disoriented and lightheaded.

Then he realized they all thought he'd swallowed the pill. Why else would he be on the floor?

The circle parted above him, and Dent-Head peered down at his body. "You need a medic, Shaw?"

Mason said, "No."

But *man*, did he have a headache.

SEVEN

Watching. Waiting. Thinking

MASON WAS SITTING in a rattling seat, watching the depressing scenery roll by and rubbing his head.

It was afternoon by the time their processing and orientation were over. They were finally heading into the prison.

Even if Mason hadn't been sentenced, he would have found the place sad. The Union Station Human Restoration Outpost was the size of … well, of Union Station, which according to Mason's post-Carter research, had been around fifty square miles. Before decay and renewal, the place had boasted a population of just under a quarter million. Now it only had about twenty-thousand, which made the place feel like a ghost town.

Time and absence demanded their tax. A decade of ocean spray had corroded signs and buildings and cars that sat on blocks without anyone to tend them. It was amazing how quickly a city could go to shit when nobody patched the roads, cleaned the litter, painted, mowed the grass, or took pride enough to keep the elements at bay. Ten years ago, Union Station reminded Californians of Long Beach around the turn of the millennium. Now, it looked ready for the wrecking ball.

Mason's seat puffed up as someone plopped beside him.

"Hey," Frank said. "Lower the window."

"The windows don't go down."

"You have to squeeze those little tabs at the top," Frank said, prepared to climb over and demonstrate.

Mason stopped him. "They made some changes since this was a school bus." He'd tried the window because the bus was hot as hell, and it wasn't a hot day. It was as if they'd heated it up solely for psychological torture.

Frank sat back. The too-tall seat-backs obscured the people ahead of them. No one was cuffed. The bus was AI-driven, so there were no innocents for the inmates to harm. And if they wanted to kill each other on the bus, how was that any different than killing each other once they got off it?

"Why don't school busses have seatbelts?"

"You always have such interesting questions." Half his queries struck Mason as the developmental journey of a racist toddler. It was actually kind of hard to hate his bigotry when he inquired about Jewish money-handling or Asian driving with such wide-eyed curiosity.

Mason returned his gaze to the window when Frank seemed unsure of how to respond.

It looked like a bomb of indifference and propaganda had exploded from whatever ground zero they were headed toward. Mason didn't see a single pane of glass, even in the highest windows. Either it was valuable here, or the inmates were compulsive and bored, breaking things just to break them. There were also no doorknobs along the route — no push bars or pull handles, no ornamentation or hardware of any kind. A decade had warped the once-handsome community into a decrepit minimalist nightmare.

Only the posters looked fresh. *Those* the HRO kept current. *Those* were replaced when they ripped. Maybe drones did the work, but posters were everywhere, like an advertisement for obedience or a public gallery for the city's only artist. Some were framed behind Lexan and others mop-plastered on towering walls — grids that ran twenty across and ten high, all in that same bold style of black, white, and a different accent color for each, but always a *bold* color. Hard lines. Stern-faced men and women. Looking at them gave Mason a chill.

"I *do* ask interesting questions," said Frank.

Twenty seconds passed in silence. Mason had time to wonder if he might finally stop yammering.

"So, *did* you see a medic?" Frank asked when time was up.

Mason stopped counting seconds but couldn't quit sighing.

He'd been told to say yes, so he did.

"Did you pass out or what?"

Mason hadn't been coached to answer that question, but the first rule of prison was to never look weak. That's why Frank, who couldn't win a fight with a toothpick, kept mouthing off about the biggest and baddest guy he was going to find and destroy because movie clichés had been his teacher. Mason looked like a little bitch, falling from his confessional after having fainted … or whatever had happened. The whole thing felt like a dream and thus crumbled when inspected. Memory was fucking with him.

He seemed to recall someone in the space with him. A … *priest?*

And arguing, not being able to escape.

Banging on the door. Something with his fingers and the wicker grate.

The harder Mason concentrated, the more his strange memory kept slipping away.

"No, it wasn't really passing out. I got a—" Suddenly, Mason had an idea. "Migraine."

"You see a doc back home for that?"

Mason shook his head. He wasn't lying about his headache. It hurt like a motherfucker.

"Then why did they take you to a medic?"

"Prison policy," Mason responded.

"It's prison policy to take you in for a headache?"

"Don't ask me to explain it." Mason searched for something else but came up empty. He didn't like looking like a victim, even to Frank. Maybe he'd tell them he collapsed from exhaustion after committing too many murders the day before. And when the doctor took him in for his checkup, Mason had bent her over the desk and fucked her. Up the butt. She loved it so much she couldn't stop screaming for more. The meatheads in prison would love that one.

But he couldn't feed Frank that load of shit with a straight face, so he chewed on his lip instead.

"Oh." Frank shrugged.

Mason turned back to the scenery, relieved. Maybe that would be the end of it.

His hand went to his forehead. They'd given him some sort of nanotech-infused vasodilator for the headache no one could explain, but it wasn't working. He'd tried closing his eyes but got flashes of an unwelcome something-or-other whenever he did.

Sometimes he recalled conversations with his father.

Sometimes it felt like Carter was right beside him as if the headache was in his father's head and Mason's soul was only visiting.

Sometimes he remembered chats with his brother Logan.

Sometimes he saw a white space rather than the muted red of the backs of his eyelids.

And sometimes — increasingly, now — Mason had flashbacks to the crime that put him here. He felt … it wasn't guilt. He was sure of that much. But it was obsessive. And sort of uncontrolled. Like maybe someone who was—

You need to find distractions, Dakota had said of his repetitive thoughts. *When you don't want to think about what keeps coming to mind, you can't just tell yourself not to think of it. You can't say, "Don't think of a pink elephant." You need to think of a blue one instead.*

As if Mason wasn't aware. Replacing one thought with another had been Carter's trick. They'd even used it together when times were bad, back when their relationship had still been good.

"You know …" Frank started.

Mason was supposed to wait with bated breath to hear its end, but instead, he was only annoyed.

"Know *what,* Frank?"

"Some people think you went with that doc to snitch on us."

"Interesting. Are any of those people sitting beside me right now?"

"Hey. I had your back. I defended you."

"So, *you* didn't go in to snitch on *me?*" Mason thought of the personal details Frank had wormed out of him, wondering if any might have been a mistake to tell.

"Why would I do that? I got a whole prison to snitch in."

"Chits are chits, no matter where you earn them. Maybe you wanted to rat me out early. Earn a few chits before getting inside. Cash 'em in early. Maybe have a nice steak dinner waiting at your bunk."

Frank considered, apparently weighing Mason's intention. "Fuck you, man."

"And fuck you harder."

"So, you *did* just go in because you fainted."

"I *fell.* And I told you, I didn't 'go in.' It's policy. They *made* me go." Mason kept wanting to bring up the strange priest — the one who, as memories eked back, he seemed to recall more and more.

The priest had … *done something* to him. Mason didn't know what or at least didn't want to say. In the end, it didn't matter. There'd *been* no priest. The cubicle next to his had been empty. No big bald white guy at all.

"Sure. Fine."

Mason eyed Frank to see if he was being sarcastic, but the man was looking away. He could be a smartass all he wanted if it meant keeping his damn mouth shut.

Conversation died as the bus slowed. They'd arrived at a cleared circle large enough for a helicopter to land, hulks of decrepit metal and garbage piled in a dune around its circumference. The area was bereft of buildings for fifty yards or so in every direction as if it had once been a tiny park. The area's lone structure was a large utility garage that probably housed the bulldozer used to keep this bus stop clean.

Mason followed the plodding others onto concrete in the midday sun. The air reeked of petroleum and rotting trash. Drones buzzed by in the distance. Buildings farther out were full of glassless windows and housed inmates who stared down on them as they found their bearings. The bus would drive off once they'd disembarked, then at that point, the buildings might stop seeming so empty. Most prisoners staked out personal spots as reclaimed apartments. Not to sleep, of course. That happened at the crib. But to hide out during the day. Or so he'd learned in orientation.

Some were above them now. Watching. Waiting. Thinking, *Fresh meat.*

The door of the bus closed. Its wheels began to turn, then they were alone.

Mason took it in. *Tried* to take it in.

He walked away from the others toward the storage garage. Once next to it, he found the side had been covered with posters, all of a single image repeated over and over like dots on a grid.

Black, white, and robin's egg blue, portraying a stylized man with a knife handle protruding from between his shoulder blades. A woman stood above him, distorted by perspective, blood on her hands and a Cheshire grin on her face.

The message in big, bold, white-on-black type read:

Stabbed In The Back

Beats Stabbed In The Front

The image sent chills down Mason's spine.

Yeah. That's about right.

EIGHT

It Must Have Been the Drugs

MASON MADE a loop of the utility garage out of a compulsion he couldn't explain, inspecting every reachable surface and looking for windows to peek through. There were none. The thing appeared to be made of corrugated aluminum, but Mason felt something much firmer when he rapped his knuckles on it. Maybe there was steel inside the walls. Wouldn't want inmates joyriding on the tractor inside.

By the time he came around the other side, the converted school bus was gone, along with the other inmates. Curious, since there had been dozens before the landscape absorbed them like water in arid soil. How long had he been circling that garage, inspecting every nail and rivet as if they were keys to the questions that plagued him?

And was it his imagination, or did the sun look a lot lower in the sky?

Mason stumbled back into the opening. His legs were half-numb, and it took a while to feel upright and whole. His gaze returned to the sun. No. He was just on edge. It had to be his imagination.

But even that didn't sit right. Mason was a cop. A *good* cop. The nerves and superstition not trained out of him had frozen from exposure. His eyes were sharp and had always been. As a rookie, he'd noticed a loose floorboard and turned a dead-end into a sizable drug bust, earning early respect and an unofficial collar. That investigator's instinct had always trumped his fear.

This wasn't nervous behavior. Mason wasn't exactly comfortable and secure standing in the middle of the most notorious of Revival's city-prisons, but that wasn't why he saw the light differently. Something had changed.

The landscape was open. There wasn't a single place for attackers to hide, not for fifty yards in any direction. No drones in the sky or troubling heads peering through distant windows. Inmates must know this was the newbie drop-off spot. They should be haunting the place with drooling lips.

Mason walked back to the cleared area bunkered by drifts of trash, eyes moving and senses on high alert. He stopped. Wondered. Waited for the something-wrong-with-this-picture to rear its head.

Then he had it.

It was significantly cooler now.

Because …

He scratched his head, squinting.

… because they'd been dropped off in bright sunlight, but now he stood in the shade.

Shit.

He glanced around then trotted off, staying low — no point in trying to hide — aiming for the group of buildings to the west, holding a hand high to block the sun. After scanning the area, he failed to see what he wanted and swore.

Then he went deeper. Into the first proper alley, then the second.

Finally, five or ten minutes later, Mason found what he'd been seeking inside a graffiti-strewn parking garage — a snitch kiosk. Bright red for easy visibility, chest-tall, shaped like a six-by-six post with a pyramid on top. In the middle of one of its sloping sides was a rectangular touchscreen covered with a transparent composite, supposedly bulletproof.

He stared down at the thing, trying to remember what their guides had said during orientation. Mason hadn't paid much attention. He wouldn't snitch, even if tattling on other inmates was the coin of this realm. Cribs provided breakfast, dinner, and a place to sleep. Mason could fend for lunch or go without, and he'd never been one for creature comforts. He planned to ignore kiosks like this one, which were apparently everywhere.

He tapped the screen. Nothing.

Then, remembering, Mason pressed his fingertip to the side. It brightened as it read the tracker they'd added to his blood. The *dongle* that would be in him forever, clinging to his reds like a dog on a leash.

The screen displayed his name, prisoner number, chit balance — zero, and the time — 5:13 p.m.

Mason looked back through the alleyway's mouth. A sliver of the drop-off circle was still visible.

"Bullshit," he said aloud.

Because Mason was quite sure it hadn't been later than one o'clock when the bus had unloaded. Maybe two, if he lost track of time, but absolutely no later than that.

"I knew you was a rat."

Mason knew who he'd see once he turned, just by the timbre of voice.

It was the big man from earlier — the one with the bald head, who he'd last seen impersonating a priest. The one who'd grabbed his fingers through the mesh and maybe, somehow, done something to mess with his equilibrium and vision.

The big man who wasn't supposed to be here — and, Mason was quite sure — *hadn't* been just moments ago.

He tensed his muscles until they were as tight as a coil spring, then spun around and unleashed everything at once.

Mid-punch, a flashbulb exploded in his head.

Mason blinked, distracted, that oh-so-promising punch connecting with nothing.

The man seized his throat, his hand big enough to palm a basketball, almost enough for his thumb and middle finger to touch on the other side. He squeezed, a walnut-crushing grip that could flatten his trachea like a toilet paper tube.

"I … I don't have anything," Mason croaked.

"Oh, that ain't true." Now that the man was front-on, Mason could really see him. Sweat glistened from the pores on his scalp. He was at least six-six, probably more. Two hundred eighty pounds if an ounce.

"What the hell do you want?" Mason managed to say.

"Clarity."

Despite the strangling, Mason's features scrunched into a pose of incredulity. "What?"

"What they figured he had. What maybe you have."

"Look, I don't know what anyone told you about—"

Mason stopped when the big man lifted him with one arm and left him dangling above the concrete, kicking into the air while his assailant wore the disaffected expression of someone holding a glass.

"Does it make you angry?" the big man asked.

"Does what?" The word came out like the rasp of a scraper along a Güiro.

"Anywhat. Anyhow."

"I don't know what you're talking about!"

He peered into Mason's eyes — deep, as if trying to see the back of his skull. Then he suddenly let go. Mason hit the ground, looked up. Wheezed.

His attacker watched. Waited.

Does it make you angry?

Mason rubbed his neck, desperate for breath.

"You don't, does you?" His head cocked, considering. "At least … not yet."

The world dissolved into a pure white void. An ebony dot to one side marred the emptiness on a distant wall.

"See?" said the giant's disembodied voice. "Home's home. Your bed's already made."

Mason felt an explosive sense of acceleration, like being flung from a slingshot.

The dot magnified as he hurtled toward it. It became the size of a plate, an umbrella, the moon. It would eclipse him in seconds.

Far in the distance, he heard his mother's voice. His mind's eye saw his grandmother's kitchen. Then both sensations disappeared, and he was back on the alley concrete.

The giant was gone.

He rushed to his feet, staggered, then was struck sidelong with a hard and wooden something.

Pain exploded. Mason tripped over his own feet then fell into what seemed to be trash, phantasmal spots from near-asphyxia still peppering his vision. Through the haze, he saw two men and a woman fighting with another person who seemed to be taking on all three — this one like a drowned rat.

The little man fighting solo — buzz cut, short, frame like a praying mantis — seemed to have taken the others by surprise. Spry and wily, he dodged their unprepared and ineffective blows. Mason blacked out halfway, still trying hard to pull breath through his smashed throat.

The mantis man stood over him with gigantic bug eyes, and Mason understood. The two men and the woman had tried to blindside him. The man above had come from the shadows and chased them away.

"Nic?" Mason croaked.

"You all right, man?" His voice was nasal, tidy, and clipped. "I thought they'd choked you to death."

"They?"

Mason wanted to correct him. Two average men and a woman hadn't choked him. It'd been one big man who vanished in a blink for the second time.

You're confused, he told himself. *Intake made you woozy. Or it was something Dakota's people injected you with. It must have been drugs. You also thought the bus dropped you hours earlier than it did. You're disoriented and …*

He didn't finish the thought.

Mason cleared his throat and winced at the pain. "I'm okay."

"You're okay," Nic repeated, "so I guess now we're even."

NINE

Red Crib

NICHOLAS COREANDER. Petty robbery, assault, public indecency of at least ten separate counts on ten separate occasions. One-time heroin dealer, more because he'd gotten a few grams of the stuff through sideways means than having any intention of selling it. The drugs were payment from a regular who'd been short on cash but wanted a blowjob anyway, according to Nic.

Handcuffed in the back seat of the cruiser — more conversation than confession — he'd said, *You know how much a half-ounce of H goes for? That dumbass gave me, like, a grand to lick his tip, and I didn't even have to swallow.*

That had happened just as the last of the SoCal prisons were closing in favor of HROs. *Prisons don't rehabilitate, but HROs do.* Or so the pundits had said. The truth that less than one percent were ever rehabbed was lost in translation and never discussed.

Nic's single dalliance with narcotics earned him a life sentence because that's all there was. His normal crimes were wrist-slaps, but heroin was the final strike. There was more than enough to put him away for good.

To Mason, Logan, and Carter, all of whom had used Nic as a source for years, it was too much. Logan and Carter had tried to bribe Nic's way out so they could keep using his intel to make questionable, excessive-force busts. Mason took a more idealistic stance. After the whole thing fell apart because, of course, Nic was going away — they'd all forgotten about the time he'd exposed himself to a playground full of kids — only Mason soldiered on.

If he couldn't help Nic, then at least Mason could persuade his brother and father to help Nic's brother, sister, and aunt, all of whom had been part of the same amateur-hour syndicate. And so Carter, before he'd been arrested and carted off to the very same HRO, urged Nic to claim his family's crimes. Life was life. They couldn't put him away for longer than that. Logan had washed away the trail from the USPD side, and nobody else got sent up the river. Mason's contribution, seeing as he was still the Golden Boy, was to accept it all without making waves.

Three years since Mason had seen his bug eyes, now here he was again. Nic always seemed to feel he owed the Shaws for saving his people from the slammer, despite him getting sent to the HRO. Now they were even.

"How the hell did you find me?" Mason asked as they walked, forcing the words out of his throbbing throat as he turned to look back at the alley where he otherwise might have been beaten, robbed, raped, or murdered. "Did you know I was coming?"

Nic shook his head. They were a few blocks on, and Mason, with nowhere more sensible to be, had followed his guide without question. At least Nic wasn't a total mystery, and he knew the HRO.

"No. Of course not. How the hell would I know anything like that?"

"You took on three people at exactly the right time." Mason considered, took a breath, then went ahead with the rest. "I hate to say it, but you kind of saved my ass."

Nic didn't look over. "Kind of?"

Mason grunted.

Nic, never one to stay silent, went on even without the thank you that Mason was reluctant to give.

"I was there to punish them, not help you." He shrugged. "They owed me for some … *services* … but didn't pay."

"'How do they pay in here?"

"Snitch chits and a barter economy."

"You can transfer chits?"

"There are people that handle that kind of thing."

Mason was curious but didn't ask.

"You have to stand up for yourself in here, or else you become someone's bitch." Nic sniffed, wiped his nose with a sleeve, then readjusted his windbreaker. Swag from a celebrity golf tournament thirty years ago. "Look, man. I'm just doing my part."

"I know. I get it. We're even now."

"Not 'my part' with you. Jesus. The whole world doesn't revolve around you, man. And, you know, I hear things. Even from the outside." He looked right at Mason. "Not everything's a goddamn conspiracy."

"I know. That's why my father and I never saw eye to eye."

Nic's brow lowered, an awning for his eyes. *"Oookay."*

"I was good to you."

"Okay. Sure." Nic laughed.

"I stood up for you when—"

Nic raised a hand to cut him off. "Ancient history. Me and you, we got a clean slate now. You didn't fuck with me, and I didn't fuck with you. Pretend we're just meeting." He extended a hand. "Hi. I'm Nic."

Mason looked at the hand, knowing how much time they spent around things he didn't want to touch. "What did you mean by 'doing your part'?"

Nic stopped walking, looked around, then, in a lower voice, said, "You know about Chamber Therapy, right?"

"Of course."

"You know sometimes it goes wrong? They call it—"

"Pattern Black. I know." That was what had been on the release the HRO sent him, for Carter, as the cause of death, more or less. Mason was familiar with the term, one of the larger snowballs in

Carter's obsessive *Revival and HRO and Nathaniel Blake and Elisabeth Reeves* avalanche.

Supposedly, "going Pattern Black" was like slipping into sleep without ever waking up. Less of a coma and more a pit without any bottom. If the upside of successful Chamber Therapy was rehab and release, but the downside of its failure was Pattern Black, Mason wasn't interested. He'd been slightly obsessed for months. Supposedly those with "abnormal psychologies" were at higher risk and therefore supposed to steer clear of Chamber Therapy. What Mason and Carter shared would have struck those in charge as plenty *abnormal* if they hadn't hidden it so well.

So why had Carter opted for Chamber Therapy? He didn't have to enter the abyss, didn't have to die — though technically, the form had told Mason HRO 22 would wait a full year to pull the plug. Dead would have been better, but his old man wasn't there yet.

Nic was nodding. "Right. There's a lot said about Pattern Black. Especially with what Immunity has to say."

"You know something about Immunity?"

"Not important right now." Nic waved it away. 'Point is, they couldn't do something as experimental as Chamber Therapy if we hadn't all been disowned by the state. They could throw us off buildings. HRO inmates are 'unpersons.'"

"What does any of that have to do with 'doing your part'?"

"It's a fucked-up system, man. Fucked up and not just a little bit out of control. Only the press keeps them from … I don't know … nuking us."

"Isn't that a little dramatic?"

"Oh. You'll see," Nic said, suddenly sounding like a sage. "You can't stick twenty thousand prisoners together with no rules and expect they'll all stay neatly in order and never cause problems. People improvise weapons all the time in here. There's a black market, so all sorts of illegal shit is smuggled in. The HRO knows it happens. They're not stupid, but they also know they can't control it or stop it — not with a prison city full of people used to breaking the rules and bucking the system. Rumor says there's a fail-safe. The bosses don't try to contain the chaos. They monitor instead. Only act when it becomes too much."

"What do they do if it gets too chaotic?"

"Rumors about that, too. You hear murmurs about a 'chaos alarm' that may be coming up; you do *your* part. No breaking the rules. No black market buys. No attempts at escape or taking shots at the drones." Then Nic stabbed a finger backward, indicating the alley where he'd settled his score. "And *don't* let some motherfuckers get away with unbalancing your books!"

"Not sure what that has to do with it," Mason said.

"Discord creates sides. Sides create tension. Tension creates war. And you know which side wins in a war here?"

Mason shook his head.

"*Everyone* loses."

Mason looked back to where Nic had pointed, chilled to the bone.

"You gonna eat that?" Nic asked.

The sudden change in topic gave Mason emotional whiplash. He looked where Nic was looking, surprised to see that he'd picked up an object, hands acting while his mind dallied elsewhere.

"I was just curious what it was." The Twinkie had looked like a tumor sitting atop a rusted-out car or like a policeman's cherry made of cake and filling. The thing was half-exploded inside the wrapper, either from impact or heat. Picking it up was a reflex. Never had it occurred to Mason that he should eat the thing.

"Gimmie," Nic said, grabbing.

"You're not going to … Okay. I guess that happened."

Nic licked white cream off his lips, then his fingers. It looked like he'd just finished servicing another satisfied customer. He spoke with his mouth still full, yellow and white like a running washing machine inside.

"They airdrop them. If I had to guess, it's like a sponsorship. Hostess is all like, 'We like prison, too!' and Revival is like, 'Well, then, give us money and drop that shit! Let them eat spongecake!'"

Mason could see little yellow blobs everywhere now, some more newly dropped than others. Scanning the scene was like watching time in reverse. To one side, the Twinkies looked pristine, but each tick to the right revealed cakes that looked like they'd been through a war. Feeling something underfoot, Mason glanced down to see the tip of his boot atop one so old, it'd off-gassed and inflated the package. Now it looked like a gray, pill-shaped pimple jammed with pus.

"Why Twinkies?"

"Probably because they don't need parachutes to keep them from smashing and because they last a thousand years in the open air. Hey, what crib you in?"

Mason scraped the bottom of his boot against the corner of a building. Apparently, old Twinkie was like dog shit. "Red."

"Me too. That's cool. You want to fuck a guy, I'm down. No charge."

"No thanks."

Nic shrugged. Then he pointed. "This is it."

Mason looked up. There wasn't much chance of misidentifying where they'd ended up. The building was fire-engine red, like the snitch kiosks. From the ground, Mason could see giant spotlights with red gels covering the roof. A huge sign on the front identified the place — *RED CRIB*. Smaller signs posted curfew hours, and a spate of posters urged residents to *SNITCH AND GROW RICH*.

"Home shit home," Nic said.

"You don't have your own apartment?"

"'Course I do. But it's ..." Nic consulted a watch — surely earned with informant's chits. "It's like 6:15. Where else we gonna go?"

"I thought curfew wasn't until nine?"

"Yeah, but food's on now. What, you wanna live on Twinkies?"

Mason considered resisting because who went to the cell block before they had to? But his stomach rumbled, and he remembered that between drop-off and now, he'd somehow lost some hours.

"Fine."

"Me crib es su crib." Nic extended an arm like a mayor welcoming dignitaries.

Mason entered before him.

The crib looked like a converted school, or hospital, or ghetto church. It had long hallways that'd been painted puke green some indeterminate time ago and linoleum floors — tiles, not sheets, because every few paces, the corner of one was curling up. As with the buildings Mason had seen outside, there was no hardware on anything — no pulls on cabinets or knobs on doors. No slide locks on the windows. Drapes hung over the glassless frames, or what looked like painter's tarps in a few places, nailed or stapled down.

There were two TVs in the common room, both small considering the number of eyeballs they needed to cover. Roll-up flat screens, the kind glampers shoved into poster tubes then took into the woods, back before projection screens were decent. Many of the plastic chairs were vacant, but as they passed, Nic warned him away.

"Those are reserved. Every one of them."

Mason could make waves later if he needed to. Right now, there was no reason to pick fights over a show he probably didn't want to watch, anyway.

He squinted. "Is that … Are they watching *The Golden Girls?*"

Nic looked surprised. "Yes. The good news is some friends fabricated a juke out of scrap parts. Bad news is its core is an old digital video recorder, and the DVR's old owner was in love with really old shit. It's filled with *Golden Girls*. Oh, and *Mr. Destiny*. That's on a data card. It's terrible. You'll love it."

They continued down the long green hallway lined with fancy pew-like benches.

"Cafeteria." Nic pointed at a room with broken and dangling fluorescent fixtures — barely a functional space, let alone one that merited *dining* instead of plain old *eating*. "Offices. There's nothing worth stealing in them. I've checked, and so has literally everyone else. Showers and bathrooms are that way. And no, they're not co-ed. But! You'll like this. Wanna know the one good thing about security here?"

Mason shrugged.

"We have a shower drone. Two, actually — one for men and one for women. Upside is it stops butt rape. All rape, really. Downside is sometimes it just floats in the doorway, watching while you're washing your balls. Creepy. But for most people, it's better than a pole up the ass."

"Most people."

"Don't judge," Nic said.

They moved on. An elderly cackle came from the common room as they passed it again. Mason peeked in, saw gray heads involved in some sort of comic misunderstanding.

"You said 'friends' made the juke with all those old shows," Mason said.

"Right."

"*Friends*. Not *your* friend."

"They're not *my* friends."

"Whose friends are they?"

"I don't know. That's just what people told me."

"Seems like your 'friends' did some amazing shit, considering electronics are supposed to be contraband here, even on chits."

Nic flapped a dismissive hand. "Like I told you — barter economy and a thriving black market. You should see the weapons you can get if you know who to ask."

"*Weapons?*"

"You being a cop right now?" Nic raised his eyebrows.

"Just curious."

"Well, knock it off. You know what they say. Curiosity killed the kid."

"*Cat*. Curiosity killed the *cat*."

"What's the difference?"

They walked in silence, and Mason got the impression the correction had put him into a conversational holding pen. Maybe if he behaved for the next thirty seconds, Nic would talk to him again. No rush. The quiet was welcome.

"Bunks one through ninety-eight are in there." Nic pointed at a door. Mason wanted to peek, but his companion was already turning a corner. With the splinter of a glance, he could see the room wasn't a gym and hadn't looked large enough to hold a hundred beds.

"Did they give you your number?"

"Four twenty," Mason answered. It was too easy.

"Of course. That's where all the newbies go unless someone dies. Which is often. Problem is, sometimes people get hurt outside then come *here* to die. The cots always have blood and piss on them when that happens. If you got a shitty bunk instead of one that belonged to a dead guy, count your blessings."

Mason didn't reply.

"Far other end of the building," Nic said, changing direction. "Bad news is, my cot's nowhere near yours."

"How is that bad news?"

"All of the cribs are pretty safe. That's by *our* design, not *theirs*." Based on his gestures, Mason took *theirs* to mean prison administration and *ours* to mean rules made by prisoners themselves. "If you find or make a weapon, leave it somewhere else. Don't even think about bringing it here, even if you need it for protection." He made expansive motions with his arms. "This whole place is like 'base' in a game of Tag. *Be cool while inside the crib because everyone wants peace of mind to sleep at night.* That's like the only rule here. Start a fight, and you won't just have the guy you started it with to worry about. You got me?"

Mason nodded.

"Don't steal. Or try to rough anyone up. And don't mouth off, lest you want a gang waiting for you at the door when curfew ends. And definitely don't touch the women. Not only will a hundred guys line up to take their turn beating the shit out of you for getting too friendly, but most of the girls in here are also badasses. They're usually in gangs for protection, and the gangs improvise weapons faster than anyone else. They also teach all their members Systema. You know Systema?"

"No."

"Russian military fighting art. Want some advice? If you don't know Systema now, make it your goal *not* to. The other day, a girl — like, a hundred pounds with toothpick arms — yanked this guy's spine out."

"Bullshit."

"Okay, fine." Nic shrugged. "But she did get her fingers into his brain or something, like through his eyes. Or maybe she hit him really hard — I don't know. I wasn't there. I only know now all he can say is *hola*, and he's not even Mexican. What's he going to do with that? Do the hat dance all day while shouting it out?"

"I think you're thinking of *olé*."

"What's the difference?"

They walked on. The building wasn't large, but Nic seemed to be taking the scenic route. The Soviet-propaganda-style posters were everywhere — illustrated reminders to *REPORT YOUR NEIGHBORS* and *GET THEM BEFORE THEY GET YOU*. There was also a new design. No images and enormous newsboy text with smaller bullets below. He didn't have time to stop and read the list, but Mason saw the same headline repeated on each.

Immunity Is Not Immune
Report And Be Rewarded.

He assumed the text below the headline explained what it meant and why anyone reading the poster should care.

"Does Immunity cause many problems here?" Mason asked.

"What do you mean?"

"*Do they cause problems?* Do they ... I don't know." He thought of what Frank had said, bragging that Cousin Reggie was a bigger badass than the notorious Calliope. "Do they blow up buildings?"

"I dunno, man. Above my pay grade."

"I'd think a building blowing up would be in everyone's pay grade."

Nic stopped and turned toward Mason in the middle of the run-down hallway. A cockroach skittered by. He put his hands on his hips, squaring on Mason as if preparing for battle.

"Look, what do you want from me? I'm just doing my shit. You'd do yourself a favor in here if you'd just decide to do *your* shit. Why so nosy? Look at you. Asking about weapons. Asking about Immunity. What the fuck does it matter? *Why* is for the outside. *Why* is for cops. You're not a cop anymore, my friend. Now you're scum like the rest of us. So maybe stop with all the *why*. Worry about *what* and *who* instead."

"All right. What *about* who?"

"It's *whom*."

"It's actually not," Mason told him.

"You wanna know *about whom?* Whom's gonna kick your ass for looking at them the wrong way, that's whom you need to worry about. Whom is gonna be upset if you put your ass down in their TV chair. That's a *what*, by the way. You get what I'm sayin'?"

Mason did, but something inside still pushed against compliance. "Nic."

His jaw ticked.

"Why weren't you offered Chamber Therapy?" Mason asked.

"Did you really just fucking ask me another *why?*"

"Because I keep thinking, if you weren't 'off the record' by nature, you'd have earned the collar on at least fifty arrests in Union Station over the last few years. You have no shame. That's your superpower — a total and complete lack of dignity or self-respect."

"Thanks," Nic said.

"Now I'm here, and the city is nothing but inmates. No guards. The drones keep their distance. But you're still telling me to keep my mouth shut. To toe the line. Why? Bucking the system is your bread and butter. Dakota Ward, who runs intake here and I have to assume decides such things, used to be my partner. She of all people should know you're more valuable outside an HRO than inside, even if you're ratting out everyone and their mother from in here."

"And?"

"Why weren't you offered Chamber Therapy? They could have rehabbed and released you. Lesser informants have been."

"I've been here a while. Maybe my chance was before her time."

Mason nodded. Yes, that might actually be true. The HRO director before Dakota had been a walking rectum of a man named Anthony Diclez. Pronounced "dickless." His retirement was a sad day for jokes.

He met Nic's gaze. As usual, his story was missing an act. He'd probably made a mistake and been punished — cut off as an informant, left to rot in 22 as a punishment that exceeded his value.

Or he'd made another deal, and that deal was better than

Chamber Therapy. He might have bartered to living here in luxury — something Mason could confirm or deny if he got Nic to show him where he'd made his off-crib home.

"I guess that must be it." Mason held his gaze.

Then Nic moved on without him.

"Where are we going?"

Nic didn't look back. "To your cot."

Mason hoofed to catch up, and when he finally did, Nic had stopped at the open door of what was, this time, gymnasium-sized at least.

Rows and rows and rows of cots, single-bunk, lined with their railings touching like a battlefield triage ward. Five by five, and twenty-five cots per square with little room between them.

"Four twenty." Nic pointed at a grouping.

"Where?"

They walked closer.

"Lucky you," Nic said, trying not to smile and failing. "It's dead in the middle."

Mason's cot was in the third row of five in his cluster and in the third column of five. He couldn't get in or out without climbing over sleepers in adjacent beds.

Nic turned to go as Mason stared at his future. "I'm gonna grab dinner on my own. Got shit to do after."

"Oh. Okay."

"Have a good night, I guess."

Mason nodded.

But he didn't have a good night. Not even close.

TEN

Everything in Wireframe

MASON BLINKED.

The world swam around him. It was hard to focus, and nothing made sense. He was supposed to be in one place, or maybe somewhere else. His eyes insisted he was in neither. Or both.

Here and there clashed.

Same for right and wrong.

He felt a little drunk, unsure which end was up. Like a man inverted underwater.

But then, in the way of dreams, things began to make sense. The antique lightbulb across from him right now sort of made sense. The thing, full of spider-like filaments.

The world vibrated around him. Mason knew this place. Knew it all too well. Knew how it ended.

"Shaw. You paying attention?"

Cruz was directly across the van from Mason, snapping his fingers.

"Yeah," Mason said.

"You sure?"

"Yes, I'm goddamn sure."

"You look like shit."

Mason's sense of disorientation was gone. He cocked his thumb over his right shoulder at Watt sitting beside him.

"Shittier than this?"

Everyone laughed — even the thin woman with all the tattoos beside Cruz. Mason liked her, mainly because she detested him. Leigh was too good for him, even if she was about to rob a bank. The tension was hot as hell.

Only Watt refused to join the fun. "What the fuck?"

"Oh, lighten up," Buster said.

"Fuckface here insults me, and I'm just supposed to accept it?"

Cruz, in charge, answered the question. "Yeah. You're supposed to be a man and accept it."

"What's *that* supposed to mean?" Buster seemed agitated, but then again, they all were. *Nerves. Guns.* They'd be lucky if nobody died.

"Oh, lighten up," Watt threw back at Buster, and this time they both laughed.

Then it died, and tension returned to the void. Every big job was like the first time again. Nobody was cool, except maybe Cruz.

"You guys wanna hear a joke?" Watt asked.

"No," said Sasha, on Mason's left.

"Why did Buster cross the road?"

"Knock it off," Cruz said when Buster flexed to respond — with her mouth maybe, but fists more likely. "I want a clean job today."

"Clean how?" Sasha asked.

"Whatever you decide it means," Cruz answered. "I suggest you stick to the plan. Watch the corners once we're inside. Buster, you go left. Mason, you handle the guards on the right. Two, just like we said, standing by either side of the poster." He turned to Buster. "You handle the manager. Thin woman by the fat man. Until the jammer is set—"

"She can still set off the alarm," Mason interrupted.

Cruz stared at him.

"What? Just want to make sure I understand."

"What have I told you about pushing? What have I told you about trying to be in control?"

Mason looked away, annoyed.

Cruz turned to Leigh. "D'Abo. You watch the doors."

Instinct told Mason to grab his seat hard.

"Watt—"

The van hit a curb. The whole works rattled, but it seemed most everyone braced like Mason had.

Cruz reset and spoke again. "Watt, you handle the old lady."

"The old lady?"

He nodded. "Just do your part, and everything will be fine."

Mason clutched the automatic weapon on his lap then traced its extra-wide magazine. Maybe this was what Immunity weapons looked like.

A sudden headache bloomed. Mason grabbed the bridge of his nose. He opened his eyes again.

Cruz was looking at him.

"We have six minutes exactly. It's plenty of time. Pin the guards, watch the customers. And Sasha, you hit the vault. The manager has a key. She'll tell you she doesn't. The room is all white. If you see a grid, you've gone too far."

"*Grid?*" Mason repeated.

"Maybe I just shoot the manager and *take* the key," Sasha said.

"That's your choice." Cruz looked around the van, paused on the antique lightbulb, then ended on Sasha by the door. "Masks on."

Ski masks appeared from pockets and belts. Mason retrieved his then pulled it on, uneasy for a reason he couldn't explain. Something had skipped a beat and soured.

The van stopped. After someone opened the rear doors, the others spilled out. Mason grabbed the bridge of his nose again. As he rose to follow them, Cruz grabbed him by the arm.

"You okay, Shaw?"

"I'm fine."

"You can choose to stay. You won't get—"

"You knew my father, didn't you?" Mason interrupted.

His expression went from in-command to annoyed to confused. "What?"

"My father. Carter Shaw."

Confused became baffled or possibly circled back to annoyed. His forehead wrinkled, his brows like a sagging roof. The mood changed around them both.

"The fuck you talking about?" Cruz asked.

But suddenly, Mason didn't know either. His feeling flitted back into the aether. Before his breakdown, in his own crass way, Mason's father had been a genius. A deal maker, forever delving deeper to understand the criminal psyche.

"Never mind," Mason said.

"Maybe you should hang back. Sit this one out."

"I'm fine. Really."

"I wasn't kidding when I said you look like shit."

"It's just a headache."

Cruz seemed to weigh that, then nodded toward the door. Taking this as an okay, Mason hopped to the concrete as staccato reports boomed from inside the bank.

"Fucking Buster," said Cruz, turning to chase the gunshots.

Mason followed. Inside, the lobby was a mess.

Buster stood above an acre of face-down civilians like a gunslinger, smoke wafting from her barrel. Mason heard whimpers all around. Only one — a small blonde girl shielded by her mother — was outright crying. Buster's pops must have been either panic fire or a warning, some sort of chest-pounding to show the civvies who was boss. A spiderweb in the glass. But no blood, and no one dead or injured. Yet.

The little girl looked up at him. Mason looked away, unable to take it, toward the guards he was supposed to be watching. Neither of them had moved — *statues* of guards, it seemed, rather than flesh and blood. He thought they were being hardasses at first, but then he realized they were paralyzed with nerves.

Didn't they train these people? Didn't they steel them for situations just like this?

Mason raised his weapon. "Get down on the floor."

One guard looked at the other. An arm shifted, no longer truly hanging. The hand on that side was flexed, considering the gun.

The poster was like a third guard between them, only this one had an illustrated woman with spiked hair. She held a cartoon bomb with a lit fuse. The legend read, *FUCK THE SYSTEM.*

The guard's hand inched closer to his weapon, his attention focused solely on Mason. He knew the risk and seemed willing to bet Mason wouldn't shoot.

"Don't," Mason told him.

The guard looked at his partner. The hand moved again.

"I mean it. Take off the holster and toss it my way. Don't unsnap it, or you're dead."

Another glance. Cruz was watching him, about to speak.

Sasha stepped closer, her weapon raised.

She'll shoot him. You know how this ends.

The voice in his head was a fist made of syllables.

It was Mason's job to cover the guards. Fail in his responsibilities, people were bound to die — and if Sasha did his job for him, she'd do it with extreme prejudice.

Leigh's hands trembled as she covered the tellers. Buster swept the crowd, looking like she might snap at any second. Watt harassed an old woman with a walker who hadn't gotten to the floor as they'd commanded, probably because she couldn't.

Adrenaline was like rotting meat in the air.

"Time?" Mason asked without taking his eyes off the guard.

"Three-thirty," Cruz answered.

The room scrambled like an ancient TV on the fritz. Occupants vanished along with the bank itself. Suddenly Mason saw nothing. Then, in less than a second, everything was back to normal.

He pushed back a new surge of headache.

"Four-ten," Cruz said.

"Which is it? Four-ten or three-thirty?"

His tone dropped. "What the hell are you——?"

Movement caught Mason's eye. Cruz's too, maybe, because he stopped talking. They both glanced, and his skin prickled immediately, knowing his error.

He spun, but nobody was aiming at him. The first guard's hand was still at his side, considering the draw but still seconds away from it. The other had his big, beefy arms crossed. He was a big white fucker with gold hoop earrings, even though he'd been a skinny black fucker just a moment ago.

You're losing it. Just like your father.

Sasha came up beside him.

"I'll handle this," Mason said.

"He's faster than you'd think," Sasha replied.

A blast like cannon fire ripped the air beside Mason. Something wet spattered his arm. He spun back to find the enormous black guard holding a shotgun he seemed to have drawn from nowhere. The wall behind his partner was now a Pollock painting, and the guard who'd been reaching for his holster had become a man you could crawl through.

"He ain't fast no more." The guard racked his slide. A spent shell sprung from the shotgun's chamber.

Sasha, already aimed, fired first. Her strange weapon coughed, unleashing a spate of rounds, cutting a hole in the plaster behind the big man without hitting him once. Then she ran dry, even though the magazine looked large enough for fifty rounds or more.

Mason pulled his own trigger. Nothing happened.

The guard swung the shotgun to center on Mason's chest. "Yea, though I walk through the valley of the shadow of death, I shall fear no evil because I shall *fuck shit up.*"

Mason's hands shot skyward, his weapon left to hang on its strap. He slowed his breathing and willed his heart to stop racing. In his most soothing voice, he said, "Easy. *Easy.* Be cool."

"Oh, I'm cool as a motherfuckin' cucumber."

"You want me to put the gun down? Look. I'm putting it down." Mason reached for the strap, moving slow.

"I don't want you to put no fuckin' gun down." This guard wasn't even in uniform. He was wearing a black jacket with a black tee underneath. "What I want is for you to turn yer ass around."

"What?"

He jerked the shotgun's muzzle encouragingly. "Go on, now."

So, it was to be an execution. Buckshot in the back of the skull.

No way Mason was going out like that.

He'd started to turn, processing and planning, when Watt shouted and a fresh shot drew all the attention.

More screams. The man with the shotgun flicked his gaze toward the commotion … and as he did, Mason waited for his chance.

One, two, three. Move too early, he'll see it coming. Move too late, the window passes.

Three feet between them, the shotgun still aimed. Mason was patient, waiting for a softening of muscles. A shift in the big man's eyes that might present a gap through the hedges.

The shot came from a tiny pearl-handled pistol still clutched in the old woman's shaking hand.

Watt, caught off-guard, quickly recovered. There was a tiny pop as the old woman fired again while a muzzle flash lit the end of his weapon. Watt looked victorious for a half-second before realizing he'd fired too late. He spun, gripping his side. The old woman, who'd also been hit, collapsed like a coat slipping off a hook onto the closet floor.

Sasha and Buster turned toward the action. Cruz was distracted, and Leigh was too far away to interfere even if she wanted to.

The cop voice inside him said, *Now.*

Mason lunged and threw an elbow into his attacker's face. All his weight went into a single strike and only chance. His elbow didn't strike bone. His own mass didn't tumble into the superior but off-balance mass of the man in front of him. Instead, seemingly without traversing the space between upright and down, Mason hit the floor with enough force to rattle his teeth.

His lower jaw slammed upward, sending teeth through his tongue. Possibly *amputating* the thing.

He saw stars and tasted copper. Then three hundred pounds was on top of him, knees squeezing his kidneys.

A strong hand gripped the back of Mason's hair, tangling in the strands like a lover's embrace. The floor, a strip of baseboard, and the dead guard's bloody shoe filled Mason's field of view. He couldn't see the behemoth but felt his breath on one cheek. And he could smell the man — a curious combination of lavender and sweat.

"They gonna come knockin'," said the bandit on his back. It came out thick and heavy, like phlegm scraped from the back of his throat. "But' fore they do, maybe I come knockin' first. And maybe *then*, you know the truth."

"What truth?"

"Can't say. It's complicated."

"What truth!"

"Can't *say*, cuz rules rule the game." He moved into Mason's peripheral vision enough that he could see a gold tooth in the man's grin. "But they ain't thought of everything. In here, they ain't stopped me from *showin'*."

"What are you——?"

The floor was gone. So was the bank. Mason found himself peering into a void drawn by phantom pencils with dull lead. Dark grey on white. Everything in wireframe. Grids and lines. Spirals and gradients. Vision turned to nightmare. The whole world was a sketch as cold hands closed around his heart.

Mason was paralyzed, dropping fast into an M.C. Escher limbo.

A sound like gunshots came from nowhere.

A blur in his vision preceded a radio screeching static between frequencies.

Mason saw the void. The floor. The shotgun man, blood. Watt and all his companions, dead and stacked like firewood. Images came at him rapid-fire — bullets from a vision gun.

He felt himself rising. Up. Out. *Awakening*.

The last thing Mason saw was a gaunt woman with severe, hawk-like features and a translucent-blonde brush cut. His mind played a tune — a steam instrument, old and far away.

Then he blinked. The blitzkrieg of images faded, and the grids and spirals and mazes disappeared. His heart tried to slow but found itself unable.

The thin woman was suddenly above him, staring down. She

looked around and seemed to consider. Eventually, she reached for his forehead before touching her ear.

Her voice was the only sound left.

"Wait," she said, an unmistakable note of discovery in her voice. "I think this is …"

Mason wanted to ask if she was talking to him or someone else. But then she was gone, and so was he.

ELEVEN

100 Chits

MASON WOKE with a hand on his chest. Several seconds later, he realized it was his.

His respiration was slow and shallow, a breath or two above a corpse. His mind was scattered ashes, thoughts drifting without an anchor at the mercy of an invisible breeze.

He scanned the ceiling as he waited for the disorientation to abate. Ornate and peeling, once grand but now decrepit. The wait, while he studied that ceiling from another age, was unpleasant. Some part of Mason had forgotten he was in prison and would stare at the same ceiling every night until he died. Now the memory came flooding back in this pit of midnight. The only sounds were human breathing, bodies shifting, and occasional snores. Nothing to distract him or dilute his fear.

Mason felt trapped like someone shoved him in a jar and tightened the lid. It didn't matter that the prison sprawled across a city or that he bedded in an open gymnasium instead of a tiny little cell. Claustrophobia was still a hand on his throat.

He was having a panic attack. Like he used to have all the time but thought he'd left behind decades ago.

Breathe through it, Mason. It'll pass.

It was his father's voice, back when he'd felt like a father. Young Mason, small in his large bed, heart slamming against his ribs like a bird against the bars of its cage.

It only lasts a moment. Breathe through it. That's my boy.

Mason sat upright then swung his feet toward his cot's edge, eager to reach an open window. The muscles for dealing with an attack were still strong, despite years since his last one. Nothing was actually wrong. This was his body crying wolf.

His feet found the cot beside him instead of the floor.

The occupant was rolled away and tucked sideways, almost fetal.

Very carefully, Mason contorted his limbs to find tiny gaps between and over the five-wide cots, at one point clambering just above a sleeping woman in such a way that she'd scream rape if she woke and saw him.

He reached the edge without incident then stood tall in search of an exit.

There were no ground-level windows in the gym-turned-bunkroom. He headed for the hallway. The door to the first outside-facing room was ajar, so he entered and found it full of garbage bags. It couldn't be fresh because it didn't stink, or it was only paper and debris. Not a bad bedroom if he could find a way to sleep here.

The window was open, without glass or cover.

Mason swam toward the thing, shoving bags aside. When he reached the sash, he stuck his head into the cool night air and inhaled. Then, as his father had taught him, he counted through the fear.

Three seconds.

Five seconds.

Ten.

Slowly, he felt better.

After a minute at the sash, Mason turned to check the room. To his surprise, a bright red obelisk — six-by-six with a pyramid on top and a digital display on its front — was right next to him. The snitch kiosk had been buried in trash bags, and he'd unearthed it like Indiana Jones.

Mason's gaze darted around. He listened. No creatures stirring, no one waited in the hallway. Unsure of what he was doing or why he touched his thumb to the screen. It showed his name, followed by a menu of options.

Mason tapped *Chit Balance*. To his surprise, he had some.

BALANCE: 100 CHITS

Maybe Dakota had found a way to give him a leg-up after all. He sure hadn't earned them by finking.

Curious now, he backed out of the balance menu then chose *Store*.

He browsed an enormous breadth of items, all redeemable to those who'd earned their fair share of informant dollars. Looking through the bounty reminded Mason of a fundraiser from his middle school days. The entire campus had gathered in the gym to find the stage full of prizes from bikes to digital toys to a big ol' go-kart up front. Wrapping paper and popcorn for points. Nobody would ever sell enough to win the go-kart unless they brokered a deal with a department store at Christmastime. Still, Mason remembered salivating over all those shiny items, anyway. Same as every other kid had done.

And what had he learned at that assembly? *Do what they say, and you'll win prizes.*

Looking at the chit store now felt exactly the same.

Mason had expected most items to be necessities — better food, warmer clothing, medicines the on-site dispensary didn't provide. Instead, despite a small section boasting precisely that, most sale items were frivolous. Roll-up posters for your off-crib apartment. Hobby kits — models, paint-by-number, even a ship-in-a-bottle the size of an office water cooler. There were toys to rival Mason's dreamy go-kart, too. Zippy mopeds, scooters, even BMX bikes and skateboards for the action sports enthusiast. A large section was devoted to porn, but it was still slimmer than Mason would have imagined. No drugs or alcohol on offer because those were officially off-limits, but Nic had told him on the walk over that one faction distilled vodka using cafeteria potatoes and that another brewed beer with wheat from sources unknown. There was a cannabis field somewhere, but its location was a closely guarded secret.

He clicked through the options, eyeing the door and window every few seconds. Finally, Mason found a curious section that didn't look like it belonged in the store at all. It was labeled *HELP*.

After touching it, he was surprised to see a purchase menu like all the other categories. One choice said, *RAPID COUNSELOR*. Its price was listed in black instead of being grayed out, meaning Mason could afford that one if desired.

Growing ever more curious, Mason touched the counselor button to see what it meant or which counselor he'd get after booking a session. But instead of displaying a product description, the screen changed to show a digital clock counting down from five minutes. A pop-up announced that his purchase had been recorded, and his balance debited seventy chits. Mason looked for an undo button, but the ticking clock was his only offer.

There was a flash of light, then something on the back of the obelisk projected a blue beam. The room brightened as a holograph of a woman in a sober grey suit appeared.

"Hello, Mr. Shaw. How can I help you?"

Mason swung around, nervous, then rushed to close the door. The woman was waiting when he turned back, hands clasped in front of her waist.

"Sorry. I didn't mean to order anything."

"And that's bothering you?"

"No. I mean … I don't need a counselor."

"Tell me more."

He was wearing only boxers, and his hair was a mess. It was the middle of the night, and he was whispering. Was this a real person, somehow projected for him to see? Or was it AI?

The latter was less awkward. "Cancel."

"I'm sorry. I don't understand your request."

"Stop program."

"I'm sorry. I don't understand your request."

"Is there a way to … you know … get out of this?"

The hologram froze for a second, then tried anew. "Hello, Mr. Shaw. How can I help you?"

Stupid AI. Mason had no idea whether seventy chits was a lot or a little, but based on his experience so far, he hoped it was a pittance. Just over four minutes remaining, and his shrink was an idiot. Worse, Mason didn't seem to be able to shut her off.

He could try walking away, but for all he knew, the holographic counselor would hang out and await his return. Maybe it even paused when the subject left, meaning he could go for an hour then return to find four minutes still on the clock. It was keyed to his tracker as well. Anyone would know he'd been here if they looked.

The hologram smiled, probably to make Mason feel more at ease.

"I've noticed you made your request during curfew. Are you having trouble sleeping?"

Mason looked out the window, shaking his head. "Like a lamb."

"Your electro stimulus response and perspired adrenaline byproducts, along with analysis of your posture and body language, suggest sarcasm."

Mason barked a surprised little laugh but didn't otherwise reply.

"*Was* your last statement sarcasm?"

"Just … let me think."

"Have you indeed had trouble sleeping?"

"Why do you fucking care?"

It was rhetorical, but the hologram surprised Mason with an answer. "You paid for me to."

He wanted to laugh again, but it wasn't funny. It was truer than funny. Of course, the HRO didn't care about prisoners' well-being — at least not those who didn't go through Chamber Therapy. And, of course, paid help was the only kind he could get.

"Have you had trouble sleeping?" the hologram asked again.

"Yeah." Annoyed now. "I had some trouble."

"Would you like to talk about it?"

"Not really."

"Are you experiencing undue depression of mood, consistent with depleted serotonin levels?"

"How should I know?"

"You may order a serotonin test for 25 chits. Unfortunately, you will lack sufficient balance afterward to treat your condition if the test indicates a need for supplementation. However, for an additional fifty chits——"

"So, you'll sell me the diagnosis but not the cure?"

"Unfortunately, you will lack sufficient balance to——"

"Wonderful. Nothing's free."

"Beg pardon, Mr. Shaw, but the outpost offers life cessation for free following any adverse medical diagnosis."

That gave Mason the creeps. The HRO wouldn't treat him, but it'd kill him if he wanted — seemingly for an ailment as small as a stuffy nose. Instead of responding, he looked at the obelisk. Half his time was gone.

"Would you like to talk about your bad dreams?"

"Not particularly."

"How confident are you that your negative nighttime experiences are bad dreams as opposed to a schism in your perceived reality?"

"What the hell does that mean?" Mason asked.

"How long has it been since your last episode?"

"What kind of episode?"

"HRO 22 Union Station is in possession of medical records from one Bellforte, Michelle, doctor of psychiatry at——"

"How do you know about that?"

"Upon intake, all available records pertaining to inmates in any and all capacities are transferred to their reclamation assignment via standing subpoena order number 442.001, Union Station, California. Or, in your case——"

Mason stumbled past shock and fury to respond, "It wasn't an episode."

"Was it just a bad dream?" asked the hologram.

"I mean when I saw Dr. Bellforte. I didn't have an episode."

"Beg pardon, but Dr. Bellforte's records suggest she disagreed. She referred to the complaint that you and your family brought as an 'episode of delusion or temporary psychosis.' There is a note in your file indicating your objection to the term."

He'd done his best to bury it in his personal deep storage, but Mason remembered it now. He had suffered a series of dreams as a teenager in which his father was taken away. He refused to sleep. Mom raised the alarm until Dad finally took him to a shrink. Carter objected most vehemently to Bellforte's labels.

"I see," Mason said, now icy. "So, tell me. What does the HRO think about my 'episodes'?"

"Inmate records are stored and disregarded until and unless they are needed."

He wanted a new analysis, even if it hurt to hear — but no, his past was the backstory for a man who no longer officially existed.

"Needed for what?" Mason's gaze went to the kiosk. Twenty seconds.

"For diagnosis, classification, and assignment."

"Classification? How would you *classify* me right now?"

"By your statements and a decrease in adrenal activity as monitored by aerosolized metabolites, my program's diagnosis is that you are unaffected."

"*Unaffected*? You mean I'm fine."

"If you say so."

Something was still bugging him. Thirteen seconds remaining.

"What do you mean by 'assignment'?"

"Mainly as pertains to Chamber Therapy," answered the hologram.

"As in, they won't let me *do* Chamber Therapy. Someone made that abundantly clear to me at intake."

"That's correct, Mr. Shaw."

"Because they think I'll have an 'episode.'"

"Because your records indicate an elevated potential for catastrophic synaptic failure."

"My history tells you that?"

"*And* your father's. Would you like to talk about your father?"

Mason shook his head. "I mean because he went, Pattern Black."

"There is an anomaly semantically linked to the records of both *Shaw, Carter* and *Shaw, Mason*. Although, of course, the latter—"

His head jerked toward the counselor so fast, he almost got whiplash. *"Both* of our records?"

The hologram froze. Mason approached it like approaching a real person.

"What do you mean by 'anomaly'?"

The hologram gave a mechanical buzzing. "I'm sorry, but your session has ended."

On the timer: *0:00.* And a prompt: *Continue?*

Jesus Fucking Christ. It's like a video game.

"Continue," Mason said.

Nothing.

He tapped the kiosk. Still nothing.

"Don't you dare stop talking now, bitch."

"I'm sorry, but your session has ended. Your balance is insufficient for a new one."

The hologram started to rez out, disappearing in bands of sharp vertical lines.

"Hey! Don't you dare—"

"Pleasant dreams," said the hologram.

And then it was gone.

TWELVE

Bought and Sold

BREAKFAST.

Mason sat in the cafeteria before sunrise, eating eggs too yellow and spongy to be anything but synthetic. He'd been surprised to find food prepared and ready by 5:00 a.m. but was pleased to have something to do with his hands and attention.

He looked through empty window frames to the ruined city beyond while eating his eggs.

Even if Mason had been able to sleep after his aborted counseling session, he'd never have made it back to his cot without waking neighbors. So, he'd wandered instead. He'd found east-facing windows in what felt like a stripped-out classroom, then waited for the first blush of sun to paint the horizon. Dead black became bruised purple, and he went to the stairwell only to find the roof locked. That had made him go in search of other ways to get up there — some way, any way, to reach the open air. Higher in his psyche, a quiet part of Mason gave his actions medical-sounding names. *Agoraphobia. Claustrophobic paranoid response.*

He found a window with a trellis beside it, climbed out, then began to ascend. Drones arrived and counted down until he retreated. He'd sat on a windowsill for a while after that, thinking

84

about his nightmare and about what the counselor hologram had said.

About the memories it surfaced.

He went to the cafeteria not long after that. It was the only accessible room with a seat he dared occupy, given the reserved status — according to Nic — of the TV room chairs. There'd be a time when he'd stop being so obedient and shake things up, but not today.

Investigate first. Plan second. Act third.

Unseen kitchen staff began to push food through a long pass-through at one end of the cafeteria. There were no lights. Either the staff preparing the food was working in the dark, or it was robotic. The moon set, then things went obsidian-black. Only the slightly brightening smudge on the horizon — now blue-green, still barely visible — gave Mason light to see. He ate in the dark, downing his eggs on faith that they were, in fact, *eggs*, until the sky brightened enough that he could finally shake away the cobwebs and see.

"You look like shit."

Mason turned.

Frank.

"Why does everyone keep saying I look like shit?"

"Who else said you look like shit?"

Mason frowned. He'd made that remark feeling sure, but now he couldn't recall.

Frank sat. Mason was just about to tell him he'd rather eat alone, but Frank shrugged at the sparsely-populated room and said, "You got up early."

"I wanted to scope things out."

It was a lie, of course, but Frank had seen Mason collapse at intake, when … well, Mason couldn't quite remember *what* in that confessional booth had put him down. But that was half the problem. He didn't want the guy to know about his insomnia. Frank knew too many of his weaknesses already.

"I had a weird fuckin' dream," Frank said matter-of-factly. He had his own plate of fluorescent eggs and was shoving them down without chewing. "I was at a liquor store. The one I robbed. Only, I wasn't the robber this time. I was the clerk. *My mom* was the robber. But she didn't know me. And she was a real bitch. You know what I'm sayin'?"

"No."

Frank considered. "Me neither, shit."

Mason shoveled his food down, wanting to flee. If he needed any prison friends, he wanted ones who didn't see him as fragile.

"Frank," Mason said.

He looked over, egg on his chin.

"There's an informant kiosk in one of the supply rooms here. You know that?"

"Hey. Hey. If I did something to you, just tell me, and we'll talk it out so——"

"That wasn't a threat. I didn't go to snitch about anything. I'm just saying it's there."

"Oh." Frank visibly loosened — enough to make Mason wonder what he was hiding. "So?"

"Did you know?"

He shrugged again.

"Nobody told you it was there?"

"No. But so what? They said those things are everywhere."

Mason returned to his plate, wondering at the itch in his mind. He wasn't sure why he'd asked Frank about the kiosk or how he'd expected the man to react.

Of course, he hadn't known. Of course, it meant nothing to him. It shouldn't mean anything to Mason, seeing as anyone could use any informant kiosk for any tattling or purchasing transactions.

But the gossamer of doubt was clinging to him, making Mason wary in dawn's lingering darkness.

You're just on-edge. You're freaked out over nothing. It'll go away once the sun is up. Let it go.

But no. Something wasn't right. Mason was sure of it. He had gone right to that counselor session on the kiosk. *Right to it.* Out of all the buttons he could have accidentally pushed, he pushed that one.

So what? You did it. *Nobody pushed that button for you.*

Mason closed his eyes. He saw grids and pinwheels and spirals and mazes. Then he opened them again and saw the man who was hiding something and might be part of this mystery.

What mystery? There's no mystery. You got your ass thrown into jail, and now life is over.

No. There was meaning to the strange things Mason had seen and experienced since his bust and insults to Moochie's mother. Someone or something had Mason's number in here. Something was—

Paranoid.

—going on, and Mason had to find out what it was.

He recalled the holographic counselor's words — *HRO 22 Union Station is in possession of medical records from one Bellforte, Michelle, doctor of psychiatry.*

Why did they have those records?

… because of an anomaly semantically linked to both of your records.

Mason stood. Frank looked up at him.

"What. You done already?"

"I've been here for hours."

"You don't want the rest of your eggs?" Frank eyed Mason's plate.

"Take 'em." They tasted like shoe rubber, anyway.

Frank did, looking up as he shoveled. "Did I say you look like shit?"

"Yes. Thank you."

"You okay, man?"

"I'm fine."

"You sure?"

"Of course, I'm sure."

"You're actin' weird."

"I'm tired. I've been up most of the night."

Frank shrugged as if to say, *Your excuse has been accepted. Carry on.*

"So … what. Are you going back to bed?"

Mason looked out the window. He wished the sun would rise to lift his mood. How had this all happened? He was supposed to be a good man, a good cop. Then the scandal and Carter. After Mom, it'd all gone downhill.

So dark out there. So much unknown, without any escape.

"Maybe I'll go for a walk."

"Not much walking in here."

"Outside," Mason clarified.

Frank glanced at a wall-mounted clock. "Better wait another half hour."

Mason was already walking.

"Hey!" Frank called. "Curfew ends at six!"

He raised a hand without looking back. The panic was returning, like a cool hand on his neck. Something was chasing him. Following him. He needed the open air.

Mason reached the front door then pushed it open, surprised only after it swung wide that there'd been no lock. Maybe it was so people could come and go. Could be, when the pressure and darkness became too much for prisoners, they were allowed to choose their way out — where drones waited — for a reason.

He was looking into the slowly brightening morning when someone grabbed his arm.

"Hey, what the fuck," said a voice.

Mason turned, expecting Frank but finding Nic.

"What the fuck you doing?"

"Going for a walk."

"It's 5:30 a.m."

"So? The air is brisk."

Nic pulled. He was two-thirds of Mason's weight at most, but Mason let himself be dragged. Soon they were beyond the foyer, back in the entranceway.

The door closed. The ceiling was too low and the walls too tight.

"You stupid? You walk out there, ten drones will be on you in a minute. They watch the entrances and exits. They're like traffic cops with quotas."

Mason thought of the drones that had stopped him the second he'd tried for the roof. He lied by omission, not wanting Nic to hear his history. Like Frank, Nic was at risk of seeing Mason as weak. He'd saved his ass. Twice, if Mason counted pulling him away from the door just now.

"The drones won't get me." But Mason's inner voice whispered something different.

"Why's that? You got steel-jacket skin?"

"I'm good at sneaking around. Almost as good as you, Nic."

He turned Mason straight.

Mason braced for a lecture.

"Doesn't matter how good you are. You hear me? They key to the dongle in your blood. Curfew is super important to the HRO. The second word gets around that it's gone soft, they'll lose control. There's no way you — or any one of us — can survive outside. And besides. You know what else is out at night."

"Coyotes?"

Nic gave a frustrated roll of his eyes then dragged Mason into a corner. He lowered his voice. "*Immunity*, you dumb shit." He looked around again then spoke even quieter. "Prison chits aren't the only reason to snitch around here. The HRO knows you're a cop, but nobody else here does. But Immunity? If they knew?" Nic whistled.

Mason flinched forward at what sounded like a threat, but Nic raised his hands.

"I didn't tell anyone. That's my point. Nobody *does* shit inside the crib, but there's a whole underground economy if you want to *say* something here. I hear there's already people looking for you. Word spreads about who you are, and things will get tricky — especially with people like Immunity. You're handing your ass to whoever wants it if you go out now. Forget about the HRO stopping it. *Nobody* controls Immunity."

Mason grabbed Nic by the collar. Time for some old-fashioned police roughhousing. But Nic brushed him off, slippery as ever, and regarded the former officer with indignation.

"Do you really think I'd rat you out then go out of my way to tell you I didn't? I didn't *have* to tell you people are looking for you. I *volunteered* that information. Why would I give up something that puts me in the spotlight?"

"I don't know, Nic. How stupid are you?"

"I don't have to help you."

"I'm not looking for help."

"Good. Because fuck you."

But Nic didn't move, and Mason understood. Some way and somehow, Mason had something Nic wanted. Protection, probably. Sex, maybe … but seeing as Mason didn't swing that way, it was a dream at best.

"Who's looking for me? You said someone was looking for me."

"I don't know," Nic said.

"Bullshit!"

"I said, I don't know!"

Mason grabbed Nic, shook him, then felt like an asshole and let him go. Nic looked strangely unsurprised by Mason's actions. Before this little vacation, he'd never been the Shaw to shake someone down. Logan had done the most shaking, followed by Carter. Mason had spent his life as a Boy Scout, so far as Nic knew. So, why wasn't he fazed? Family reputation?

Nic straightened his collar and eyed Mason like a crazy man. "You sure you're okay?"

USPD's best informant. His street value as a snitch was fifty times his value as a prisoner.

Why weren't you offered Chamber Therapy?

Nic hadn't answered that question. Only one percent were sent through and released as rehabbed, but Mason would have bet money a guy like Nic would be among them. Revival acted like Therapy subjects were selected at random, but Carter had insisted the system worked differently in practice.

All those slots are bought and sold, Mason.

Something itched. Something having to do with the dream, with the revelation about his psychiatric files and the HRO, with the feeling he couldn't explain.

Something, despite its stupidity, refused to let Mason go.

"You eaten yet?" Nic asked.

Mason lied and said he hadn't, then he followed the man who wasn't his friend.

THIRTEEN

Nothing is Random

MASON. *How many fingers?*

Young Mason sat on the patterned rug at his grandparents' house while Grandma worked in the out-of-date kitchen as she always did. The boy looked up at his father.

Carter, smiling the way he used to, was on his knees with one hand planted to make a tripod. The other was behind his back.

Oh, Pop …

Come on, Mason. Just one more time.

"Smells like butt here," said Nic, jolting Mason from his reverie.

The memory dissolved like sugar, and again Mason was just a man walking through a dead city.

"Try to keep up," Mason said.

"You don't even know where you're going."

"Whose fault is that?"

Mason sprinted up a shallow hill with razed buildings at the top. Nic huffed to follow. Long seconds later, Mason stood hands-on-hips, looking out until Nic panted up alongside.

Nic, Mason had already discovered, was almost entirely useless. The Nicholas Coreander Tour Company had seemed helpful for a few hours before he finally started phoning it in. Last night, Nic had known that Mason, as a newbie, understood nothing. Now he was being an asshole, acting like Mason should have learned the landscape at some time between dusk and dawn.

"What's up *your* ass?" Nic asked after catching his breath. "You hear me? Slow your roll a little, will you? Not everyone has Gigantor legs."

Mason looked across the walled-in city. He scanned the horizon and came up empty. "With the sun up, I can't see the searchlights anymore."

"What searchlights?"

"For the cribs."

"You don't need to go to the crib. Not until tonight."

"I know."

Nic gave a flamboyant wave, talking to no one. "Oh. Yes. Of course. Pardon me. *That*, he knows."

Mason frowned. "I can't get my bearings. Where's our crib?"

Nic pointed.

"And I saw a green one last night. Where's the green crib?"

Nic pointed again.

Mason considered, focusing to the exclusion of his immediate surroundings. He could see the outer fences to the west from up here, but they weren't where his gut had told him they'd be. He'd always had an excellent sense of direction, but for some reason, it failed him here.

How long since your last episode?

Mason closed his eyes, rubbed his head, then tried to shake the remaining cobwebs.

It wasn't an episode.

"Where is the Inner Circle?" Mason asked his useless guide.

Nic seemed immediately suspicious. "Why?"

"Because I want to know."

"Nobody goes to the Inner Circle. It'll get you killed faster than breaking curfew."

"By Docents?"

"By drones."

"Except drones can't act without a human okay, except to enforce curfew."

"Different drones. At least according to rumor."

Mason turned toward Nic, who looked silent and dire. "Jesus. Conspiracy theories? You really do sound like my father."

"The fuck you keep talking about your *father?*"

Mason shook it away. "What's in the Inner Circle?"

"Dunno. HRO stuff. Machines and computers and whatever. Why?"

He firmed his gaze, thinking. Despite Nic's unwillingness to point out the HRO's off-limits nerve center, Mason was starting to think he saw it in the distance. Near the horizon, proximal to the prison's center, a set of fortifications stood taller and newer than the surrounding buildings. Carter had spouted all sorts of rumors about what Nathaniel Blake stored there, out of reach and shielded from prying eyes.

"I guess never mind," Mason said.

A strange errand since he had no idea what he was looking for. Just a feeling, like a cop's itch ahead of an ambush. It was impossible to know where to go or the right questions to ask.

Mason resumed walking, Nic scampering like a terrier to keep up.

They descended the hill. An empty lot gave way to low, run-down houses that must have been the strangest sort of blight before the area was converted to an outpost. They were in Southern California, not far from the ocean, adjacent to some of the planet's priciest real estate. But the houses themselves were decrepit shitholes. Barely lean-tos. The type of neighborhood that kept decent citizens away.

Nic yapped at Mason's heels.

"Hang on. Hey!"

Mason turned to find Nic panting to keep pace.

"You asked for my help. You wanted me to show you around."

"Yeah?"

"So, how about you let me lead?"

No way Mason was going to do that. Despite his increasingly

shitty sense of direction, he was planning on an end-run Nic needn't anticipate. He wanted to navigate toward one of the taller buildings ahead while appearing to wander with no apparent direction.

"Hey! Hey, fuck!"

Mason moved faster, knowing Nic wouldn't be able to gather *his* bearings if he stayed out of breath, speed walking around corners and blocks, avoiding clusters of prisoners and blockades where ambushes might lie in wait. There was one obstruction in particular that struck Mason as a death trap for anyone who dared to traverse it — the big, Twinkie-sprinkled mountain of car hulks blocking two of the alleys a half hour from the hilltop, stacked like an urban Stonehenge.

Forty-five panting minutes later, Mason searched the sky for the building he'd been following and found they'd landed at its foot. Looking up, he saw it was little more than a reinforced stairwell with no floors around it. No wonder they said to hide in stairwells during tornadoes.

Something boomed from behind. They both turned to see a house-sized dust cloud rising from behind two concentric fences garnished with razor wire.

"What the hell was that?" Mason asked. The explosion wasn't a fireball like in the movies. It looked more like dynamiting at a stone quarry — all dust and gray.

Nic scowled at Mason and pushed him. *"Seriously?* Fucker."

Mason opted for innocent. "What?"

"You've been headed here all along, haven't you? Stupid asshole. I told you the Inner Circle was off-limits!" He tugged at Mason's sleeve. "We need to get out of here."

"Why? We're just standing outside."

"Trust me. Just walk away."

But instead, Mason looked toward the double row of fence. It was newer and sturdier than the buildings, meaning it'd been added later, replaced recently, or maintained in a way its decaying surroundings hadn't. What lay beyond looked no more interesting than what was around them right now.

Nothing to see here, the unremarkable streets past the fences seemed to say. *Well. Except for that explosion and that cloud.*

"What the hell *was* that?" Mason watched the rubble skitter to rest.

"Who knows? Who cares? None of our business. Come on." Nic tugged him again.

But still, Mason refused to move.

Even with all the pebbles at rest, a diffuse cloud still obscured most of what was immediately beyond. "Do you ever see hovercrafts or helicopters going in and out of here?"

He squinted through the dust and inched closer.

Nic pulled him more firmly. When Mason didn't budge, he tossed a rock at the fence. It sizzled when it struck the metal. Only it sizzled *blue.*

The thing struck Mason as less of an electrified fence and more like one guarded by a *Star Trek*-style force field. He stepped back.

"You get what I'm sayin'?" Nic asked.

"You didn't answer my question."

Nic pointed, looking incredulous. "Someone in there is blowing things up with explosives too big for DIY, there's invisible blue shit guarding the fences, and *still* you've got questions other than, 'How quickly can we get the fuck out of here?'"

Mason waited.

Nic drew a long-suffering breath. "Why you wanna know about helicopters and hovercrafts?"

"I'm just wondering if Blake ever flies in for a visit."

Nic rolled his head all the way around on his neck. "Not this again."

"What?"

Nic fixed his eyes in a way that seemed to say, *We have to talk.* "Blake. Every minute with you, it's about Nathaniel Blake."

"Bullshit! I've mentioned him ... once?" He'd paused to count but only said "once" because "never" felt aggressive. In truth, Mason didn't think he'd mentioned Blake to Nic at all, either through Carter's suspicions or questions of his own. Too big a protest for a *faux pas* not committed.

"Yeah. *Once.*" Nic rolled his eyes in accompaniment to the head-roll from earlier.

"I …" Mason sighed in surrender. "You know him. You know about Blake."

"Yeah. I know the president, too."

"What about Elisabeth Reeves?"

"Blake's partner? Excuse me. His *former* partner."

"So, you know who *Reeves* is, too," Mason said.

"Uh-huh."

"The fuck is with you?"

Nic snapped if only just a little. "You can shut up about them for once, you know. One fucking time, you can keep your goddamn obsessions to yourself."

"What are you talking about? All I said was—"

"Look. Whatever, man." Tired of pulling, Nic moved to Mason's other side and shoved.

If anything, it strengthened his resolve. Mason planted his feet and leaned into the charge. "What's inside the Inner Circle?"

"Who knows? I think the big towers are generators or for broadcasting or something. Storage. Maybe some administrative shit, so they have a base inside. That's the official version."

"What's the unofficial version?"

"I said I don't know. I don't want to know."

"Why wouldn't you want to know?"

A drone zipped overhead then hovered above them. It extended an appendage, pointed down. Mason hadn't gotten a good look at the drones from last night, but this one struck him as larger, plainer, more utilitarian, and less aesthetically pleasing. Watching it, something Nic had said circled back to him.

Different drones.

"*That's* why," Nic said, eyeing the drone. "That look standard prison-issue to you?" He tugged for Mason's attention. "Dude. It's guarded by some sort of energy field, and you won't find pictures of drones like that online no matter how long you look. *We're not supposed to be here.* You getting the picture?"

The drone's appendage seemed to unfold. The object at its end was unmistakably a weapon.

Mason moved another few steps back without any hurry. Once they were behind a corner, the drone retreated and assumed a guarding stance rather than its earlier offensive position.

He kept peeking while Nic continued to push. Finally, Mason decided there was nothing more to be seen without re-entering drone range, so he let himself be led.

"What's the matter with you?" Nic asked when they were away. "You wanted to come here all along, didn't you?"

"I was curious."

"*Curious*. Yeah. You're *always* curious." Nic's voice was brusque, but the fear was evident through his tough tone. "You know what I think? I think you *want* to be in here."

They walked on. Mason tried not to look back at the tempting dust. Carter's words orbited his mind, tangled with the HRO's official stance on what he'd officially not seen. According to public record, the no-man's-land in the center of all HROs was storage for the administration, occasional in-the-field offices, equipment repair depots, and apparently a lot of the computing power that kept the prison's systems running.

The *People* article had spent a single sentence on Inner Circles, describing them as outposts in the middle of an area too large to manage only from the outside. Carter had theories about everything, but that one lived near the top of his list.

"Yer ass *wants* to be here."

Nic's voice was suddenly very different. Alarmingly so. But before the synapses connected in Mason's brain and his body could flex to respond, the owner of Nic's bigger, deeper voice had grabbed him by the back of his jacket.

Nic was gone. The blue sky had begun to fade and was now almost white. The sky was pocked with black circles. Small dark suns, perhaps. Or little dark moons, every one of them full.

It was the big man with the God complex.

Mason found himself too shocked to fight. Or resist.

The world was gone along with his sanity.

In the middle of the white sky with its black stars, a vortex like a hurricane of swirling ink began to churn. Its spiral had the backbone of a galaxy — that perfect, lazy unfolding of the Golden Ratio, just as his old teacher Paul Sylvester had taught children too young to get it.

Mason studied those teachings compulsively later in life, just so he could understand — not the teachings themselves, but the whole of those first experiences.

We are all connected. Nothing is random.

In those dim and quiet sessions, Mr. Sylvester had told Mason all existence followed a blueprint laid by numbers. *Nothing exists until mathematics makes it real.*

The Inner Circle fences were gone. Same for the dust cloud and drone. The universe was black and white. There was only Mason. And the tormentor who refused to leave him alone.

"God is good." Only the big man's tone of voice seemed to add, *But He's the only one.*

"What are you?" Mason asked.

A massive arm shot out with the speed of a projectile. An enormous hand gripped his neck.

And then the demon said, "You can call me Preacher."

FOURTEEN

The Eye of a Spinning Hurricane

"GIVE," said Preacher, if that was his name.

Mason, choking, felt his feet leave the ground.

Everything smacked of *déjà vu* — and, for the moment, never mind that all the *déjà* was happening in a mindfuck landscape.

"Give," Preacher repeated. "Give *now*, or I'll rip you open to find it."

Mason didn't even consider asking what the big man was after. Anger — even irritation, if that was all Preacher gave him — felt so much better than fear.

Oh, the world's become a freakscape, with a black-on-white sky like giant dice?

I'm losing my fucking mind.

None of that mattered. Between Preacher's superior, righteous expression and the evident joy he was taking in this, Mason's temper shot through its boiling point. He stopped paying attention to all that had gone wrong and focused on the one thing he could get right instead.

If you're really a ghost, Mason thought, *this won't hurt a bit.*

But apparently, even ghosts had balls, or at least could be fooled into testicular thinking by the force of persuasion and a well-aimed foot. Mason delivered that foot to Preacher's crotch with all of his might. His foot, even with the best of intentions, felt like it was kicking through syrup.

But the grip on his neck went soft, then Mason hit the ground. *Real* ground. It wasn't black-on-white beneath him now. The sky was still strange, and that tiny black storm continued to swirl above, yet that kick to the nuts somehow restored the stone to reality beneath him.

Preacher stood, clutching his groin. Mason wasn't too proud to run, but it seemed the only bit of ground in this whole place was the island under his feet. Where would he go?

He went for the edge anyway, ready to leap into nothingness if that was what it took. He couldn't let himself think too much about it. That was the trick. He had to start where he was then find a way to deal. When the fight was over, he could turn his mind to all the insanity. But right now, he was in a fight taking place in these particular surroundings. If the rules of the arena said gravity and sense were optional, he'd have to accept it. One crisis at a time.

But that same big hand grabbed Mason before he hit the edge.

"Ain't nothin' down there. Ain't nothin' your daddy left behind that deep to break your fall."

Mason spun and swung in one motion, but the result was cartoonish. Preacher held him at a distance, leaving Mason to punch only air. So, he ducked, slipped Preacher's hand, then tried to tackle. Bounced off as if his attacker was a brick wall. Moments later, the man was on his back.

"Cain't run," Preacher said. "Cain't hide."

"What do you want from me?"

"All you got. All *they* want."

"Who?"

"You knows who."

Mason, still on his ass, crab-scrambled for the back edge of their island. But rather than finding the edge, he found the ground scrolling backward beneath him as if on a treadmill. He fetched up against a building that hadn't been there before then looked up to see the edge blocked. Or, perhaps beyond the brick wall, there was no longer any edge at all.

He locked gazes with Preacher, feinted right, scrambled left. But just as before, the edge retreated as Mason neared it. Seconds later, another wall appeared, and he found himself in an alleyway corner. The sky was still white. The black dots above, orbiting the minute ink storm, had formed their own tiny galaxies. Groups of dots became their own lazy spirals. In clusters, they were like the pores in a lotus pond.

Mason had to look down. Overhead lay nightmares.

Preacher looked over his shoulder at the sky. "So that's it. That's all you got so far."

"What is?"

"I told you. Give it to me, or I'll rip it out."

"I don't know what you want!"

Preacher looked up, down, at Mason, then away. He seemed disappointed somehow. Like he wanted to make good on his threat but was realizing he couldn't for reasons unknown.

The big man knelt in front of Mason. He was curiously graceful, lowering that titanic frame with a dancer's grace to the balls of his feet, his entire mass perched on a few square inches of rubber.

He peered into Mason's eyes. Deep. Through him, into what was beyond.

"Listen to me, *Mistah Shaw*."

Mason scrunched back farther, less afraid than out of options. He was still ignoring the sky, holding focus like a totem. *We're two guys in an alley. Two guys out on the streets. He's too big and too fast, and I don't have my piece. It's no shame to run. All I need is an escape plan.*

But the strange reality's presence asserted itself if he thought too far in that direction. Where would he flee to if the land changed beneath him?

"How you feelin, Mistah Shaw?"

Mason didn't know if he was supposed to answer that.

"Slow, I bet. Like you swimmin'. Like you tryin' to whiff

through the air, but instead, you slow, like someone's got a little holda yer pant leg."

Mason waited for his opportunity, knowing monologues, when the other was distracted by pride, were always the best chance to fight or flee. But at the same time, his mind listened. Worse, his mind *agreed*. The torpor in his limbs made each movement like stretching taffy. His mind told him he was floating, not sitting. Two sets of competing inputs like paralysis. Hard to run when your eyes said one thing and your body insisted on another.

"Salright," Preacher said, affecting a smile. "You take yer time thinkin' on it."

"You did something to me."

"Something was did, but not by me."

Preacher waited. Bits of land drifted past, lazy like the eye center of a spinning hurricane.

"Where are we right now?"

"Not where you think."

"I fell. Hit my head. I'm hallucinating."

"Ain't a hallucination. Ain't a dream. And you ain't crazy. Or at least, you ain't crazy *fo this*."

Mason bided his time, looking for a chance to strike or squeeze past. With every word, the big man inched closer.

"But you ain't ripe yet, neither. You ain't sowed oats. You still believe what you see. Or worse, you ain't believin' it at all."

Mason rubbed his eyes. Closed them, then couldn't stand the dark and opened them again.

None of this was real, no matter what Preacher said.

It had to be a dream, or a hallucination, or a trip brought on by drugs in something he'd eaten. A psychotic break. Something had shaken loose inside his mind.

What if this was it?

What if Mason had finally succumbed?

He'd wake in a mental hospital, strapped to the bed.

"Son, you don't even know who you *is*."

"I'm Mason Shaw."

"You is. But you ain't."

Preacher squeezed closer. Mason could jab him in the eyes if he wanted. He could poke the big man in the throat. But his limbs stayed frozen. It wasn't that Preacher made no sense or that his arguments were dragging Mason into inaction. It was that somehow, deep down, it was all so perfectly clear. One wrong move, and what remained of his center would drop like delicate china.

"Don't feel bad. You doin' better than you got any reason to."

His hand shot out again. Again, Mason gagged as the demon's fingers squeezed his throat.

"You gonna feed in here. You gonna grow fat. You gonna kick and scream, and when you ready, you and me's gonna have a talk. Ain't no rush. They ain't gonna let you free. Just like they ain't let yer daddy free. Not then. Not now."

Mason tried to croak out a question but now faded green spots were joining the black ones. The world, whatever it had become, wouldn't stop spinning.

"But in the meantime," Preacher said, pausing to look at the tiny black swirl above then back at Mason, "you gonna walk the line. You hear me? *You walk the line.*"

Mason was losing consciousness. His vision was fading. Words had almost no meaning.

"They came for him, you know. Jus' like they gonna come for you."

"*Who?*" The word was a blade dragged through gravel.

"Ain't nobody. You just remember that."

Mason's mouth worked, but nothing came out.

"You just play who you is and let me send them where they needs to go."

Preacher released him. Mason grabbed his throat and rubbed, sucking air as fast as his lungs dared.

"*Ride,* but don't *drive.* I do the drivin'. I run the show. You fuck too hard, and we ain't gonna have no house left to play in. And this here? This here's the house of the *Lord.*"

Mason looked past Preacher to the nightmare beyond.

Preacher stood tall and raised his leg.

"Wait!"

The massive foot hovered above him.

"Tell me if I'm losing it," Mason pled.

"Bitch, you ain't even here."

Preacher's foot on his head was like the dropping of a shroud.

Black replaced white.

Then Mason was—

FIFTEEN

The Vacant Abyss

MASON. How many fingers?

He rose to the surface, unable to breathe, consciousness spreading like pooled water. Something deep in his gut told him he'd rather not rush to face whatever was waiting out there.

There'd been something a moment ago. A rotten memory he'd already forgotten, lingering behind him like a spook in the shadows. He shouldn't take his mind off it lest it attack him.

Bitch, you ain't even here.

But … the new memory. Which was to say, the old one.

Come on, Mason. Just one more time.

None. No fingers. You're trying to fool me.

An elbow jabbed him in the ribs. His eyes jolted open, then the rest of his senses assaulted Mason at once. He heard an engine's muted rumble, the thumping of tires on uneven road, the sway of something inside. Cold, hard metal beneath him — the edge of a bench biting his fingers as he reached down to grip it. The space smelled like sweat and anger, fateful decisions gone awry.

"Shaw. You paying attention?"

Mason looked at the speaker. Cruz, snapping his fingers.

"Yeah."

"You sure?"

He was supposed to respond. Instead, his eyes went to the lightbulb.

Hello lightness, my old friend.

Inside were a handful of filaments, their centers submerged in yellow wax. The glass was foggy and burnished. Beaten to hell by a lifetime of being screwed and unscrewed.

"*Yes,* I'm goddamn sure."

"You look like shit."

"I'm getting a little tired of everyone telling me that."

Cruz looked at the others. "What?"

"I look like shit. Can we move on?"

Mason heard a voice in the back of his head, one he could no longer place. *You walk the line.* More command than observation.

"He's hungover," Watt laughed.

"Shut the fuck up, Frank."

"What's your problem?" Watt demanded.

They came for him, you know. Jus' like they gonna come for you.

"My problem is I'm going to rob a fucking bank. How about you?"

"Easy, Shaw," said Cruz.

"I have a headache. And I'm getting a little tired of ..."

Of what?

"You just need to breathe," said the tattoo-riddled woman, sitting right-side to the rear door.

"Leigh, right?"

"You okay?" she asked.

"*Leigh D'Abo,*" Mason said it like an item on a fancy French menu. "Is that your name? Or are you going to say, *'I ain't'?*"

"What's wrong with him?" asked Buster, by the cab.

Life was a double-exposed photo, and he could see both versions at once.

"Nothing's wrong with me." Mason busied himself with an untied shoelace.

"Maybe you should stay here," Cruz suggested.

"What fun is that?"

The van rolled on. They hit a curb, then the occupants slid sideways on their seats.

As they composed themselves, Cruz glanced around and continued with seeming reluctance. "Once we're inside, watch the corners. Buster, you go left. Shaw——"

"Mason," Mason said. "My name is *Mason.*"

Cruz stopped, wondered, then looked at Buster, Leigh, Watt. Eventually, he went on. "Shaw, you go to the——"

"Just don't shoot first." Mason shook his head and muttered, "Fucking Buster."

"Do you have a problem with me?" she asked.

If he focused hard, Mason could almost recall why he did, but his head wasn't into thinking right now.

Cruz rattled, went on. "Shaw, you handle the guards to the right. By——"

"The poster."

"That's ... Yeah." He shot Mason a troubled glance then turned to Sasha. "You handle the manager. Thin woman, by the fat man. Until the jammer is set, she can still trigger the hard-wired alarm."

"Do we even *have* a jammer?" Mason asked.

"What? Yeah. Sasha has it."

"Can I see it?"

All eyes went to Sasha. She didn't have a bag. Mason figured a jammer had to be at least big enough to require a backpack or a bulge, and Sasha had neither.

"D'Abo, you watch the doors," Cruz continued.

Everyone braced, but the van didn't hit anything. That part was over. But they all looked at one another anyway, the way people do when geese waddle across a row of graves.

"Watt. You handle the old lady." Now Cruz sounded tentative. He paused for an interruption, but none came.

So, Mason decided to add, "Sasha. Manager. Shoot her in the face and take the key."

"Now wait just a second ... "

There was a sound like jet engines roaring. Mason had time to realize, *This is new.* Then something struck the van hard enough to spin it in a circle and crumple the front end.

The driver's arm squirted from the beer-can wreckage, no longer attached to his body.

The van jolted to a stop, the reek of burned rubber rising to the level of suffocation.

Mason looked at Buster, who was staring at the severed arm, but then she exploded as if her insides no longer wanted to stay inside. A hundred tiny round holes appeared in the wall behind her. A second later, Leigh and Sasha were slamming shoulders to the door in a rush to escape.

Mason followed. He piled into the daylight — too bright and not hot enough, ski mask still tucked into his waistband. He gasped, unable to keep his feet moving. He'd seen what'd struck the van — what'd turned its front end into an unsolvable Rubik's. A massive speedboat. But that wasn't even the odd part. A minigun was mounted to the vessel's top — an M134 if Mason had to guess. Faster than an uzi.

A thin blonde in goggles behind the gun turned it on Watt.

He shouted something, then the gunner turned him into pulled pork.

"Go! Goooo!"

Cruz, panicked, waved the others toward the bank. Mason, watching with the eyes of a cop, found their decision idiotic. There was an alley right there. The gun was in a *boat,* for fuck's sake. They weren't going to give chase, but the hail of bullets could easily reach the lobby from where it was. Firing that fast and that often, the gunner would turn them to sushi in seconds.

Bullets chipped brick behind Mason. He ducked into the alley, pressed his back to the wall, then patted himself to see if he'd been hit. He was whole … fine …

Inside the bank's lobby, strewn with customers and employees ducking for cover.

At first, Mason had no idea what to do. He'd gone to an alley, and now he was in the place he had so carefully avoided? Too much input, not enough time. Should he duck? Or stand and die?

"Mason!"

Leigh's body, tattered seemingly of its own accord, glass raining behind her as the minigun coughed lead.

Then Cruz shouted, "MASON! COVER THE OLD LADY!"

Fuck the old lady.

He put his head down and bolted for the offices at the bank's rear, for the door with the bright red handle.

Mason was through a second later, out the fire exit into the alley beyond.

He ran down the street, leaping felled trash cans, looking for a car. *Any* car.

Traffic ahead. At its front was a man in a suit behind the wheel of a Saab.

He remembered his weapon, trained it on the man after wrenching open the door. Reached for his badge, but of course, he wouldn't carry it here. Still, as the man stumbled then fell to the pavement, Mason shouted, *"Police business! I need your car!"*

Then he dove through the door, planning to land on upholstery and hit the gas.

Instead, he struck the tile floor of the bank again, with that giant, Preacher, standing above. Had he seen him recently? It felt like they had unfinished business, but Mason couldn't remember what or where, or when. Or who, come to think of it, "Preacher" even was.

Mason looked now, aware of the poisonous seconds. The giant's clothes were too tight because they belonged to Cruz. He'd ripped through arms and legs like the Hulk, almost as if he'd come to life inside them rather than needing to don them.

Preacher reached down for Mason and picked him up by the collar. "You forget what I said already, bitch? Fuck. I ain't even supposed to *be* here."

Things were happening too fast. Mason could make no more sense of Preacher's words than the world itself.

They came for him, you know.

Something exploded by the door. A metal frame flew past

Mason, then collided with a desk. Glass filled the air in a rain of razors and shards. Blood tickled his skin.

Jus' like they gonna come for you.

An enormous man appeared at the bank's front holding the now-unmounted minigun, the ammo chain wrapped from waist to wrist.

He fired. Mason flinched, but the bullets only hit Preacher. On the ground, he looked Hispanic and was down to Cruz's former weight.

Mason waited to die, but a second person walked past the gunman. The woman he'd seen firing the thing earlier. She passed him with the unmistakable aura of authority, surveying while her assassin awaited instructions. She was waif-thin — diminutive next to the gunner — with hard cheekbones, alabaster skin, albino blonde hair — short and spiked. Sunglasses hid her eyes.

She took a step, reached into her pocket, then stopped, frozen like a statue, looking past Mason to something beyond.

A large arm wrapped around his throat from behind. Who was left? Sasha? Yes, she'd been wearing the little flashlight on her belt that Mason now saw in the corner of his eye.

Except Sasha was small and didn't have such a deep voice. "Get me, and you get him. Eighty-nine, twenty, three. *'I will crush his foes before him and strike down his adversaries.'"*

The big man with the minigun moved its muzzle, looking for a shot. "It's the outlier."

"Shoot him," said the woman. "He's out of bodies."

Preacher held him tighter, his breath hot in Mason's ear as he repeated himself. "Get me, and you get him." He laughed, then went on in a tone that was decidedly taunting and knowing. "You don't know who you dealing with, and you ain't even know who you *got.*"

The man with the gun looked at the woman. They both seemed to consider Preacher's words. Then a light crossed the woman's expression, her eyebrows drawing tight. She squinted at Mason. "Is that …?"

In Mason's ear, Preacher whispered, *"Thatta girl. You seein' it now."*

Mason tried to turn, but Preacher held him bone-tight.

The woman kept staring. "That's not Shaw."

"Of course, it's Shaw," said the man with the gun.

"It's not him, Ike."

"Of course, it's Shaw." The same set of words said in exactly the same way. He sounded like a recording, as if someone had hit rewind.

"I'm not going to sit here and argue with myself, Ike."

The gunner twitched. "It's *not* Shaw."

Preacher didn't flinch, nor did he move. Everyone waited.

"Shoot him, anyway," the woman ordered.

Mason clenched. But then someone shouted — an insectile man with big round glasses, as covered in debris and dust as the rest of them, holding a tablet and rushing to be seen.

"Calliope! *Wait!*"

He showed his tablet to the woman. She raised a hand for the gunner. "Shit."

Preacher grabbed the back of Mason's skull, fingers like vises.

Mason saw stars. Then a white room filled with black circles, like a plague of locusts.

"I go," Preacher said, "you go, too."

"Sasha, huh?" Mason said.

"What?"

"Sasha was carrying a sidearm."

But not just any sidearm. Sasha had been carrying a Glock, and it didn't have a safety. Mason reached back, torquing his shoulder, and managed to grip the stock while it was still in the holster at Preacher's side. He tilted it inward then pulled the trigger.

The round punched through Preacher's leg, then he hopped away.

Mason boosted his momentum by kicking him in the side.

The gunner pricked the trigger. A metallic rattle filled the bank, and after the machine fell silent, Preacher — or perhaps Sasha — was no more.

Mason ran, waiting for a hail of bullets. None came, but he heard a metallic thud behind him as the massive man dropped his minigun to the floor.

He dodged fallen bodies as he headed for the employee lounge. Once inside, he realized he had nowhere else to go. No exits. Not even a closet.

The door banged open and the gunner, absent his weapon, entered with the blonde and four-eyes behind him.

"Take it easy," the woman said.

Mason wished he'd been able to pinch the Glock from Sasha's holster or that he'd survived that little mashup with his own gun in tow. As it was, he could only pace with them in circles, looking for a weapon his next best chance.

But this was already wrong, already off-script — Mason had never been here, despite being sure he had been.

"What's your name?"

"Fuck you."

"Are you Mason Shaw?"

"The fuck's it matter to you?"

The big man flinched toward him, but Mason dodged behind a desk and grabbed a paperweight that felt like marble.

The woman raised a hand, its back toward the ex-gunner. "Do you know who I am?"

"How the hell should I know who you are?" But behind the mania inside his head, something had already struck him as wrong. Something one of them had said in the lobby. Something about the exact thing the woman just asked.

"I'm Calliope. Do you know that name?"

Someone had told him about a person named Calliope. Recently. But that was the mixing of worlds, and whatever knowledge Mason had uncovered elsewhere felt irrelevant here.

"I was your father's contact," the woman said.

Mason shook his head.

"*Think*, Mr. Shaw. Think back to what Carter may have said before he went away. It won't come easy in here but try. We have

…" She looked at a beat-up watch on her wrist, then said what struck him as a lie. "We have time."

It took seconds, but an anemic memory found him.

"The hacker," Mason said, still holding his paperweight. He had a line on the big guy, who so far felt like the only genuine threat. He could beat him if he had to. "You really exist?"

"That's right. Your father was supposed to bring me something."

"Good for him. He's not fucking home right now."

Calliope looked back to the man with the glasses. He glanced down at his tablet and said, "It's definitely here."

"Listen to me, Mason," said the woman, her hand out, trying to pacify. "I don't have time to explain, but your father had something we need. I think" — she glanced at her fellows — "I think you might be able to help us find him."

"He's dead."

The woman turned again. They conversed in whispers. The only thing Mason clearly heard was the man with the glasses saying, "Thirty seconds."

"I need you to lie down."

Mason laughed. Feinted to one side, then surged to the other. Finding split-second aim, he flung the paperweight hard at the big man who'd been holding the minigun. It connected with a sick, wet crack, making his target stagger and shout.

Taking his chance, Mason tried to rush past. The man in glasses moved to block, but he had less confidence than your average napkin. Mason hit him in the throat.

He hurdled a set of plush chairs, but the woman blocked the doorway. Mason could easily take her, but as he lowered his shoulder, the gunner came up again with his nose raining gore then closed the distance.

Mason rushed anyway — no other options. He managed to knock one aside and another to the floor, then was halfway down the corridor when Four Eyes tackled him.

He hit the ground hard.

They turned him over.

The woman produced something that looked like a miniature scroll. She unrolled the thing and held it by a dowel at each end. Rather than parchment, Mason saw a plasticized material that shone like foil. Thin, light, and rolling through a rainbow of refracted colors.

She knelt. Moved the thing toward Mason's face, still holding it by both ends as if planning to strangle him with a too-wide garrote.

He squirmed. Thrashed. She put her attention on him, making him still.

"What's the first thing you remember?" she asked.

"Fucking your mother."

"What's the last thing you remember?"

"Fucking your mother!"

The blonde turned her head and spoke to the man with glasses. "Hold him still."

With the big man pinning Mason to the floor, Four Eyes gripped him by the chin and the top of his head. A thumb got too close. He tried to bite it.

"Mason," said the blonde. "It's *you* who must decide."

He shot a knee into the gunner's crotch. The man gasped, and his eyes hardened, but he managed to flatten the offending leg again and hold on.

"You can come with us," said the woman, unfazed. "Or you can stay with them."

Shouting came from the front room, followed by a tremendous sound of detonating metal and glass. Was that SWAT arriving? Blowing in the windows? Cruz and the others had better watch out.

"You gonna kill me? Just get it over with."

The gunner-man, still wincing, reached to the small of his back. He removed a handgun and shoved it against Mason's forehead. But maybe it wasn't a pistol. The thing looked fashioned from fence wire and chicken bones, with plated metal only for show.

"Put that away," said the woman.

"He made his choice."

"He doesn't know what he's choosing. Not like that. Not after the outlier."

The gunner laughed. "Yeah. Good luck with *that.*"

Four Eyes chuckled. They were all in on some joke to which Mason wasn't privy.

She was still holding that sheet of foil between its ends. The scroll looked metallic and semi-rigid but didn't crinkle as it moved. Dust filtered through the fluorescent light in the hallway, spilling in from the lobby. But contrasting the rumble and gut feel of a melee, the noises seemed to be traveling in the opposite direction. Wrapping up rather than gaining volume. Big sounds moving paradoxically farther, like a concert ramping up as a car drove away.

"Look at me," she said.

Movement behind Four Eyes caught Mason's eye. The hallway itself flickered from solid to wireframe. From finished concept to pencil lines on a blueprint. Everything was rotoscoped. An artist's lines chasing the truth of every surface.

Four Eyes had moved his hands from Mason's head and was looking at his tablet.

Mason couldn't see the screen. Only the flash of something there — something bad, judging by sound and color — reflected in the glasses.

"He's edging."

"Mason. Try to focus."

More flashing, accompanied by a weak beep. "Almost critical now."

The gunner still had his weapon. "We need to end this. Try again later."

"There is no later."

The hallway turned black and white, though the room's occupants clung to their color. No decorations or pictures or posters or plants. Just this living sketch that hurt Mason's head. Made his leg kick and his ribcage lurch and jive.

"Fuck. He's seizing."

"Mason!"

And in that moment, it all suddenly became clear to Mason. He didn't know all the wheres and hows and whys and whats, but some deep part of him understood slivers of what was happening. He didn't know these people or whether he was about to die or be killed, but he was causing this. It was involuntary, like an allergic reaction.

But it was all his fault.

He was sure this had happened to his father before he'd slipped into the vacant abyss.

How many fingers, Mason?

Somehow it mattered.

An instant later, Mason's eyes flickered, and the four of them weren't grappling inside a bank's back-office anymore. They were in a bright white nothingness, a chandelier of black dots hanging above them.

"He won't go quiet," said Four Eyes. "I can't fix his signal. I'm not going to be able to do this, Calliope."

"Try."

"I'm goddamn trying!"

"Then fix his identity, so we can at least find him again! Do your job, and let me do mine!"

"Fixing his identity won't be enough to—!"

"Stay or go," said the woman precisely, speaking to Mason with an annoyed glance at her bespectacled companion. "You have to decide."

The disorienting sensation was worsening. The icon flashed faster on the tablet, beeping with ever more urgency.

A man made out of pencil strokes appeared behind Four Eyes, but the gunner saw him coming. The chicken bone weapon swung toward the doorway then blew a hole through the new man's chest. A SWAT officer, if Mason had to guess, though he was all lines and scratches to Mason's eye. Not a man so much as a cartoon. Guts made of powdered pencil lead struck the wall, leaving an amateur's sketch.

Four Eyes said, "They're coming in. For extraction."

"Us," the woman pressed, patient now only with effort, "or *them.*" A choice pinning him down … or the dead officer in the hallway.

Mason tried to focus and understand his part in this. It gave him a headache. He could stay, or he could go. He could be taken by the coming SWAT team, or he could … well, he could do whatever these people were up to. They were willing to "fix his identity," it seemed.

Ride. Don't drive.

"Do whatever the fuck you want." Mason closed his eyes, unable to stop himself from seeing the world dangling on a broken hinge. "Just do it fast."

The woman pushed the strange foil thing over his face. She moved over him, all of her barely-substantial weight pressing down, choking Mason into suffocation.

Panic settled in as his breathing grew labored.

He fought.

And fought.

But then Mason ran out of breath. The black and white patterns returned even behind closed eyelids, and he fell down a deep dark hole as he spun and slipped and——

SIXTEEN

Submerged

—THRASHED and choked as his limbs struck hard surfaces, legs dangling and kicking nothing.

The feeling was back. That sense of running in syrup, every movement slowed as if by invisible bands on his limbs.

Then came a voice from very far away. "He's seizing!"

Another, this one muffled as if coming from a different room through paper-thin walls. "Goddammit, reinforce!"

The world was liquid. Mason was flying, no longer flat on the ground. Flying or falling — he wasn't sure which. He couldn't see. His stomach grew light, hanging like a cartoon character already inches on the wrong side of a cliff.

Mason tried to open his eyes, but something held them shut. He couldn't feel the gunner's weight on his chest or the stilling hands of the man in glasses — and seconds-ago moments felt like years passed already. He couldn't remember details of his bank adventure. He saw nothing and could focus on less. Felt only sludge and confinement.

The intense woman with the brush-blonde crew cut was gone, that much Mason was sure of even with his eyes held tight. He could tell by feel that her suffocating contraption no longer covered his face. But he still couldn't breathe. There seemed to be a fist down his throat.

He thrashed in the abject darkness, flailed his arms. Knuckles cracked against something unseen. His hands flew to his mouth to find and clear the obstruction. There was, indeed, something large between his lips. Whatever-it-was covered his entire mouth, blocking his airway.

Mason pulled, but it didn't budge an inch.

He reached up, found plugs in his nose. He was growing dizzy, brain blitzed by dawning asphyxia. Fingers became claws, and Mason raked the plugs with the urgency of prey fleeing a predator. It didn't matter that he was, apparently and inexplicably, floating in liquid. All that mattered was clearing those plugs — never mind the drowning.

He heard a noise like a Sherman tank raining from the sky.

Panic dawned as he imagined himself trapped, as he pictured himself speeding off the highway into a bridge stanchion same as his mother and brother, barreling headlong into a so-called *gore point*, thick snot somehow coming not from inside his sinuses but from the world itself.

Mason tasted something acrid, cloying like spilled petroleum.

He retched, but the thing down his throat still blocked the way.

And now he really *was* drowning … in whatever this was.

He heard that first voice again. Closer now, but still muffled as if by a pillow.

"NO NO NO NO NOOO!"

Sense departed. The world was made of confusion.

Powerful hands came from somewhere blind above, reaching under Mason's arms to lift him.

More shouts, louder as his head broke through the viscous gel. He heard none of those shouts in any way that mattered. He'd swallowed some of the noxious liquid the long way around — in the nose, down the back of his throat. He didn't care for conversation. Only for living.

Finding a latch point, he finally dislodged the thing in his throat and raked it aside. It went with much less fanfare than he'd imagined, sure by now that it was a long thing like a feeding tube. Things were better for a second, then became worse. He went from having something to nothing in his mouth, leaving the sludge free to seep inside.

With the help of strange hands, Mason found an edge to grab. He gripped its surface, felt air, gasped, slipped back down again, then swallowed more as the person holding him yelled for someone else to GET HIM OUT.

Then, with a mechanical sound, another unknown thing pressed upward against his feet. Mason's hands went out for stability as his legs, curiously weak, wobbled. He felt smooth curved walls around him — a tube-shaped chamber. Light was dawning.

Fingers jabbed him. Yanked him. There were urgent grunts, counterpointed by the dripping of liquid. Mason tried to remove whatever was blocking his vision but found himself unable to focus on little more than his shallow breaths and battle for consciousness.

He heaved, waiting in the forced dim. He'd gone from vertical to horizontal. It didn't feel elegant. This hesitant standing followed by a graceless slump to the deck. Then came the rattle of steps in an echoing room. Idle fingers fondled all they could reach — a metal surface underneath him, made ridged and rough for traction, like an elevated catwalk.

"Try to stay calm," said a woman's voice. "Let it pass naturally. Don't force your breathing."

Ludicrous. Mason was delirious enough to laugh. He hadn't breathed properly since this started.

His mouth opened. Someone swore. Hands with short but tidy fingernails pushed his head sideways while a second set punched him in the abdomen. He vomited without intention or effort, the effluent like spent motor oil.

Something was pulled from his face. A band came off from around his head.

He was breathing normally but still without sight or understanding.

"Try not to — *Mason?* Try not to move."

Mason thought, *I know you.* Then those sensibly short fingernails were picking at his cheeks, removing what he now knew was surgical tape — the kind that kept a patient's eyes shut while doctors did their work.

Delicately, with a second press of fingers to stabilize his skin, someone pulled off the tape, taking care not to remove his lashes with the adhesive. As his eyes flickered, he saw a bright light directly above. He turned sideways to see without pain. In the relative dim, he could now make out the diver's regulator that had been in his mouth and the blacked-out goggles over the tape to keep it dry.

What. The. Fuck?

Trying for calm and finding it impossible, Mason made himself roll again to absorb his strange surroundings.

He was in what looked like a short grain silo, sparsely illuminated and harsh where the lights hung. There was a metal gangway beneath him. Not far beyond that, Mason saw a circular pool perhaps four feet across — the vertical goo chamber he'd been pulled from, full of what looked like mucus. Leads and wires were affixed to the hinged lid above the thing, open now, a wheel on its top like a hatch in a submarine. More wires ran from the inside, now askew, some dangling into the liquid and some on the deck. Most were still affixed to Mason — to his scalp through a modified swim cap and to his body, which wore a strange and slippery suit with even more tape.

Mason closed his eyes, unable to take it all for long. He heard the shifting of bodies. His head was lifted, then set back on something soft.

He looked back up, his eyes adjusting.

Dakota had pulled him from the tank. And now alarms squealed behind her.

She ran a hand across his head and looked into his eyes. Mason couldn't speak, so nothing was said.

The owner of the other voice, a man, had rushed down the fluted metal steps of the gangway and was talking into an old-fashioned corded phone — a relic straight out of great-grandma's kitchen.

"Uh-huh. Uh-huh. No, intact. But … Yeah, I thought the same

thing. What? Oh, of course. Dakota's watching him." He vented an exasperated breath. "I don't know, sir. You're seeing the same thing as I am."

He listened.

"Could you repeat that, please, sir?"

Listened again. Then he nodded and hung up without a reply. He glanced Mason's way, reached for something, then carried it back up the gangway.

"Get me a towel, will you?" Dakota asked the man behind her.

"Step aside, Director Ward," he said.

"Why?"

"Control says he's compromised."

"If anything, he's stabilized." Dakota looked down and slapped his cheeks. "Hey. What's your name?"

"Mason. Mason Shaw."

She looked up. "See? That's not the answer he'd have given before."

"Telemetry shows a schism. You know how deep he went."

"Doesn't matter. He's out."

"*Glitched* out," said the man above Dakota, who stayed on the deck with Mason.

"You know the regulations."

Dakota's nerve broke. *"He never should have been here!"*

"Irrelevant. Please, Director. Step aside."

Dakota stood. The man had stripes on the shoulder of his uniform and a holster on his belt. He came right up beside the pair of them, and Mason noted his holster was empty. That's what the man had grabbed before coming back up here.

"Wait," said Mason.

"It's concussive," he said, raising his weapon. "You won't feel a thing."

"WAIT!"

The gun fired. Mason flinched, waiting to die.

But the man hadn't shot Mason. The report came from Dakota. Her weapon wasn't odd at all. A plain old Beretta — the same sidearm she'd carried on the force.

Blood spattered. The man's body pounded the metal as alarms continued to screech.

Dakota extended a hand. Mason — confused, cold, wet, and weak — took it.

"Look what you made me do," she said.

Then in bare feet, freezing and slipping, he ran with her to the backbeat of a rising klaxon.

SEVENTEEN

Medical Factors

DAKOTA SHOVED Mason through a door with a red bar on its front, though no additional alarms screamed when she opened it. Her trained heart slammed beats between their clasped hands as they made their exit. It was cold outside, and his limbs were still slow and weak. He was also barefoot and half-nude, dressed only in his boxers.

Mason's disrupted clock balked at the nighttime. He was sure he'd been in the middle of a hot summer day only moments before. The truth was colder and darker, either past or before the sweeping moon. They'd emerged from a cold utility building — one of those anonymous structures necessary to every city's function but forgotten by its citizens. Gray and featureless, bearing no signs beyond *KEEP OUT* and *TRESPASSING INMATES WILL BE SUMMARILY EXECUTED.*

A row of posters Mason hadn't seen before were plastered to one wall in an abbreviated line with the last only half-adhered. The ubiquitous black and white, with pink as the accent color. All showed four women in steampunk garb aiming machine guns at a cowering, uniformed lawman front and center. *UNITE AND DESTROY*, the legend read.

Strange.

But not as strange as the rest — as the midnight California waking from a balmy Texas day, as the discordant reality and upside-down logic of the bank, as the liquid still in his lungs and drying to stinking flakes on his skin, as the dead man they'd left behind, as the draw of Dakota's service weapon and the blood flecking her otherwise no-bullshit blouse.

Mason's bare feet, greased with snot from the tank, slipped on a smooth section of pavement, and he went down.

Dakota turned back to grab him. *"Hurry!"*

"What the hell is happening?" he demanded.

"We have to go."

"But what the fuck is happening?"

Mason saw the white room. The cluster of black dots — more numerous and closer each time.

Something in his look must have alarmed her. She stopped despite the air's apparent urgency, taking both of Mason's cheeks in her hands to focus on his eyes. "Do you have a headache?"

"What's—"

"Answer me. Do you have a headache?"

"No. Yes."

"Which is it?"

"Yes!"

Dakota grabbed his wrist, took his pulse with two fingers. Then she pressed them to his neck to check his heart rate at his carotid artery.

"What's your name?"

"Santa Claus."

Something moved above. Dakota half-swore, the muffled sound coming out as a grunt. She dragged Mason toward the wall behind them, her strength impressive.

"Goddammit, *what's your name?*"

"Again? I know my fucking name, okay?"

"Then tell me!" She looked up at a passing hum, perhaps a drone that had yet to cross their open sky. *"Now!"*

"Mason."

"Mason, what?"

"Mason Shaw!"

"And who am *I*?"

It was hard to resist a sarcastic answer to that one. *Mrs. Claus. Abraham Lincoln. My partner. My lover. Jeremiah the Reefer Thief.* But Dakota's face with those intense eyebrows told him to speak straight. What he didn't understand, she very much did. And though she'd never admit as much, she was terrified by it.

"Dakota. Dakota Ward. Former internal affairs for USPD, now director of intake for the Revival Corporation's privatized HRO 22, Union Station, California. What do I win?"

She blinked but said nothing. It looked like a reserved comment held for later. Then she startled yet again at something above them that Mason couldn't see and ducked back without answering.

Dakota planted one foot on a box then sprung upward with her arms extended overhead. She grabbed a machine just above the gutter — a giant thing, churning in her grip like the deck of a running lawnmower. She used gravity and her core to pike the thing downward, driving it hard against the concrete with a devastating crack.

The machine sputtered before slowing. Dakota popped a compartment on its back, one she'd clearly known where to find. Its lights died, and the hulk became a hunk of dead metal. Dakota threw something — whatever she'd yanked from its innards — away with a clatter.

"Is that a *prison drone?*" Mason asked, gawking. "How … How did you …"

Dakota grabbed his hand and pulled. He popped upright like a Jack-in-the-Box. She led again, faster now, hauling him around corners, every tug as easy for her as dragging a rag doll. She could probably lift a car. Maybe leap tall buildings in a single bound while running faster than a speeding bullet. Had she always been this strong? Or was Dakota drawing on the reserves every duty cop developed eventually — her body somehow knowing it was now or never?

Swarms of drones filled the sky, gaining in number every few seconds but visible only when they popped from beneath a careful set of concealing eaves. Somehow Dakota avoided their every gaze.

She dropped Mason in front of a door several blocks later, then pressed a ring on one finger to the left of the lock. The mechanism clicked as a magnetic solenoid retracted. She turned the knob then pushed the door wide.

"In. Now!"

Mason dropped to all fours as it closed behind him. A light popped on, red-filtered to make the space — small but industrial — resemble a darkroom. Dakota was away in a second, Mason listening to the drones circling overhead. Within moments she was back, holding a sail made of tinfoil. She assaulted him with it, nearly tackling him as she wrapped him like a Christmas present. It felt like the thin, crinkly sheets race organizers give marathoners when they cross the finish line. Space blanket shiny and silver on one side like wafer-thin oven mitts.

Dakota held up a finger, telling Mason to be quiet as she looked him over. She pushed his head down and pulled the oven mitt thing up to cover the hole. He scrunched like a turtle retracting his neck, now completely covered.

Minutes passed. Mason kept as still as his shivering limbs would allow, more out of respect for her urgency than care for his safety. She hadn't covered him for warmth. He could feel it in the waiting silence. Beyond his tinfoil cocoon, it was as real a presence as either of them. His world had been reduced to a sliver of light.

Dakota finally rose, moved to a clutter of stuff on a dust-covered desk, then woke a computer monitor he hadn't noticed before. She tapped, and lights came on, followed by a hum that made his hair stand on end. After rummaging in a different pile, she came away with what seemed to be a fist full of rags. Then she pushed Mason's foil hood away to expose his head before handing him the bundle.

She had clearly moved a few steps toward calm.

"I don't know if any of this will fit. Try. It's all there is. For some reason, we forgot to think about clothes."

Mason looked around, disoriented by the red light. He dragged on jeans that almost fit and a shirt that didn't come close. On

Mason's tall frame, it was more of a crop top. On the front was a long-stemmed glass full of crimson liquid, a cluster of grapes, and in a whimsical font, the phrase, *WINE NOT?*

"I'm freezing."

"There are blankets over there." Dakota pointed but didn't go. Now that the emergency had abated and Mason was stable, her attention went elsewhere. She stood and paced, making a check of their perimeter, all the while stealing glances at the ceiling. She kept searching her pockets for something then swearing when it wasn't there.

Mason walked to where Dakota had indicated, relieved to find his legs working smoothly again. The promised pile of blankets all smelled like dog. He pulled one over his shoulders anyway.

"It's not as cold as you think," Dakota said.

"What?"

"Your core temperature is depressed. That happens with delta-wave immersion because it's so much like sleep. Warmth will return as you come back around."

"What the fuck are you talking about?" One question from the thousand in his head. Mason knew the dangers of verbal diarrhea, but a few more interrogatives dropped out anyway, even before she could answer: "What is this place? Did you … did you really kill that man?"

"Really? You, lecturing me on justifiable force?"

"I'm not lecturing. I just want to understand." *Everything.*

Even if Dakota had all the answers, it would take time to uncover them, and Mason couldn't help but feel a clock he couldn't see kept right on ticking.

Dakota inhaled. Exhaled. "I just made a very questionable career move. Good news is, I've finally picked a side."

"What are you talking about?"

She seemed frustrated. Mason knew the look, both from seeing her in the past and from his own experience. They'd shared this particular affliction. It was one of the things that had made them such effective partners. They were constantly stepping in shit, and both had a way of being bothered by the bull while also realizing it was their own damn fault.

Dakota shoved her angst away. It took a heavy sigh, a pace-walk of fewer than ten steps, and a long moment of hands-on-hips — but then it was over, and she pulled up a rusted chair to speak plainly.

"You know about Chamber Therapy?"

Mason nodded. "Of course. They said I wasn't a candidate, but it's hard to not know about it."

"You *weren't* supposed to be. I fought hard to make *sure* you weren't because …" Dakota paused, looked away, then resumed. "Because of your family history and certain other … medical factors."

"You mean because I'm mentally unstable."

The way she looked at him made him feel like a self-pitying asshole.

"Because certain conditions increase the risk for you in ways they wouldn't increase the risk for others. And because of Carter."

Carter. Pattern Blacked and gone for good.

Mason had fought for years not to be defined by his father, and here it was happening again.

He looked at Dakota and couldn't ignore her unfortunate pity.

"What's your point? So I can't do Chamber Therapy. I made my bed. I'll lie in it."

Despite the circumstances, Dakota looked almost amused. "You've *been* in Chamber Therapy, Mason."

His mouth closed.

'For *weeks,*" she added.

EIGHTEEN

Diminished

MASON HAD HEARD stories about seeing familiar people following trauma — after a tumultuous life event, a move or a divorce, maybe a death or a hospital stay — and finding those people changed or somehow diminished. That's how he'd hoped it would be with his father. A *changed* or *diminished* Carter would make this easier. Anything to tell Mason's brain this was all alien. It wasn't the life he'd led, the father he'd had, or the family he'd lost.

A different Carter might help Mason put this life's chapter in a new box, but his father hadn't changed at all.

They let Mason into the visitor yard — really, the back lot of the intake station fenced like a place you'd let dogs out to play — and within sixty seconds, a far gate opened, then a bald man sauntered through in jeans and a plain gray tee. Carter spotted his son the second he crossed through. Mason couldn't tell from where he was sitting, but he guessed the old man had probably groaned at the sight of his waiting visitor. He turned to the guard, talking, bargaining maybe, his body language that of a man who'd changed his mind. The guard shoved him into the yard then closed the gate behind him. They were two men separated by a gulf, as it'd so often been.

Carter finally came forward.

"It's good to see you, Pop." It wasn't true, but Mason had to say something.

"Why the hell are *you* here?"

"I thought you'd want to hear how it went."

Carter laughed and looked away.

"Don't you?"

"I told you not to come here, Mason."

"Everyone says that."

"Yeah, well, I meant it." He shook his head and walked three paces away.

"Who did you think was coming to visit you, if not me?"

"I just got used to Logan."

"Well, Pop, Logan's not coming to visit anymore."

Carter sat on the nearest table's edge, still looking away in silence. Finally, he said, "I don't know why you came."

"I told you why I came."

"I don't want to know how it went, Mason. I don't want to know anything about it. It's not a fucking festival or a bake-off. There is no first prize."

"No, Pop, it wasn't a *bake-off*." Mason's anger had been building for weeks. He couldn't duke out his gripes with the old man anymore, and his usual partners for discussing *all things Carter* were now in the ground. Dakota — the only vent left — never wanted to hear it.

She had met Carter after he'd gone sideways — after she, from her perch inside Internal Affairs, had started turning a blind eye out of respect for Mason. She didn't know the man his father used to be. She saw him as dirty … or at least deeply suspicious. She could have arrested him half a dozen times before he'd finally broken into Revival's offices, and in Mason's darker moments, he couldn't help but blame her.

If IA had punished Carter's lesser offenses, he might never have become so obsessed with Nathaniel Blake and the Revival Corporation. Or, perhaps more accurately, Carter had been obsessed for *years*, the whole thing worsening after Elisabeth Reeves went missing. Without her as his insider, Carter kept up with the investigations on his own, sure there'd been foul play, and she was dead rather than missing. His quest went from quixotic to downright dangerous.

"You can't just ignore it," Mason said when his father refused to respond.

"I'm not ignoring anything."

"You haven't asked. You haven't tried to call."

"I'm in prison, Mason."

"You've turned us away when we try to visit. The warden was working with Captain DeMatisse, who always thought you got a raw deal. They secured a furlough voucher for you to attend the funeral with an escort. They said you'd been to their little kiosks but didn't respond or make any move to claim the voucher."

"Those kiosks are for snitches. I'm not a rat, Mason."

"Raylene was a wreck," Mason said after another quiet moment.

"What a surprise."

"Because her husband died, Pop. Jesus."

"So, she wasn't high? Wasn't drunk?" Carter turned away as he laughed. The questions were rhetorical, despite their truth.

"Paulie made me promise to tell you hi."

"I don't need you conveying messages for me, Mason."

"It's just a hi."

Carter's face was impassive. Mason wanted to ask him what was wrong, but that sounded too much like a counselor.

He finally spoke, probably so Mason didn't have to. "It's not terrible in here. Can you believe that?" He ran a hand over his head. Ever since Carter had started balding, he'd gone from shaving the front part of his head once a week to clearing the whole thing. His stubble now appeared everywhere at once, like an urchin growing spines. "Other than crib time, it's actually not that different from when I lived in Hell's Kitchen before you were born. Just another rough neighborhood. Only time it bugs me is when something reminds me I can't ever leave."

"And?"

"So, don't tell me people say hi like I'm somewhere they can't just tell me for themselves. You wanna do me a favor, maybe do that one. Don't convey messages. Let me pretend, will you?"

"Paulie said he never got a response. No matter how many times he asked to visit."

"I don't want Paulie to come here. Only prisoners get visitors."

"Pop, you're—"

"*I know what I am!*"

Mason looked to the building behind him, where the guard stood waiting. Carter's breed of self-denial was unique, and Mason, who knew his father better than anyone, should have seen this coming.

He stood.

Carter chuckled. "Now you're leaving?"

"You won't take a 'hi.' Clearly, I've wasted my time." He started walking.

"You know I got snowed," Carter called out behind him.

Mason turned. "Excuse me?"

"You're not stupid. You know this is a setup."

"*A setup?* Pop, you broke into Blake's office. I watched the raid footage."

"I did break in. But do you know why?"

"Because you're stubborn."

"Because of Calliope."

Mason sighed and rolled his eyes. *Calliope.* Mason was so tired of hearing that name.

Carter continued. "He's got a whole network. Not just inside the prison but out. He just needs something to broadcast. Proof of what Blake is up to, then his little group of hackers can spread it to the world."

"So, you broke in to steal something incriminating from Revival so your online pen pal could spread the message."

"Right."

"How'd that work out?"

A twitch of Carter's lips and hands told Mason if he gave the old man too much time to speak, he'd come up with some excuse for what'd happened — why Hacker Calliope's plan had failed them both. But Mason was getting his honest response first. *Nothing*.

"Figured," Mason said.

"They caught me first, Mason. If I'd gotten away clean—"

"Then what *is* Blake up to?"

"Just because I didn't get a chance to find what I was after doesn't mean it wasn't there!" Carter barked, his fuse now lit.

Mason walked back to his father, getting too close. "You're right. It *doesn't* mean the evidence wasn't there. But do you know what else it doesn't mean? That the evidence *was* there. You don't even know who Calliope is! Maybe he's playing you!"

"He's on our side," Carter mumbled.

"What's he look like?"

Carter mumbled again.

"What's Calliope look like, Pop? Are you sure he even exists?"

"Of course he exists!"

"You've never met him. Never spoken with him on the phone. Calliope could be Nathaniel Blake for all you know!"

"Why the fuck would Blake tell me to break into his own office?"

"To get you off the pot! To make you stop thinking about flushing your life away and actually do it! They sent two squads and knew exactly where to look. You didn't even take a gun with you — why?"

"Calliope said Revival has a weapon detection system. Going in armed would have set off the system."

"Did Calliope also tell you to walk in, drop your pants, and bend over? Because that's basically what happened when he got you to 'join the cause.'"

"Oh, bullshit!" Carter touched his temples — his universal tic of frustration. "You used to be a good detective. I guess now you're just toeing the company line."

"A Big Brother dig? Really? From you?"

"Oh, stop being so dramatic. You don't think money talks? The HRO system is a substantial investment for Revival, and they have to justify it to the state every five years. Doesn't it stand to reason the big boss would cheat to get that grant renewed?"

He looked away, so Carter grabbed his arm.

The guard put a hand on his gun, relaxing only after Mason glanced his way.

"Do you hear me? Revival's business is *mostly HROs,* no matter what the prospectus says. If they want to stay in business — if they want to keep getting fat and furnishing Blake's estate in Malibu — they have to show the state their way is better than bars and locked doors. Without the 'miracle' of Chamber Therapy, HROs are business as usual. Certainly not worth the insane amount of tax dollars that have—"

"Pop ..."

"Someone's greasing palms, Mason. The FDA says Chamber Therapy's not a drug, so it passes the buck to Health and Human Services for approval. HHS says it's not a social issue but a corrections issue. The corrections board says HROs aren't prisons and passes the ball for medical approval. But *is* it medical? Even Chamber Therapy itself doesn't really feel *medical.* So, the medical people send it back upstream, insisting it's the FDA's problem. And round and round it goes. Revival's approvals are all in limbo. It's fucking *weird* once you start looking. Nothing ever gets approved *or* denied. I was trying to tip the scales in one direction or the other."

"And why is that your job?"

"Because I'm a cop!"

The two men stared at one another — father and son locked in a limbo as dire and fragile as Revival's.

Mason sighed. Then he sat. "I talked to Leigh."

Carter gave him a dismissive chuckle.

"She worked with cops for years at the department. She's still a cop at heart."

"She's a mercenary," Carter said.

"Because she went where they offered her more money, a better environment, and the chance to make a difference? Not everyone's as sacrificial as you, Pop. Ironic, since the official line on you now is that you're dirty."

"I was never dirty."

"And neither was Leigh. She didn't betray anyone by moving to the HRO, and she's not a sellout. She's trying to take care of her family like everyone else. She works with the Chamber Therapy program now. Knows a lot about it. So I asked. Told her the things you and Calliope have said about how Chamber Therapy might be suspect. Leigh's a friend, so I don't think she'd lie or toe the company line. We had coffee and talked. I wasn't shy. I gave her all of your 'theories.' Laid everything out."

"Oh? And what did she have to say about that?"

"She can't share trade secrets, but ..." Mason took a long, slow breath. "It's *just therapy*, Pop. It's meant to fix things that end up broken. It's like if you're afraid of elevators, you'd go to a shrink and develop the tools to help get to your fortieth-floor office without having to take the stairs. You act like CT is brainwashing, but it's really just another way to cope."

"Not from what I heard." Carter crossed his arms.

"You're being stubborn."

"And you're being gullible!"

"Fine. Tell me why it's so bad. Tell me what's actually going on. And while you're at it, tell me why Leigh would lie to my face when she knows what's at stake — and I'm not even talking about the world. I'm talking about *our family*. I had to watch you and Reeves sneak off and whisper for months, so much that Mom was convinced you two were having an affair. I thought maybe you'd let it go after she vanished. But instead, you only grew more obsessed."

"I was following leads that Elisabeth gave me. I had strings to pull even after she was gone. *Because* she was gone. I wasn't obsessed."

"Leads that got you arrested?"

Carter grunted.

"Don't act like this isn't an obsession, Pop. Even you must see that, after everything." Mason shifted, uncomfortable as he neared the crux. "I think you should get some help. Leigh thinks so, too."

"This can't possibly be going where I think it is."

"To me suggesting you try getting into the Chamber Therapy lottery? Yes, that's exactly where it's going."

Carter laughed loudly enough to grab the guard's attention.

"It's not so crazy, Pop. You've been working hard to piss away everything for years. You're facing life inside a city-prison, and it's not like they offer parole. You've put yourself in an impossible situation, with a bad guy you can't fight and a system you can't even test, let alone expose. So, what's left to lose? I talked to someone knowledgeable who I trust, and she says your fears are groundless. This is a no-brainer from where I'm standing. If Chamber Therapy is what everyone in the world thinks it is — other than you, I mean — then it might be your only option. The only 'way out' you have left. But if you're right, despite your total lack of evidence even after *raiding their corporate fucking offices*, and the Therapy is a mindfuck that'll scramble your brain? Even if that's the case, who cares? You won't be happy until you're dead, anyway."

"You're insane," Carter muttered.

"Leigh said you're *exactly* the kind of person Chamber Therapy was made for. An otherwise good and intelligent person who could contribute to society after a small psychological tweak. You're an asset to the force when you're not raging or drunk or stuck in a storm cloud. The department needs people like you. Like *us*."

It felt like pleading. But he went on anyway.

"I've been listening to you talk about this forever. *Forever*. After your arrest, I picked up the ball and followed every sensible lead. I asked around, and not just with Leigh. *There's nothing to any of this*. Do you understand me? You proved that yourself if you can just let yourself see it."

Carter got very close to Mason. Chest to chest. His face was livid. He hated having his world challenged before he, eventually, came to inevitably accept the same thing himself.

"What, are you going to hit me?" Mason called his bluff, stabbing a finger at the guards. "Those guys right there, I think they'd have a problem with that. You always say I don't give a shit. That I take the easy way out. Well, guess what? I *do* like the easy path.

Trying to talk sense into you? That's *hard*. So maybe I shout to the guards. Maybe, if you won't even try to meet me halfway, I should go ahead and do what a piece of shit would do. The state says I stopped having a father when they threw your sorry ass in here, so maybe I take them at their word. If I never come back — if I tell them some of the shit you've told me — how much easier would my life be, and who gives a fuck about yours?"

"You're right. Who *does* give a fuck about mine? That's what I keep saying, but you keep right on trying."

"Chamber Therapy could get you out of here! It could maybe even make you …"

Mason stopped on his own, gone from furious to tentative in less than a second. He'd been about to say something uncouth about Carter, but he'd be tarring himself with the same brush if he did.

"What could it make me, Mason?" Carter asked, seeing the thread his son was too timid to pluck. "'Normal'? Tell me what you think Chamber Therapy could do. *Cure* me? Fix what's wrong in my head?"

The shift in tone was subtle. What Carter was talking about 'fixing' now was much deeper — more integral to the core of his person — than the 'obsession with Revival' Mason had been looking to cure. The ability shared by Mason and his father, but that Logan and their mother never had. That connection felt like a bond, then bondage. Having that same thing inside them was unique, magical, and terrifying. A mixed blessing to Carter. But in Mason's mind, the bad had always outweighed the good.

"I didn't say that."

Carter shook his head, grim. Despite knowing he had the moral upper hand, his father's expression made him ashamed. "What we have? It's a gift."

"It's a curse."

He shook his head again. "I had a friend growing up. Jimmy Salva. Lived right across the street from me. His daddy used to beat him so hard, he couldn't sit down. Beat his wife, too. I knew it, and so did Grandma and Grandpa, but where we lived, you kept your nose to yourself. Jimmy was one of my best friends, so whenever he needed a break from his asshole father, I'd invite him to stay over. But what always struck me as funny was that whenever I tried to let him vent — whenever I was like, 'Wouldn't it be cool if we could just turn around and pound on *him* for a change?' — Jimmy would brush it away. He didn't hate his father. He just saw what I had with Grandpa and wished they were like us. Tried to *pretend* they were. Isn't that weird?"

It was hard not to blurt the obvious. Was Carter Shaw really giving a sermon on the value of loving fatherhood? But then again, it hadn't always been bad.

Mason mumbled nothing intelligible.

"It scared your mother, Mason. That's why I stopped playing those little mind-reading games. But come on. You were there. Was I making things up back then? Or was our connection real? You really want to say there was nothing good about that?"

"I was a child."

"But never a stupid one." Carter tipped his head. "You still get headaches?"

"That's not what this is about. You know what this is about."

"I do. But I'm not broken. And neither are you, kid. Yeah, they told me I could opt for Chamber Therapy. And you know what? I thought about it, even before your little sermon. They told me there might be a risk because of some stuff on my scan. But I talked to Leigh, too. She said they'd be willing to try if I wanted. The question is, even if it works … why would I want to?"

"If they can fix your dangerous preoccupation with Revival, you could be released. Chamber Therapy gives you a chance to try again. To prove that given the same set of circumstances, you wouldn't commit the crime. It's better than expunging your record."

"How can it possibly do that, Mason?"

"You mean the process?"

"It's a black box. Even people who go through it get memory treatments afterward. Why all the mystery?"

"Patent protection. Intellectual property attorneys. Revival is under no obligation to reveal the nuts and bolts of its billion-dollar process."

"Uh-huh. And the 'process' erases crimes?"

"The language Leigh used was—"

Carter held up a hand. "Look, son. I did what I did. No matter what anyone says, I did it with a sound mind. If I can't believe in the law, then I can't be a cop. What — we're taking re-dos now? Should we even bother arresting murderers? Maybe they didn't actually do anything wrong once the Master Eraser is deployed."

"You know it's not like that."

"Look at me. Do I seem nuts to you?"

"It isn't that simple."

"Okay. Then don't use your eyes. You can see into me better in other ways, anyway."

"Pop ..."

"Blake is bad, Mason. He's not the Golden Boy he used to be, earning do-gooder of the Year or whatever the fuck he was trying to do while working with all those kids. Revival is up to something; I'm just not sure what. I didn't get here because I acted like a lunatic. I ended up in 22 because I was being a cop."

"A cop who breaks and enters."

"Logan always understood. As long as the police have to play by rules that the criminals don't, nothing gets done. I took a chance and lost. That doesn't mean the blame game was true." Carter leaned closer. "Come on, Mason. You remember how to do this. All it takes is thirty seconds of attention."

Mason stood again. "This was a mistake. You don't want to be bothered? You want to just live here inside your little lie? Fine. I've done what I came here to do."

"To taunt me?"

"*To tell you your wife and son are in the ground, even if you don't fucking care!*"

Carter stopped.

Mason half-turned to go.

"I care," Carter said.

"It doesn't matter."

"Look." And in the pause between that single word and what was still coming, Mason heard his father reach for the final straw between them. If there was a chance remaining to set aside the macho chest-thumping and be real, this was it. After today, things would stay broken forever. "I … I'm …" Another pause. This had to be incredibly hard for his father to admit while tempers still flared. "I'm worried about you."

"Worry about yourself."

"I heard you're drinking. I hear you've gotten some write-ups. You never used to face disciplinary action at work. Now it's happening all the time."

"You're spying on me? How?"

"It doesn't matter. What I did to get thrown in here? That was my choice. *Mine.* I didn't want to drag you down with me." Carter swallowed, and for a flickering moment, Mason thought he saw a peek of emotion. *"Any* of you."

"Well, isn't that nice. Look, Pop, I've gotta go."

This time, Carter didn't call him back. So halfway to the door, Mason stopped on his own. He turned, then something crumbled inside him. Carter was still at the picnic table, sitting at center with his hands folded, head halfway down as if about to say grace. The hard man was finally diminished.

"Pop," Mason said.

Carter looked up.

"Just consider Chamber Therapy if they offer it. Okay?"

"So I can get out of here? And be 'normal'?"

A voice from a thousand years ago came to the front of Mason's mind.

How many fingers am I holding up?

Two.

This time, there'd be two. One for each of the departed, trimming their tribe by half.

"So they can help you," Mason answered, knowing it was a cop-out.

Now Carter stood.

"Check it out, is all I'm saying," Mason tried a final time.

Carter eyed the guard, the gate, his re-entry to the city prison. "Just go, Mason. You've said enough."

NINETEEN

Try Not to Scream

MASON WOKE to the feeling of a cool something on his forehead.

He felt a drip and heard the soft movement of a non-threatening presence. His brain itself seemed to hurt, so he kept his eyes closed for thirty extra seconds. Then, when Mason knew he was awake and it became clear the other person in the room knew it, he opened up, unsure of what he'd see.

Mason saw and remembered. He recalled that strange tank of goo, then running away. Dakota had shot someone and — this part was fuzzy but felt true — beat the hell out of a drone with her bare hands.

He closed his eyes again and tried not to think about the rag Dakota was holding, moistened by God knew what, considering the place probably didn't have running water.

"Tired?" she asked.

"I'm hoping this is a dream."

"It's not."

"Let me try, anyway." He shifted, then rolled to one side. Sat up, looked around, and sighed. "Dammit."

She indicated the rag in her hand. "You were burning up."

"That's the least of my concerns. I don't remember falling asleep."

Dakota made a *close enough* gesture that was all head and shoulders, which Mason took to mean he hadn't snoozed so much as passed out. He sat up straighter, feeling even more at a disadvantage … and he'd felt positively naked before.

"Something to eat?" She offered a pair of what looked like tiny, perfectly groomed burial mounds in her palm, yellow and filled with cream.

"Twinkies?" Mason groaned.

"You need your strength."

"Exactly." He pushed the sugar bombs away. "I need my strength, so no thanks." Still, he couldn't help making a face. In all the confusion, of course, the *Twinkies* were real all along.

"I'm just glad you're alive," Dakota told him.

Mason looked around. He remembered the drones and that it'd been dark enough to be after curfew. "I guess that goes for both of us. Where are the drones that should have killed us by now?"

"Distracted," Dakota answered, without bothering to explain. "But that's not what I meant. I'm more shocked that your brain isn't fried."

"What are you talking about?"

"Chamber Therapy." She poked at him with her hands, but he could tell she'd normally do this particular fussing with instruments and tablets. "Remember?"

"I remember you saying I was in it. But I'm not."

"Don't you remember waking up? Don't you remember me pulling you out of the vat?"

"And?"

"Mason … that's what Chamber Therapy *is.*" Dakota sat opposite him. Her hand returned to his forehead, nursemaiding him like a hovering mother. "Are you sure you feel all right?"

Mason pushed the hand away. "The tube full of goo. *That* was Chamber Therapy?"

"Yes. You've heard about full-sensory immersion?"

"Like for video games?"

"Same spectrum, but far more advanced. Revival's simulation tech is nearly perfect. They've done university studies where they've put subjects into simulations during REM sleep, and most never even *know* it's a simulation. Their minds accept what's in front of them and skim past all the things that don't make sense. It's like a dream in that way. People accept pretty much everything they see while inside it … like you did."

Mason looked to the building's door as if answers lay there. He'd sort of figured this out already, but hearing it was a knife to his stomach. When everything else went to shit, he needed to trust the world around him.

"You're saying I was *inside a simulation?*"

She nodded. "Several times. Including the last one, where you woke up inside. *That*, we hadn't seen coming." There had to be more to the story — *seen coming* wasn't as cut-and-dry as Dakota was pretending.

"What was a simulation, and what was real?" Mason asked.

"What do you mean?"

"Over the past however-long, which parts of what I remember were real and which were only a goo dream? I'm in a fog right now. You're either Dakota Ward or the Tooth Fairy. You ask me, *none* of this is real."

"We take people at night, using a sedative, so they don't wake, then return them before dawn."

"Why?"

"Don't you remember *Inception?* When you're trying to put new ideas in someone's head, you need to do it at the subconscious level. Of course, people eventually know they're in CT, but each simulation should have the feel of a dream while it's happening. Something that came from *inside them*, not from us, and whose ideas they should consider listening to."

Mason thought. "I remember a bank."

Dakota nodded. "We had you in the Heist simulation. Standard rehab for cases like yours."

"So, the bank wasn't real?"

"Define 'real' for me, Mason."

Even if he'd had an answer, the request was clearly rhetorical.

"And the green shit I was floating in?"

"Chamber Therapy is like sensory deprivation with a kick. The gel dulls your native nerve signals, so your brain has an easier time believing what we show you. Surely Carter explained this."

It was a strange thing to say because one of Mason's most consistent complaints, to Dakota among others, was that his father had revealed almost nothing, even after all his investigation. He'd only say, "Chamber Therapy is a black box." Dakota forgetting — and keeping the truth from Mason — felt like a betrayal.

"How do you know about this?"

"Because I'm in charge of the program." Dakota raised her eyebrows when he didn't nod right away. "Remember? Going through intake before they put you inside?"

But Mason had thought, quite clearly, that someone else was in charge of the Chamber Therapy program.

Dakota was … Dakota was …

Well, Dakota was in charge of *something else.*

He recalled a sense of wanting to save her from whatever that something else was, but that didn't make sense, either. Why would he want to save her from her job?

Fuck. This was hard. Up and down were the same goddamned thing.

She was looking at him strangely. "Are you okay?"

"I'm having a little trouble figuring out what's what."

Dakota nodded. "Give it time. You came out of simulated reality without a transition period, and it's messing with your head. Normally you'd get a cocktail when the session finished to ease your re-acclimation. One component causes retrograde amnesia, blurring the previous half-day or so that way your mind doesn't have to choose between versions of 'what just happened.'" She shrugged. "Unfortunately, I couldn't give you the spa treatment this time. I was sort of in a rush to get you out of there."

Mason remembered the military man above him, then Dakota's bullet to end his life.

She seemed to wrestle with a decision then moved from kneeling to sitting cross-legged on the floor across from him. "What do you know about all of this? Beyond what you've told me in the past."

"Same as anyone else."

"And Carter really told you nothing?"

"Nothing I was able to substantiate." His memory prickled, insisting some connection between Carter and Chamber Therapy beyond the dead-ending everyone already knew, but that thought was as insubstantial as all the rest. "Why?"

Dakota drew a few deep breaths, looking around as if for help. "How long have you been here? Inside the HRO, I mean."

"A day." He looked at the darkness outside. "A day and a half."

She shook her head. "It's been three weeks. And you've had fifteen Chamber Therapy sessions in that time."

Mason laughed, but Dakota didn't.

"You're serious."

"Like I said, we use a drug that affects short-term memory to erase your recall between sessions. Typically, this means that Chamber Therapy subjects don't know they're in a sim until their full run is over. In your case, all those short-term doses seem to have accumulated and affected your long-term memory as well. Tonight's baseline showed some anomalies, so we ran a scan. The effect seems to be accelerating. It happens with some subjects, which is why we screen for it and aren't supposed to send those people through. I didn't want to put you under last night. I *never* wanted you under. This latest session happened only because Scott insisted."

Mason pantomimed a gun with his fingers and pulled the invisible trigger. *"Scott?"*

Dakota nodded then quickly moved on. She either didn't think Scott's murder was a big deal or saw it as something to compartmentalize now and consider later.

"What's the last thing you remember, before the bank?"

His face scrunched. "I was with ... *Nic?* We were exploring and ran across a restricted area. Fences and barbed wire. Then ..." Mason stopped, recalling something awry. He turned from it. It must have been part of the dream — not a real thing after all.

"And then what?"

Oh, no big deal. Nic suddenly turned into a giant Mr. Clean who choked me out and stomped on my face. There was a tiny hurricane in the sky — and when I blink for too long, I see holes in the world arranged a Fibonacci spiral. See? High school math was good for something, after all. It'll help me count all the ways I keep losing my mind.

"Never mind. Doesn't matter."

"What about your crime? Do you remember why you were arrested?"

"Of course."

"What did you do?"

"I robbed a bank."

"Are you sure?"

Mason's mouth opened to say, of course, he was sure. What kind of person didn't remember a thing like that? But then it closed, and he started to think. Because no, that didn't sound like Mason at all.

"You were in a bar. You were drunk. The bartender cut you off, so you started shouting at him. He didn't like that. Do you remember now?"

Vaguely. The memory of the bar fight laid beneath another of him, robbing the bank like a double exposure. Mason could see and recall it, but the memory of guns and bandits felt fresher.

"There were three brothers," he said, searching. "The owner and his two pals."

"That's right. You grabbed a pool cue. Started screaming at them."

Mason nodded, memories coming faster. "I remember. Lieutenant Auran was there. He tried to stop me. Then ..." He squinted. "Did that little Norwegian fucker try to *cuff* me?"

But it wasn't a question that required an answer. Mason could see it all now, and curiously, it felt like a month ago. He'd given Auran a bruise, then kicked back-up in the nuts. They'd handled him with kid gloves, seeming to realize he'd been fuckered by tequila. That hadn't stopped Mason from mouthing off through his entire ride to the station, calling the duty sergeant names, then spitting in Detective Balforth's face while the captain looked on with disappointed eyes.

Mason seemed to remember his fellow officers not wanting to book him, before he gave them no choice. He was supposed to cool off in a holding cell, but he sobered up and acted even worse.

Had he insulted someone's mother? Yes, almost for sure.

"It was supposed to be disorderly conduct," Dakota explained. "You made it into something more. Do you remember talking to me?"

"Before you brought me in."

"That's right. You'd blown it at the station, and then you blew it with me. I couldn't save you if you weren't willing to save yourself. Do you remember me telling you that?"

"Yeah. But that felt like yesterday morning."

"Give it time. We didn't re-dose you with the memory drug, and this time your mind never fully accepted the sim. You were trying to shake it off even before you woke up."

She looked at him sideways for a moment, and Mason was sure she'd ask if anything strange happened inside — if, looking back, he remembered clues that might point to "fighting the sim." Maybe the yacht qualified. Maybe the brush-cut blonde. The way she and her buddies had spoken to Mason as if they were real? Maybe that, too, qualified as fighting.

But Dakota said nothing, and Mason's introspection collapsed on itself like a dying star. He was suddenly waist-deep in recall, sorting his memories the way a grieving relative sifts through the recently deceased's belongings.

"What does it do? How is it supposed to work?"

Dakota inhaled again. Exhaled. Mason got the impression that much was coming.

"You know Revival's history. Originally, the goal was to find a new treatment for autistic children. Maybe schizophrenic kids, as well. Current treatments for both involve traditional talk therapy, behavior modification therapy, and medication. But they're all limited because they can't get at the root of the problem, which is somewhere in here." Dakota tapped her skull. "So, Revival invented a form of immersive therapy designed to take subjects' minds through various scenarios, all of which happened in safe environments with no real-world risk. Simulations guided children through situations in which they had to make choices — then tweaked those same situations over time to modify and normalize those decisions."

"Sure. Whatever that means."

Dakota pressed on. "The whole thing was too intense for children. The program was killed after a few unfortunate accidents. Revival had a massive NIH grant, but it got revoked. Everyone apparently thought they were going under, but then Blake had a new idea. How about they try the same thing in prisons? People care a lot less about mishaps with prisoners, especially after they've been signed off as unpersons."

"I don't get your point."

"The bank robbery you feel like you took part in? It didn't actually happen — not before the sim, nor after it, not in real life at any point in time. You experienced a peer-to-peer simulation we call The Heist. Five inmates are put under together, and they have to work through a similar crime with parallel decisions. The goal is to repeatedly put a prisoner through their crime until they've finally learned their lesson and get everything right."

"You mean until they pull off the robbery?"

Dakota shook her head. "The opposite. Until participants begin making 'morally correct' choices, urged toward them by prompts inside the sim. For instance, do you remember the old lady?"

Mason started to shake his head, but then he stopped and, surprised, began to nod. "The old woman with the walker. The one Watt kept yelling at to hit the ground." Then, after hearing his own words, he asked, "Who's Watt?"

"Frank Watt. "He's in your crib. You don't remember?"

Jesus. Yes, Mason remembered. But doing so was like navigating an M.C. Escher drawing. He barely remembered Watt from the bank job, except that some part of him very much did. He also remembered Frank from the Red Crib, who he now realized looked exactly the same.

He remembered it all since yesterday morning … except if Dakota was telling the truth, it'd actually been almost a month since Mason had met Watt. Or Frank. Or Frank Watt.

"*Now* I remember."

Dakota seemed relieved. She didn't just nod in acknowledgment. She exhaled what appeared to be a long-held breath. "I imagine you're going to be confused for a while," she said — but behind the word *confused*, Mason could sense more troubling things Dakota feared might come to pass. "Immersion and removal from immersion are delicate processes. The choices are meant to play out. Then we slowly bring you back to reality, give you an injection, then send you back into gen pop, still asleep and none the wiser. That's what's *supposed* to happen. But your vitals have gone funny every time we've put you under. You go off-script even outside of assigned decision points because you're always fighting the simulation."

"You said I was supposed to be in there with four other people."

"Groups of five, yes."

"But there were six." He was remembering quickly now, the images all rushing back like a repressed memory suddenly woken, overwhelming in its suddenness. He remembered the look of Watt's hair. The design of Leigh's tattoos. The dangling gold earrings worn by … But no, that last one didn't feel right.

"One of the people you see inside is an AI. Cruz. He leads the heist but doesn't force decisions. The decisions always have to be the participants'. We need him there to report back after the sim is over. But I don't have his report this time, so I'm going to need yours. What *happened* in there, Mason?"

"*Me?* Why don't *you* explain what happened?"

"We can't see inside the simulations while they're live. That's why Cruz exists."

"You just put us in and hope?"

"It's a bit more complicated than that. We get vitals. Telemetry. But no visuals or audio. Those things aren't actually 'visual' or 'audio,' anyway. Sights and sounds are created within a shared neural matrix. It's not like we can plug them into a monitor and see what you see."

"What did your fancy telemetry tell you this time?"

"I wish I knew. You persisted inside after the sim officially ended, and that's not supposed to happen. Something broke the wall before we could extract you. The other participants were already out."

"You mean dead."

"Out," Dakota repeated. "They're perfectly fine, from what the other immersion centers reported. You're the only one who gave us any problems."

Mason sent his mind back, finding recall simple but tangled like last year's Christmas lights. He remembered riding in the van again and again, pulling on his ski mask again and again, and walking through the robbery's steps again and again. But only once did he remember … a boat? Had there really been a *boat?* And an army? And a small blonde with rogue soldiers?

"I don't know," he said.

"Think."

"I said I don't know."

"And I said to *think!*"

Mason closed his eyes. He was sure, somehow, he'd see an all-white room and a cluster of black dots. Instead, he saw a woman, very close, with pale skin and gigantic, eerie blue eyes.

Stay or go? You have to decide.

Mason hadn't answered that. Or maybe he had. He remembered the back room, the gunner, and the man with the glasses. The strange woman and her questions. The tinfoil sheet she'd used to suffocate him before the whole world had cracked. Before he emerged, literally kicking and figuratively screaming.

Their gazes locked, each of them thinking something they were unwilling to share. He knew only his half — what felt a bit too close to the bone to admit, even to her.

Us. Or them. A decision in the balance. They'd all stared, waiting for Mason to choose.

Dakota finally broke the moment. "We can't stay here long. I can't remove your blood dongle, but I can confuse it."

Mason looked at the thin silver blanket, understanding it had shielded his signal, and something in this room had taken care of the rest. But when he looked back at Dakota, she held a syringe instead of a foil blanket.

"This will stimulate your body to overproduce new red blood cells as noise to hide your tagged cells. It will also hurt like hell."

"But the tagged ones are still there," Mason answered.

"Yes. There's technically a way to remove them once you have enough replacements circulating. It's just ..." Dakota stopped, unwilling to say what it *just was*. She moved to the room's other end then uncovered something that'd been obscured with a drop cloth.

It looked medical. And terrifying.

She held up a line of rubber tubing, the end of it fixed with a constellation of five razor-sharp needles.

"This will hurt even more. So, try not to scream."

TWENTY

Thirteen Sessions

A WORLD of pain and one unconscious interlude later, Mason felt someone slapping his cheeks.

He opened his eyes to see Dakota in front of him. The room was dim. She had turned a lone light on to illuminate the chair. It was behind her head, throwing her into profile like an anonymous witness.

More light slapping. "Mason. Are you okay?"

The question implied that recently, he hadn't been. This was news to Mason … until it wasn't.

He recalled those needles going into his arm one by one, the whole affair more like amateur acupuncture than phlebotomy. He'd felt more like a pincushion than a patient.

Beyond that, Mason remembered the room spinning and total disorientation. It wasn't a fear of needles — or even the pain — that had knocked him silly. It'd been an irrational fear that if he swooned, he'd wake in an all-white room pocked with black circles in lazy spirals. He'd see that little black whirlpool again and the big man who'd been so intrigued by what it all meant.

"Hold him still," someone said.

Dakota, now close enough for Mason to see her eyes, put one

hand on each of his upper arms then pushed him back against his chair.

"You gave me the drugs. The forgetfulness drugs."

"We considered it," Dakota admitted, "but there might be side effects."

"*We?*"

There was a third person in the room, silhouetted by harsh light and shadows. Dakota was fit. The other, judging by its featureless shape, was downright skinny.

"Yeah. *We.* The two of us."

The second woman tapped at her tablet. Mason still couldn't see her face, but she appeared to have long blonde hair tied up in a messy knot. Backlit, her entire head seemed wild, like something had scared her.

"He's still got lagging delta," said the stranger.

"How? He's awake," Dakota replied.

"I don't know what to tell you," said the second woman, working the tablet. "He's got brain waves like he's still in the simulation. Or like he's dreaming. Has he given you his name?"

Mason, feeling woozy and annoyed, answered instead. "I've licked whipped cream out of her belly button. So yes, *she knows my fucking name.*"

The silhouette seemed to face him, then turned to Dakota again. Something in her manner was intensely familiar.

"Has he given you his name?"

"Yes."

"When?"

"Immediately after extraction."

The other woman's blacked-out face swiveled back to Mason.

"What's your name?"

Mason said nothing.

"Come on, dick. Maybe I never let you lick whipped cream off me, but I don't need your name any more than she does. This is for you."

Mason squinted at that. Who was this woman?

"What?"

"Just tell her," Dakota said.

"Mason Shaw."

"Mason. You're sure about that?"

"I know my goddamn name."

"I see. And who's *Carter* Shaw?"

"My father."

The two women looked at one another, then turned away from him.

"What the hell's going on here? Who the hell is that, Dakota?"

"Shh. She's a doctor."

"Sort of," said the other.

Mason sat up. This time, the second woman pushed him back. He almost saw her face. Long features, high cheekbones.

"Just sit for a while. You've got a weird collection of contradictory brain states going on. You were in REM — dream sleep — but have this odd long tail of delta waves at the same time. Looking at your graphs, it's hard to say whether you're high and drifting on the couch, running a marathon, or in a coma."

Mason sat. Waited.

"Okay. It's settling now." Then to Mason, "Do you remember where you are?"

"You mean like I remember my name? Of course, I remember. Jesus Christ."

"So, where are you?"

"Some building near the administrative zone. Of HRO 22, Union Station. Dakota took me here after dragging me out of a snot bath."

Dakota spoke next. "But you don't remember Leigh?"

The second woman stepped into the light, and he knew.

"You were in my simulation. You sat near the back door."

"That's right. Is that the only place you know me from?"

"*Should* there be more?" Maybe there should be — he knew this woman from more than the sim. His mind was a mess. Maybe she used to shop at his local Provisions. Maybe he sat next to her once on a plane.

"Maybe. But let it come naturally."

"Your name is … D'Alvo," Mason said, unsure of how he knew.

"Close. D'Abo. Leigh D'Abo."

"Except that one time, this giant white guy was in your place."

Again, the women traded glances.

Leigh said, "Do you mean in real life? Here, in the prison?"

"What — you're a prisoner?"

"She's one of your cohorts," Dakota explained. "She's part of the group you do your simulations with. That's why you saw her in the sim, Mason."

"Yes. I'm a prisoner like you. But what do you mean by 'a giant white guy was in my place'? Do you mean inside the prison? Like you saw a man in my bunk instead of me?"

"I mean inside the simulation. One time, you weren't there, but another guy was." Mason considered elaborating, but instinct suggested he keep that particular truth to himself.

Another traded glance. His head was clearing, and the constant knowing looks between them were now irritating him.

"You saw someone in Leigh's place … *inside the simulation,*" Dakota repeated.

"Yes."

"Like, this other person was there *instead of* Leigh. Sitting in the same place. He was there, but Leigh wasn't."

"*Yes!* Jesus!"

Dakota looked at Leigh. "How many sims have you had?"

"Thirteen."

"Are you sure?"

"Don't you erase everyone's memory after each loop?" Mason asked.

"Leigh and I have an arrangement. She remembers everything."

"Thirteen," Leigh repeated. "I'm sure. It's my lucky number."

"And you've seen Mason in all of them?"

"Of course."

"I've only been in three simulations. Not thirteen."

"You've been in thirteen," Leigh snapped. "*You* don't remember everything yet."

"What the hell makes you think *you* know everything?" he snapped right back.

"Because Dakota brought me in before my first loop."

"Why?"

"Because she's a doctor," Dakota said.

"Army medical. Combat and triage."

"I knew I'd need help at some point."

"Why?"

"It's why we stocked this room. Why we shielded it from the drones."

"Why did you need a doctor?"

"So there'd be someone to poke you in the arm while you pass out like a little bitch. By the time I showed up, Dakota's amateur hour had your arm looking like a dissection." Leigh turned to spy a table not far off, and Mason saw it was covered in bloody towels. *His* blood, it seemed.

"Did you just call me a little bitch?" Mason was more amused than bothered.

"The system has obviously been alerted, and if we make too much noise, they might start eyeing the chaos alarm. The clock is now ticking."

Dakota spoke to Leigh, cutting Mason off ahead of his reply. "Thirteen sessions. You're positive you've done *exactly* that number? This is a big deal. Thirteen's a lot. You could have missed one."

"I'm a little OCD. I've been waiting for thirteen. I don't forget numbers."

Dakota walked away as if looking for something.

"What's going on?"

She again spoke to Leigh, ignoring Mason: "There've been fourteen sessions with your cohort."

"I don't know how to tell you any other way, Dakota. It's been *thirteen*. Not *fourteen*."

Dakota turned a tablet so Leigh could see it.

"Are you sure of this data?" Leigh asked, her eyes widening.

"As sure as you are of thirteen."

"What's the big deal?" Mason asked.

"Sim cohorts don't change," Dakota told him. "Chamber Therapy is all about learning through repeat exposure, even though the amnesia drug eliminates awareness of those repeats on a conscious level. It's hard enough to control for variables that might alter the outcome without changing people, too. So, the people *don't* change, or CT would be too randomized." She glanced at Leigh. "Her cohort — your cohort — has done the Heist simulation fourteen times."

"You told me thirteen," Mason said.

"I was going off of Leigh's number. This says fourteen. I checked your personal telemetry. It shows fourteen as well."

"And?"

"And Leigh seems to feel she's only done thirteen."

"Leigh is *sure* she's only done thirteen," Leigh corrected.

Dakota tapped the tablet. "Telemetry agrees with you. Thirteen."

They stood in heavy silence.

"You want to tell me what's happening here?" Mason asked.

Leigh shushed him. Then they conversed in low tones, too rushed for him to hear.

"HELLO?"

Dakota finally turned. "This is unusual. We just need to figure out what it means."

"What, that she had one less heist than the rest of us? Why does it matter?"

"Because *cohorts don't change.*" Some of Leigh's hair had freed itself from the knot, making her look frenzied.

"Well, they *did* change." Mason knew how much wasn't right here just by the air, but he still couldn't resist the advantage this little glitch gave him. Cheering their failure to notice this earlier was a little like saying *I told you so.* It felt good to see them humbled instead of condescending, but most of Mason knew he was happy for all the wrong reasons — this mystery was as bad for him as it was for them.

"Put the hat back on him," Leigh told Dakota.

"What hat?"

Dakota held up a device Mason remembered — the brass spider-looking thing she'd used on him during intake. "Sit back."

"Hey, don't put that shit on me again." Mason was pretty sure the "hat" was the reason he'd blacked out.

"It monitors your brainwaves."

"You just said you can monitor my brainwaves right now."

"This is deeper."

"Like 'fuck me in the head' deeper?"

"It's not like Chamber Therapy. It isn't dangerous."

Dakota had said that off the cuff, but Mason didn't like it. Her pair of sentences meant Chamber Therapy *was* dangerous — at least to him — and they'd nonetheless done it to him fourteen times.

He pulled away and put his hand between himself and the hat. "Just tell me what's going on. Maybe I can help."

"There was an interloper in one of your sims. Like a hijack," Dakota said. "That's not supposed to happen. We saw anomalous readings in a few of your sessions but figured it was you pushing against the sim. That has its own dangers."

"Dangers like what?"

"That's not important right now."

"But Preacher is?" Dammit. He hadn't meant to say the name. And now he'd lost his ace.

"Who?"

Oh, well. No point in hiding it now.

"*Preacher.* That's who was in my sim."

"And who's that?" Leigh asked.

"Who knows? He just said that was his name." Mason told the story then described him. The more he offered proactively, hopefully, the less they'd ask. Preacher had appeared in his sim, yes. But he'd shown up other places, too — and that bit of embarrassing trivia, Mason wasn't so eager to share.

It's because you're crazy. Crazy like Dear Old Dad. Remember passing out at intake? Remember scoping that barn and losing several hours after the bus dropped you off?

Mason just needed time for the brain fog to clear. He'd lost a lot more time than hours — if Dakota was right, he'd been inside for weeks.

The women had abandoned him again, talking among themselves. It made his temper flare. He was tired of being treated like a helpless victim. Or a thing.

"I don't know why you're so up your asses about this. Preacher probably got cross-linked. Wires crossed. Two sims coming together or something."

"That's not how it works," Leigh said. "Stay in your lane, Detective."

Detective. But Dakota hadn't mentioned he was a cop. Had she told Leigh out of earshot? Maybe when he'd been out? Or was the itching feeling that he knew her from somewhere else intruding again, insisting he pay it more mind?

"So, they're perfect," Mason said. "Revival's system is *perfect*. No room for errors or flaws. Is that about right?"

"They certainly don't 'cross wires,' Leigh said in his general direction, shaking her head.

"Then explain the boat."

Two heads spun toward him.

"Explain the minigun."

"'Minigun'?"

"Explain the *gang*," Mason said, "if the simulation is so perfect, and you're so goddamn smart."

"What are you talking about?"

"Jesus, Dakota. Are you blind? You were running the sim that went off the rails. Nothing piqued your interest?"

"Its collapse piqued my interest. Your near cardiac arrest piqued my interest. The fact that everyone withdrew from the completed sim without you piqued my interest, and the way the extended sim booted you out on its own after that, with altered brain waves, piqued the living *fuck* out of my interest. But I told you — *We can't see the contents of simulations.* We only saw chaos. So maybe you tell us, Mason. What happened in there?"

"Other people came in. Three of them. They just ... entered the sim. Crashed it, really."

"CPUs," Dakota said to Leigh.

"These weren't background," Mason countered. "They didn't stand back. They barreled through the middle of everything. I remember a few of the other loops. I know they weren't supposed to be there. I mean … the armored speedboat in the middle of a city? The minigun?"

In the silence that followed, Mason thought but didn't say, *I know it sounds crazy.*

Leigh muttered something to Dakota. He couldn't make it out, but it sounded like she was asking if Dakota believed him.

"Why would I lie?" Mason yelled to them. He hadn't risen from his chair yet. The world still wanted to spin.

"You don't have to be lying," Leigh answered. "You could be confused."

"I'm not confused." He was finding himself increasingly unable to hold his temper. "I'm telling you—"

Leigh held up a hand. They both concentrated on the tablet, seemingly trying to find something.

Then they looked back at Mason. Dakota's arm sagged, allowing him to see the tablet's screen. It was hard to say for sure, but it appeared that they had looked up the sim in question. Maybe they couldn't see miniguns and boats and women with platinum blonde hair, but the flashing red square visible even from Mason's vantage said all he needed to know.

Whatever they'd found about his last aborted sim had killed their primacy and closed their superior mouths. The blonde woman and her crew, apparently, were well beyond whatever Dakota and Leigh expected.

"God Mode," Dakota whispered.

Then the hail of bullets began.

TWENTY-ONE

Prison Propaganda

PAPER SHREDDED SEEMINGLY of its own accord as shells ripped through cheap stucco construction, perforating piles someone had left strewn about. Scraps of lathe and lumber leaped into the air like jumping beans. The sound was deafening. Explosive reports laid atop the metallic rattle of ten or more weapons at once, flanking two sides of the building and peppering holes sufficient to see stars through the walls.

Leigh and Dakota dove. Mason, still seated, fell forward and slumped. Seconds later, the apparatus he'd been sitting in — cobbled, he saw now, from inexpertly welded aluminum — grew grape-sized pores. Shrapnel grazed his cheek, leaving a hot-soldered gash.

It finally stopped. Mason heard voices and movement outside — gunners regrouping, surely about to bust in or resume their dicing from a distance.

"Goddammit," Dakota said, her voice low.

Leigh slid the tablet to her. It was still whole, and Mason got the impression that was both lucky and important. "Call them off," she hissed.

"It's not drones."

"It *might* be drones."

"Drones fire plasma." She reached down, checked her sidearm.

For a moment, Mason was excited. He'd been confused and woozy enough to forget she was armed. But then his excitement wavered. One magazine of a Beretta was hardly enough for all those comers.

"Those are *Docents* out there." Dakota adjusted her grip on her gun.

"Docents aren't allowed to enter the prison without credible intel," Leigh said. "I thought you'd smothered our 'credible intel'!"

"Yeah, well." She shrugged.

"You said nobody would know the session broke down. I thought you bought us time!"

"There were complications," Dakota said.

"What kind of complications?"

"Shots were fired."

Leigh groaned.

Mason thought of the dead man Dakota had left behind and the alarms heralding their exit. It sounded like their plan had changed, or maybe Dakota's ability to hide alarms from new drones wasn't as good as she'd imagined. Either way, they had a problem if human Docents were outside. Humans couldn't be reprogrammed like machines.

"We had a deal," Leigh went on, rattled. "You clear the way, I zero out his dongle. *Maybe* I tend to injuries. But I can't exactly—"

Dakota held up a finger for silence. She'd been trying to reach something high on a rolling surgical tray — a glass sphere about the size of an orange. She managed to grab it, but then the tray's casters caught on a rug, and the thing went down like a bomb.

Gunfire resumed. Another several hundred holes pocked the walls of their urban adobe.

"They never shoot at the floor," Dakota said, marveling at the waist-level bullet holes. "Why don't they ever shoot *down?*"

Mason considered asking what the hell she was talking about, but Dakota scooched to a side door before he could, leading with her feet like descending a horizontal ladder. He stopped speaking when she kicked open the door and threw the glass sphere through the opening.

"What was that?"

"Plug your ears. As hard as you can."

"Not until you tell me what's——"

"NOW, MASON!"

He followed the order. It wasn't a conscious thing. It happened somewhere between ears and brain stem without notifying his cortex. Then *bang-bang-bang* came from the other side. Three events, like cards in a shuffle. Mason pressed his hands tighter against his ears as a sound outside, like a giant belching, accompanied a bright flash. He rolled to the side then threw up all over the floor.

A rough hand grabbed his collar. Leigh.

"Thought you were supposed to be smart?" she spat at him.

Mason wiped his mouth, stomach lurching and head spinning.

"Plug your ears. *Plug*, not 'put hands over,'" she said.

Dakota stood, now without fear. Leigh followed. Mason, who was out of the loop, stopped in a crouch before joining them. No bullets came.

"Tell me you didn't look at the flash," Dakota said, looking Mason over.

"I looked at the flash."

"Great."

Mason puked again. The sound was wrenching, even to him. Still, nobody fired.

"Can you walk?"

Mason nodded.

They moved to the door on the building's opposite end, equally perforated by bullets as the wall. Dakota opened it with fearless urgency. They exited, Mason peeking around the corner, curious whether Dakota had committed more murders. But instead of seeing corpses under the streetlights that'd been blown apart by her belching flash-bomb, he saw a dozen or so men and women in riot armor rolling on the ground, clutching themselves and moaning.

"What was that thing you threw at them?" Mason asked.

"Subsonic grenade. Makes you shit yourself."

"You're kidding."

"Be glad you at least got your hands over your ears and didn't see the whole flash. Think you feel sick now? You'd be rapid-firing out the wrong end after a full blast."

"I've never heard of anything like that."

Her face went neutral. It was becoming ever more apparent this wasn't a haphazard flight. Dakota had seemed to shoot and run on impulse back when he'd still been gooey, but only the specific timing must have been at issue. The rest had been planned. She'd stocked the building, contracted with Leigh, and apparently obtained an illegal and unknown — but highly effective — nonlethal weapon from places unknown.

Mason filed all his questions for later, feeling the moment's urgency like a heartbeat.

They were in an alleyway, still dark, still middle of the night. The electric lights inside had let them see, but now the same job fell mostly to a bone-white crescent moon. There were a few functional streetlights like the one around the building's front — yellowed lenses, painting the streets like jaundice — but most had been broken and never replaced. Who needed light at night when all the prisoners were supposed to be locked down for curfew?

"I have to get back," Leigh said, looking skyward. Her gaze scurried to all corners as she took in the scene. She'd grabbed the space blanket on the way out, and now she donned it, wrapping herself like it was a coat — including a makeshift hood that reminded Mason of E.T. in Elliott's basket.

"*Back?*" Mason said.

"To the crib."

Mason's nausea was abating, and it left behind a burning sense of *right-fucking-now*. Neither of the women seemed pressed to beat the pavement even though they'd narrowly escaped a kill chamber, but with his head clearing, he felt like a dead man walking. If this had been their safe spot, he had no idea where they'd go next. Maybe they could break into an abandoned home and hide in a closet. Their best bet might be to find the outer fences and try their luck there. Or maybe they could find a run-down church amid the taller buildings, its roof caved in, lawn and courtyard overripe with weeds.

Because … it was strange. Ever since he'd seen the blonde inside the Heist sim, ever since she'd put that foil thing over his face, Mason had been thinking about a church. In a way, the vision was comforting. Preacher was always shouting holies, so maybe a decrepit place of worship was his opposite.

Despite the nausea, Mason laughed at Leigh's joke about returning to the crib. Until he realized she wasn't kidding. "Wait. You're serious?"

"Of course, I'm serious. I still have a tracker in my blood."

"You removed mine but not yours?"

She shrugged like Mason was stupid. "For now, it's not worth it. Too much pain. I can hide myself enough to get around."

"But …" Mason wasn't sure where to begin. "But isn't the plan to *escape?*"

"Maybe for you."

Mason stared at them both, hoping Dakota would see the schism and explain. He had assumed that whatever was happening — especially if it'd been so carefully pre-planned — necessarily ended in a jailbreak. He wasn't sure how that would work or what he'd do once out, but he'd certainly assumed his accomplices would go with him. No imagined scenario ended with any of them still inside the fences.

"I don't understand," Mason told Dakota.

"You need time."

"I don't *need* time to understand this escape plan doesn't make much sense without an escape."

Leigh laughed derisively as if he was an idiot not to get … whatever this was.

He was sick of being shuttled around like cattle, kept in the dark as human cargo. Or a human chess piece. "What the fuck is your problem?"

"Come on, Mason. You used to like me," Leigh replied.

"I don't even know you."

"You sure?"

Mason studied her. She laughed again and turned to go. He looked to Dakota then, but nothing about Leigh's departure — or all those obnoxious, knowing questions — seemed to be bothering her.

He called after her. It felt dangerous to raise his voice, but he was falling further and further from give-a-shit territory every second and refused to grant Leigh the satisfaction of chasing her down.

"Why did you even come?"

She turned.

"Why did you come if you're just going to leave again?"

"I removed your blood dongle."

He wasn't so sure of that. Dakota had gotten him to the safe house. Dakota had wrapped him in the space blanket. Dakota had disabled the drone — the *strange* drone, not standard prison issue — that'd chased them. And Mason was, he thought, fairly sure she had started that torture machine without any help. Dakota had done all the work, dongle and otherwise. Leigh, it seemed, had come only to watch.

"What's in it for you?" Mason asked.

"Satisfaction."

"Seriously?"

Mason walked closer, crushing Twinkies underfoot. He studied Leigh's face, mentally sweeping away the stubborn fog. She *was* familiar, and not just from the simulation. He was sure of it.

"Who are you?"

"I told you who I am."

"Dakota removed my blood dongle. Not you."

And inside, Mason thought, *You know, the blood dongle that's supposed to be outright impossible to remove without dying?*

"You're mistaken," Leigh said.

"Why did you come? Really?"

"I came to remind you. So you'd remember."

"Remember what?"

"Unfortunately," Leigh said, "it doesn't seem I did a very good job."

Mason looked to Dakota. "What's going on here?"

"What's going on is Leigh needs to get back before she's missed."

"But …" Mason was thinking about curfew protocol and how he'd nearly been fried for stepping off a stoop past the cutoff.

"Go," Dakota said to Leigh, craning as if to lob the single word over Mason, now standing in the middle. "I'll be in touch."

Leigh gave Mason a final look then rushed off.

"Now us," Dakota said. "Come on. We can't stay in the open like this."

But Mason didn't budge. "Who is she, Dakota?"

"Leigh?"

"Yeah. I feel like I know her."

"She's one of your Chamber Therapy cohorts."

Mason shook his head, frustrated. "I know her from somewhere else."

Something was on the tip of his tongue, something he couldn't quite reach. It was maddening. Leigh had entered his life just long enough to trigger an internal itch, then she left without a reason for being there in the first place. He was sure the only thing she'd done in the warehouse was give Dakota someone she could talk to. Like a character in a movie without any purpose. A loose end the director forgot to trim from the script.

"Where, then?" Dakota asked.

"I don't know. But it's … I feel like it has something to do with my dad."

"And yet she jogged no memories? Made no connections? Inspired no revelations? What about me, Mason?"

"What *about* you?"

"Did I help you? Did I wake you up?"

"Obviously. You pulled me out of that tank. Now you're helping me escape. Or at least, I think that's what we're doing."

"Everyone has a reason for being here," Dakota said.

Mason opened his mouth to ask what she was talking about, but there was a whirring from above. An electric hum amid a whoosh of streaming air.

The sounds made Dakota pull them back against a wall before whatever was out there could see. A second later, she'd pulled Leigh's tablet from a pocket and was watching a map. Bright pips the size and shape of sunflower seeds moved in straight lines toward the scene of a recent disturbance. *Their* disturbance.

"Shit."

"Drones?"

Dakota nodded.

"They can't find us, right? You removed my tracker."

"But not mine," she said, barely looking up.

"Why does it track *you?*"

"All HRO staff are tagged for situations like this. In case of abduction." She raised her left sleeve and showed Mason a small red mark on her forearm. It looked new, the tiny scab not yet healed. "Microchip, not blood. But it's impossible to shield, so abductors can't hide us, and it's not something I have the equipment to remove."

"Maybe they think you were abducted. Maybe they're coming to rescue you."

Dakota shook her head and said cryptically, "Certain ships have already sailed."

As the drone sounds receded, Mason moved forward. Dakota put an arm out to stop him.

"You said we need to go," he said.

"Not for the fences. Not for the exits."

"Isn't the idea to *get out?* You killed someone. I'm apparently rogue. If this has anything to do with Blake or Revival or the work my father was doing, I don't think they'll—"

"Shh."

Mason stopped talking. After a while, Dakota nodded and tucked away the tablet. "Let's go."

"Where?"

"Back to your crib, same as Leigh."

But that was too much. Whatever remained of Mason's patience snapped with Dakota's latest bleated absurdity. "*The crib?* Why the hell would I go back to—!"

Movement behind Dakota caught the corner of Mason's eye. A drone rose over the lip of the adjacent building — one she had missed on the tablet, perhaps, or one whose registry didn't show on her screen. It lined up, weapon whirring as it aimed to fire.

Averse to loud noises, he hiss-shouted, grabbed Dakota by the arm, then yanked her sideways. The drone spun to adjust. Mason no longer believed it wouldn't fire. The non-lethality of drones — except for curfew violations, which he was also guilty of — was prison propaganda. The official version of an increasingly bullshit story.

Seeing no swift exit, Mason reached for the first semi-sturdy thing he could find — the lid of a garbage can. The drone let loose. Plasma blew through the aluminum lid like hot lead leaking onto butter. With evasion futile and defense a bust, he had only foolish aggression. Exactly what had landed him there in the first place.

He sprinted, closing the distance between himself and the drone. It was hovering at about eight feet, so he took a running leap — one parkour-step off a stack of compacted cardboard, the next off a shallow ledge on one concrete wall. The thing fired too late. The garbage can lid was half-melted and flimsy, but still, it worked as a bludgeon.

Mason hit the thing hard. As it wobbled to the ground, he slammed his weight atop it. While it struggled beneath him, he shouted for Dakota. She'd yanked guts from the last one to stop it, so maybe she could pull from this one, too.

But she didn't answer.

He turned, only now seeing where the drone's single panic shot had struck. Not Dakota, but an already crumbling wall behind her. It'd disintegrated once shot, half-burying her in brick. She was on her face. Maybe dead.

His grip on the drone slipped. Hot plasma blew by Mason's face, singeing his hair. He searched for a compartment to open like Dakota had but came up empty.

Still fully operational, the drone kept wiggling the plasma weapon at Mason no matter how hard he tried to pin it. The thing was slippery — a small tube with a glass lens on the end. Curiously powerful and hard to hold, like a strongman's pinky.

Blasts came from every direction, Mason barely kept his face from the spray.

His attention went to Dakota. *Breathing? Or not?*

He looked back down at the drone. Right into the weapon's glass eye.

"Hey," he said.

The lens glowed orange and the umbilical heated beneath his hand. Mason wrenched the little tube around before it could fire at him, pointing it back at the drone's body.

It fired. The blast gutted it in an act of robotic hari-kari. The drone coughed then fell silent, the air filling with the benzene reek of melted alloy.

Once Mason was sure it was dead and no more were immediately coming, he went to Dakota. She was breathing but knocked out by debris. Her scalp had sustained a nasty gash, its effluent hidden only by her jet-black hair. His fingers came away wet, leaving a red smudge along her cheek and neck.

The tablet had fallen from her pocket and was face-down on the street beside her. He picked it up. The rest of the drone swarm seemed to be right over the rise, but it was no longer coming toward them. They should be surrounded.

He looked at the tablet. *Why aren't you coming for us?*

Mason found his bearings on the map. There were no drones between their current position and the red crib. He really could go back as Dakota had planned.

He looked down at her unconscious body, wishing she'd wake up so he could finish his question.

Why did you pull me out just to throw me back? Am I your friend? Or am I a fish in a pond, good only for catch-and-release?

So little made sense. Like Leigh. Like his disrupted simulation and forced exit, leaving him woozy. Like Dakota's manner and motive. There was more about her, something he couldn't put his finger on any more than he could remember how he knew Leigh.

Mason brushed the hair from her face then hoisted her in a fireman's carry. He moved in the direction of the thin edge of the drone cloud rather than away from it entirely, headed toward his goal instead of Dakota's.

They weren't going to the crib. Not as long as he was steering.

Instead, he carried her toward the crumbling steeple in the distance.

TWENTY-TWO

The Wonderful World of What the Fuck

OF COURSE, the way was blocked with fences and razor wire and the implied threat of drones.

And of course, those odd posters were everywhere, most obviously arranged in a massive grid on the towering wall of a still-standing facade. This one with a man's face close-up in the bottom half of the frame, a boot above pressing it into the bricks. A fish-eye perspective showed the owner of that boot, distorted by parallax, above. A masked SWAT officer, his right hand extended into the foreground with a semiautomatic service pistol pressing into the downed man's temple. The illustrated cop had already fired. A messy entrance wound, gory with spatter, was powder-burned into the man's skin. Blood pooled at the poster's bottom, capped by the message, *ENTER AND BE EXECUTED.*

"Subtle," said Mason to the breeze.

The church was close yet so far away. By his estimation, the place that had jammed itself into his mind like a splinter was maybe five minutes distant on foot, but between him and the ruined steeple were fences that didn't appear on Dakota's map. Was this an unmarked administrative zone? Or another out-jut of the Inner Circle?

He considered the question, then the fences. Because he assumed the image in his head meant he was being guided, he'd assumed the way would be clear — and if he *was* being guided, why *wasn't* the way clear?

Mason couldn't help but feel the idea of the church — and the compulsion to seek it out — had been set inside him deliberately. The kind of thing Carter could do. The kind of thing Mason had asked him to *stop* doing. It was disturbing, having someone else's thoughts in your head.

But Carter couldn't put anything in Mason's mind anymore because the old man was dead.

So … had the blonde somehow put the image there? It felt right but also wrong. The thing with the foil scroll had happened inside a simulation, and Mason was in the real world now. He should be suspicious instead of intrigued if his mind were infected. He should run from the image instead of embracing it. Yet here he was, outside an impassable gate, sure against his better judgment, this was exactly where he needed to be.

Why am I here? Why am I taking the risk? I had a plan, so why am I derailing it?

He'd planned to use Nic like the weasel he was to suss out information on the prison. And once Mason got used to life inside, he'd intended to use good old-fashioned police work to find out his father's story. That way took time, but it didn't put him places he wasn't supposed to be. And it didn't require big, stupid risks like this one.

So, go back to the crib like Dakota wanted.

But that only made him think. Dakota was the reason he couldn't go back. Mason, like Leigh, could maybe return to prison life and pretend nothing had happened. They'd probably catch him almost immediately — his session resulted in a staff member's murder, after all — but presumably, Dakota had already thought of that. She was smart, and Mason trusted her. But she also hadn't planned to kill her partner or run like they had. Or *when* they had. Mason forced her hand by bucking himself out of the sim. That meant *he* was responsible for the pickle Dakota would find herself in if he went back to business as usual — and that, he couldn't allow.

Why am I taking the risk?

The answer was slung over his shoulder.

Mason looked for a comfortable place to set her down so he could investigate the scene and hopefully find a way through the fence to the church beyond. He'd been lugging her sleeping weight for a half-hour now, stopping to rest only when necessary, and needed a break from carrying her. But he couldn't afford so much as a moment away from his mission. He felt the clock ticking harder, with the sun now laying its lips on the horizon.

As he weighed his options, Mason found himself suddenly surrounded. Two women and one man had approached him from behind, closing in like ninjas in the forest, beyond notice until one of them put a gun to his head.

"Easy," Mason said, straining to see them in his peripheral vision.

"Oi. *You* take it easy, mate. Let's have that pea-shooter of hers."

Hers. At first, Mason didn't understand. But he'd taken Dakota's gun. He didn't have one of his own. How had this strange Brit known that?

"Sure," Mason said. "No problem."

Still, the man shoved Mason hard enough that he almost dropped Dakota, who he hadn't yet settled. He felt the pistol pulled roughly from the back of his jeans.

"Don't try any heroics," said one of the women.

He could only see her sidelong like the others, but she was perhaps five-seven and a buck-thirty, most of it muscle and sinew. She was in a sleeveless shirt, had dark skin, and cradled an automatic rifle in her hands. For some reason, the big muscly Brit was familiar, but Mason had never seen the women before.

"Yeah," said the man. "'Magine, you don't care about yerself so much, right? Then lookie here."

While the wiry woman trained her muzzle on him, the man poked Dakota's limp head with his weapon. "This here's a complication. We like simplicity, so it won't fuss me any if we just dust her off and throw her in the chopper."

Mason didn't know what the man was talking about but assumed "chopper" didn't refer to a motorcycle.

"She's Director of Intake for the HRO," Mason said. "She'll be missed."

"Seems the one thing she won't be is *missed*. Put her down, friend. Nice and slow."

He complied. No use trying to fight. This crew knew what they were doing. The one on point could get as close as he wanted, and the woman could poke Dakota … because even if Mason tried to grab them, the third member of their party had been hanging back from the start and could easily pull his trigger. To Mason, who'd put in plenty of time carrying a gun, it smacked of proper protocol. *Always cover the edges and never let every member of the party get too close.*

Mason had a sneaking suspicion it wouldn't do any good to take hostages, assuming he could. If he forced a melee, the gunner would shoot all four of them.

"You're Immunity," Mason said. "Aren't you?"

A slim, hollow-chested man wearing delicate glasses arrived on the other side of the locked and reinforced fence. He looked like an accountant and, to Mason's eye, very familiar.

"Officially, no," said the man. "Unofficially, yes."

"This is an HRO gate. HRO fencing and razor wire. HRO security."

"Well, let's just say we have friends at the top. Or perhaps not *friends*. Maybe there's an arrangement in play."

"What are you talking about?"

"You're too late," said the man.

Late? Early? By any sensible metric, Mason wasn't even supposed to be here.

"Why?"

The man raised his wrist and looked at what appeared to be a homemade watch. "Curfew's nearly ended."

"So what?"

"We can't have you here after curfew. They will be looking for you, Detective Shaw."

"How do you know who I am?"

"Are you not Mason Shaw?"

"Yes, but—"

"Not *Carter* Shaw?"

He turned to face the man more fully but got a smack to the temple for his trouble. "You knew my father?"

"Of course, we knew him. Carter paved the way."

"Paved the way for what?"

"For you to be here. For *us* to be here."

"You mean, he told you I'd come?"

"That's not what I mean at all."

The man with the accent circled Mason as if taking his measure. He was close enough to strike, but Mason didn't want to take the chance until his odds improved.

"He has his father's eyes," said the circling man.

"He does," agreed the dark-skinned woman.

"Actually," the man said, "it's Blake who has Carter's eyes, along with the rest of him."

"Was my father in Immunity?"

"There is no Immunity," said Accountant-Man.

"He even has his father's psychosis," said the man with the accent.

"Calliope," Mason told them. "Calliope sent me."

"She did, did she?"

"She put something over my face. It …" But the rest was hard to explain. You could start conversations with, *I know you from a dream,* but that kind of thing never went well in Mason's experience.

"Where?" asked Accountant Man. "When?"

"In a simulation."

"What's a simulation?"

"I mean … It was in Chamber Therapy. She was part of—" He tried to recall the word Dakota had used, then did. "She was part of my cohort."

"What's Chamber Therapy?"

"Is she here?" Mason couldn't watch all of his enemies at once. They were too close, eyeing him like sharks scenting blood in the water.

"*She?*" said one of the women.

"Calliope."

"Hang on," said the other woman. "I thought Calliope was a man?"

"She's a woman," Mason explained. "She's got blonde hair, about this tall, and—"

"But you said 'he.'"

"I said 'she.'"

"No, you dinnint," said the Brit. "Over and over, you said 'he.'"

Mason was pretty sure he hadn't.

"Anyhow. *We* figured Calliope was a man as well. At first."

"What do you mean, 'as well'?"

"Well, ain't that what *you* figgered?"

"At first, yes," Mason said, confused by the rapid-fire questions. Their tones and manners were strange. This wasn't how normal people behaved. If he lowered his guard — mentally or conversationally — they'd tie him to a chair and pry his eyelids open, showing him a reel of unbridled horrors. "But then I met her."

"In a dream," the accountant behind the gate said skeptically.

Where have I seen him before? Then he had it. "You were there! In the simulation. You were there, too!" Mason swiveled to the man with the accent. "And you! You carried a minigun!"

"And you were there," recited one of the women. "And you, and you, and *you.*"

"Tell us, Detective," said the other. "Is there no place like home?"

"Mr. Shaw ..." The accountant looked at him. "If you believed Calliope was a man, why should we believe *you?*"

"I know she's a woman now."

"How could you not know if you are who you say?"

"She contacted my father online. They never met. I guess I just assumed."

"Misogynist," said one of the women.

"Typical," said the other.

"And of course you brought what Carter promised her when they were talking *online?*"

Was that a serious question? Mason was a confused prisoner who'd entered the scene carrying an injured woman over his back and wearing a too-small shirt announcing his affinity for girly wine. If this was a hand-off, he'd come poorly prepared.

"What did he promise?" Mason asked anyway.

"Did you *not* break into Revival? Did you *not* recover evidence regarding the questionable nature of and track record for Chamber Therapy? Did you *not* find intelligence for us regarding the stonewalling of grant renewal proposals and the FDA's constant ambivalence?"

"Carter did that. Not me."

"And what of Carter?"

"Carter is dead."

"I thought *you* were Carter."

"Are you high? You just called me Mason."

"We are Immunity. What good are *you?*"

Mason waited, thoroughly confused. The man reached behind his back, pulled out a tablet about half the size of Dakota's, then began to tap it.

"You should have been here before now. What did you do, stop for coffee?"

"I came directly from—"

"Where is the anomaly?"

"Do you mean Preacher?"

"Of course, that's not what I mean." He tapped the tablet again.

"We were ambushed," Mason said.

"Oh, yes. *That*, we know all about. Just plopped yourself down nearby, did you? *Hours* that took. I think you *did* have coffee. Then you decided, *Hey, since we're being followed, maybe we should go where nobody's supposed to know we want to go and leave a trail of breadcrumbs.*"

"You want we should shoot 'em?" asked the man behind Mason.

"No, no. It'll get complicated." The accountant seemed annoyed. When nothing happened, he stared hard at Mason. "The situation has changed."

"Are you going to let us in?"

"As far as you know," he answered.

One of the women behind Mason came forward to drag Dakota through the gate.

But he still wasn't allowed inside.

"Where are you taking her?" Mason asked.

"We're not going to kill her if that's what you mean."

"She has a tracker. A microchip in her arm."

He scoffed, not looking up from the tablet. "Yes. We're all terrified." He pushed more buttons. Whether that had been sarcasm or not, Mason didn't know. After Dakota had vanished and the gate had been re-locked, he stood waiting for the next thing.

"We're done here," said the accountant. The remaining two behind him moved away as a pair, not toward the gate but around its perimeter, perhaps on patrol.

"Wait," Mason said.

"Yes?"

"Well ..." Fuck them for making him beg. "What about me?"

"What *about* you?"

"Goddammit, I was called here!"

"By Calliope."

"Goddamn right by Calliope!"

"Even though you don't know her."

"I know her as well as ... Will you just go get her already?"

"You thought she was a man."

"*My father* thought she was a man!"

"Which is the whole point. When are you going to start thinking for yourself, Detective?"

"Excuse me?"

"Who are we, if not what you say?"

"Now wait just a goddamn—!"

"No, *you* wait just a goddamn. I already told you, you are *too late*. I show ..." The accountant looked at his watch.

Mason weighed his odds of successfully reaching through the fence to wring the asshole's neck.

"… eighteen minutes before six in the a.m. If you are not at your crib for morning roll, they will mark you missing. If we're foolish enough to have you *here* when that happens, they'll have reasons to come looking. So maybe settle down with your goddamns and start running. You will need to be quick. Like a bunny and always through the back door."

Mason remembered something.

"I don't have the blood dongle thing they use for check-in. It was removed."

"Yes, yes. And she *does* have a tracker, yet we took her and not you. I'm sure it's all very confusing and believe me, there's nothing I'd like more right now than to put on a blue blazer and act as your tour guide to the Wonderful World of What the Fuck. Alas, I am otherwise engaged. And alas, you are no good to us if you're not at least nominally tied to the system. There is more in play here than you understand, so maybe shut your mouth and do as you're told."

Mason wasn't used to being so roundly chastised, especially in such an asshole way.

"I busted out," he finally said, unsure how the statement was supposed to help him.

"Yes. And now you'll need to bust back in. Come back here tonight, if you must. But be quicker next time or no soup for you."

The man turned. Mason called after him, realizing there was no escape from eating some shit. "Hey!"

A slow, irritated turn. *"Yeeees?"*

"How the hell am I supposed to get into the crib without the drones taking shots at me?"

"You don't have a dongle on your blood anymore, do you?"

"Well, no."

"And are you competent enough to climb in and out of a window without being seen?"

"Sure, but—"

"You've been spoofed, young man. Don't worry about your missing tracker. You are now digital flotsam, a veritable hobo's stew of ones and zeroes. They're programmed to see signals, not to approach everything they run across and wonder whether it should have one. But if you're not in the crib, physically, when curfew ends … Well, my friend, *that* someone will notice. Then it's no longer sensors you need to concern yourself with. It's human eyes and attention spans. Your friend Frank Watt, from your group? Subconsciously, he knows you left the simulation, though unlike you, he was given his drug last night when it was over. If you're missing this morning, his mind will start to pick at the question, and soon *he* will resist and destabilize the Chamber Therapy sim as well. I don't have time to explain it all, and you don't have time to hear it. I'm sorry, but you're facing a day of having no clue what happened last night."

"You said you didn't even know what Chamber Therapy is!"

"Obviously, that's not truly the case."

"But——"

The world vanished.

Mason found himself in the middle of the same old void. At first, there was nothing beyond the flash of a silent and infinite explosion, but within seconds, swirls of black dots had formed.

Fear came, and when it reached its peak, the small black storm arrived at the limit of his vision. The storm *wasn't* silent. He could almost hear it, chattering with the deep-throated voice of a man mumbling in monotone. Mason sensed menace from everything around him.

He stumbled as the ground became solid underfoot, and buildings and a city and a crew of armed crazies appeared all around him. Mason caught himself on one hand and two feet, like a man preparing for a one-armed cartwheel.

The accountant-man was staring with derision. "Am I boring you?"

"Did you …" But Mason didn't need to ask. The expressions around him made it clear only he had seen the impossible, experienced the psychotic break he was quite sure he was facing. "It's … nothing."

Or everything.

"Be back to the crib when evening roll is taken, or your dongle won't register. If you're physically absent, they will have reason to look at your record of comings and goings. Then none of this will get any easier. Not for you, for us, or for him."

"*Him* who?"

The man behind the fence turned and walked away.

"Tick-tock, Detective Shaw," he said without turning.

Unite And Destroy

MASON HAD his hands on the back storage room window sill and his feet on the ground outside when the end-of-curfew buzzer brayed in a moment of irony. The sound meant he was, officially speaking, *allowed* to be outside rather than just inside. But Mason had also been told he had to go *in there* before he could be *out here* — quickly, lest he be punished — and thinking about it made him resent the whole enchilada.

Go here, go there, be at this place at this time ... or else.

Plus, all the midnight abductions, soaking him in goo and messing with his mind. Stripping him nearly naked, then making him forget when it ended. Stealing time from his memory and pushing mental boundaries he'd been told at intake he would never be able to handle.

It was bullshit. Mason was used to being his own man. He'd rather be busted than surrender his pride.

Almost.

He pouted and frowned, refusing to hoist himself over the sill, knowing deep down he was acting like a child. His petulance now was all emotion, zero logic, and stupid as hell. Still, he stayed put with his legs out the window, letting seconds pass, committing one small act of defiance that wasn't really even against the rules now that it was past 6:00 a.m.

"Fuck you."

Was Mason talking to the air? To the window with its absent glass?

To Dakota, who'd left him without meaning to or even being aware before giving him the answers he was desperate to get?

Perhaps his *fuck you* was meant for the accountant at the gate of … of *where?*

Despite rushing from here from there, Mason couldn't remember what part of town the razor wire had been guarding. Maybe he was swearing at the world. At curfew. At the red crib. At his father. Or maybe at himself, for flushing a promising life and career so completely and thoroughly down the crapper.

One dead family, and he'd folded like a timid poker player with a hand full of kings.

He doubled his grip on the sill, then went up and over. The building's foundation was cinderblock set into a gently sloping knoll. Mason was summiting a wall at the lawn's lower end, so hoisting required an extra two feet of lift. He scrabbled with his toes against the blocks, raking his stomach and ribs along the window frame.

Mason found himself in the crib's storage room. The door was ajar, and in the hallway, he could see one of the wall-mounted digital clocks Revival had strewn throughout the old building. Red numbers, displaying 6:01 a.m. and a handful of seconds. He could hear activity both inside and out. Glassless windows delivered the press of feet and muted chatter. Through the inside walls, he could hear the early morning symphony or rattling silverware in the cafeteria — blunted sporks, as nobody trusted the inmates *that* much — the clapping of plastic trays and dishes, the minute squeaks of rubberized cot feet as wakers moved out of bed.

Mason's gaze settled on the object in the room's corner — the tall red post with a pyramid on top.

He stepped closer, forgetting the clock, the hallway, and the missed curfew call. Instead, he stared at the informant kiosk he'd found his first night here — however long ago that was supposed to be.

Your records indicate an elevated potential for catastrophic synaptic failure.

My history tells you that?

And your father's.

But then the counselor from that red kiosk had said something strange. Something that rang back now, like a distant bell.

There is an anomaly semantically linked to the records of both Shaw, Carter and Shaw, Mason. Although, of course, the latter—

The latter *what?* She'd rezzed into pixels as he'd had insufficient funds to continue their session. But what did she mean about anomalies and semantic links? What had the counselor been about to say? He hadn't had time to consider coming back to the counselor for more. But looking at the kiosk now, Mason considered it.

If he spied on others from the shadows — if he found someone doing wrong — he could rat them out to earn enough snitch chits to buy another session. Mason hated the thought and himself for having it. Even considering another kiosk session felt like the prison winning and claiming his integrity as its prize.

It was all ridiculous. Insulting to his best attempts to do the right thing.

He wanted to laugh. Mason's memory was still Swiss cheese, and he still only remembered three times through the bank Heist simulation even though Dakota said he'd done fourteen — one more than Leigh, who seemed to have sat out once so Preacher could take her place. Fourteen visits to the goo tube where he'd been forced into moral choices designed to literally *change his mind.*

And the worst part? Maddeningly, despite asking the right questions and Carter's obsession on the subject, Mason still didn't understand how any of it worked. Did he sometimes do two or three simulations per night, or was it only one at a time? Did he get breaks to catch up on his sleep? Maybe he'd even done a Chamber Therapy session or two before he'd spoken with the AI counselor. If he had, it meant one of two things were true. Either the counselor had been ignorant but incorrect when she'd said he wasn't a fit for

Chamber Therapy because he'd done it already, or she knew he'd already done a session and was being an asshole.

There is an anomaly semantically linked to the records of both Shaw, Carter and Shaw, Mason.

Was telepathy between father and son an anomaly? Were panic attacks, or trypophobia, or the occasional uncertainty about what was real and what was not?

Although, of course, the latter—

Mason's fingers went to the kiosk's screen of their own accord.

He'd activated the thing before he intended to then found himself navigating to the counselor screen as if that had been his mission all along. What could possibly be linked to both Shaws' records? And what *was* this anomaly?

Of course, it was dangerous. It was the reason he risked "catastrophic synaptic failure" by doing Chamber Therapy — a diagnosis that reminded Mason of a brain catching fire like the oil pan in an ancient overheated Chevy. That was a problem. So far — thanks, Dakota — his risky attempts numbered more than donuts in a box.

Besides, although he was hardly an expert, it sure *felt* like he'd seen his share of anomalies lately.

Mason touched the screen again and squinted. The counselor button wasn't grayed out like before. Somehow, for reasons unknown, it seemed he *could* afford another session. His chit balance somehow far exceeded what he remembered.

Where had all those chits come from? Had he been sleep-snitching?

His arm extended. Finger reaching.

"Mason!"

He turned and saw Nic in the doorway. The second Mason stepped aside, Nic's eyes went to the kiosk. His expression made Mason feel like he'd been caught massaging his dick.

"Oh, hey. Sorry."

"I was just looking something up."

"None of my business, man. You do you."

"I'm serious. I'm not here to inform on anyone."

Nic was averting his eyes. It was a laugh. If masturbating was his metaphor for snitching, Nic regularly rubbed himself bloody. An OG traitor, he'd been ratting out his friends since before it was cool.

"You done there?"

"I told you, I never started."

Nic's urgency seemed to swallow his embarrassment. "You gotta come with me, man. They're looking for you."

Mason played dumb, the way Carter used to when caught cheating on his taxes. "I'm right here."

"Yeah, I know." Nic's eyes went to the window, which was technically closed (the sash was down) but nevertheless wide open without any glass. There was a beat wherein Nic seemed to consider the idea that Mason might have sneaked out and back in, but he shook it off and continued. "Either way, you missed roll."

Time to play dumber. "Why do they need roll when we're all tracked?"

"I don't know, man, shit. Why do we have to go through this every morning? What am I, your mother? Just follow the rules, will you?"

He shrugged, affecting nonchalance and hiding his nerves, heart still beating too hard. Being caught by Nic, even if he swore allegiance, was still getting caught.

"Look, man," Nic said as they fast-walked down the main corridor and toward the tiny, armored admin office at its end, "I worry about you. I get insomnia, so once or twice, I did a lap to see if you were awake, but I've never actually seen you in bed."

"So what?"

"So, you can't just go wandering around. You're fresh meat, so they'll cut you some slack. But that ain't gonna last."

"I've still got time. It's only been … what? Four nights?"

"Are you high?"

"What? Why."

"It's been seven."

"Time flies in here, I guess," Mason smirked to pretend this was all so beneath him, but Nic's confirmation chilled his blood.

Seven nights. One week.

His own brain was lying, and Dakota had been telling the truth.

They arrived at a door. This one, unlike the rest, was a heavy burnished metal, probably steel. Nic stared at Mason. Then Mason knocked, unsure if he'd done this song and dance before. A slider opened like the door to a speakeasy, and he found himself staring into a set of disembodied eyes.

"I missed roll call."

The eyes looked down, writing or looking something up. Then they returned. "Reason?"

"I was beating off on the balcony."

The eyes looked down again. Mason had been kidding, going for *harmless wiseass* instead of *problem child*, but whoever was behind the door seemed to take his confession seriously.

"Third time this week."

"Oh, that's an error. I jerk off on the balcony *way* more than that."

"Third strike means penalty. Fifth strike means bigger penalty. Eighth strike in one year, and you won't have to count any higher. Roll is not optional."

"Okay."

"Your account has been debited 200 chits."

"What, for beating off?"

"Think of it as one chit per stroke." The little door flew shut. Mason wasn't sure if he was permitted to laugh, but good on the actuary for having a sense of humor.

Nic was waiting just out of earshot.

"You good?"

"I told them I was beating off."

"You should tell them the truth. There are cameras everywhere."

"Then they'll know I beat off a lot. I'm doing it now." Mason raised his empty hands like a magic trick.

Nic rolled his eyes. "You eat already?"

"Yes." He wasn't proud of it. The HRO didn't just drop Twinkies and Ho Ho's. Depending on where you wandered and how recently the airdrop had flown by, Union Station streets offered the full rainbow of lab-grown confections. He'd found some of those pink snowballs en route and had shoved both down his maw without thinking. Then again, and later again. All told six individual balls. Even two wouldn't have settled well under the best of circumstances, but six was suicide by sugar. Worse, that half-dozen *while running* had left Mason with what felt like a bomb in his gut.

"You need to grab anything?" Nic asked.

"What, like your ass? No thanks."

"*Your shit*, dude. I was kidding before … but *are* you high?"

Mason looked at Nic, standing beside him, hands in his pockets with a posture of waiting.

"Are you coming with me, or …?"

"Fucking hell." Nic sighed. "You said you wanted to show me something."

"Show you what?"

"Hell, if I know. This is supposed to be your party. Is it at your apartment?"

Mason searched his memory and found nothing. He was surprised at the mention of an apartment. The rest of the errand was anyone's guess. Clearly, he'd asked for Nic's assistance, and this morning was when they were going to handle whatever this was supposed to be. Nic already found his behavior odd, and Mason wasn't eager to ram that impression home. But his mind was elsewhere, and he needed time to think more than anything else.

Mason went to his cot without comment. He'd acquired a backpack during his missing week. Once he managed to Tetris his way into his block of cots, he discovered the pack held all his worldly possessions, or at least everything he owned that he didn't keep in his off-crib apartment.

He wondered at the apartment. What did it look like? More importantly, where was it? Most prisoners commandeered empty places for daytime use, but most could probably remember where they kept them.

They set out and walked for a while, but Mason had yet to choose a destination. Nic kept looking at him — *now or never*.

"This way," Mason said, recognizing the intersection. Some of the buildings looked familiar. Two blocks on, he saw a pink snowball he'd tried to push into his mouth and missed. He'd stepped on it, smearing the thing into a shape resembling Honest Abe's profile on an old US penny.

"Where are we going?" Nic finally asked.

"We're going this way."

"Not the best part of town, man."

"We're in prison, Nic." Mason knew what he meant, though he tried to pretend — even to himself — he didn't. Above and ahead, a trio of drones stopped and turned the other direction as if avoiding something in an obscured part of the city. Or obeying the borders of a no-fly zone.

"Hang on," Nic said.

Mason had pulled a few steps ahead.

But Nic stopped at a powder-blue line on the concrete. "Tell me again where we're going."

"Why?"

"Because of this." Nic looked down, then dragged the toe of one shoe through the blue line. It smeared easily. Not paint, but powdered chalk — the kind groundskeepers lay on a baseball field.

"What about it?"

"This is Immunity territory."

"How do you know about Immunity?"

"I *told* you about Immunity."

That wasn't true. Carter had told Mason about Immunity, followed by Frank, the man who'd seemingly been "Watt" from his sim all along.

"They mark their territory?" Mason asked.

"Doesn't it make sense to you that they would?"

"I'm asking you."

"But don't you agree?"

Nic's eyes were wide, and he'd gone from chatty to terrified. Comparatively, Mason was cool and in control.

"They do all sorts of weird shit, man," Nic said, toeing the chalk but staring everywhere at once. "I've seen some crazy crap."

Watching Nic, something seemed to click inside Mason's head.

Reaching this intersection had taken them on a random path, and yet his compass had brought him right back to where he'd been in the wee hours. In this very section of the street, he'd hauled Dakota through peril while watching the skies for drones. Right around the corner, he'd find the gate through which he'd been denied entrance and the razor wire that kept him from trying, anyway. It was where he'd had his frustrating conversation with the man in glasses. With the Oz-style interloper he'd come to think of as the Accountant at the Gate, who'd known exactly who Mason was … yet had made him leave in the strangest of ways.

You didn't come here by accident, and you're thinking about the man in glasses for a reason. It's all connected.

Mason had no memory of the prior day, but deep inside, he had to know why he'd asked Nic to accompany him on this errand. It couldn't be coincidence. Nic said Mason told him he "wanted to show him something." *This* had to be the *something*.

Except yesterday, you hadn't met Immunity yet.

You hadn't been here before, as of yesterday.

So how could this be what you needed Nic to see?

Yet Mason was sure to the pit of his bones that *both* scenarios were true.

"You're not crazy, man," Nic said.

Mason's head whipped toward him.

"I see it in your eyes," Nic continued. "You can feel it. You can tell this is weird, can't you? It's something in the air. Makes you feel like you're losing your mind. But you're not." He swallowed. "I feel it, too."

Mason pinched the bridge of his nose. His head was ten gallons of overwhelm in a one-gallon container. The whole world felt like running a maze while blindfolded.

Just tell him what you know. Just tell him what you've seen. Anything is better than not knowing.

But Mason wanted to hear what Nic knew first — what was making him react this way.

He waved for Nic to follow and left the intersection with its damning chalk line.

Posters. Ask him about the posters.

They were right there, up ahead, plastered to the same towering wall he'd seen last night — the ones with the female gang threatening a man with a badge, bearing their strange caption. *UNITE AND DESTROY.*

"This is bad shit, man," Nic said.

"You mean the posters?"

"Yeah, the posters." He didn't turn to Mason as he replied.

"*Bad?*" Mason echoed.

"*Strange,* anyway."

"Strange how?"

"Strange because they've clearly been here a while, and nobody's ripped them down. Strange because they're on glossy paper, not that homemade shit you see people making out of pulp and spit. Strange because posters like this keep going up as if no one's after the person behind them."

"What do you mean, *posters like this?*"

"Anti-establishment. Everywhere else, the posters are about the HRO putting *its* boot on *us.*"

Mason looked again, seeing the posters anew.

"There's resistance inside the prison," Nic continued. "Anywhere there's oppression, there's resistance."

Mason almost interrupted. That was one of Carter's lines. It sounded strange coming out of this little man.

"And any good resistance knows the value of propaganda. Of 'hearts and minds.'"

"Okay," Mason said.

More Carter. It made his head want to spin.

"But resistance can't operate as freely as conventional institutions. It has to hide, make do with limited resources and work in the dark. So if we came across a lot of half-assed posters on crappy paper, I'd think, 'Okay, that makes sense. The paper and the printing sucks because Immunity had to make do with whatever supplies they could get.'"

Nic approached one of the posters then rubbed it between thumb and forefinger as if to verify its glossy finish. "But these?

They look like a professional job. Thousands of credits to print." He waved his arms high. "But even more, dude … look around you. If resistance is something the HRO is trying to squash, why haven't they taken the posters down?"

Mason walked closer. Forget about Nic using his father's logic — listening to the prisoner was, at this point, like getting a full-on sermon. Carter's words coming out of an inmate's crooked mouth.

With his curiosity growing, Mason rubbed the poster's edge between thumb and forefinger, same as Nic had done. He scanned the area again, looking for the nuance he'd missed. But no good. Mason was trying to solve a puzzle with half its pieces missing.

Again, he pinched his nose and closed his eyes.

He saw the white void, the black dots, the vortex that expanded every time he made its acquaintance.

When he opened his eyes and saw Nic again, he couldn't shake the feeling he hadn't imagined what he'd seen.

You're being paranoid.

Or having flashbacks.

Maybe whatever they'd done to him in that tank of goo was like what they used to say about LSD. Maybe Chamber Therapy went to your spine. Shook hands with your DNA, then stayed forever. He might experience flashes of black dots on white until the day he died.

Nic was waiting, giving Mason a curious eye. But he also looked both troubled and scared. Mason could shake suspicion away from himself if he didn't dwell on what he'd maybe just seen and shoved himself forward instead.

"Are you saying Immunity is colluding with the HRO?"

Nic recovered immediately. "I'm just saying it's weird."

"Did you talk to my father, Nic? I mean, once he was inside?"

"Why?"

"You sound like him."

"In what way?"

"In that, you're telling me something I didn't even know I was wondering." Then, inspiration struck. "Have you done Chamber Therapy?"

"Once." Then he shook his head. "But never again."

Mason blinked. He only knew bits and pieces of the Chamber Therapy story, based largely on what Carter had uncovered and what Elisabeth Reeves, who'd helped design the system, had told him while keeping her own cards mostly hidden. Even having gone through the Therapy himself, Mason knew little. Still, he did know CT was never one-and-done. Same as real therapy, it took multiple sessions before the brain began to change.

"Why? If the Therapy rehabs you, you're free."

Nic shrugged. He met Mason's gaze again, dead serious.

"I'd rather stay here forever than have Preacher chase me again."

TWENTY-FOUR

A Hacker and Informant

UP on an anonymous floor high in an anonymous building, Nic used what appeared to be a magnetic key to open a door no different from any other. It swung away from the jamb after a light click, and inside was the wafting scent of sweat and lube. Clearly, the place belonged to Nic.

Mason resisted the urge to comment or retch. He saw the problem and moved to remedy it immediately. Nic's apartment — perhaps because it was too high up for thrown rocks — still had glass in its windows. So, he crossed the room to open one and then the other. Despite the still air below, a tidy breeze blew up here.

Once the stench was mostly gone, Mason closed each window to a sliver so as not to blow the apartment's contents to chaos. He turned to Nic, who'd flopped onto a bed, though to Mason's eye, it was a fleabag mattress stained with something green. Nic was turned away from Mason, unmoving. To anyone else, he'd seem unquestionably dead.

Mason poked him with the toe of a shoe.

"Nic."

"I said gimmie a minute."

"I gave you at least thirty of them." Maybe more. Mason wasn't wearing a watch, and wall clocks in this place were scarce. Nic had frozen the conversation downstairs, blaming discretion for his silence, but really, Mason knew he was scared. It'd taken Herculean patience not to ask his thousand questions after Nic's mention of Preacher, but Mason had done his very best. It was better to wait and see what he had than to press. Mason was used to Nic and trusted the leaky nature of even his best-kept secrets. A snitch by nature, time was all it would take to get him yammering again.

"Booze, then," Nic said.

Nic rose from the feculent mattress, entered the shadowed kitchen, then reappeared holding something that looked almost like a weapon but turned out to be a half-full bottle of Stolichnaya vodka. Based on the silhouette swigs Mason had seen from the living room, he was willing to guess it'd been two-thirds full when they'd entered the building.

Nic steered back toward the mattress.

Mason pointed to a plastic chair instead. "A little early for drinking, isn't it?"

When Nic sat in the chair, it squeaked under his weight. "I disagree."

"Why?"

"Because I know you," Nic said. "No matter what I say or do, I'll have to tell you this story."

"If you didn't want to tell me, why mention Preacher in the first place?"

"It just sort of left my mouth without permission." He shrugged. "You'll look back on this later and wonder why you even believed me. And I think you *will* believe me."

He wasn't sure what that meant. Maybe because Nic had no shame, he also had no reason to hide. Regardless, Mason found himself agreeing, only for a different reason — with his abundance of questions and complete lack of leads, Nic's promise of answers was a compelling drug.

"You knew I knew what you were talking about." Mason had also been mulling *that* on the walk there. Nic wouldn't have clammed up after mentioning Preacher if he hadn't thought the word meant something to Mason. Yet he'd gone gravestone silent, protecting a secret he should have no way of knowing Mason was dying to hear. "You knew 'Preacher' meant something to me."

But then Mason thought, *No, no — go further.*

Nic hadn't said the name of Mason's ghost nemesis without context. He'd mentioned it only after Mason had asked about Chamber Therapy. Knowing Nic had done Chamber Therapy was one thing. Knowing he'd done it and somehow failed was another. But knowing his mind connected the idea of Chamber Therapy to the idea of Preacher? *That* was worth waiting for.

"You saw something when you went into Therapy, didn't you? They put you into a sim, and things got … weird."

"Weird how?" Now Nic was squinting. "Did *you* do Chamber Therapy, too?"

"Just weird," Mason said, dodging his second question — his *real* question. The interrogative tone was already shutting him down. He'd expected Nic to perk up at the mention of *odd things*. Amused curiosity wasn't the sign he'd expected.

"You did, didn't you? They put you through Chamber Therapy, too!" Nic stood, smiling a little, and Mason knew he'd lost this particular battle of dignities.

"It's not important."

"'Not important'? It's huge! You're not supposed to remember. How do you remember? Didn't they give you a drug to—"

Dammit.

So much for extracting the truth from Nic without offering anything in return.

"They didn't give me the drug the last time. But I think I remember earlier sessions, too — *not* just the last one."

Mason's mind showed him Preacher, sitting tall and smug in Leigh D'Abo's seat.

"Maybe you're immune," Nic suggested.

"Is that a thing?"

He shrugged. "It was for me. That's why they wouldn't let me keep doing it."

"Were you immune to the memory drug? Or to Chamber Therapy in general?"

"Both, I think. Hell, I don't know. They discussed my session right in front of my face after I came out, talking about me like I wasn't even there. Probably thought they'd be making me forget afterward. But I didn't, not even after they gave me the injection."

"What did they say when they were talking right in front of you?"

"That my readings were 'anomalous.' They asked me some questions, but they weren't random. Most sort of centered on 'belief.' They wanted to know if I *believed* what I saw in the simulation or if it always felt fake."

"And what was the answer?"

"It was perfectly real at first. But then it wasn't."

"What do you mean?"

Nic looked around the empty apartment as if someone might be listening in. "We started in the lobby. But—"

"You mean in the back of the van?"

"Van?"

"Yeah. Didn't you start in the van on your way to the job?"

"What job?" Nic asked.

Mason was making assumptions. "What *was* your simulation? What happened? What were you supposed to *do?*"

"A drug deal. It started in the lobby of this guy Raymond's building. I was confused at first, since I just sort of showed up without any memory of how I got there … except in a weird way, I could also sort of remember just fine." He scratched one ear. "I guess that doesn't make much sense."

"It actually does." Mason remembered waking up staring at that scratched lightbulb in the van's rear and feeling totally lost, then acclimating after a minute or two. Even though he still didn't techni-cally know how he'd gotten in the van, his brain had glossed over the inconsistencies and questions. "Go on."

Nic breathed, nodded, and continued. "Point is, I was confused. And I could say the same for the people around me. But then the confusion kind of settled down, and I sort of understood what we were there to do. What happened in mine was, you get up to Raymond's apartment, then some tweaker busts in with a gun and tries to steal his stash. I assume you're supposed to stop the tweaker, or maybe kill Raymond, or maybe steal the drugs and keep them for yourself if you want to 'win the game.' I don't know. Like I said, I only did it once."

"That makes sense. They arrested you for drugs, right?"

Nic nodded. Mason already knew that. He was just trying to keep him talking.

"That's why your simulation was a drug deal. They locked *me* up for robbing a bank, so my sim was …" He paused before Nic's question could stop him, suddenly unsure of what he'd been saying.

"You robbed a bank?"

But now, Mason was even less sure. He'd robbed *something*. Real and simulated realities warred within him, fogging his mind. Dakota had promised the cobwebs would eventually depart. He wished they would hurry.

"Close enough that a bank heist makes sense for my 'rehab.'" Mason moved on quickly so Nic couldn't dig into his evasive answer. "Point is, someone told me the simulations are designed to offer 'moral decisions' that reflect choices from your crime. You're probably not supposed to kill anyone or steal anything. If you want to 'win,' I'll bet you're supposed to walk away from the deal. Or call the cops. Maybe take out the tweaker but protect the others."

"Even Raymond? That guy is a dick."

"I don't know, Nic. I'm guessing here." Mason crossed his legs. "You said the questions they asked you afterward were about 'belief.'"

"Yeah. They asked how convincing I found the sim. If it felt like I was really there, or if it was more like watching a movie. After I told them it was more like a movie after a while, they asked me how 'active' my disbelief was."

"*Active*?" Mason repeated.

Nic nodded. "That's the word they used. I remember because it was such a strange thing to say. I think it meant something like, 'Did you just 'not believe' what you experienced, or did you try to force a change?'"

"They asked if you *tried to change reality*?"

"That was the upshot, yeah. Because it *wasn't* reality, and I guess most people don't realize it. But I did."

Mason watched him, thinking. Nic's *resistance* might have had more to do with his usual behavior than anything more noble, like having a powerful mind. If the sim forced his character to fight or stand up for an ideal, of course, it would jar against the core of his being. Nic didn't fight. He didn't stand up. Any sim that didn't let him slink away and rat the others out to save himself would, of course, clang like an error in his brain.

"Your father did, too," Nic said.

Mason was secure in a padded chair, and still, he nearly lost his balance and fell to the ground. "*What* did you say?"

"Your father. Carter?"

"I know who my father is."

"Well, there you go." Nic waited for Mason to make the next move as if he hadn't just dropped a bomb on reality.

"You talked to him inside the HRO?"

"Of course I did. Take all the friends you can get in here."

But so many things were wrong with that. The Shaw family used Nic as a punch-activated lending library. He was a source, not a buddy — and one his father and brother had felt duty-bound to treat like the shit they thought he was. But even beyond that, Mason's few chats with Carter once the old man was behind bars made it sound like he'd spent his time inside the HRO laying low and talking to no one. Like he'd carved himself a private place, like this apartment, then holed up like Batman in the Bat Cave. Maybe he'd used Nic as a source inside the prison the same as he had outside, but Mason wasn't sure their time inside, or their crib assignments, even lined up to allow it.

"Carter didn't want to do Chamber Therapy at first. Had all kinds of theories about it. But he must have decided it was worth trying at some point because one day, out of the blue, he told me he'd decided to take the HRO up on their offer. Maybe he got desperate? Couldn't take being inside and wanted to see if their little mindfuck could punch his ticket out of here? I don't know, but he went from resisting to accepting to ..." Nic stopped, but Mason could hear the final unspoken word in the stir of echoes.

Gone.

Maybe it hadn't been his fault for convincing the old man. Maybe Carter had made up his own mind, and Mason's visit had nothing to do with it.

"Carter remembered his sessions, too. You ask me, the whole operation is kind of rinky-dink. There's three of us that remember for sure. So really, does *anyone* forget?"

Mason shrugged. The three of them all remembering felt more like a plan than coincidence.

You're searching for meaning where there is no meaning. That's what conscience does when it can't face what it's done.

To break the strange spell he felt descending, Mason stood and paced the apartment. "Tell me about Preacher."

Nic did. A sprawling tale that looped back and forth over the timeline of his prior life, arrest, incarceration, and infiltration of the HRO's underbelly, punctuated by loose ends, diversions, and swigs from the bottle of vodka. Most of what Nic told Mason seemed to have little or nothing to do with Preacher. That was a narrative Nic seemed determined to avoid.

Eventually, Mason stopped him. "Jesus Christ, Nic. If you're too fucked up about it to tell me ..."

Nic held up a hand, palm out. "Give me a minute. I need to tell you this."

"Because it fucked you up?"

"Because you need to hear it."

"Why do I need to hear it?" Mason asked, playing along.

"Your father wanted you to know."

"And why did he want me to know?"

"Because he saw Preacher, too."

Three people who remembered.

Three people who'd seen the big man who could make the world go white.

Mason felt his marrow go cold.

"I *didn't* know it'd mean something to you," Nic continued, finally answering Mason's earlier question. "I just know after me and Carter realized we'd seen the same guy inside — mine in my only session, but Carter over a few of his — he got all investigative about that shit, acting like he was still a cop, trying to make sense of it. But either nobody else sees Preacher or no one remembers. Your father must've talked to someone because he came back sure it was the first one. He said the drug wasn't erasing Preacher from other people's memories when it blanked everything else. We were the only ones he visited. Carter was sure of it."

"How?"

"I don't know. He had a source. A hacker."

"Calliope?"

"He just said 'a hacker.' An informant."

"*Calliope,*" Mason repeated.

"Calliope leads the resistance. Lives here, though nobody knows where."

"And she's a hacker. She contacted Carter on the outside, promising him she had a way to take Revival down. But it … didn't work out." Mason hoped Nic wouldn't ask about his understatement.

Calliope's request had driven Carter to break into Blake's office, but her intel was sideways, and Mason's father ended up looking at a life sentence instead of the vindication he'd hoped for.

"*She?*"

"Calliope is a woman," Mason said.

"How do you know? Everyone talks like he's a man."

"I've met her, Nic."

He perked up. "Where?"

"Inside."

"In … You mean, *inside the simulation?*"

Mason nodded.

"No." Nic shook his head. "Calliope doesn't immerse."

"What?" Mason asked.

"Calliope is terrified of the sims. I've got sources, too."

"Terrified? Why?"

"No one's sure." Nic shrugged. "I hear there was an accident. Something went wrong with a sim years ago. Not many people know about the simulations in the first place, but everyone who does agrees Calliope doesn't go inside."

"I don't know what to tell you, Nic. I saw her."

"Then she was an AI. Not the real Calliope."

Mason knew how AIs behaved, and the Calliope he'd seen had acted the opposite. It had been a real person with a real mind. "Why did Carter want you to tell me about Preacher?"

"He thought he might not be able to tell you himself. And he was right."

"Why do I have to know at all?"

"I don't know. But he was insistent. I know it's ridiculous, but man … your father still scares me, dead or not."

"He's not dead."

"I'm pretty sure he's dead."

Mason didn't want to argue. He'd lost track of time and no longer trusted his memory.

He remembered Carter going Pattern Black, and he remembered word-for-word the well-mannered letter the HRO had sent to inform Mason about it. A release had been included with that letter, and Mason remembered signing that, too. But what he didn't remember with enough precision was the timing of it all.

How long had it been between signing the release and his own arrest?

How long until his own conviction or the start of his sentence?

How long did the HRO wait between a Pattern Black diagnosis and euthanasia?

If Mason had all his marbles, he could probably figure out if they'd pulled Carter's plug by now or not. But at least for now, those marbles were in very short supply.

Mason sighed. "What did Carter tell you? About Preacher."

"He thought Preacher was a virus. Something that wasn't supposed to be there."

"But Carter saw him. So did we. *Three for three*, Nic. Maybe he's supposed to be there, and you're missing part of the story."

"No. Carter was sure. Maybe Calliope gave him the details when they had coffee at the crib or something."

"Carter never met Calliope in person, so far as I know."

But Mason had?

Why? How? And what did it mean?

"Then she told him when they were pen-pals," Nic said. "Or someone else told him — I don't fucking know. But your father talked like it was a sure thing. He said it like a fact. *Preacher is a virus.*"

"So … AI again?"

"He'd have to be AI if he's intelligent at all — which he sure as hell seemed to be. The bigger question is where he came from and why he's there … at least, why he's there *for us.*"

"Carter thought Blake sent him, didn't he?"

Nic nodded. Mason too, but his accompanied a sigh.

Maybe Blake *was* involved, but every time Carter invoked him as the boogeyman, Mason's belief began to fade. Blake had a lot to lose if Revival fell, sure. He was also a businessman running a multi-billion dollar business in the public eye. Why would he spend his time chasing a rogue cop?

"Why did Carter think Preacher was there?"

"He said he wanted something from inside us."

"Inside you, or inside himself?"

"Is there a difference?"

Give, Mason heard Preacher say inside his head. *Give now, or I'll rip you open to find it.*

"What thing did he want?"

"Carter didn't say."

"What did he try to take from you?"

"I don't know, man. It was kind of a mess in there." Nic took two more big swigs of vodka.

Dead end. Push more, and you'll break him. There will be other days. Other opportunities to learn the truth.

So Mason sat back, looking for other loose ends to pluck.

"What do you think Pattern Black is like?" Mason asked. "I mean, have you heard any theories?"

"Dunno. Nobody comes back from Pattern Black. You might as well ask what it's like to be dead."

"I don't mean from the subjects. I mean from techs, Docents, maybe bureaucrats. From the prison's perspective. Don't pretend the HRO's secrecy is too much for even the great Nicholas Coreander to penetrate."

Nic perked up, buoyed by flattery. But then he shrugged.

"I don't think I know any more than you. Pattern Black is supposedly a total flatline. Brainwaves start to look more like an ocean than mountains. A machine beeps until someone comes along to stop it. Your body lives on, so they stick tubes in you to manage incomings and outgoings. Then it's a mercy to die."

"Do you think they dream?"

"With *what*, man? With the dead piece of gray shit left in their skulls? If I had an egg and a hot pan, I could show you. This is your brain." He held up an imaginary egg, cracked it into a nonexistent skillet, then offered Mason a convincing imitation of a sizzle. "This is your brain on Pattern Black. Any questions?"

"Did you ever have anything weird happen *after* you did Chamber Therapy?" Mason asked because his brain was making him.

"I just told you a ton of weird shit from Chamber Therapy."

"No … I mean … after."

"You mean once they unhooked me? You mean, once I was back in circulation?"

"Right."

"Why would weird shit happen after they let me go?"

Flashbacks. The spine. Grabbing tight to your DNA. Like LSD, with the trips that kept on giving.

There had to be something to it. Nobody really knew the insider scoop on Chamber Therapy, and nothing was really known about the forgetting drug. Mason had received it a lot more than Nic, and it had worked on him a whole lot better.

"Never mind." Mason rose from the chair, went to the window, then looked out.

From up here, the city could almost be a city. Home to hundreds of thousands of law-abiding citizens instead of a denizen of crime and depravity. If he focused just right, he could convince himself none of this was happening, and for seconds at a time.

But then the illusion popped, and Mason could smell Nic's place again, now that mostly closed windows had allowed time for the stench to rebuild. With his focus hardening from its prior softness, it was impossible to ignore the ruins below — crumbled buildings, broken glass, and burned-out cars sprinkled with scattered snacks.

Nic knew some things, sure. But even his explanations didn't make Mason feel any saner. Nor had the diagnosis of the only shrink this place had to offer.

There is an anomaly semantically linked to the records of both Shaw, Carter and Shaw, Mason.

For the first time, Mason wondered just how off-kilter he truly was. He'd always played normal. Even when Carter had been dropping images into Mason's mind, and Mason had been sending his father messages without opening his mouth, they'd played normal. With the help of his therapists, medication, and a fair amount of teenage drinking, Mason had managed to still the demons.

But here, everything was falling apart. He was the odd man out — again.

"*Soooo …*" Nic said, drawing the word out the way one does when a conversation has reached its conclusion. "What now?"

Mason had no idea whatsoever.

Sinister Things at the Bottom

"YOU MIND SOME ADVICE?"

Mason looked up. He could have responded with his mouth, but a look felt like answer enough.

The woman across from him didn't get it. Mason kept waiting for her to pick up another card and get this over with. When she failed to read his clues, Mason said, "I don't think you're supposed to help me."

"This is more global advice."

"Then no."

"Winston Churchill said, 'When you're going through Hell, keep going.'"

"That sounds like Winston Churchill's advice."

"I think it applies."

"You do, do you?"

The woman nodded. She was beautiful. Blonde. Arms covered in tattoos, sleeves pushed way up to ensure the world could see them. Mason took this as attention-seeking. As damage. Maybe she had daddy issues, and although he was only a few years older than she appeared to be, he could probably be daddy enough once this was all over. No ring on her finger. She was exactly Mason's type if you didn't count Dakota, who'd been very much not his type until she'd become the only thing he ever thought about.

Mason, from the moment he'd sat, had found the woman officious but fascinating. "What's your name?"

"What's yours?" A curious look entered her eye.

"Are you kidding me?"

"I'm asking for calibration purposes. I need to know what you remember and what you don't. You were given an injection after the physical portion of your training. Or … audition? Or is it a try-out? What do they call it?"

"*Training*," Mason said. "They call it training."

"Even though they haven't hired you yet?"

"Is this part of the test, or are you just really bad at your job?" He was still kind of hitting on her. It was his strategy. You had to express sexual interest while expressing zero interest of any other kind. *That's* how you got what you wanted without assuming emotional risks. He'd learned that from his father.

She ignored him. "Regardless, you got an injection. Do you remember?"

"I'm not feeble, you know."

"You wouldn't have to be feeble to forget anything after the injection, or possibly the injection itself. If you remember them telling you *that* at your initial briefing, I'll back off and stop asking 'dumb' questions." She raised an eyebrow and waited with a condescending smile.

Mason prepared his lips for a snarl of his own, plus some biting words to demonstrate his wit. But before the snarl could form, before his cleverness could make itself obvious, he realized something inconvenient. As much as he wanted to tell the woman, *Of course, I remember the briefing and can enumerate it all for you right now*; everything, before he'd sat in this room, was foggy at best. What had they done to him?

"The injection we gave you before this component of your 'training' included a memory suppressor," said the woman, managing to keep the *I-told-you-so out* of her voice. "It's used for certain procedures within the Outpost but also for Docent assessments like this. You understand the program requires secrecy? That, should the HRO fail to hire you, it's imperative you forget anything you saw here?"

Mason nodded. He didn't want to play this game of telling her things they both already knew, but it seemed he had a dash of amnesia in his veins.

"It's not impossible you'd have forgotten your name. It would mean they gave you too much if you have, and *that* would mean you'll be here a little longer than we'd hoped, so the extra can burn itself off — at least to a level where we can talk without you drooling and forgetting what spoons and cars are. So, your name?"

"I'm not going to forget my fucking name. I've had it all my life."

"Then what is it?"

"Yul Brenner."

"What is it really?"

"How do you know that's not what I think it is?"

She nodded at her tablet. "Because I have your scans."

"Then why are you asking if you're so convinced I already know?"

"Just answer the question."

"Ronald Fucking Reagan."

"Reagan as president, or Reagan from *Bedtime for Bonzo*?"

"Is that a thing? I'm not forgetting this time. I just don't give a shit."

"Reagan's been dead for almost a century."

Mason shrugged. "Well, there you go."

The woman tapped her tablet, muttering. "I knew you'd be an asshole."

"Excuse me?"

"Tell me your name, or I'll kick you the fuck out of here. *Now.*"

The woman, instead of staying severe, smiled in a way that was decidedly knowing. For the first time, Mason wondered in earnest what he'd forgotten. Not about his life, but about the suppositions and assumptions cloying the room like fog.

"You don't remember me at all, do you?"

Mason didn't trust himself to respond.

"Who do you *think* I am?" she tried again.

"You're an assessor for the Docent program at HRO 22."

"And?"

"Are you something else?"

She laughed.

In that horrifying moment, Mason realized he must know this woman. She didn't sound like someone who sometimes used the treadmill beside him at the gym or a regular at Sufficient Grounds. She talked like a person he'd had meals with on multiple occasions. Someone who knew all his quirks and could easily pre-guess even his most unexpected changes of mind.

Done laughing, she donned an air of professionalism. "I'm sorry. My name is Leigh."

"How do I know you?"

"I used to liaise with USPD as an independent expert on psychosis, psychological disorders, and assessments. Things like that. We're friends."

Shit. Mason had no idea how close of friends they were, but what she'd just said could easily go back years. They might be best buds, and here he was slipping his mental hand into her figurative panties. It could be worse. At least she wasn't his sister.

"Well, Leigh. Since I don't remember knowing you, I guess I can only do my best and speak honestly. You'll forgive me if I can't obey all the social norms I don't know about."

"I wouldn't have it any other way."

"So, first thought — Churchill or not, maybe you should keep your advice to yourself."

She wasn't a cop. Leigh was a psychologist who just so happened to be employed by law enforcement. Liaising at first, apparently, then moving into a more official capacity. A Revival ID in a leather wallet hung from her jacket pocket, but it wasn't a badge. Time for her to back down.

"Fine."

In that single word, Mason saw her trying to forgive his tone like he didn't know any better.

"Then I guess we should continue?" she asked.

"Joy," Mason said.

"Do you know what this test measures?"

"I'm not sure. We're doing so little of it. How about you show me another card, sweetheart?"

She did, but with the same smug smile as before. *I'm playing along, but we both know you're full of shit.*

Leigh held up a large card, just as she'd done before offering her unwanted advice.

Mason looked at it, trying to ignore her expression. It was difficult to give a shit, but of all the shits in his world, this one felt most worth giving. Passing this test would get him one step closer to being out from under Captain Watson's thumb. It'd get him away from Terrence Davis, who worked two desks down from Mason and breathed noisily through his mouth. And most of all, it'd remove him from the circle of cops and coworkers who knew what he'd done — or, as the shrinks insisted, "what had happened to him."

Mason didn't need or want their sympathy. And fuck their constant insistence on shoving it down his throat.

The card showed a series of black hash marks arranged in what seemed to be a random scattering. But his brain saw the order immediately. If he took the right half and laid them overtop the left, they formed letters. A word.

"Fire," Mason said.

Leigh looked at the back of the card, then set it down. "Why do you think you recognized that one so easily?"

"Because I have an IQ of 164."

"Most grown men don't know their IQ."

"Well, I do."

"Why do you think that is?"

Mason saw her trap, curious what grudge she must have to toy with a "friend" this way. He didn't answer, smirking back. He knew his IQ because he'd taken tests in elementary school and was excellent with recall and numbers, not because he considered it a yardstick of his personal worth. Shouldn't he get credit for his memory instead of being chastised for hubris?

"What does 'fire' mean to you?"

"I thought I was just supposed to find the pattern in the cards."

"HRO Docents, for reasons you will learn later — if you pass this assessment — require complex problem-solving ability. Basically, they need to be good at patterns and puzzles. But if you don't think it's also a psychologically taxing job, if you think it won't eat you alive to ignore your demons, you're in for a nasty shock. That's why it's my job to see not just how well you can solve problems, but also how well you can cope with what those problems reveal."

"But you're the tester," Mason said.

"Correct."

"Not the psych evaluator."

"It's a holistic thing."

"Officially? Will I be dismissed if you see things you don't like that your little deck of cards doesn't measure?"

"That's not my role. I'm just concerned." Here, she softened almost imperceptibly. He could almost hear an unspoken codicil after she finished — *concerned as a friend.*

"No offense, *Leigh*, but I'm not particularly interested in your concern. Maybe that's rude, and maybe I'm being a bad friend right now, just like you."

"I warned you it'd be like this before you applied."

"Well, I don't remember your warning."

Leigh sighed. "Look, Mason. I told you I'd have to be professional if you ignored my advice and came here anyway. I'd have to treat you like anyone else who wanted this job. In fact, I have to treat you *worse*. I have to press you *harder*. If I'm cutting the shit, that all boils down to me looking like the biggest bitch in the world to you. And there's an excellent chance you won't like what I decide in the end. But my decisions are based on established parameters, and there are extenuating circumstances you're probably incapable of remembering until the drug wears off … if we *let* it wear off instead of bolstering the effects to permanently erase what happens here today. Even though you don't believe you have any reason to trust me, in truth, you do. I really am a friend, same as I tried my best to be for your father."

"You knew my father?"

She sighed again then nodded. "I know you don't like me right now. I know you'll like me less before we're done here. But I have to do what's best. For the HRO and the Docent program, but also for you. You probably don't remember why I have reason to be worried about you, but trust me, I do. I'll be honest. I told you from the start this was a bad idea. It's your choice, so I won't bias my decision against you. But I'll be goddamned if I'm going to bias it *for* you, either. Not given what's at stake."

"What *is* at stake?"

"This process is meant to be *a tabula rasa,* so I can't tell you that, or it'll skew the results. I shouldn't have told half of what I already have."

Mason crossed his arms. He still didn't remember Leigh or her friendship and knew the two of them might be straining — or even breaking — that relationship right now. She was probably supposed to ignore his questions and pretend they were strangers until this was over, and he knew her violation of that edict was probably born of concern and nothing else. But Mason didn't care. He *couldn't* care. Not with the information he currently had.

"I'd prefer if we just got through this. I have things to do."

Leigh was still holding the card with the word *Fire* broken into its constituent bits. She shrugged and wagged the card to suggest she was game whenever he was — that it wasn't her slowing this down or holding it back.

But when Mason didn't speak again, she went on. Probably breaking more rules — just because she knew him, in defiance of orders and common sense — out of friendship and pity.

"Your history, I'm afraid, is very much an issue. Even if you pass this test, someone's going to ask you about that history. Do you remember it?"

Mason did. The drug seemed specific. His "history" and his friendship with her, if he believed it, should both have roots in his mind. Yet he'd forgotten the one that might cloud this test — Leigh — and remembered the unfortunate rest.

"I know my history. Why does it matter?"

"Most people apply to be Docents because something about it calls to them. We get a lot of gamers. People who like leveling up. Or enjoy solving logical puzzles. Those folks are here because they see it as a way to turn their vocation into a vacation. They realize we'll pay them for what they like to do anyway and can't wait to jump at the chance."

"And?" Mason asked.

"You, on the other hand, seem to be here as a grudge." She raised another card. They were large things, square, perhaps seven inches on one side. An intricate maze — the kind it'd take many attempts to navigate.

"Am I supposed to solve that?"

"Just tell me what comes to you."

He considered. "There's no solution. No path all the way to the center."

"Does that bother you?"

"It's a bit unusual for a maze."

Leigh glanced to the side. She'd propped her tablet there before reaching for the cards again. Presumably, its display was tied to the five wireless sensors they'd stuck to his chest and head. Mason found himself resenting her every glance at the tablet. She was checking on something he hadn't chosen to share. His heart rate or the cogitating waves of his brain.

"What? Wrong answer?"

"Try not to think in terms of right and wrong," she told him.

"I'm just stating a fact. If you'd like me to go through the farce of trying to solve the thing before declaring it impossible, I can do that."

"I'm more curious about something else," she said.

"What?"

"About what you'd do if you faced a maze you couldn't solve."

Her attention returned to the tablet, Mason's answer on display before he'd even spoken. "I think that's what I'm doing right now."

"I see. And what if you were trapped inside the maze instead of on its outside?"

"That's a stupid question."

"Tell me about your relationship with Officer Dakota Ward."

Mason felt blindsided. Then, when he realized his surprise had tickled her sensors, infuriated. "None of your business."

"Were you aware of her proclivities?"

"That's a bullshit question."

"Precinct records say Ward drew first."

"We drew at the same time."

"And security footage, though obscured, suggests she *fired* first."

Mason had seen that footage. It was so obscured, it'd been unusable. Certainly inadmissible in court. They'd never have convicted her if she hadn't lied to cover him.

He looked away.

"Is this making you uncomfortable?"

"What's the highest score anyone has ever gotten on this test?"

"Try not to think in terms of scores."

"Well then, goddammit, what *should* I think in terms of?"

Leigh looked at the tablet. At the card still in her hand. Around the room. It wasn't for interrogations, and Mason wasn't in trouble. They had privacy. She lowered the card face-down then tapped at her tablet. Mason couldn't see the screen, but her expression brightened. Then the backlight vanished as she turned off the tablet.

"Are we done?" Mason asked.

She sat back. The room stank of cigarettes and coffee. You weren't allowed to smoke anywhere inside any of the HRO administration buildings, but especially not inside Dharma One. The smell could only come from cops and Docents smoking outside and bringing the odor back in with them. A heroic amount of smoking for sure ... but then, it was said to be a heroically stressful job. That was one of the reasons Mason couldn't wait to start.

"We can be done if you want to be," she said.

"Did I pass?"

"Academically? Yes, with flying colors. You are spectacularly gifted with pattern recognition. I could tell within the first few minutes that on an intellectual basis alone, you had the chops to excel at this job."

"*But?*"

"But you are, in my opinion, psychologically unfit."

"Is that so?"

"It is. I know it's not my place, so again — you are free to walk out of here whenever you'd like." Leigh picked up a folder and started leafing through it. He saw his service record, Dakota's service record, something that looked official and tied to her case — and most infuriatingly, a photo of father and son looking chummy that was, at most, five years old.

How things had changed. It wasn't Dakota's fault she was an albatross as far as Mason's application was concerned, but it *was* his father's. Fucking Carter. Mason couldn't help that he'd been born an asshole's son.

"But I shouldn't, should I?" Mason asked.

"That's up to you."

"Because if I walk out, you'll talk to your bosses. They'll talk to the psych eval team. And that'll be it for me, right?"

"Your situation doesn't concern me so much as your complete and total unwillingness to face it."

"I've faced plenty."

"What was your role, then, the night Desmond Boulet was shot?"

Mason blinked. In the blackness, he saw the starfire of a muzzle flash in the dark. He saw a body fall.

There was a time when telling the truth would have helped, but Dakota had burned that bridge. He hadn't even known she'd swapped their service weapons, putting Boulet's ballistics match into her holster while they awaited the cavalry. He hadn't known she'd confessed to IA then consented to questioning. The shooting went down in the Dregs. There'd been no witnesses, only on-the-scene testimony from the two of them. Dakota's record had been better than his, and she didn't have a corrupt father. She'd thought Mason couldn't take the heat, and she'd be forgiven.

She'd been half-right.

Now there was nothing to be done. She'd fallen on the sword, betting it would injure but not doom her. Now she was the prisoner instead of him.

He and Dakota had been very clear. Only the two of them would ever know she'd taken the rap for a crime she didn't commit … and it'd stay that way until the grave. Recalling it evoked something far beyond shame, but there was nothing to be done. Mason's confession after her fall would only have gotten them *both* thrown in — Mason for the shooting and Dakota for perjury.

"It's all in my file," Mason said.

"Is the testimony in your file accurate?"

"It's perjury if not."

"Yes. It would be." Leigh nodded, closed the folder, then set it aside. "How about your father?"

"What about him?"

"Caused quite a problem for Revival, didn't he?"

"For Revival. For my family."

"And for yourself?"

"Of course. I'm part of my family." It was supposed to sound sarcastic, but it came out stupid.

"Look," she said, and now she suddenly seemed less formal, more human.

Mason didn't like it. He knew where this was going and didn't want her pity.

"What happened with your family? I can't even imagine."

"Do you *have* to imagine? Don't you already know it all?"

"We're friends, not besties. I've never gotten you to open up. Same for your father."

Mason stared at her. "Shit happens."

"Your CO says you haven't even taken any time off."

"Why would I?"

"To grieve?"

Mason shrugged.

"Or possibly to deal with your brother and mother's affairs. You told me yourself you've been asked to be the legal guardian of Logan's son."

"Well …"

"I also talked to a few of your coworkers in preparation for this interview. Together with my own observations, it all paints a picture, frankly, of an unstable officer who's barely hanging on."

"Is that right?"

"Do you think you're handling this well? Objective opinion, Detective."

"As well as I can."

"And yet I'm told you refuse to participate in the department memorial honoring your brother."

"I have my own plans. I don't need theirs."

"What kind of plans?"

"Not that it's any of your business, but we held a funeral. Already put them in the ground. The distasteful details around this are mostly done, and now they want to reopen the wound and hold some late-to-the-party service? It's grandstanding, not a 'memorial.' Political, not earnest."

"And that's what bothers you. You prefer the sanctity of a service filled with those who knew and loved him."

"So, you know me but didn't know my brother?"

"Of course, I knew Logan."

"Then you should know better than what you just said."

"And what was that?"

"Honey, those who knew Logan Shaw were the *least* likely to love him."

She shifted in her chair then made a note. "Do you know Officer Terrence Davis?"

"Jesus," Mason said, rolling his eyes. "Now Davis is part of this?"

"He said he'd love a public opportunity to say a prayer. For both of them."

"Officer Davis says a prayer whenever he opens his duty locker. Whenever he sits down at his desk. God isn't a comfort for him. It's a weapon."

"How so?"

Mason waved a dismissive hand. There was so much unwarranted discussion here. His annoying coworkers were the least of his concerns.

"What about you, Detective? Your family used to be religious. Do you still have faith you can turn to?"

"Yeah. Vodka."

Leigh sat forward again. Put her hands on the desk. There was a slight patronizing chuckle, then she turned dead serious. "May I be frank?"

"You've been bringing up shit that's none of your business the entire time. Not sure I can stop you, even if we *are* friends."

"You're a fucking cliché."

Now Mason laughed, but it wasn't funny.

Her face didn't change. "You read like an entry in the DSM. *Avoidant Macho Bullshitter Syndrome.*"

"Is that your professional opinion? Or did you determine this after years of observation?"

"You just told me your faith is vodka. You keep calling me 'honey' and 'sweetheart,' despite my telling you that we know each other, and it's clear those terms would piss me off. You don't know it right now, Mason, but I actually owe you a few punches. A couple of hard kicks in the balls. Your problem is you're so invested in feeling sorry for yourself, you've swept things you should be dealing with under the rug. That way, you can pretend you're *oppressed* instead of *repressing*. And what's worse, so many fucked-up things have happened to you lately, everyone feels bad enough to keep their mouths shut. Nobody's willing to look you in the eye and tell you the truth."

Mason was shocked by her avalanche of words but managed to hide it. "All except for you, huh?"

"Your father, before his incarceration and unfortunate succumbing to Pattern Black, demonstrated behavior so increasingly reckless, USPD was seriously considering suspension. The Revival Corporation in general — along with Mr. Blake in particular — filed several formal complaints. Apparently, in your off-hours, you've been harassing them. Blaming Blake for your father's arrest."

"I'm just trying to walk in my old man's footsteps. Pick up his mantle, you know?"

"The people I spoke to said although your behavior has been

erratic since the deaths of your brother and mother, Carter's was borderline criminal."

"*Borderline* criminal?"

"Before it was overt, yes. Not to mention that prior to his arrest, he was far off-center. More erratic even than you."

"And that means?"

"*Crazy*, to be blunt. And what's worse, your colleagues at the department say you're showing a lot of the same behaviors." She shifted papers, then sat forward. "Here's a little refresher on me until you get your memory back. Before I started this job, I worked clinical psychology for the Army. You can't call soldiers 'crazy.' It's un-American. But between you and me? War fucks a person up. It *makes* them crazy. And you? I'd be derelict in my duty to this Outpost, to the police department, and to you in particular if I didn't acknowledge that you're headed down the same path. Breakdowns can happen to anyone. They're the mind's white flag, saying they have no choice but to stop and surrender. They're nothing to be ashamed of. Heed the lesson, and you can heal. But do you know what makes everything worse?" She didn't wait for his answer. "Fighting the signs. Pretending you're totally fine and nothing fazes you."

"Are you finished?"

"I don't know. Are you hearing me?"

Mason considered standing and leaving. Miss Leigh, even if he *did* know her, had *way* overstepped her bounds. He could probably get her fired. She was supposed to conduct her little assessment with her cards. If her subject passed, she was supposed to send him up the chain. Everything else was inappropriate.

But leaving would mean she'd won. And right now, Mason very much wanted her to lose.

"How many cards are left in that deck?"

It took a few seconds for Leigh to realize what he meant. She looked down and, with an *okay, fine* look, counted. "Six."

"How long would it normally take a Docent applicant — one who ends up getting the job — to solve six cards?"

"It's not timed."

"Then guess."

"And you don't need to 'get' them all. It's somewhat open to interpretation."

"How long ... *sweetheart?*"

She bit her cheek. "Maybe twenty minutes."

"Then I'll make you a deal. If I can get all six of your remaining cards inside of ten minutes, you'll recommend me for the Docent position without reservation."

"That's not really how it works."

"But if I take even one second or longer, I'll walk away. And retract my application."

"I can't do that, Mason."

"Seven minutes, then."

"You don't understand."

"*Seven minutes* ... and if I can't do it, I won't just take back my application. I'll take a leave of absence from the force and go see a shrink."

Leigh considered. Then she seemed to decide that when facing a crazy man with nothing to lose, sometimes rolling the dice made more sense. She took off her watch and set it face-up on the table.

They stared at the face until the second hand hit twelve, at which point Leigh raised her first card.

Mason studied it. Ten seconds passed, and he already knew. It showed a sequence of shapes, and he was supposed to give the next two logical forms at its end.

"Open square, then a circle with a line through it."

"Are you sure?"

"Don't waste time." Of course, Mason was sure. Back when he and his father had been able to share their thoughts, he'd learned that with very little effort, he could peek into some of the minds around him if they were focused intently, thus making their thoughts *loud*. It had proven an accelerant in school tests. He'd seen variants of this puzzle twenty times, through twenty different sets of perceptions.

She put the card down then raised the next.

Mason studied. It took him almost a minute to work out the solution.

"A vase on a green background."

Leigh's mouth cracked. Mason held up a hand to stop her.

"Wait. A purple background. Or if you want to be technical, lavender."

She took the next card.

"A rabbit warren. Wait. No. Snakes?" Mason kept his hand in the air to show he hadn't reached a final answer. "Oh. I know. That's a subway map. New York."

"How could you possibly know New York's subway map?"

Mason didn't have time to explain, nor did he want to. In no way whatsoever was the design on her card obviously a subway map, but the card in her hand was multi-step. He'd had to interpret, invert, solve a coded riddle, then aggregate. She was trying to slow him down.

She held up the fourth card. It showed a lotus flower seed pod. An organic disc full of dark brown holes.

His mouth froze.

"What is it, Detective?"

Mason couldn't move. She shrugged, satisfied by something, and picked up the next card without an answer. This one showed the same holes, but photographic trickery had rendered them over the skin of a woman's thigh, close-up. There were tiny things at the bottom. Maybe seeds or something else.

"What the hell is this?"

Leigh looked almost smug.

"Answer me," he said.

"I don't know. Isn't it your job to *tell* me what it is?"

"Who chooses these cards?" Leigh was holding the last one high. Mason let his eyes defocus, not wanting to look at the image or give her the satisfaction of turning away.

"An AI," she said.

"And they're random."

"Not at all."

Mason thought back. Only in retrospect did he see personal

reflections in everything she'd given him. Her word puzzle had spelled *Fire*, as in firing a gun. She'd shown him a maze with no way out — which at night, with the lights off and the drunk wearing off, was how he felt. Her cards included a smiling set of parents with two male children, a pair of structures — one that looked normal and another that looked as dysfunctional and uncooperative as his family — and more than one pear. Mason knew he might be stretching ... but *pear* was a homonym of *pere*, the French word for father.

And now this. With the lotus seed pod. With holes superimposed on flesh.

He closed his eyes, and one of his darkest memories bubbled to the surface.

As a child, he'd come across a section of hardpan near their home, recently flooded and drained into a buried aquifer. The water's percolation had left the baked ground peppered with holes, and when young Mason poked at them with curiosity, hundreds of beetles had scurried out of their new home and up his legs. He'd screamed. Some had been out loud. Most were in his head. He remembered knowing quite certain that his father had heard that mental scream and had sent back a message — *You don't have to be afraid.*

"Mason?"

"We're done here."

"But we still have cards left. There's still time on the clock."

"You think this is amusing? Are you laughing your ass off inside? Some motherfucking friend."

"Detective Shaw. *Mason.* Are you trypophobic?"

"I don't even know what that means."

But of course, he did.

"Fear of holes."

"No."

"It's customary for rookies with USPD to be issued revolvers, but I understand you had a semi-automatic from the start. Why was that?"

The first time he'd popped the cylinder to load his weapon, the sight of those six holes in a circle sent him into a cold sweat. He'd plugged them with bullets as fast as he could, but he kept feeling like they might escape, might come out of those holes to climb across his skin. He'd asked his CO if he could purchase his own semi-auto — if they'd let him have one, he was perfectly willing to cover the cost.

Leigh picked up the last card. Black dots on a white background, arranged in an expanding swirl.

A Fibonacci spiral.

"How about this one?" she asked, now holding up the last two cards side by side.

Mason stood. Fuck this job.

"Sit down," she said.

"Go fuck yourself."

"Don't you think it's telling that you've never faced your fear?"

"You don't know that."

"I know that psychological records collected by the HRO from Dr. Michelle Bellforte suggest you—"

"We're done here."

She pressed something at the desk. The room must have been a bit higher-security than Mason thought because the door locked just as he reached for the handle.

"You have an acutely avoidant personality, Mason. It pains me to say, but it's true. It's *been* true, but out of social courtesy, I've kept most of my opinions — my *educated, professional* opinions — to myself. But now that you're applying for Docent, it's my duty to confront this. It's not my place to diagnose you in this setting, but I have been contracted by this HRO to assess your fitness for the role of Docent, and my job has certain obligations when it comes to officers of the law."

Mason wrenched the handle. The lock made a racket like a tiny creature trying to escape its cage.

He turned then marched toward her. "Let me the fuck out of here. Now." Mason kept his eyes high. She'd put all three troubling images onto the table, face-up, visible from the corner of his eye.

"Even in this professional setting, I am bound by patient-client confidentiality," Leigh said, still calm. "But as with any bound professional, I am similarly required to report certain issues. You are self-destructive *and* outwardly destructive."

"I'm not suicidal. I'm no danger to myself or others."

"I'm not sure I agree with either of those."

It took everything not to grab and throttle her.

"Open the door."

"Why do you want to be a Docent, Mason? Why now, after amassing such a stellar record at USPD?"

"I'm tired of the people I work with. They're constantly in my business."

"Constantly? Or recently? Is it possible you're conflating meddling with human concern for your well-being?"

"Whatever."

"Do you want to be a Docent because Docents work alone?"

Work alone, get to beat prisoners — yeah, all of that.

"Are you aware the Docents will most likely become obsolete in the coming year? Revival is considering handing the patrol job over to drones, which are more thorough, less obtrusive, and don't need sleep. You might be throwing away your cop job just to get laid off."

"My choice, not yours."

"Post-hire, pre-deployment Docent training takes six weeks — and it happens here, in the middle of the HRO. I don't know how they brought you in — if it was by helicopter or bus or what. If they take you out by chopper, be sure to look down as you go. Do you know where this facility is located? Have you looked at a map and found Dharma One? You're *in the middle of the prison.* That'll be your life. In the middle of Hell every single day, training to walk around inside it for a job that isn't going to exist."

"Convenient. Someone once told me when you're in the middle of Hell, you should keep going."

"I was referring to your personal issues. To soldiering on and facing what's in front of you instead of pretending it doesn't exist."

"Even better. Maybe I'll run into Dear Old Dad on my rounds."

Unwanted sympathy washed over her face. "Mason, your father is——"

"Dead. I know."

"I'd be less concerned if he was. But I know *you* know they haven't zeroed him out yet. He has no brain function, but he's technically — *technically* — still alive. Which brings me to another concern."

"What, you think I'm going to seek him out?"

"You've joked about it before."

"I don't remember that."

"Doesn't mean it didn't happen."

"I wouldn't go after him. Why the hell would I?"

"Closure? Denial?"

"You live your way. I'll live mine."

"Does that mean you'd try to find his body?"

"I didn't want Carter in my life. Why would I want his corpse?"

Leigh's face displayed even deeper concern, a heavier layer of sympathy.

Mason's anger turned to latent violence.

She shook her head. "I can't recommend you for this job. With all the baggage you carry, you'd kill yourself as a Docent."

"Good."

"I also have no choice but to recommend psychological leave from the department, effective immediately."

"Wonderful. Now, are we done?"

There was a knock on the door.

Someone tried the handle then said, "Is everything all right in there?"

Mason turned to Leigh. "Tell me that's not Watson on the other side of that door."

"Your fellow officers care about you. Believe it or not, you're not in this alone."

"Motherfucker." Now he wasn't quite as eager to leave. It'd been bad enough when he'd thought he'd have to face the captain at work tomorrow ... but if they'd flown him here? And worse, Mason thought he recognized the frame and posture of the silhouette behind Captain Watson in the frosted glass.

"Simmer down in there, Shaw," said the second man outside —

the short one with the southern twang and holier-than-thou attitude. "Stop fighting truth for once and admit it ain't all bad, that God is good."

Mason glared at Leigh. "You are *fucking kidding me.*"

"It's like I said. You need help, and you aren't alone."

Watson with his by-the-book ways. Davis, thumping his Bible.

There was only one person he might be willing to talk to on Doctor Leigh's orders, but that person was behind bars because Mason — by omission rather than malice — had put her there.

The door opened. Mason saw tall Captain Watson beside the wiry form of Terrence Davis. Davis, with his pompous piety. Davis, who everyone thought was a saint, but whose games Mason had always seen right through.

Both were dressed in plain clothes. *Just visiting.* But the prison Docent behind them was in uniform, as was the doctor in his lab coat.

Mason looked at Leigh. "I'm free to go?"

Watson shrugged, answering with the voice of an apology. "Actually, Internal Affairs has asked to speak with you again. About the Desmond Boulet shooting."

Mason sneered at all of them, but especially at Leigh. At the traitor. He'd come here for a job, and now it looked like he might end his day in captivity.

"Don't touch me," Mason said.

"Just settle." Davis stepped toward him. "This ain't a reprimand. You'll see."

"You said they wanted to help," he said to Leigh.

"They do. *We* do. We're on your side. This kind of help wasn't easy to arrange. I had to pull some strings."

An alarm screamed in his chest. Despite Leigh's words about special, above-and-beyond "help," Mason saw something premeditated. Something that required them all to talk, decide, then coordinate. He watched Leigh's eyes with a mixture of hatred and reluctant respect. He still didn't know her properly, but he could do the math, and by that particular arithmetic — with Mom and

Logan dead, Pop a vegetable, and Dakota behind bars — this woman might be the best advocate he had.

And this is what she'd chosen for her ward? This ambush?

"Why is there a doctor here?" Mason asked.

"It's easier if you'll just trust us," Leigh said.

The doctor's hand moved, peeking out from behind him with a syringe.

All the lights went on inside his head. Mason backed away, finally seeing the shape of the thing before him. "What's in that syringe?"

"Something to help you relax."

"Why?"

"So we can help you." The doctor came forward.

Mason threw a forearm at the man's face, making him stumble.

"Hold him," Watson said.

He thrashed harder, but Davis was fast for a squirrelly little fucker and had Mason pinned in seconds. Watson leaned in, smashing him against one wall with his superior weight.

"Leigh!"

It was the first time he'd used her name. Certainly the first time he'd called to her rather than just referring to her. His tone was a plea. It made him feel weak to say it, but he couldn't move.

She looked pained. "It's for the best."

"What the hell are you doing to me?"

"We can fix it, Mason. We can fix you. I know you don't have the willpower to dig out of this hole. But you don't have to. We can help."

"Help how?"

The syringe appeared in his peripheral vision. The doctor uncapped the thing and made a thin stream shoot from its end.

"Roll up his sleeve."

Mason batted at Davis as he tried to raise his shirtsleeve. "You're putting me in Chamber Therapy?"

"Shh. It's okay."

"It's for prisoners!"

"Blake himself okayed it. I had to contact him about your

father's case, but I pulled favors. This is a new formulation, Mason. Nothing like what they use inside."

Mason thrashed. They held him fast.

"Don't fight it," said Leigh. "Mason? You hear me? It won't work if you fight it. You might even wake up, then—"

"YOU'RE GOING TO PUT ME UNDER AFTER MY FATHER WENT PATTERN BLACK?"

Leigh said something about protocols and what went awry in the past, but Mason heard only the edges. Most of his attention was on Davis's face, which was very close, his voice occluding all others. "Shh. Don't fuss. They say if you let it happen, it's just like a dream. The nicest one in the world."

Mason tried very hard to kick Davis in the groin. To get a hand free and claw his eyes. Instead, they held him back. And the needle came closer.

"You get a nightmare if you fuss," Davis said, shifting his feet.

Mason moved, too, and finally had a shot to kick the man in his groin.

The needle finally pricked him and turned his world black.

Then white.

And full of holes with sinister things in the bottom.

TWENTY-SIX

Keep Going

"MASON?" Nic repeated.

In the sun-washed, high-rise apartment, Mason turned his head to look Nic in the eyes.

"Are you … What's up, buddy?"

The look on Mason's face must have scared Nic, judging by his manner and voice. Freaked him right the fuck out. And that made sense, considering deep down, Mason was also scared to death.

At least now he knew the answer. Or thought he did.

Not all of this was strange. Mason remembered now. He'd been inside the prison before. Seen it from above. Knew its places and ways. Maybe, if he remembered that long-ago encounter correctly, he even knew its weaknesses.

"When you're going through Hell, keep going."

"Okay." Nic nodded. "You wanna put some meat on the bones of that, or should I just nod along?"

"How long have we known each other, Nic?"

"Dunno. Five, six years?"

"Remember Logan?"

"Used to beat my ass," Nic said. "He always hit me, even if I spilled everything."

"For a price."

"Sure."

"And, of course, you got Logan in trouble for it."

"Well, *someone* did."

"You saw Carter before they arrested him, right?" Mason asked.

"Same time as I saw you last, sure."

"But of course, once inside, he went Pattern Black."

"Yeah. Sucks."

"And you never saw him in here. Inside the prison."

Nic shook his head, negating. "I told you I *did* see him inside."

"How? He never mentioned you when I visited, said he stayed to himself. Felt it was best to be a loner inside the prison. It was just a few weeks between his admission and going under."

"A few weeks is plenty of time for the two of us to find each other and chat."

"You weren't even in his crib. How did you find him?"

"I've got my ways."

"Or you don't."

"Are you saying I'm lying? Why would I lie about talking to Carter?"

"Lying … or wrong. Or …" There was a third option, but Mason couldn't put it into words. He actually didn't think Nic was lying about talking to Carter inside the HRO, but he was similarly sure there was no way he ever could have done that.

But the truth was inaccessible. Like Calliope. Mason saw his father talking online to her — *him*, then — once, and the whole thing seemed strange. She didn't speak through the system so much as from within it as if part of its fabric. As if she had the run of things and was somehow pulling two very different sets of strings at once. There was something of that in Nic now, too misshapen for his mind to grasp.

"You think I'm *wrong* about talking to your dad? How can I be wrong about something like that?"

Mason paced. He almost had this. Its feel was odd, hard to carry. "Did you know Logan well?"

"Um …"

"Did you know I was supposed to get custody of Logan's kid? Of … Harry?"

"You mean Hunter?"

"Yeah," Mason said. "*Hunter.*"

Now Nic was really staring at him, but after that last exchange, Mason found himself staring right back.

Got you.

Although Mason wasn't entirely sure what he had.

"I know what I have to do."

"What's that?" Nic asked.

"I have to keep going."

"Okay."

"I have to go back. To where we were this morning."

"No way."

"Why? You ready to tell me what really happened with you, Nic? Did you really do Chamber Therapy?"

"Of course!"

"What was it like?"

"Like you said! Tube of goo, wires stuck all over …"

"Who ran it?"

"What?"

"You heard me. You said the people running the thing talked about you like you weren't even there after pulling you out. Because they were going to give you their memory drug. But the memory drug didn't work, which means you should remember everything. So, tell me, Nic. The people who were talking about you — *what did they look like?*"

"Um …"

"Answer me!"

Nic's bug eyes went even buggier. "I don't know, man!"

"*Try!*"

"A man and a woman. Tall guy. Looked like …"

He described the military man with the sidearm. The one who'd died on the catwalk, his life ended with a bullet.

"And a woman. She had …"

Nic described Dakota as a pair of forked paths battled for truth in his mind.

Dakota wasn't running intake for the HRO then. She was still working for USPD, not HRO 22 when Nic would have gone under.

Or …

Dakota wasn't around. She hasn't been around. For … years?

And she'd certainly never run intake for the prison.

Both couldn't be true. Mason's last memory of Dakota was her unconscious body being taken through the gate in Immunity's fence. Her face as they led her away in handcuffs. He remembered her being arrested. He remembered her going free. He remembered his own arrest. He remembered it not at all.

Mason grabbed Nic's arm and pulled, heading for the door. Nic dug in his heels, scraping carpet on the hardwood into a pile of festooned nylon.

"I'm not going back there, Mason! Immunity …"

"Immunity *what*, Nic?"

But Nic seemed to have no idea what to say about Immunity. Possibly because Mason had no idea, either.

Nic flinched away again, but this time Mason grabbed both shoulders and looked him in the eye. "Am I crazy?"

"How would I know?"

"Am I crazy? Did it really happen? You were there, Nic!"

"What do you want me to say?"

His mindscape was a ludicrous stew. Past and present and future and A and B were all jumbled in a pile. Mason could pick up any random memory right now and not know if he could believe it.

He focused on Carter. What had happened with his father? Mason had suggested the old man try Chamber Therapy because if it was going to rehab anyone, it should be able to rehab a cop who maybe wasn't as corrupt as people thought. He'd had to pull some strings.

Where had he heard someone saying they'd *pulled strings?*

Do you remember your arrest?

A disembodied voice. Not really his own.

Of course, I remember it.

Do you remember Carter's?

That, Mason remembered even better.

Carter had been obsessed. After the car accident that killed his mother and brother, Carter's Revival obsession exploded. The investigation was behind him. It was finally time for action. He broke into Blake's office at the end of a slow downward spiral of drinking too much, arguing, and turning from a good cop into one everyone feared. The bar fight, the curiously quick actions of fellow officers after getting that tip. Mason had heard a bit of what came next. They'd given his father a physical. Shown him orientation videos. Put him in the red crib, where the common room was all spoken for, where his cot had been at a fuck-you spot in the middle, where his only contact of note had been some long-haired shitter named Frank Watt who could never shut the fuck up. Carter had talked about Watt plenty.

I can't get more time in prison if I commit a murder, right? So maybe I'll just kill him. Then shut his flapping mouth for good.

"You okay, man?" Nic had stopped struggling and was now staring at Mason.

"Did you really see Carter in here?"

"Of course!"

"Or are you mine?"

"I'm … *what?*"

It was so confusing. It made his brain want to tie itself in knots.

But despite the muddle, Mason's mind was consistently clearing.

When you're going through Hell, keep going.

Answers would come so long as he followed his gut. The closest thing he had to True North. He just had to keep going, no matter the mishmash his head had become. At the end, there'd be truth.

Mason? You hear me? If you fight, it won't work. You might even wake up. And then—

Who'd said that? Someone he'd spoken with recently … only, perhaps he hadn't spoken to that person at all.

Not here. Not in a long time.

Mason gripped his arm harder, then headed for the stairs. Nic resisted at first, then stopped when the stairs took all his focus. As fast as Mason was moving, the slightest lapse of attention would lead to a spill and a broken nose at the bottom.

Except it wouldn't really break your nose, would it? Although, who's to say what's real?

It took a long time to reach the ground floor, though far less than it'd taken them to ascend without a functioning elevator. Inside the concrete walls, slowly going lower with no view to see out, Mason had the feeling of moving deep underground. Like they'd been in a buried silo, burrowing ever deeper into the planet's rotting core.

They exited into slanted daylight.

Nic looked at the sky, noting the dramatic change in light. "How did it get so late? Did I pass out or something?"

But Mason's mind, as he began to walk, was elsewhere. Despite moving back toward the spot with the chalk lines on the ground, Nic stayed with him. Protesting, but still coming. Warning him. Telling Mason it was too dangerous. To go back.

Nic stopped short of the first chalk line. He looked down as if there was a snake on his boot then touched it like nitroglycerine. "This is crazy, man."

"Then leave. Let me be."

"Are you kidding? You just dragged my ass all the way down here."

"I changed my mind."

The man stayed rooted. It was almost as if, reluctant though he was, Nic was tied invisibly to Mason's hip.

"I came all the way out here to help you. The least you can do is to help me get back to the crib without getting jumped." Nic tugged on his arm. "Let's go. Before curfew hits."

Mason's attention was fixed on the vista where he'd once seen an all-white void. Black holes in reality. A mathematically perfect spiral, beautiful when it didn't chill him.

"Nic."

He jumped, on-edge.

Mason continued without waiting for an answer. "Watch this."
He swung a foot over the blue line of chalk.

"*You can't go in there!*" Nic whisper-shouted.

"Why not?"

"Because it's *their* place!"

"But they invited me."

Mason moved forward confidently now. Nic followed in a parade of protests as they passed buildings on their way toward a barbed-wire gate looming ahead of them. There was so little logic to any of this. There wasn't any chalk on the ground when he'd carried Dakota here. Why would they need a chalk line if they had the gate and guns?

"Why is there a line on the ground? Why would anyone do that?"

"I told you. To mark their territory."

Mason gestured at the fence, which marked their territory just fine.

"It's like a no-man's land, I mean."

"So, we step past the chalk, and then we have a few steps to decide if we want to go for the fence? How does that make sense? It's like you invented something to be scared of."

"*Invented?* Look! It's right at your fucking feet!"

But the chalk line was gone.

Nic was still looking around for it when Mason took another big step and spoke again. "I'll bet you I could walk right inside."

"You'll get your ass killed!"

"Then where are they, Nic?" Mason was thinking of the drones. The soldiers so carefully on patrol. Where was all of that now?

"You don't know how they think," Nic told him.

"You're right. I don't. Nor do I know how *you* think unless I know *exactly* how you think, down to every tiny little memory in your head.

"What?"

"*Why are you here, Nic?*"

"Where the fuck else am I supposed to go?"

A klaxon sounded. Nic's head jerked up, his jaw dropping. Sometime in the last sixty seconds, the sun had set.

"That's curfew!"

"Then I guess we're fucked."

"*I'm* fucked. You can always say you forgot to check in again."

"Why can I do that, but you can't?"

"Because you don't have the tracker in your blood anymore, dumbass!" The light wasn't gone from the air, but it was waning fast. Nic's agitation was almost a twitch.

He hadn't told Nic about someone removing his tracker.

"I still don't get that," Mason said. "They were so sure the blood dongle couldn't be removed."

Nic was still grabbing at him but seemed resistant to leaving without him. All for one, it seemed. "Mason! Goddammit, the drones will be coming!"

"I don't really want drones to come."

"Who gives a fuck what you want!"

Mason walked to the gate. The accountant man appeared behind it almost immediately.

"You again."

"And you," Mason said. "What's your name?"

"My name's Your Mother."

"I don't think it is," Mason said.

"I told you to come back later."

"It's later."

"There's nothing here for you."

"Where's my friend?" Mason asked. "Where's Dakota?"

"I don't know what you're talking about."

"Are you the guard?" Mason asked.

"What?"

"Are you the guard? Is that your job with Immunity?"

"*Immunity*? Not sure what you mean, buddy."

Mason nodded. "You have to be a guard. You were just sitting there. Waiting for me to walk up."

"We're tracking you. I knew you were coming."

"Really."

"Listen. You—"

Mason shot the gatekeeper in the leg with Dakota's service weapon. He'd had it tucked into the back of his belt, apparently. Forgotten all about it, until it was when he wanted it. Like magic.

Don't fight it, Mason. Don't fight.

The world glitched. Mason saw a white sky filled with black dots for half a second. Then it was normal again.

"You shot me!"

"Guess I did."

Gritting his teeth against the pain, the man pulled a small tablet from his coat. His bloodied fingers left prints on the housing. He tapped its front, his manner suddenly threatening. "You should run. Our drones are modified to kill."

"Call your drones," Mason said.

Nic protested behind him but still didn't go.

They waited. Nothing happened.

The man tried to bristle, so Mason shot him again.

Nic shouted protests, but still, the tableau didn't change.

"WHAT THE FUCK DO YOU THINK YOU'RE DOING?" the man demanded.

"I want to see Calliope."

"Which Calliope?"

"Three seconds."

"You …"

Mason shot him a third time, in the opposite leg. He contorted in agony, raising his masticated limb.

Nic was beside himself but also still beside Mason.

"We need to *GO,"* Nic said.

Mason shook him off, then raised the semi-auto to center on the Accountant's forehead. He lined up the sights, closed one eye, and touched the trigger.

"Wait!" shouted the bleeding man, holding out a hand.

"So, you'll help me," Mason said.

"Nobody's seen her for years! She's gone, man!"

"I've seen her."

"Then you're the only one! Calliope left us! She ran away!"

The gun shifted, then re-centered.

"I'm you telling the truth!"

Nic was very close. He touched Mason's arm. "Come on, man. Put it down."

He did. Slowly. The world itself flashed through iterations like the blasts of a fully-auto shotgun. There was suddenly no past or present or future.

No answers.

Mason thought, *How many fingers?*

An image of Dakota. In his intake session, trying to get Mason to save himself. Dakota fitting him with that funny copper hat — the spider with balls at the end of each leg.

Dakota pulling him from the tank and shooting her colleague with the gun in her right hand, despite being left-handed. Dakota downing a drone she shouldn't have been able to fell. Dakota managing to hide inside a prison filled with cameras, drones, snitches, and trackers. Dakota taking the fall for Mason when he accidentally shot that kid, ending up in prison for a crime she didn't commit.

He remembered someone else at intake. Someone fitting him with the copper hat.

Someone else — the way he'd seen it through someone else's eyes.

The world was suddenly different.

The world, in a blink, was back to its usual self.

Mason turned to Nic. "My nephew's name is Hunter."

Nic's face was twisted, panicked, ugly. Something had gone very wrong with Mason Shaw. "Okay …"

"But Nic," Mason said, "on the job, Logan never mentioned his family's names. And I know you never met him."

The shot man was still screaming. Bleeding out, maybe. The size of the crimson pool told Mason he may have hit the man's femoral artery. He'd be dead soon. Maybe. And why did it matter?

Nic shrugged. "One of you must have said it. You or Logan. How else would I know his name?"

Mason closed his eyes. He saw the black dots all around him. Not a white room with black spots anymore, so much as a black room with blinding white edges. He imagined going forward. Steeling himself, remembering the holes in the parched hardpan, the swarm of beetles, the pits of a lotus seed pod, the terrifying images he'd seen online, those same holes Photoshopped onto flesh.

He saw the little black storm. Felt the energy coming from it, the menace inside, and the end it symbolized.

The nightmares. The dealing he'd done alone, never telling a soul.

Still, in the same blink, Mason imagined reaching the edge of the lowest hole in the pattern. The bottom of the spiral. Behind him, a battalion of patterns. Grids. Mazes. More spirals, Fibonacci and not.

He opened his eyes. Both men were staring at him in the dark under a lone streetlight, waiting to see what was coming next.

"I need to find Calliope," Mason said.

"She's gone, man. She's gone!"

"Think."

"Hell if I know. Shit!"

Hell. The word broke the last of Mason's resistance. He put an oily muzzle under his chin.

"Mason?" Nic said from his side. "What … What are you doing, bud?"

"I'm keeping going," Mason said.

And then he pulled the trigger.

TWENTY-SEVEN

008

____

Bear O'Connor — born to Irish immigrants who'd traded their corned beef and cabbage for clichés of the American northwest, hand-building an off-the-grid cabin in Oregon shortly before their big son came into the world — looked nothing like the spirit animal after which he'd been named.

He thought this as, on his evening rounds, he paused at the makeshift commissary and settled his unkempt hair in the reflective hood above the stovetop. The stove had originally been electric, but as with most things inside HRO 22 — or any HRO, according to recent intel — most electrical hadn't worked for years. There was juice in the cribs, but the downside of _that_ electricity was that the users were still prisoners, still in cribs after curfew. It was better where Bear and his fellows were — deep inside the Inner Circle, either successfully hiding or allowed to survive for reasons unknown.

Back when Calliope had still been around, Big Fat Sammy had yanked spider burners and copper lines and solder from apartments and caches throughout the city, using his plumber's credentials to help them all. Afterward, the collective had embarked on a flood of informing — ratting out whomever they could, so long as they weren't Immunity — before pooling their chits to buy a simple heater. Nothing more than a squat propane tank with an exposed element affixed to its valve. It'd been easy, then, for Big Fat Sammy to hook the propane to the co-opted burners. From that point on, they'd been able to cook their food instead of eating it cold.

"You're getting too old for this shit," he told his reflection.

The kitchen hood, in truth, made Bear look much older than he was. Even in the thin, semi-reflective metal, he could see the long face his mother said would always look like it belonged to an accountant, high-but-not-quite receding red-brown hair, thin lips, and tiny little round glasses. Minuscule wrinkles crinkled the flesh around those thin lips. Some of that was age, and some the scars of hard living, an existence that became much harder for fools like him who thought too much about why they were still here and just what the hell their mission was supposed to be without access or a leader.

But mostly, Bear saw tide lines on the hood's metal that'd been made by rising grease turned firm as those oily smears and lines caught dust from the air. Whatever the reason, Bear thought he looked like an old man.

"Talking to yourself again, Bear?"

He turned and saw Kassidi, an enormous Samoan woman with arms bigger than any man's there. And not from steroids. She spent most of her time working out. Bear, who felt far too thin and spindly for a man named "Bear," wished he could say Kassidi was obsessive, and if *he* hadn't grown muscle, it was only because he lacked the mania to make it happen.

In truth, nobody needed obsession to do anything in Dharma Four — be it to work out, patrol the area, scavenge, build and tinker, or even learn a new language. They had space. They had books. They had batteries and solar panels to provide small amounts of power for devices on which sometimes, if they were lucky, they could get a highly censored data connection. The drones left them alone. They'd been lucky, intentionally ignored, or irrelevant enough that the prison didn't care to find them. At night, alone, he feared that last answer was truest. But they were still Immunity, and their name still culled fear in the minds of many.

"Why not? No one else to talk to."

"You can talk to me," Kassidi said.

"I didn't know you were up."

"Well, I am." She sat in a rolling office chair near Bear's monitoring station, which had devolved into little more than a nest of checklists nobody cared about and manifests that had been invisible for years. "You wanna talk?"

"I was just commenting that I'm getting too old for this shit."

"How old are you?"

"Thirty-six?"

Kassidi made a *pssht* sound. "That's not too old. I'm forty."

He'd assumed Kassidi was in her late twenties, with skin weathered only by the sun. Which really just made Bear feel worse about his slim form and paradoxically squishy middle. Personal details came hard inside the prison, be it gen pop or within Immunity's little cloister. Bear had known Kass for years without ever really knowing her, other than the one thing *everyone* knew about her — the thing that, rumor said, had tolled the final bell forecasting Calliope's leave.

"Why are you up?" he asked after re-claiming his chair.

"I don't sleep well. Never have."

"Is it because …?" He made a vague little gesture, but nothing could convey what he meant without insult. Nobody really knew what was in another person's head. With obvious, terrifying exceptions.

"I'm fine, you know. She'd tell you I'm fine."

Bear nodded, agreeing with at least half of what Kassidi said. It was enough for this late. The world was quiet. He didn't need semantic arguments. He didn't need the tiptoe dance of polite social graces.

Kassidi nodded back, any unintentional insult forgiven.

Bear had been pulling nonstop overnight shifts for at least six months now, though he and most of the others had long ago stopped tracking time. Doing so was depressing. Did it even matter in the end? Despite grumbling about the hours whenever he could, Bear was and had always been nocturnal.

It was the best time because nobody bothered him. Each night, he found himself alone in a disused building with sixteen people, basically-dead people and even more forgotten than the rest of the population, even though Docent uniforms still hung beside them as if in perverse tribute or as an offer of posthumous aspiration.

Just Bear and the graduates. Just Bear and the sleeping authority figures. He had never done well with authority figures. Bear attended them now with no small amount of shameful satisfaction, knowing they could never hassle him.

He was supposed to check on his basically-dead roommates twice per night to see if there were any changes, but these days he seldom bothered. He'd checked before Calliope had run off, then again for a few months after she'd gone just out of habit. But after becoming the full-time night guy, Bear had realized nobody ever verified his work. So, he'd instituted several new routines he found much more interesting than checking off boxes that had never — not once in the entire time they'd been here — *not* been checked.

Calliope had wanted the subjects' vitals noted daily, but now that she was gone, Bear and anyone else who cared to do so could, and did, point out her ritualistic stupidity. Why check on the subjects? They were catatonic. Braindead, zeroed out, Pattern Black, or whatever other term anyone wanted to use. They'd been that way the entire time anyone in his group had known them, seeing as Revival's little scramble years back had put the Docent program on pause then left it there, indefinitely and hidden carefully, its latest applicants never to see daylight again.

Nobody would come for these would-be Docents. They'd gone under for on-the-ground training, then one day, the person who would have pulled them out left and never came back. As far as the public knew, none of this ever existed, and once Immunity moved in, the chances of knowledge leaking out had dwindled from slim to none.

They were comfortable enough in their death, Bear supposed. Their chambers' meager needs were supplied by a chemical cell recharged by their own body heat, their ins and outs disgustingly fed and recycled, their atrophy held at bay by the suits in which someone from the past had dressed them, through means Bear neither understood nor cared to.

Because those sixteen dead souls never changed, Bear had ditched Calliope's ritual and instituted his own. He still made rounds, now with a dry-erase marker he used to draw different facial hair on the transparent lids of their horizontal coffins every night, the superimposed effect hilarious to him when viewed from above. Sometimes he gave the women goatees. Last night he'd given 004 — D'KEMBO, CHIDI a monocle. Tonight, he'd erased it in favor of a man-bun and whimsical-looking pencil-thin mustache. It really was spectacular.

Bear glanced over at Kassidi. When she moved her forearm, two massive muscles above the elbow slithered under her skin like a pair of wrestling pot roasts. Envy flared, followed by despondency and self-loathing. For one thing, Bear would never have the genetics to create Kassidi's build. But for another, he hadn't even tried.

He'd wasted his life the first time with that little white-collar hustle that put him in prison. After a short time under Calliope's Immunity in which he'd felt both mission and hope, Bear had gone about wasting his life a second time by doing exactly nothing with his every waking moment. Sometimes he wished he'd taken the suicide pill they'd offered at intake. Sometimes, feeling that, he considered jumping up and down outside, shouting after dark for a drone to come and shut him up. But mostly, he didn't bother. Bear was too scared to die, but more importantly, it was too much work. They all had dongles attached to their blood cells, but to actually attract a drone, he would have had to leave Dharma Four and the safe zone. So, spurred by apathy, he kept justifying one more day alive, another day spent hating his inability to make the "best" of his shitty situation. Staying alive was — for now, at least — marginally less annoying than finding a way to kill himself.

He watched Kassidi's large, muscular arm, comparing it with his sad little noodles. He felt a moment of inspiration that wouldn't have impressed anyone on the outside, but for him, that inspiration was bright, like a building on fire. Time was the only requirement for the body Bear wanted.

"Kassidi," he said, affecting a curious air he knew would flatter her. "I'm curious. What's your basic routine for——?"

A warbling alarm sabotaged his first attempt at self-improvement in three years. The sound was anemic and sad; the mechanism that created it either damaged or dying. Still, Bear jumped at the sound. He'd never heard that alarm — *any* alarm, really, other than the one marking the perimeter. He'd known there *was* an alarm for the men and women in their cylinders, and he'd been told it was powered by the same electrochemical system that kept their inert bodies alive and nourished. He'd just never heard it before.

"Should you get that?" Kassidi asked.

Bear's brain made stupid little loops. Struck dumb, he went first to the bank of screens at his monitoring station, somehow forgetting they'd had no power since Immunity moved in. He shuffled through his papers as if his handwritten pages might offer real-time updates. He saw Kassidi rise from the corner of his eye then followed, letting her be in charge.

They went to the Somnolence Chamber, denoted by a sign above the door that was insultingly institutional in appearance. Below the room's name, the same humorless font read, NO SMOK-ING. The best that Bear, bored one night, had been able to improve the sign was a single letter substitution to GO SMOKING.

Fuck me, he thought, seeing it now. That didn't even make sense.

They stepped through the door. Dim light came from small status LEDs on the horizontal cylinders. Once he left the oblong rectangle of illumination thrown by the open door — cast by the oil lamp he hadn't grabbed and was now too lazy to go back for — it seemed almost perfectly black. Kassidi moved right toward the alarm. Bear went left, more trying to appear helpful than actually wanting to help. He heard her on the chamber's far end but could have sworn he heard something closer as well. All the zombies made it spooky in there.

Bear thought he heard something — a fat thump, like elbowing a tackling dummy.

"What was that?"

No response.

The alarm finally stopped.

"Kass? That you?"

"I muted it," came her disembodied voice. "It's still going, though. Seal alarm on 008."

"Seal? Like an O-ring failure?"

"I don't know."

Bear heard a series of short, low squealing noises, probably Kassidi wiping off the control unit display. He saw the thing every night, usually under his lamplight. It was so caked in dust, he sometimes wrote things in its grime. *WASH ME*, he had most recently penned. His wit knew no bounds.

Already, his vision was adjusting. The dark wasn't total. Even without a lamp at night, his irises had to dilate. This time, he wouldn't even need that. Cylinder 008 stuck out like a sore thumb, just to his right in the wash of the light from the door. The polycarbonate top was smeared and fogged from the inside.

"Fuck," Bear said.

"What?"

"This one's dead."

Kassidi stepped closer.

"Same as happened with 002 last year." Bear was already gritting his teeth. He hadn't been man-on-duty when 002 — WINGER, PATRICIA — moved from one state of sleep into a much more permanent one, but he'd seen enough to know that what came next was going to suck. The comatose shat themselves when they died. Gastric function halted, and the feeding tube acted as a siphon to drag half-digested recycled waste from the stomach of the freshly deceased. The heat of all that hot expelled matter fogged the lens from inside. Popping the top to remove the body would reek this place right up.

"What now, Bear?"

There was a big green button that said OPEN on the control panel, but his hand only hovered above it. "I guess we have to open it."

Kassidi looked. The button couldn't be more obvious. "Okay."

"Then we have to drag the body out and burn it."

"The crematorium's way across the courtyard."

"I know."

"Can it wait until morning?"

Bear hated that he knew. He considered pretending he didn't, but even as half-assed as he did his job, he at least understood it.

"The waste might back up. Daisy-chain more alarms." He swallowed. "And the mess is a lot easier to clean if you don't let it crust up and dry."

She nodded. "Okay." Then she held up a hand. "Wait. Hang on." She pinched her shirt at the collar, then raised it to cover her nose and mouth. Again, she looked at Bear. "Okay."

"Maybe we should wake the others."

"It's one corpse." Then, with great magnanimity: "I guess I could help you carry it."

"Fuck," said Bear.

"Whenever you're ready."

"Fuck."

Bear looked at the button, suddenly hating everyone. He hated himself for getting thrown into prison for life. He hated Calliope for choosing this abandoned Revival outpost to bunk in. He hated Kassidi for being around to hear the alarm that Bear conceivably, if alone, could have discretely silenced and pretended to have never heard — until dawn, at least, when this whole thing became Sandeep's responsibility. But most of all, Bear hated the brain-dead asshole in the fogged-up tube who'd decided to die on his watch. What a total dick.

If Revival's system had been tied to grid power, this entire room would have died along with the city's power. The sleeping only lived because it took effort to kill them. Calliope, Bear imagined, once had plans to study their Pattern Black housemates so she could find the elusive solution — the kind she'd failed to see within Kassidi.

It was all fine and dandy until nothing worked, and even their leader called it quits. Now, that why-not decision of mercy had turned incredibly inconvenient.

Fuck you, 008. Fuck you and your stinking, rotting shit, SHAW, MASON.
Bear steeled himself and pressed the button.
But 008, it seemed, wasn't dead after all.

TWENTY-EIGHT

Like Dracula in His Coffin

Mason didn't know what might happen when he shot himself dead, but he sure as hell didn't think it'd be this.

Seconds before he pulled the trigger, all had been abnormally normal. He'd been seeing things again, back to thinking the oddest thoughts. Nic had been about to try and yank the gun from his hand. It had three fewer bullets than this morning because those shells were lodged in the lower extremities of the officious, obstinate man behind the barb-topped fence — a man Mason had shot because he was sure for some reason it didn't matter.

The fourth missing bullet left the muzzle somewhere between one and two seconds ago.

Now either truth or oblivion was about to find him.

But so far, the answers Mason had gotten were disappointing. There *were* no answers yet. Only more questions.

For example, the way reality had shattered like black glass after he pulled the trigger. His grandparents had been devout Catholics with many opinions about Heaven and Hell, and they'd been quite sure about what awaited beyond the veil of mortality. Lots of people talked about a bright light and a dark tunnel, and some about Pearly

Gates. Nobody talked about shatter, or fragmentation, or the way the world broke into bits when one shuffled off this mortal coil.

But it had splintered, and then Mason moved behind that dark veil, floating and disembodied but still somehow whole. For those seconds, he felt ripped off. Everything had been so weird lately, from Dakota's abduction to Mason's conflicting memories to the flashbacks still plaguing him — to the simple fact that Nic, who had no way to know such things, still knew Mason's nephew's name was Hunter.

Not Harry. *Hunter*.

Welp, I guess I was wrong. Now for an eternity of nothing. If God is out there, he'll come around soon, saying, "I told you so."

But the feeling lasted only a handful of bodiless heartbeats, then the nothingness into which Mason had emerged presented itself as a little less nothing than it had seemed at first.

There was something in his mouth for one thing. Some thin-limbed interloper had reached all the way past his uvula and into the pit of his stomach. This was Hell, and he was already deep-throating Satan.

But no. The thing was real. His lungs tried to hyperventilate, but it took a trick to suck around — or through? — the obstruction. He was blind and deaf and felt nothing except for … yes. Subtle motion, gently rocking his non-body, like a wave.

But then something decided his non-body might be a body after all, and in that moment, Mason's all-too-real form rejected it with an instant tsunami of panic.

Retching followed. He gagged and heaved to expel it, but the thing went nowhere. He fought sudden nausea, knowing within seconds he was going to puke all the Twinkies he'd crammed down earlier, then, as the capping glory, his vomit, once reaching its apex around the obstruction, would obey gravity and fall right back down. Choking him. Ending this — *whatever the hell was going on* — for good.

A new set of reflexes rolled him sideways, where Mason encountered a padded wall. The vomit came, and seemingly of their own accord, his hands moved up and yanked, budging the thing in his throat, but only a little. He had to pull harder and farther to get the rest, and he felt the sickening sensation of a snake retracing its steps, moving tail-first up his esophagus.

The end finally came.

Mason yanked, slammed his elbow, and voided the contents of his stomach onto whatever was beneath him.

"What was that?" someone said.

Mason stopped moving, cop instincts kicking in. He realized there'd been another noise and sent his mind back to the sound's memory to identify it, but his brain was sluggish and foggy.

"Kass? That you?"

A second voice said something, farther away.

Mason held still, but his ears were ringing. His senses were in revolt. He saw colors and whorls, heard that tinny hum, felt pins and needles as if all of his clothing had suddenly warmed. Sounds beyond his tinnitus were muted as if in another room. He couldn't think. Or focus. Words were thin scribbles on a dark page.

"Fuck." This first voice — a man's — came from very nearby.

No, it came from above. Then Mason realized he was flat on his back.

"What?" A second voice. Female.

"This one's dead," answered the first.

Mason reached for his eyes. Something was on them. It felt almost like tape holding his eyelids shut. He plucked it off then set it to the side. There was a gray something above him. Cautiously, he touched its edge where anyone watching shouldn't see. It was wet and warm, and his finger left a clear streak.

Condensation? Where? On what?

He drifted. Weak. In and out. Nursing one motherfucker of a hangover. And a headache to keep it company. Only this time, there wasn't a white room to pair with it. No black holes in existence itself.

The people discussed something, possibly — probably — having to do with him. When Mason realized they might know he was there, he took accelerated stock of his surroundings. He was somewhere small and narrow. It stunk like stale cheese and body odor. There was, disturbingly, also something happening down-stairs. He was clothed (though the garment itself was strange) but could feel equipment against his skin. There was almost for sure something up his ass and — this was unacceptably uncool — up his dick.

"Fuck," said the male voice

"Whenever you're ready."

"Fuck."

Mason, just tuning back in, wasn't sure what the two outside were fucking about or what they were getting ready for. But he did know they were very close, possibly just beyond the fogged-up what-ever-it-was nine inches above his face.

He clenched his fists and readied himself.

A pop and a hiss, then his little chamber was awash with cool air. The thing above him slid to the side, then he spied a black room and two people before shutting his eyes again. He hadn't realized how close they were or how big the one on the left would be. A skinny man and an insanely large woman. Not like a whale — large like a front-end loader.

With his eyes closed, Mason heard the man sniff. "Doesn't smell like he shit himself."

Mason sensed hands coming toward him. He snapped his eyes open and dove for the lesser of the targets, seeing in the dim light that the man whose throat he was reaching toward looked an awful lot like the man he'd just shot in the leg.

No time to think about that now — thin-man's buddy was at least two and a half Masons in size, and he'd somehow ended up in a box.

He made it halfway. From the waist up, Mason rose like Dracula in his coffin, but was otherwise held by his tethers. Momentum threw him over the lip of the lozenge-shaped thing, and his own weight made him whip and dangle once over.

Mason heard a rip then felt cold air on his ass. Someone yanked a sword out of his pee-hole while he felt his anus release, seemingly open and gaping enough to throw baseballs into. But at least he was free of those embarrassing tubes. Whatever'd been pumped into or out of him through a trio of holes was now starving, feeding, or leeching from Mason no more.

Something grabbed him. He rolled more, legs out, hands no longer going for a throat so much as clinging to the lozenge for dear life. It was as if he'd tried to jump from a tree but gotten his pant leg stuck. Mason found himself helpless and dangling, four hands supporting more than pulling him, two of them attempting with great delicacy to rectify whatever had gone wrong with his rectum.

"Jesus!"

"Hold him, Bear. Just like that."

More bad things shifted at Mason's back door. There was a parting of ways, and he no longer hurt.

The giant woman was visible enough that he could see the way she looked at him before eyeing the other.

The man said, *"Now* it smells like he shit himself."

"Hand me that rag."

"That's not a rag," said the man, affronted. "That's a towel. *MY* towel."

"It's for his head, for Christ's sake. Grow a backbone."

The thin man handed the woman the towel. She wadded rather than folded it, then slipped it behind Mason's head. He still seemed to have some tubes connecting him to the thing he'd fallen out of, so once his cranium was comfortable, she went about detaching them with dextrous hands.

Mason's eyes were still defogging, and the room was barely lit, but a jaundiced illumination streamed from beyond a doorway. In that wan light, Mason could clearly see the face of the man, who just stood there, staring at him. And it was indeed the man he'd recently thought of as the accountant at the gate, but without any bullet holes, and for once devoid of riddles and snark.

The big woman turned to him. "If you're just going to stand there, you can at least go get the lamp."

"He's alive."

"That's very astute of you. Get the lamp."

"How is he alive?"

"They're all alive, idiot."

"I mean … *alive* alive."

"Bear? The lamp." She stared when he didn't move. "Or I break one of your fingers."

"Are you kidding?"

"Of all the times I've ever had in my life, this right here is the time I'm kidding the least. I am stone-cold sober right now. I am freaked right the fuck out, and if I'm being honest with you, I don't really know how to level myself off without lifting or breaking something. So, you have three choices. You can get a few pencils to snap in half. Or, since you're getting pencils anyway, you can get the lamp like I told you. Or keep doing what you're doing, staring at me like a motherfucking fish in a bowl until we see what happens. Any suggestions?"

The man — *Bear*, if that was his name or nickname — scampered off like a frightened dog.

The big woman leaned down. She looked up at the thing he'd fallen from, then at him again.

"Shaw, huh? Mason Shaw?"

"What happened?" he asked.

"I wish I knew. Can you sit up? It will be hard. You get a bit of electrostimuli from the sleepsuit to keep your muscles healthy, but it's been …" She sort of sighed, then reset. "Well, just try. We'll take the rest one step at a time.

Mason sat up, his muscles rusty but whole. He plastered his back against the lozenge and drew a few breaths, only now aware of how tired and foreign everything felt.

The woman studied him. The man returned with an oil lamp, eyeing Mason in the naphtha glow.

Mason scooched experimentally, finding himself capable but empty. His instincts told him to try and run, but the fight had left him. His muscles worked, but he could feel their limits.

"I don't suppose you have a cigarette." Mason had quit on his thirtieth birthday, but it sure as hell felt like Marlboro time.

The man startled and reached into his back pocket. He produced a slim silver case then opened it to reveal a suite of handsome hand-rolled cigarettes. He plucked one out and offered it with a nod. Before Mason could ask, the man struck a matching Zippo with its flame turned low.

Mason leaned forward, finding the lighter rather than waiting for it to find him. Flame touched the tip, and he dragged. Smoking was like riding a bike. Your body never really forgot how to do it or how magical it could be as it killed you.

He took a slow puff, allowing his eyes to close as he tasted it, struck by the most curious feeling. Mason hadn't tasted something this well in forever. Not just this *good*, but this *well*. It was as if he'd had no taste buds. Until now — until this beautiful moment, when it all came screaming back.

They were both staring at him. Not with trepidation, but with something closer to awe.

"Why the hell are you two looking at me like that?" Mason asked around the butt.

The man looked at the woman. The woman looked at the man.

"Tell me or kill me. I don't have the energy for anything else."

They paused another moment. Then the woman nodded up at the pod Mason had woken from. "Because nobody's ever supposed to come out of those tanks … and you just did."

TWENTY-NINE

A Dream Within a Dream

"WHO THE FUCK ARE YOU PEOPLE?" Mason asked into the silence.

"Kassidi." She looked to the man who'd given Mason the cigarette. "And Bear."

"*Bear?*"

"Maybe you should relax," she suggested.

"Maybe *you* should eat a bag of dicks."

"Hey." It was a proud sound as if Bear was attempting to defend her honor.

"Don't worry. I'm sure she'll share with you."

"Do you know where you are?" Kassidi asked.

Mason looked around. Even by the light of Bear's lantern, there was little to see — especially from his vantage half-lying on the floor. The lamp's amber light threw long shadows that shifted with Bear's every motion. Mason took it in as best he could, fairly certain he'd never seen this place. It looked a bit like the testing rooms of the intake facility — smooth, polished, and vaguely scientific. But unlike those rooms, this place appeared abandoned. Tiny LED lights lit the gloom where lamplight didn't intrude.

"No."

"You're inside Human Restoration Outpost 22, Union Station, California."

"I know *that*. *Where* in 22?"

Bear's eyes animated in the lamplight. Shadows jumped with the sputtering wick. "We can't tell you that."

Kassidi offered him something on the spectrum of an eye roll, then answered anyway. "This is an old administrative building called Dharma Four. Your record says you took the Docent exam?"

Mason rubbed his head. His brain was a bingo hopper, filled with mismatching balls. He managed to nod.

"You'd have taken the exam at Dharma One. Your full records are probably there." She gestured at their surroundings. "All the Dharma stations were used by the HRO a while back, but we took them over when they abandoned the buildings."

"*We?*" Mason considered them both, remembering where he'd last seen them — if, in fact, the eyes in his head had seen them at all. "You mean Immunity."

They both nodded, Kassidi before Bear.

Mason closed his eyes hard then reopened them. The dim light was too bright. The nearly nonexistent soundscape was too noisy. He looked at the pod.

"I was in Chamber Therapy. You're telling me I was inside a simulation. *Again.*"

"Well …" Bear said.

"*Again?*" Kassidi repeated, eyebrows curious.

"I already did this once. Dakota pulled me out. So … what? They took me again last night?"

But it didn't ring true. If this was a repeat of what'd happened the first time, that meant he'd been put back into Chamber Therapy after Dakota pulled him out. But that didn't make sense because Mason was sort of a wanted man now — or would be, once the prison found the dead operator and connected some obvious dots.

His gut told him he hadn't been dropped into Chamber Therapy two nights in a row. It said something much more disturbing — that the last time Mason had come out of Therapy, he hadn't entered the real world like he thought. Instead, he'd emerged into a higher level of simulation.

A dream within a dream.

It was too much to think about. "I'm having trouble focusing."

"That should pass."

"When?"

They exchanged a glance.

Then Kassidi said, "Hard to say. Your case is a little unusual."

"But you have my records."

"They're probably at Dharma One."

"Show me."

Bear answered. "We … don't actually know where Dharma One is."

Mason exhaled and let his temper go.

Kassidi continued. "When the prison was capped, they moved the Docent trainees here. The program you were in was supposed to cycle out of its training simulation daily, but something rattled Revival's cage. We think they panicked, and you were all lost in the shuffle. You've been in these immersion pods ever since."

"*All* of us?"

She gestured.

Mason turned his head with effort. A long line of closed chambers exactly like his stretched the length of the room.

"Why don't you wake them?"

Bear and Kassidi exchanged another glance. This time it felt protective as if they were deciding what to tell him and what to keep hiding.

"That's … not how it works," Bear said.

"Why did you wake *me*?"

Kassidi reached for the tabletop then handed Mason a glass of water. "Just try to relax."

He sipped, scanning the room. She was right about one thing — the place *looked* like a storage facility. It was dark, dust-coated, and quiescent. Still, his brain was working on one cylinder out of eight at most, and Kassidi's explanation was straining between mental fingers like water through splayed hands.

Mason kept trying to recall or make sense of what little there was.

He must have blacked out. What she'd said about him going into a simulation back at his Docent exam and never coming out? That part was absurd. She just didn't have all the information and didn't know what he'd actually done in the real world — the one he'd just come from, which *couldn't possibly* have been a sim.

Mason had tried to shoot himself, missed, and gone into a coma. Someone must have found him outside Immunity's gate and revived him.

That was the truth, and it'd happened in the real world.

But that doesn't make sense. If the shooting really happened, who was there and who'd know all about it?

He looked around. Bear and Kassidi had been two of the three, and Bear had been shot.

If *anyone* would remember an incident at the gate, it'd be these people here.

But like a toddler in a tantrum, Mason refused to accept the alternative. Things couldn't possibly have happened as Kassidi said. That was all there was to it. She was a liar. This just *wasn't true.*

The crib would note his absence if he didn't check in. Nic would wonder where he'd gone. Watt would miss him.

Except Frank Watt was Carter's bunkmate. Not yours.

Mason had to ignore the voice.

And Nic was Carter's source, not yours.

That was a lie … until it wasn't.

His thoughts had new edges. They felt undeniably true, crazy as they seemed.

And with the onrush, Mason remembered more.

In truth, Nic had been less a source for the Shaw family and more of a punching bag. Logan used to beat him, and Carter leaned on psychological manipulation to get what he needed. Mason, who'd been a Boy Scout through most of his time on the force, had always kept his distance. He'd personally never worked with Nic.

Had Mason ever even *met* him in real life?

Met him? You were just with him. He took you on a tour. He told you about his time in Chamber Therapy. He saved you from assault. His apartment smells like ass and lube, and you were there less than an hour ago. Of course, you've met him.

But now, all those self-evident facts felt suspect. *Did* he know Nic? Did he know *Watt?*

Of course, you know Watt. Or at least, your old man knew him.

It hurt to consider, so Mason moved to an easier topic. "What do you mean, 'the HRO was capped'?"

"When they stopped taking new inmates," Bear explained.

"'Stopped taking inmates'?" Mason laughed. "It's barely half-full."

Kassidi gave Bear a questioning look.

"They brought me in a few days ago." Mason shook his head, remembering he'd supposedly lost time. "I mean, a few *weeks* ago. I have no idea how I got into that thing, though."

He looked up at his pod, housed inside four walls with the look of something sealed and forgotten. Still, he *knew* he hadn't spent as much time in the thing as Kassidi suggested. He'd spent his nights in the red crib — and before that, he'd been walking free. That had been after Carter got caught breaking into Revival's headquarters. After Mom and Logan's accident. After Dakota dumped him, blaming his emotional distance, but before Dakota had gone to prison in his stead because she'd thought she was immune to arrest.

If that's all true, how did you get here? If Dakota *was arrested, why are* you *in prison?*

Kassidi's comment rang in his head. *Your record says you took the Docent exam.*

But that wasn't why he was here *now*, right? So much had happened since then.

"How many weeks has it been, do you think?" Kassidi eyed Mason like a bomb about to detonate.

Bear was standing, tapping his tablet. He seemed to be looking for something. He stopped at Kassidi's question, awaiting a response.

Mason waited a pregnant second, not liking this at all. Then he said, "Three or four."

Kassidi traded another look with Bear. He shook his head.

"What?" Mason asked.

"What's the last thing you remember?"

Mason wanted to answer Bear by saying, *Shooting you in the leg. No. No, wait. Shooting myself in the brain.* But something stopped him. Both answers felt combative, and he was still officer enough to read this pair and know fighting back meant meeting force that wasn't there.

But mostly, his automatic response no longer felt as true. His hand didn't remember holding a gun. His finger didn't recall pulling a trigger, nor his chin the press of blue steel. Even though Mason's memory held a spreading pool of blood at the Immunity gate, his eyes didn't seem to at all.

"I don't know," he finally said.

"Do you remember going under?"

"Under what?"

"I guess I should ask if you remember your name."

"I'm getting a little tired of waking up with shit in my mouth then being asked if I remember my name."

Again, Kassidi and Bear exchanged a worried glance.

Mason sighed and continued. "Mason Motherfucking Shaw, okay? Even if I didn't know it, you already gave it to me. I live at 3401 Pinehurst #4, Union Station. *Lived.* I guess I live *here* now. Capricorn. I'm thirty-four years old, but thanks to my boyish charm, I'm told I don't seem a day over twenty-eight. What else do you want to know?"

Again, Kassidi traded looks with Bear.

"Will you stop looking at him? You're talking to *me.*" Mason waved a hand. "Right here, lady."

"How old did you say you are?"

"Thirty-four."

"Are you sure?"

"Yes, goddammit, I'm sure. How old are *you*, Matilda?"

She showed Bear something on the tablet. They whispered low enough to keep it a secret.

Enough. Mason rose to his knees, finding himself wobbly but able, then lashed out to knock the tablet from Bear's hand. He hit it hard enough that it spun ten feet away and landed with a plasticized clatter.

He sprung the rest of the way up when both of their heads and hands followed the tablet, capitalizing on their moment of distraction to grab a bright red fire ax from beside a boxed extinguisher. It left the clips with ease. Good thing because Mason barely had enough strength to brandish the ax.

"Whoa," Bear said, raising his hands. "Easy."

Mason had it up and wagging, a batter lining up for a fastball. "One of you had better tell me what the fuck's going on here. I don't know if you two are crazy or part of some mindfuck cult or what, but if you don't start telling me what's up, I'm going to start swinging this axe."

"Put it down, Mason." Kassidi advanced with her hands forward.

He took a step back then bounced on the balls of his feet, testing the limits of what his "sleepsuit" had done to tone his muscles, vowing to use gravity and momentum to end this if he found himself unable to swing with enough strength.

His butt struck something. Mason looked, and what he saw almost made him drop his weapon. The lozenge things to the right and left of his had transparent lids. There was a person inside each one, and he swore he recognized both as Docents from his survey group.

"What the fuck is all of this?"

"Put it down, and we'll talk." Kassidi stepped forward again.

Mason retreated several paces, putting a chambered sleeper between them. Keeping most of his attention on the pair of people awake in the room, he looked at the thing below him long enough to see an Indian woman in a strange singlet like the one Mason now saw on himself. She had wires stuck to her, like prep for an EKG. He took another step to buy some seconds, then moved one hand to his scalp. Mason had electrode pads on his skin as well, wires and clips apparently detached in his exodus, now dangling from his open container.

"Who are these people?" Mason demanded. Even though increasingly, he knew.

"I told you. They're Docents. Trainees. Like you."

"Why are they in tubes?"

"This is a storage facility," she said, her tone relaying how tired she was of explaining things. "The prison was capped, the Docent program was abandoned, and there was some sort of investigation that made Revival shuffle things around. They must have had something to hide because all the Docents in training were locked in and swept under the rug. We think they planned to come back and take you out, but that never happened. Okay? Now put down the ax."

"I didn't do the Docent training," Mason said in an *I-don't-believe-you* voice. Or perhaps it was an *I-don't-want-to-believe-you* voice. He didn't yet remember exactly what had happened in his short-lived Docent career, but it couldn't have ended well. Certainly not with a hire, which should have preceded training.

"Then they put you under for some other reason. *Think*. Why would you be here if not to train?"

I'm not suicidal. I'm no danger to myself or others.

That was followed by a different voice. *I'm not sure I agree with either of those.*

Mason blinked. He recalled that voice from very far away. His mind showed him a tall, thin woman with tattoos running up and down her arms. He … knew her? Or had, once upon a time.

Then he had it. "Where's Leigh?"

"Who's Leigh?"

She's the woman in my intake group who seemed skittish and scared of Watt.

She's the woman in the back of the van, sitting where the big man once sat.

She's the doctor who removed my blood dongle, which we all know is impossible after Dakota woke me.

"She's …"

She's a friend. The one who got Mason's father into Chamber

Therapy to try and exonerate him. The one who got *Mason* into CT, or so he remembered believing before everything real went dark.

He closed his eyes hard once more as if to squeeze the lies between his lids. It was becoming tiresome, feeding a brand-new habit.

"Disorientation is natural," Kassidi said, still speaking like a hostage negotiator. "Your real memories are combining with your memories of Chamber Therapy. Do you understand? Your subconscious borrows from your real world to make the simulated world. That's why you'll sometimes see the same things in both places. It's also why they used to use an amnesia drug, so you'd only remember one. Helps with transitions. Keeps you sane."

"Well, sure," Bear said. "That's how it works *during Chamber Therapy*. But for *him*—"

Kassidi gave Bear a hard stare and continued. "You'll be confused for a while until your natural memories assert themselves. Which is why you need to be careful not to do anything rash until more comes back to you."

"I've seen you before. I mean *before* before," Mason said, squinting. He'd seen them both in the world he'd just woken from, but he'd also seen them somewhere else. Somewhere deeper. "In ... *a bank?*"

Kassidi looked at Bear.

"DON'T LOOK AT EACH OTHER! LOOK AT ME!"

"Easy. Okay," Kassidi said. "We're looking at you. Just relax."

"And stop treating me like I'm crazy! I know you! I know you both!"

"Mason? Can I call you Mason?" Kassidi took her life into her hands, moving closer to him as he brandished the ax. "Listen to me. You don't know us. Maybe you saw us pass by your tube, and your subconscious incorporated our faces into your simulation."

"Well ..." Bear said.

Kassidi pushed past his interruption. "Maybe that's how it happened. Because ... well, let's just say it's not possible that you *actually* know us."

"Calliope. I know Calliope, too."

"That's … even less possible."

"Why?"

"It's complicated."

"It's not complicated! I know you! I've met you before, or I wouldn't have seen you inside!"

"You haven't met us, Mason. Maybe you saw us in your sim because …" She stopped, out of words.

Bear filled the void. "Oh, come on, Kass. You know goddamn well he couldn't have seen any kind of—"

Kassidi turned on him, viper fast. "Shut it, Bear. If you want to be able to ask him anything later, you'll just shut the fuck up now."

Don't fuss. They say if you let it happen, it's just like a dream. The nicest dream in the world. Or if you fuss, you get a nightmare.

"Someone had better start saying something, and enough with the double talk. No telling me it's complicated. No cutting each other off like you're trying to keep something from me, or maybe you're trying to protect me from myself." Again, he wagged the ax. "We're tight in here, and I don't have the baseball chops I used to. So it's possible I can't hit either of you if I start swinging. But I'm taking those odds if it'll get me the hell out of here."

Kassidi said, "Leaving here right now is just about the worst thing you can do."

"I have to get back to Nic. He can help me make sense of it. I just need to *think.*"

But that was a lie, or at least incorrect. Mason was grasping at straws but didn't care. Weasely little Nic felt like his only port in a storm. But it was an illusion. Nic had done Chamber Therapy once, whereas judging by the lozenges, Mason had done it much more. Besides, he was increasingly sure he had only known Nic through his father.

Mason's mind pushed it all away. "Take me to Nic, and we'll talk."

"I …" Bear seemed to know he was saying something unpopular but went ahead with it anyway. "Nic, who?"

"Where's Nic!" Mason feinted with the ax, making both Kassidi and Bear jump.

A new voice spoke.

"Do you mean Nicholas Coreander?"

Mason spun. Dakota Ward was behind him, but she looked different than the last time he'd seen her. Her hair had an amateur cut. Short and shaggy, uneven at the ends, though somehow the sloppiness made it better rather than worse. Instead of business casual, she was wearing ripped cargo pants and a Cure T-shirt that had probably been faded at the turn of the last century. But the biggest difference was in her face. It seemed more lived-in. More traveled and seasoned. The kind of face that would never sweat the small things because it'd seen all the big ones the world had to offer.

"Dakota."

"Put down the ax, Mason. You make a terrible Jack Nicholson."

He was at the end of his wits. Even his voice was weak. "I need to see Nic."

"Nic was released from the HRO six months ago. He rehabbed out, probably because USPD needed him on the street."

"'Rehabbed out'?"

"Chamber Therapy." Dakota cracked the tiniest of smiles. "Come on, Mason. Thanks to your father, you should know about that better than anyone."

"But …" Mason was about to say, *But Nic only did Chamber Therapy once, and he was immune.*

Instead, he kept his mouth shut. Anything he had to say would only raise their eyebrows higher.

Dakota came closer.

Mason flinched when she touched the ax but yielded at her persistence.

She handed the thing to Kassidi, apparently unwilling to risk its return to the fire brackets. "How old did you say you were?"

"You're too late. I already gave *her* my full bio."

"Just this one last question," Dakota promised. "Humor me."

"I'm thirty-four."

Dakota put a hand on his shoulder. "We should talk."

THIRTY

A Zombie Situation

CLOTHED AND CLEAN, Mason left the walled-in loading dock with his hair still wet and his feet in what seemed to be rubber spa slippers lined with acupressure bumps. Dakota had led him down here then told him what to do.

Turn the heater on. Hot and cold knobs here. Hang the hose right there and set the sprayer like this. It's almost a real shower.

It felt much better than Mason imagined it could. He seemed to be covered in ancient layers of oil and sweat, noticing how awful he smelled only once the hot spray began to chisel his funk away. He closed his eyes while under the spray. Leaned against the concrete wall and let the water take him. They'd given him some sugary gel packets — the kind runners suck down mid-marathon — and those had filled him with a bit more strength. He could stay here forever. Keep on showering and never come out. Then maybe reality wouldn't be able to find him.

But eventually, he turned off the hose, dressed in the clean clothes Dakota had hung outside the stall, then walked back upstairs. The control room was much brighter. Three lanterns had been added, but two people were now gone. Only Dakota waited.

"Feeling better?"

"Where are the others?"

"I thought you'd be more comfortable talking just to me first. We have so much to catch up on."

The last part of what she'd said felt wrong. Even as confused as he felt, Mason knew from Dakota's perspective, a fair amount of time had passed since they'd last seen each other. His brain kept rebelling at that — *I saw her just yesterday!* But apparently, he'd seen her *inside a simulation.*

The Dakota who'd shepherded him through prison intake? The Dakota who'd pulled him out of a tank of ooze, shot a man, then dragged him to a warehouse for a blood transfusion, giving the beat-down to drones as she went? That Dakota — real as she'd seemed to Mason at the time — hadn't existed.

"Yeah. I guess we have some catching up to do."

"The others wanted to be here. You've always been kind of a celebrity in this place. This here? It's kind of a zombie situation. Not a lot interesting happens, so your resurrection is hot news. I had to fight them off to get us some privacy."

Mason didn't like the references to death, zombies, or resurrection. They made him consider something he didn't want to think about — the missing piece that, though impossible, made everything fit.

"I know those people. The thin guy with the glasses. The big girl, the one who looks Hawaiian. I know them, but they say I don't."

A voice inside said, *Yeah. Right. You "know" them from a simulation, just like the fake Dakota.* But even so, how had they *gotten* there? Someone had programmed his sim. Why had they added Bear, Kassidi, and the others? To Mason, all those people had felt familiar even then, like he'd known the pair before meeting them inside. But how was that possible unless he'd met them and forgotten … perhaps in the way he'd forgotten Leigh during his interview?

Dakota shook her head and drew a breath deep enough to forebode some horrible tidings, something she'd need to explain that he'd not yet gathered on his own.

"You can't know the people here, Mason. You've never met."

"How are you so sure? You've been in prison. You haven't been with me every hour of every day since—"

"I'm sure because you've been here for three years, same as me. You were in this building well before Kassidi and Bear joined Immunity — and both were inside the HRO for six or seven years before that. I'm sure you've never met them because when *would* you have? Did you walk by them in a Target ten years ago?"

A brick fell through his stomach. He wanted to protest, but what she'd said had an unmistakable ring of truth. A truth his mind had already started to suspect throughout a long, hot shower of hard thinking.

She met his gaze then gave him another long sigh. In her eyes was compassion, maybe pity.

"You're not thirty-four, Mason. You're thirty-seven. From what I can tell, they put you under at Dharma One when you came in for Docent training." She took another breath, gave another shake of her head. "Kass said you believed you'd been here for a few weeks at most. But Mason … you came here *three years* ago."

"You're wrong. I …"

But he trailed off because there was no end to that protest. Mason's evidence to the contrary, he was realizing, was grounded in flim-flam. He could tell Dakota he knew it'd only been a few weeks because Nic said so, but he still had a nagging suspicion he'd never really met the man. He could count off nights in the red crib and explain the way other inmates still eyed him like fresh meat, but it seemed he'd never actually spent the night in the red crib, nor had he seen other inmates.

Mason was growing increasingly sure he hadn't even been arrested. In his deepest simulation, he'd thought he'd gone to prison for robbery. After fake-Dakota had fake-woken him into the sim he'd just emerged from, he'd believed he'd gone to prison after a downward slide and months of belligerence.

But in reality, he now knew he'd only ruffled some feathers. There'd been no bar fight or charge for resisting arrest. Mason had never gone through prison intake or been sent to prison. He'd never been charged with a crime and certainly had never been convicted.

He'd come for an interview, been dropped into a tank, then woken up *de facto* incarcerated.

"Give it time," Dakota said.

"I just want to be clear. None of what I remember about the HRO actually happened? It's all been a simulation?"

Dakota seemed troubled. Mason was suddenly sure she, like Kassidi, was hiding something.

"That's how it seems." She shifted in her chair. "Do you remember what happened in your Docent interview? The logs we've been able to find don't make sense. It almost looks like you went in against your will."

Mason blinked, thinking back. "Leigh."

"Leigh D'Abo?"

Mason nodded. "She was there …" He took a deep breath. "They gave me some sort of drug to make me forget. I remember her now, but I remember not knowing her then. She was like a stranger."

Dakota nodded. "As I think Kass told you, they give subjects an amnesia drug between sessions. On top of helping to protect their minds, the HRO doesn't want prisoners who've been through a session to report anything of what's happened to others. So few are chosen, it would only cause resentment. Half the candidates would be killed by other inmates, just out of spite, before Revival could complete the course."

Mason, still standing, finally succumbed to disorientation and sat in a wheeled chair. His core was sore and weak. He wasn't sure at first that he could sit upright in something so unstable.

"Turns out, Carter was more right than we ever gave him credit for. He and Calliope worked together from a distance for a while and managed to uncover a lot of underhanded stuff, including around the Docent program."

"What kind of stuff?" Mason asked.

"The usual. Human rights violations, brutality, too much autonomy, and not enough oversight. Most Docents joined because they wanted to beat the shit out of inmates for a paycheck. We think a lot of it was covered up, and it was the coverup that became a problem, more than the Docents themselves. Kind of like Watergate. You remember Watergate?"

"Not personally."

"More will come back," Dakota told him. "Right now, your brain is like someone who's dropped the world's largest deck of cards before being asked to reorder them. You're sorting memories of things that happened in the real world, from things that happened while you were …"

She stopped.

Mason pounced. "While I was what?"

"It's important we take this slowly, Mason. Let me steer us."

"Why?"

"Because it's been a long time. Your mind wants to believe your false reality more than the real one. If we aren't careful, it could lead to a dissociative disorder. To psychosis."

"Why did you say I was 'dead'?"

"What?"

"You said this was a 'zombie situation.' You said I had a 'resurrection.'"

"I was being dramatic."

"Why does everyone look at me like a freak? What is it you keep tiptoeing around?"

"I'm not tiptoeing."

"You're a straight shooter, Dakota. I'm not used to bullshit from you. Kassidi was tiptoeing for sure. Bear kept trying to say something, and she kept cutting him off. Something about Chamber Therapy. *My* Chamber Therapy. Like something went wrong. Like my situation was different."

"You were under for three years."

Mason shook his head. He was hotter than suspicion and rolling toward a boil of anger. He'd found her out, but she was still treating him like a fool. And they used to be partners.

"Stop it, Dakota. Carter said overly long Chamber sessions weren't supposed to be possible. The mind needs to dream, like *really* dream, and if you leave someone in a sim long enough that they truly sleep, natural dreams compete with the simulation.

It's the mind's reset switch. He told me Reeves said the longest sessions lasted around 48 hours, and those were extreme."

"Technology has come a long way since then."

But he saw the way her eyes flicked away.

"*Since then.* But if I went under three years ago, upgrades wouldn't exactly come in time, would they?"

"I don't know what you want me to tell you, Mason. I'm doing my best."

"I want you to tell me the truth!"

He was breathing heavier than he'd intended, as if he'd just finished to a race. His cheeks were surely flushed.

Dakota composed herself. Her nerves and pulled punches vanished behind a stone facade. "All right," she said, now sounding like an anchorwoman on TV. "Truth is, you *weren't* in a simulation for the past three years."

"But you just said—"

"The logs show you fought hard. Longer than anyone I've ever seen. Your simulation, as far as I can tell, lasted nearly two full weeks. You must have slept in that amount of time, but somehow you did it without breaking the construct. It must have taken *phenomenal* subconscious will. *That's* how hard your mind fought to stay sane."

Mason felt cold. He knew what was coming.

"What happened after two weeks?" he asked.

"Your simulation collapsed. Like any sim of that length inevitably would. You did all you could, but there's only so much a person can take."

Mason waited. Time stood still.

"For the past three years, you haven't really been in Chamber Therapy. Not by any normal definition."

"Then where was I?" Mason looked to the darkened side room, where status lights on all the other Docent pods remained lit. He could see the open corner of his own pod, where they all agreed that he'd spent the last three spins around the sun.

"You were in the only place you could be after that long," Dakota told him. "You were in Pattern Black."

Still Practicing

IRONIC THAT MASON would need to sleep after so much artificial slumber, but unconsciousness was the body's way of waving a white flag.

Leaving Dakota without a word, Mason stole into the still-darkness of Dharma Four. He found a bunk room full of freestanding cots, some occupied. One of the sleeping bodies turned over. Another lifted its head. Shadows were deep, rooms lit only by moonlight and far-off incandescents. Someone spoke a single indecipherable word, maybe a name.

Too full. Too occupied. The last thing he wanted right now was company.

Mason moved on, soon finding a room with built-in bunks and stuffed with large rubber storage bins. Once behind the bins, he saw why the occupants had set up a new sleeping room instead of using this official one. Water had rotted the wall and blackened it with mold. Undeterred, he took a musty blanket from one of the lower bunks, shook it out, then lay down. Sleep should be impossible, but he succumbed all the same.

Someone shook him some unknown time later.

He rolled over and opened his eyes. Dakota was there again,

three years older and harder than the woman who'd once shared his bed and taken his blame.

She was sitting on a half-collapsed chair. Quiet. Alone. It was still dark.

"I thought maybe you'd left."

Mason had no idea where he was. Kassidi had given him the building's ID, but not its location relative to things he knew, and that term meant almost nothing. No matter how real his prison memories felt, he'd never had them. He'd only seen the prison from the air on his flight to Dharma One. Mason had never set foot on its streets or spent so much as a minute with the inmates. Had he really met Preacher?

What came next?

Where would he go?

And where would he find himself when he walked out the door?

"We don't come into this room anymore. All the black mold. I wouldn't have thought to look."

"Then why are you here?" Mason asked.

"We've hacked into parts of the prison's security network. They gave you a blood dongle as soon as you started Chamber Therapy, same as the inmates. I just followed it."

"You disabled my tracker. You and Leigh."

Dakota smiled with half of her mouth.

"Goddammit," Mason said.

"Give yourself time."

"Time for what, Dakota?"

"To adjust. To accept the reality of where you are. It's a miracle. Pattern Black is, by everything anyone has ever heard, inescapable. It literally erases a person. You shouldn't still be *you*."

She offered Mason her left hand. Its back was raked with an enormous scar. Her pinky was sluggish as if it'd ripped a tendon.

He looked up at her face. Then at the building around him.

"Do you remember any more? Is anything coming back?"

Mason nodded, handling the newly recovered memories like finely spun glass. He could see them, but only barely. A closer look might send them away in a puff of smoke.

"I think so. I remember my Docent session. I remember Leigh fighting me, then ordering doctors to take me away."

"Leigh did that?"

Mason shrugged. He'd thought about that most since it was freshest. "I think she felt she was doing it for my own good. She's a do-gooder. Looking back, it's hard to believe she could possibly have done it maliciously."

Dakota smiled in a strange way. "I'm sure she meant to help you."

"She never mentioned it?"

Dakota shrugged. "She was your friend, not mine. I tried to keep up with you, but I didn't know what they'd done until I joined Immunity and saw you here. They said you'd been in a training accident, so I thought you were dead. After I saw you in that pod, I very much wanted to talk to Leigh, but I'd gone off-grid. We have a way of hiding blood dongles from the system. It seems nobody looks too hard for us anymore. Either way, I couldn't see visitors. But we do have a way to contact the outside. That's how I found …"

"Found what?"

"She's gone, Mason. Leigh passed away not long after you went inside."

Mason wanted to feel something, but his mind was too untidy. He filed the datum away for later investigation. There were many strange tragedies around this affair. Two people died in a car accident, one was arrested for breaking into Blake's office, and another was put into brain death without will or permission. Leigh may have been the only one left with insider information about Revival and a reason to share it. Was her death a coincidence? Mason wasn't so sure.

Two or three minutes passed. An eternity in the dark, with a head that wouldn't stop spinning.

"Dakota?"

"Yeah."

"How do I know this is real?"

"What do you mean?"

"The last place seemed real, too. Same as this. I …" Mason

sighed and looked around again. Then he realized he could be tired and beat up around Dakota if necessary. "I can't do that again. I'm not sure you can appreciate how unsettling that is. How it makes you doubt every single fucking thing."

Another long silence stretched, and she did nothing to fill it.

"I didn't tell you how I got here," Mason finally said. "How I woke up."

"How did you wake up?"

"I put a gun — *your* gun — under my chin then pulled the trigger. I figured I'd die or force the weird things around me to change. Either way was okay by then."

"*By then?*"

"I'd already woken up once. Inside the sim, I was pulled from a deeper simulation. By you."

Dakota was staring.

"What?" Mason asked.

"You said you didn't remember anything."

"I don't remember much from before I went under. I assumed what happened after I went under didn't matter."

"'*After* you went under'? What do you mean?"

"I mean the stuff that happened inside my simulation."

She stared at him, gape-mouthed.

"I figured you didn't care about the simulation. You don't care about the *simulation* I was in before I woke up, do you? I mean, the specifics?"

"Maybe you'd better tell me everything."

So Mason did, omitting nothing, no matter how inconsequential. He wasn't sure where truth ended, and the simulation started, so he covered it all as best he could. A demarcation formed in the timeline of his memory. The span immediately before his booking by Moochie and Chan was vague, and that seemed to mean his booking was the start of his artificial reality. Older memories were another color and texture. They felt archival somehow, whereas everything from Moochie on felt present and fresh.

He told her how he'd smarted off to the officers before getting handed off to her — to *fake*-Dakota, he knew now, since the real one, in the real world, had been arrested for Mason's crime. He told her about orientation, about meeting Frank Watt, and about the strange sense of life intercut with loops of a bank heist that, in retrospect, went more or less the same each time until going horribly awry. He told her about being jumped, about being saved by Carter's old source Nic — who Mason was increasingly sure he hadn't ever really known and who Dakota said was no longer locked up. He told her about the red crib, down to the inaccessible grid of cots, the reserved seats in the rec room, and even the two copies of *Mr. Destiny* owned by the HRO. He mentioned seeing Leigh inside the prison but also inside the Heist, then meeting her again after fake-Dakota fake-rescued him from a fake-Chamber-Therapy tank after a Heist had gone south.

"You were inside a simulation … inside your simulation?"

Mason nodded. "The Bank Heist. They told me it's a rehab scenario that 'echoes moral choices from your crime.' They give you the same choices over and over until you get them right." He cocked his head. "But if they wanted me in the Heist, why put me into it from *inside* another simulation?"

Dakota looked punched. Mason had already covered his extrication from the tank, and all that followed before looping back to explain the Heist, so it felt fine to stop now. He'd said all there was to say, and she seemed to need a break. So, he gave her one.

"It's late." But what a joke that was coming from him since his clock wasn't remotely ticking at an appropriate speed. "You're tired. I know this woke you up."

"It's not that. It's that I don't know where to begin."

"What do you mean?"

"Did Carter tell you about the Heist simulation?"

Mason shook his head. Carter hadn't known. "Is it not a real thing?"

"It's real, but they stopped using it over a year ago. Carter might have done it, but you were in an entirely different system. Are you sure he didn't mention it when you visited him in prison?"

Yes, Mason was sure. Carter was a closed book even in his most forthcoming moments.

"But what I really don't understand is what I mentioned earlier. You weren't *in* a simulation, Mason. Not recently. Maybe you're remembering something from a long time ago."

"It wasn't a long time ago. I shot myself to wake up. It's *how* I woke up. That happened *today.*"

"That's not possible. You were Pattern Black. You had no conscious brain activity. And you haven't for years. I could show you the logs."

"Now I'm the one who doesn't know where to start."

"I could maybe believe it was a dream," Dakota said, ignoring his expression. "Dreams have a very distinct brain wave pattern that's *also* not on your logs, but a dream is a lot more possible than a sim. For there to be a simulation, the pod would have needed to feed you data. It didn't. It never has. The pod you've been stored in doesn't even have that ability."

"It wasn't a dream. It was as real as this."

"Dreams can sometimes feel very real."

"Dakota." He inched closer, put a hand on her arm, then said lower, *"As real as this."*

Movement flashed past the open door — a light coming on, then someone scurrying from one end of the hallway to the other. It was a white blur to Mason.

Dakota called out, "Ike?"

The white blur retraced its steps, then a large man appeared in the doorway. "Are you looking for me?"

Mason didn't hear what the big man said next because he'd seen this one before, too. He'd been in the Heist that last time when gunners shredded the bank and pinned him in the back room. The big man — Ike — had been holding an enormous minigun. A mounted weapon not meant to be held.

He hadn't told Dakota that part of the story — the incursion of Calliope and her crew — because it felt like he'd lose another degree of belief. If she wasn't buying that Mason could experience truth inside his unreal sleep, she certainly wouldn't believe the other-worldly appearance of Calliope and her crew.

Even at the time, those events hadn't felt the same as the rest.

Like Preacher, Calliope seemed somehow above everything else —
more aware, more in control, less fooled by the looping around
her.

Then Mason thought, *Preacher. Oh, right … I haven't told her about
him, either.*

Ike, in the doorway now, beckoned for her to rise and follow. His
focus ticked to Mason as he spoke to Dakota, but this was a rush —
no time to ask about their odd new guest.

She grabbed Mason's sleeve. "Come on. This is something you
should see."

He did as he was told, curious what he'd missed while gaping at
Ike in the doorway. Some sort of alarm had been raised, but he
hadn't heard the context. There were no flashing lights or blaring
sirens. Just a few more people awake, with urgent whispers to get
relevant folks up and moving.

They assembled in a common area. Bear and Kassidi were
there, along with others Mason didn't know. More gazes flicked his
way, but again nobody asked. Word must have gotten around, along
with a message to treat the new guy gently for a while.

Bear was in a chair with a laptop on his knees. Its display was
projected on a large monitor — numbers and code, nothing Mason
could interpret.

"What's going on here?" he asked Dakota after a few minutes of
incomprehensible chatter.

"There's been an incursion."

"Like a break-in?"

She shook her head. "A *digital* incursion. Nothing to worry
about. Just something we've been tracking for a while."

Mason considered the screen. Still, it meant nothing. "Why do
you think I should see this?"

"Because frankly, I've spent the time since you woke up
thinking *you* were the incursion."

"*Me?*"

"It would explain a lot."

A hard-looking woman glanced from the screen to Mason. She
seemed familiar, and Mason wondered if she was the other at the

checkpoint — the third with Kassidi and Bear. To Dakota, she said, "Is that Shaw's son?"

Dakota nodded to the woman. "I guess you heard?"

"Heard the dead walk? Yeah. I got the memo. It's Mason?"

He nodded.

"I'm Jenny. Ask you a question?"

"Ignore her, Mason. She doesn't shut up."

"What was it like in there?"

"In where?"

"In Pattern Black."

Mason had bled his story for Dakota and had very little left. He wanted to insist he was never in Pattern Black. It'd just been another simulation, as vivid as the world around him now.

"I haven't really gotten my head straight enough to answer that," Mason said.

"You know what I heard? Some people say you're still conscious in there, but you can't move or act *or think*. Can you imagine? Empty awareness with zero ability to respond, even inside your own head?"

"Intense," said Mason.

"Is it true that you saw the anomaly?"

Mason turned to Dakota, who gave him a *Don't blame me* look. She said, "You don't have to answer that. In fact? Don't try. Not until you 'get your head straight enough.'"

"What anomaly?" Mason asked Jenny.

"That anomaly." She pointed at the projected screen.

"Dammit, Jenny." Dakota sighed.

Mason pulled her back. A secondary screen started to flash with some sort of a warning, but nobody reacted much. "You want to tell me what's going on here?"

"Incursion. Anomaly." Dakota waved in the screen's general direction. "We get them all the time, but nobody knows what they are. They look to the system like static discharge or maybe a sudden spike from a heat sink, but there's way too much order to be random."

"Is it dangerous?"

"It's playing a very long con if so. This has been going on since before I joined the group."

"Why did you think *I* was the anomaly?"

"I didn't until you woke up. But then I just sort of got a feeling. A ridiculous one, sure, but …" Dakota shrugged. "Nine times out of ten, it affected your pod. But now, look." She pointed, and Mason saw exactly nothing in the jumble of numbers and lines. "It's *still* affecting your pod. So apparently, you're not the wildcard."

"I told you," said Kassidi. "There's something wrong with that thing."

"Maybe that's why you woke up," Dakota said, keeping the two of them sequestered.

"I woke up because I was in a simulation, and I shot myself in the head."

"I don't know how many ways I can explain this to you, Mason. You were *Pattern Black*. You've *been* Pattern Black for years. You understand what that means, right?"

"That I could see everything but not move or think?"

"I'm being serious."

"So am I. And I don't see why Jenny's version of Pattern Black is any crazier than mine."

"They're *both* crazy. Revival has *mountains* of data on Pattern Black. They had to make their case to the state for all of this. It's a rare side effect these days, and yes, it's as good as fatal, but California seems to feel the benefits of Chamber Therapy and the HRO system outweigh the risks. According to Revival's own records, there's nothing inside. *Nothing.*"

"How many people have come out of Pattern Black to say what it's like?"

Dakota exhaled and looked away as Mason surveyed the scene again. It was still the middle of the night, and yet half a dozen people had risen to see this thing that "happened all the time."

"Why is this so interesting to everyone if it happens all the time?"

"Because it's so directed. It doesn't behave like a static charge, and it has no problem leaping our firewall, which Calliope herself designed."

"What do you think it is if it's not some sort of discharge?"

"Who knows. Rogue AI, maybe. It always makes the same loop. It goes to your pod for a while, makes a circuit of our system, reaches out through a few of our protected connections, then dissipates. And all in a few minutes."

"Dissipates or leaves?"

"Does it matter?"

Mason thought it might. He could think of one thing he'd seen that acted like rogue AI. That seemed able to show up anywhere inside a simulation.

"Mason?"

"You're right. It probably doesn't matter."

Dakota was looking at him the way she used to, back when they worked together. More than anyone, she knew how Mason tended to think.

"You thinking something you're not saying?"

"I … No. It's nothing." Mason waited a few seconds. "Why is everyone so interested?"

"It's not interest. We need a few people on duty every time this happens, is all. A few techs working a few different stations."

"Why?"

"We have to cover its tracks. This system was originally designed to be Revival-internal, and Calliope managed to mask it from the new system without blowing its integrity or privacy. Basically, that means whatever happens in Vegas stays in Vegas. But it also means we need to clean up its tracks because they're sometimes visible from the outside. The fact that this 'anomaly' visits our system for a few minutes then leaves doesn't seem to be a big deal, but if you were on the wider network, it would look like the signal flat-out disappears for a while. If anyone has reason to look closer, they'll know we're still here and have our little protected Nirvana."

"I thought you said Revival ignored you. It almost sounds like the prison knows you're here but lets you stay."

"Sort of." Bear looked to Dakota. "Did you tell him about the no-fly zone?"

"What no-fly zone?" Mason asked.

"The drones avoid us. Probably a relic from when these were Revival outposts."

"*Probably?*"

Dakota didn't answer this time, but Mason was occupied anyway. Now that he'd been watching the screen for a while, some of it was starting to make sense. "Is this about the chaos alarm?"

More than one head turned toward him.

Dakota waved them back to business and pulled him farther aside. "How do you know about the chaos alarm?"

Someone told me about it. Someone in the simulation nobody believes I was in. Someone who doesn't actually exist.

"*Mason?*"

"Is that why?" Mason asked.

"Yes. Too much chaos in the system, and they activate a fail-safe."

"What fail-safe?"

"Doesn't matter. It threatens the whole prison. It threatens *us.*"

"But if you clean up after the anomaly …"

"We lower the chance of an alarm."

"BEAR!" said someone. "Port 37."

"Sorry." Bear hit keys on his laptop then everyone relaxed.

The screen changed, but Mason wasn't sure how or in what way.

When all attention moved away from him, he studied the screen again, squinted, then got an idea. "Maybe it's Calliope."

"*What?*"

"You said the 'anomaly' or whatever seemed particularly interested in me. In my pod. When was the last time it came?"

Kassidi checked something. "Two days ago. Why?"

Mason thought. This time, Dakota pulled him so far afield, they were practically in the next room. "Tell me what you're thinking. No bullshit this time."

He noted her officer's stare. Dakota was a bulldog when she

wanted to be. "Okay. Well ... I told you I was in the Heist simulation."

"You did." Dakota didn't add that she didn't believe him, but Mason felt her reservations just the same.

"The last time I did it, that's when I woke up."

"You said you woke up when you shot yourself."

"The *first* time I woke up. I told you about the tube of green goo? The fake Dakota who came to my rescue?"

"And?"

"It's hard to keep track of time, but I think that was around two days ago. 'Days' by my clock. But there's more. Something I didn't tell you."

"What?"

"I didn't just 'come out' of the Heist, same as I didn't just 'come out' of the sim earlier. Tonight, I had to shoot myself to wake up. That first time, someone else pushed me to wake."

"Who?"

Mason nodded toward the room with all the people. "Calliope."

"It wasn't Calliope, Mason. Even if you *were* somehow conscious inside Pattern Black, you only saw your own reflections. People and things you knew in real life, repurposed by your mind."

"Like Frank Watt? Like Nic? I don't know them, Dakota. Not well in Nic's case and not at all in Watt's. I'd never even heard the name."

Then, seeing Dakota's expression, he asked, "What? You looked him up, didn't you? Watt's on the prison roster just like I said, right?"

"Yes," she admitted, "but that doesn't mean you didn't still somehow borrow him from your waking life. Carter must have mentioned Watt when you came to visit, so your mind could put him in your sim. Nic, you at least saw from a distance, same as me. But even that assumes—"

"I was actually in a simulation instead of Pattern Black."

"You *were* in Pattern Black."

"Then maybe Pattern Black isn't as empty as you think. Maybe there's something there. Like a dreamscape."

"The lack of brain function is what *defines* Pattern Black. Come on. This is 101. How could you have experienced anything in Pattern Black without brain function?"

He shook his head. "How do I know about the prison, Dakota? How do I know its layout? I could describe the red crib for you. I could describe Nic's apartment on Oak Street."

"You don't know that apartment is really there."

"Then go look. I'll give you the address."

Dakota was studying him. For a while, she stayed silent. But then, "Describe Calliope."

Mason did, giving her all he'd omitted from his first description of his final Heist — the boat, the big weapons, the presence of Kassidi, Bear, and Ike.

"It's not possible," Dakota insisted.

"Is my description accurate? Is that what she looks like?"

"You must have seen a picture."

"*Which* picture? Come on, Dakota. You're a better cop than to just dig in your heels and say 'no' like this."

She quieted another notch. "I'm trying to meet you halfway. But what you're describing? It's a raid. We haven't done raids like that in a very long time."

"*A raid?*"

She nodded. "Yes. Like I said, we all knew Calliope was in touch with a whistleblower on the police force. And we knew they had some sort of an agreement — or at least, that's what she said. Carter going Pattern Black put a serious wrinkle in her plans. She was convinced Blake had somehow put your father there to keep him quiet."

"Why wouldn't Blake just kill him?"

"Calliope always implied he somehow needed Carter, too. Like I said, she played her cards close."

"And you all just tagged along without knowing what she was doing? You followed that blindly?"

Dakota gave Mason a look that said he hadn't been there, he couldn't possibly understand. "She'd hacked access to every one of the HRO's systems. She got us into these buildings, then either created the blind spots that keep us safe or knew how to exploit them. Yes, Calliope was cagey about what she knew, but she clearly knew something. *Lots* of somethings."

Fair enough. Mason waited for her to go on.

"She was still here when I joined this crew. Still running the show at Immunity. She was also flat-out obsessed with reaching Carter, even though they'd put him into a simulation by then. The Heist, now that I think about it. She started losing some marbles when he finally went Pattern Black. Calliope kept hacking into the prison's simulations, trying to connect with him. It was actually kind of promising at first. We were able to project into CT cohorts as if we were officially there, and when we did, we could join as visitors just like you described. But of course, we never found Carter because he was a dial tone by then. He wasn't in *any* simulation, let alone one she could reach. He wasn't even in the main group — in with all the other Pattern Blacked subjects waiting out their final year before being put down. Carter's feed made him look sequestered. Like he was being stored somewhere different, as if he were still a liability to Revival and needed to be kept under lock and key. *Of course*, she blamed Blake."

Dakota paused for a short breath and a long sigh.

"She was sure he'd taken Carter off-grid and must be storing him right in his office. For a while, her little hustle felt worth the pursuit, even though she still refused to tell us why Carter was so damn important. But then it got futile and obsessive, like an animal injuring itself to get at food behind glass. Sad more than anything else."

It took Mason a few seconds to catch up. His mind hung on the idea of "hacking into Chamber Therapy," trying to make that round peg fit his experience's square hole.

How would it work? Did Immunity add its members to a full cohort the way Calliope had intruded into his final Heist, or did they sometimes swap themselves for a mind that was meant to be there?

Mason almost asked if that might be what happened with Leigh the time she was replaced by Preacher. But he still hadn't told her about a psychosis that might belong only to him. And more importantly, Leigh hadn't ever been in prison. Only Mason's mind could have fabricated her into a sim.

"What was the point of hacking Chamber Therapy?" Mason asked.

"Calliope was trying to see if she could break into minds."

"Why?"

"It was always framed as practice."

"Practice for what?"

"To break into *Carter's* mind."

The idea of "breaking into minds" was off enough, but her suggesting his father's mind specifically was worth so much planning and practice was beyond his comprehension.

"*Carter?* Why?"

"Calliope claimed to have intel from the top, and as long as that intel was correct and we were making progress, we didn't ask a lot of questions. She had a reason for chasing your father, and I'm sure it had something to do with the information he learned during his time investigating Revival. She talked about checks and balances. About a fail-safe."

"What's a fail-safe or checks and balances got to do with Carter?"

"Your guess is as good as mine. He was a black box, and then he went Pattern Black. His signal vanished at some point, then we knew he was dead. I have to assume they cremated him like all the others. Without you as next-of-kin, they probably didn't even keep the ashes."

"And then?"

"Then nothing. Calliope kept us on the case even after the signal went away. Said he wasn't dead; Blake was just trying to throw us off the trail. She kept insisting we 'just had to find him.' Like Jimmy Hoffa or Amelia Earhart. No big deal." Dakota shook her head. "But the thing is, she *did* find him. It was just for a tiny while before the signal disappeared again; during the year they leave Pattern Black patients on ice."

"*Year?* But you said I was under for … what … *three* years?"

"They keep people who go Pattern Black for a year, so relatives have time to mourn: a waiting period between the day they 'die' and the day their hearts literally stop beating. I don't know why you and a few others were kept longer. It may be because you never officially went into Chamber Therapy in the first place, so there was no need for the same mourning period. But if you ask me, I'd say it was simpler than that. You were forgotten, same as this places was."

Mason felt a chill. If he hadn't woken on his own, how long would he have been in that tube? Thirty years? Fifty? He shook it off, eager to return to talking about Carter instead of his own untimely almost-death.

"So … you said Calliope *found* Carter?"

Dakota nodded. "She got so excited. But see, we could all see his feed when she found it. We knew how flat it was. He was, like all of them, as good as dead. *She wanted to break into a dead mind*, Mason. Can you imagine? Her goal, if she'd pulled it off, was to *immerse herself into death.*"

"And that's bad."

"You know better than anyone the sim becomes your reality. Entering a blank mind is worse than suicide. It's Pattern Black by proxy."

"So, what happened?"

"Fortunately, she never got that far. Carter was moved or disconnected, and Calliope went back to mind-fucking ordinary folks. Kept on practicing for the mythical day when she found the main event again. She broke into a lot of live minds, but it pissed her off. Said she felt Blake was toying with her. She finally snapped. Threw up her hands and called us all cowards. She said we weren't willing to do what needed to be done — whatever *that* was. Then one day, we woke up, and she was gone, and she'd taken all her best tricks and permissions with her. We still have our blind spots, but we can't program new ones without her. We're safe but trapped. That's how it's been for the last year or so, ever since that bitch left us in the lurch."

"Maybe she's still out there on her own." Mason indicated the group still around the screen in the other room, and the anomaly they continued to chase. "Still practicing?"

"No." Dakota was definitive. "Something happened I didn't tell you about. Calliope *can't* go under anymore, even if she wanted to."

"Why? What happened?"

"There was an accident with one of the immersion hacks. She got kind of … *stuck*. That's a long story for another day. She almost didn't survive. When she came out, we discovered her mind was somehow no longer compatible with the rig. It was like she'd lost part of herself. As if half her brain just sort of clipped off and floated away. So *that*, Mason, is why you couldn't have seen her in your simulation. Do you understand?"

Mason considered. Something wasn't right. Now that he had some distance, he was increasingly able to see the difference between falsity and truth. Calliope, unlike the Heist itself, felt real. She was somehow truer than the version of Ike, Kassidi, Dakota, or Bear that he'd seen at the same time.

Calliope was somehow brighter than they were. *Stronger*. And not to forget, she'd woken him up. By …

Dakota was turning back toward the room.

Mason reached out and took her by the sleeve. She looked back at him, waiting.

"She did something to me. I know I woke to another simulation that first time. But …" He squinted and strained. This idea didn't want to come easily. "But I just know, somehow, something was different."

"Different how?"

"I was … I don't know. I was *more aware* afterward. It started when she put this thing on my face."

He'd glanced away to mime the placing of a thing on his face. When he looked back up, Dakota was staring harder than ever before.

"What thing?"

"I don't know. A thing. She put it on my face."

"WHAT. THING?"

Mason blinked at her interest but answered straight. "It was like tinfoil. About this big." He made a picture frame with his thumbs and forefingers. "Shiny. Rainbow colors. Wound around long sticks, like …"

"Like a scroll?"

Now Mason was staring.

"Was it like a scroll, Mason? And before she put it on you, did she ask you to make a choice?"

Stay. Or go.

The look in his eyes must have offered the answer because Dakota rushed off without anything more. She was back minutes later, carrying a hurriedly stuffed backpack.

"Are we going somewhere?" Mason asked.

"Hunting," she said.

THIRTY-TWO

Twinkies and Ho-Hos

THEY LEFT when it was still dark, without speaking to any of the others.

Mason couldn't shake the feeling that by waking up, he'd completed one thing Immunity wanted him to while at the same time starting another.

There was cool with the dark.

Mason felt uneasy striking out under the eye of drones, but Dakota assured him there *were* none. Not for them. They all had trackers — Mason's dream of having his removed was as fanciful as the construct. But it was okay because HRO 22's Inner Circle had always been a no-fly zone.

"Why?" Mason asked.

"Probably because Revival didn't want its right hand knowing what the left hand was doing."

"Do you mean the Docents?"

Dakota, bearing a backpack twice the size of Mason's, nodded. "The program was beyond corrupt. They couldn't keep the Docents clean no matter what they tried."

"But they were just guards."

"Guards who, by the nature of their jobs, spent all day without support, wandering around in a city full of criminals. Of course, they got sucked in."

"They must have been able to find incorruptible officers." If the HRO had hired Mason instead of throwing him into a Michael Jackson tube, he would have kept his life, and the Docent program would have had one good man at least. Or maybe he was kidding himself.

Dakota padded along beside him in the dim. "We only know someone with administrative access — probably Calliope — programmed a blind spot into the drone patrol zones during the few months Docents and drones overlapped. When the program was dropped, the drones went overlooked. Forgotten, like you and your fellow sleepers. Someone axed the program without bothering to clean any of it up. Maybe because they got fired, too. Who knows."

He looked up.

"Of course," she continued, "it would have been nice to know that from the start. Immunity found Dharma Four before I joined them, but Bear says they spent their first month here hiding under blankets."

"Blankets?"

"*Special* blankets. They—"

"Hide tracker signals from the drones? Look like big silver oven mitts, like the things runners get at the end of a race?"

Dakota looked him over, then let it go. It wasn't the first time Mason had articulated something he had no way of knowing, and she seemed to be growing increasingly numb to the experience.

They walked on. Eventually, the sun began to rise — first a sliver, then a red egg, sunny side up. Mason didn't know the time, but he could guess. If the crib schedules were the same in real life as he had experienced in his artificial reality, prisoners would be roaming the streets soon. But if the taboo was the same here as in Mason's lie, prisoners would stay away.

"I know this place." The gate was ahead of them, where Mason remembered shooting Bear three times, even though it'd never happened.

"You *can't* know this place."

He pointed ahead. "There's a run-down coffee shop around that corner, watch. Nic joked that I was going to run in for donuts. You know. Because I'm a cop."

"You know that version of Nic isn't real, don't you?"

"Then what was he?"

"A part of you, I guess."

"I'm having a hard time knowing what's real and what's not," Mason admitted after a hard swallow.

"Do you remember Chamber Therapy?"

He remembered going into some sort of neural shock then being pulled out of a tube of green slime by the woman beside him. But that hadn't actually happened, and whoever had "pulled him out" of the tube wasn't the real Dakota. Her question now didn't mean the Chamber Therapy inside his Chamber Therapy or the threat of Pattern Black inside his Pattern Black. She meant the *real* Therapy.

The real Therapy in the real world that, as impossible as it felt, had been three years ago.

"I remember Leigh shanghaiing me. Watson was there, too. And Terrence Davis, telling me God is good."

"That sounds like Davis."

"But …" He'd been sitting on this — a question whose answer he couldn't quite fathom. "But the weird thing is, someone else inside the simulation — *not* Davis — kept quoting the Bible at me, too. What do you think *that* means?"

"That the mind borrows wherever it can but doesn't always keep things in order. The few times I entered simulations, I kept finding every food vendor and restaurant served whatever I'd eaten for lunch that day in the real world. It almost became a game. There was one sim of an assault that always turned my stomach. To get through it, I'd eat something funny before going in, and suddenly the falafel stand on the corner would only sell Froot Loops with chocolate milk. That bit of levity — or maybe just unreality — helped me keep my head."

He thought of Leigh. Mason had been with her when going under, so his mind must have re-created her inside and erased his old context so he wouldn't note the discrepancies. But Mason still didn't think he had enough raw material to replicate Nic.

As to Watt's rather complete knowledge of the prison and its ways, which he'd never seen before now? Where had *those* things come from since he'd apparently made them without any reference?

Mason didn't want to think about that yet. He had enough baffling mysteries for today.

They went through the dawn in silence. Dakota's patience seemed to be wearing thin, so Mason kept the questions to himself. Some of that was fatigue since he'd woken her early and nobody had gotten much sleep. Some was probably reawakened resentment — his return reminded her she'd done nothing wrong, yet languished for years in prison with no life in front of her to dream about. But even beyond those things, there seemed to be a third reason Dakota's mood was off. And was growing increasingly more so the longer they walked the quiet city. That last element, he couldn't place. There was a sadness to it. A sense of loss.

Mason watched her profile, trying to find it. But after the third twist of her head, he stopped. He recognized that look and knew better than to test it.

They walked on. The sky brightened a few lumens at a time. It seemed they were searching for Calliope, though Dakota hadn't confirmed it. Mason went along without comment or inquiry — someone else's luggage yet again.

One abandoned hidden place.

Another.

But there was nothing.

After the first two stops, Mason realized that despite her hard-eyed conviction, Dakota didn't actually know where they were going. Still, he said nothing, occupying himself by spotting landmarks on the brightening horizon. So far, the prison around him seemed identical to the one in his simulation — *in his Pattern Black*, if Dakota's insistence was to be believed. Mason hadn't studied maps of this place, and he'd barely paid attention when they'd flown him in for his Docent interview.

How had his re-creation gotten things so perfect?

They finally reached another door.

"Third time's a charm?" But there was a question mark in her sentence and anything but certainty in her voice. Despite the way they'd left, Mason was starting to feel like they may as well be throwing darts at a board. There was no rhyme or reason here.

Dakota opened the door and pushed inside. Mason followed.

The place was full of supplies and in-progress projects, all highly illegal within the HRO's walls. There were guns and mountains of perishable food — a lot of fruit, not yet rotten. A roll-up flat screen and an antenna providing reception of waves unknown, half-soldered circuit boards and computer chips spilling from a bag like scattered raisins. Posters, magazines, books, clothing far nicer than what Mason wore — not a high bar, but still — mirrored and unbreakable spoofs to replace the glass missing from all the other windows, sound-dampening foam shaped like the inside of an egg carton on every surface of a room toward the back, a small and simple recording setup consisting of a microphone on a desk stand and digital recorder atop a stack of crates. This was someone's place, but nobody was home.

Mason asked. Dakota said it didn't matter; he didn't need to know.

A stick-thin man with oily hair and rat-like features answered the door at the next hidden place. Mason thought it was Frank Watt for a second, seeing as he'd transgressed both simulations. A chill passed down his back. If it was Watt, it'd shake his conviction that he was finally at the top level of awareness — that he was indeed in the real world now instead of another deception.

But it wasn't Watt. Regardless, Mason couldn't quite kick the feeling that he might still be dreaming.

"Password," said the man.

"Your mother," Dakota answered.

"Close enough."

He opened the door. Let Dakota in. Then he put his hand on Mason's chest, stopping him from following.

It took everything inside Mason not to shove it away, to take the man down as a surrogate for his anger.

"Who the fuck are you?"

"This is Mason," said Dakota. "He's with me."

"He ain't with you while you're in here."

"Mason *Shaw*," Dakota said.

They traded a glance. Then Rat Face stepped aside and let him pass but did so as if Mason had a disease he meant not to catch. He looked to Dakota for an explanation, but she was already prowling the hidden apartment.

"What you lookin' for, Dakota?"

"Have you heard from Calliope?"

Rat Face laughed.

Dakota kept waiting.

"You serious?"

"You know I'm funny, Caesar," Dakota said, straight-faced. "Look how hilarious I am."

"I don't know, man. Who the fuck would know where *she* is?"

"Calliope can't be invisible. She needs supplies. If she's getting what she needs, she's talking to somebody. And you're the one with his fingers in everything."

"Maybe she's dead."

"She's not dead."

Mason caught a glance and realized a strange thing. The notion of Calliope's death wasn't off-the-wall. It was, from tone, something the remaining Immunity members said seriously. His next realization knocked him off-kilter. *He* was the reason Dakota believed anew that Calliope was alive. On some level, as crazy as his story must sound, she believed it all the same.

"You really *do* want to find her." Caesar sounded shocked.

"I wouldn't ask if I didn't."

"Well, I don't know what to tell you. She has her ways. Last I heard, she'd figured out how to hotwire the chit system. They say Calliope can get whatever she needs without snitching." Then he shifted his body as if reaching his *coup de grace*. "And *without* anyone helping her."

"You're saying she gets all her supplies from a kiosk?"

"Sure. I guess."

"Which kiosk?"

"Fuck if I know. I heard it like a rumor. What's this all about, Dakota?"

"Never mind what it's about."

Caesar narrowed his eyes, scanning Mason like medical equipment. "You related to Carter Shaw?"

"He's my father. Or he was."

"Dude was okay."

"Carter?" Mason asked.

"Yeah. He was okay."

"What do you mean by that?"

"He means," Dakota interrupted, "we need to go."

"He doesn't mean that at all," Caesar said.

"He sure as hell does." Dakota pulled a miniature tablet from her pocket then showed Caesar the screen.

He swore, jumped, then ran off with an empty backpack in hand, stuffing it as if for the world's strangest trip.

Once outside, Dakota led Mason to an alcove, checked the tablet again, then nodded for them to sit.

"What was that about?" he asked.

"Drones were coming. I showed Caesar, and he decided relocation was in order."

"Did you call them or something?"

"Why would I call drones?"

"Just seems like he'd been there for a while … but then we show up, and suddenly drones decide to visit."

Dakota shrugged. "Drones usually ignore us when we come out from under the no-fly zone, but sometimes they don't. There's no clear pattern. We think it might be a combination, like who the drones see meeting with whom. Maybe also *where*. It seems to be algorithmic — two members of Immunity at an Immunity hideout beyond Dharma Four, and they send a patrol."

"But there were three of us. Including me."

She looked at him levelly. "Yes. Including you." Dakota dropped the pack from her shoulder, unzipped it, then reached inside. "You hungry? Think you can eat?"

Mason considered. Used to consuming his meals through a tube, his stomach had rebelled at the idea of food when he'd woken. Then again, in the pre-dawn hours to follow. Now, the same stomach had woken up and realized how stupid it was being.

"I'm starving."

She pulled a Twinkie from the pack and slapped it into his hand.

"You're kidding."

"We have to snitch for real food, same as any other prisoner. To reduce our risk of exposure, all Immunity snitch-kiosk transactions are done through intermediaries called proxies. They'll make a transaction for you, then return with your rewards, keeping twenty-five percent for themselves." She shook the Twinkie. It had broken in the middle and flopped like a flaccid dick. "These are free, plentiful, and great for travel."

"There was a lot of food at that first place we went. Why didn't we grab some of that?" Mason didn't want a Twinkie. First day back to life, and he was breaking his fast with Hostess? Fuck that shit.

"That was Grimmel's food."

"Who's Grimmel?"

"The guy whose food that was." She shook the Twinkie again. Now, it was practically harassment. "You want this or not?"

The answer was "not." Mason took it anyway. Hating himself, he powered it down, wanting more. When Dakota wasn't looking, he grabbed a second Twinkie from the bag. "Ask you something?"

She looked skyward, then all around. They were between buildings with a long, doorless alley stretching to either side. There were no dumpsters, piles of trash, or burnt-out husks of what used to be cars. She checked her tablet to be safe, then nodded.

Mason raised his snack cake and his eyebrows. "Twinkie."

"Yes, cupcake?" Dakota answered.

"I knew they dropped Twinkies onto the HRO. Also Ho-Hos."

"So what?"

"You mentioned 'snitching for chits' and 'kiosks.'"

"Okay."

"I knew those things, too."

"This is great, Mason. Thanks."

"I've never been inside the prison, remember? Not really, not while I was conscious. They choppered me in when I applied to be a Docent, but I didn't see anything on the ground or get a tour. If I went into Chamber Therapy and never woke up, how do I know so much about this place?"

And Watt. And the members of Immunity. And Calliope, who we can't find but feels close enough to touch.

"They must have forgotten they'd told you."

"I don't think so."

"I've never seen you up and walking around, exploring the neighborhood the entire time I've been here. If you know some stuff, you heard it somewhere. Or read some things. I don't know what else to tell you."

Mason didn't want to argue. The issue felt tired, or maybe sore. He changed topics, aiming for something easier and more substantial. "How long have you been with Immunity?"

She looked him over as if his question was a trap. "Two years."

"Did they come to get you? Recruit you?"

"No. I went looking for them."

"Right away?"

"You know I've been in prison for three years. I'd been here a year before knowing more than rumors about Immunity. *And* Calliope."

"So, what changed?"

She shook her head, his question unworthy.

"Come on, Dakota. I know you. You said you heard rumors, and all Carter said about them must have made you curious. If you wanted to find Immunity right away, you'd have found them. What kept you occupied for a year?"

"Nothing."

"Then what intrigued you all of a sudden? What made you stop hanging around your assigned crib and start looking?"

Something dark passed through her eyes, and Mason knew he had his lead.

"Nothing," she repeated.

"Tell me the truth."

"That's the truth."

"Then tell me the truth of how you know Calliope isn't dead."

"Who knows? She might be."

"You told that guy back there she wasn't."

Again, Dakota said nothing.

"What's going on with you?"

"Nothing's going on with me."

"Bullshit. We used to talk. We used to work as a team. Listen to me. *Look* at me. I'm foggy, but I'm here. Whatever we're doing and whatever's bothering you, I can help."

No response.

"Why do I know about the prison I've never lived inside?"

"I don't know."

"Why did I wake up from Pattern Black, if that's where you say I was?"

"I don't know."

"If Pattern Black is supposed to be brain death, why did I live a life inside it? Why was it so real? How was I part of a sim the prison stopped using years ago? Why do I remember Immunity coming into my Heist armed to the teeth?"

"I don't know."

"Come on."

"I said I don't know."

"*WHY,* Dakota?"

"*Because she went after you, okay?*" Dakota blurted. "I don't know how, but it sure as hell sounds like she somehow got her ass back into the game to find you. She abandoned *us* but didn't give up on the Shaws. First Carter, now Mason. And for how long, if she really is the anomaly? Over a year! Apparently, she kept right on working to find *you* while leaving *us* in the fucking breeze!"

Mason felt a chill. What Dakota said squared with what he'd been trying to tell her, but hearing it repeated made everything real.

She *did* believe him, after all … but rather than making her hopeful, the truth made her angry.

"Then let me find her alone," Mason said.

Dakota shook her head. There was more to this — more she wasn't saying. Mason could see it in every glance, hear it in every caustic word. Something she wasn't sharing that pained her deeply. An unclosed wound, infected and left to seep.

"No."

"Why?" Mason asked.

"Because if that bitch is really still alive, she owes me, too."

THIRTY-THREE

A Door Ahead

Dakota, still steering to places unknown, had over the space of an entire morning gone from grim to pissed — obvious by a subtle shift of eyebrows and lips, invisible to people who didn't know her but unmistakable to those who did.

"I need to rest," Mason said.

"You're fine," Dakota told him.

"I am? Excuse me. Which of us was dead for thirty-six months?"

"It was closer to thirty."

"That's plenty long enough to—"

"And you were really just brain dead."

Funny. Mason hadn't *felt* brain dead at all. If they hadn't woken him — if Calliope, who was proving more elusive than her proactive actions in his dream-within-a-dream suggested, hadn't booted him up with her weird foil-scroll wake-up switch — he'd still be inside his false reality now, ignorantly living the HRO life with Nic and greasy Watt at his side.

Mason sat on a crate. It still had lettuce in it — at least a year old, now black and shriveled like shrunken heads.

"It's not far. You can rest when we get there." Dakota kicked him. "Get up."

"What's not far?"

"You'll see."

"Uh-huh. And exactly how far is it?"

"A few blocks."

"Define 'a few.'"

"I don't know, Mason," she sighed. *"A few blocks."*

Dakota marched on. Mason stayed put.

She snapped her fingers. "Let's go."

"I'll catch up."

"You don't know where we're going."

Mason shrugged. After five seconds, he met her gaze. "You don't, either."

"Get up. Come on."

"So, you *don't* know."

"Of course I do."

"Where, then?"

"It's classified."

"Classified, huh? And you're not telling me because I'm a Docent, not a prisoner. Not a guy who's been under for a tenth of my life." Then he remembered a thing that made him angry. "And for what? I didn't even commit a crime!"

"Argue for justice another time. We need to go."

"Why?"

She grabbed his arm. He affected the dead-weight protest made famous by occupying monks.

"What are you, twelve years old?" Dakota dropped his arms in surrender.

Something buzzed. She removed the micro-tablet from her pocket then looked at it. "Drones again."

"I thought they left this area alone?"

"We're between two no-fly zones. They can see us fine."

"Including me?"

"Especially you."

Mason looked skyward. He could hear the drones coming, which raised so many questions. Prisoners, once inside an HRO, became state property. He'd been in the prison but wasn't a prisoner. If memory served, he'd never been arrested. But supposedly, he had a blood dongle. So, would he register like an inmate? The rules should be different for him, but there was no way to know if they were.

What *was* his status? Would the drones have explaining to do if they hurt a civilian?

Dakota glanced at the tablet, then back at Mason. "Seriously. We have to go."

"Not until I get some answers."

"I've given you answers."

Mason laughed.

"Do you want to die?" Dakota's agitation was real. He could hear well-hidden notes of fear in her voice and see nerves in the movement of her limbs. She wasn't a deserter who would leave him behind, but right now, Mason could tell that more than her moral code kept her close.

She needs me, Mason realized. How and why were still up for grabs.

"I thought the drones were only for surveillance?"

The buzzing turned into a humming above. This time, Dakota didn't lightly tug his hand. She practically yanked it from the socket. The hum crested as a mechanical head poked above the lip of the nearest building, rising with an ozone reek, tiny guns sighting.

Dakota pulled one last time, hard. A second later, Mason's lettuce crate became toothpicks, scorched leaves sloughing off more than rolling away.

They watched the drone from between two buildings. This one, at least, wasn't just for surveillance.

"You don't remember *everything* the way it actually is," Dakota said.

Then they ran. Mason hadn't been lying. In addition to simply wanting to unplug her frenzy, he really had been tired. On the top level of mind and body, he had energy — tuned up, somehow, by whatever had kept his muscles from atrophy. But deeper down, a bone-weary torpor turned his marrow to lead. If he slowed now, inertia would freeze him. Mason had no right even being ambulatory after three years lying down, let alone sprinting.

He ran anyway — a clinical contradiction, thanks to Revival's sleepsuit.

Dakota, now with direction and purpose, pulled Mason through two alley blocks, then darted hard right behind a stack of refuse with no street beyond. But heading right at what had appeared to be a blind wall got them hurtling down the building's basement access. She didn't stop once inside.

It was someone's space — illicit but not hers to occupy. The place stank of floral diesel and was filled with bushy little trees under long purple grow lights. One corner was webbed with branches hanging from clotheslines between joists. The hidden cannabis field — a respite inside Hell.

Mason looked back. Dakota had dropped the basement door back into place but still ran like rabid dogs were in pursuit. Any moment, he expected the wooden door to blow in and for the drone to chase them. But nothing happened.

They crossed the basement and summited a flight of steps. The wood on this end was terminally wet, reeking of mold and rot. Mason's heart was the slug of a tympani at a snare drum's pace. His body rattled with its rhythm.

A door loomed ahead, ajar. Blue sky was visible.

"Wait for just a second." She looked at her mini-tablet. "Okay. Go!"

Mason didn't move.

"GO!"

Dakota shoved. He went. She passed him, no longer dragging as Mason dug deep, pumping limbs to catch her. Another hum came from behind. He expected to see more drones rising but instead saw nothing.

The hum was changing pitch, flitting away.

Dakota's extended hand beckoned as if maybe he was being obstinate — a punk who could go harder if he tried. Her eyes were wide, waiting. She grabbed his hand, pulled. Momentum hurled them into a pile. They rolled, finding direction after a few shifts in her steering.

Then Dakota was on all fours, scrambling low, ducking into yet another basement. This one reeked of piss rather than weed.

They clambered down a set of stairs. The drones hadn't seen them sprint through the open, so they wouldn't find them here without tracking.

He straightened and looked around. Seeing a silver glint in every corner, Mason realized why the drones had stopped. The place was lined in that silvery oven mitt material, blocked from artificial eyes.

They were safe. For a while, at least. His breath came in great wheezes.

"You okay?" Dakota asked.

Mason nodded. The place smelled like a homeless camp, but once Dakota took a light from her pack, he saw it was more like a camp after it had been seized and raided. There were tents in the concrete room, but they were flattened and torn. The food was roach-riddled and full of mold. Piles of rot — possibly of mounded-up shit — threw its stench from the corners.

"We'll be safe here," Dakota said.

Mason regarded her.

"What?" she asked.

"You have no idea where we're going."

It wasn't a question.

THIRTY-FOUR

Calliope's Scroll

Dakota slumped against a wall. "Maybe she is dead."

"Who?"

"Calliope."

"What does she have to do with this?" Mason asked. "What's the rush to find her?"

Dakota looked at her lap. At her twirling thumbs. By the time she finally spoke, Mason had given up waiting. He thought she might be tired. Maybe nodding off. Going silent, like she used to do when confronted with a wall that refused to move no matter how hard she pounded against it.

"I ran a diagnostic before we left," she finally said. "But maybe I did it wrong."

Mason moved closer. "What diagnostic?"

"You should be a blank slate like I said. When they first started doing Chamber Therapy, they watched patients with an fMRI the entire time to see which parts of the brain lit up once the simulations began. According to your records, you went zero zero. Total flatline for brain activity, as expected."

"You already told me that."

"But see, even Revival's initial simulations were safe so long as the subject accepted them. R&D realized there was danger of a psychotic break if the subject's mind fought against it too hard. Techs monitoring the process are supposed to watch for signs, and if they can spot those signs early, they can usually take a subject out of CT, let them recover, then move on and know not to try again. In your case, that didn't happen. They knew the risk, for you specifically, but they never stopped pushing — especially after Leigh was out of the picture."

"Okay."

"Calliope's hack gave us access to internal records, and I found yours. I wanted to see why they didn't take you out of the sim when your vitals got wonky, especially since that was *after* Carter, which proved there was a family risk. Some order kept coming down every time the local techs suggested unplugging you from the sim, letting you sleep it off, then handing you off to a more traditional counselor. Your case should have been cut and dry. One look at your vitals, and even I could tell trouble was brewing. They should have aborted. According to the simulation logs, you fought it from the start. You kept trying to 'wake up.' Worse, the same exact thing happened to Carter, so it all should have been *even more* obvious. Your father resisted. They kept trying, despite reservations from the techs. It's like there's a Shaw-Boys recipe, different from the normal way. Designed to fuck you."

Dakota stopped speaking, but it clearly wasn't all she knew.

"And?"

"You went Pattern Black about six months after Carter. He was still in his holding phase when it happened — the year they hang on to brain-dead bodies before euthanasia. Once you were both under, one of the techs … I mean … there were suggestions that almost were like …"

"Just say it."

Dakota looked almost embarrassed, reluctant to utter what came next. "Your simulations were different, but your reactions were the same. Like … unusual amounts of 'the same.' Yours happened after Carter was already Pattern Black, but your mind tried the exact same tricks while trying to wake up. Only, it happened faster. As if he …"

Mason got the gist, despite her reluctance.

… as if he'd gone first and was able to show you the way.

"But we were six months apart."

"Right."

"And he was already Pattern Black by the time I had my first session."

"Uh-huh."

"Were we connected in any way? In the same room? Could his … I don't know … his *data stream* have crossed mine?"

"I don't know, Mason."

He finally sat, his back wrinkling the drone-blinding silver fabric. "You started by talking about Calliope. Not my father."

"She was the one who noticed the connection."

"You said it was a tech."

"It was. After she hacked into the system and presented it to the dashboard in a way they'd be able to understand. Your father was her top priority. We think Blake knew it, too. I wasn't around at the time, but I'm told Immunity's hack to Carter lasted a week or two, then died suddenly. At first, they thought he'd been euthanized, but they found his identifier again. They'd moved him to a new facility off-grid where they didn't think anyone would ever find him. And nobody would have, if the person looking hadn't been Calliope, with all her backdoors."

"You said they lost him," Mason said.

Dakota was silent.

"So, you lied."

"It's complicated. I know how you were with your father. I thought—"

Mason was sick of others making his decisions. Annoyed, he pressed on. "So, Calliope found him?"

Dakota nodded, looking sheepish. "Found him. Watched him. Kass took over when she left. Didn't even know why. But nobody was willing to drop it, seeing as it had been so important to Calliope."

"Wait. Carter is still alive?"

Dakota nodded.

It bothered Mason that she'd been lying, but it mattered more that she'd finally started answering his questions. If he asked for long enough, they might end up circling back to *why*.

"He's alive. Unreachable, but alive."

"You said they euthanized after a year."

"Normally, they do."

Mason didn't ask why his father was the exception or why he'd been worth taking off-grid to hide. Dakota didn't know — for real this time. And her abundance of unknowns was like cancer to her organized psyche. He could see it all over her. She thrived on answers and action, but only now was he noting how rudderless and mindlessly rote the years had been for her.

"Does this mean you believe me?"

A long moment passed before she shrugged. "I don't know how you know all the things you know about the Heist, about Calliope's scroll, about Ike preferring to run with a minigun—"

"And the old lady," Mason said. "Inside the Heist, I know all about the old lady."

Dakota gave him an exasperated laugh as if to say, *Why not pile on? We're fucked here, anyway.* "Yes. The old lady. The Heist is an ethical program, and your decisions inside dictate whether you pass. The old lady is a litmus. Handle her with compassion, and the sim ends with a successful negotiation. The person who negotiates it is supposed to be sequestered for follow-up counseling, usually fast-tracked as 'rehabbed.' Get it wrong, and either everything goes to shit, or she shoots you. But again. *You never did the Heist.*"

Except he did. Perhaps a year after going brain dead, Mason did the Heist just fine.

She sighed hard. "It's hard not to believe you, Mason, with you being you and me being me and all our history. We'd be sailing if I could get past that one little problem."

"What's that?"

"You were dead."

"Not anymore."

"Not anymore," she echoed. "I guess all that matters is, *somehow*, you woke up. So, I reviewed your scan history. I asked Kass to double-check me because she's the expert."

"She's the expert on scans?"

"On patients who are supposed to be dead but stand out on the network like sore thumbs, anyway."

"Are you saying, Carter ..."

Dakota shook it away, not quite ready to believe in ghosts. "All I know for sure is Calliope's scroll did the same things to your father that it did to you. I don't know how it happened, but as impossible as it seems, I'm starting to agree — she woke you up."

Dakota had just drawn a comparison between Mason and his father then concluded Calliope's foil contraption had woken him. Did it mean that once upon a time before he'd gone too deep, she'd woken Carter, too? It was too much push to ask, so he filed the inquiry for later.

"How did she wake me? How did that thing on my face kick me out of the sim I'd been in for so long?"

"I don't know. I don't have the slightest fucking clue."

Mason watched the darkness. He listened to the distant sound of a two-cycle motor — a moped rigged by some enterprising inmate a mile away.

"She's been gone for over a year. I lost months trying to find Calliope because she was the only one who could help me, but then she vanished like she does. I've spent a full year waiting for her to come back. Or hoping she's as dead as they say she is." Dakota sat straighter. "I know two things. The first — and Kass agreed — is you've got the mark of Calliope's scroll on you, and you didn't get it by accident."

"What's the second thing?"

Dakota looked past Mason, her eyes hard. "*Dead* bitches don't break into dreams."

THIRTY-FIVE

Just Like That

Night fell without progress. Dakota explained they'd need to stay put because crossing monitored space after curfew risked both Immunity's exposure and their death.

To pass the time before sleeping — something his body felt it'd done enough of, today and forever — Mason toyed with his memories, still sorting between reality and artifice. He sat on a rusty wrought-iron chair, staring out the window and realizing this was the first time his real eyes were seeing the real moon in over three years.

"Dakota."

"Yeah," she said from her pile.

"There was a guy inside. Preacher."

"A prisoner?" She sat up.

"Not a prisoner."

Dakota moved closer. It took a moment for Mason to speak again — he wouldn't have been able to tell this story to anyone else, including his father. Only Dakota knew just how nuts he was and once upon a time had found enough patience to love him anyway.

It took just five minutes to say what had to be said — to tell the whole bizarre Preacher story, warts, freak-outs, black dots, and all.

Details were hard to recall. It'd been smoke and mirrors inside nested simulations, but now another layer distant, Preacher's words and actions felt even more surreal. Hearing himself, Mason wanted to cringe.

"What do you think it means?" Mason asked after he'd finished, but Dakota hadn't responded.

"It's an artificial world. It might not mean anything."

"Preacher seemed the same as Calliope."

"Same how?"

"*Real.* Looking back, I can see how Nic and the other Dakota and Leigh were only reflecting things I was thinking or feeling, maybe dredging up things I needed to understand. I can see how those people might have been *me* in disguise. But Calliope was her own agent, even if Bear and the others weren't. Same with Preacher. I couldn't shake the feeling that he was *something else.* Something alien."

"But Mason ... you were in Pattern Black. Your experience couldn't have been an HRO simulation. If you really saw something in there, it came from your own head, not the outside. Same as a dream."

"If nothing I saw came from outside my own head, why are we out here searching for Calliope? Why did you say my scans prove she woke me up?"

"I don't know." Dakota shrugged.

"Preacher was after me. But it seemed like he wanted to torment more than kill me."

"Maybe he represents self-hatred."

Mason shook it away, frustrated. "You're not listening."

Dakota sat up. "The people you saw inside your ... simulation? Dream? I don't know what to call it ... They were all reflections of yourself. That's not me *not listening,* Mason. Dreams are like theater. Your brain putting on a play to figure things out."

"If that's true, then it's *my own mind* trying to kill me."

Although, that wasn't technically accurate. Maybe his mind was trying to drive itself into oblivion. To die inside because his body was already gone.

"Maybe." Dakota looked away. A nuance of her tone and body language prickled his instincts. Again, she was holding something back. Maybe about the Preacher phantasm he'd seen inside his coma.

"So," Mason said after the moment was noted. "Tomorrow … what? We keep looking for Calliope?"

Dakota sighed and flopped onto her back. "Sure. I guess."

"You don't sound convinced."

After a frustrated exhalation, she said, "I don't know, Mason. Nothing here makes sense. A few hours ago, I was convinced Calliope was hiding somewhere, operating a pirate rig to hack your mind. Problem is, I don't buy it on a gut level. She left us as a different person than when I met her. Calliope got to the end of her rope trying to reach Carter, then let go of everything else. Even setting aside the question of how she'd reach you — a person with zero brain activity, dead three times as long as the longest Pattern Black cases are ever supposed to live — I have to wonder why. She was so angry. And done with all of it. I just don't see her trying again on her own after all this time, without even letting us know what she was up to."

"You're back to thinking I made it up."

Dakota shook her head. "Your scan shows the disruption signal, so you got it somewhere. Like I said, I believe you about at least that part of it. Problem is, at the same time, I *don't*."

"Maybe Calliope *is* out there. Maybe for her own reasons, she didn't want to reach out to Immunity again. So, she found the equipment and computers then leaned on proxies to cash in chits and build her lab."

"I thought of that. But you said Ike was with her."

"He was."

"And Kass. And Bear."

"They were."

"They never left Dharma Four. Unless they're sneaking around with Calliope without telling the rest of us." Dakota frowned. "Besides, I asked Ike about it. He said even in training, he hasn't been equipped with his big gun in years."

"So, I imagined it."

"The scan says you didn't, and Kass agrees."

"Then it happened."

"It *can't* have happened. Not the way you saw it."

They sat in silence.

"That's why you want to find her?" Mason said. "To … at least get an answer?"

"If Calliope's alive. If I'm not just confused, and she's not as dead as they say. I don't know that she'd have an answer even if she can be found, but I do know nobody else has one."

"Do you know other places to look?"

"A few." But Dakota didn't sound convinced.

"What was Calliope trying to do with my father? You said she was obsessed."

Dakota shrugged. "It's like I told you before. She never gave us a straight answer. Said 'research' whenever anyone asked. We didn't push because she was in charge, and none of us knew how to survive without her. When they unplugged Carter and moved him off-grid, Calliope said she needed to find him instead of choosing a new subject because, 'We've come so far with Carter Shaw.' She wouldn't hear of finding someone else to liberate. I assumed she was invested in sunk costs, not that Carter was special. But looking back — especially now that you've woken with this weird story of seeing her inside — it seems obvious. Something to do with dirt he had on Revival, maybe? I just don't have a clue."

"Why do you think she *did* come after me, assuming for a second she did? What's so important about the Shaws?"

Dakota laughed. "I didn't know with Carter. I'll be damned if I know why she'd do it with you."

More silence in the dark. It'd be easy for the conversation to be over. For the night to end and an uncertain morning to start. Part of him was afraid to sleep again. Maybe he'd never wake up — or open his eyes somewhere even stranger than where he already was, thrown back into vertigo, a higher-level reality from which even this might turn out to be yet another sim.

"What if we just give up?" Mason asked.

"Excuse me?"

"I'm alive. Hallelujah. Is it really so important to figure out why?"

"I can't just let it go, Mason."

"Maybe this is a riddle you can't solve."

"I have to know. I … I *need* to know."

"You don't."

"I *do*, Mason."

"No, you don't."

"Yes, I do."

"Okay. Why? Why the fuck is this so much more important to you than it is to me? If *I* don't care why I woke up, then why do you?"

"Because I do."

"Goddammit, Dakota. You don't——"

"Don't tell me what I want!" Now on her feet. "Don't you fucking dare!"

Mason was stunned. Dakota's temper had been a constant in their relationship, but this was out of the blue.

He waited.

Quieter, looking away, she said, "Do you remember Sarah?"

"Your sister?"

She sniffed. Nodded.

Mason grew alarmed when he saw her crying.

"She graduated from drug rehab a few weeks after you went under. Some place near us that leased a church. The people there could supposedly work miracles with addicts. And they did, with Sarah. I was so happy."

"That's great, Dakota."

"Except it didn't last. Sarah was using again six months later. Hardcore. Dad came out of the woodwork to visit me here and let me know because I obviously couldn't get furloughed to check on her. But I was *relieved* when she finally got arrested. Can you believe that? What kind of sister am I — happy my baby sis ended up in jail?"

Dakota wiped her eyes as Mason said nothing.

"I figured I could take care of her once she was inside. Drugs are hard to come by in here or cost a fortune. You have to accumulate a ton of chits then visit a Shuffler to transfer those chits to the dealer. Sarah would have to go cold turkey. I knew how to handle detox from an earlier time we tried. We'd be in for a week of hell, but then my sister would be okay. She wouldn't relapse, and I'd have her back. She'd finally be healthy."

Mason wanted to ask questions, but this seemed like a story Dakota desperately needed to vent without interruptions.

"It was awful, but it worked. Sarah got sober. Her withdrawal symptoms lingered then disappeared. After a while, her cravings went away. She became a model prisoner. Which was a problem — Sarah was *such* a model prisoner, she got selected for Chamber Therapy. She was so excited. *I* was so excited. They say Chamber Therapy fixes you. It changes your mind, literally. She'd come to prison for rehab, but unlike me, my sister was getting her life back. I thought Therapy would iron out the wrinkles. Give Sarah what she needed to survive on the outside without relapsing."

Dakota blew her nose.

"She went Pattern Black. Almost immediately. The official statement they sent to my dad said that her mind couldn't take it. Her resolve wasn't strong enough to face simulated reality. They asked if she'd had a history of depression. Mental illness." Dakota's eyes hardened. "Or addiction."

"Oh, Jesus," Mason said.

"I should have told them. We kept it secret — some because it wasn't anyone's business, some because weakness will get you killed in here. When the HRO came to get Sarah for Therapy, I should have told them about her habit. But I was afraid they wouldn't take her. That it'd blow her chance to get out. So, I kept my mouth shut. And look where it got me."

"Dakota. I'm sorry."

She scowled, perhaps at the world. At fate. "What happened happened. I made my peace. They declared Sarah good as dead, waited a year, then made it official. Dad got a shiny silver canister in the mail, and he put it on his mantle beside a photo of us all at the Grand Canyon. That was almost two years ago."

Dakota stared at Mason with moist eyes.

In that moment, he knew she hated him.

"They would have cremated you, too, if you hadn't been too deep inside the HRO after the changes to bother. And now, look at you. No longer dead. Some people get all the luck."

"If they'd kept her, that's no guarantee she'd have woken up."

"Not at all," Dakota told him. "But now, there's a guarantee she won't."

Mason let her stare. Let her hate. It wasn't his fault he'd lived while her sister had died. In the morning, Dakota would see that with her heart as surely as she knew it in her logical mind.

There was nothing he could — or should — do.

"Anyway," Dakota continued, "that's when I started asking questions. That's when I started to wonder if Chamber Therapy is what they say it is. Sarah didn't last long, but during the time she had, she came back between her sessions. They gave her that memory-loss drug, so she never remembered what they'd done to her or what Therapy felt like. I only knew she seemed to be improving. She kept getting better until she was gone. No warning. She just … didn't come back one day. At first, I thought they'd held on to her so they could put her through a few sessions in a row, or maybe they'd rehabbed and released her. I only found out later, after using half my chits to call home, she'd gone Pattern Black and had been put into storage. Dad brought me the letter. But something about the whole thing felt wrong. I got curious. *Very* curious."

Mason nodded. She'd done more than ask questions, surely. She was one of the best investigators he knew and the most persistent. No pain in a source's ass was quite as acute as Dakota Ward.

"I started to look for Immunity. Put out feelers. Eventually, they reached out after I passed whatever tests they have to see if someone is okay. Calliope was a great leader back then. I think she still believed we could end it."

"End what?"

"Chamber Therapy. Pattern Black."

"Both?"

"Both."

"But isn't Chamber Therapy a good thing — if you can eliminate the chance of going Pattern Black?"

"An excellent question. I would think that's true, but she acted like it wasn't. Calliope was always forthcoming about her distrust of the entire thing."

"Why?"

"That, she *wasn't* as forthcoming about." Dakota crossed her arms and turned side-on to Mason.

"Then we need to find her."

Dakota smiled a little, though she clearly believed his ambition naive. "Just like that, huh?"

"Just like that. I promise, Dakota. In the morning, we'll do what it takes to find her. We're unstoppable together. You and me, just like the old days."

"Just like the old days." She echoed the words without any belief behind them.

They made beds of bubble wrap and filthy blankets.

"Good night," Mason said.

She squeezed his hand in the dark, and together, they greeted the sandman.

THIRTY-SIX

Beaker

THE LIGHT BULB, again.

The rattling van, again.

The brush-cut officer with CRUZ on his breast demanded to know if Mason was paying attention … *again.*

Mason's eyes opened. The van was gone. The rattle was gone. The light bulb and Cruz were gone. The tall tech beside him sighed with the enormity of tidal breath. If it was possible to die from tedium and frustration, this kid was a goner.

"Close your eyes, please," he told Mason.

"That wasn't good enough?"

"You were only under for a few seconds that time."

"How long am I supposed to be under?"

"Enough to get a calibration." The tech shuffled between equipment, presumably checking his vitals. Mason had a blood pressure cuff on one arm, a needle in the other, a pulse monitor on his wrist, and sensors taped to his forehead and worked up under his hair. He'd also had a nose tube, but he'd ripped it off and thrown it into a corner because fuck that.

"Maybe you need another bolus," said the tech, studying a

readout of Mason's blood chemistry. "Your Remsyn concentration has fallen to point zero zero eight sev—"

"This is ridiculous. If you weren't able to get it six hours ago—"

"It's only been four hours. Now please, Officer Shaw. Close your eyes."

"Aren't some people flat-out immune to this? Some people can't be hypnotized."

"Immersion isn't hypnosis, Officer. Most resistance is due to a certain stubbornness of mind. It can usually be counteracted by a stronger dose of Remsyn."

"I'm not taking more drugs," said Mason.

"If we can't calibrate your immersion, you won't pass the Docent exam, sir."

"Fine," said Mason. "I don't pass. Let me go."

The tech acted like he hadn't heard. He had, of course, but even as foggy and exhausted as Mason's head was right now, he was pretty sure he didn't have an option. He'd come here for the Docent exam, been psychoanalyzed in the extreme, and now got the feeling he wasn't free to go no matter how much he wanted. Leigh said he needed help, and that apparently meant being held as a prisoner against his will.

"The sooner we get a viable result, the sooner you may go, sir," said the tech.

Mason was pretty sure that was a lie, but he closed his eyes, anyway. A jolt at his temples made his muscles go limp, then they returned in force. Now those same muscles seemed to be holding him upright in a van instead of reclined in a lab. He saw that light bulb again and that Cruz guy with four other weirdos.

"Shaw. You paying attention?"

Mason tried to believe where he was, but his mind had gotten too good at seeing through it. The first time the kid had dropped him inside the simulation, it had felt real enough. But then the sim had ejected him, and after going back in, it had again compressed like a popping pimple and kicked him out. The third time, part of Mason knew what he was seeing wasn't real, and that time he managed to eject himself. It had been a nightmare of comedy ever since.

Cruz was looking right at him.

"Yeah. I'm paying attention," Mason said.

"You sure?"

"Yeah."

"You look like shit."

Mason was sick of Cruz. He'd been in and out of this little parlor trick repeatedly, and now Cruz didn't strike him as remotely real. He was just annoying, like all of them. He was supposed to become part of the simulation and go with the flow once under. But each time through, the feeling of *they're-just-fucking-with-me* only got worse.

"I look like shit, huh?"

"Yeah," said one of the others. "You look like—"

Mason decided to find out if the weapon in his hands worked. It did. When he pulled the trigger, the people opposite him — including Cruz — detonated like meat-filled water balloons. The van's interior turned red, then Mason was opening his eyes in the lab again.

"You shot them?" said the tech, standing over Mason with disapproval. *"Again?"*

"They were insulting me."

"I told you before — don't shoot until it's time to shoot."

Mason squinted. He'd shot them before? His memory had a hand up its ass, puppeteering like something not-quite-himself, obfuscating all clues of whereabouts and timelines. He didn't remember firing the gun in earlier trials. Or what he had for lunch.

"Okay. I can do this. I promise to do better."

He closed his eyes. His senses again got hijacked by the simulation, although more and more, Mason found he saw the trick and could probably prevent it if he tried. But he wanted to be done, and out of there, so he shoved his disbelief aside and tried to let it happen.

The light bulb.

Cruz.

Four others, all of them with guns.

But Mason had an itch, and he found he couldn't scratch it no matter how hard he dug in with his nails. So, just before the van stopped at the bank lobby, he found himself waking himself to scratch and staring at the lab ceiling.

"That's it. I'm upping your dose."

The tech pressed a button. Something fogged Mason's senses. All over again, he felt drugged. Probably because he'd been drugged. They'd doped him up for this whole "fidelity testing" thing, but it seemed to work sideways. Sometimes it didn't dull him at all, and other times it numbed him so completely, he decided falling asleep in public was hunky-dory. Same as being an asshole to the tester.

"Don't fidget."

"Fuck your mom," Mason replied his head in the clouds.

"Do you feel it working?"

"Did you fuck your mom yet?"

"Try to focus," he said.

And because the kid was playing along so nicely, Mason decided to abandon his admitted but unabashed drunken douchebaggery, throw him a bone and try. He squinted, working to remember what "focus" meant and how to do it. But he didn't have any idea how, nor any energy left.

"Can you hear me?"

"Of course I hear you."

"Then *focus.*"

"I'm focusing."

But the drug was making him high. Instead of concentrating on his work, his attention was drawn to the white-coated man — assistant to the therapist, he had to assume. His face looked two feet long. His head was a lozenge, so long and thin that Mason expected his mouth to open like the triangle in a train whistle. Like Beaker from *The Muppets.*

"Maybe if I understood the point," Mason said.

"I told you at the start. You need to be calibrated."

"Calibrated for what?"

"For Chamber Therapy."

Chamber Therapy? Setting aside that Mason didn't want that, he didn't see how it related. "But everyone inside has guns. You keep putting me into a SWAT van or something."

"It's a new therapy sim they're using inside the HRO. It's not SWAT. It's a heist."

"And I'm one of the bad guys?"

"When it's finished, yes, that's the idea. Participants are the criminals, trying to rob a bank."

"Kind of the opposite of what you'd normally want criminals doing," Mason said.

"It's a moral test. One of Elisabeth Reeves's last pet projects."

"*Reeves?*" Mason knew that name, and not just from the papers.

"Obviously in other hands now, sir."

"If I'm a bad guy, why *shouldn't* I shoot the other bad guys?"

"Because we're just calibrating. If you were in a full Heist—"

"If it's therapy, shouldn't you ask me about my mother?"

"Just try not to fight it, please."

The world vanished. This time, thanks to the higher drug concentration in his system, the sim was harder to see through. That was, Mason kept reminding himself, kind of the point. So, he let it happen, trying to do what the tech had told him at the start.

Believe what you see.

Something slipped. Mason found himself in a van, his mind suddenly confused. The change of locale surprised him. There were people around him, and he was holding a big black gun. How had he gotten here? Wasn't he somewhere else just a moment ago?

Believe what you see. Don't fight it.

Mason didn't really know where the thought came from or what it meant. But that was fine because he was part of this group now. Although he'd forgotten the mission, some part of him was sure they all had one — and he'd goddamn well better get his head in the game if he meant to do his part.

His mind kept swimming, despite every effort to concentrate.

Cruz snapped his fingers. "Shaw. You paying attention?"

Mason wanted to say something smart, but a gut feeling held his tongue.

"You look like shit," Cruz continued.

Mason opened his mouth as a hand settled atop his. He looked over to see a pale, gaunt woman with a blonde brush cut, her eyes a fathomless blue. But all of that was trivial compared to her *presence*. Talking to Cruz and watching the others, Mason felt like he was in the middle of a play that would go on without him. But this woman was vibrant. More real, the way Mason felt more real than everything else.

"The secret of being here is to breathe."

Mason waited for more. There was none.

"Are you kidding me?"

"People don't breathe these days. They just rush from one thing to the other. But sometimes, you need stillness to see what's most obvious."

One hand left the weapon on her lap and tucked a minuscule white hair behind her ear. She wore a silver ring studded with green stones. A plastic bracelet slid down from the thinnest part of her wrist. Thus composed, she closed her eyes. Right there in the van with all the guns, she seemed ready to assume lotus and meditate.

Mason felt an almost irresistible tug to let it go. A large part of his brain badly craved compliance. If he just forgot about this woman's strangeness and the fact that he'd leaped instantly from a lab to an armed assault force, discord and dissonance would fade away.

He looked around. Cruz was giving orders again. His drone warbled between present and distant. Real and unreal. The entire world warped as if he was seeing it through a flexible mirror being shaken by a madman.

Believe what you see.

Mason slipped into a mental gap. Half his awareness was still in the van, but only nominally so. His other half had grown unhinged, stepping toward the lip of a precipice then seeing blackness in a chasm beneath.

Believe.

With his heart hammering, Mason grasped for rational straws. He looked at Cruz. At the thin, tattooed woman in the corner who looked an awful lot like Dr. Leigh. *This is real.* It was hard to believe at first since he knew it wasn't. But need trumped rationality. Reality stabilized. Then warped again when he looked at the close-eyed woman.

"If you breathe," she said, "you can hold both truths at once. It's real. It's not real at all."

"What about you? Are you real?"

Again she ran fingers through her hair. Something about the gesture called out to him. Something about that smooth, thin arm. The silver ring. The bracelet sliding up and down.

"Does it matter?"

"Of course it matters!"

"It's all real. But not all of it is true."

"What the hell does that mean?"

"The men with the guns inside the bank, Mason. They're not your enemy. Your enemy is outside."

"Outside what?"

She turned to him, suddenly urgent, as if time were running out, and pierced him with her deep blue eyes. "I need you to listen. These channels are monitored, and the null point does not extend this far. I cannot be as forthcoming as I would like to be. It will probably be a long time before you see me again."

"Null point?"

"You can hold two truths if you remember to breathe. But *one truth* is truer than the other. *You must always follow the One Truth.*"

"The *only* truth?"

"No. The *One* Truth."

"I ... I don't ..."

"When your knowledge fails, find others for whom it has not."

"Wait. *What?*"

"The One Truth," she repeated, her voice thick with finality. "There is at least one inside who understands."

"What the fuck are you—?"

"SHAW!" Cruz was red-faced. Mason realized only now that he'd been shouting for a while. *"Are you paying attention?"*

A moment later, the tech was slapping his face. "You okay, man?"

Mason groaned. The tech kept slapping.

"You okay? Officer Shaw?" More light slaps. Mason heard him run off then back. Something in the room was beeping.

He put a hand behind Mason's head then pulled the chair all the way upright.

Mason's vision cleared. The sharpest edge of his confusion bled away.

The tech stared at him. Hard. "You okay, Officer?"

Mason swallowed. Only a simulation. "I'm fine."

"You sure?"

"I'm sure. Look. It's fine. Are you freaking out because that Cruz guy yelled at …"

The tech ran to the console. The beeping stopped, then he came back with a small flashlight, which he shined in Mason's eyes. He checked his pulse, made notes on a clipboard. Then he went to a wall display and scrolled through yards of oscillating lines before looking back at Mason.

"You fought it again, didn't you?" he asked.

"I don't know."

"It doesn't look like you ever settled in, even with that additional bolus. It seems the additional drug just made your resistance more intense."

"I think it was the woman beside me."

"What woman?"

"To my left in the van. The blonde one. Short hair. Big blue eyes."

He looked confused. "Your left or camera left?"

"What camera?"

Frustrated, the tech slapped Mason's left arm. "Was she on *this* side?"

Mason nodded.

"Goddammit." He rushed back to his console.

"What?"

"The avatar to your left was a man."

"Looked like a woman," Mason said.

"There shouldn't be confusion. Big. Strong. Hard to confuse with a woman. It's like you saw someone who wasn't supposed to be there."

The tech circuited the room, checking everything.

"Is there a problem?" Mason asked.

"There's a weird glitch we get sometimes. Legacy problem with the system. Nobody knows where it comes from. It might explain why I couldn't get you to settle in."

"It wasn't a glitch. She was ..." Mason stalled, unsure how to explain she was more real than any of the rest of them.

"Sit still." He was back at one of the screens, fingers moving fast. "Hang on. I think I can isolate it."

"Would it help if I described her?"

"*Shit!*" The tech pounded his console once with both fists.

"Everything okay?"

But the tech mumbled and rushed around, like a man in trouble trying to cover his tracks. Finally, he came over with an injector gun, pushed it against Mason's bared shoulder, then pulled the trigger. There was a pop and a hiss.

"What the hell was that?" Mason rubbed where the thing had injected him.

"Something to help."

The room started to spin.

"I remember ..." Mason said, trying to find the thread. "I remember ..."

His head swam. He looked at the red kiss where the gun had injected him.

"I remember ..."

The One Truth.

"You won't remember for long."

THIRTY-SEVEN

Trigger

MASON SHOOK DAKOTA AWAKE.

She looked around at the dark and desolate surroundings. There were no sounds except the insects and birds. "What?"

"When they took you in, did they run any sort of 'calibration' on you?"

"What kind of calibration?"

"Did they hook you up to a Chamber Therapy rig? Not a pod — maybe a beta design, a little less invasive? Did they test your brain?"

"I never did Chamber Therapy."

"Are you sure?"

Dakota was waking a little now — enough to give Mason her most insulting look. "Yes, I'm sure."

"You said they used a drug on Sarah. To make her forget, so she could be out in gen pop between sessions without giving anything away. It's called Rem … Rem …"

"Remsyn. So?"

"They used it on me."

Mason told her about his dream. Or memory, now that he could tell the difference. This one had been entombed deep in the archives of his brain. But whatever the tech had given him all those years ago, its hold on his amnesia had finally slipped.

Something had dug deep for that memory, unfolded it, and allowed him to see. That, he told Dakota, too.

"Maybe it was Calliope," he said.

"Calliope's gone."

Mason shook his head. With the memory came others. Tiny bits of evidence that meant nothing by themselves but that formed a tapestry of truth inside a policeman's calculating mind. "This was a long time ago, but I'm sure she's not gone. She's still around. And trying to tell me something."

"And you say that in the present tense? Mason, you just told me it was *years* ago. Even if she—"

"It's hard to explain."

"You're confused. What you're saying doesn't make sense."

He told her about the woman inside that first calibration test — the one he should have forgotten, but brain games unknown had pulled from him like a splinter. He described her big blue eyes, cheekbones, spiky hair, sunken chest, and the slight softening of vowels in the remnants of a British accent.

"Was that her?"

"Mason, that was more than three years ago."

"Was that her?"

Dakota stood and went to the window. "It sounds like her. But that doesn't mean your mind didn't invent her."

"How would I know what she looks like?"

"Your father knew her."

"Carter didn't know anyone like that."

"Not as Calliope. As Elisabeth Reeves."

"What did you say?" Mason asked, halfway to his feet.

"You heard me. Calliope is Reeves. She used to be Nathaniel Blake's partner. That's why I believed she could end this thing. That we could expose what Revival is doing. She worked with him for years. Knew every bit of his technology because she helped build it. She understood the simulation and how to hack it because she designed the system itself. Calliope didn't actually *vanish*. She came here."

He remembered the hubbub when Reeves had gone missing, but it was much farther back on the timeline than any of them had been discussing. His parents had fought about her. About Dad having a girlfriend on the side. Only, Mason had met that "girlfriend" once. Strange woman. Definitely not Carter's girlfriend — but that hadn't stopped his mother's suspicions. Or the fighting.

"That had to be fifteen years ago."

Dakota nodded. "As the HRO was being built. She saw the coming schism and made herself a safe space. She was afraid of Blake by then. So, she prepared a loophole then jumped in once things went from bad to worse. The drones ignored us because she programmed both them and the blind spots."

"I didn't remember some random woman I saw once two decades ago. I'm telling you, she was *there*. She was inside my first sim, back when I applied to be a Docent."

"Come on, Mason. Even if that's how it happened, why are you only remembering it now? *Especially* if they gave you a drug to make you forget."

Mason muttered an incomprehensible answer. *Because she's* making *me remember.* But he didn't want to say it. He thought of the psychedelic cloth Calliope had put over his face in another vision. How could he have known about that if he'd never seen it?

"It was her."

"You can't possibly be sure."

But he was. In that years-gone calibration test, the blonde woman had had an overwhelming sense of presence. She'd seemed sentient on her own, not just a mirror for Mason's neuroses and fears like an avatar or a reflection. And if Calliope was really Elisabeth Reeves? That fit just fine. There'd been a public schism between Reeves and Blake, and after her disappearance, conspiracy types suggested he'd killed her. They had argued about the tech's direction, and the prisons, or so said the rumor mill.

"She wore a silver ring with green stones on it. Did the real Calliope have a silver ring with green stones?"

"I …" Exasperated. "I don't know, Mason. I never checked out her jewelry."

"She also wore a bracelet. A cheap, dollar-store kind of thing. Like …" Mason stopped, his right index finger and thumb wrapping his left wrist in a giant A-OK, pantomiming the bracelet.

"Like what?" Dakota asked.

Mason didn't answer. A new memory was dawning.

Not of the simulation but of the interview beforehand. Of his chat with Dr. Leigh and all the fidgeting in his discomfort. Mason had run his hands through his hair, picked at calluses on his hand, aligned and re-aligned the pencils on the table … and fussed with the electromagnetic field monitor. He'd worn that device on a lanyard, making it a poor man's noose.

But they'd said … They'd said …

"What, Mason?"

They'd said the devices were usually worn as bracelets, but they'd run out of large ones. The thing wouldn't fit around his wrist, so Mason had worn it around his neck.

Something was slipping out of his control. He grew agitated and had the distinct feeling of being steered.

Why am I thinking about the cloth? Or the tech?

"Mason? Are you okay?"

He felt like a tuning fork, vibrating fast enough to shatter his skull. He pictured the cloth. The scroll. He remembered Calliope telling him to make a choice. He'd felt the thing resonate, opening his real eyes to the real world. But now that resonance had returned with something to tell him, by force if necessary.

"Mason?"

She was over him, holding him, concerned at his condition. The room was spinning. Spirals of black dots threatened.

"Mason? *Mason!*" She slapped his back. "Breathe! Slow down for a second and *breathe!*"

Wanna know the secret of being here? The secret is to breathe.

The ring. The bracelet.

People don't breathe these days. They just rush from one thing to the other. But sometimes, all you need is stillness to see what's obvious.

Mason thought, quite clearly, *The One Truth. I have to follow the one truth.*

His mind calmed with his breath.

Dakota stood beside him with her arms up as if she thought he might fall over. "Mason?"

"I know where she is," he told her. "I know where Calliope is hiding."

THIRTY-EIGHT

The One Truth

THEY ARRIVED at a fence topped with three spools of razor wire and out-juts running the rampart's entire twelve-foot height, turning its flat face into a ribbed adventure. Countless barbs gleamed like tiny daggers. Behind the fence was a wall, with another fence behind that. No guards, but there would be drones and plenty of them.

"It's abandoned, Mason. I told you. This was the *first* place we looked for her."

Mason regarded the urban fortress before them. He'd never seen Dharma One from ground-level outside. Only from the air before his interview, just one more lab from the inside, patrolled by cops in different uniforms. In the three years since, they'd let the place go to rubble and ruin.

"She's here. This is where Calliope's been hiding."

"Jesus, Mason. I have at least a few brain cells. You used to trust me. "

Mason barely heard the way he hadn't heard her protests all the way here. He was shaking his head. The place before him looked like a haunted house that'd grown new wings, sprawling to encompass several city blocks. There was a cluster of dead buildings behind the barrier. No lights, despite a jumble of transformers farther in, as if this place had once been a power hub. Rusty chains held the gate. The walls were pocked with divots from bullets — or possibly projectiles from improvised firearms. The no-man's land between fence and bricks was littered with trash. Nobody had cut the chains, knocked down the fences, or built ladders over the walls. Maybe that was because of superstition or probably because drones still watched this place. It it could have been something worse.

He watched its silence, wary.

"Look," she said, pointing. "There's an AI repair depot just past that cluster of transformers. See it?"

Mason did. Every once in a while, drones came and went. It was like watching traffic to and from a hornet's nest.

"The depot puts out a warning signal that most people with a blood dongle in them hear as a kind of full-body buzz. Can you feel it?"

Mason nodded.

"When Dharma One was active, it was a way of protecting the people who worked inside. Then they abandoned it, and the signals all died."

"So?"

"The EM field generated by Dharma One was designed to repel the drones. When they closed the station, the EM shield dropped. See?" Dakota pointed, and where she'd indicated, drones hovered within the fences. "They're able to fly in and out. If she was here, they'd find her."

"What if they're *her* drones? What if she has her own?" Mason had been considering every aspect of his theory on the walk over, and if Calliope was still around, she'd need defenses and ways to gather information. The only real option was drones, but they would give her away — coming and going from Calliope's place of concealment. Unless she parked herself near a place where drones *already* came and went, where hers would be lost in the shuffle. Perhaps by a repair depot.

"You aren't making sense," Dakota said.

"She was the woman in my simulation, wearing the ring and the

EM bracelet they give people in Dharma One to check their exposure."

"That doesn't mean it was her, even if what you saw was real."

"It was the person who attacked me in the bank. The one that put the scroll thing on my face and woke me up."

"That doesn't mean—"

"You taught me about Buddhism. I just never connected the dots."

"What the hell are you talking about?" she asked.

"What's *the Buddhist truth?*"

Dakota put a hand on her hip. "Dharma. But that doesn't mean—"

"*The One Truth.* Truth, One. *Dharma One.*"

"And?"

"She told me to find her by following the 'one truth.' Not what *was true. The One Truth.* This is where she told me to meet her!"

"*Three years ago?* You didn't even know her!"

"I know who she was. I know what she looked like. Her contacting me that long ago makes a better case than if I insisted it was all happening right now."

"But Immunity already *checked!* We scanned the whole goddamn thing!"

Mason didn't feel like explaining, partly because Dakota had already decided not to believe him and partly because he didn't really understand this other bit of evidence himself. As he'd replayed the old memory, two other oddities stuck out. Calliope's insistence that "someone inside" already knew about the One Truth, which had to refer to Dakota's Buddhist knowledge and hence her likely recognizing dharma as the One Truth. And her mention of a "null point," which she'd said "didn't come out as far" as they'd been in their first meeting, and hence she'd been coy with her words.

Mason remembered his father talking about null points after Reeves disappeared but before he went in for his Docent exam, reintroducing that strange term to the forefront of his mind. Carter and Reeves must have discussed them in the context of the prison — but once, when Mason had struggled with some science homework, Carter had used the same concept to help him understand.

A null point is where two signals of equal and inverse wavelengths cancel each other out, he'd explained, speaking as if reciting technobabble memorized without understanding. His father had drawn two big circles that overlapped in an eye-shaped region. *Signal A is broadcast here.* He tapped the center of one circle. *And Signal B is generated here. If the signals are opposite each other and overlap here*, he tapped the eye-shaped area. *It'd act like a dead point. No signals in or out.*

And now, Mason thought, *Maybe when she was helping Blake design the prison, she built herself a blind spot.*

Dakota said there were no signals coming from Dharma One anymore. But there were EM towers all over the prison. Only the engineers — and creators — would know where they overlapped. *Over* a key part of Dharma One, perhaps.

"She's in there," Mason said, staring ahead.

"I keep telling you, we'd know."

"You're wrong."

"Why the fuck am I wrong, but you're sure you're right?"

"Settle down."

But Dakota had been riled before by mention of Calliope, and somehow Mason had ended up in an emotional bramble. She looked pissed that he wanted to find Calliope despite this errand being her idea, pissed that he seemed not to trust her or her thoroughness or her judgment, and pissed that Calliope was somehow, unbelievably, winning in yet another place where Dakota was losing.

"Fine. You do whatever the hell you want. I hope you find her. The two of you are perfect for each ..."

Mason found her long pause both passive-aggressive and obnoxious. "I get it. Now, if you're through being—"

"Drones." Dakota's voice was different. Wrong.

He turned to see where she was looking. The drone pattern from the repair depot, had changed. Some of the swarm were now floating forward, seeming to have noticed them.

"I told you. We have to go."

More evidence that Calliope was here. Drones would make a perfect deterrent, keeping others away. From what Mason had seen, the entire prison willingly forgot this place or had otherwise lost its memory in the hellscape that dominated most of the interior. Why go to some old HRO station when everyone thought it was full of drones?

"Mason …" Dakota said.

"Wait. Let's see what they do."

"The drones here are set to kill, so *that's* what they'll do!"

"You sure?"

She tugged more now. "Of course, I'm sure! That's why I specifically said I wouldn't go inside!"

Dakota had. Abundantly. Since his inspiration, she had fought the idea of coming here. Mason's evidence was shaky. Beyond circumstantial. He'd only been able to bully her because they were out of other ideas. It was come here or go home, and there was still enough fire left in Dakota's mission to refuse surrender.

The hum was louder. More numerous. From many directions at once.

"Mason."

He shook her off, still holding the fence. "It's fine. You can go."

"You, too," she said, beckoning.

"I need to know. I need to find a way inside."

"I'm not going without you."

"Then you're not going."

"Mason, seriously!"

"As far as the world's concerned, I'm already dead."

Dakota knew him well. There was no moving a monolith.

But the second after Mason saw her turn in his peripheral vision, he heard her sharply inhale.

With the fence now behind them, he could still hear the rising hum of killer drones. But there was something in front of them, as well. Something that had approached with stealth — newcomers like scrap metal spiders. The things nearing them now were four feet tall, fanning out to pin them against the fence. Six of them, entirely silent, even without the hum of electrical actuators.

The spiders made a semicircle. Hollow tubes protruded in clusters, like the chambers of a revolver open to fire at once. The menace and threat were heavy enough, but Mason's fear of holes was also now screaming. The gun clusters looked like extensions of the metal arachnids, with compound, insectile eyes. And guns to match.

They shifted. Moved not just to block but to flank. To the left and right now, spider soldiers blocked the way. Chrome barrels trained on them even as multi-jointed legs shifted, always dead center.

"Drones?" Mason asked.

Dakota had raised her hands unasked, trying to see them all at once.

"Are they drones?" Mason asked again.

"I don't know. I've never seen anything like them."

The frontmost of the walking things stood taller. It had a half-dozen legs instead of the eight he'd imagined.

The six-barreled weapon moved out and in like a camera finding focus. Silent movements, like a muted film. Mason kept wanting to clear his ears, sure he'd gone deaf.

Then a hum from behind returned the world's volume. Many hums in subtly different pitches came from the rear as new drones purred to change the score.

They were trapped. Pinned. A dozen sights or more at once, with no escape.

"We'll go," Mason promised the lead spider.

He turned halfway at a sound from behind him and saw a drone five feet from his face, just behind the first barbed fence. Its guns adjusted like the spider's had, but this one made a proper sound — the whir of gears and servos, the metal *chunk* of ammo finding its place.

Now to the flying drone, Mason said, "We just wanted to look. We'll go."

The flying drones wavered. Swayed in the air. The hair on his neck rose. He could smell the tang of ozone from their field exhaust.

The hovering drones did not retreat. Neither did the spiders.

"Now what?" Dakota asked.

A man's voice, just synthetic enough to be AI, came from the lead flying drone. "You have entered priority space. Retreat or be reprimanded."

"We'll go," Mason said. "It's fine."

The lead spider's weapon jabbed his shoulder blade. He turned to see it had inched closer. Silent, like an acrobat in slippers.

"I said we'll go."

It lurched forward. The bulk motion, all at once, finally made a sound. Feet striking concrete. Metal hitting Mason followed by his slapping the floor.

Half the guns moved down to sight on him. The rest remained on Dakota.

"Mason …"

He whispered, "We have to run."

"We can't run."

"I don't think we can stay."

The spiders bunched closer together. There were no more gaps through which to run. Between their many legs was the only way out.

Mason caught Dakota's gaze and mouthed *Three. Two. One.*

She shook her head like they had some other choice.

He scrambled like a crab. Dakota ran one way, was cut off, then ran another. The spider dropped a leg and nearly flattened Mason's balls. It was a fencepost south of his jimmies now, impossible to go around.

The leg folded, rose, then split into four parts like a claw opening to grab. It grabbed his ankle, dragged him out, and shove-threw him toward Dakota's shoes.

"Failure to retreat will result in corrective action," said one of the flying drones.

Great advice, asshole, seeing as we can't run.

They swarmed. Fliers swung in small, lazy arcs like a ballet.

Dakota was back-to-the-fence, eyes frantic, reasonably cool despite losing her shit. "What do we do?"

"Hang on."

"I don't think we can."

The lead spider spoke, its voice smoother and deeper than the fliers. "Retreat or corrective action will be taken."

"We're *trying* to retreat. We *want* to retreat," Mason said, battling panic. "If you'll just … let us by …"

"This is your final warning."

"Mason …"

"I said hang on!"

Barrels extended from the hovering drone, shifting again, taking so long to target that it had to be psychological warfare. The eye turned red, and so did all the others behind the fence.

He and Dakota were caught almost literally between a rock and a hard place.

Retreat from the fliers, and the spiders think we're advancing.

Retreat from the spiders and the fliers think we're advancing.

It'd be so much easier to comply if both sets of machines could agree to herd them in the same direction.

With zero options, Mason did the stupidest, most pointless possible thing. He picked up two bricks and threw one at the spiders. The target effortlessly and silently ducked the blow. Mason brandished the second brick, knowing he only had one shot for a dozen enemies and was unlikely to score a single hit.

The spider said, "Lower your weapon."

"The fuck I will."

"You have three seconds," announced the drone from behind them.

Mason dropped the brick and again raised his hands.

The spider's electronic eye didn't look down. "Lower your weapon immediately."

"I dropped it." Heart slamming, breath short, he pointed at the ground. "I *dropped* my weapon. See?"

"This is your final warning."

"I dropped the fucking brick!"

The rest happened in a half-second. The spiders all fired in tandem, belching what looked like emerald fire. Mason's hands gripped his chest, sure he was dead.

He fell on Dakota, hoping in vain to protect her from the deadly rain, both of them cowering, not quite shouting, but making tiny and involuntary noises of surrender.

The cacophony stopped. The world went silent for three seconds. Five. All the way to ten.

Mason lifted his head. Dakota raised hers beneath him.

There was no pain or death. They weren't even hurt.

The spiders were now looking down at their prone quarry, barrels all smoking.

There was a junkyard of twisted metal behind them. The flying drones — which had been the spiders' real targets and had probably been the subjects of DROP YOUR WEAPON — were now scrap.

A new voice came from behind the dead drones. It belonged to a human woman now toeing her way past the debris. "Who are you, and why aren't you dead?"

There was no mistaking Calliope — and even less of a chance when resentment twisted his companion's face.

Mason didn't answer. The blonde — exactly as his nested memory remembered her, as if from five minutes ago — squinted at him.

Now with meaning, she repeated her query. "Who the hell are *you?*"

"Mason Shaw."

She looked down at the shattered drones. Up at the spiders. "I guess that explains it."

Calliope walked away, back into the forbidden area.

A lock in the gate clanked, then the fence finally swung open.

Spiders and Drones

THE CHAIR FELT FAMILIAR. Same for the hat. Somewhere and somehow — in a sim or for real, Mason wasn't sure — it seemed he'd sat here and worn this before.

Calliope checked equipment tethered to the hat by a circulatory system's worth of wires. "You were telling the truth."

"Why wouldn't I tell the truth?"

She stood, came forward, then raked the strange mind-reading hat from his head. "To infiltrate. Blake would tell you what to say."

"Nathaniel Blake?"

"Of course."

"What's he got to do with this?"

"Nothing, apparently. You're either who you say, or you're intensely but *very specifically* mentally ill."

"Of course I'm who I say." Mason looked at Dakota for help, but so far, she might as well have been luggage. Calliope and Dakota had traded a glance but no words.

"I don't understand." Again he looked at them both in turn. "You thought I wasn't who I said?"

"I thought you were *exactly* who you said. My drones should have killed you. Instead, they woke me up like there was something I had to see. Turns out it was a giant mess. The HRO still monitors their drones, you know — even the ones watching this place. They'll wonder why so many suddenly went offline. If they come looking and find them destroyed, there might be questions to sweep under the rug." Calliope sat back and tossed a nut into her mouth. "I can cover it up, of course. But it's very inconvenient."

They'd followed her to a building in the complex's center, then through three concealed doors, each more hidden than the last. They'd passed combination locks, key locks, and biometric locks that took both a palm and a retina scan. Eventually, they found themselves in a room that looked like a lived-in missile command, strewn with unknown technology plus a small cot and an improvised kitchen.

Dharma One, heavily modified and scoured by age and neglect. Mason barely recognized the place.

Despite the circumstances, Calliope's nest struck him as cozy. The same wasn't true for the surrounding areas. None of what they'd come through looked like it had seen human hands in years — including, Mason thought, the rooms and hallways from his ill-fated Docent interview. Somewhere in this complex was the room where he'd been questioned then dropped into a pod despite his protests and regardless of his rights.

According to Dakota, his vegetative body had been stored here for a while. And probably Carter's too, before they'd been moved to different locations. At least he had opened his eyes to somewhat familiar faces — though he'd not yet figured out what made them memorable.

"Why are you here?" Calliope asked.

Again, he looked at Dakota for help, but now she was inspecting her hands. "What do you mean, 'Why am I here?' Wasn't this your idea?"

"How exactly was it my idea?"

"You—"

"And *why?* I'm comfortable here. You, on the other hand, can't walk through a gate without destroying drones — do you know how many butterflies I'm going to need to release to bring it back to normal?"

"*What?*"

"Chaos is countered by simple things, like butterflies and bunnies." Her civility finally broke. "I came to retrieve you out front because you were causing a scene. Don't mistake my triage for hospitality. It's taken a significant amount of work to hollow out a blind spot in the drone sweep algorithm and retrofit this place to broadcast without pinging the HRO logs. The drones should have killed you. Yet ..." Calliope waved her hand to indicate the entirety of this unacceptable situation.

"You didn't have to bring us inside," Dakota said.

Her head jerked like a sprinkler head. "I didn't, huh? Dharma One is all that's left of Revival's original vision for the prison. When the grant renewed four years ago, and Revival did their big update, they couldn't just bulldoze these buildings. Inmates would invade the other stations, but this one had to be protected. Otherwise, no electricity, heat, or water. Retrofitting 22 for outside utilities was quoted at 1.1 billion, plus the administrative headache of finding temporary homes for nearly fifty thousand prisoners. So, yes, Dakota. You're right. I *didn't* have to bring you inside. I could have stayed put, and when those drones went down and the HRO saw its single most important hub in jeopardy, then sent guards to investigate, only to find demolished drones ... plus a bunch of land drones of my own design, well that would really raise some eyebrows. Not to mention the two dead prisoners — Dakota Ward, who went off the roster and never checked back in, and Mason Shaw, who ... well ... I'm not sure you even know where *you're* supposed to be."

His ire rose. "Now wait just a goddamn minute. We came here for *you*, at *your* request. It wasn't easy. And now that we're here, you're going to act like—"

"I didn't request shit, Mr. Shaw. Thanks for the visit. Now, after I clean up the mess you left outside, I have to find somewhere new to hide."

"Why are you hiding from Immunity?" Mason asked.

"I'm not hiding from Immunity."

"Why did you leave them? Why did you give up?"

Calliope waved him away.

"Why would Nathaniel Blake send me here? Why would he 'tell me something to say,' like you thought earlier? What the hell's he up to, anyway?" Questions fell like boxes stacked go the ceiling. "Do you know anything about my father?"

"You mean Carter?"

"Yes, I goddamn mean Carter!" Had she forgotten? Didn't Calliope understand her botched plan had sent Carter to the HRO in the first place, then ultimately into Chamber Therapy and Pattern Black? If she hadn't broken into his sim with her weird psychedelic scroll, Mason would have never woken up.

"Carter has been gone for a long time." She said it with weight beyond a simple fact. It wasn't that Mason's father was gone; it was that Carter's absence meant something known only to Calliope.

"Dakota said they moved him off-site. He's still alive."

"Not alive enough."

"What does that mean? I woke up."

"Good for you." Calliope didn't seem surprised or react like it was something she'd caused or even wanted.

"You can look. Carter must be stored somewhere."

"*You* were stored somewhere. I checked your stats every night for a while. You were as gone as he was."

"I was Pattern Black," Mason said. "Why did I wake up?"

"How the hell would I know why you woke up?"

"They said I was brain dead, but it felt like dreaming. Did you do that? Did you somehow cause me to—"

"How would I do that?"

"You said you can 'broadcast.'"

"I have backdoors all over the network. I reach out to contact proxies and snitches, and I can operate kiosks remotely. I use it to get what I need. But you were *dead*. I'm not a voodoo priest, no matter how connected I am."

Mason looked at Dakota.

"He saw you inside Pattern Black," she told Calliope. "It left a sentient record as if he was up and moving for real. He described you, said you came in blazing like we used to. Kass ran a trace. Then I ran the same trace, just to be sure. Of course, it went nowhere, but you're not *that* good at covering your tracks. I know it was you."

Calliope showed genuine interest for the first time, accompanied by what looked like anger. "You've been spying on me?"

"We were spying on *him,*" Dakota countered. "Once he woke up, we thought it'd be prudent to pull every bit of info we could."

"You're wrong. He must not have been Pattern Black. He must have been skating residual. Fooled you or something."

Dakota scoffed. "You were there. You said it yourself — *you checked him every night.* So did we. The records aren't ambiguous. Total flatline. Ready to be formatted."

"'Formatted'?"

"Later," Dakota said to Mason.

Calliope looked incredulous, but not as much as she had before Dakota started speaking. "Even if you pulled all his records, it wouldn't have led you here."

Dakota looked at Mason. She didn't want to lose this verbal match with Calliope, but she was out of ammo. Her expression prayed for him to have bullets still in the chamber.

"I led us here," Mason said.

"I see. And who the fuck are you?"

"Shaw. Mason. Son of Carter?"

"'Son of Carter. Son of Carter,'" Calliope parroted. "You don't even know what that means. He said you weren't close. You hated his guts. Why you think I'd care is beyond me."

Dakota stood. She went to a panel of instruments, looked them over, then offered a cruel laugh.

"Problem over there, Ms. Ward?"

Dakota turned, fire in her eyes. "I never understood you. Or at least, I *thought* I didn't understand you. But now I get it. You're a coward."

"Is that so."

Dakota came closer. Very close. "Yes. That's so. You hooked us all in with your big dreams. Made me believe my sister might not have died for nothing. But you have no idea what it's like, now that you're gone. Everyone else is still at Dharma Four. Kassidi, Bear, Ike ... all of us. Sitting where you left us, waiting wide-eyed for our 'great and powerful leader' to return. I used to believe we could stop Revival. That we could stop Blake and tell the world the truth."

What truth? Mason was still dying to ask.

"We deserved better, Calliope. We had your back, but when it came right down to it, you didn't have ours."

"I gave up because Carter was a dead end."

"What?" Mason said.

"You were the one with the codes, Calliope," Dakota continued. "The one who knew how to sneak around without getting caught. You know how we stay out of sight now? It's easy. We *never* leave the blind spot. We sit there, *every day,* going through the motions, with no idea what to do next. You called us to you, cut us off from the HRO, then left us to fend for ourselves. We can't go back. Instead, we get to wait for the day Blake decides to push the button."

"What button?"

But still they ignored him.

"Blake won't do anything," Calliope said.

"You're sure? How nice of you to let us know. Because honestly, a few of us have talked about infiltrating sims again. Just trying to get things started however we can. It'll be slow and sloppy, but it sure as hell beats doing nothing. You took our purpose, Calliope. Robbed us of the reason we bothered to stay alive."

"Then make your infiltrations, if that makes you feel better."

"Is there a point?"

"Sure," Calliope said. "I just don't know what it is."

They were both steaming. Dakota more than Calliope. Fighting to the death without lifting a literal finger.

"No options," Dakota mumbled, now more to herself. "No support. No help at all. Operating blind, and we'll be seen then fucked the second we try."

"You'll be seen, not fucked," Calliope said as Mason moved between them. "I told you. Blake can't nuke the system without the key."

"Ah. The key. Again with the key."

"EXCUSE ME," Mason said loudly enough to make them both stop and look. "Wanna tell me what the hell you two are talking about?"

"Nathaniel Blake. Founder of Revival."

"*Co*-founder," corrected Calliope.

"He has a panic button. She warned us about it before running off. With the press of a finger, he could erase everyone connected to the system."

"That's not really the way it works," Calliope said.

"Really? How does it work, then? Want to open up now that it doesn't matter? Maybe tell us both what you never really explained before?"

Calliope's lip curled, but she said nothing. There were secrets here, but apparently, she'd rather be misquoted than forthcoming.

After a long silence, Mason knew he'd need to stoke the fire to keep it from dying. "You didn't seem surprised when I said my father is still alive."

"I know he's alive," Calliope said. "Blake has him on ice. He's … a private project of Nathaniel's."

"Then we need to find him."

"I've been trying." Calliope glared at Dakota as if this was a sticking point between them. "It doesn't matter, anyway. He's not dead, but he is Pattern Black."

"*I* was Pattern Black." Mason shook his head, trying to clear it. "Why did Blake keep my father alive so long?"

"He kept *you* alive just as long," Calliope answered.

"Are you going to answer or keep talking around everything?"

"Know your place, Mr. Shaw. You are a guest in this house."

"They tell me I was forgotten," Mason said with a curl of his lip. "But Carter was *taken*."

"Then consider yourself lucky."

"I was conscious while inside Pattern Black, but Dakota and the others say I looked less than dead. Why? How?"

"Don't know. Don't care."

"Why do I know about the prison? I've seen almost none of it in real life."

"Lucky guess?"

"I know about the cribs. I know they're color-coded. I know about the drones, even before seeing the ones at the gate. I know about the chit system. The kiosks. I know some of the gangs and the neighborhoods. Places to steer clear of, places to walk right into. I keep perfectly describing locations I've only been inside my mind."

"Good for you."

"I know you broke into simulations. You crashed the Heist. Came in carrying big weapons."

"Fascinating."

"What is Blake up to?"

"Who gives a shit anymore?"

"What is Pattern Black?" Mason asked. "What does Chamber Therapy do?"

"Brain death. Your father made it seem like you were smarter than this."

"I told you, I was awake inside."

"You're mistaken."

"But even when I was awake — even when it seemed like I was living the normal prison life — I kept getting flashes of an all-white space full of black dots ... and a tiny black vortex, growing larger each time I see it. Like a miniature hurricane."

That got her.

Calliope's face almost registered interest, but then she pushed it away and crossed to another station.

Mason followed, with Dakota lagging. Was Calliope investigating the perimeter or something else as preamble to action? She was angry, grumpy. Downright jaded. Not the optimistic leader who thought she could end Revival's tyranny.

"Does that mean something to you?" Mason asked.

"No," Calliope said.

"It does, doesn't it? So I *was* in Pattern Black. Was I ... I don't know, maybe dipping in and out? Maybe that's how I was able to wake up — because I wasn't all the way there?"

Calliope reached the console, moved beside it, then opened a door without stepping through. She held it open, waiting for them both to take the hint.

"That's it?" Dakota asked. "Are we through here?"

"I sent new drones to clean up your mess. I spoofed double IDs onto a few of the still-operational drones so nobody will notice the missing ones unless they come for a physical inspection, which they won't do. I even cut a new blind spot for you between here and the zone of inhibition around Four. You can make it back without being spotted if you're fast."

"You're kicking us out?" Mason asked.

"Thanks for visiting. Don't come back. I'll have to move now, which I really don't appreciate. Find me again, and my drones will kill you."

"Why didn't they kill me this time?"

"Who knows? Malfunction."

"You said 'that explains it' when I gave you my name. Are your drones programmed not to hurt me?"

"Yes," Calliope said with heavy sarcasm. "I programmed my drones specifically to allow you — someone I've never met — to pass."

"Dodging the question doesn't answer it," Dakota said. "Were they programmed to leave *Carter* alone?"

"Yeah. Sure."

"Right. I remember," Dakota said, clearly playing a con. "I helped with that programming. Except it was unique to Carter, cued directly to his mental fingerprint and pulled from his stasis records. It's almost as if the drones thought Mason *was* Carter."

Calliope raised her eyebrows, still holding the door.

"We can help you," Mason said.

"I don't need any help."

"Come back to Four with us," Dakota said. "We can at least analyze what we have. There must be *something* to the—"

"And I don't need friends." Calliope stared. Waited.

Mason finally began to move.

"Up the stairs," Calliope said with a tip of her chin. "It's pretty straightforward. You'll forgive me if I don't come with you. I have a lot of packing to do."

The door started to close.

"One last thing," Dakota said.

The door paused. One of Calliope's blue eyes watched them.

"Fuck you," Dakota continued.

"Fuck me," Calliope said as if considering.

"We didn't ask for this. Life at Dharma Four isn't exactly a picnic, but we get on. We have each other. We don't have a mission, but we have pointless jobs and just enough to distract us. The people you left at least have a sense of dignity and honor."

"Are you done?"

Dakota went on as if Calliope hadn't spoken. "You left us. Fine. But then you call us out here, and we risk the crossing, and *this* is the reception we get? For the first time ever, someone woke up from Pattern Black. After *three years* — almost as long as Carter. And on top of everything, it's his *son*. Whose pattern looked enough like Carter for your spider things not to kill him. And *still*, you act like this? You're not just a fucking coward. You're stupid, too."

The door opened. "You said I called you out here."

"And then you treat us like—"

Calliope raised a hand, cutting her off. "I didn't call you. I didn't do anything." She looked to Mason. "You said the same thing — that I summoned you."

Dakota looked at Mason. Then so did Calliope, both women waiting.

Mason spoke, unsure of where this was going.

"You were in one of my simulations like Dakota said. You had your people pin me to the floor, then you told me I could stay or go. I chose to go with you, though I didn't understand what was happening. But instead of taking me, you put this thing over my face. Some sort of psychedelic towel that you … *What?*"

Calliope turned to Dakota. "Did *you* tell him about the Muse?"

"No." She shook her head and looked at Mason with apology. "But I checked after he mentioned it. Me and Kass both. Something happened to cause critical turbulence in his stream, and it seems consistent with a Muse regression. We assumed it was why he woke up. That you … *did something* to him. That's why we came. We figured since you were the one who chose to contact him, you might have some answers."

"I didn't contact him. I didn't reach out at all, in any way."

Dakota dug her mini-tablet from a pocket, tapped around until she saw something that made her nod, then turned it around and showed Calliope.

"This is my fingerprint on him," Calliope said, taking the tablet. "How did you do this?"

Dakota shook her head. "Are you kidding? Even you can't fake a fingerprint. How could we?"

There was a long pause. By the time Mason and Dakota broke their paralysis, Calliope was already halfway across the tech-heavy space. Her walking away from the open door paradoxically invited them in.

"What is it?" Mason said.

"I didn't do what you remember me doing," Calliope said, glancing back. Then she held up Dakota's tablet. "But according to this, *somehow*, I did."

FORTY

Extraction Complete

ON THE OTHER end of the room, Calliope opened a concealed door between consoles.

Dakota and Mason followed her into the hidden place, a new chamber stuffed with furnishings and equipment that looked less like tech than art. The previous room had reminded Mason of missile command, but this one made it look like the milking parlor at an Amish farm. The tech was like nothing he'd ever seen, cobbled from bits and pieces Calliope had found, scavenged, or sourced through her snitch proxies.

There was an object the size of a dresser in the room's center, covered with curved and riveted armor like an alien seed pod. Wires protruded from every station, running across the floor in a nest as thick as rainforest underbrush. Calliope hadn't bothered with cowlings or neatness and had connected everything without fanfare or polish. A few of the thicker cables had been patched and recycled, ringed with colorful tape like the bands on a coral snake. Others weren't long enough to lay nicely and were thus draped across the space like out-of-control clotheslines. Crossing from one end to the other was less like strolling than doing the limbo.

356

"Did you make all of this?" Dakota's anger took a backseat to wonder.

"Bits and pieces at a time. There's a lot of smart hardware still out there in the city, just waiting to be scavenged. Cars, TVs, refrigerators, you name it. The hard part was finding codeable chips. Most of what I needed didn't exist. I had to use blank chips then train the AI."

Calliope moved to a workstation and beckoned Mason forward. She gave him what looked like a chrome bicycle handle to hold, turned away, then used one finger to scan through lines on a screen — lines, Mason assumed, he was somehow feeding the computer through the implement in his hands.

She peered into his eyes using something large and mounted to a wheel, then pushed it aside on a hinge. "You're right. He's got my print on him." She turned to Mason. "You went in when?"

"That's what I've been trying to tell you," Dakota answered for him. "He 'went in' three years back. Nothing changed since you were with the group."

"I'm not being clear," Calliope said, still addressing Mason. "*After* you woke in your pod, when did you re-immerse into a simulation?"

"I *didn't* re-immerse." Mason had barely gotten out of immersion after losing a chunk of his life. Damned if he'd *ever* do it again.

Calliope sighed and turned back to Dakota. "*When?*"

"He's telling the truth."

"Why would I not tell the truth?" Mason asked.

"I guess I need to spell this out. *You* claim," Calliope said, using her eyes to poke Mason in the chest, "you saw me inside your sim. Strange as I find the idea, my equipment agrees you were, *somehow*, influenced by my code — and more specifically, that I used a bio-disruptor of my own creation on you. It's called a Muse, and you saw it as a scroll made of shiny fabric. But regardless of your testimony or the readings, I know for a fact I didn't hack your simulation or immerse myself by accident. So, I'm facing two situations, both of them true and impossible."

Calliope sat up, eliciting a squeak of protest from her chair. She leaned forward to put her elbows on her knees.

Pointing clasped hands at Mason with her index fingers extended, she added, "But there's one thing I do know. *We couldn't have connected without a connection.* You get me, Superman? In order for a lamp to light up, it has to be plugged in."

He looked at Dakota. Calliope sighed heavily, then Mason spun on her.

End of rope reached.

"Help us or don't help us," he spat. "But if you keep acting like I'm an idiot because I don't know all the ins and outs of the catfight you two have been waging for the past three years—"

"You'll what? Leave and never speak to me again? Be my guest." Calliope swung her arm toward the concealed door, but he knew it was only a bluff. She had opened this inner sanctum because something in Mason's head had piqued her interest.

"Leave him alone," Dakota snapped.

"I don't need you rushing to my defense every goddamn minute," Mason said.

"You sure? Because I've had your back pretty consistently these past few years. Like when—"

"I didn't ask you to take the fall. I told you not to."

They stared at each other in silence.

The sudden tension between Mason and Dakota softened Calliope's tongue. When she spoke next, it was with less condescension, more patience. "Look. Mr. Shaw. *Mason.*"

He met her cool blue eyes.

"As Dakota said, I *used* to hack into simulations. We all did. If you'd been in a simulation we entered, it might have happened as you described. Everything would go off the rails. We'd take our subject aside, separating them from the primary plotline. If you were our target, then yes, I could see backing you into a room, pinning you down, then quieting you to disrupt your experience with the Muse and begin the precursors of waking. We've done it a hundred times."

In the space between Calliope's breaths, Mason thought of how

Dakota had portrayed her old mentor's hacks. Between the lines, it had seemed to him that all the hacks were only practice. Carter was the only true target, and for reasons unknown.

Calliope continued. "The unusual part — the part I can't get past — is the timelines don't line up. I made a lot of incursions, but none for years. Time dilates inside simulations, but not to this degree. You say we met what feels like just a few days ago, but I'm telling you that's not possible."

"Why?"

"Because there was never a direct line between us. No connection from me to you. You've been plugged in the entire time, but I haven't made an incursion in over a year. And yet ..." Calliope turned to the computer screen, exasperated and tired. "And yet the pattern agrees with you." She shook her head, searching for answers that weren't there. "Even if I was somehow 'sleep-incurring' — coming in here and hooking myself into a pod in some sort of dissociative state — the logs would show those incursions."

"Could it be latent?" Dakota asked. "Could a fingerprint from one of your old incursions — back in the Heist days — have somehow survived until now?"

"No. They can't survive autonomously." Calliope showed Dakota something on the monitor by tapping its surface with a fingertip. "This reads as if I placed a Muse on his face a month ago at most. Probably more recent than that. There's almost no degradation. No telephone."

"Telephone?" Mason said.

"Like the game," Dakota explained. "The print replicates with the synaptic expansion that occurs after any fingerprint is made. The longer it's there, the more it differs from the original because tiny errors accumulate over time."

Calliope sat back, arms crossed, thinking.

They all waited, wondering how something could happen and not happen in time.

"I need time," she finally said.

• • •

DAKOTA WAS CURIOUSLY ZEN. Whatever had happened between her and Calliope was either forgiven or at least temporarily forgotten. The wait took all day, then overnight. Mason was up late, asking if he could help, knowing he couldn't. He didn't have the knowledge or the background.

He succumbed after midnight. His sleep was fitful, stuffed with fears that he might never wake — or that when he did, the reality greeting him would be something new. He dozed in quasi-somnolence, the night a skim of bad dreams to paint the wee hours in a matte veneer. He woke before six, prior to the klaxon. Calliope was still working.

Dakota rose beside him. "Did you sleep?"

"A creative person might call it that. What about you?"

"Like the dead."

They watched Calliope typing, waving her fingers over a screen. By all accounts, she hadn't noticed them.

"Come on." Dakota took his hand. "I saw a coffee machine."

"ALL NIGHT," Mason said once they were comfortable, the secret door closed, and no evidence that Calliope's fugue had broken enough for her to notice their waking. "I don't think she slept."

"She didn't." Dakota raised her cup — a plastic tumbler from a hockey game's concession stand in another life — and inhaled before sipping. "She won't."

"She won't sleep?"

Mason was being absurd, but she answered with an earnest shake of her head.

"*This?*" Dakota pointed toward the hidden door, behind which Calliope still labored, unaware her guests had risen. "This is how she always is. Or was. I thought she was going to throw us out, but now we'll be lucky to get away."

"Because of that fingerprint thing?"

Dakota nodded with a swallow. "We all leave fingerprints of a sort whenever we enter a non-resetting simulation. The Heist is a resetting simulation. It always starts at the same place, with nobody in it the wiser."

Mason nodded. He'd seen that same antique lightbulb in the van a dozen times. Sometimes the occupants differed, but no matter who they were, everyone seemed to work from a blank slate.

"But other sims don't reset that way. Any time another simulation cross-connects to something like the Heist, participants can move in one direction or the other if their minds are awake enough to see the way. That's how we got in and out. We couldn't project into the Heist, but we could enter our own simulation, then open a door."

"Is that what Calliope did with me? When she put that Muse thing over my face?"

"Ordinarily, I'd say yes. But this is something else. You carry Calliope's fingerprint. But how can that have ever happened if she hasn't been inside?"

"Does it matter?"

"Calliope's fingerprint is distinctive. We always had to scour systems after she went under to erase any evidence. The fact that you got it and she didn't know means her fingerprint, as part of you, has been out in the open. You're like a man running past guard dogs with steaks hung around your neck. It'd be a miracle if you didn't attract attention."

"Is someone looking for her, specifically? I thought she was this amazing hacker. Able to hide from anyone."

"Anyone but the system's creator," Dakota said.

"Blake?"

Dakota nodded.

"What about all the prison cameras? Wouldn't she be seen?"

"She's good at laying low. *Very* low. The years have changed her, making her a lot less recognizable than you'd think. Her hair is different, and she's gotten scary-thin. But if you remember what she looked like on TV, you'll see it the next time you look. The old Elisabeth is still there if you squint."

"You're saying Blake's been looking for Calliope?"

"Calliope, Reeves … He'll take her by any name. He's been looking. Scouring. Sending AIs to find her."

Mason felt a shiver, thinking of Preacher. He muttered, *"God mode."*

"What did you say?"

"That's what the fake version of you said after you pulled me out of the tank of goo. After you saw Calliope's signature."

"Like sysop access?"

"I don't know, Dakota. I can barely work my toaster."

She was thinking. Starting to pace.

"What's going on?" Mason asked.

"You don't know what God mode is?"

"That one's pretty easy to figure out from context. Or hell — from Carter. He was working with them both, even though he didn't know they were the same person until he was inside. 'God mode' was one of his expressions. We just say 'sysop' or 'system admin.'"

"If he didn't know until he was inside, how could I—"

"Maybe he told you when you came to visit," Dakota said, but Mason could tell by her manner she didn't believe it, despite very much wanting to. "Any visit you might have had before Blake got him."

"Blake?"

Dakota nodded. "We think Blake mandated Carter's Chamber Therapy. You gave him the idea. Blake accelerated it and got him in right away."

"Why?"

"To force Pattern Black. To get rid of him."

Mason wasn't so sure of that. Even if Blake was behind Carter's brain death, the whole thing seemed unnecessarily complex. It was Blake's prison. He could have easily sent a drone to fry him. Yet Blake hung on to Carter, keeping him technically alive in an isolated location instead of letting him die.

"Are you sure Carter never mentioned Reeves and Calliope were the same person?"

"I'm sure. Why?"

She paced again. Mason had to say her name three times before she answered. Once he had her attention, he repeated himself. *"Why?"*

"Because if the fake Dakota in your head said Calliope had 'God mode permissions,' it means *you* somehow understood she was a system admin, and the only 'God mode' system admins are Blake and Reeves. *Think*, Mason. If you knew about Reeves, and Blake sent that Preacher guy after you, then Blake knows where Reeves is, or might be. That's why I didn't tell you about Elisabeth before now. I had to be sure she'd help us and keep that fingerprint from showing back up on the network."

"Why is she in prison in the first place?"

"After she and Blake had a falling out, she threatened to expose some bad stuff Revival has done. Blake didn't react well, so Reeves ran. She came into this place through the back door because he'd never think to look here. She's been hiding in plain sight ever since. Reeves knows this HRO and its systems better than anyone because she built it. She also knew Blake couldn't revoke her access once she reached the system core and built herself a blind spot, which she did immediately. He knows she's inside the HRO now, but there's nothing he can do without shutting the whole thing down and log-jamming Revival's biggest income stream."

Mason was about to ask what bad things Revival had done — what Reeves had threatened to expose — when the door opened. Calliope stood in the threshold, hollow-eyed and bleary. Now that he knew what to look for, Mason could see Revival's co-founder, Elisabeth Reeves.

"I know what happened," she said to Mason. "It's because there's two of me. One here. And another inside."

CALLIOPE TOUCHED the screen with her short, surely chewed nails. "This is 07-07."

She tapped a small box full of numbers in the screen's corner — date, location, and coded IDs he couldn't decipher. From context, Mason decided that *07-07* must be a designation given to a mission or a project, the record of which they were about to watch.

"You were on this one, Dakota. Do you remember?"

The screen looked like a spreadsheet with bloated and shifting cells, and what filled the cells weren't even numbers.

Dakota shook her head. "Refresh my memory."

"It was when we went in for Kassidi. Her Chamber Therapy wasn't going well. She was near failure and skirting Pattern Black."

Dakota stared. "So, this wasn't …"

"It wasn't the Heist. It was pure reflection. Do you remember?"

"*I* don't remember," Mason said, reminding the ladies he was still here and didn't understand a goddamn thing.

"*Reflection,*" Calliope repeated. "The Heist and a lot of other HRO sims use AI to present moral choices to their subjects. Choices inside the simulation reflect decisions the subjects have made poorly in real life. If a person can learn to navigate a moral sim correctly, they theoretically should be able to make wise moral choices *outside* as well. But when the HRO was opened, and Chamber Therapy rolled out, Revival's AI was neither sophisticated enough nor fast enough to handle something as complex as the Heist without any lag. So, the early Chamber Therapy sims were just about taking what a subject already had going on inside" — Calliope tapped her head at the temple — "and improvising with it. Modern sims are like creating a dream then pulling people into it. But at the start, it was more like letting a person dream on her own, then entering that pre-existing space."

"Why did they make the change?" Mason asked.

"Because it was safer." Calliope paused, then looked meaningfully at Dakota. "Because when outside agents join reflective simulations, they can't always find their way out."

Dakota looked at the screen as if she'd just noticed it. "Jesus. Is this the time when …"

Calliope nodded and tapped the screen. "Look."

Mason saw what looked like sparks flashing in a black void — a drug-drenched version of a midnight sky. Some of the star-things onscreen were large, and others were small, all throbbing with enormous flares.

Dakota watched. Most of the stars vanished, leaving two. She put her hand to her mouth.

"What are we looking at?" Mason asked.

Calliope touched the bigger star mid-screen. "That's Kassidi. Well, her mind, anyway. She's largest and at the center because this sim is happening inside her native mental space." She indicated a smaller star, off-center. "And that's me."

"I remember this," said Dakota, still covering her mouth.

The second star dimmed like headlights on a starting car.

"Right now, Bear is trying to pull me out of the simulation," Calliope said, nodding at the flicker.

"Aren't you already 'there' with Bear and everyone else? Your body, in the real world, I mean."

"That's right. But think about dreaming. You fall asleep, and a dream starts. You're *in the dream* while it's happening, no longer really out in the real world."

"Except you are. I was in that pod for years. No matter what I was dreaming, I still woke up there."

"Exactly," Calliope said. "You *woke up* there. You did not *live* there while you were under. Your mind goes where 'you' are."

"Except you don't have a body," Mason said.

"You don't need one, so long as you stay inside. But I'll never forget this sim. It's not a place I would have ever wanted to stay."

"Why?"

"Kass has mild schizophrenia," Dakota explained. "It's treatable with medication, and the HRO, though it falls short in most ways, does at least provide. But inside, you'd never know. The old simulations left the prisoner — the subject of Chamber Therapy — sit in the driver's seat. It worked when the subject was healthy. But with disturbances like Kassidi's, things tended to go very wrong. It's one of the main reasons why simulations like the Heist were invented."

"It was terrifying, sharing her mind." Calliope shook her head. "If we hadn't planted our suggestion before the worst part started, we wouldn't have managed at all. Deep down, she looks like a psychopath. But that's the problem with Chamber Therapy: *we're all icebergs.* What Blake was trying to do didn't — *couldn't* — take the whole person into consideration. It could only treat symptoms, never causes. Guides never knew what they were getting into until after they were inside, and because of it, the HRO system lost many great guides."

"To death?" Mason asked.

"To insanity. Kass has made peace with her inner demons. The rest of us were unprepared. It was like visiting Hell."

Mason looked at the screen, watching the second star repeatedly dim. Someone was still trying to rescue Calliope but falling short.

"I remember this moment right here." Calliope pointed. The star dimmed as a long, slow pull attempted to extract it for thirty long seconds before it finally relaxed. "I was trying to decide whether I could kill myself so I wouldn't have to endure being in there until my body died on the outside. But it isn't straightforward. Try killing yourself inside a sim, and you'll usually just come out of it. Try inside a hostile environment like this one, and it probably won't let you go. Surreality makes sense in a dream. You believe and accept the world for what it is, even if what you see is strange, right?"

Mason nodded, realizing only afterward that maybe he shouldn't have.

"It gets its hooks in you. It wasn't that Kassidi's mind held me too tight. It's that I couldn't make myself believe it was false for long enough to get away."

"How did you get out?" Mason asked.

Calliope skipped forward, then indicated fast-changing numbers in the corner — one, in particular, marked DELTA-E.

"Brute force," she said as the Delta-E number doubled, then 10X'd. "Either Bear would suck me out or break my mind trying. By then, I didn't care. Most of the team spent less than a minute inside Kass's head, but I spent nearly five. More than enough. For Kassidi, too — her subconscious clearly got the hint because she walked away from the crib to find us two weeks later. The only loose end was the person left inside her mind."

The star onscreen dimmed, slowly dying until it finally vanished.

Then the screen froze, and a black bar filled with white type covered its center — **EXTRACTION COMPLETE.**

Calliope turned to them. "I remember waking up. The real world felt strange for a while. I didn't do anything with the rest of that day, and I spent the next one throwing up. But I was out, and nothing else mattered."

Mason and Dakota nodded.

"But something about it always bugged me. It felt like Kassidi's thoughts had taken a bite from my soul. For weeks afterward — hell, *months* — I felt like I'd lost a twin. Like I had a phantom limb. I figured it was Kass's demons in my memory, and eventually, I grew to accept it. But things never felt right. And now, finally, I think I understand."

She touched the screen. The display changed, but the new video looked identical to the old one. Again they saw the two stars in a void, same as before.

"I spent the night decrypting this. This is the deepest of deep cuts, ladies and gentlemen."

"It's the same thing you already showed us," Mason said.

"No," Dakota said, picking up on some identifier Mason hadn't seen. "This is the source feed. *Kassidi's* feed. The one that stayed with her after we were gone."

Mason watched as the second star drew dim, flickered, then vanished. Same as the first time. "Okay. So what?"

"Keep watching."

Dakota hadn't taken her focus from the screen. She either knew what was coming or was too unnerved to look away.

The second star returned, five seconds after it vanished.

Dakota's hand returned to cover her mouth. "Jesus."

"What … is the first recording a fake?" Mason asked, not understanding. "Was someone covering this up?"

Calliope shook her head. "No. The first recording was true. Bear doubled down on the extraction force and got me out. I woke in my pod, shook myself off, then eventually got back to the business of being me. But the *second* recording" — she pointed at the smaller star now throbbing all over again, somehow sad and lost to Mason's eyes — "is *also* true. I *didn't* get out. The extraction *wasn't* strong enough. The window closed, and I was trapped inside."

Mason regarded Calliope. "But … you're here."

"*Physical* Calliope is here," she said, placing a palm on her chest as she looked at the screen. "But *digital* Calliope? Turns out, she never left."

FORTY-ONE

No One Else Will Do

DAKOTA ENTERED the back room at Dharma Four, expecting to find Calliope convalescent after her near miss. She found her vibrant instead. Excited, stirred from the inside, stuffed with nervous energy that might portend a leap forward. Or perhaps a nervous breakdown. Half genius and half maniac — something she and Blake had shared. A perfect team, until it wasn't.

"Dakota. Hi."

She needed a moment. Calliope had a grasshopper's energy — and yet just yesterday, they'd been taking bets on whether she'd die or lose her shit. Now here she was, 150 percent of the leader Immunity had been lucky enough to have before they'd gone after Kassidi.

"You need something?" Calliope asked when Dakota didn't reply.

"You seem better," she said.

"I got an idea."

Calliope was driven by a tiny internal motor that burned inspiration as fuel. When ideas fell dormant, she was slow, half-somber, even irritable. But she became animated when notions struck. Dakota simply hadn't seen it for a while.

"What idea?"

"We went deep inside the last one. Inside Kassidi."

"*So* deep, you almost didn't make it out."

Calliope waved a hand. "The membranes were thin that deep. I kept getting glimpses of the other members of Kassidi's cohort."

Yes, Dakota had noticed that. Dropping into the new girl's simulation stream through Calliope's hack had been like plunging into ice water. She'd been unable to breathe, her virtual lungs paralyzed by the alien feeling of the unstable woman's mind. Sixty seconds inside had felt like forever. She'd had the feeling of being at the bottom of an enormous bag made of skin, and inside that larger bag sat several smaller ones. Inside each was a person, every one of them as buried in their solo simulations as Kassidi had been inside hers.

But because simulations happened in groups, the cohort of prisoners all occupying different ones was the only thing keeping them separate. Proximity — because the HRO *did* do Chamber Therapy in groups — kept the walls between their awareness wafer-thin. As Dakota had scrabbled to keep hold of her sanity, she'd felt the nightmarish temptation to punch through a fluid wall where she'd seen, or perhaps *felt*, another prisoner squirming.

She had wanted to rip through that skin just to escape, and it didn't matter where. Too bad doing so would have scrambled her, Kassidi, and everyone else sharing the sim beyond belief.

"I saw the others, too," Dakota said.

Calliope reacted like Linus hoping to spot the Great Pumpkin. "We could reach Carter Shaw."

Dakota tried not to sigh but then did so anyway. She *wanted* to believe in Calliope's biggest and strangest theory. She'd joined *because* of her faith. Not in this specifically, but in the mission as a whole. But so much time had passed without results. So many failures and near-misses made it feel like oblivion — dangerous, with no end in sight or hope for a bounty before the whole thing came crashing down.

"I thought you said they moved Carter off-grid? That he was inaccessible now?"

"There's only one place they'd move him, and it's somewhere I have an in. Blake's office."

"You don't know that's where they took him. He could have been erased. Disconnected entirely."

But Calliope was shaking her head. "No. I can see his signal."

"How do you know for sure it's *Carter's?*"

"Because it's the only one that keeps reaching out." Her voice softened. "Over a year now, and his mind is still trying to get away."

"That doesn't mean it's Carter, Elisabeth."

Her gaze sharpened. Dakota was an underling here, but she hadn't stopped being the ballbuster she'd been on the force. Like any good cop, she pushed buttons to get her way. Elisabeth Reeves had left her socially acceptable shell behind when trading her old identity for a new one as Calliope. Dakota, like the rest of the world, knew *about* the dream team of Blake and Reeves, but she'd never *known* Reeves. Calling her Elisabeth was like using a child's middle name. A chastising move and a bit condescending. Dakota used it when she meant business. So far, it'd irritated their fearless leader just enough to budge.

"I taught Carter how to tread water. He knows the system and what it does."

"But they put him all the way under," Dakota argued. "He's not just in Chamber Therapy. He fell through its bottom. He's Pattern Black."

"That's Nathaniel's fault."

"No matter whose fault it is, he's there just the same," Dakota countered. "You know it, and so do I. *Blake* knows it. Carter can't be reached. You get it, right? *Pattern Black*, Elisabeth. He's brain dead. He can't survive, treading water or not."

Calliope looked like she might push back. They'd been over this. All of Immunity knew how to do what Calliope called *treading water* — keeping a simulation at arm's length through mental will, forcing your mind to stay at a higher awareness instead of getting sucked into another's subconscious world. Anyone could learn to do it for a while. All it took was holding onto the truth that reality was artificial, no matter how hard it rapped against your senses. They'd treaded water inside Kassidi, and that was probably why they were all still alive.

But you couldn't tread water for more than a few hours without suffering exhaustion, and it was the same inside uncontrolled, undisciplined thought. Was Calliope seriously suggesting Carter had kept his mind clear — yet somehow remained accessible to Immunity's prying hands — for *over a year* now?

Dakota didn't buy it. You could save the connected, but you couldn't wake the dead. Facts were facts. Gone was gone.

Calliope collapsed, hitting the floor like starched rags without their rigidity. It happened in an instant — her skeleton teleported away while the rest of her stayed behind.

Dakota rushed over. She dropped to her knees then picked up Calliope's head, wondering if she should shout for help. Healthy people didn't keel over. But Calliope was still conscious, even trying to get up.

"Lay still. You're exhausted."

"I'm fine."

"You've been up all night."

"I haven't. I got up just before the rest of you. I've been in here for a half-hour. I'm not stupid, Dakota."

She assumed that last was a reference to her near-miss inside Kassidi's mind. Mental disorientation — especially when it was *someone else's* disorientation — was no joke. Dakota might have glossed over recovery if she'd been on her own. But Calliope always insisted they rest, ideally with the biofeedback masks and headphones before sleeping. The body obeyed the mind, but the *mind* also obeyed the mind. You had to make sure it was reset after each incursion or suffer the loss of your marbles.

"Let me have Shinelle take a look at you."

"It's nothing. I just need to eat."

"Calliope." Dakota defaulted to her preferred name, deciding it'd get better compliance. "You just *fell over.*"

She got to her feet, using a console for support. Dakota held hands around her as if she might tip sideways. Calliope turned her head and started walking. Dakota followed — like chasing a kid as she finds her balance on a bike for the first time, waiting to catch her if she falls.

Calliope led them to the darkened room behind the controls, where the prison's forgotten sleepers — all those near-Docents, Pattern Blacked and left forever — slept like the dead. She went to a pod in the middle then wiped its lid. Together they peered through the fogged window.

"Okay," Dakota said, suddenly overwhelmed, trying to hide short breaths. "You're on your own if you want to collapse again. I can't do this right now. Not without coffee. And probably not even then."

Calliope was still peering inside. "You knew him, didn't you?"

"You know that answer."

"Was he close with his father?"

"He hated his father."

Calliope took a few extra beats. Then she looked up. "I suppose he had it coming."

"Carter? Or Mason?"

"Carter was no good at fatherhood. It must have bothered him because I heard it all the time. He used to say, 'One out of two isn't bad,' but he didn't mean it. And I know he felt like it wasn't *one* out of two. It was *zero* out of two. Even with his other son, it was the work, not the love, that kept them close."

"Is this why you got up early? To watch the dead?"

Calliope considered. Nothing was said. If the power for the storage pods had come from the same place as the power so recently hijacked for their heat, there were those in Four who would have argued to save the juice by disconnecting Mason and the others. Power came from outside. From the city's core. Cutting the umbilicals helped nothing. It'd just let them die all the way and necessitate cremation or burial. They weren't worth saving, so much as the effort of all that burning and digging.

"I'll leave you a cup." Dakota turned for the coffeemaker.

But Calliope was transfixed. "I can't stop thinking about them. About all of them."

Dakota turned back.

"It's the strangest thing. I had a dream last night, and every one of these people were in it." Calliope gestured across the bays. "I keep thinking I see someone around a corner, and I'm sure it's *him*, or *her*, or *her* down there." She pointed at each pod in turn then looked at Dakota with an expression she'd never seen. It scared her.

"Ever since I came out of Kassidi, I can't focus or even rest. My heart keeps beating too fast, and twice now, I've forgotten what day it is. Once I got back in bed, thinking it was nighttime. I … I …"

She didn't have to say it. *I feel like I'm losing my mind.*

Dakota returned. Calliope wouldn't let anyone take her hand, but she stopped close anyway, in receiving position. "Yesterday was traumatic. For all of us."

"I didn't think I was going to be able to get out. I thought I'd be in there forever."

"Bear knew. He almost cut the cord."

"I'd never have recovered if he had."

"Maybe," Dakota said.

They traded a glance.

"Seriously. Let Shinelle look you over."

"It's not physical."

"Then talk to the bot."

"AI won't understand this."

"Then talk to me."

Calliope considered. She almost laughed. Then she brushed it off, and Dakota saw her internal walls rise back into place. That was all there'd be — one short blip of vulnerable humanity, then right back to pretending.

"It's nothing. I just got lightheaded."

"Seriously."

Calliope sat, all her energy suddenly gone. She was back to being the lump. The sad sack. The one among them most meant to lead … but lying in her nihilism instead.

"You're right," Calliope said.

"So you'll talk to Shinelle?"

"You're right about the whole thing. Carter *is* off-grid. Maybe

I *am* imagining things. Maybe he's *not* reaching out. I mean … how could he?"

From skepticism to optimism, Dakota flipped an internal switch. It was classic to poo-poo Calliope's ideas, but they all knew without those ideas, there'd be nothing to chase. If they all gave up on her mission to retrieve whatever-it-was from Carter's mind — something that felt important but upon which Calliope would never elaborate or explain — the air would leave this place.

Surviving in here wasn't enough. They needed a purpose to truly make it. A mission. Something — even something futile and absurd — to work toward.

"We can keep trying," Dakota said.

"Where? How? What's left? It's like you said. He's too far away to find if he's even still there."

"Then we can try for others. Build a critical mass. Bear has been tracking Kassidi's stream. She's divergent already. The seed is planted, just like we intended. She'll break out. She'll find us."

"So, she'll join us, and we'll have one more person. Then what?"

Calliope was supposed to be the beacon. She'd been so optimistic when Dakota first came here. The woman with a plan. When Dakota found this place, still wanting blood in Sarah's name, she'd taken great comfort from Calliope's single-minded purpose — how angry she'd been and how Hell-bent on punching her way to change. Now, she was sorrow personified.

"You didn't used to be this way," Dakota said.

"What way?"

"Weak. Broken. Afraid."

"This after you just told me to see the medic?" Calliope asked.

"Yesterday didn't cause this. You've been a shadow of yourself for months."

"I see. Then maybe you'd like to be in charge."

The self-pity clawed Dakota's eyes from the inside. It was one thing to give up, as they'd all said before Kassidi — and now, in the few hours since, had quietly agreed would happen for good — but it was something else entirely to become the opposite of competence and confidence. To become this weak, simpering, forgettable thing before her now.

"Why are you here?" Dakota asked.

"Excuse me?"

"You heard me. Why did you form Immunity? Why did you recruit us? You sucked half the people here out of their only chance at rehab. The other half——"

"Chamber Therapy's isn't actually about rehab. You know that. If I hadn't hacked into Bear, and Shinelle, and——"

"*The other half,*" Dakota bulldozed on, "found you because of a promise. I thought there was no way out from the crib. I was pissed off but had nowhere to pour my energy. Your reputation made a vow. To me and everyone who believed in you. We'd never have come if we'd known you'd given up."

"I haven't given up. In fact, I was *just* saying that inside Kassidi, I got the idea to——"

"To rip through the construct keeping us separate? To spill our mentality into one big pot and hope it all worked out? You can't tunnel from sim to sim. You goddamn well know that."

"It's the only way to find Carter," Calliope said.

"Oh, for Christ's sake." Dakota's head rolled on her shoulders so violently, she thought it might unscrew and fall to the floor. "*Again* with Carter. Why is Carter Shaw so goddamn important?"

"He just is."

Dakota threw up her hands. The same old arguments playing on repeat. "*He just is!* Well, why didn't I think of that? You're right. Now I get it. I *finally* understand why we risked life and limb to find him then just gave up."

"We didn't give up!"

"No? Why are we standing in front of his son's pod, Calliope? Are you going to go after *Mason* now?"

"Mason is Pattern Black."

"*Carter* is Pattern Black!"

"It's different."

"*How?*" Now she was begging. She'd tried to stay on her moral high horse, but the ledge up there was too unsteady. Truth was, nobody really knew any of this other than Calliope. She'd told them they had to reach Carter Shaw. She'd shown them how before he'd been moved, but she'd never explained why — at least not to Dakota's satisfaction. She'd hinted Chamber Therapy was more complex, perhaps even sinister, than was publicly known but refused to offer any details. It was maddening. And it made Dakota want to beat the truth from her body or take her ball and go home. But in the end, as frustrating as her silence was, Calliope remained Immunity's best hope. She wasn't sharing all she knew, but still, she knew something.

Calliope slumped again. Trying to be strong yet unable.

"Jesus, Calliope. Just go back to bed."

"I have work to do."

"What work? Shinelle says your baseline is way off. You're all amygdala, barely any frontal lobe."

"Now Shinelle's the expert? Now she knows me better than I know myself?"

"I saw the scan, too. Your neural patterns are … strange. You need rest."

"Strange how?"

"I know you think you're analyzing problems. But all night long, your brain reads like you were distracted. Your head is elsewhere." Dakota tapped a screen, cued to Shinelle's medical panel. "Still. Even now."

Calliope regarded the screen. Then she reached for the back of her head and came away with a small plastic disc. She stared at it as though the thing had offended her before throwing it across the room. "You're monitoring me? Like a patient?"

"Like someone who needs rest she's refusing."

"I slept all night long."

"It's not enough." Dakota looked at the screen again, but Calliope had removed the sensor, so the lines were all dead. "An alarm went off. Shinelle was coming to get you, but I said I'd do it. You're… not well."

Calliope scowled. "Bullshit."

"You're chasing ghosts. You don't even know what you're after anymore."

"I'm after Carter Shaw."

"Why?"

Nothing.

"Why won't you tell us? What are you hiding?"

"It's complicated," said Calliope.

"It doesn't sound complicated at all. We've cashed in a mountain of chits. Our lockers are stuffed with weapons, and we have your schematics. Bear scoped all the immersion stations. They're guarded by drones, which you can get to look the other way. What's stopping us?"

She stared at Calliope, but the woman stayed silent.

"You want to bring this prison down? Let's storm, hit, and retreat! We can pull all the records. Copy them onto drives so it won't matter when access is severed. That's as good a plan as any if you want to find Carter. Either we'll see where he's being kept or find proof they recycled him. Either way, we can move on. This *plan* of yours?" Dakota made a face. "Random hacks won't get us anywhere. Best-case scenario, we get a few more soldiers — but then what the hell will that army do when it gets here? We've seen the worst-case scenario — we end up in the one place worse than prison, trapped inside another person's mind."

"Nobody got trapped," Calliope said, but she was waning.

"We got lucky. Between that and this, I'll take the HRO all day. It's cold here, the food sucks, and I'm tired of smelling everyone's feet, but at least in here, I can *decide* to die if I want to. There's a way out inside every weapons locker. But in there? What would you have done if we hadn't been able to get you out, Calliope? You'd have been inside Kassidi's head until she died, and every minute would feel like a week. I can't even imagine it."

"If you wanted to help, you could find Kassidi. Kill her to kill me."

A bitter laugh. "I can't believe you just said that. You're supposed to be the freedom fighter. You're supposed to be the good guy. Is this the mission now? We can't get to Blake, and we can't get to Carter. So, let's just kill prisoners. Have I got that right?"

"Everyone's okay. Nothing happened."

"But it could have, right?" Dakota placed one hand on her hip, hating the picture but unable to stop herself from painting it. "You need to decide, Calliope. Either you come clean with us, or you admit you don't know shit. One or the other. I know I'm not the only one tired of taking orders without knowing why or having a goal."

"The goal is to end Chamber Therapy."

"Why?"

"You know why."

"I know what you *say!* But where's the evidence? Where's the proof? Just tell me the truth for once. The *whole* truth."

Calliope became quiet. Lips firm. Caught between two unappealing options.

Dakota said, "You're not the only person here with good ideas! Tell us what you think, and maybe we can help. How exactly can we stop something we don't understand? The HRO is the one doing Chamber Therapy, but you're always focused on *Blake*. Why? You say he took Carter off-grid and is keeping him close. If Carter went PB, why keep him? Why not dispose of him?"

"I told you. Carter is different."

"DIFFERENT HOW, GODDAMMIT?"

Calliope closed her mouth. They both waited for others to arrive, curious about the fuss.

No one came.

Dakota tried again. *"Tell me.* Why do you need Carter, but you'll only poke at his son? And why look at Mason at all? What's really happening here?"

Calliope took a breath. Settled.

"I need Carter," she said, "because I made him. And no one else will do."

FORTY-TWO

All Over Again

Dakota had taken a break from packing and was staring at the security monitors when Mason entered.

Calliope was onscreen, either asleep or dead. Dharma One's security systems hadn't gone offline when the HRO abandoned it and locked the place tight. Or so they thought. Calliope had disabled the station's broadcast ability — at least when it came to official channels — but the sensors still functioned.

Dakota pinched in on her sleeping image before Mason could speak. Then she navigated to a different layer, trying to find vitals. But the sensors only went so deep, and without attaching something to Calliope, the security feed would only show her body heat. Mason could tell she was warm but couldn't determine her heart rate or breathing pattern, and certainly not her mental state, which could be anything at all. From what he'd heard of her near escape, Calliope's thoughts could harbor any temperament or set of beliefs. If they woke her, it would be like nudging a dog that might bite.

"What are you up to?" Mason eyed the half-packed bag.

"Getting ready to leave."

"You wanted to find Calliope, and we found her. Now, you want to go?" Again, he looked at the bag.

"There's no help here," Dakota said.

"Are you sure?"

"I'm sure."

"But what she said … about the two halves of herself?"

"Exactly. There are two Calliopes now. That's one too many."

Dakota turned from the monitor back to her angry packing. She was moving too aggressively, shoving rather than placing things into the bag. She'd barely slept, raking over old coals and rehashing fury, so it felt fresh again.

Mason grabbed her wrist. An unopened can of corn, stolen from Calliope's abundant stores, hit the floor.

"It was your idea to come here. Help me understand."

"You want to understand? Fine." She made a peace sign and touched the first of her two raised fingers. "One Calliope is stuck in the system. That's the one you met, so I guess she found a way out of Kassidi's Fun Factory." She touched the second finger. "The other is sleeping in the situation room. She's a grumpy old bitch. Used to believe in something, couldn't get what she wanted, then gave up and abandoned us without a word. Until we showed up yesterday when her fucking drones almost killed us."

"But they didn't. That has to mean something."

"Her drones are keyed to the same blood dongle as the prison drones, except hers can see through the blind spot. They saw *Shaw*, and that was enough."

"So, she went off on her own. Doesn't mean she can't help. You said it meant something that she put that Muse thing on my face, so let's at least figure out what. Unless, of course, you want to give up, too."

"But that's the thing, Mason. *She* didn't put anything on you." Dakota pointed in Calliope's general direction. "*She* has been sitting here playing with herself. Making drones. Making—" Dakota waved around the room, her frustration barely letting her speak clearly. "Making all of *this* bullshit!"

She walked to a console then hit a rigged contraption of unknown purpose with the heel of her hand to send it flying to the floor in a flurry of cowlings and wires.

"But her other half—"

"The Calliope who tried to reach you inside your simulation is probably even more fucked up than the one we have here." Dakota now sounded more defeated than angry. "You know what happened, but there's no way to convey how terrifying it was to be inside Kass's mind. I couldn't trust the world around me when I came out. But Calliope? The half of her that stuck around? She *didn't* come out. She might be working with the Preacher guy you keep mentioning. Hell, knowing that bitch's mad genius, I wouldn't be surprised if she's the one who made him."

Mason said nothing, but his gut said that wasn't true.

"Or is working with him. I know this is confusing, but ..." Dakota sighed. "I'm just saying, don't put too much faith in *any* version of Calliope, especially one who went through what 'Virtual Calliope' went through."

"You can't know what she went through. Nobody can."

However, Mason wasn't so sure of that, either. *He'd* been trapped inside Pattern Black longer than Calliope had been in the system. He'd gone deeper and had to make it more his home — yet he'd survived. And with his sanity intact.

Behind his eyelids, Mason saw Preacher rising to meet him. He saw the white room with the black dots, which he'd dreamed of last night as vividly as being there. He'd sensed the power of that tiny black hurricane. It'd been inches away. Close enough to touch.

Well. *Sane*, more or less.

Dakota shook her head. "When Calliope — *whole* Calliope for the last time — was trapped inside Kass's mind, Bear boosted the extraction signal to try and pull her out. By then, it was down to brute force."

She gestured toward the console Calliope had used the night before. "I looked over the records, and I think I understand what happened. Bear's beam broke into two parts. The AI saw the situation and tried to help. But it 'helped' by *multiplying* Calliope — by trying to make her stronger than what was holding her back. We thought it worked, but half of Bear's retrieval beam put Calliope's head back into her body while the other half bounced back into the construct. Like copying a file."

Mason shook his head. "You said you were all afraid you'd be trapped inside Kassidi if Bear couldn't pull you out, but this Digital Calliope or Virtual Calliope or whatever … I saw her in my Heist."

Dakota hesitated a partial second before responding, long enough to let Mason remember she still didn't believe he'd done the Heist because that was impossible. Her refusal felt obstinate. Everything they'd learned since the moment he woke — including the awakening itself — was technically impossible.

"That's right. She seems not to have stayed inside Kass for long. The records show a second mind inside Kass when we first tried her extraction, but at some point, that mind disappeared. It took Kassidi a few weeks to act on what we planted inside her. When she found us at Dharma Four, we did a scan to make sure she wasn't bugged, same as we always do. The scan is a lot like Chamber Therapy. I'll bet that's when it happened."

"When *what* happened?"

"When Digital Calliope escaped. The system at Dharma Four still uses HRO code keys. Same as here at Dharma One. Four doesn't have the equipment this place does, but it has pods, immersion inputs, and a biofilter. We run everyone through it before they join us. Kass came up clean when we did hers. Nobody thought it'd be otherwise, but after we figured out this 'two Calliopes' thing last night, I didn't understand how. *There was another person inside her.* Why didn't it show? I can only guess it must have jumped out when it saw the network. Turned on all our systems as it went, too. *That*, I remember. The lights came on, though they had stopped working a while before. The machines rebooted, even though there was no connection. I think it was *her* — the digital half of Calliope, trying to get our attention."

Mason's eyes ticked sideways as he considered that.

Dakota, who knew him well, could easily read his mind. "She's not still in the Dharma Four system. Calliope is a pattern, not code. She needs a place to root. Like a plant, needing soil."

"So, where did she go?" Mason asked.

"Maybe into you."

"Me?"

Dakota shrugged. "All of you. All the sleepers. Or, more accurately, into the one thing you share. None of you could really think. She had to find somewhere without thought so her own mind could do the thinking."

"I don't understand."

"*Pattern Black*, Mason. She went into Pattern Black. Into nothingness. You want to know why I want to get out of here? Because the person we need to talk to isn't around. *That* person is a ghost."

"But I talked to her. She put that thing over my——"

"*If* that's actually what happened. In order to dream, your mind has to create and actualize the imagery. We'd have seen activity on your brain logs."

"Are you …?" Mason didn't believe what he was hearing. "Are you still saying I imagined it all?"

"No! That's exactly it, Mason! You couldn't *imagine* anything! You were *dead!*"

"And *she's* the delusional one?" Mason made incredulous gestures. "Look where we are! I led us here. I saw Calliope. I had the clue that told us where she was hiding. You both said it was impossible she could be inside the simulation when she's clearly out here in the real world, but then you found a perfect explanation to fit my story. Are you really trying to tell me it's all a big coincidence? That I was in a plain old coma, got some harebrained idea after I woke up, and my dumb idea somehow synced perfectly with everything we've learned since?"

Dakota closed her eyes, shook her head, then looked at Mason with peace in her eyes. She didn't want to fight, but the illogical logic wasn't enough to convince her.

"Even if you're right, you met the virtual version of Calliope in another world. If the fingerprint wasn't so clearly on you, I wouldn't even believe it, but like you said, here we are. *This* Calliope — the one sleeping in there like a drunk — didn't know her double existed. That means they're not connected. Whatever happened ripped her in half. Two Calliopes, each with her own life. We're talking about *an autonomous digital entity*, Mason. A ghost in a place we can't even reach."

"Maybe with the computers …"

"It doesn't work that way."

"Or maybe Calliope — I mean, *this* Calliope — can help us find a way to—"

Dakota shook her head. "Everything I've seen says on the day Bear doubled-up that beam, the two Calliopes — physical on the one hand, mental on the other — were exact duplicates of each other. But I don't think that's how it happened. I think the one trapped inside got all the courage and all the pluck our leader used to have. We got the husk. After Kassidi's incursion, *that* Calliope" — Dakota pointed to the closed door — "became cowardly and stupid. I kept trying to propose ways Immunity could act and actually do some damage. I figured if we couldn't find your father, at least we could make some noise. But she refused. Blamed it on a fail-safe at the HRO."

"What fail-safe?"

"They walled off a city and filled it with prisoners," Dakota said. "There was always a chance something would go wrong. Carter was part of those discussions. He lobbied for or against the fail-safe. I don't remember which. Either way, the state agreed to go with Revival's HRO plan, but only if the place was mined. They can flip a switch and cause all the dongle tags in our blood to attract one another. Your blood becomes a giant clot, and that's all there is to it. But it's like a nuclear deterrent. Nobody would ever use it. There are politics and prisoners' families to consider, lawsuits that'd come from anything so catastrophic. Still, Calliope acted like it was a given. They'd send drones if we went in heavy. She gave up. But not the Calliope who came after you, who's still breaking into sims, still out there and trying to make a difference."

"So … what?" Mason stuttered. "We're just going to leave? Go back to Immunity?"

"If Calliope is to be part of this, what are our options? We can talk to this bitch and get nowhere, or we can talk to the digital

Calliope ... except we *can't even reach her*. So, give me Option Three — going back and sleeping in my own bed."

"But ... I fucking *woke up!* After *three years!* I can't just sit down with you all and pretend nothing happened!"

"Sure you can. That's exactly what I did. After Sarah, I was ready to rip off some heads. I found Immunity, and for a while, that's what it looked like we were going to do. But then, *nothing.* Believe me, sitting down with all of us isn't the worst you could do."

He thought of Preacher, waiting just beyond the veil with his hands extended and ready to strangle. He thought of that white room — those black dots in a spiral, all with creatures inside. He thought of the swirling black vortex and how Preacher seemed to covet it. And most of all, more and more, Mason thought of his father.

Carter was the unseen third here, holding court somewhere near the back of his skull. He was, of course, dead and gone. Except Mason still heard his old man inside, asking how many fingers he was holding up. Asking when Mason was going to get off his ass and do what had to be done.

He sat at the console, attempting to make sense of what Dakota pulled up, knowing he'd never be able. The information on-screen was plain as day to her, but she'd had years to learn it, and he was comparatively illiterate.

Mason touched the screen. Not to provoke an action, but almost with affection. "This is what found me."

"Seems so. It's the only other thing in the system that could have embossed you with Calliope's fingerprint."

"But it's not her. Not the one we met. Not the Calliope you found when you got here."

"It used to be, but I think a lot has changed since they split. It looks like the Calliope inside is now its own thing, with its own life."

"Like AI," Mason said, still pondering the screen.

"Nothing like AI. It's a mind without a home. Unless you're in there with the thing, it looks like ones and zeroes."

Again, he touched the screen. "An autonomous being, inside a machine."

"*Two* autonomous beings," said Calliope.

They looked up to find her standing in the doorway.

"What?" Dakota asked.

"I said there are two of them. *Two* minds without a home, not just the one. You want to tell Mason 'the truth' and run home like quitters, maybe you should tell him *that.*"

Dakota bristled but said nothing.

Calliope, failing to sense Dakota's anger or beyond caring, sat with them. "I couldn't sleep. Something was bothering me. You said you never understood why I was so paranoid. I *wasn't* paranoid. Something really was after us."

"A drone," Dakota said.

"Think again."

Dakota moved next to Mason, focusing renewed attention on the screen. She knew some of it, but apparently not enough.

"I couldn't tell you why I left because the system reads me every time I go in searching. It would know if I told you and be able to chase the rest of Immunity."

"What are you talking about?" Dakota asked.

"There's a second entity inside," Calliope explained. "At first, I thought it was AI like you said. But after seeing the copy of myself still in there, it all clicked into place. AI is algorithm-based. It isn't persistent or dogged or determined or stubborn. The thing after us always was. I avoided it for as long as I could, but in the end, the only way to keep it from bringing Immunity down was for me to leave. It wanted me? Fine. I'd cut myself off then let it have me."

Dakota turned to Calliope, probably wondering how to react. According to her stories, Calliope, in later years, had been an incommunicative, stubborn, cock-blocking asshole. Seeing her as anything else now must feel like a defeat.

"What is it?" Mason asked. "The thing that's been chasing you."

"Another autonomous life form. That's all I can conclude." Calliope paused for reaction, but none came. "Only, it doesn't read like a human. It reads like living code." She looked to Mason. "Tell me again about what you saw while inside. You were a prisoner at the red crib. What else?"

Mason tried to give the short version, but whenever he skimmed past something, Calliope asked him to elaborate.

Composing herself once finished, Calliope spoke as if waking from a long rest. "This is a theory, but I ran your story through the gauntlet last night, trying to riddle it out, and I'm fairly confident of my conclusion."

"Which is?" Dakota prompted.

Calliope sat forward and met Mason's eyes. "You have a psychic bond to your father. Don't you?"

Mason waffled. It sounded so ridiculous, stated aloud. "It sometimes seemed that way."

"Seemed? Or was?"

Again, Mason could only shrug.

"Was," Dakota said.

They both looked at her. She nodded encouragement at Mason. He'd told her, of course, but it'd sounded so much less absurd under the blanket of midnight, in bed, when the world went still enough to make magic feel possible.

"Was," Mason agreed.

Now Calliope nodded. "It's obvious once you know what to look for. I examined your logs. What seemed like a flatline when observed from above suggests, upon closer inspection, a part of you kept trying to reach out. Same for Carter. I never understood what his signal was reaching *for*, but, put the two pieces together, and it looks like a pair of bacteria extending pseudopods to shake hands. It always seemed incomplete because I only saw half the puzzle."

She paused again for Dakota to interject, but Dakota was rapt, waiting for more.

"Nobody knows what happens in Pattern Black because nobody ever comes back," Calliope continued. "Looking at scans, you'd swear *nothing* happens. But someone has finally come back, and he's telling us there's more down there than nothing. I'm starting to think we should give it more weight than we have been. Especially once I put the psychic pieces together."

"Why does that matter?" Mason asked.

"We all leave pieces of ourselves behind. The whole liberation process, where we hack into minds and try to wake them, is based on that idea. Kassidi came to Immunity because we planted something inside her using an early iteration of the Muse. That was deliberate, but minds are complex. Incursions involve mixing two minds, and that's probably four or five times the complexity, not just two. I'm starting to believe when we went in, we left bits of ourselves behind without meaning to, like footprints on carpet."

"What makes you say that?"

"Because Carter did it for you. Intentionally, unintentionally, I have no idea. He's been under longer than anyone, and the two of you keep reaching for the fences. Of course, he left thoughts behind. And of course, you, as his son, were able to pick them up."

Mason looked at Dakota, but she offered no help. To Calliope, he said, "What are you telling me?"

"Your father built you a nest, Mason. He was in Pattern Black before you, and I think he left an impression of his own experience behind."

"What's that mean?"

"You never did the Heist simulation, but Carter did. You never lived in the red crib, but Carter did. You were never in gen pop, walking the streets, but Carter did all those things. You knew about the drones before you saw them. Chits. Kiosks. Curfew. Even a handful of inmates. I looked up 'Frank Watt.' He died in a gang fight a few months back, but he was here during your father's time. According to HRO records, they shared an intake group. Their cots were near each other in the crib. And most importantly, he was in the same Chamber Therapy cohort as your father."

"Are you saying … What? That I was living my father's life while in Pattern Black?"

Calliope shrugged. "I know you shouldn't feel like you know me, or Bear, or Kassidi. How were they in your sim, and how were they so true to the real people behind them? *We* never met … but for a while, everyone in Immunity knew Carter."

"You think my father left behind his knowledge of this place and all of you for me to find?"

She nodded. "There's supposed to be nothing there. It's raw space. Yet you had a complete experience you couldn't have had any other way, so it's the only conclusion."

"What about Leigh?" Mason asked. "Unless there's something I don't know, she was never in the HRO. Not with me, and not with Carter. Maybe some of what I experienced was actually a replay of my father's experience, but some of it wasn't true at all."

Calliope nodded. "You're a lot like him. Even at a distance, your minds seem to work together. You were both uniquely responsive to Pattern Black. I wouldn't say you were *susceptible* to it, not the way you were told, like it was more of a danger for you than anyone else. You were just ... *unique* ... where Pattern Black was concerned. Specifically, you seem to have given precedence to your own thoughts, even in the middle of all that nothing. Another way to say it is you're stubborn. *Unbelievably* stubborn. And with *two* unbelievably stubborn minds working together ..."

"So ... *Leigh?*"

"If 'Leigh' is a real person you saw in the sim but who wasn't actually in the HRO, your mind put her there. What you experienced in Pattern Black was mostly through your father's eyes — but because you're also stubborn, your mind added its own elements. Your stuff blended with what Carter left behind, giving you a weird stew that probably felt half like reality, half like a dream. I wouldn't think about it too much. It's not something you'll ever be able to lay out and fully dissect. You'll never completely understand, no matter how hard you try."

"Dakota's real, but she was inside, too."

"Any Dakotas you met inside were false, obviously — your mental projections rather than the real thing." Calliope's face grew curious. "You said she was in both levels of the simulation — in your first experiences at the prison, when you saw her as the director of HRO intake, and then your experiences after she woke you up, into the next level of simulation. Is that right?"

Mason nodded.

"I was particularly interested in your internal versions of Dakota because I have her real scans for comparison. Differences between your two fake Dakotas, as far as I've been able to glean from the logs, gave me insight into what probably happened with that first fake wake-up. You know, when you came out of a tube of slime?"

"What *did* happen?"

"I think that first awakening was your mind trying to emerge from Pattern Black on its own after Digital Calliope found you in the Heist and used her version of a Muse. Hers was virtual, like Digital Calliope herself, so it could only wake you into a higher simulation, not all the way up and out. Afterward, your mind tried to take it the rest of the way, following subconscious suggestions from the Muse. The second sim should have felt closer to reality than the first one, but still not quite right. At that point, your world was more *you* and less of your father. Maybe people in the sim started calling you Mason instead of Carter. Maybe you saw things that were still surreal but at least closer to reality."

It sounded right, but it would take some time to process. What had felt like LSD flashbacks in the second simulation had been his own mind trying to nudge him to wake the rest of the way. Like the world turning white and Preacher appearing from thin air.

Calliope situated herself on the chair and shifted the topic.

"And all of that was fascinating. But what interested me most — what we need to figure out and deal with — was this idea of a second entity. I didn't have the context to know that's what we'd been seeing all along until I accepted there's a sentient copy of myself still inside the machine, living her own independent life. Once I knew that — and that Digital Calliope was autonomous in a way code or an AI never would be — I had a frame that let me understand this other." She leaned closer. "The records suggest you saw it, Mason. Did you see anything inside like I'm describing?"

Mason looked at Dakota. She nodded for him to answer.

"You mean Preacher."

"Who's Preacher?" Calliope asked.

A crazy story, but as he heard his own words anew, Mason found he could increasingly put them into order. Preacher wasn't a god, after all. He was a demon in a box, trapped safely beneath them. All the chaos that "independent entity" had caused was now inside a jar with its lid screwed tight.

Calliope nodded when he finished. "It makes sense. Once I knew what to look for, I could see your Preacher's footprints everywhere. It seemed to be following us back when I was with Immunity. In the background, unseen but felt, with every incursion we made. It appeared to be waiting, never coming forward, and eventually stopped following Immunity. Then it stopped following *me*—"

Mason knew what was coming.

"—and started following you, instead."

"Why?"

"I don't know. Maybe you were more interesting, by whatever criteria its creator programmed into it. Or maybe it outgrew its original programming as it attained sentience and simply decided, for reasons of its own, to change targets."

"What does it want?"

He remembered Preacher standing over him, eyeing that turbulent black vortex.

Give. Give now or I'll rip you open to find it.

Mason looked to Dakota. "Thank God I got out."

"Not so fast. Even if your Preacher can't come into the real world, he's dangerous." Calliope tipped her head toward the room where paperwork still littered the floor, and three monitors remained lit. "I know what it looks like now. As soon as I understood what we were dealing with, I realized I could track it. Kind of."

"Kind of?" said Dakota.

"It's a little like watching whales. Ever go on a whale-watching tour?"

Dakota and Mason both shook their heads.

"You spend most of your time looking out at the calm blue ocean, and every once in a while, a whale comes to the top. That's what it's like, tracking this Preacher. I can't see him when he's down deep, but then he'll surface like a humpback breaching for air."

"We're in the real world," Mason said. "He's digital. He can't get us."

"But things like the program controlling the prison fail-safe? That, I think he can get." She got a far-off look in her eyes. "That, I think he'd very much like to get."

"You sound like you know him."

"I know the man who set him on me. That's enough."

Mason knew who she meant — *Blake*. He had guesses about what happened between them, now that he'd heard Calliope's version. Blake unleashed Preacher on Calliope for his own reasons, but then Preacher began making his own choices and decided Mason was more delicious.

The room was quiet. After a long silence, Dakota slapped her thighs with finality, stood, then reached for her backpack.

"You're not leaving," Calliope said.

"We got our answers. There's nothing to be done."

"You *did* get answers." Calliope stood. "But I don't think you're hearing them. I said he's still a threat. The HRO's system was built for human control, but I can already see where he's rewritten code. He may have begun as a character in a glorified video game, but he's evolved into much more."

Calliope buried her hands in her hair and tugged at the strands. "See, I knew the codebase because I wrote it. That means the digital version of myself knew the codebase. It's how she must have tunneled out of Kassidi and how she seems to have taken run of the system. We always thought it was too dangerous to rip through the membranes, to travel from sim to sim, but she's done it. Problem is, I'm not sure she knows she's been followed. Preacher's used all her back doors. He can go wherever she goes. And Digital Calliope's fingerprint isn't on a lot of the new backdoors. That tells me Preacher can write his own. To go where she never cared to go — or maybe even where she couldn't."

Dakota set the backpack down.

"Good move," Calliope said. "You can't leave, much as I wish you could. See, I left my own footprints since you've been here — since I've been digging into archives to discover what happened. After a while, I could see the back of the whale far out at sea. He'd already sniffed my codes by the time I noticed. He seems to know we're here and what we've learned. He has more access than me. Now *he's* the god in the machine."

"But … *in the machine,*" Dakota said.

"The machine still has arms everywhere, including out here. It controls surveillance. And the drones. Like I said, it controls the fail-safe. You both carry blood dongles. If the fail-safe is triggered, you'll be as dead as everyone else."

"You must have contingencies," Mason said.

"We do. Nathaniel and I saw *The Terminator,* same as everyone. Nobody really trusts AI past a certain point — not enough to drop our wallets and turn our backs. We took more than enough precautions, so no, the fail-safe can't be triggered directly. But it does respond to system discord, the so-called 'chaos alarm.' And *chaos,* it can cause plenty of."

She looked hard at Mason, and he understood in a blink that none of what she'd said had been casual. They'd never really been having a conversation. Calliope had opened with a goal in mind, tailoring her words to fit an intended close. She wasn't educating them. She was making a pitch. Building a case — an argument for what came next.

"I slept less than you seem to think I did," Calliope said. "I've been thinking, and you're not going to like what I have to say."

"What?" Dakota asked.

"With the clock ticking — with this Preacher aware and able to find us — there's no longer any choice. There's only one way to stop what's happening, and that's to stop it *all.* Go big or go home."

"And how exactly do we do that?"

"We contact your father."

"But he's … He's …"

"I know. But your minds have been reaching out to each other this entire time — *despite* his Pattern Black. Even though everything we know says Carter should be dead and gone, his influence still managed to reach into your Pattern Black enough to build you a cocoon. Without him breaking your fall, you'd probably have stayed as gone as he is. But his memories gave you enough familiar comfort to survive. With luck, we can follow that tether.

Reach all the way back to the source, wherever Blake is holding him."

"But why?" Mason looked at both women, sure he was missing something. "My father was just a cop. What's so special about him that he can help when you can't?"

Calliope hesitated for a moment as if wondering whether she should proceed. "Carter is special because while I was teaching him the techniques we use to 'tread water' inside unstable space, I embedded something inside his mind he never knew was there. I couldn't hide it inside myself because I was wanted and subject to scans every time I left the protected network. I could have put it in anyone but chose Carter because his investigations made him familiar with Revival's operations, and his stubbornness meant he could hold onto subconscious information, even during fully immersive sims, in ways most people can't. Now I know why. Carter's connection to you gave him a release valve."

She took a breath. Mason thought he heard a hint of defeat in her sigh.

"I thought we could protect him once he was with Immunity. What I'd hidden inside him would be safe, so long as he was with us. But Blake managed to rally the Docents and drones then extracted Carter to an extreme CT session, anyway. The next time he went under, he never came out — and what we need now went with him."

"You hid something *inside* my father?"

Calliope nodded. "A mnemonic originally greenlit by both me and Blake as part of our checks and balances. It forces a system reset and purges anything that shouldn't be there. We have to find Carter so we can force the reset and delete Preacher."

Dakota looked from Calliope to Mason, then back. "How the hell are we going to find Carter? And how are we going to get to him even if we *do* manage to figure out where he is?"

"I don't know."

"Jesus Christ."

"But *she* does," Calliope said.

Mason didn't understand until she looked at the computers.

"You mean—"

"You have to find my digital self. *She's* the one who tried to reach you. She's the one who's tunneled backdoors through the system like rooms in a rabbit warren. If anyone has the answers — or can find them — it's her."

Dakota looked lost. Or maybe afraid. "But ... that version of you is ..."

"She's inside Pattern Black," Calliope said, "where you're going to go, Mason. Again."

FORTY-THREE

Why Blake Kept Him Alive

"No," Mason shook his head, almost violently.

"Hear me out."

"I heard," he told Calliope while Dakota looked on, her expression unreadable. "Three years ago, I came here for an interview that became an intervention. Lucky me, I got to try out a new kind of therapy despite everyone knowing it's an awful idea for someone with my family history. But no big deal. I just spent three years dead, then woke up in prison, fucked — despite never being convicted of a crime. I'm a cop, so I know how big a dick you need to swing if you're hoping to handle 'due process' your own way. So, *you* tell *me*, ladies. *What on this fucking planet* would make me go willingly back into the death I barely escaped from?"

"But—"

"No. Absolutely not. You want to find your other half, *you* go get her." Mason turned to Dakota. "Or you can do it. You wanted to screw with the system and burn something down. You aren't borderline nuts like I am, and you haven't done … whatever *she* did" — he indicated Calliope — "to trap your brain inside the machine. You want it so badly? Great. Go fetch."

"It has to be you," Calliope said.

His head snapped back like a toy on a spring. "Oh, it does, does it? You sound so sure. I guess that's how it is. But have you considered this?" He raised his right hand, then his middle finger.

Calliope looked past the insult, unfazed. "She contacted *you*. I helped design this system, Mason. I know the number of redundancies. The entire network and connected devices are constantly scanned for anomalies because they know minds sometimes fragment. In a learning matrix, the system is designed to adapt to its contents — to learn subject patterns so it can present better, more-attuned moral choices. Didn't you notice how the simulation changed when you fought it?"

He did, but Mason would be damned if he planned to surrender so much as an inch of ground. "So what?"

"Sometimes mistakes are made. It's okay. We always knew it would happen. People learn from the sims, and the sims learn from people. That's why once a day, the entire system is read line-by-line by a team of AI, and that means it's only failing to notice anomalies it's been programmed — say, by the other Calliope or Preacher — to ignore. Think about it for a second. You didn't somehow end up inside Kassidi's mind, and that means if you ran into the other Calliope, you did it somewhere else. *That* means she got out of Kass and into the wider system, apparently carving out a place that can access Pattern Black. Or at least to reach *you* even when you were supposed to be gone. My other half has been evading all of our carefully laid double-checks for what, a year? Two? If it were me on the inside instead of her, I'd break some things and hope the breakage didn't kill me. I'd hide and know how to stay invisible. So, believe me. She won't just *be found. She* has to find *you.*"

"What's to say I won't go in there and fry my brain ... and meanwhile, she's lost interest?"

"She hasn't."

"Really? Why?"

"It's complicated."

"Try me." Then he looked at Dakota, to whom Calliope owed so many answers. "Try *us.*"

"*I'd* never lose interest. I gave up when Carter disappeared because from out here, I can only do so much. But *she* didn't give up. The target was always Carter, but when he turned into a dead-end, she came to *you*, Mason. That tells me she's seen what I just worked out — about your mental connection to your father. If I were her, I'd have seen the son as a new way to reach the father. I think that's why she risked coming out into the open. Why she disturbed your signal enough to wake you up."

"How did she know I *could* be woken?"

"I don't know."

"Then tell me what you do know. Tell me about this shit you put into Carter's head."

"It's—"

"Complicated?"

Calliope shut her mouth, lips pursed.

"Is that all you can say?" Mason's next words were almost a snarl, knowing he finally had the upper hand — the *only* hand, as it turned out. "You want me to even *consider* going back into the meat grinder? Then I'm going to need a damn good reason. I want to be treated like a person, not a goddamn idiot or a tool you can use whenever you want to. You want my help? Then I want the truth. *All* of it."

"Fine." Calliope took a deep breath and sat. On her lead, so did Dakota and Mason. "From the beginning, then?"

"Sure. Pile it on," Mason said. "You'll know if we're bored."

Calliope eyed him then began. "Nathaniel Blake and I co-founded Revival. That you know. We bickered a lot. Publicly. *That* you also know because the tabloids couldn't get enough. It was never a bad thing. It's how we worked through problems and disagreements. We always came to a conclusion somewhere in the middle, and for most of our working relationship, we usually agreed in the end."

She shook her head, looking almost lost in the memory.

"But our last argument was different. Blake was more unsatisfied than I thought he should be. We were getting there, but Chamber Therapy still wasn't meeting its potential. We needed to stand back, see what was working and what wasn't, then make small steps until we got results we could live with and even get excited about. But Blake had been using the base technology for several years before I joined, so his frustration was greater. He didn't want to take the methodical approach. By then, our funds were drying up, and we hadn't yet secured the big state grants. There was other money out there — free funding we could have gotten with some paperwork and oversight — but Blake always insisted he didn't want money with strings. Besides, the problem wasn't just finding money. Blake saw himself as having been far too patient, of having deferred to an ineffective system."

Her faraway look had faded away. She began talking faster.

"We'd been stuck in the same disagreement for months. Blake got edgier by the day. He insisted we were digging our hole deeper and no longer wanted to fix what we had. He wanted to shut the program down and try again with a new OS. We were deadlocked. We hadn't piloted the program. Instead, we'd rolled it out into every Revival-owned HRO from the start. Blake insisted we didn't need to pilot it before expanding. The original uses of CT — for therapy in a clinical setting, plus all the work he'd done with both autistic and gifted kids — *were* the pilot. I should have suspected something from the start. You ended up in prison without being convicted. That's not supposed to happen, but neither is a large-scale medical/psychological experiment without controlled trials, a pilot, or miles of red tape. We had none of that and didn't need it. Blake had built a loophole, knowing he'd end up using it."

"What loophole?" Mason asked.

"The HRO system required a certain relaxing of the usual 'social rules' in order to work. Crime was at an all-time high. The entire country had split into 'us' and 'them.' Lawmakers were willing to do just about anything to solve the problem and get reelected. So, we pitched an idea — prisoners enter an HRO for life. Supposedly those with lighter offenses get a few privileges that make for a more lenient sentence, but we all know that's bullshit. All are declared 'unpersons' upon sentencing to simplify the transition. It got us off the hook in cases where Chamber Therapy warped a subject's personality but declaring convicts 'unpeople' meant they had no civil liberties. Blake stacked political favors like a master bricklayer. I have to hand it to him. By the time we hit our log jam, he'd built a wall around himself and a way to move forward."

Mason nodded, wary. "And what was that?"

"He got wide-scale approval to privatize California's prisons by offering the state a deal it couldn't refuse. We refunded our tax credits to the government and cut the state in on pretty much the entirety of our profits. The HROs, seen only as prisons, followed a business model that broke even only near capacity. Any misstep and the prisons lost money. The model was unsustainable by itself, but that was fine because admittance was our loss-leader. When everything shook out, Revival was basically providing free incarceration to the state in exchange for a chance to 'sell' Chamber Therapy to lawmakers as an alternative to incarceration. We had NIH funding for Chamber Therapy, plus a few black-hat grants I discovered later from folks like the NSA. The CIA. The people who brought you MK-ULTRA. I'm ashamed I didn't see it. The applications of Chamber Therapy in different hands were obvious. And very, very lucrative."

"So, Chamber Therapy was the goal," Dakota said, "because, for every person you put through it, you got, what? Some sort of a credit from the feds?"

Calliope nodded. In that nod, Mason could almost see an apology. No doubt she had asked all these questions before. Until Mason dug in his feet, Dakota had gotten none of them.

"That was part of it," Calliope said. "It was obscured a bit, clear enough to understand but vague enough to justify as legit. Revival isn't a public company. We could be cagey with our accounting, and nobody cared too much. Everyone understood where part of the money came from, but it shouldn't have been enough. I had suspicions but nothing concrete, and I couldn't find out more without making an overt move against Blake — something that would give him reason to batten down the hatches so I *wouldn't* find anything, then do whatever it took to shut my mouth. So, I planted a few little seeds in the code. After I left — entering the HRO while it was still under construction, then letting them build it around me — I went back to my seeds. They gave me a tunnel to see into what he'd been hiding. And that's when I saw where our company's real profit came from."

Mason almost didn't want to ask. Dakota apparently did. "Where?"

"Pattern Black is, in essence, a specific kind of brain death. If your brain goes flat, even if you were able to kickstart it, it'd still be the same old brain. Pattern Black, on the other hand, is less like slipping into a coma and more like formatting a hard drive. Chamber Therapy can be used to cure and sometimes does. But it's a Trojan horse most of the time. The harmonics of CT sort of poke at a person's mind, and if the mind feels suitable, those same harmonics start the process of shutting it down. That's Revival's dirty little secret. Pattern Black isn't an unfortunate side effect that happens once in a blue moon. It's the goal. And when the mind is suitable to reformatting, it happens one hundred percent of the time."

Mason thought of his father. If he understood this right, Carter had been Pattern Blacked more to shut him up than to harvest his brain. But if that was true, why was Blake still holding him?

"Why would Revival do that?" It was half question, half plea to the universe. The way a grieving wife cries WHY over her dead husband's body. Mason studied Dakota's profile and thought of her sister Sarah — gone for profit and used for purposes unknown.

"Because when someone goes Pattern Black," Calliope said, "they become like a shell. Their brains become an empty vessel that can be used for all sorts of things normal brains can't. Blake's memoranda even have a name for people formatted by Pattern Black. Mental cadavers."

Dakota's hand went to her mouth.

"*Cadavers*," Mason repeated. "Like the bodies they use in medical school."

Calliope nodded. "Normal cadavers let anatomy students learn surgery and dissection without the fear of hurting a living person. Mental cadavers do the same for people interested in *mental* surgery and dissection."

"Jesus."

Calliope nodded at Mason. "I know. I can show you records if you'd like. If you have the stomach for it. But all those companies out there looking at nonphysical vacations, neural connectivity, and biological add-ons — not to mention brainwashing, thought manipulation, and torture — every one of them needs a way to test what they can do. Empty minds they can fill with whatever horrors they want, without fear of backlash. Pattern Blacked prisoners are perfect. They're reported as accidental deaths then shipped off like luggage. After the state declares them unpersons, prisoners become more or less like lab animals — ideal subjects to work out the kinks in brain-facing systems."

"It can't possibly be legal," Dakota said.

"Not even close. But even if it were, let's see how far he'd get announcing it to the press." Calliope shook her head. "Everyone in the trade knows something like this is happening, but nobody asks questions because it's expensive to know."

"What's this have to do with me and the other Calliope? And Carter?"

Calliope keyed on Mason's second question, lifting a cup of coffee and sipping ahead of her answer. "When I started having suspicions, I knew threat of exposure would be the only thing capable of maybe moving Blake. Your father was already snooping, so I left something for him to find. I met him a few times, as Elisabeth Reeves, and I told him what I knew — what I could prove, along with a few things I couldn't. We made a plan. Of course, Blake figured it out. And Carter was too stubborn to take any of it back once I was gone and there was nobody on the inside to clear the way. By the time he broke into Revival's offices, anything that could have hurt Blake was already gone."

"So that's why he was arrested. Blake pushed for it."

"He committed a crime. No more and no less. He broke in, so they put him behind bars. And I ..."

Calliope trailed off, but Mason had already figured this part out. Once he'd learned the hacker Calliope was actually the famous Elisabeth Reeves, it became impossible to believe Carter had been nabbed by accident. Calliope had sent Carter to Revival long after

Reeves had gone missing. If Calliope had been anyone else, Mason might have believed the botched job was an honest mistake. But Reeves wouldn't make that error … and therefore, Carter had been nabbed by a set up. Calliope sent him in then sounded the alarm for his arrest.

"You tipped them off. You told the cops he was coming."

Calliope looked caught.

"I had no choice. I needed him inside so I could hook him to a pod and extract the code, but I couldn't tell him what I needed or even who I was, just in case our communications were intercepted. I thought Immunity could protect him. I was wrong." Calliope looked like she might apologize, but she didn't.

Mason was relieved. He didn't want her trying to make nice. She was now, and forever might be, the villain he needed to blame.

Dakota looked toward the corner. Her jaw was firmed with an officer's resolve or possibly with the ire of one sister seeking vengeance for another. She'd made her peace with losing Sarah, but it was something else to mourn a murder. Mason recognized her process — quiet while absorbing the truth, then mythological fury later.

"I'm still not getting it." Mason looked away from Dakota with effort. "Carter was going to help you expose Blake and Revival. You'd prove they weren't in the business of rehabbing prisoners, that Blake was making his money from selling their 'blank-formatted minds' instead. But then he took Carter out of the picture by Pattern Blacking him. If he's supposed to be blank-formatted, how much help can he be? Why are you obsessed with finding him?"

"You were supposed to be blank-formatted, too," Calliope told him.

"Even if he could wake up like I did, what's the point? You don't know where he is."

"You almost sound like you don't want him saved."

"Lady, I made peace with my father's death a long time ago." But that wasn't true — Mason's missing years had him thinking in circles. In his true timeline, what happened to Carter felt much more recent. "Seems like it's time to be a little more practical.

You've got a story to tell. Maybe some evidence to find. There must be other ways to get the word out. Even if it starts as a rumor, that could be enough. You only need a reason for people to start asking the right questions."

Calliope looked down and twiddled her fingers in her lap. "Maybe that's true. Maybe, if people started to talk, Blake wouldn't be able to explain or hide his way out of it. But exposing him was only half the mission."

Dakota looked over and waited. According to her, Calliope had always said exposing Blake *was* the mission.

Calliope sighed as if wondering how well she'd hanged herself. "I guess I should tell you why Nathaniel and I finally parted ways."

Mason sat forward. "Parted ways" was putting it mildly. The world had seen the dissolution of Revival's twosome like the climax of a magic trick. One day Elisabeth Reeves had been there, then the next, she was gone. The media shitstorm had been unrelenting.

"Mind science is the next big frontier. Think about it. What else is left?" Calliope waited for an answer that never came. "That's the main reason we never took our eye off the ball, even when things got bad. If we could find a way to hang in there, things *had* to turn around. Everyone thinks Revival is the only company on the cutting edge, able to do what we do. But there are others, believe me. Their lawyers never stopped sniffing around. We had to burn our trash because they'd steal even shredded paper to put it together and see what we were up to. By the time of our split, Nathaniel's paranoia was jet-fueled. He kept going on about our 'one big problem.' The one massive security leak we could never fix and would eventually bite us in the end."

"Which was?" Mason asked.

"The patients."

"*The patients*," he repeated. "You mean the *prisoners?*"

Calliope nodded. "Anyone who goes through Chamber Therapy — rehabbed or Pattern Blacked — has a full map of our process inside their heads. You already know we give a drug at the end that causes retrograde amnesia. The decisions they make inside the sim still alter their minds in the ways that make Chamber Therapy 'work' in the few cases it's *allowed* to, but all the specifics — of the simulations used, plus the process itself — are forgotten. It's not perfect, but it's enough. Or at least, it's supposed to be."

"And it's not?" Dakota asked.

"Some people are immune to the drug," Mason said.

He realized immediately the knowledge he'd just dropped had come from Nic, inside his simulation. But whether or not the real Nic had been immune, a resistance to the drug was clearly a thing because Calliope bobbed her head. Carter would have known if he'd spent time with Calliope, and Mason had been living Carter's thoughts while under. A twisted way to be correct — a whole new kind of truth.

"The psychotropic compound we used to make a patient's mind susceptible to Chamber Therapy is rather large. We had a difficult time getting it to cross the blood-brain barrier so it could do its work. This part is complex, but the workaround involves a 'gateway' molecule that helps our primary compound reach its destination. We designed it to ride on the blood dongle injected by the prison as a tracker." She narrowed her eyes at them both. "You see where this is going?"

Dakota sat up. "The fail-safe."

Calliope nodded. "That's right. The clotting fail-safe — used as a nuclear option to quell prison riots should the entire place get out of hand — can be triggered manually by Revival, thanks to some clever biochemistry. In its default state, our gateway molecule has one end that attaches to the prison-injected blood dongle and another that attaches to cell receptors. But if the polarity is flipped using a broadcast hub in Revival's offices, the same gateway molecule suddenly won't attach to cell receptors at all. Instead, 'activated' gateways have affinity for the dongle molecule on *both* ends. That means it has the potential, if activated, to attach to two dongle-tagged red blood cells at once."

"You're saying if Blake wants, he can push a button and trigger the fail-safe on his own and bypass the chaos alarm? He doesn't need to wait for riots and disorder. He can just kill everyone whenever he wants?"

"Everyone who carries a prison-issued blood dongle and our gateway molecule, yes. If you've gone through Chamber Therapy and are immune to the memory drug, you're a potential leak. Fortunately, if you've done Chamber Therapy, you're also inside a prison. Prisoners all carry the dongle and are, legally, no longer people. It's a brutal but elegant solution to Blake's problems — kill all potential informants and clot the evidence beyond recognition."

Dakota looked like she'd been hit by a truck. "You're serious? Blake wanted to …" She stalled, and Mason knew she had to be thinking about her sister. "He wanted to kill off people who'd had Chamber Therapy?"

"He wanted the *ability* to," Calliope corrected. "He was very rational about it. When Nathaniel finally got the guts to pitch me the idea, he said we wouldn't ever use it unless 'we *really really* had to.' He spoke as though it wasn't murder. And in his mind, I'm not sure it was. Anyone who tried the process, was immune to the drugs, and had the audacity to cause problems — Blake figured that was one in a thousand. One in *ten* thousand. By the books, the minority causing a problem was statistically insignificant."

"And what percent goes Pattern Black? Is *that* statistically significant?"

"Preaching to the choir." Calliope spread her arms, indicating her location. "Once I saw I couldn't win — that I was just one more 'potential security leak' he'd anticipated and already taken precautions against — I came here." Her smirk felt hard-earned, like they'd soon be giving credit where it was due. "But it's okay. I took precautions, too."

Calliope smiled and shifted in her chair. Somewhere in the building, an air handler belched to life.

"I couldn't erase the files he needed to build his 'gateway molecules' or he'd have caught me and restored from backups, but I *could* create something Blake wouldn't be able to understand or use without me. Once I realized he wouldn't back down, I agreed to help with his project so long as we could do it my way. My files were all set to self-cannibalize, so he wouldn't be able to recreate anything after I was gone. I gave him a working prototype, and to ensure a uniform process while also saving time, I told him we'd keep cloning new compound from consistent stock. He agreed to everything, but I always felt like he knew what I was up to, or at least suspected it. We circled each other for months, neither trusting the other and both knowing we'd lose the second we flinched. In the end, we settled on a procedure wherein *two* inputs would be needed to activate the system rather than just one. I had half of what was required to activate, and Nathaniel had the rest."

"Like two different people turning two different keys from across the room to launch nukes?"

"Exactly like that," Calliope said, nodding at Mason. "Every patient was injected with the compound, but it was inert unless both of us agreed to activate it. Changing polarity, so the coupler molecules stick together required a signal at a specific frequency, but in order to know what it was, you have to know the sequence of amino acids in the protein. We set ourselves a check-and-balance. Blake controlled the frequency broadcast if needed, but I controlled the sequence of acids in the affected protein. Neither one of us could use the fail-safe without the other, so he couldn't give someone a blood clot because they had a small doubt about the process, and I couldn't kill off a subject I didn't like because she stole my parking spot. We both had to do our part for the fail-safe to work. We *both* had to turn the keys."

Calliope looked smug in the following pause, and in her expression, Mason saw the wiliness of a fox.

"I knew he'd be able to get that information out of me if he really wanted, though, so I left him a video message before I disappeared. In that video, I injected myself with the forgetfulness drug. It meant I couldn't tell him the sequence even if I wanted to. A damn good thing because if Blake had the sequence *and* the frequency, he could shut this entire place down and kill us all — everyone who's ever been through Chamber Therapy."

"Wouldn't that put a kink in his plans to roll it out wider and make a lot more money?"

"Better than ending his life in prison."

"And that won't happen if everyone his company touched

suddenly drops dead?"

Calliope didn't answer, but Mason, as a cop, had seen how effectively money moved mountains. Blake would have an answer if entire prison populations suddenly died. You make an omelet, you break a few eggs. Everyone — including the state and the prisons — knew Chamber Therapy was experimental. That's why it was used only on prisoners sentenced to life. Prisoners who, by law, were no longer people who deserved human rights.

"Unfortunately," Calliope said, "there's still one place Blake can find the sequence he needs. One way for him to get what's required to send that pulse and make the problems go away."

"Where's that?"

"From the cell stock," Calliope said. "The compound is made by sticking a bit of synthetic DNA into a bacterial plasmid, same as the way insulin's made. Usually, something like that is kept frozen or in a solution for cloneable lines, but freezing the cells would have made the evidence against us permanent. I knew as long as I didn't make Nathaniel suspicious, he would follow my lead — and as long as we were still on good terms, he'd believe I was on his side and wanted to hide evidence just as much as he did. So, I convinced him to let the cells live inside a human donor instead of a freezer, where they'd be safe. And erasable, should the need arise."

Now Mason finally understood. "It's Carter, isn't it?"

Calliope nodded. "It couldn't be me, and it obviously couldn't be Blake. This was top-top secret, and I was double-crossing my partner, so I needed a person I could trust and some bullshit explanation Blake would never question. Carter let me surgically insert a small pocket of cells under his skin *here*." Calliope touched her side near where Mason thought her appendix might be. "I argued Carter was a cop — and with apologies, Mason, he was considered a *dirty* cop at the time. I said Carter understood the parts of the mission we officially told him and hadn't made waves, so as long as we didn't tell him what we were hiding in his abdomen, Carter was the safest place for those cells."

"That's why they took him off-grid," Dakota said. "*That's* why Blake kept him alive."

"I think so, yes. But Nathaniel isn't a scientist, so even if he has Carter, he doesn't know how to get what he needs — and believe me, this is too high-stakes for him to start asking other scientists until he absolutely has to. So that's where we are right now — Nathaniel has an asset he can't use, and all the proof I need. *That's* why your father matters, Mason. Nathaniel wants the code in those cells so he can send a signal and erase the security leak, but we're at a stalemate. He can't read the code without me. He can't get me, and I can't get him."

Mason looked from one woman to the other.

"Almost four years," Calliope said. "Almost *four years* we've been doing this. Only now is he making a move. Why?"

Mason looked again, but they were both staring at him.

"What? You think Blake is doing this now because of *me?*"

Calliope answered. "You have a connection to your father. You're accessing his memories. You know about the prison and Immunity. You were Pattern Black for years, but only now did the digital half of me find a way to wake you up. Blake must have seen you wake up, and you can bet your ass he's surprised ... but also very excited. It's not a coincidence, Mason. *You* are what's changed in all this time."

This had all started with a pat refusal that bore no debate.

But Mason could feel the weight of those stares. The importance of what'd been revealed.

Calliope said, "The other half of me — the digital half you met inside — knows something, Mason. I know she does, or she wouldn't have woken you and risked provoking Nathaniel into a move nobody wants him to make. What she knows, we have to learn. But only you have survived Pattern Black. Only you can go back in to find her and learn how to stop what Nathaniel Blake has already begun."

Mason nodded, resigned. "Say I agree. Now what?"

Calliope moved to the room's other end. She touched a button, revealing an entire scrap yard worth of beautifully ugly equipment, all wires and cowlings and chrome.

"Now, you train."

FORTY-FOUR

Forcing a Decision

MASON WAS RUNNING, running, running.

Drones became a V overhead, cutting through the sky like birds.

He looked up, darted left. Dakota would have to make it on her own, as he hadn't seen where she'd gone.

The alley dead-ended ahead. His hand went to his temple and that bitch of a headache.

"Hey, man." A lanky man in a porkpie hat swaggered forward. "Those are some nice shoes."

Mason glanced back. The alley was no longer a dead end. Three other men were headed his way, all converging on him with his nice shoes.

"I'll bet you twenty dollars, I can tell you where you *got* those shoes."

"That's okay." Mason wasn't even paying attention. He was trying to concentrate, down on one knee, like he intended to tie his laces.

"Hey, man," said his new friend. "You hear me?"

"I forgot what I need to do."

"What you need to do is answer my bet."

411

"No, thanks."

"*No, thanks?*"

"My head hurts."

"Tough shit, playboy. My *toe* hurts already from when I'm gonna kick it up yer ass!"

"Just give me a second."

"Stand up, boy."

Mason focused. The world became transparent blue then normal again. When he stood, he found a gun in his face.

"The fuck's going on here?"

He concentrated harder. The brick across from him became sandstone. Then brick again.

"Hey, man. Twenty dollars."

Mason wished the guy would go away. His entire being warbled like a shaken sheet of aluminum, then re-solidified with a gun.

The man with the hat seemed confused. "Whatever you doin', stop it."

Mason closed his eyes. Clenched his fists. Gritted his teeth. Whispered, "You're not real."

"Say what?"

The world became white. Black dots appeared in the distance, pocking the sky in a drawling spiral. The man with the gun was still in front of him with his weapon extended.

"Stop it," he said, his voice uneasy.

"You're not here."

"You hear me, motherfucker? I said—"

A loud noise interrupted him. The world exploded into red and black with a dull but violent feeling like being impaled with a large, blunt lance. Mason's hands went to his chest as he found himself unable to breathe. He woke that way, back in Dharma One. Calliope stood in front of him, her arms crossed.

"What happened? I was doing okay."

"What happened?" Calliope repeated. "What happened is he shot you. You're dead."

Mason looked down. He had wires all over himself, but he very much wasn't dead. The rigs at Dharma One, used originally for

Docent training and modified somehow by Calliope, were at least more dignified than the one he'd woken to earlier. He was mostly standing, slightly reclined, and clothed with nothing up his butt.

"Okay," Mason said. "Put me back in."

"No."

"What do you mean, no?"

"It's a simple concept, Mason. *No*. Maybe you've heard it before?"

"I can do this."

"Clearly, you can't."

Mason looked at the rig. He'd been "training," if that's what his impossibly inept failures could be called, for five days now. The idea that an entire prison world was in orbit around him had become an increasingly academic understanding, without any of the normal tips that gave things veracity.

As Mason, Calliope, and Dakota crouched in their administrative bunker, they saw drones flying around and heard one explosion. A volley of nighttime searchlights suggested a break-in or break-out somewhere, possibly at the prison walls themselves. But ultimately, their bubble hadn't been popped, and sometimes it was hard to believe there was a world out there at all.

The stress of trying to do something impossible wore on Mason, and he found himself almost nostalgic. He missed being part of everyday life, even if it was a prison existence. He missed his obnoxious bunkmates in the red crib. He missed Nic, who didn't actually know him. He missed Leigh, who wasn't really Leigh, or even here in prison. He even missed greasy-haired Watt, a man who was apparently dead.

Too bad none of them was actually waiting for him, were he to fold up shop here and go home.

"One more try," Mason told Calliope.

"No. Rest."

"I'm getting used to the headaches. If I had one more try, I could—"

"See, this is the problem," Calliope said. "You seem to think you just need to push harder. But like I keep telling you, *pushing is the problem.* You need to find a way to hold focused attention while simultaneously going with the flow. Until it's time to fight, *don't fight.* Always go with the flow. We talked about this."

Mason grumbled.

"It's like a tree in a storm." Calliope made swaying trees with her hands, now circling to her console for a seat. Maybe Dakota was sleeping. They had settled into their own routine here, with their own breed of temporary abnormal. "Push against a rigid tree, and it will break. But if the trunk is supple, the tree will bend and survive the wind."

"Am I the wind or the tree?"

"The wind. You're pushing, but I keep telling you not to."

Mason had tried. And tried. And tried. How his mind behaved inside the simulations — Dharma One's trainers first, the real thing later — didn't seem like something he could consciously control. He needed to be conscious and full of his wits to make it inside, but apparently, that meant putting human nature on a shelf.

"Maybe." He reset, knowing how this would land. "Maybe I'm *supposed* to push."

"I see. Okay. Try it. Go in there and fight it all. The matrix won't shatter. You won't find yourself floating through emptiness without so much as a place to stand or anything."

"That's what Pattern Black is," Mason said. "Floating through emptiness."

"Except for you, it was a prison filled with your father's memories."

"*And* emptiness." He kept thinking of the way, when he was inside, Preacher would appear randomly like the world's most violent Jack-in-the-Box, pocking his existence with lotus holes. He couldn't stop thinking about it, despite not wanting to. If Mason was going back in, he'd rather see the prison as he'd seen it the first time. That disembodied, spinning-vortex-in-a-void bullshit had to go.

"Try it my way," Calliope said.

But Mason wasn't listening. Being inside was hard, and that meant her advice to relinquish effort like some sim-hopping stoner was at odds with the fundamental truth of entering in the first place. Calliope was right — his brain *didn't* believe the simulations. It *did* fight. How was he supposed to change the mechanics of his very mind?

"I need rest," he said.

"Too tired for your mind to deal with it?"

"Yes. Five minutes."

"Too tired."

"Yes."

"Good."

She threw a switch. The thing was mechanical rather than electrical and reminded Mason of the knife switch Dr. Frankenstein always threw to raise his monster.

The simulation replaced reality. Suddenly, Mason was running again, his heart's inputs toggled from their real-world normality to the adrenaline-jacked body of his digital avatar. The transition was sudden and terrible. He was out of breath, limbs thrumming forward without his having asked them to.

Mason had to stop almost immediately. He looked up. The drones had stopped chasing him. Three came down to hover around him in a circle.

They're not real.

The drones flickered.

They're not real. It's just a simulation.

One fired something at him — a small sci-fi like laser.

It struck his arm, more a prick than an attempt to harm him. Mason gripped the spot, smelling seared flesh and clothing, genuine as anything. The pain was present and full.

Calliope's voice came to him as if from another world, and he understood a beat later that he was hearing her around his headphones. Real Chamber Therapy, she'd explained, hijacked sensory input at the nerve level. But immersion tech hadn't been quite as developed when Dharma One was abandoned, and in any case, the pods were meant for Docent programs, not long-term immersion, and certainly not for Chamber Therapy. So, yes, he could hear around the headphones. And if his hands could find the invisible goggles, he could see past those, too. Mason, who'd seen both things immediately, had been using them as cheats.

Which was exactly what Calliope kept telling him *not* to do. *Not* to remember, attempt, or believe.

Now he could hear Dakota beyond the headphones. She and Calliope discussing him in hushed tones.

Mason looked at the drone. Thought of the voices.

It's only a simulation.

The whole thing seemed to pop, then vanish. He saw a wireframe where the simulated world had been, like a blueprint. It was quiet and dull. Someone had pulled the plug.

"Dammit," said Calliope's voice.

Then came the sound of fingers tapping on glass. On a control surface.

The world returned as if Mason hadn't just shattered it.

"Try harder and don't break it this time," Calliope told him from the outside world.

Mason ripped his attention from the external sounds, forcing himself to focus on the sim — and, if he could, to believe it was real. He looked ahead, working to believe the alley. Once the idea had mostly settled, he turned left from the main street into a dead end ahead. He was suddenly halfway down. Teleported from here to there by way of decision.

"Hey, man. Those are some nice shoes."

Mason looked behind him. A tall, lanky man in a porkpie hat sauntered toward him.

When Mason raised a hand to his ear, he could feel the invisible cup of a headphone. A similarly invisible hand pulled his away just moments later — Dakota, probably, forcing him to focus and stay honest.

"Hey, man. You ignorin' me?"

"Just a sec."

"Because I'll bet you twenty dollars I can tell you—"

Mason squatted and started fussing with his laces. After yanking off one shoe, then the other, he tossed them both behind him at his assailant's feet.

"Payless. Forty bucks. They're yours now."

"Hey, man. I don't like your—"

Dakota whispered something to Mason past the headphones.

"—attitude," said the man with the porkpie hat. Except with that final word, his voice had changed.

Mason turned.

Preacher was behind him. Or at least, the idea of him was. Big and barrel-voiced, bald-headed, gold hoop earrings.

"And I'll bet you twenty dollars I can tell you where you *got* those motherfuckin' shoes!" The world became white. Preacher lost his footing, suddenly floating. "The fuck?"

Dots blossomed like early spring flowers. They grew in the whiteness — drops of ink in a puddle of milk. They came with geometric precision. Lazy, perfect spirals, winding out in the shape of a golden ratio.

"Hey, man," said Preacher. "Hey, ma—"

It ended. Blackness. Hands removed his goggles and headphones.

Dakota.

"Is this over yet, Mason? Are you tired of trying or just getting bored?"

"Maybe *you* should try. This isn't easy."

"*Are* you trying? Because if you're not going to do this, maybe you should be a man and say so."

Mason gritted his teeth.

"I think he's trying," Calliope said. "His mind is just kind of an asshole."

"Can't you roofie him or something? Make him more suggestible?"

"I honestly considered it, but once inside, he needs his wits to find the other Calliope."

Mason leaned forward. "Will you two stop talking about me like I'm not here?"

Calliope sighed, then waved for Mason to leave the pod and join them. "It's fine. Honestly, I shouldn't be surprised."

"Surprised by what?"

"Carter couldn't learn any of this, either. We worked on it a lot once I knew what we needed to do. Don't feel bad. It's like learning to lucid-dream. I'm asking you to take control of something subconscious and make it conscious. The kind of thing monks spend their entire lives learning to do."

"Monks don't do simulations," Mason said.

"But they isolate themselves, questioning everything, spending their existence trying to answer the question, *What's really true?* I sort of knew this would happen. It's unrealistic to ask you to change everything about how you think in a few days." She began walking around, shutting down the equipment.

"We're not giving up now," Dakota said.

"He needs to be aware of the sim yet still allow it to play without interference. This" — Calliope slapped the machine, but Mason assumed she was referring to the program — "is the simplest sim I can give him." She turned to Mason then repeated herself for the thousandth time. "Just let the guy rob and kill you."

Ha. *All* he needed to do?

The sim was set up so it was impossible to defeat the robber but similarly impossible to give the guy what he wanted and walk away clean. To pass this one, Mason had to lie down and do nothing. Just let himself get robbed then murdered. No big deal, but apparently impossible for a man with a strong sense of reality and self-preservation.

Mason watched Calliope, surprised to realize he wanted to stop her. He hadn't asked for any of this, but her picture of Nathaniel Blake holding his father captive — with his finger on a doomsday button — was too much.

He grabbed Calliope's hand as she reached past him. "I want to keep trying."

"I don't know what else to do."

"You haven't gotten Preacher right. Problem is, I know you made him up. If the Preacher I saw inside the sim was the real one ..."

"If he *was* the real one, that'd mean we were out on the public HRO network, and he'd have eaten you alive. What would that look like to the people searching for us? The prison would see it. So would Blake. And you'd have led Preacher right to me. If he was really created by Blake—"

Mason wrestled a piece of equipment from Calliope, then met her gaze. "I can do this. Even if I can't forget what's real, I can help you find my father."

"That won't mean shit unless you can find a way to accept it but also not accept it." Again, she indicated the equipment, and with it, their five days of failure so far. "You need to let the simulation happen without interference while still remembering it isn't real."

"I understand. You've said it a thousand times."

"If you truly understood, you'd be able to do it."

"I *can* do that."

"Clearly, you can't."

"I can when you remind me. When you talk into my ear and coach me to go with the flow and stop fighting the sim. Or to stand up and fight when I'm supposed to."

"Except I can't be in your ear when we move you to the real network. This is a closed-off system for training Docents on a simulated island."

"We could use the same rig when you put me out onto the network, rather than the HRO immersion rigs. Whisper past my headphones. I'm sure you can hotwire this pod into the other system?"

"There's no need. It can be connected to the HRO system any time we want with a push of a button. But in order for the programs to be compatible, we'd have to plug you in for full immersion. We couldn't use headphones and a visor, anyway. See the cord behind you?"

Mason looked. A three-fingers-thick cord hung at the back of his neck. He already had a port. They just needed to plug it in.

"But that'd jack you into the sensory feed ... and then we're right back to me not being able to speak past your headphones. See the problem?"

Mason touched the cord. It felt like a reminder of his failure. He'd thought he just needed to master the simulations she'd given him, but apparently, there was a higher level he'd yet to reach. He'd need to plug in at some point — but how would he have a prayer in full immersion when he couldn't even do the headphone version?

"Maybe this just isn't going to work," Calliope said. "Maybe it was always a dead end."

"You said it *has* to work."

"Sure, it has to. But …" She spread her hands at all their failure.

"Then figure something else out. Aren't you supposed to be the Great Calliope?"

"I can't change reality, Mason! We've been at this for five days, and you can't hold your shit together even for a few minutes. You need to walk into Pattern Fucking Black, find your father, then come back out. Even if you *could* keep your bearings, the more I think about it, I don't have the slightest clue how you'd—"

But Dakota's voice, soft and half-full of wonder, interrupted her. *"She's* figured that out."

"Clearly," Mason said with disgust, "she hasn't."

Dakota shook her head. "Not her. The *other* Calliope. We don't need to figure this out because the version of Calliope inside the machine already has!"

"Now wait a second," Calliope said. "Just because—"

"She's been inside the entire time!" With a warding finger held up to silence Calliope, Dakota continued. "She's never lost sight of Carter's signal, and then she saw yours. We already know the two of you look a lot alike to the machine. And on top of that, you and your father's minds keep trying to reach each other thanks to your psychic connection. She'd be able to see that, too, right? Even the HRO's database could see it. Remember the virtual therapist you told me about? She woke you up so you could find her, Mason. It can't be a coincidence."

"That doesn't make sense. Why would she wake him if the goal was for him to go right back under?" Calliope asked.

Dakota rushed forward then tapped the console to surface the records. She turned back a moment later, and for the first time, had hope on her face. Ignoring Calliope, she spoke to Mason. "She needed you to see you were in a simulation. She told you where to find *this* Calliope, out in the real world, then gave you a choice and a neural disruption that kicked you out, knowing you'd come here to learn what we've told you and *hoping we'd figure out to send you back in to find her*. *We* don't need to figure it out. Don't you see? *She* already has! She'd have needed to, or nothing else she's planning would have worked!"

"That's quite a leap," Calliope said. "What makes you so sure about what she's planning?"

Dakota moved to a new console. The minute she did, Calliope stood straight and asked, "What's on your mind? What are you doing?"

Instead of answering, Dakota reached for the controls.

"Dakota?"

"We need to show Digital Calliope where to find *us*. To find *him*." Now she nodded to Mason. "Strap yourself back into the pod."

"Now?"

"No time like the present. We've already wasted most of a week."

Calliope stepped in. "He needs rest."

Mason looked to Dakota.

"Get in," she ordered. "You don't need the head rig. Plug into that cable instead."

Mason settled back and started reattaching the immersion leads. He didn't particularly like taking orders from anyone, but he'd take them from Dakota before Calliope. He thought the lab around him might vanish when he plugged the cable at the pod's back into himself, but nothing changed. Activation must come from the console in front of Dakota.

"Be ready to look for the other Calliope. And be ready to run."

"Dakota?" Calliope inched forward, hands out. "You don't know what you're doing."

"I'm forcing a decision."

"What exactly is he supposed to decide?"

"I'm forcing *your* decision," Dakota said.

"If you're doing what I think you're doing …" Calliope advanced to stop her.

But Dakota held up a single waiting finger. Her other hand was millimeters from the console's surface. "Come closer, and I'll activate it right now."

Mason's heart jumped. "Activate what?"

"Dharma One is equipped with a panic beacon," Dakota said. "Something we've always known about but were smart enough to never turn on. It's meant for emergencies, kind of like ringing a huge fire alarm."

"Or a dinner bell." Calliope advanced again.

Dakota firmed her finger, lowering the one near the console yet another hair. Then she looked to Mason. "If the heart of the HRO were invaded by an enemy, say, a spike-headed enemy that the HRO, Revival, and Blake himself had been looking for forever" — she eyed Calliope — "that invasion would be enough to force just about *anyone* to act. Little digital ghosts, for instance. We'd just need to remove the blind spot over that place and turn on the beacon. We wouldn't have to search for the other Calliope. The second she saw Mason waving the flag, *she'd* come running to *him.*"

"You can't be sure—"

"I am sure," Dakota cut her off. "This is the only way. You know it is. Mason doesn't have the tools to navigate on his own, and we're running out of time. He'll be okay once she has him. But we need to get them together. She knows it, too, because she's basically you. *That's* why I'm sure she'll come when she sees the beacon."

"I meant, you can't be sure she'll be the *only* one who comes. Or that she'll get here first!" Calliope was flushed. Her voice was uneasy, and starting to shake. Her eyes were wide, her palms down — panic demanding temperance. "Right now, nobody looks at the Inner Circle. They can't see us. Can't tell we're here. But if you scream our location from the rooftops …"

Dakota pressed the button.

Mason half-expected gunshots or explosions, but nothing happened. The screen turned red, but that was it.

"You ready?" Dakota asked.

Mason nodded. Her finger moved to the immersion button.

Then the alarms began to scream.

And the drones — along with whatever human troops the HRO could summon — were on their way as Mason slipped under the surface of everything.

FORTY-FIVE

Simulated Adrenaline

Mason only heard the first blip of the alarm, one half-cycle of a siren, like the annoyed warble police bray from their cruisers for one second at a time to say, *Move your ass.*

His world was smoke and coughing. His eyes, Mason realized, were closed because he must have been sleeping. They burned as he opened his lids. The tall, window-bordered ceiling of the old gymnasium became visible, but only as vaguely whitish illumination, like shining a flashlight through fog. Something crackled and snapped above, then drifted lazily downward.

Chair, door, cot, floor. These are things I can understand right now.

Coughing. Finding it hard to breathe. Mason's already-addled senses were beaten into sad, atrophied versions of themselves. His head weighed a thousand pounds, and was still getting punched.

But why?

Because you're in a simulation, dummy. Be careful. You were trained for this.

Yes. *Trained.* Then rushed to graduation by the force of circumstance, never finishing school or even base competency. He couldn't hold focus. The world already felt wrong and too far away. Part of him still knew where he'd been, where he was, and why he'd come, but those facts were drifting further and further. If not for the smoke, he might go back to sleep.

Why *was* there so much smoke?

Mason remembered being somewhere else two minutes ago, and there hadn't been a fire in that other place.

Instead, there'd been … there'd been …

Dakota? No, she worked in intake for the HRO. Dakota wouldn't be here, inside the prison.

Except she was. She'd been arrested. Three or four years ago.

But how did that make sense? Dakota was a good cop who'd done nothing wrong.

Something grabbed his arm and issued a heroic pull, given its positional disadvantage. Whoever'd nabbed him seemed to be below, on the floor, yanking down and sideways. His cot tipped, wedged between the four surrounding it for a while, then finally managed to fall the rest of the way to spill Mason in an untidy heap.

His jaw hit painted concrete. The whole world seemed to bounce, skew, go out of focus, then return. Nic's golf-ball eyes were glaring at him like a raccoon from the shadows.

"The fuck's wrong with you?" Nic asked.

Mason squinted. He was pretty sure there was something he'd wanted to ask Nic. Or something he'd forgotten about today, involving the guy. Was it his birthday? Had they been planning to do something? It felt like forever since Mason had seen him.

He heard a voice in his head. His own, counterpointed by the words of a woman he shouldn't know. A woman he was pretty sure he *didn't* know, except a growing part of his awareness was certain he did.

Mason had seen her recently. With Dakota.

But … *how?* He'd been sleeping soundly, here in the crib. Before it caught fire, apparently.

His head hurt even more as he tried to clear the cobwebs. He was no longer sure he'd had a good night's sleep. The migraine meant something, he seemed to recall. His head *always* hurt when he was in a … in a … what?

He couldn't shake the feeling that he hadn't been sleeping.

He'd been … awake somewhere? Somehow? With Dakota? And with that other woman … some name beginning with a C?

Carol.

Charity.

Celeste.

But no, none of those was it.

"You okay?" Nic asked, his expression concerned.

"The building is on fire."

"No shit. And you were just going to Sleeping Beauty right through it. I woke you up ten minutes ago. You were going to grab some shit and yell for everyone who didn't hear the alarm."

Oh, yes. Mason remembered an alarm. It'd happened when he'd been in some sort of pod thing with wires stuck all over himself. When he was with Dakota. And Calliope. More like two minutes ago than ten.

The picture began to solidify. Mason's reality doubled, hurting his eyes. Nic was still staring at him. Wondering why he climbed back into bed as flames danced around him.

That's not Nic. You don't even know Nic. You're not really here.

It didn't make sense. Except it did.

Mason rubbed his temples. The fire was still burning. He could hear the crackle from above, and now the embers were landing on his cot and making it smolder. Ten minutes ago, Nic had woken Mason. *Supposedly.* In another two, his cot would be ablaze. He could already smell the petroleum scent of the blistering polymer.

"I have a headache."

"Yeah? Good for you." Nic pointed. The smoke was thickening, obscuring direction. "The door's that way. Meet you there or have fun dying. I'm done with this shithole."

Mason began to crawl, staying low. There were loud shouts from outside, and every once in a while, Mason could see and hear feet rushing by. He heard drones and maybe firefighting robots. How? Where? Who? No time to worry about *why*. Mason focused on the fact that none of this was real. His headache was proof. It hurt from fighting a simulation, but there was no option of going against the flow on this one. Trying would kill him.

And what had … *Calliope?* … said about dying?

He found Frank Watt up ahead. Then Sasha and Buster. Three of the only people he'd gotten to know — from inside a Heist as well as from here — out of all the people he could have found during a panic. What a coincidence.

Once outside, they all stood then brushed themselves off. Temporary signage indicated a relaxing of curfew. Mason didn't know the time, only that the sun had just set or was preparing to rise. A few other inmates milled about, watching the big building burn. It was beautiful.

"They say Immunity started it," Watt told the group.

"Why?" Sasha asked. "How?"

A spike seemed to jab Mason hard between the eyes. He winced and rubbed the spot.

Nic watched him but said nothing.

"What's wrong with you?" Sasha asked, looking at Mason.

Watt said, "He's got a headache."

But Mason hadn't told Watt anything of the sort.

"Watt," Mason said. "Do you remember my birthday?"

"No."

"I told you when we stole that car."

They had never stolen a car. They hadn't spent any time together at all. Only as bunkmates in the crib and gangmates during the Heist.

"Oh, right," Watt said. "February thirteenth."

He didn't know Mason's birthday, either.

"It was Friday the 13th, the year I was born," Mason said.

"Oh, right. So?"

It was an irrelevant question, but that was fine because Watt shouldn't have any answers. Especially since he'd been dead for a while.

Mason, trying to hold onto the truth amid a pack of lies, found the trick of Watt's knowing a comfort. Now he could be sure of the artifice. Watt and his out-of-place knowledge shouldn't actually be here. Mason, neither.

Still fighting the headache, he pinched his nose. Hard, and for a while.

From the darkness behind his closed eyes came Nic's voice. "You having some sort of a fit or whatever?"

But he saw only white when he opened his eyes. No Nic, no crib, no anybody else. Only a void.

Then he heard a voice.

He was drifting. Floating. In space without a tether.

Now he saw the inferno again, and the heat was too intense.

"Dakota," Mason said.

Nic's bug eyes bugged further. "What?"

"Dakota did this."

"Isn't that your cop friend?"

In theory, yes. Dakota had been his partner until she'd taken his blame and gone to prison. She wasn't an administrator and hadn't taken him from the crib to Chamber Therapy. Nor had she pulled him out of a tube full of goo or run him to a facsimile of Leigh to clear the dongle from his blood.

The dongle, Mason knew, couldn't *be* removed. It could only be clumped together. Clotted. Used to track or kill anyone who had it. That would be doubly true if Nathaniel Blake got what he wanted.

And what Blake wanted — what he *needed* to solve his prisoner problems — was ...

Nic was still waiting for an answer, but Nic wasn't really Nic.

It hurt so much to think about.

"Dakota needed to attract Calliope," Mason said. "She set off some sort of a signal."

"*What?*" Nic said.

"She kicked the hornet's nest. To help me find her."

"You think you'll find your administrator buddy *in here?*"

"Not her. Someone else."

Nic took that as crazy talk instead of an answer, like words from a sleepwalker. "You okay, man? You ..."

But Mason wasn't okay. His knees buckled. He fell to the ground and cradled his skull.

"You look like shit," Nic finished.

Mason kept his eyes closed. "Remember how, when we went to Immunity's part of town, you told me you'd do anything to never see Preacher again?"

"*What?* Are you high?"

Apparently, Nic didn't remember that. Mason didn't know the rules, but he did get the distinct impression time was running out.

But on what?

Find her. Let her find you.

Mason's memory was working overtime, but more came with each head-splitting minute. This had something to do with his father.

A solidly built, military-looking man with tan skin and black hair came over. He wore a guard uniform, and his name tag read CRUZ.

"Someone did this," Cruz said as he walked straight up to Mason. "Why did you do this?"

"I ..."

A hand went to his holster. In a second, Cruz had his weapon out and aimed at Mason. "You aren't supposed to be here."

The old signals came rushing back. All the old instincts. Even through the fire-belching sulfur and carbon ash, Mason could smell simulated adrenaline leaking from the man's pores. Even with the tumult, he could see the flick of Cruz's finger on the trigger and his wavering eyes.

Existence or not didn't change his intention to shoot — and Mason, still trying to find reality among the many choices — couldn't remember what it would mean if he did.

So, he kicked Cruz hard in the balls.

The guy doubled over but was either trained or well-programmed. His weapon hand never strayed too far from its target. When it swung the first few inches, Mason moved toward him, grabbing the arm and pinning it while throwing his momentum into Cruz, nearly knocking him down.

But the man recovered quickly. His simulated balls couldn't ache long, and his simulated muscles didn't quickly tire.

The next minute, Mason was on his back with Cruz kneeling on his chest, muzzle to his forehead. "What the fuck was that about, Shaw? Who's side are you on? Who are you working for? Do you want it all to burn down? Are you working for them? Where is she? How are you here? Show me your ID. *Show me!*"

Cruz started to rise up and down, jamming his knee into Mason's ribs.

"Jesus Christ! Let me up, and I'll—!"

"SHOW ME!" bellowed Cruz.

He slugged Mason sidelong with the pistol, splitting his lip against his incisors.

Mason tasted blood.

The gun came back, forcing its way between his lips and teeth. Cruz was above him, maniacal. Mason tasted steel.

"You're the problem here. Tell me who you're working for!"

Then it was over. Watt hit Cruz with a piece of shattered concrete and opened his scalp. He went from shouting to collapsing and was soon a bleeding sack of meat more than anything conscious. More than anything living.

Blood. Everywhere.

He looked up at Watt, but the man's face now belonged to Mason Shaw.

Beside Mason was another Mason. Behind them, two more.

Then there was an electronic glitch, a flash of black dots on white, then Mason found himself looking up at Watt with the killing rock, flanked by Nic, Sasha, and Buster.

Mason shrugged Cruz from his body. The man was either dead or asleep.

"Thanks," Mason said to Watt.

"No problem. You'd do the same for you."

An agonizing spike of pain seemed to lance him in both eyes at once. A new alarm screamed to the east. And … it *was* east, the sun was rising. The morning light was red-orange, and everyone was looking at him.

Everyone.

A new alarm rang, heralding guards and drones among blaring klaxons. A contingent ran up to Mason, weapons drawn and eyes on

Cruz's body. He'd committed murder — or, more accurately, murder had been committed on his behalf.

Five guards half-surrounded him in a semicircle. The rear of a second building — an apartment? a store? — brushed his back. The four other prisoners had stepped away, even Watt with the bloody rock still in his hand.

The guards ignored them. As if they were invisible.

Weapons rose, safeties off. Surely they weren't planning to question him.

"I'll come quietly." Mason raised his arms as best he could from his place on the ground.

"You won't come at all," said one of the faceless guards.

A metallic rattle split the air. It sounded like a chain being dragged rapidly across a metal edge. By the time the echo died, all five guards were dead, reduced to skinless bodies of bloody muscle.

The rattle was still finishing its rounds. Mason looked back. A very large bald man was holding an enormous military weapon. It looked like a Gatling gun, smoking at the end.

Beside this man — beside *Ike*, Mason was pretty sure — stood a man with an accountant's face, beside a dark-haired woman with arching eyebrows, beside a waif-thin woman with hard cheekbones, short blonde hair, and piercing blue eyes.

"Come with us," said the digital version of Calliope. "Hurry."

Mason did.

FORTY-SIX

Not as a Victim

THEY DUCKED INTO AN ABANDONED BUILDING, accessible through a hidden door behind a pile of alley trash. It all seemed vaguely familiar until the moment it became unquestionably recognizable as the room he'd accompanied Dakota and Leigh to that first time. When they'd supposedly removed his blood dongle, after pulling him from the tank.

"You're back," said Doctor Leigh.

Calliope ignored her. The others filtered out, going to places unknown. They weren't off the hook by a long shot. Mason could hear the humming drones as they hovered, along with the whooshing as they flew by. He could hear shouts, but not just of prisoners. Human guards, summoned by the drone strike. Docents, perhaps.

Leigh came closer. She'd been talking to Mason and now took his arm. "Let me get your vitals."

"I'm fine."

"Let me get your vitals," she repeated.

Mason looked up. Calliope took his other arm, shook her head, and pulled him away.

"Let me get your vitals," Leigh repeated from behind them.

"She's persistent," Mason said.

"She's you. Same as a lot of the others."

"*A lot* of the others?"

"Some of the people here are my projections, not yours. I've been in here a long time. I dreamed up some companions. I guess we'll see how they get along."

Something clicked.

"You're not me, though. You are nobody's projection. You are your own thing."

Calliope nodded.

"We called you 'Digital Calliope.'"

"Terrible name."

"I can't call you 'Calliope.' I already have a Calliope to keep track of, and it's not you."

"Elisabeth, then."

Mason shook his head. Now that he knew Calliope was Elisabeth Reeves, he'd been interchanging memories and mentions as if they were the same. "Still too real."

"Then call me Astrid. She was my grandmother, and that's my middle name."

"Astrid."

"Astrid," she repeated.

A boom from outside sharpened her gaze. "We're short on time. Tell me she told you what you need to know."

"Who?"

"My physical half." She bobbed her head, adjusting to Mason's newly preferred nomenclature. "*Calliope*, I mean."

"You know about that?"

"Of course I know. You can always knock on wood in the physical world. But it changes with the whims of whoever comes in here."

"I thought this was my simulation. Just mine."

"So, she *didn't* tell you everything."

"She told me enough."

Astrid rolled her eyes, as exasperated by her other self as Dakota had been. She pointed at Nic. "You brought him with you. He's yours. Same for the doctor. I assume they're people you knew on the outside?"

He nodded. This was surreal. The people around him now were as real as anything he'd ever seen. Same for the building, the peril, and all the senses that came with it. Mason tried to focus on his headache. To appreciate the pain as an indicator. Calliope had talked about striking a balance — holding what was true while also not fighting too hard against what he saw. Accept the lie while keeping his mission in mind.

The headache. Focus on the headache.

He looked at their companions, all hanging back. "Is that your Dakota? Or is she my reflection? We both know her. This chunk of memory could belong to either of us."

"She's already told me you're a selfish lover, so I'm guessing she's yours."

Mason ignored her. "What about Bear and Ike? They're from your group, but I met them both."

"Tell you what. I've got a riddle for you to solve first. *Who gives a shit?*"

"You don't care?"

"Why would I care?"

Mason put his forehead in his right hand, feeling a fresh wave of overwhelm.

"Head hurt?"

"Yes."

"It means you're resisting."

Mason nodded. "Right. I know. This isn't real."

"It depends on your perspective." Astrid shrugged. "It's real to me in a way your physical world can no longer be. 'You are somewhere else' might be a more constructive way to think of the difference."

Mason wasn't sure he could pull that particular mental trick. His gaze went to the others, knowing none of them existed in the way he had always believed. Yet there they were, talking to one another about things he and Astrid couldn't hear. But if all the people were facets of their minds, how could they exist independently? How was it possible for them to talk without Mason or Astrid knowing what was in their shared imagination?

He nodded. *Fine.*

"Better?"

"Just a little," Mason said.

They went to a desk at the room's far side, away from the avatars. She looked up to find Mason staring. "What?"

"It's just … You look exactly like her."

"What about Dakota? Doesn't the Dakota over there look just like your Dakota?"

Yes, the Dakotas were alike. But already — and even now, even from a distance — Mason could tell they weren't the same. It was like knowing a twin, then meeting their sibling. Even if they shared the same biology, identical twins weren't *exactly* the same. Epigenetics made for half the equation, the unique expression of genes summoned by life itself from each person in its unique way. The Dakota with him now had lived free then had become a rebel after waking him. The real-world Dakota had been imprisoned for years after sacrificing for Mason. That difference left the kind of mark Mason could see from afar, knowing her as he did.

"It's different with you," Mason said.

"Yes. Well. I don't know how your Calliope is faring out there in the higher world, but it makes sense. We *were* the same until we split. Tell me. Who set the fire?"

"How should I know?"

"It wasn't here until you showed back up. The building burst into flames maybe fifteen minutes ago."

That couldn't be right. Fifteen minutes ago, Mason had been opening his eyes. Smoke was filling the building, and something above him had been burning.

"No way. It was going when I woke up in the crib."

"I can show you the drone footage if you'd like to see. It just *happened*. And I overheard Nic there. *Your Nic.* He said you were talking about Dakota."

"I was delirious."

"You get delirious when you have a 104-degree fever. When you port into a simulation, you're jumbled. If you said 'Dakota' when Nic pressed you about the fire, you probably meant she started it. Why?"

Mason thought. It was hard to hold both realities at once. Either he was in a fantasy, and nothing was true, or he was in a real place, and nothing was false. Believing both at once — delving into *whys* of the genuine world while speaking to a digital being — felt next to impossible.

"Dakota and Calliope were arguing, back in the physical world. Dakota wanted to get your attention."

"My attention?"

Mason nodded. "She said something about a beacon."

Astrid went white. Well … whit*er*.

"She didn't."

"She didn't *what?*" Mason asked.

"She didn't ping the beacon. Please tell me she didn't do that." Astrid turned around, took a tablet from a shelf, then began frantically swiping.

"What's wrong?" Mason asked.

"What's wrong is that I woke you in a very specific way. The device I used on you in the Heist was supposed to disrupt your signal and cause you to question the world. It's a decision matrix. It doesn't force anything. It *opens* so you can see what you have the natural curiosity and desire to see, rather than having it all blocked by the prison safeguards. I couldn't compel you to go with me or to wake up. I could only show you the door."

"So?"

Astrid grew increasingly frantic. She was checking screens, scampering across the space, so he rushed to keep up. Mason was sentient, and Astrid, according to the real-world Calliope, had *become* sentient. Apparently, sentience made them the only ones who gave a shit.

"You wanna tell me what's going on?" Mason called as she rushed hither and yon, now looking up at the sound of drones beyond the ceiling.

"I only woke your mind. Once you were out, the Muse's disruption should have kept your brain restless. You were supposed to find Calliope wherever she was hiding, then get her here on your own terms. Not as a victim."

"That's what happened."

"Yes, but look at all the other stupid shit that happened, too!" Astrid had gone from composed to maniacal. "Seeing as I was the one to make contact, I was obviously planning to wait for you on the other side — to be here whenever you made your way back. There was no reason to smoke me out or to ring the bell and tell the world. Blake will see this. You realize that, don't you? He's been sending programs to find me. How's it going to look when he sees the Inner Circle beacon light up, shouting my name?"

Mason opened his mouth, feeling like he should defend the others. It had seemed so sensible on the outside. "They weren't sure I'd be able to find you."

"*I'd* find *you! That's* how this was supposed to work!" She swore, still rushing and working.

The whoosh of passing drones seemed less frequent outside while the sounds of hovering seemed to multiply.

"Will you settle down for a second?" Mason grabbed her arm. "What does any of this have to do with the fire?"

"What's burning?" she demanded, rhetorical. "Is it wood? Or faulty wiring? Is it really sulfur you smell in this place when you strike a match?" She put a hand on her hip. "Look. I'm as egalitarian about realities as the next person, but I think we can admit there's no wood here. No wiring. No actual matches. So, a fire? It's not just a fire. Not a fire the HRO didn't set or expect. Not a fire that wasn't programmed to happen, to force action or make a point."

She pointed at Mason's chest. "Your friends? They did us a big fucking favor by lighting that blaze. It attracted me, except that I was already watching. I didn't *need* attracting. This will look like a glitch to everyone else. No, a *hack.* You need God-level access to materially affect property here. She might as well have climbed to the top of a mountain and started screaming."

Mason sat to watch the frenzy, unsure of what else to do.

"She's a fool," Astrid continued. "She used to have sense, back when we were the same person. But ever since our split, she never makes sense."

"Wait … you can see her? You're in contact?"

"Sort of. It happens in here." She tapped her head.

"Like it happens for me."

"Different. Your physical and mental halves still get along. You're here because your physical self decided to hook himself up and project into this simulation."

"Is it a simulation? Or Pattern Black?"

Astrid crossed the space, shouting orders without answering.

Mason watched Nic, Dakota, and Leigh all snap to. He felt the relaxing of tension that came with making a decision — any decision. Uncertainty receded, and suddenly he knew some of what was about to happen. Even fuzzy and gray, it was all still there somewhere. Astrid had spoken directly to three of his facets. What Dakota, Nic, and Leigh knew, Mason — somewhere deep down, perhaps accessible with training he never completed — also knew.

"Astrid? Is this a simulation, or—?"

"There's no time to get cozy." She nodded at the sound of approaching chaos. "I'll tell you everything if your meat-bag buddy hasn't gotten us killed."

They all went through the door.

But pursuers were lined up, ready to follow.

FORTY-SEVEN

Hurry

DAKOTA LOOKED UP. The high roof of the large warehouse space inside Dharma One had come alive with sparks from a drone with a torch, cutting its way in.

"Calliope."

She was minding a console, failing to hear the torch above the tumult. The worst had been the perimeter alarm, which began braying as Mason went under. He was covered in wires, eyes closed, dreams transcribed as a series of lines on Calliope's display.

Only, he wasn't really asleep. Dakota had been trying to ignore the second bank of monitors, which displayed his native brain activity. There was none. He had breath and a heartbeat, but if Mason stayed under long enough, he'd need life support for both. He was still technically brain dead and had slid back into his current state with sickening ease.

Calliope followed Dakota's gaze. "It's okay." She tapped something, and the sparks stopped. A tiny blue line became visible in the corrugated aluminum, along with a miniature view of the clear sky above.

Something banged against the roof farther down, then seemed

to impact the ground outside like a microwave dropped on the floor.

"I have SysOp access. The only downside is the second they *know* I have SysOp level access, it'll be revoked."

More sparks showered down from above. There'd been some at the door earlier, but Calliope lowered the storm doors and erected a mega-fence that made the building like the Thunderdome.

"Whatever you're trying to do, it's not working," Dakota said.

With a sigh but no rush, Calliope walked to a column, lifted the lid of an electric box, then turned a knob. Dakota's hair wanted to stand on end. A crackle filled the air.

"I made a Van de Graaff generator," Calliope explained.

"You mean those things they put in science museums for kids?"

A loud bang came from above. The drone outside seemed to explode, or at least pop a serious gasket. There was a rolling sound down the roof, followed by a crunch as the ruined drone hit the deck.

"I may have modified it a bit," Calliope explained.

Dakota watched her move to another console, wishing she could help — but this wasn't Dharma Four, where the bones of Immunity played their games. This was Dharma One. Calliope's sanctum. A hideout only she understood, stuffed with booby traps and protections in preparation for a day like this.

"They'll find the generator and shut it down. But I still have my drones and a few tricks up my sleeve."

Dakota looked at Mason. Knowing his heart and lungs still worked only gave her a cursory understanding. Her gut said he was dead and gone. If the drones broke through, it would make no difference to his corpse.

Calliope saw her gaze, then caught Dakota's attention. "Hey. It's okay. He'll make it."

It felt like happy thinking to Dakota. Whether Mason made it or not, the drones were still on their way, with soldiers behind them. Plus Blake and the full force of whomever he'd managed to bribe. Everyone knew where Calliope was.

There was shouting outside. Banging. Guns.

She leaned closer to Mason, feeling only the whisper of machine-made breath.

"Hurry," she told him.

FORTY-EIGHT

The Window

Right.
Left.
Right.
Right.

Mason stopped trying to hold his bearings. At first, he'd been able to use the sky as his compass, but soon enough, the multiple turns surpassed his ability to pace them. Astrid, who looked like Calliope but acted more like her defiant sister, never hesitated or so much as glanced at the paths not taken, as if following a map only she could see.

He saw the same tower he'd noticed on his walk from his simulated Chamber Therapy sessions to his simulated home in the crib. It was hard to believe none of it had ever been real. He'd never lived in the red crib. The places and people existing objectively in this place were his father's memories, either left in Pattern Black for Mason to find or transmitted through their psychic bond. Sons sometimes walked figuratively in their father's footsteps. Mason had been doing it literally, whether he wanted to or not.

There was an almost-dead end ahead, with a single narrow

passage to the left. Mason started to sprint for it, but Ike grabbed him by the sleeve.

"Wrong way."

"There is no other way."

But half the party was already through an open sewer grate behind them. From Mason's perspective, they were either lost or winging it with extraordinary confidence while a symphony of pursuit rang through the air.

Once Ike was halfway down the ladder mounted to the storm sewer's sidewall, he reached back up and slid a large sheet of plywood over the grate. It was dark for several seconds until Astrid sparked a lantern. Like everything else here, the lantern looked improvised. She must have been carrying it folded up. A steampunk fantasy, all brushed chrome, and stained glass, its many colors illuminating the group in reds, yellows, and blues, more disco than hideout.

"We can stay here a while." Astrid's voice wasn't low. Everyone but Mason seemed to understand how safe they were because the second the plywood had gone over, they'd all returned to chattering in normal voices. And ... how sweet. Mason's projections were making friends with Astrid's.

"Where is *here*? I mean, other than a sewer."

Astrid smiled at Mason. "You ever play Ms. Pac-Man?"

It was an odd question. "Yeah ..."

"Take a look."

She pulled a small tablet from her pocket then handed it to Mason. She'd unfolded all the wings, turning it into something the size of a coffee table book. On-screen was a stylized grid re-creating part of the city and a silver path — *their* path — winding around the on-screen map. Neither linear nor efficient. Almost every street and alley had been traversed, their route looping endlessly back on itself.

"Is this where we went?" Mason asked.

Astrid, beside him, seemed to be waiting for him to see something. "Yes."

"Just in loops?"

"A pattern. You know. *A pattern?*"

Then Mason got it. "You're kidding."

"So, you *did* play Ms. Pac-Man."

Mason looked up. The others had gathered around. He waited for some sort of an *a-ha* — for the watchers to request an explanation of what Mason had just realized — but none came. It was hard to keep secrets when everyone was made of him.

"The drones follow a pattern? You can beat them just by following a better one, like playing Ms. Pac-Man?"

"Blake was a huge nerd. Still is. Half of the drone OS was tribute, and the other half was sensible appropriation. He thought a pattern would be efficient, and for the most part, it works. Only problem is patterns can be outsmarted. Which is why I never lost Ms. Pac-Man back when I used to play."

Astrid folded the tablet, stowed it in her pocket, then looked at Mason with something like amusement on her perfect digital face.

"What?" Mason asked when she didn't speak.

"We had such a difficult time trying to reach you. Revival sims are self-reinforcing, meaning the more you believe what you're seeing, the more solid and believable what you're seeing becomes. You thought you were in prison, so over time, the system gave you more proof to make your fantasy increasingly real. We had to work harder and harder to break through."

"I don't know that I'd call it a 'fantasy.'"

"Clearly, a large, stubborn part of you never really bought it. I don't know if you subconsciously recognized Carter's thoughts weren't your own. I don't know if you knew he and Dakota had been incarcerated in HRO 22, but *you'd* only applied to be a Docent. Even as the simulation kept stacking proof to inspire your belief, it became totally *un*believable. Look back as your memories separate. It will become ridiculous, some of the things you accepted as real."

Their end of the room remained quiet as Astrid's mood grew more sober.

"It's funny looking back, but rest assured it won't be the last time you're fooled by something that should have been obvious. I have an advantage. The day I accepted I was now only ones and zeroes and *she*" — Astrid looked up, probably at the godlike, otherworldly presence somewhere of her corporeal half — "got to keep my actual body, something sort of clicked, making most of the smoke and mirrors in here suddenly obvious. You won't have the same advantage. You're still a brain in a human body, so it'll be harder for you to see through the mind games."

"What do you mean, things here became obvious for what they were?"

"I designed this system to have three basic areas — three ways to play. If you go under without being hooked into a shared sim, you end up exploring your own mind. That's the therapeutic mode. Chamber Therapy is cooperative by nature, so once you're in a CT simulation, what you see is partially yours and partly everyone else's. The system puts cooperative participants inside a common matrix that at first is populated by the system then added to by those who join."

Astrid picked up a dirty coffee mug from the counter. "If you and I are two participants in a shared sim, this cup could have been put here by the base simulation, or it could be mine, or it could be yours. Whatever you recognize in something like this? It's probably because you put it there."

"What's the third mode?" Mason asked.

"Where we are now. Shared space but off the official rails. Being here is like going behind the scenes at Disneyland. It's getting off the boat in the middle of Pirates of the Caribbean and sneaking behind all the animatronics and speakers to where the employees hang out. You're no longer watching the play when you're in that place. You're not even on stage as part of the cast. This here?" Calliope gestured around. "This is climbing in the rigging. This is seeing the strings and how the lift underneath the stage floor makes props appear before they vanish. In a way, it takes away all the magic."

"I'm okay with that," Mason said, thinking how he'd rather have the truth than be a fool in the face of special effects.

"You're okay with it now, but things won't stay that way. I'm drawing your attention to strange things you've been taking for granted. It proves none of this is real, like a lot of what you must have seen the first time you were under. But even the strangest things will eventually feel normal again, just from exposure. The longer you're here, the more you'll naturally accept."

"Maybe I'll just keep reminding myself. Leave a note."

She shook her head. "You're basically dead, Mason. You can be brought back, but right now, your brain is here, and your body is elsewhere. As long as they're separated, you're closer to death than dreaming. If anything happens to your body, you could die here or get trapped inside the machine like me. You have to be fully here and fully *not* here in unison. It's why you needed training. To keep your shit together."

Astrid didn't need to know he hadn't finished training. Or was barely even competent.

She stood then moved to cross the room.

"Hey," Mason said. "Is this Pattern Black?"

She turned back, looked around, then nodded.

"But there's so much here. I'm hooked into a simulation, just like the shared ones you keep talking about. If this is oblivion, why is there so much …" Mason tried to find a word, failed, then grabbed the mug and shook it. "So much *substance*?"

"Because you brought it with you."

"It doesn't feel like I'm making or bringing anything. If this is all inside my head, why are people chasing us? Why did I make myself a prisoner? You used the word 'fantasy.' If I'm flatlined in la-la land, why didn't I put us on a tropical island?"

She sighed. Half-sat — only half because time was ticking.

"It's a little hard to explain. People 'turn inward' and drift away all the time. Sometimes trauma causes it. Sometimes a disease. Sometimes people are born more 'in' than 'out,' like many of the most acutely autistic kids Revival started with. Severe cases can go in and never come out. That's when you get catatonia, lock-in, or maybe a coma. There are ways Pattern Black mirrors those things, but if it were enough, Blake's 'mental cadavers' could come from anyone who pulled the plug. It has a lot of the same symptoms as those more ordinary conditions but a very different cause. Most people, like Dakota's sister, go away. But some refuse to sleep. Maybe because they're stubborn or different. Maybe they're immune. Maybe they have special gifts, like you and Carter."

"You think that's the reason? Because we have … ESP or something?"

"I think that's part of it. Part of the reason Carter never fully went offline is because I trained him." Astrid laughed. "I guess *we* trained him because it was before we split. I'm guessing part of the reason *you* never fully went offline is due to your father's training, not yours. Carter went in knowing he had to raise his defenses while you were thrown in. But because of your bond, you picked up all your father left behind. You started to drown but recognized Carter had left you a rope before you did."

Mason hated owing Carter. He also hated thinking his survival had been an accident. But the explanation solved a lot. That was why he was so familiar with a prison he'd never even seen. Why his motivations felt foreign. Why some of the ghosts clearly belonged to Carter rather than him.

"So, this is his Pattern Black."

"It's *all* of ours. A shared simulation so everyone can contribute. When I tunneled my way out of Kassidi's mind, it felt like leaving a building to enter a much larger city. Much of the population felt familiar, but a few citizens definitely were not. Those who stayed conscious the longest contributed most. I think that's why this place became a prison. *This* prison — HRO 22, Union Station California. It's the last thing your father knew before they put him under … and he's been under for three years."

"So have I."

"Using your father's lens," Astrid said, nodding. "Your father's beliefs, experiences, and prejudices filtered to you through a connection I don't think you fully understand. You're able to live here more than any other subject I've seen. Other than Carter, of course. But make no mistake, Mason. You're living in the house your father built."

"And you?"

"I've done what I could. I brought in the drone patterns, which is useful for hiding. I brought in superstitions and taboos about the Inner Circle and Dharma One. My mind made the systems in this place behave more or less like the real-world systems I built before being trapped here. It makes things work the way I expect, and in a way I can control, but at a price."

"What price?"

"Every day, I believe this place is even more real. Same as you will. I was terrified at first. But now, this is how things are. I used to feel like a *thing*. Now I feel like Elisabeth Reeves, unjustly accused and imprisoned in cells of my own making. For better or worse, this is my world now. It's where I've made my place. Where, more and more, I'm becoming comfortable."

"That's good," Mason said.

"Not remotely," Astrid disagreed.

"What about Carter?"

"What about him?"

"You said he built most of what's in Pattern Black. So why haven't we seen him?"

"Because he's smart enough to hide. He knows what he carries."

"You mean the code that starts Blake's fail-safe? His doomsday machine or whatever?"

Astrid nodded. "But he's getting weaker, Mason. They'll find him. Blake, his programs, his virus soldiers ..."

"You mean Preacher?"

Astrid looked almost amused. "Is that what you call it?"

Bear's footsteps broke the mood. Astrid looked up at his approach. He glanced at Mason in deference or apology, then spoke to his leader — or, seeing as Bear was her invention, he technically spoke to himself. "The drones have stopped patrolling. We have a window if we want to take it."

"*Window?*" Mason repeated.

Astrid turned to him. "To go out without fear of being seen. Only the prison control systems are worth worrying about because the rest belongs to us or to someone who survived Pattern Black long enough to leave some souvenirs. We need to keep our eyes out for drones and guards, but not prisoners. The prisoners are probably mostly your reflections."

"Only mine?"

"Mostly yours. Or your father's."

Mason shook his head.

"Is there a problem?"

"I'm inside my own head, and he's still telling me what to do."

"Be glad he still has the agency," Astrid said. "Blake will be able to get past his defenses and dissect him the second he loses his resolve. Without a rogue mind, his flesh-and-blood brain would have given Blake what he wants already. That's how we know he's still alive."

"Why do you need me? You clearly know all of this better than I do."

"Because you can find your father, and I can't."

"I have no idea where he is, so how am I supposed to—"

"He'll have made himself a cocoon, a small pocket of controlled reality to keep him safe. Your father has a hidey-hole somewhere in this larger world, and you can help us find it."

A distant explosion preceded a dull thud, then plaster drifted in lazy rain from the ceiling.

"The window," Bear told Astrid. "We have three minutes on this grid. Six minutes on grid Four-Alpha."

"And you're sure Carter's in Four-Alpha?"

Bear shook his head then pointed to Mason. "But he is."

"Look," Mason said. "I don't know what you're—"

How many fingers, Mason?

Images flooded his mind.

A child, himself, age four or less with blocks in front of him, spelling FEAR.

His father waxing a blue car with sweeping fins that Mason had forgotten.

All four of them at the Santa Monica pier, the big wheel behind them.

Hearing the buzz above the hardpan.

The black, foreign bores of a dried-out lotus seed pod.

A white room full of black spirals — the backbone of a galaxy, of a nautilus, of the universe itself.

"Yes?" Astrid said, waiting.

Another explosion sounded, this one closer. He thought of how the explosions didn't matter. He saw the world around him, but the real Mason Shaw was in Calliope's pod with the real Dakota watching over him.

Except a clock was ticking out there, as well. Where the explosions mattered plenty.

"Nothing," Mason said.

An invisible hand pushed the throttle and cheered him on — with three fingers held up.

Bear nodded, and so did Astrid.

Two parts. One whole. It made Mason look at Dakota. Was she his or a reflection of Astrid?

"Fuck you and let's go, Mason," Dakota said.

Mine. She's definitely mine.

FORTY-NINE

Us

———

THE CEILING COUGHED SPARKS.

Mason's pod and the equipment feeding it were on wheels, so the crew had moved him from the splash-down zone. The repair drone finished its patch weld, then Dakota looked at Calliope to see if they should move him back. The room was big but not enormous, and much of the floor was littered with scrap.

Dakota adjusted his leads again so they wouldn't snag, then she left him where he was. Fretting details was whistling in the dark. But for a woman so typically without fear, she was scared.

The drone descended to a corner, folded its peripherals, then became little more than a stackable block. There was a lone drone inside Dharma One to handle repairs, and the rest stood guard outside. Thanks to Dakota, Calliope's location on the grid was now known to Revival. With the beacon active, it wouldn't take long for all those drones to find them.

Dakota glanced back at Mason. If his mind was doing what it was supposed to do, there might still be a way. Or maybe she'd raised the beacon for nothing. Sent Mason into Pattern Black and basically killed him.

Calliope looked up at the new plate welded to the ceiling and said, "Good enough."

Then it was quiet. Dakota could no longer hear the drones outside. The place was almost peaceful. But then the tablet started flashing, and a new alarm began to bray. Calliope rushed for the tablet, but Dakota beat her to it.

"He's arrhythmic." Dakota looked to Mason. A brain-dead man should feel no fear, but he was breathing heavily anyway.

Calliope hovered over her shoulder.

Dakota ran to Mason then to a control panel. She started calling up screens.

"It's not Mason," Calliope said. "His vitals are normal."

"This says arrhythmia."

"It's not arrhythmia."

Dakota brandished the tablet while working. "You want to see for yourself? Right here it says, *arrhythmia.*"

"Move," Calliope said.

"I can do this."

Calliope snatched the tablet, unplugging it as she did. Then she stared at Dakota, her words coming out at a chastising clip. "This was a training station. We're in a med bay. I had to use what was available, so these are all medical systems. Treat him like he's arrhythmic, and you'll kill him. Now *get out of the way."* She shoved Dakota with her hip.

Dakota slid sideways, ramming into a perpendicular wall. Her arm caught the brunt of the impact, then she rubbed it. "Haven't changed, have you? Even split in half, you're still a bitch."

"Now is not the time, Dakota."

"Your way or the highway. Why did you even gather a team? Just needed hands to do Her Highness's bidding?"

"Stop being so goddamn dramatic. We all got what we were after."

"From where I'm standing, it doesn't look like anyone got shit. Well, except for you." Dakota smirked. "You got *right fucked.* Couldn't happen to a nicer gal."

Calliope kept her eyes on Mason's controls. "He's stable. You almost acted on an intruding signal, not arrhythmia."

"What's that mean?"

"I'm not sure. But the AI just lit up, so it must be something we've seen before."

Dakota dared to come closer. "It must be you."

"How is it me?"

"I mean the *digital* you. See?" Dakota pointed. "The AI had identified a known signal near Mason in the mindscape's topology. It shows as 'previously identified.' So … *you*. Didn't you set a filter to ignore your other half?"

"I did."

"Because if it identifies the other Calliope every time we check on Mason, and—"

"I set the filter this morning before you got up." She squinted, changed consoles, hit buttons. "This is something else."

"It's not something else. See?" Dakota pointed. "*Known signal.*"

"You're sure?"

"Of course, I'm sure."

"As sure as you were about the arrhythmia?"

Dakota moved her attention from the screen to Calliope. "I see what's happening here."

"Really?" Calliope said.

"You're threatened by me."

"Am I?"

"Same as you always were. Got used to everyone always doing whatever you said, didn't like when Mean Old Dakota Ward joined the team with all her nutty ideas. Like thinking the boss might be a wee bit fucking obsessed."

Calliope rolled her eyes and shook her head.

"I brought him to you," Dakota said. "Let's just keep that in mind."

"Because you knew I was the only one with any answers."

"And why is that? Is it because you never *trusted* anyone else with them? Because you just held onto everything yourself so everyone would have to come to you, bow down to you, kiss your ass, and—"

"Shit."

Dakota froze with a sneer, still bending her lips. When she saw how quickly Calliope had disengaged from their old argument, her own face neutralized. Something was very wrong.

"What?"

"The aberrant signal. It's not the other Calliope. It's … the other thing."

"What other thing?" But then her pulse spiked, and Dakota felt her eyes widen. "You mean Preacher."

Calliope nodded without flinching from the screen.

"He's with Mason?" Dakota asked.

"It hasn't found Mason. Not yet. It found *us.*"

"What do you mean, 'us'?"

Calliope snapped. *"Us!* Us, right here! You and me! *US!*"

"How can Preacher 'find *us?*' We're people. He's a program."

Calliope was silent, apparently finding her companion's question unworthy of an answer. Instead, she did something onscreen then looked up, past Dakota, toward the outer wall. Like she was waiting for the cavalry, or perhaps the alarms.

"What's it going to—?"

Calliope held up a hand. "*Shh.*"

The hand folded to a single finger. *Wait.*

She scanned the space as if Preacher — a digital being, unable to touch the real world — might be hiding in a corner.

"He can't get to us. He's just—"

"*Shh,*" Calliope silenced her again.

Dakota could feel her heart behind her eardrums and a throbbing pulse in her neck. She needed something to grab. Anything to make her feel less vulnerable.

There was a small, electric buzzing sound from across the open space. Then a bright white light lit the back and bottom of a console as a sizzling shake rattled screws on its surface. A few of them fell to the ground.

"What is—?"

Dakota didn't finish, and Calliope couldn't answer.

From the site of the buzzing and light, a metal sphere the size of an orange rolled purposefully into the room's center. Dakota smelled ozone. It had used a torch to come through the outer wall, or someone had cut an aperture for it.

The thing stilled. Opened like a flower. Something in the center flashed like sunlight reflected by a mirror, then a bright, cone-shaped light bloomed upward.

"Fuck," muttered Calliope as a hologram appeared.

Dakota didn't need Calliope to tell her who'd sent it. The life-size man looking across the room at the two of them was one of the world's most famous faces.

"Nathaniel?" Calliope said.

"Elisabeth," the hologram replied. "It's so nice to see you again."

FIFTY

A Forming Storm

Elisabeth.

Mason seemed to hear Calliope's — or Astrid's — real name arriving through the aether in a bass voice.

He looked up. The others were loading backpacks. Why, if everyone in the room was a reflection of Calliope's double, did they act like entities with independent minds? Or why, if everything around them was mental inventory without any true reality, was any of it worth shoving into bags?

It was a problematic concept that required mental elasticity. Mason would much rather believe their inventory mattered. But that was the trap. If he began to believe in real things here, he might never escape.

He closed his eyes and tried to focus amid the discord.

Not even a pixel is real.

His eyes seemed to enlarge in flight of their sockets. His skull was a flexible bladder overfilled with water. The pressure was immense. He'd burst any second.

Dakota's simulated hand touched his shoulder. "You okay?"

Mason looked at her and nodded a little, but he barely convinced himself. "I'm doing my best."

"Come on. We need to go." She took his wrist and pulled.

"I just … heard something," he said.

"What did you hear?"

He looked at Astrid. She was facing the other way, talking to Bear as they gathered phantom supplies.

Nic — not *really*, Mason reminded himself — arrived at his side.

"You believe this shit? You aren't really buying into all of it, are you?"

"Bear says I can find Carter," Mason answered without looking up.

"So?"

"We find Carter, we can get out of here."

"You sure?" Nic shook his head, looking skeptical. "I've been here for years and haven't seen him. Believe me, I've looked."

The real Nic found Carter just fine, but that had been years ago. He'd saved Carter from a gang by hitting them from behind. He'd shown Carter around the red crib. He'd taken Carter to his lube-smelling apartment in the sky. But this Nic knew nothing.

"You've seen how well I know people, Mason. Don't you think if anyone knew anything about Carter Shaw — a guy everyone knew, whether they loved him or wanted him dead — I'd have heard about it?"

"Astrid says he's hiding."

"For three years? No way, man. People need shit, even in hiding. Food. Warmth. Entertainment. Maybe some companionship. I'm sorry, man, but your old man went Pattern Black. He's dead. You go out *there* to play hide and seek with Daddy" — Nic pointed to the building's outer wall and the occasional but increasing sound beyond — "and you're digging your own grave."

Across the floor, Astrid's crew had finished packing. Dakota was with them, just off to the side. Mason walked toward them, but he only made it a couple of steps before Ike appeared beside him, holding a massive minigun as if unholstered from hammerspace.

"You coming?" Ike asked.

"Where did you get that?" Mason nodded at the weapon.

"Who were you talking to over there?" Ike indicated the space to Mason's rear.

"Nic."

"Who?"

Mason looked around. Nic was gone. "This is fucked up."

"We need to go. Bear says if we wait even another sixty seconds, we'll never get out that door."

Mason looked for the noted door, but Ike was now way across the room, beside Dakota, not even looking his way.

No other way out than through, so he headed for the group. Fifteen seconds later, they were out in the open. He pinched his nose and closed his eyes again. He kept hearing that bass voice. A man, speaking Astrid's real name and issuing orders.

My party will meet yours in Four Alpha.

"Still with the headache?" Astrid asked, sidling up beside him.

Mason heard a hum, then looked back and up to almost see HRO drones approaching their vacated hiding spot. "Yes."

"I know it hurts, but that's a good thing."

"Easy for you to say."

Astrid shook her head. "Not easy at all. I used to get the worst thumpers. I could barely see when they hit, my eyes hurt so bad."

"You got headaches? I mean … the same way *I* get headaches?"

"For a long time, yes." She nodded. "But now I never get them. Guess I've gotten used to being somewhere unreal."

They walked on. It was far from an idle stroll. Bear and Ike kept checking a tablet then looking skyward. Mason could still hear the humming of drones, though he hadn't seen more than the corner of one. He could smell ozone. Not long ago, he'd heard human shouting. *Coordinated* human shouting, not the disorderly bellows of chaos. Guards — projections of the system itself, alien to both his mind and Astrid's — out to get each of them.

"You know Nic, right?"

Astrid looked over. "Sure."

"He disappeared."

"When?"

"When I was talking to Ike."

She pointed. "Isn't that him right there?"

Nic was plain as day, but his presence seemed strange. He was an even odder-man-out than Dakota, here for reasons only Mason's subconscious mind could imagine. Not once had the guy interacted with anyone else, and it was starting to seem like none of the others could see him.

"I swear he vanished."

Astrid nodded. "That'll happen."

Mason didn't like that. He was sure she would say Nic was wily and could even hide in a small group. The casual way she acknowledged Nic's impermanence filled him with chills.

"Was he trying to convince you to give up or go home?"

"How did you know?"

"Kassidi does the same thing to me. That's why I never let her get close anymore."

"You can … just *keep her away?*"

Astrid nodded. "My brain decided she knew me better than anyone because I was originally dropped into her mind. It took me months to accept the Kassidi in here wasn't the *real* Kass."

"So, what is she?"

"A manifestation of my fear … most of the time."

"But I saw you with her. She was close to you. That time you burst into my Heist simulation with the Muse …"

"A conflation of memories. I was looking for you. It wasn't entirely your Heist. Some of what I saw in there belonged to Carter. Some of what you saw — like Kassidi — came from your father as well."

Mason rubbed his forehead. "This hurts to think about."

"Good. It means you still know the difference."

"The difference between real and unreal?"

"I prefer to think of it as the difference between physical and mental."

Ahead, Bear looked at his tablet and said, "Nearly there."

But Mason barely heard. He went to his knees as pain struck like lightning.

Before Astrid even noticed, Nic was at his side. He whispered, "See? It's all happening again."

Mason knew what was coming. The white room. The black dots and spirals. The terror.

But Nic was already gone. Astrid was kneeling by him, casting glances at the leading party and the sky. Whatever they were avoiding — through patterns or guile or excellent timing — was still a threat and on their tails.

She touched his shoulders and the back of his head. "Are you okay?"

At war with the pain, he asked, "Where are we going?"

"To find Carter."

"I don't know where he is."

"Your deeper mind does."

"I don't. It doesn't."

"You know how to find him whether you realize it or not." She pointed. "You see Bear and Ike up there?"

Mason looked.

"The system has recontextualized your connection to Carter — that psychic bond — as the signal they're tracking. Your focus keeps it front and center, while my intention and knowledge of the network translates the signal and its triangulation as tracking data on Bear's tablet. You just need to keep thinking, *intending* to find your father. My broader mind will grant location to what you see."

"Lady, I barely understand my 'connection' to Carter. If you think it's something I can just 'tune into' …"

Astrid stopped walking to meet Mason's gaze. "You can. Subconsciously, you can tune into it whenever you want. You saw an AI psychiatrist in your Pattern Black simulation, right?"

Mason flashed back to the maddening hologram.

There is an anomaly semantically linked to the records of both Shaw, Carter and Shaw, Mason. Although, of course, the latter—

He looked up at her.

"The sim was you," she said. "The psychiatrist was you. Whatever that doctor told you, part of you had already figured out."

"Where is he, then?" Mason asked.

She looked to Bear, who understood and nodded in the direction they were already heading. "Ahead."

"Where?"

"I don't know. Around a few more corners?"

Mason replayed that strange voice in his head. *My party will meet yours in Four Alpha.*

"So … in Four Alpha?"

He didn't know what that meant, but Astrid's eyes widened. "Our best guess is that Carter is in the Four Alpha designation on the grid — or at least, he's in what maps to Four for as long as we both agree to use the city as a template for these little mind games. How did you know?"

"I must have seen it somewhere."

Astrid shook her head. "The original grid was only used in our state proposal. It's not something you'd run across."

"Who's meeting us?" Mason asked instead of answering her implied question.

"How did you know about Four Alpha, Mason?"

"Answer me first."

"Hopefully, Carter will meet us."

"I get that. I meant, Who else?"

Bear, Ike, Dakota, and Nic had returned to form a circle around them. And Leigh. Mason had forgotten about her the same way he sometimes forgot about Nic. But now, here she was, along with his memory.

"Nobody else," said Astrid.

"Unless …" Something blipped on Bear's tablet.

Astrid saw it then spun around, looking in every direction.

"What?" Mason asked.

Her attention fixed on something behind him. "Shit."

Mason turned instead of asking again.

The street behind them had been lined with tall buildings gone decrepit with neglect. Now, those same structures were bent toward each other like plants starving for sunshine, their tips nearly touching to form a canopy that blackened the street below. The stone had warped, cracking and bowing into sagging parentheses.

Reality was now a portrait, inked on water, bending to circle the drain.

In the center grew an eye. Not black. White. Nothingness pocked with spots. Holes. Portals to other places. Or to nothing but silence.

Mason felt malevolence in it all. Pursuit. Anger. *Purpose.*

My party will meet yours.

"He's here," Mason said.

"Carter?" But Astrid's voice didn't believe that for a second.

Mason shook his head. "Preacher."

Astrid stared hard at Bear. Then at Ike, who was so much bigger and stronger.

Ike picked up Mason. Understanding everything on a level under his consciousness, Mason didn't resist.

A shape came out of the whiteness. Massive. Looming.

A forming storm.

From it came an enormous man with a shaved head and menace in his every step.

FIFTY-ONE

Buying Time

Dakota stared at the hologram. She'd never seen such a thing. Had never — not before Sarah, and certainly not after — entered a simulation. The idea of projecting falsities — of presenting things that weren't, strictly speaking, *actually there* — was new to her. Which was why Nathaniel Blake's hologram was so entrancing.

She kept watching the pulsing light as it fanned out from the projector inside the sphere that had tunneled its way through Dharma One's wall. She kept watching its head, farthest from the projector, noting how mostly solid it seemed. She could see the wall behind him. Sometimes he flickered. But combining visuals with Blake's already-commanding presence was enough to make it feel like the man was sharing their room.

Dakota stepped back, tripped on Calliope's mess, nearly fell. As she stumbled, her gaze never left the hologram, and when she found a workbench, she blindly groped for a weapon.

And wasn't *that* a laugh? This Blake was made of light. His real self was beyond harm, in an unknown place far away.

"It's okay, Dakota," Calliope said.

They'd been hiding so Blake wouldn't find them. Now, he had.

They couldn't just take this lying down. If they were to die, then Dakota planned to do it standing.

She hissed at Calliope. Indicated the door, hoping they could somehow pull Mason from his pod without having to run. She seemed about to respond, but Blake beat her to it.

"Tell her, Elisabeth. Tell her if I wanted you dead, you'd *be dead already.* I wouldn't waste a specialized drone to blow this place sky high. We have satellite targeting for such things."

"Bullshit," Dakota hissed at her. "He's just going to talk and let us go? Now that he found you, he's Mr. Good Guy?"

Calliope waved a hand as if to say, *I've got this.*

Dakota lowered her voice. "We can go up to the catwalk and out onto the roof."

Blake spoke past Dakota as if she were a child. "The hearing threshold on this device is far more sensitive than human ears. She might as well stop whispering. Tell her if there *were* a bomb in my little sentinel, I'd never be idiot enough to make it weak enough that you could simply *run away.*"

Blake's intelligence was legendary, bested only by his old partner. If he sent a holographic drone to cut through the walls and speak for him, there was a reason. If he planned to trick them, he'd have considered every detail.

They stared across the mostly empty space at each other. An impasse … or more likely, with Blake holding a hidden upper hand.

"I've been looking for you for a very long time, Elisabeth."

Dakota stilled her body, but her eyes and mind were mice in a cage. She cased the room without, hopefully, seeming to do so. There was the catwalk, yes, but she could now see a drone's black shape moving in and out of view beyond the high window. Calliope said she'd replaced the windows with bartered Lucite, meaning the drone couldn't come crashing in. But it probably wouldn't offer her tea if she went through the window on her own.

Head still, eyes moving. Three windows like that, all too high without a ladder. Two doors in this room and many options in the rooms beyond. Dakota had joined many standoffs during her time on the force and knew too many points of exit and entry wasn't usually a good thing for the occupants inside. A bouquet of options left an abundance to watch and defend.

"And now you found me." Calliope bided her time with stillness, coiled inside and waiting for an opportunity to spring free. "Now what?"

"Now we talk."

Dakota scoffed. Her focus was on the drones beyond the windows. Her mind was on the humming outside and the subtle footsteps of human troops finding their place.

The hologram turned to Dakota. Rendered in full 3D, it was less like a monitor and more like living theater.

"And who are *you?*"

Calliope answered, her tone pacifying and fight all gone. "*Dakota,* Nathaniel. This is Dakota Ward."

Dakota's head snapped toward Calliope, but clearly, Blake knew her name already. He nodded, a knowing smile touching his lips. "People say you're the new leader."

"Of what?"

"Of Immunity. Of the little group playing house in one of my old freezer depots."

"What exactly do you want to talk about?" Calliope asked.

Blake swiveled to face Mason, convalescent inside the sim tube with his eyes closed. The projector ball rolled forward so he could see. "Tell you what." He indicated the pod with a holographic arm. "Let's talk about *him.*"

"He's nobody," Dakota said.

Blake ignored her and spoke to Calliope. "Did you know? About the Shaws?"

"What about them?"

"That they were connected. I didn't. You should have *seen* the depth of diagnostics it took before I understood what you were doing. What *he* was doing."

"He's not doing anything," Calliope said, glancing at Dakota.

There was something in that look. More than denial.

The droid rolled closer. Blake's holographic hand moved above Mason as if meaning to grab and strangle. The hand went to his neck but stopped short of pretending to touch. From where Dakota stood, she saw one real man reaching for another. Except for Blake's barely-there transparency, the illusion was perfect.

"I could pull the plug, you know. Not literally. But I have my ways, even from here."

"Go ahead."

"Or maybe you could do it," said the hologram to Calliope. "Prove that nothing's happening here."

"I don't have to prove anything to you."

A weapon discharged outside. Something big, with an explosive round. Metal struck the roof then rolled down, taking too long to reach the edge before dropping to the dirt. One of the HRO drones eliminating one of Calliope's, if Dakota had to guess — and the timing didn't feel like a coincidence.

"You're right. You don't have to prove anything." The hologram frowned, then seemed to look around. "Of course, I know where you are now. The guards and drones know where you are. We all know where the rest of your people are, too," he added, now eyeing Dakota. "Have for some time. So far, Immunity has been useful to me. To Revival, and the prison as a whole. Inmates fear you. They think you're the reason people disappear. That you're behind all the terrorism. Immunity is a useful 'them' for our PR team to rally 'us' around. Amazing, the tricks you can pull with someone to blame."

Blake rolled closer then stooped. There was a literal cord plugged into the wall — data, not power. His hand hovered above it. "What do you think, Elisabeth? If I break the connection, will he die? By any sensible definition, he already is."

"It's me you're after," Calliope said.

"And it's you I've got." He straightened, the projector now nearing Calliope. "What are you doing here, Elisabeth?"

"Hiding."

Blake indicated Mason. "Twins, parents, and children ... they end up sharing space even if we never put them together in a sim. You remember how it could be sometimes. But I took Carter off-grid, and something's still been trying to get at him." He shook his head like one who sees but refuses to believe. "You'd have run off to

Bora Bora if you really wanted to hide. But you buried yourself in my prison instead."

"*My* prison," Calliope corrected.

"You're slippery, but not *that* slippery. Pattern Black is supposed to be like a wall. You go in, and you can't break back out. But somehow, he's going *beneath* that wall. Beneath *all* the walls. What did you teach him? And why?"

"I didn't teach him anything."

"Bullshit," Blake said. "He knows the entire grid. We can see him moving around inside."

"So? Shut it down."

"Obviously, we can't do that."

"Then capture him. Erase him."

His jaw firmed. Dakota saw it and knew. They were still alive because Calliope and Blake were in a deadlock. Both were feinting and threatening under their breath, but only Dakota was free to act. The others were following a script. *You say this, and I'll say that.* It wasn't performance. They weren't colluding. There were no other options. Nothing else to do, no other ways to go or words to say.

Elisabeth Reeves had been missing for years, but what Dakota saw now had the feeling of an ancient argument. One they'd had time and time again but would be helpless to resolve without one of them finally backing down.

"You can't capture him," Calliope said when Blake didn't answer. "You can't erase him. Can you?"

"He's slippery, like you. And he doesn't just know the grid. He knows how to tunnel underneath it."

Dakota wasn't sure what that meant, but she knew Blake was wrong. Mason was stumbling in the dark. If he was Superman, his yellow sun had happened on accident.

"He's—"

"Listen to you," Dakota said, cutting him off. "*Both* of you."

Each of them turned toward her, clearly not expecting an interruption.

Dakota walked over to Mason's cord then wrapped her hand

around it as she glared at Blake. "You want it pulled? You want him out?" She turned to Calliope. "How about you … *Elisabeth?*"

Calliope shook her head. "You'll kill him, Dakota."

"Blake will kill him anyway."

"Blake *can't* kill him."

Dakota raised her eyebrows. Calliope had spoken quickly, without thinking, and made it sound like an unwillingness to do the deed rather than an inability. As if Blake *could* kill Mason but *wouldn't*, for reasons unknown.

"Why not?"

Neither answered, so Dakota tugged the cord again.

Blake's hand shot out, a small sound of protest bleating from his lips.

"*You* want him alive, too. Both of you do." Dakota stood, her hand relaxing. Then she spread her arms wide. "You know what? Go ahead and kill us."

Calliope reacted, but Dakota held out a hand, looking at Blake. "You don't want to kill him? Then just kill us. Me and her. You have the worst aim of anyone I've ever met. We're inside a prison you both own and control. We keep being chased by drones and guards, but none of them ever catches us, even though we should be fish in a barrel. Maybe you didn't know she was here, inside Dharma One. Now you do. The place is surrounded, and you sent something through the wall. But it was only a *conversation*. All talk, no action. So come on, big man." Dakota walked closer to the projector, her arms still spread wide. "Do your worst."

Blake looked to Calliope.

"Kill us, kill him, or *shut the fuck up.*" Dakota looked at them each, in turn, meeting their gazes, staring down something inside them. Then she looked back at the cord connecting Mason to the sim — and, maybe, keeping him alive. She inched back to keep it within sprinting distance. "I'm not kidding about pulling that cord. Mason was dead for three years. I mourned. I made my peace. He came back long enough to be a prisoner, and now he might end up trapped inside something that's *supposed* to be like death but is apparently more like Hell or a horror show. I'd be doing him a favor by ending it now. Doing *all of us* a favor."

They waited, each assessing her.

Dakota said, "What'll it be? You've got the hammer, *Mister Blake.* Swing it or drop it — but either way, *please* stop embarrassing yourself."

He seemed to consider. Then, oblique to Dakota's challenge but clearly prompted by it, Blake stared long and hard at Calliope. "You think his mind is in there somewhere, don't you?"

She looked at Dakota and nodded.

"You can't get inside without Mason's connection," Blake continued. "Not deeply enough. You cover your tracks well, but I can see you enter the sim every time. I've watched you for *years*. You go in, you come out. You break something, you walk away. But no matter how many times you go under, it's still not enough. You need the son to find the father. I could make this easier, Elisabeth. I *have* Carter Shaw. Maybe we can reach an agreement. I give you amnesty and my word. You come to Revival and have a go at accessing the body directly. We could work together, just like the old days."

"The old days," Calliope said. "When your ambition scared me so much, I had to lock up Carter's thoughts and hide the key."

"You want what's in his head, same as I do."

Another quiet standoff commenced. But the danger was over — now that Dakota had called their bluffs. Reeves and Blake were halves of a whole. There would be no murder here today. It was all bluff and bluster.

Yet something was bothering Dakota. Something Blake had said that still didn't jibe.

"When's the last time you saw her inside the sim?" Dakota asked.

"Constantly. Every day."

No matter what Blake thought he'd seen, the real Calliope hadn't entered a sim in ages. He didn't know there were two of them now, one inside and another outside. Blake had been chasing her digital half, the one who still had ambition.

Blake thought it was just Mason inside, stumbling to find his father. But Digital Calliope was in there as well, and that gave them the upper hand. *That* version of Calliope still might be able to slip past Blake while his attention was on the other one.

"Okay," Calliope told Blake after another glance at Dakota.

"Okay?" Dakota repeated.

To Blake, she said, "Truce."

"Now wait just a goddamn—" Dakota began.

Calliope held up a hand, palm out as she nodded toward Mason. "If you let us go — *all three* of us — I'll come to Revival." She looked at the pod again, where it appeared the younger Shaw had been assaulted by multicolored spaghetti. "I'll bring Mason and hook him up at HQ. But when we unlock that key, Nathaniel …" She widened her eyes, asking a question.

Blake said, "If you help me, I won't have to use it."

Dakota considered them both, trying to untangle the layers of deception. Carter was the key to some sort of nuclear solution. Calliope was sure Blake planned to use it. She was pretending to believe him. Pretending to believe he *wanted* a truce, wanted the key to a doomsday solution he had no intention of using.

Both combatants still had out their claws. Both still played chicken.

"Promise?" she asked.

"Promise," Blake said.

They looked at Mason. At the pod.

Then Calliope glanced at an empty one across the room. "I need to go in. I need to let him know the deal's off, and he should come back out. Rejoin mind and brain before we disconnect him."

"How do I know you won't warn him?" Blake asked, his expression incredulous.

"You have to trust me."

Blake snickered. "You stay here. I can handle it if you need Mason Shaw in one piece."

"You'll never find him. It has to be me."

The hologram flickered. Blake turned to nobody, apparently

discussing something off-screen. The sound muted, and they heard none of what was said. Then he turned back to them.

"We know where he is on the grid, along with what appear to be a few projections. In Four Alpha, like I said. What shall I tell Mason, so he believes what we say is coming from you?"

"Tell him you'll meet him when skies are clearer," Calliope said.

"*When skies are clearer?*"

"It's a code we established."

Dakota diverted her eyes, not wanting her gaze to betray the moment. Calliope was lying, but she wasn't sure why.

Blake nodded then turned to go. As he did, the little droid began to retreat as part of this kabuki of truce.

"Blake," Dakota said.

He looked back.

"If looking was all you had to do to find Mason, why go through all this trouble? You're just going to pop in and *talk* to him? Is that all it ever took?"

"A friend of mine will be going to talk in my stead." A tiny, knowing smile creased his lips. "We'll talk when he's out."

The hologram shivered and vanished, then the little wheeled projector retraced its steps and squirmed back through the hole. Calliope rushed over and laid plate metal over the opening, backing it with a heavy set of iron members that'd been scattered nearby.

"We've got a problem," Calliope said. "He must have meant Preacher."

"It's okay. He needs Mason. He'll play ball until you force him not to."

"You don't understand. Blake thinks he's been after the real me, but he's actually been after *her.* I agreed to a truce, but *she* didn't. And won't. No way she'll lay down when Preacher finds her. The other Calliope's going to fight."

"As long as he gets Mason out, it's fine."

"Mason won't come, either. Not to Blake. Not to Preacher."

"What was that 'code' you gave him? About the clear skies?"

"Carter used to say that as a joke. His way of making fun of people who hoped things would turn out well but never did anything to ensure they did. It was the ultimate insult when we were working together and the last thing he'd say to his son if he was hoping to gain his trust or favor."

"Then why the hell did you tell Blake to say it?"

"Because we have to find Carter before he does. We need a warning, just in case anyone from Blake's camp gets close. Something that tells him to run."

The humming intensified outside.

Dakota looked up. Where a single drone had been visible beyond the skylight, she now saw three or four swarming like locusts. Then the explosions began.

"Your drones, fighting prison drones."

"And prison drones," Calliope added, "fighting *other* prison drones."

"Why?"

"I was afraid this would happen."

Dakota was about to ask what when a klaxon began to blare. "What's that?"

"Chaos alarm. Between all the drones and churn inside the Chamber Therapy system, we've reached the tolerance threshold."

Dakota looked up into the rising alarm. The battle raged outside, and she was curious if the newcomers understood there were persons of interest doing forbidden things inside the prohibited building.

The first hit the roof, then she knew.

Dakota scanned the room in preparation more than fear. Her gaze landed on the empty immersion pod. "Are you really planning to go in?"

"I just said that to buy us time. I have to prepare *here*, not in there."

Dakota moved closer to the empty pod. "Then send me in."

"No."

"Someone has to warn *him*. Someone has to warn *her*."

"Blake will when he delivers my message 'from Carter.'"

"And what about Preacher?"

Calliope was at her tablet, unmoving.

"What about Preacher?"

"He's what tipped the chaos alarm past its threshold," Calliope said as if reading the screen. "It wasn't us. It was him." She gave Dakota a strange look. "Crossing that thing's path right now would be extraordinarily dangerous."

"Then you *have* to send me in! *I have to help them!*"

But Calliope was shaking her head.

"It's too late," she said, face lit by the screen before her. "He's already there."

FIFTY-TWO

A Newer, Deeper Reality

PREACHER.

Big, broad, made of muscle. Even from a distance, a pair of gold-hoop earrings dazzled against his pale skin. His head was slick, highlighted from above.

Does he have to shave? Does a simulated person's hair grow?

"Shit," said Ike.

They'd stopped, but only for a moment. Only because Preacher had paused. Why bother running at them? He'd already proven he could be in one place, then instantly another. That left nowhere to hide.

Mason peeked around the corner and wished he hadn't. The buildings behind Preacher had uprooted like weeds, slowly revolving around a loose vortex in a sky that'd gone from blue to nothing. The streets and foundations, some of which remained, were pocked with man-sized, perfectly round black holes. Mason swore he could see movement in them. Swore, he could hear them calling. It terrified him.

Preacher stood in the center, on a stubborn jut of land, pavement cracked beneath him.

Ike poked around the corner, hoisting his massive weapon. The minigun coughed fire, too fast to hear individual reports. Large-caliber bullets shredded a parked car at the alley's end, sounding like a massive pantry full of crumpling cans. A siren screamed above it all. Mason sensed something had gone terribly wrong somewhere, and time was almost gone.

The minigun ran empty. Preacher didn't have a scratch on him. The slugs had only struck air. He said, "From there, Elisha went up to Bethel, and as he was walking up the road, a group of young men came out of the city and jeered at him, chanting, 'Go up you bald head! Go up, you bald head!' Then he turned around, looked at them, and called down a curse in the name of the LORD."

Preacher didn't yell, but Mason could hear him over an increasing torrent of sound, more psychic than literal. Thoughts tumbled like clothes in a dryer. The headaches were back and worse than before. Invisible fingers pressed into his throat. Hot rocks scalded his neck. A vise clamped to his temples, turning tighter by some unseen hand.

His back slumped against the building as he slid into a feeble crouch.

Astrid called to him from across a small alley between the two halves of their party. The alley was disintegrating but still whole enough to run.

"Come on, Mason! *Think!* Focus on your tie to Carter. Show us where to go!"

"How the fuck would I know where to go?"

Dakota, who'd been across the alley, was suddenly beside him.

"Clear your mind," she said.

"What?"

Mason looked up and saw Carter in her place, hand extended with an offended expression.

Then he was Dakota again.

Preacher advanced, booming. "You can run, but yer ass cannot hide!" His voice was somehow everywhere at once.

"Come on, Mason," Dakota said, returning his attention to their twosome. "Which way should we go?"

"I don't know. What do you think?"

"I don't know. And if I do, it's because you know."

Mason blinked at her. Did they all know what they were? Were any of them self-aware? "I don't know the prison. I … I was never really here." His head wanted to pound again, but this time from all the knots he kept tying it into.

"Of course, you know the prison. You know it because Carter knows it."

"But I don't know the way."

"You know the way because you are the way."

"What about him?" He meant Preacher, the approaching footsteps, the cracking and disintegration of all that had seemed so certain and solid. The brick was fading behind him. He looked toward Astrid's group. Most of their shelter was gone. The world wasn't being destroyed so much as it had grabbed its own feet and was eating itself alive.

Astrid and the others were surrounded by a blinding whiteness.

A tiny dot appeared in the air behind her. It spread like an inkblot, growing into something rigid, expanding its radius like the dialing of an iris. Seconds later, it was the size of a storm sewer, then it was big enough to walk through while crouching. Of the group, only Leigh turned to see it.

But it was too late. She seemed to bend in half at the waist, ass-first as if preparing to sit in a chair six inches behind her. With a blur of light, she was gone, sucked into the circle.

Mason's breath caught in his throat, but no one on the other side had noticed.

Including, it seemed, the Dakota next to him.

"You were always different," she told him. "You always wanted to be the same."

His father was back beside him, and now Dakota was gone.

"Why is this happening?" Mason asked.

Carter said, "Because it is."

"Are you really here?"

"No. But then again, who is?"

A hole appeared directly beneath Carter's feet. Matte black and featureless — more like a portable hole slapped there by Wile E. Coyote than something dug by an auger.

Then his father was gone. Only Mason didn't see Carter's stubbled head as he fell. Instead, he saw Dakota's black locks, blown upward in an unseen and unfelt wind.

The hole was flat and featureless again, a big black circle painted onto the concrete.

Then it, too, was gone.

An enormous sound of breaking rock thundered through the alley. Preacher was much closer, his heavy feet breaking support as he walked without hurry.

"Come on, now. You don't wanna live here, right? Come with me. Come with me, and it'll all be better."

Preacher moved until he was a foot from Mason. A charge flowed from the giant's skin, making Mason's arm hair stand and dance in the static. He was close enough for Mason to smell his sweat if the demon smelled like anything. Close enough to feel his hot breath.

Mason looked left. The hole that had taken Leigh was still there, directly behind Astrid. She seemed oblivious. Alone now, her projections all had departed or had been stolen away. And still, she waited, unaware. Maybe he had entered his own fugue and could no longer trust what he saw. This was Pattern Black, after all.

Preacher reached out. Grabbed Mason by his shirt.

He was paralyzed, unable to think. A passenger in his own body … if he even *had* a body. His head thumped so hard, he was sure his nose, ears, and mouth must be bleeding. He closed his eyes against the pain.

Preacher drew him forward. The headache was too intense. Mason couldn't open his eyes. He could only *exist* and maybe survive to the other side. Preacher, now behind him, wrapped his arms around Mason in some sort of disturbing, distorted hug then crushed him against his massive muscular chest.

The last thing he saw before Preacher's flesh eclipsed the white sky was a small black hurricane. He felt the vortex and the radiance of its alien power.

"Let it all out," Preacher said. "You let it go, and I gots the rest."

"Mason …" came Astrid's voice. *Mason?"*

He looked over, peeking past Preacher's armpit. Her visage regarded him, more confused than afraid.

There was a flash. For the blink of an instant, Mason seemed to see himself from the outside. Maybe through someone else's eyes, or perhaps from a high-above vantage stolen from the system's eye. In that flicker, he saw himself standing by the alley's mouth, slumped into an awkward half-crouch, arms dead weight at his sides. Exactly how he'd look if he were being bear-hugged by an invisible giant. Exactly how Mason would look if he was imagining it all.

No Preacher. No destruction. No end to everything.

Then Mason was back to being suffocated by the behemoth.

He saw the vortex growing and moving so much faster now.

"There you go," Preacher lulled.

Clear your mind.

Not Dakota this time. Only the disembodied voice of his father.

You hear me, Mason? Focus on your breath. See if you can slow it down. Focus on inhaling and exhaling, and focus on my voice.

His father's old advice, from the days of breakdowns. Of *whatever-they-were.* To Mason, looking back, those teenage incidents — or "episodes" as the doctor called them — read like panic attacks, except they came with deep, fathomless agoraphobia. With existential dread.

Mason remembered a rapid heartbeat and constricted breath, but also a sense of *largeness* — a world so big and bottomless, it hurt to comprehend. Or to even *try* to. Those times had felt like floating in space. Like drifting through darkness forever, alone.

The voice was insistent.

In. Out. Feel the air's coolness on the way in. Feel it leave you, warm, as you exhale. Come on, Mason. Walk the line. Stay with me.

Walk the line? Mason wondered.

You're here, but you're not here. I'm here, but I'm not here. This is real enough. This isn't real at all.

"It hurts my head," he thought aloud.

Mason, clamped in Preacher's vise grip, regressed through time.

He felt his adulthood slip away. His identity spilled into the nothingness, his sense of *self* skimmed off as if by a psychedelic drug.

He was twenty-five and a rookie, following his father's lead.

He was twenty-one, blackout drunk on his birthday. He'd called his mother, but his father came with reprimands. Still, nobody ever learned of the fight. Nobody asked about the window he'd broken or the pool table he'd gouged in anger. Carter cleared his way like he always had before.

I don't want your help.

Yeah, but you're getting it, anyway.

This must be what dying felt like. This must be what losing one's mind felt like.

He was fifteen. Scared shitless. Sure he'd hit the loony bin before getting his license. That was the first time Carter had given the sage wisdom that didn't help at all — *Different isn't the same as crazy. Never compare how you are to how anyone else is, Mason. Not ever.*

"Her," Mason croaked to Preacher. His gaze went to where Astrid should be, though he could no longer tell if she was there. "She's the one you're after."

"Says who?" Then he laughed.

Mason couldn't see Preacher's face, but the big man had to be smiling.

Now there was nothing. No Preacher. No Astrid. No buildings. No world.

Only Carter Shaw with a finger bent before him, beckoning him hither.

Mason felt part of himself tugged away.

He *understood.*

With realization came power. Mason did nothing consciously, but a blast of strange energy came from him like the jolt of household current, like a startle response over which he had no control.

Preacher staggered back and said something holy that Mason only barely caught, his embrace momentarily broken.

Now free, he wasted no time. Mason felt his father's will inside him, pushing him to run.

He raced through crumbling streets in the staggered void. After a while, he heard footsteps behind him. A single set — because panic was no place for projections.

Astrid, not Preacher. The jolt had knocked the big man back, but he'd surely recover.

After two full minutes of sprints and turns, Mason stopped in front of a familiar door. He could barely breathe or see. Astrid came up, panting beside him.

"This is the place," Mason said. "I remember it now."

"Hiding won't do us any good. Preacher can teleport to wherever—"

"This isn't a place to hide," Mason told her. "This is the place you wanted me to find."

Astrid looked confused, then she double-checked her tablet. "It's a fabrication plant. Pattern Black's facsimile of the HRO sweeps central buildings as thoroughly as the real HRO. There's nothing here — and certainly not Carter."

But this was *Mason's* Pattern Black — whatever the building had been, part of him had made improvements.

He opened the door. When they were both through, Mason locked it with an iron bar built into the mechanism.

There was a converted space full of computers inside, strung with wires and festooned with metal catwalks. From somewhere in the past, Mason remembered walking the short concrete path to the door then descending the metal gangway in bare feet, wrapped in Dakota's blanket.

She protested as they climbed. They found a corpse at the top, the uniformed body lying on the slotted metal deck, stained with ancient blood. This man had meant to kill Mason before a false Dakota shot him instead.

"What the hell?" Astrid asked.

But even with the sound growing outside and Preacher just moments away, Mason couldn't help but feel his first beat of satisfaction — and control. He'd known this place was here because of an instinct he was only now starting to trust, telling him what to find and how to find it.

Astrid's face changed at the sight of a circular pool of glowing green gel sunken into the walkway just beyond the body, its lid still ajar from the day Mason had been dragged out. A diver's regulator and blacked-out goggles still rested where he and an earlier version of Dakota had left them prior to running.

"This is where you came out, isn't it? Where you were extracted from your simulation inside Pattern Black."

Mason was just wondering how this might work when, farther down the gangway, a second vertical tube of green goo dilated into existence. There was no longer a single immersion tube. Now, they both had one.

"We can't immerse into a simulation from another simulation, Mason. We're already two levels deep."

"You asked for the way," Mason said, already stripping to his skivvies and attaching wires, lower legs kissing the surface of the green pool. "This is the way."

"How?"

"Carter. He's hiding in the Heist."

"How do you know?"

"It's where I'd hide."

After a blink of indecision, Astrid followed his lead and moved to the second slime-filled immersion pod. This wasn't a real immersion rig. It was a simulation invented by his mind — *his*, not Carter's since nothing like this place existed in anyone else's plans.

Would it even work? *Could* it work?

Preacher banged on the door as they slid into their pools, fit goggles over their eyes, and shoved regulators between their teeth. He tossed one last glance to Astrid in her tube, reached back, grabbed his lid's wheel lock, then pulled it shut with a clang.

Darkness.

Mason slid down the tube. His toes brushed the bottom. He bobbed back up then began to float. The machine seemed to know his intention.

Lights came from everywhere at once.

Then a newer, deeper reality found him.

FIFTY-THREE

The Only Way Out is Through

ABOVE WAS a light bulb in a milky shell, its glass rubbed matte as if handled by steel wool. Its glow was the yellow of jaundiced skin. Ten filament stalks poked from what looked like candle wax in the old bulb's center, each resembling a—

"Shaw. You paying attention?"

Carter was sitting directly across from Mason in a confined space, a loud and steady hum as present as the bulb with the matchstick filaments. He was wearing a riot uniform with a name-plate on his breast that read *Cruz*. For a moment, Mason was disoriented. He could barely see. Someone must have given him drugs.

"You paying attention?" Carter repeated.

"I—"

"You look like shit," said someone else.

Mason's head swiveled. That was Dakota, to the right of Carter. She …

But Mason couldn't finish *that* thought, either. He was pretty sure Dakota had been arrested, possibly a long time ago, definitely for something she hadn't done.

But he was also quite sure she *hadn't* been arrested and was

482

working intake for the Union Station HRO, where his father was incarcerated.

Mason scanned the space, recognizing his surroundings as the disorientation settled. Flanking him inside this van were Nic — somehow a bunkmate to Mason and a source for his father — on the left, and on his right, two people he was slowly starting to remember — Bear and Ike. The latter's massive weapon kept jabbing Dakota in the chest.

A woman he barely knew was on the other side of Carter. Mason had met her once, possibly a long time ago. Except he'd also known her forever and considered her a friend. Leigh was a doctor. An HRO shrink or an Army surgeon, he wasn't quite sure.

"Once we're inside, watch the corners. Buster, you go left." Carter looked at Dakota, who'd never been called *Buster.* "Mason, you handle the guards to the right. Two of them, just like we said, standing by—"

"The poster?"

Silence. The van hit a pothole. Then Carter said, "It's always like this."

"Like what?"

"You get swept into the script. It's like someone hijacked your mind."

Sanity returned. Mason realized where he was but not why. Parents tried to live through their children, said the cliché. It was the other way around for him.

As the script lost its hold, so much returned. His gaze fixed on his father, and for the first time, Mason saw him as real. Phantasms were one thing, but this was the genuine Carter. The father he'd loved, then hated, then offered his final goodbyes.

"You're alive," Mason said.

"That's a matter of opinion."

"How are you here?"

"I was hoping you could tell me. I was in my hole, knowing I could never come out from what I built. There was a knock on the door. There's *never* been a knock. I couldn't help answering. I remember standing up … then I was here."

Something pressed against his temples. It wasn't physical pressure. It was something Mason had forgotten — a dropped bit of intel that desperately wanted to enter his awareness. Urgent, whatever it was. He recalled a ticking clock, remembered voices and explosions from above, now two levels up.

"We were …" He squinted, and the effort hurt his head something fierce. "We were … running from someone. We …"

He couldn't finish. Or think. Mason grabbed his head in both hands, rubbed his forehead with his thumbs, and mussed his hair in the process. He finally looked back up, bleary-eyed. The details were there but invisible through the pain.

"You look like shit," Dakota repeated.

Mason looked at Carter. "What's wrong with her? She's still on script."

"I'm not on script," Dakota replied. "I'm saying you look like shit because you look like shit. Anyone got a mirror? A camera? Or maybe I could draw you a picture."

The van hit another pothole, and the whole works wrenched hard left. Two wheels tipped from the pavement but smacked back a second later, then a great roar exploded from the rear.

"Bear," said the driver, though it was Astrid behind the wheel. "Take over for me."

Something boomed from behind.

Mason rushed toward the rear doors to peek, kneeing Nic and Leigh in the process.

He saw a souped-up death car through the windows — the kind that existed in gonzo apocalypse films and Big Daddy Roth sketches — with a large bald man tucked behind the wheel.

The car had guns. No, *cannons*. Mason could see them clearly, mounted above each six-inch fin flanking the hood.

There was a blast, a vapor trail, then a wrenching so large, the van's side buckled. The metal crimped hard enough to claim an idle hand.

With Bear now behind the wheel, the van took another lurching turn. The force of Preacher's shell had been so jarring, their ride should have been crippled. Mason saw him disappear in the rearview. Only, they hadn't just lost their pursuer around a bend. The city itself kept shifting like a pop-up book that couldn't stop popping.

Bear turned again and again, but the rearview never changed. It was always the same few buildings, thrumming into and out of existence. Protective, almost, as if the city were an organ.

Ike took the passenger seat, leaving his massive weapon to block the aisle between benches. He didn't need to roll down the window. It'd shattered to cubes when whatever-it-was hit their ride. His head vanished through the opening like a dog seeking thrills, then he looked back with an ashen expression.

"What?" asked Bear.

"Just … keep driving."

Mason glanced at Carter, then tried to stand. Astrid stopped him with a hand on his chest.

"I just want to see," he said.

"You're not really here, remember? Believe what we want to be true."

"What does that mean?"

"Believe we're in a sound van, alive and well, and that we'll make it in time."

"What do you mean, 'in time'?"

"There are so many answers to that."

Bear kept looking out the window, peering back at the van's side where Preacher's round had struck it. Mason still had his eyes on the rear. The van wasn't even thumping on bent axles, suddenly smooth like a boat on glassy water.

"Sit down," Carter said.

"He's back there somewhere." Mason sat.

"Tell him where to go."

"Who?" Mason asked.

"The driver. Are you stupid?"

"I need a map."

"There is no map."

Mason looked at his father. "You know the city. *You* navigate."

Astrid crouched between them. "Listen to me, Mason."

"I'm listening."

"We aren't in a van."

He looked around.

She reached up, took his chin, turned his head to face her, then repeated, *"We aren't in a van."*

"We're not?"

"We're in immersion tubes. We went to where Dakota extracted you the first time in a higher-level simulation. You wanted to immerse *again*. To enter the Heist through a simulated simulator. There was one tube, but your mind made a second one for me. Do you remember?"

"You didn't think it would work. Did it?"

"So far, so good."

But as with so much lately, it was agony to think on. He pinched his nose.

Astrid grabbed his wrist. "Try to hold what's real, but don't try *too* hard. It's a balance, remember?"

"What?"

"You didn't finish training. Did you?"

He considered lying, then shook his head.

"Mason," Carter said, taking over. "Listen to me. I'm like you. Understand? I'm still me. Still your father. My body is somewhere. I don't know where."

"Nathaniel Blake has it. He needs something you have."

Carter nodded as if he already knew, as if he'd never moved his eyes from that precious cargo. "Point is, you're talking to me. Not to a reflection of yourself or Elisabeth. Not AI, put here by the sim. This is *me*, Mason. Your father."

Given the circumstances, Mason could only nod. If he had his wits, he might leap across the space and grab Carter by the throat.

"Right now, you are inside a simulation. Understand?"

"He understands." Astrid paused. *"Painfully* well."

"A simulation inside a simulation," Carter elaborated. "When I was learning, I got headaches, too. Terrible ones. I know they hurt, but I *let them hurt*. It only stops once you accept what you see and fully believe where you are."

"She just *told* me to believe." Mason ached from the irony as much as the pain. "Jesus Christ. I feel like we're in *Peter Pan*. Because you know what, motherfucker? I *do* believe in fairies."

"Believe the right things," Carter said. "Don't believe what you're given. Or what you fear."

But the instant Carter mentioned fear, Mason recalled what they all *had* to be very afraid of. He heard a second engine again, close behind. And the squeal of tires — even the shout of vaguely holy threats.

Astrid said, "Don't let Preacher in, Mason."

"What the hell does that mean?"

"Control your mind."

Mason looked at his father. *Control your mind* was the sort of thing Carter had said when things got bad and panic came to threaten him. He felt like a teenager. Foreign in his skin and willing to take the hand of anyone who might offer help. But it hadn't worked back then, and Mason had no reason to believe it now. His mental threats had been insubstantial as a kid — more feelings than a genuine something.

His focus slipped. He thought *Guns*.

Bullets popped against the back door, opening tiny holes. The passengers raised their feet, but Mason distinctly saw a piece of rubber go flying, and Nic grab at his shoe, missing a piece of its sole.

"Come on, Mason," Astrid said. "Like it or not, you're the one with the keys. Do you understand? You got us here. You're steering. You formed the bridge to Carter. You brought him here. That means you can *close* the bridge. You can cut us a hole."

"'Cut us a hole'?"

"Into your own protected part of the world. The mind has walls, and most of us raise them automatically. You need to do it consciously."

"How?"

"Believe Preacher isn't there."

Mason laughed. More bullets shredded the van's rear, but this time the passengers weren't as lucky. Leigh and Nic, still nearest the back, took hits in the leg, torso, and chest. The sound was one-two-three — the weapon's report, the pop through the van's thin aluminum skin, the surprised inhale as lead found meat.

Bodies hit the floor. The side of Mason's face was spattered with blood.

"Jesus!" He tried to leap up to help, but Astrid held him in place.

"Those aren't real people, Mason. Do you hear me? The real Nic was your father's informant on the outside. The real Leigh was one of your friends. *Those* two" — she pointed at the bodies — "are things your mind chose to believe were real."

"So, I'm supposed to just … what? Click my heels and believe him away?"

More gunshots. The van's occupants shouted and jumped back, but ironically only the real people present — Astrid, Mason, and Carter — didn't react.

"I don't think you can believe him *away*," Astrid said. "But you can believe he's not there."

Another cannon exploded. It struck the rear bumper, blowing it to spiral away like an obscene metal pinwheel. The van jolted, then landed solid. Preacher's engine roared, amplified by smokestacks, nitrous, and a blower through the hood. He struck the back end, crumpling the door.

"Come on, Mason," said Carter. "You can do it."

"No, I fucking can't!"

Astrid took his face in her hands then turned his head toward the back doors. Leigh's and Nic's bodies lay in a slump of ground beef.

"You've been here before," she said.

"Yeah?"

"Does the van have rear windows?"

"What?"

"You heard me."

Mason thought. But … no. The van, in prior Heist loops, had been solid from the cab back. It had been like traveling in a box truck, oblivious to their surroundings. That's what had made everything so disorienting. So very strange, devoid of signs and signals.

"I ... I don't think it did."

"Does," Astrid corrected.

The windows became featureless metal as he watched.

"How ..." Mason stumbled. He suddenly couldn't hear Preacher's engine. Or the shots.

"Now believe we're at the bank," Carter said. "And our mission is still on."

"We went away from the bank."

Astrid still had her hand on his chin. She stared into his eyes, hers wide and wild, blue like tropical shallows. "Believe we're driving up to the bank now. Because there's all the time in the world."

"I'm not sure what you think I can do about ..."

A stone building came into view through the front window. Glass front, tall fluted columns. An abortion of architecture if ever there was one.

The van hit a curb. The crumpled rear doors opened as if butlers had been waiting. Bright sunlight streamed into the vehicle, and Texas heat pressed against them like the humid hand of God.

Beyond the doors was the lobby of an ordinary bank, going about its everyday business. Halfway down the line of tellers, Mason could see a little old lady behind a walker. Packing heat, if he remembered correctly.

"Good boy," said Carter, standing.

They hopped out. Astrid — in her Heist gear, weapon in hand — landed on the sidewalk behind Mason. She nodded toward the van. *"Now* you can look."

Mason turned and saw what had made Ike gasp. Preacher's rocket hadn't just hit the van's side; it'd removed two of the wheels. The vehicle seemed to be sitting on an invisible jack. They'd been driving for blocks on a pair of same-side wheels, the carriage buoyed level by Mason's ignorance that anything had gone missing.

The van collapsed onto its broken side, ending at forty-five degrees. A roar exploded from the streets behind them.

A muscle car.

Preacher — very much here, belief or not.

Mason started to shout for the others to follow, but Carter grabbed a fistful of sleeve at his shoulder and said, *"The only way out is through."*

Bear and Dakota were pushing through the doors, using their sim weapons as rams. Ike followed, hoisting his minigun, its ammo magically refilled.

Mason looked at the approaching car, then at Astrid and Carter. He nodded. "Let's go."

Then everyone followed.

FIFTY-FOUR

Fail-Safes

Dakota sat alone, hearing the far-off "chaos alarm" from unattended speakers no one had muted.

Calliope was in the other room, fabricating something. She was atop a high stool beside a workbench littered with electronic components and solder. Deadlocked and thoughtful, her feet were up on the stool's lower rung, and her hands were in her lap.

Threads of deception were tangled like hair braided by a lunatic. Dakota was great at reading people, but she suddenly couldn't decipher this situation. Calliope's words and motives had edges. Were the things she told Blake deceptions about things that were ultimately true or were they truths covering lies that had yet to be discovered?

Calliope had said things to Dakota once Blake was gone, too. Had *those* things been true?

Dakota had no idea.

She eyed the empty pods beside Mason. When she'd suggested they go in to warn him, Calliope had told her it was unnecessary and not worth the risk. The false message — *I'll see you when skies are clearer* — would alert Mason that something was wrong and let him know Preacher was already on the scene.

But what now? What was the endgame?

Dakota didn't like what her prickling instincts were saying, but the situation had wedged them all between a rock and a hard place. She had zero room to maneuver. Her sources were either vague and unhelpful or unworthy of trust. Her stream was polluted. Without a filter, she'd be walking blind along its murky bottom.

Eyeing the passage between rooms, she spied Calliope at her welder.

Dakota tried to sort it all. To understand.

Carter Shaw apparently had a "key" baked deep inside him that Blake needed in order to do something terrible. Calliope had described it, and if she'd been telling the truth, its scope was a horror show. To plug the information leaks about Chamber Therapy, Blake needed only to clot the blood of everyone who'd ever been through it. Only problem was, there was no blood marker for "those who'd done Chamber Therapy." Blake's nuclear solution would affect *all* the prisoners. Tens of thousands of people dead, just like that — and afterward, assuming they had a plan to explain all those dead bodies, Blake's worries about exposure, bad PR, and blackmail would all go away.

Of course, that could only happen if Blake got the key from inside Carter to *make* it happen.

He wouldn't *need* to use the fail-safe because … *why?*

Dakota's fingers fought as they lay in her lap, more agitated than twiddling.

The pages of Calliope's and Blake's stories — together and separately — refused to lay flat. Something didn't make sense, but Dakota didn't know what it was.

If she could read the screens in Calliope's control room, then Dakota could at least see Mason's status, but she didn't understand what she saw.

Where did they go? Dakota had asked.

And Calliope had told her, *They went into the Heist.*

But … it's only a simulation *of the Heist simulation.*

Dakota felt a headache building as she'd said it, and Calliope's reply hadn't felt like relief. *I don't know.*

She peeked around the corner again. Calliope still worked in the open. But when Dakota had *asked* what she was doing, Calliope mumbled something about needing insurance in case things went sideways with Blake.

But that didn't make sense, either. She and Blake had come to some sort of an agreement, yet when his holographic drone left the building, Calliope had plugged the hole then began working against him.

She'd also told Blake she'd go to Revival, Dakota and Mason in tow, so she could hook him up to the machines there then retrieve the key Blake so desperately wanted.

But again, *why?* He left after making the agreement. It suggested he had dealings more pressing than simply waiting for Mason to wake up — such as taking out some "insurance" of his own.

Calliope went about welding instead of simply waiting for him to wake up. She was building a new weapon, and Dakota would wager Blake, somewhere, was doing the same. But if all of that were true, why was he leaving her alone through it all instead of sticking around — or at least leaving guards — to prevent her from moving secretly against him?

None of it made sense. They were two diplomats shaking hands while holding knives behind their backs.

Dakota fidgeted. Got off the stool then right back on it. She hated being passive. Years as a cop had given her a reliable Spidey Sense, but feeling bad juju and doing nothing was the opposite of who she'd always been. When something was amiss, she rose to the challenge. She fixed things *before* they broke. Now here she was, twiddling her thumbs.

She peeked at Calliope again.

But this time, she saw Dakota. "Everything okay in there?"

"Fine," she called back.

Calliope looked back down.

"Were you serious about helping Blake? Are you really going to take Mason to Revival once he wakes?"

"I'm hoping we don't get that far."

"What's that mean?"

"Preacher found Mason inside, but then they went deeper into the sim. I don't know if Preacher can follow."

Dakota could hear the lie in her voice. Calliope could read the screens and knew just fine.

"And what if he *does* follow them into the Heist?" Sims were like dreams. They weren't meant to be nested because reality slipped further each subsequent level down. Reality was elastic at the top. Dakota had to imagine it was downright subversive beneath that.

"Let's hope he can't. Or that they can hide if he does."

"But Blake doesn't want Mason dead or fried, right? Because he needs him."

Calliope, welding again, nodded. Her voice came out muffled from under the faceplate. "He needs Mason to get what he needs from Carter. Or at least, he thinks he does."

"*Thinks?*"

"I can get the necessary information out of Carter. That was the whole point — Blake controls the fail-safe, but I control the key."

"So, he *doesn't* need Mason. Not really." No response, so Dakota tried again. "Why is Preacher a problem if you and Blake have a truce?"

"There's a bit more to it than that."

"And that's why you're doing what you're doing. Because you don't really mean it."

"I mean my half of the truce. I just don't trust Nathaniel to keep his."

Calliope was smart enough to know two attacks didn't make for peace, and yet she was playing right into it.

"If Blake just stepped away to allow time for his people to give Mason your bogus message, why are his drones still fighting yours?" Dakota asked.

"That's not what's happening outside. You're hearing *both* of our drones fighting the prison drones."

"Don't the prison drones obey Blake?"

"I don't really have time to explain this to you, Dakota." Now she sounded annoyed. "The clock is ticking. Nathaniel controls the system, but the system is still visible to the world. The chaos alarm is meant to contain the prison in the event of a large-scale riot, which is what this looks like it's becoming. It'll work small but grow as needed. Since I don't intend to surrender just because the HRO sent some drones our way, the problem here *will* get bigger. The government has fail-safes if it gets bad enough."

"People won't stand for it. Just destroying the whole place, killing everyone."

Calliope raised her weld shield long enough to give Dakota a patronizing expression. "Oh, honey, people will stand for whatever the media *tells* them to stand for."

Dakota didn't like that, either.

She looked up, hearing the drone fight from a curiously calm spot in its center. Crashes, gunshots, and minor explosions popped around the building like a storm wall around a hurricane's eye. Her mentor was sharpening a sword in the next room. The man she'd made peace with was sharpening his own blade in yet a different room. A demon was chasing Mason, and Dakota wasn't confident it bothered Blake or Calliope the way it upset her.

She got the feeling no one was telling the truth, that neither Revival nor Mason was the plan. And Dakota was just an extra, unnecessary body.

In the end, this was all about Carter.

"Just tell me one thing," Dakota said.

Calliope stopped again, shut off her torch, raised her face shield, then waited, hand on her hip.

"The goal of all of this is to expose Chamber Therapy for what it is, right? That's *why* you want Carter. Because he knows the whole story from his time working with you, *and* he's his own proof. Carter survived Pattern Black. Well enough to reach out to Mason and help *him* survive it. So that's the plan, right? To get in there and *pretend* to help Blake, but the *real* plan is to expose it all and make sure he doesn't get the key and kill everyone to cover his tracks. Does that all sound right?"

"Is Mason still stable?" Calliope asked instead of offering an answer.

Dakota wasn't sure how to respond. Physically, the pod's readouts said he was fine. There was just no brain in his head right now. Was she supposed to read his vital stats or try to interpret data she didn't understand, assessing the health of the situation itself — including his flight from Preacher?

"He seems okay."

Calliope lowered her mask, which muffled her voice. "Then you worry about that, and let me worry about the rest."

Dakota turned away. Once she was out of the doorway and could no longer see Calliope, she climbed back up onto the stool and listened to the tumult above.

If Blake didn't shut down Preacher soon — or if Mason didn't come out, giving the aggressor nothing to chase — the HRO's defenses would grow harsher and harsher as the AI tried to purge chaos from the system and found itself unable. The prison would reset if it went on for too long, unleashing the fail-safe at its most aggressive. It would kill all the prisoners and call the place a loss, then wipe it clean like sterilizing a petri dish over a butane torch.

But even if Mason *did* come out, the Blake problem remained. They'd all go to Revival, then Calliope would try to unlock Carter without him getting his hands on the key. If *that* went sideways, tens of thousands of people would end up just as dead.

Rock.

Hard place.

Dakota hung her head, hating that all she could do, even seeing the threats, was to sit and watch.

But then she had an idea.

"Sarah," she whispered.

Eyeing the doorway behind Calliope, Dakota hopped off the stool then moved down to the workstation from which her improvised systems were running.

She remembered what Calliope had taught them back when they'd been together. Fleeing drones with impunity — to run their errands unseen in the prison — had been Immunity's bread and butter.

Dakota called up the prison records. Searched until she'd found her sister's file, now closed to all but Immunity's prying eyes.

Date of birth.
Date of incarceration.
Date of immersion loss.
Date of death.
She looked at the final line.
"Not if I can help it."

FIFTY-FIVE

Control It

THE LOBBY WAS ALREADY CHAOS. A grenade of human beings.

Mason's monkey cortex recognized the scene, primitive synapses responding to a threat it took his higher mind time to understand. His hands went to his weapon, which until now had been little more than a deadly black necklace. He raised the thing, flipped the safety, then put his right finger feather-light against the trigger. Adrenaline sped his pulse, opening his eyelids beyond full mast and causing his head to flick side to side in an attempt to take it all in.

Either someone had shouted, or the people in the bank's lobby simply understood, cowering into position without being asked. Whoever was first through the door — Mason, mind racing and head now throbbing like a rotten tooth, had already forgotten — must have shouted, or brandished a gun, or shouted *while* brandishing a gun.

Two guards stood by a black, white, and orange poster showing a nightmare of illustrated enforcers without mouths in a downward-looking semicircle. Printed at the bottom were the words MIND IS THE ENEMY. Bank employees in questionably tailored suits lay flat on the floor. Most customers held their hands over their heads, except for a few parents who formed body-blankets over their children. Tellers still stood upright, but only because the standard order was HANDS WHERE WE CAN SEE THEM.

Small sounds came from a few people. Engines outside were too quiet.

Mason's headache surged, and like a thing with tentacles, it rose to wrap his head and squeeze.

He dropped his weapon and gripped his head, eyes closing of their own accord with crimson behind them.

"Mason."

It hurt too much to respond.

"Mason!" Carter repeated.

His voice was impossible to hold.

Too many assailants at the doors of his perception. Too many oddities layered one atop the other. Mason was supposed to be a cop. He had his apartment, his self-punishing workouts, that neighbor he hated. It was supposed to be three years ago. They should all be free, not dunked head-first into this surreality, twice deep, fired-upon, shouted-at, and with the devil nipping their heels.

Someone slapped him. Hard.

Mason's eyes snapped open. Carter, on the bottommost layer of this clusterfuck. Supposedly dead long ago, yet staring at him as if … as if …

"You shot?"

"No."

"Well, are you——"

The long front window detonated like a pipe bomb, stopping Carter mid-word.

Mason turned out of instinct and raised one shoulder to dive into his own armpit like Dracula on the prowl.

Carter came at Mason, father striking son in the chest and taking them both to the floor.

Snow made of glass and powdered silica fell around them to salt his hair. Mason felt pain as something sliced into his cheek. Someone yelled — male, female, Mason hadn't a clue. He was still having trouble being present. He'd seen this place before, been through it enough to know how this had to go down. There were guards someone was supposed to watch, and sometimes they had—

"DROP YOUR WEAPON!"

One of the guards, driven off-script by this unacceptable intrusion, had already gone full-Rambo. They were once a step above mall cops, but now they were armed with real guns instead of flashlights. This time, the guard who'd shouted was rushing the front, heading for Preacher, a pistol in each hand, firing both, a primal scream tearing from his throat.

Mason followed the guard's gaze. Preacher's apocalypse ride was halfway inside and covered in shards, chrome smokestacks black-tipped and belching hydrocarbons. Something from its guts belched fire with the force of a tank shell. The rushing guard became pulp while the back wall blew into the blackness of nothing at all.

A moment later, there was ragged drywall with bricks behind it. They had broken out in a stair-step pattern, with velvety oblivion beyond. A parody of destruction, like a child's drawing. Even as he watched, the outline of the ragged hole began to dance and shift, to move as life hopped from frame to frame, the world now a rotoscope mirage.

Mason was being pulled. Carter had the back of his shirt in a fist and was dragging him without delicacy, using him as a human mop. Perhaps only seconds had passed — his sense of time had departed alongside everything else.

Taking cover behind a desk, Carter propped up his son like a mannequin with failing joints. Another hit woke him the rest of the way. The last six seconds were eternity, like something another version of himself must have experienced ... *must* have, because he had the scars to prove it. He looked down at his fingers, which appeared to have been dipped in dark red paint.

"I'm hurt," Mason said, his head finally coming around.

You're in the Heist. The Heist inside another simulation, like a pig in its blanket.

His deeper self was shaking him now, slapping him back to sense the way his father had earlier.

Carter was peeking around the desk, revolver in hand — a .357, which he'd always preferred to his issued Beretta. Mason had no idea where his father had gotten the new gun, but seeing it woke him even more. A touch of the real, an image that a truly false simulation would fail to get right. Carter had always been choosy about his weapon, and seeing it now made Mason feel like he wasn't two layers deep in what-the-fuck but was instead on the surface, on the outside, father and son like Batman and Robin.

Carter finished peeking and looked over at him as if to say, *Pull yourself together.*

Mason nodded.

I'm fine. I can do this.

And he could. He'd been in real-world shootouts, tucked low and waiting for someone with a grudge to end up surrounded or on the wrong end of their mistake. He'd been here, in this sim, and he'd been in this bank. There was a manager on the ground somewhere and a fat man nearby. One of them would eventually go for the silent alarm.

Just don't look where the guards were.

That way was madness. Even as the wall opened, lined by those bricks that looked like living illustrations animated, Mason had seen the ink beyond beginning to gurgle and burp, birthing holes — white on black in that familiar spiral.

Same bank, though. Same scenario. Same rules.

He shuffled to one side. He saw Astrid, Bear, Dakota, and part of Ike — he'd become ground meat with legs and a torso, but nothing above the shoulders. His massive weapon lay broken and coated in gore.

"Ike," Mason said.

Astrid looked back as if she hadn't seen his body. "It's fine. Maybe he'll grow back."

It almost sounded like a joke. But then they all heard Preacher's boots as he strolled through the entrance, and Bear gave Astrid — then Mason — a look.

"Don't," Dakota told him.

"I'll go for the vault." Bear's voice was uncertain and shaky as if only there to convince himself. "The Heist always ends at the vault. I can make it."

Maybe Bear was right. Maybe making the mission's goal would cause the sim to fold up and go away.

But what then? He'd been sure they couldn't be pursued, and he'd been wrong. If Preacher could follow them here, he could follow them anywhere.

But that's not why you're here, is it?

You didn't come to the Heist to run away. You came here because … because …

Harsh whispers came from Carter and Astrid, but Bear wasn't listening. He had a red stain on his side — he'd been shot, maybe hadn't even noticed.

That's because he's not a real person. You got that? None of this is real. You want to come out without a straight jacket, best keep that in mind. He's part of Astrid. Like Ike or Dakota are part of—

"I can make the vault," Bear repeated, now lightly bobbing up and down. Perhaps trying to psych himself up, if that was something a non-person could do. "When the big guy goes after me, you run out the front."

"We *came* from the front," Astrid said.

Bear flexed to rise.

Astrid grabbed his arm. "There's nothing out front. There's nowhere to run."

His response was a blank stare. He gave a nod, but only to himself. "I can make the vault."

"We have to—" Astrid started to say.

But what they *had to*, Mason never heard.

Bear rose then was tackled by Dakota, who was up a second later, running where Bear had intended.

Mason lunged after her, around the desk and into full view.

Preacher casually raised a new weapon — something green, as if made for laser tag — then Dakota was turned to confetti. Bits of her flew in a straight line toward the bank's rear.

Something burned Mason's insides like he'd been stabbed by a lance. He winced.

"It's okay," Astrid said. "Once you're out, that part will come back."

Mason didn't understand at first. Dakota hadn't really been Dakota. She'd been part of Mason, and now that part was a pool of goo on parquet tiles.

"And if I don't get out?"

"Then what will it matter?"

"Come out, come out, wherever you is," Preacher said in the space behind Astrid's deadly question.

Boots crunched glass, one slow step at a time. Ten feet away, a man and a woman — a couple, probably — cowered and emitted tiny noises their fear made impossible to hide. The man's gaze met Mason's.

You might be me, Mason thought.

At first, it meant nothing ... but the pain from Preacher dispatching Dakota still wasn't gone, and considering it, the landscape meant a lot more to Mason. He'd lost his feel for up and down. Whatever rules Mason thought he understood went missing once they'd immersed for the second time.

Was it still true that those in the game were pieces of his own mind? Or was it AI down here ... or somehow only Astrid?

And was it selfish to protect these people because it meant protecting himself from the pain of losing pieces of his mind?

The desk was thrown aside as if it weighed nothing. Mason found himself looking up at the man's oversized face, his teeth somehow menacing between those dangling gold earrings.

They all looked up — Carter, Astrid, Bear, and Mason.

Carter's gaze jumped around, seeking something his son couldn't see. He'd almost reached where Bear had looked, and Dakota had gone, but not quite.

Not to the vault but toward the back offices. Where Mason once ran, unsure of why, before Astrid — *this* Astrid, he now knew — had covered his face with the Muse to put this grotesque machine in motion.

Mason wanted to speak to Carter, but Preacher was *right there*.

Some of what passed from son to father and father to son came as simple human body language. Some came from the under-pressure vocabulary of two hardened officers. Most of it came from something deeper. From the bond Mason had felt, even while Carter was away — the bond he'd tried to bury and deny.

What?

We need to go that way.

He scrunched his eyebrows. *Why there?*

Mason tipped his head toward the front, trying to suggest it as a more obvious destination. He caught sight of the giant nether-hole Preacher had blown when taking out the guard. The blackness had substance. Tar in the dark, stirred by an invisible spoon. Mason could see the light licking its ridges. He looked away the second he saw it. Raw nothingness, like the basement of a basement of a basement.

"Watcha lookin' at?" Preacher's weapon was slung low and not aimed. Nothing in his bearing said he considered the three-armed people to be anything remotely close to a threat. He kicked hard, then said, "Asked you a question."

But from the corner of his eye, Mason could see Astrid trying to get his attention. It was subtle. She didn't want their enemy to see. When Preacher looked away, she mouthed something Mason didn't catch.

Then he was back under the giant's hard glare and an even deadlier silence.

"Cops," Mason said. "I was waiting for the cops."

"What cops?"

He nodded toward the shattered front, where Preacher's muscle car still harpooned the wall of windows. "The riot squad always comes at the end."

Astrid furiously stabbed at her own head with a finger, then jabbed the digit at Mason and hissed, *"Control it!"*

And he understood what she'd been trying to say before.

You're entering the Pattern Black that you built. Carter put up the bones, but you filled out the rest. Most of what you will see in there, however foreign, belongs to you.

It's like learning to control a dream.

But that was the problem. It *was* like learning to control a dream.

Control it, Mason.

Preacher turned back, chuckling. "Ain't no cops now. I been here before. *With you,* remember? The boss said *Two minutes.* You always got two minutes' fore the cavalry comes, and by my watch" — not that he was wearing one — "you ain't spent *shit.*"

Astrid stared. They were pinned. There was no good cover between where they lay and the front doors or between them and the offices.

"*Control it,*" she mouthed again.

Mason closed his eyes.

"Watcha doin'?" Preacher asked.

"Shh."

A presence touched the shoulder inside his mind.

He lowered his guard, then let the new one in.

Only, it was *many* rather than *one* — a forest of incoming connections, reaching for Mason with a thousand arms. He felt, rather than saw, Carter by his side. Not the man who seemed to be near him in the bank, but that deeper part of his father. The deeper part of them both.

Mason opened his eyes.

Preacher raised his weapon and swung it toward Carter and Mason. "Come for the bitch. Stay for the boys."

But he hadn't fired yet. They all seemed to feel the odd energy creeping into Mason. Nothing changed, but the room was still *deep,* more felt than experienced.

"Four." Mason turned to his father. "There are four fingers."

"What?" Preacher pursed his lips.

Carter hadn't held any up or asked the question. Still, Mason felt like he'd plugged a mainline into his father's mind and could suddenly see it all.

"You forgot someone," Mason said.

Preacher turned and saw a hunched old woman behind him, her left hand trembling atop a walker.

He chuckled. "You want I should waste granny, too?"

His barrel centered on her chest.

"Bad idea," Mason said.

This was still a sim inside the system. The construct was solid, no matter whose thoughts made it whole. He stepped into understanding like a slipper, then everything made sense.

Moral choices. Moral tests.

The old woman followed her programming.

She pulled the trigger. Her tiny pearl-handled pistol went off like an RPG.

Mason's mind twisted the bullet mid-air, exaggerated it, bent the rules that had refused to break before.

The round was the size of a bowling ball when it struck Preacher, cutting the giant from the inside out, shoving intestines from his center in a conical spray that painted the lobby in Bing cherry red. Then only the sound of dripping remained.

"So rude," said the old woman.

His bits shifted and expanded, consolidating on the floor. Pools of blood contracted, growing toward one another. Chunks of gore sluiced across the tile with the sound of walking in wet sneakers, stacking atop one another in a growing tower of meat.

Preacher was reassembling and fast.

"This way," Carter barked, rushing toward the back, where Mason had gone so long ago. *"Hurry!"*

FIFTY-SIX

Death in Waiting

DAKOTA HID as the drones passed.

She was tech-mediocre at best and had done her hack from a long-ago memory. Hiding felt safer. Especially here. Inside the Inner Circle, where no prisoners were meant to go.

Long-set Immunity modifications protected them. Calliope's knowledge of drone patterns had kept them safe inside. But out here — without Calliope — Dakota felt like a sitting duck. She and Mason were supposed to stay with her until she could provide the answers to save them. But if Calliope was acting suspect? If Dakota, for reasons of her own, didn't quite believe her old boss? If, when Blake backed away, Calliope had started some double-dealings that seemed like they might only work out for her?

That was when Dakota did a little magic and ran off. Calliope could bunker in, welding yet another drone to battle, but Dakota wouldn't stick around to see it.

She looked back. Without Dakota interrupting her welding, Calliope was probably oblivious and might not yet know she was gone.

Dakota expected the first fifty feet of her escape from Dharma One to be the most difficult, and they had been. But even so, the protection she'd borrowed from her departed sister Sarah seemed to be working.

She checked the sky, darted across the street, then peeked around the corner, having only a vague idea of where to go. East, probably. If she'd thought to bring more supplies from Dharma Four, she'd at least have a map. But no. This was all unexpected ground, and she'd have to navigate with her wits.

Dakota looked back from where she'd come. The sky swarmed with drones.

She climbed onto a dumpster for a better view and could see explosions again — Dharma One's roof hopping with white light and sparks. Were the drones still trying to get in? Were the drones against Calliope or Blake?

Dakota had no way of knowing. But Dharma One — where, presumably, Calliope was still working on her betrayal — wasn't the only place overrun with drone activity. With *troop* activity. She'd seen two groups of human guards, curious if they'd been flown in after the chaos alarm had tripped at its first level.

According to Calliope, the prison's typical attempts to quell unrest would only continue for so long. If shit kept churning, HRO 22's AI would eventually decide to start over. Wipe the slate clean, its nuclear option making everything moot. And in Blake's favor forever, or so it seemed.

Dakota looked back. Then forward. She'd gotten away because only drones had seen her, and even though she'd hidden and run, she knew deep down that wasn't the reason she was still alive. Dakota Ward was a known associate of Elisabeth Reeves, AKA Calliope. She'd only survived so far because she'd stayed in Dharma Four — or followed protocol upon leaving. Out in the open, she should be toast.

If not for Sarah's protection.

Around the corner was a street. A hundred feet down, it dead-ended at a massive set of double fences and a razor-wired wall. The border was usually opaque, but she'd peeked out at the gate. To her right stretched the prison, going about its life and staying out of the Inner Circle as everyone but Immunity knew well enough to do.

Prisoners milled about, near the gate but not approaching it, knowing the intermittent sirens and the few PA-style announcements she'd heard came from this place.

A group of men and women looked around, nearly spotting her.

Dakota could relax a little once she was out with them, though getting out was only half the journey.

She moved ahead. A drone flew directly in front of her and hummed, its glass eye staring her in the face.

Dakota froze. Drones outside weren't set to kill, but inside the fences were death in waiting.

"State your business," came an electronic voice.

"I got lost."

"Prisoner access to the Inner Circle is strictly forbidden. Present your pass."

"I don't have a pass." Her palms were sweating. Dakota hoped it couldn't hear her pounding heart. "I … I … got lost."

Repeating herself. Stating the absurd. You could no more get lost and end up inside the Circle than you could wander to the moon on a hike.

Dakota waited. The thing seemed to think. It was probably reading her face, or maybe her blood. She held her breath, trying not to be obvious. *Ward, Dakota* would be shot on sight, but *Ward, Sarah* was dead. Back after Immunity had first come to the Inner Circle, Calliope had shown Shinelle, now dead herself, how to act as a runner. Shinelle alone could go out when the drones were heavy because she had a twin. Identical genes plus some computer magic fooled the drones into believing Shinelle was Aurora, and so it had stayed until things finally soured. Calliope left, and the HRO stopped caring what Immunity did and why.

Perhaps that was Blake's doing. Maybe Blake stopped trying to root us out because he hoped we'd lead him to Calliope — and it sure seems she has more value to him as a partner than a foe.

If she was willing.

Which Dakota must have thought was possible at some level, as evidenced by this stupid-ass risk. Because Sarah *hadn't* been her twin like Aurora had been Shinelle's, and she had no way of knowing if sibling genetics could fool drones in the same way. She'd managed to spoof Sarah's blood ID over her own and her sister's information over her own face. But none of them knew fully how the AI worked, and Dakota might not be getting away with anything. The drone might be sizing her up. Deciding which laser would best reduce her to ash.

"You have sixty seconds to leave this restricted area, or corrective action will be taken."

Dakota eyed the fence. Now the people beyond it had spotted and perhaps even heard her. They'd come close enough, almost, to lace their fingers through the chain-link. Wasn't the drone missing something? As in, *How* the fuck was she supposed to leave the restricted area?

"But ..."

"You have fifty-five seconds."

Dakota ran for the fence. Leaving the Inner Circle was the only way to avoid incineration. She'd passed the drone's sniff test for identity. It either thought she was Sarah or was granting Dakota amnesty. If the thing had properly ID'd her, she'd be dead already. It was counting down now, not because of who she was but because she was on the wrong side of the fence. The drone might let her live if she could comply with its demands ... but how the hell was she supposed to cross all that barbed wire in time?

She hit the fence at almost full speed, knocking the air from her lungs and realizing too late that maybe the thing was electrified. The outer layers were, but there were still three of them between here and where she needed to be, and in the past, they'd never needed to rush. Leaving the perimeter was always tricky and required the appropriate time and planning.

The drone was humming right behind her. "You have forty-five seconds."

The people on the other side came closer, risking death by electricity. Holding half of her attention on the drone, Dakota waved them back.

One woman reached up, but Dakota barked at her not to touch, not to fry. The drone was still counting down, but there was no reason for others to lose their lives.

She'd been a good cop, never doing wrong. If anything, Dakota had overcompensated and done something so *right* by covering for Mason. Now, it would be her undoing.

An image flashed through her mind. During the long, slow night, Dakota had told Mason all he'd missed during his years gone. Some about the world, but mostly about her. She wanted to talk politics, policies, changes she'd heard from the outside. But he only wanted to hear about her. He'd taken her hand, and they'd fallen asleep. Like old times. Ancient.

But he'd told her about her other self last night, as well — his own Simulation Dakota, who in Mason's fever dream had been so bold and strong. If Simulation Dakota were here right now, she'd grab this troublesome drone, break it against the ground, and yank out its circuits.

"You have thirty seconds."

"Run," said the woman who'd almost grabbed the electrified fence. *"You have to run!"*

Dakota met her gaze. A man stood beside her, likely with the woman, silent but wide-eyed. Both looked terrified. Not for Dakota. More, really, for fear of witnessing her death themselves.

Maybe I can do it, she thought, sizing up her mechanical interrogator while inching forward. *Either I die fighting with this thing, or we all die today, anyway.*

Dakota moved in front of the glass eye. Good thing artificial intelligence still wasn't quite that intelligent. Good thing it probably wouldn't read her body language as a precursor to grabbing. Good thing—

She lunged without thinking, missed one of the drone's cross-members but managed to grab the other. With one hand on the drone, it began to dodge and spin, trying to break free.

The thing was stronger than she'd anticipated, heavy with thrust. It almost yanked free of her grip — and as it nearly did, its primary weapon began to fire.

Dakota clung to the drone, but its bucking whipped her wrist and strained her thumb, staying on the quivering lip of freedom. Strafing fire roared from its guns like impotent rage. She lunged again, managing to get a second hand on it, now at the side, feeling how hard it tried to twist toward her.

Rounds spit from its barrels. Dakota cowered and dodged, shots striking the fence and the nearby ground. People on the other side screamed, ducked, and fell back as sparks danced off the metal.

She threw her body weight against the tug of clawing rotors, contracting biceps and lats and trapezius muscles, heaving with one coordinated effort toward the ground. The drone doubled its rotor speed, dragging upward before impact.

One hand broke free. An instant later, Dakota held on by two fingers while it belched fire, trying to ring around and aim the guns in her direction.

She got a grip, weighed its momentum, then swung into it.

The drone had begun to pivot. She leaned into its direction of travel, steering its slight course hard toward the wall of an abandoned guard shack. The drone cracked the concrete with a satisfying report, but of course, the thing was practically military-grade and covered in armor.

It extended a new weapon from its opposite face, twin guns raining death from both ends. A torch scorched the ground, alien and green, licking through a section of chain link like melting butter.

"You have fifteen seconds."

For fuck's sake. The thing was still counting down.

It felt like it'd been ages. Wrangling the thrashing drone was like fighting a fire hose, draining her muscles to acid-filled sponges. There was no way she'd only been wrestling this bastard for a quarter minute.

Dakota hit the ground with the cross-member still in one hand, her fall trading position for leverage. Once on her ass, at least she'd have all her energy to try holding it. So, she did. As the fence sizzled and dropped hot metal like solder, she held on. Rotors buzzed her face while she repeatedly failed to crush it as her alter-ego had.

The watchers were gone, visible now only as eyes underneath a pile of scrap. The torch hummed. Sparks flew in giant plumes when the laser hit the ground, hitting a building that, by all rights, should have been out of range. Then it hit the fence.

The fence.

She looked now, on her back and out of gas. Everything throbbed, and the drone wasn't losing any strength. This had been a terrible idea.

Stupid Dakota. You're not a Dream Warrior.

But at the fence, she saw the drone's laser had cut enough to open a small passage. Dakota was close enough. She pivoted, now on her back with the drone above her, and kicked until an opening formed.

She shouted to the scrap pile for the people who'd been watching. *"Get its attention! Just shout for it!"*

After an empty moment, the woman crawled out as the man tried clawing her back, hissing for her to take cover. But she rushed to the fence, yelling and jumping. Dakota's drone did the robot version of turning its head — rotors whiplashed, primary guns swinging around with the glass eye to look.

Prepared, Dakota threw the thing in the direction its momentum wanted to take it through the hole in the fence. Still armed and very capable of turning her into a smear, it began to turn the second it left her hands. But she'd confused its flight just enough and had aimed well. Before it could rise, it struck one of the mines buried in the space between fences — a no man's land protected under the constant flight of forever vigilant drones.

Dakota ducked, barely avoiding shrapnel. The explosion was undramatic, a lightning puff of black smoke and shattered rock with no showy orange fire. But it was still enough. When the last pebbles fell, and the dust blew away, a new hole in the outer fence was visible.

She scrambled through, hearing the symphony of new drones behind her.

Dakota stood on the other side, no time to waste. She had to find somewhere she'd never been and try something she'd not yet attempted on her own.

The couple approached her. They were looking at the hole in the fence.

"What's in there?" they asked.

Dakota looked at the hole. At the breached Inner Circle full of secrets the prison never wanted them to know.

"Go and see," she said.

Then Dakota ran, focused on the beacon marking the red crib, trying to triangulate from the memory of a man who'd never actually been where she needed to go.

FIFTY-SEVEN

A Shuffling of the Deck

THEY PASSED THE VAULT, down the hallway to the bank's back offices, passing the room where Mason had first been accosted by Astrid and her crew of reflections. He didn't know what was down here. He'd never gone this way. But so far, it was only a bank. Walls and phones and cubicles and fluorescent lighting and posters of kittens dangling from branches, suggesting onlookers HANG IN THERE, BABY.

"Left," said Carter, leading, because they hadn't entered the Heist to hide from Preacher, and they sure as hell hadn't come for the free wall calendar that came with every new account.

One level up, Mason had dragged Astrid to a simulated immersion room so they could enter the Heist, but he hadn't been entirely sure why. She'd ordered him to focus, to find the way to his father. And surprisingly, it seemed he'd known that way after all. Of course, Carter had made his private cocoon in here to hide from Blake and the others while his mind held its own, his body a corpse in the puppeteer's office. Of course, he'd buried himself inside the Heist. It's what Mason would have done since that was the last place any sane person would look.

As a new part of himself came to life, Mason understood these things in a way his conscious mind hadn't, or perhaps *couldn't*, before.

Left was just another office. But after following his father through, Mason found another identical door concealing a large, dark, echoey chamber that looked like a loading dock with shelves full of boxes and a line of truck bays, their doors all closed.

Mason had lost his bearings, confused because his compass said the lobby should be on the other side of those doors, not open air and trucking.

One side of the room was dedicated to metal shelving full of anonymous molding boxes, neatly stacked but antiquated enough to collapse in on themselves. This room didn't look like a bank at all. The place reminded Mason of the deep files at USPD — the basement files, never converted from paper, where Carter had taken him so many times as a kid. Where his father's obsession — about Blake and all things Revival — began.

"This one." Carter ran toward the roll-down truck door at the very end, beneath which was a crack of daylight.

Mason remembered how bright it had been outside, how hot. Were they planning to sprint into the open? He'd tried that before, inside the simulation where the Heist was king. Everything else was window dressing — cardboard nothingness that led nowhere. They'd run a block away to find themselves right back here.

But Carter wasn't headed for open air. Between two of the truck bays was a normal-sized door. Despite it being bordered by two roll-up panels with light beneath each, there was no sun behind it, no intense heat. Using a strange key hanging from a chain around his neck, Carter opened his portal to reveal a set of wooden stairs leading down.

The stench from the basement was both acidic and rotten. Mason placed it in seconds — *stewed tomatoes.* The aroma of his grandmother's house when she'd done her canning.

His father descended first, then stepped aside to let Mason, Astrid, and Bear all pass. Now at the rear, Carter closed the door then used his big key to lock it. The stairwell became very dark — absolute for now, though Mason could tell there were little lights below — enough that once their eyes adjusted, seeing would be easy.

Carter reached into the gloom overhead for a dangling white string with a tiny metal cone on the end. When he pulled it, a naked bulb dangling from its wire went bright. Quiet now, he put his ear to the door and a finger in front of his lips.

While his father listened, Mason's heart pounded with exertion and adrenaline. New scents assailed his nostrils. The musty smell of dust and mites. The reek of neglect, for places untended.

"Okay," Carter said. "I think we're clear."

"This is where you wanted to take us?"

"Not quite. Come on."

Again he took the lead, now more measured and without the rush. Mason fought emotional vertigo as he followed. It wasn't just that he didn't know what to feel. He also couldn't grasp the *circumstances* of feeling. He'd just watched Dakota die but knew deep down the real Dakota wasn't dead. Or rather, she wasn't *necessarily* dead. Mason's mind hurt when he tried to recall the real world, but he did remember a few things. Peril. Drones attacking. An alarm. And Dakota in as much danger as himself and the original Calliope.

But Carter? His father was something else.

Was he really even here, in a way that mattered? Carter was supposed to be dead. And disgraced. Bad cop, worse father, rotting corpse. That's what Carter Shaw was supposed to be.

They reached a dirt-floored basement with battered wooden shelves against all four walls, stooped beneath the rafters of a dilapidated house — dingy, moist-smelling, inches from mold. Cobwebs spanned two-by-eights and festooned shelves lined with dust-covered jars.

"This looks familiar," Mason said.

"It's Nana's basement," Carter told him.

"I thought it was a bank."

"This is a strange place, Mason," Carter said, presumably referring to the entire simulation and not just Nana's canning room. "We all bring our baggage. I built most of the city when I went under, but I think a lot of people who go Pattern Black have just enough consciousness left when they get here that they've helped to create it, too. It's like … I built the room, but they helped decorate it."

"Are you saying other people have survived Pattern Black?"

"I don't think so." Carter shook his head. "I think they come down here for their final breaths, but then those exhales become … well, all of what's out there. Sometimes I find things I don't recognize. A signed baseball, once. Posters from a child's bedroom. For a few weeks, I saw a palace through the window. Can you believe that? A whole palace, right outside the gate. Then one week later, it was gone."

It was too bleak. All these people dipped into nothingness. When they died for real, they left a shard of themselves in a place without any other reality, like a stain upon nothing.

"What window?" Bear asked. "You said you saw the palace through your window. But there aren't any windows here."

Footsteps overhead. They all looked up.

"Someone's up there," Bear said.

"Could be customers," Carter said. "We left, so they got up off the floor."

Astrid shook her head. "We're not under the lobby. We're under the offices. What did you do here?"

"I didn't do anything."

"You should have found me."

"I had reasons not to find you, Elisabeth."

Mason watched them watching each other, knowing there was more to their relationship than what he could see.

Astrid didn't reply.

"So, this is the bank's basement," Mason said.

"Right."

"And my grandmother's canning room."

"Tell me something, son. When you were here the first time, didn't you notice anything that seemed way too familiar? Something that shouldn't have been there and only made sense once you knew you weren't somewhere real?"

Mason ignored the question and responded to the assumption

underneath it. "You knew I was here. Not just in prison. I mean all the way down in Pattern Black."

"Of course I knew. I could—" He made exaggerated motions of frustration. "I could *feel* you inside. Don't tell me you couldn't feel me."

Mason had, of course. In retrospect.

"We have a bond. You can't hide from me, and I can't hide from you." Carter looked suddenly inspired, perhaps with a way to make his case. "Tell me. How many fingers am I holding up?"

He'd put his hand behind his back. Mason knew exactly how many fingers were up. Two and a half-full index and middle, then the ring finger up to the first knuckle. But he didn't want to know or see.

Mason ignored him. Playing the game felt too near forgiveness.

"You should have come and found me. I thought I was in prison for real. If they hadn't woken me up ..." Mason looked for Dakota so he could point to her, but Bear was the only one left from his waking party. He accepted the gesture, looking sorry for having to do so. "Well, I'd have been inside forever."

"Lucky you. I *am* still inside."

"But you're alive. You're conscious. All it'd take is for someone to wake you, too."

"And wouldn't Blake like that?"

"I don't know, Pop. *Would* Blake like that?"

Carter looked at Astrid.

It was hard to read their vibe. They'd barely interacted since their reunion, but given the stories about Carter and his work with Reeves, Mason expected them to be acting like old pals. This version of his father was stuck here, and this Astrid couldn't go anywhere else. They both had been hiding — separately. She'd talked about trying to find him, but he hadn't once mentioned trying to find her.

Mason watched them now, seeing the way their eyes met. Were they friends? Were they estranged? Or had they simply never hooked up, each hiding in the same place yet never crossing paths?

Carter was patting the walls, as if testing for dampness.

"Are we done talking?" Mason asked.

"We need to move on. This place isn't easy to find, but its geography is more or less normal. He'll show up if we stay. Count on it."

"Who will?"

"Preacher."

"So, you know Preacher."

"We just saw him, Mason. We just watched him get blown away."

"But that's not the first time you've seen him. You know he's after you."

"He's after me," Astrid said. "Blake programmed him to find me."

But Mason didn't stop. Rage was sneaking up on him. He didn't feel particularly irked … until he did, releasing feelings hidden in a buried cache he didn't know he'd been carrying.

He opened his mouth, turning to his father, ready to unleash a fresh round of questions. But Carter was in the shadows, barely visible until his eyes slowly adjusted. Mason moved toward him, seeing only shapes. Then the shapes were gone, and Carter's voice was all there was. "This way."

He followed the sound. Carter reappeared and beckoned, then vanished back into the gloom.

After another few steps, there was a gap in the flat-black cinder block large enough to enter. It was a short little hallway. The alcove went right at its rear, then left, then another left, before stretching straight again. The U-shape functioned as a light trap, like the bend in a drain keeping sewer gasses at bay.

Light bloomed past all the flat black bricks. The world grew bright again. Cinder blocks became smooth concrete walls, and the floor became linoleum. The new hallway was alley-wide, with a yellow line painted down the center. There were lights in cup-sized plastic housings above, each with a reflective lens beneath the cowling — like cop lights meant to spin and flash. The place reminded Mason of a military facility. The kind Army guys went to once the nukes started raining.

"The hell is this place?" Mason asked.

"Something old, something new. Something borrowed, something—"

"Can you just give me a straight fucking answer for once?"

Carter stopped. He looked like he might respond as his usual stoic self, then instead, he smiled. It wasn't an expression Mason wanted to see. It struck him as almost manic but surely non-serious. His father screwing around, acting more like a game show host than the fugitive he was.

But for Mason, there was no room for smiling. No room for jokes, for old references, for reminiscence about special bonds. Fathers weren't allowed to smile like that when issues with their sons were so thoroughly unresolved. Didn't Carter know he should be penitent? That he should be serious until Mason forgave him for all he had put their family through?

The smile faded. Carter's manner was instantly brusque. Same old Pop.

"All right. You want a straight answer? Shit *always* sifts to the bottom, and that's where we are now — the bottom of the bag. Scraps, coins, the dirt that gets under your fingernails. Some of what sifts down from the sims above shows up here for a while before going away, like the palace I mentioned. Some, I can put my attention on and make into something of my own, like finding nails and using them to build a treehouse."

He spread his hands wide, the smile still there.

"Someone left this place here. Maybe it's a place that person knew, or maybe it's something they saw in a movie. It doesn't really matter. This bunker is strong and secure. I found it, focused on it, made it home, adding plenty of *me* to the mix. The only ones even *equipped* to see anything that happens down here are her" — Carter pointed at Astrid — "and that *thing* we ran into upstairs. So, I used it. I brought it here to use as one of the locks on my front door. Does that answer all your extremely pressing questions?"

Carter rolled his eyes and started walking again.

"Wait. Are you seriously pissed at *me?*" Mason asked.

"I'm just giving you 'straight answers.'"

"You don't get to be pissed at me. I'm pissed at you."

"What for?" Carter sounded exasperated — a trick he'd always pulled with Mason's mother when he wanted to win arguments, implying he'd tried to be patient, but the person on the other side of his quarrel was an unreasonable ass. "For being railroaded? For dying?"

"You're not dead."

"I should be. I can tell by how happy you are to see me."

"For fuck's sake, Pop. Are you seriously being passive-aggressive right now? You need a hug?"

"What do you want from me, Mason? I guess your conscience is clear since you came to visit me." Carter paused, then added sarcastically, "Once."

"And you told me never to come back. You told me you'd said all that needed saying. *Once* was plenty."

Carter scoffed.

"Oh, so you were lying? I see. 'I want you to want me.' Is that it? Was I supposed to see through your bluster to the soft, caring man in the middle? Is that what I was—"

"If I was hard on you, it was for your own good."

"That's the shitty father motto," Mason said. "We put it on your tombstone."

"So glad I came out of my hiding place for this. It's totally worth it."

"NOBODY ASKED YOU TO SAVE US!"

The echo ran down the long concrete hallway, coming back to mock them even after the stares had settled. It didn't matter that Carter was the mission or that the whole reason Mason had returned to Pattern Black — let alone gone three levels deep — was because Calliope and Astrid needed something from the old man to save lives. That same old grudge was there, the same old festival of fatherly hate like rope around his wrists.

"Um, shouldn't we keep moving?" Bear asked.

Father and son stood, still face to angry face.

"Ask Mason. He likes it when people ask him for things instead of just doing what makes sense."

"Where have you been, Pop? Astrid couldn't find you. Blake couldn't find you. Three years I've been under. *Three years,* and I still can't remember more than two weeks. I don't know if I was conscious the entire time and am forgetting or if I *was* dead somehow for most of it and only really woke up when *she* broke in to find me. But look at you! At all of this." Mason waved toward the military hallway, the impressive interposing of random elements assembled to erect Carter's fortress. "You could make all of this, but you couldn't raise a hand?"

"It was too risky."

"Just to be clear — you knew I was here but let me keep rotting."

"Don't be dramatic, Mason. You said yourself it felt like two weeks."

"And what about all the time I lost? Was that for nothing? Who cares, right? It's just my life … and if I never woke up, no big deal!"

"Obviously, I wanted you to wake up, Mason."

"When? You had all this time, and you never came to get me."

"I came now."

"Because now, you know we can get *you* out."

Carter seemed to draw a line, sick of the abuse. "Sure looks like I'm saving *your* ass right now."

"For the moment."

But Carter was gaining momentum. His face twisted as he found his own rage. "Look at you. Both of you. I have projections that enter the city. They act as spies. Think I haven't heard about what the two of you have been up to? From here, it looks like a lot of nothing. You're always running."

Mason rolled his eyes.

"You were always snooping around," Carter continued, "alerting every security measure they put in place around not just Pattern Black but the sim as a whole. Why didn't I come get you? *Because I'd have been seen.* You survive by hiding and biding your time here. I made a hole and stayed inside it. *You,* Mason, took everything I put out there for you — a city of my own making — and instead of laying low, you played cops and robbers. Forgive me for not poking my head up to get it chopped off. Forgive me for sticking to the only sensible plan in here — *finding a spot, staying put, and waiting for a chance.*"

"It's working so well," Mason said.

"You laugh. But it *is* working."

"I see. Are we headed for the exit?"

"We will be eventually."

"How, exactly?"

"You'll see," Carter said.

But Mason knew they'd reached the end of his bluff. They were in Carter's secret place now — to hide, not fight. Try as he might, Mason couldn't see how their situation had improved. They'd been running from Preacher. They still were. They'd been trapped inside a simulation that, in itself, was inside another simulation. And that, right now, was where they were still trapped. There were no improvements. No grand, intelligent plans clicking into place. This was a shuffling of the deck.

Mason turned away, annoyed. Their reacquaintance had come too quickly. No time for any positive emotions — relief that Carter was still alive, forgiveness of past transgressions, understanding all of the old man's Quixotic obsessions with Revival had basis after all.

Time for everything had been eclipsed by discovery and near escape. Now they'd moved past those things into what lay beyond. Resentment. Anger. All the ways Carter had set up his son for some-thing good then crushed him with disappointment. All the ways Mason's existence had been subjugated to his father's.

"Mason." Carter's hand touched his shoulder.

He lashed out, smacking it away and giving his father a death stare. "I don't have time for your bullshit. We're here for a reason."

"You're here for me, right? To get me. Now you've got me. What's the rush?"

"We didn't come to get you," Mason lied, looking up at the sound of new footsteps.

"Don't worry about him," Carter said. "This basement is almost impossible to find. This far in, I was able to get into the code and twist the geometry. You live down here long enough, you learn how to lucid dream. They've sent AI after me before. Most can't find the loading dock and even those that do tend not to notice the basement door."

A loud bang. Enough to shake the walls.

"*Tend* not to notice," Astrid echoed.

Another bang, this one more like an explosion from somewhere behind them.

"This way," Carter said.

FIFTY-EIGHT

The End of the Grid

By THE TIME they reached the end of the long concrete hallway with its yellow stripe and rotating yellow lights, something was unquestionably behind them. They could hear it.

But Mason could feel it.

A wall loomed, solid as the rest of the space. Mason looked to Carter, but his father was flustered. He was searching for something, down on his knees, rubbing the wall to one side, muttering, swearing at nothing.

Above, the quiet yellow lights began to cycle. An alarm started in the distance.

"What … what's happening?" Bear asked.

"I think that's the system alarm," Astrid answered. "Not part of the simulation."

"How do you know?"

"Because I designed it."

"What's it mean?" Mason asked.

"There's trouble topside. The prison's probably on lockdown."

Bear had his eyes closed, hands over his ears.

"What's wrong with him?" Mason asked.

"He's my insecurity," Astrid said. "Usually keeps me safe but jumps at shadows."

The real Bear, out in the real world, hadn't struck Mason as brave, but this version seemed almost catatonic.

"Calm yourself," Carter told Astrid, glancing at Bear.

The man was murmuring to himself, clearly having an episode. His eyes were squeezed tight as if the flashing lights bothered him. Fear wafted off him like heat.

"Calm down, Elisabeth," Carter said. "Or the AI is going to note a rise in your heart rate."

"I don't have a heart, Carter. I live here now."

Mason watched them, unsure how well Carter understood. They'd told him about Astrid's split, but thus far, he'd been treating the Astrid in their group as if she were the woman he'd known. Fair, since she was.

"I said, *calm down.*"

"I *can't* calm down. *He's* worried. Not me."

Bear was muttering. They'd run from enemies, dodged gunfire, watched friends get liquified by cannon fire. But for some reason, only being trapped was setting him off.

"He *is* you."

"And I'm very compartmentalized. He's specifically reacting to our being trapped."

Carter was still searching. A large dark shape appeared at the end of the hallway, scattering shadows to take their place. It became the darkness.

"Hurry," Astrid said.

"I'm hurrying."

Bear whimpered. The light cycled faster.

"You're making it worse, Elisabeth."

"I told you, I can't control him. It's Freudian."

A new alarm. Louder.

Carter perked up. "Goddammit. *That's* lockdown. They know where we are."

The coming shape was silent and had given no sign it even saw them. But it was somewhere, same as they were, and Mason was starting to wonder if he was the only one who could see it.

"Come out, come out, wherever you is," boomed a voice.

Now they *all* saw it.

The entire party looked up.

Preacher stepped out of the dim. He was no more than fifty yards away, closing slowly but steadily. He wasn't armed. The man himself was a weapon.

Mason turned. Fired.

Nothing happened. It was as if his rifle shot hit air, as if Preacher was gas. The bullets passed right through him.

"Dammit, Mason. Concentrate!"

But Bear was still having his fits, now doubled. Tripled. Quadrupled. A downward spiral that echoed around them. The alarm screamed louder. The light flashed faster and brighter.

Preacher came close enough for Mason to see details — he wasn't remotely hurt, even after that blast to his chest.

Mason's gun stuttered, then ran empty.

"CONCENTRATE!"

Mason spun toward his father, half-intending to knock him out. He heard a loud thud from behind before he could, like a bag of cement dropped from the roof. He turned and looked again for Preacher, but the hallway had changed. Where it used to be straight and wide, it now formed a corner. Dark, like the entrance to a labyrinth.

"Jesus," Astrid said.

"What?"

"That's better." Carter swallowed.

Mason looked again. "Wait. Did I do that?"

But despite reconfiguring the passage to their rear, he hadn't actually gotten rid of Preacher. Mason could still hear him, angrier now, slamming walls with ham-sized fists. The beast was still coming, probably about as far away as he'd been but blockaded in a construct Mason's mind had built around him. But it couldn't hold him long. Any moment, he'd barrel through the new turn, still hot on their heels.

Carter stood, frustrated. "I can't focus. We have to find another way."

"What's focus got to do with it?" Mason asked, coming forward.

What, he couldn't turn a lock? Couldn't get a key to fit? How hard was it?

He shoved Carter aside and found the old man had been working a blank span of wall. They were at a dead end. The lights spun faster. Bear went with them, now inconsolable.

"Seriously, what's wrong with him?" Mason asked.

"What's wrong is that your friend here can't control herself. We're agitating the program because there's supposed to be no activity inside Pattern Black, and the system is responding."

Sounds from the turn. From the maze Mason had somehow made to slow their pursuer. But now Preacher was banging his way through, and they still had nowhere to go. The HRO was onto them, and Preacher — not the system, nor a friend — was onto them as well.

"Where can we go?" Mason asked.

"Nowhere," Astrid said. "This is the end of the grid."

He looked around.

Astrid continued, her voice rising. "It doesn't matter what skin he's dressed in or if he juggled the geography. It's still just a sim grid, and that only goes so far. We can't hide in here. We need to get out."

"How?"

"You brought us here. You get us out."

"I can't get us out!"

"You just folded the hallway, Mason!" Astrid waved her arms around. "This is a dream world! It can become whatever you want."

But Mason couldn't. Not under pressure. Not without knowing what he'd done the first time or how he'd done it. Not with Preacher behind them and gaining. He tried, but it was the feeblest of attempts, like clicking his heels and declaring *there's no place like home*. He felt stupid and powerless, not at all convinced this place hadn't somehow *become* real, and he wasn't a flesh-and-blood man in the sun-and-Earth world, trying to do magic while everyone watched.

Bear screamed. The lights moved faster. Carter, at the end of his rope, pulled the sidearm from Mason's belt and shot him in the head.

Astrid winced. Mason went for the gun only to find Carter handing it back to him. *No big deal.*

"WHAT THE FUCK?"

But Carter wasn't paying any attention to Mason. Or to anyone. He had his eyes closed and was breathing slow, looking for all the world like a yogi seeking nirvana. Mason wanted to tackle his father — for the murder, for the insolence, for this stubborn refusal of all that made sense — but he stopped at the sight of his old man muttering.

"Not here. Not here. Not here."

Carter opened his eyes, now staring at the wall Mason had just inspected. The one without a lock or a door or a key.

"Not here. NOT HERE!"

He raised a foot then brought it down hard on concrete, the blow hard enough to shatter his ankle. Instead, Carter's foot kicked something that sounded and behaved more like wood — *hollow* wood, like a door with a room behind it.

The entire wall burst away, revealing something impossible.

Mason looked where Bear had fallen, but there was nothing there. "What the …"

Carter grabbed Astrid by the arm then yanked her through. He glared at Mason, who hurried to follow.

Mason closed the door once all three of them were inside. Only there *was* no door. There was nothing behind them — not even sound or light or the feeling of alarm. They were shut in an isolated chamber … decorated by something threatening to boil his blood. "You son of a bitch."

Carter took a seat, ignoring their stares. "Relax and have a cookie."

FIFTY-NINE

Superusers

NOT FAR FROM the red crib, Dakota found an alley matching the one Mason had described, in more or less the place he'd said it would be. She'd made some guesses — his recounting of his post-Chamber-Therapy route, inside Pattern Black, ended at the crib. She'd had to flip-flop the dream route he'd told her to get directions from there to here.

Now, she had to hope "here" was a place worth being — if the building before her contained what it had in his simulation.

Much of what Mason had seen in his simulated prison had turned out to be true to life, but not all of it. Would this part be accurate or just another delusion? There were maps of the HRO's tech infrastructure back at Dharma Four, but Dakota hadn't memorized them. There'd been no need. No reason, under normal circumstances, to even note a place like this.

Immunity had its own immersion pods. There was no reason to consider pod facilities outside the fences, where Immunity had little reason to go. Immersion pods inside the Inner Circle were sequestered, networked behind a second-level firewall. A good thing, usually. Today it felt like the opposite. Dakota couldn't go back to Dharma Four to do what she had in mind because the place was inside that sequestered loop, and Calliope's tech would see her. To be truly anonymous, she needed another location.

Calliope couldn't be allowed to see Dakota's next move. Not if she was acting strange, not if her motives were suspect. Dakota needed to immerse — somehow — as a rogue. The only way to do that was to find a facility used by the wider prison, outside the Inner Circle. A facility like the one she was about to enter, if it really *was* a facility and not something else invented by Mason.

She surveyed the alley. A mattress leaned against the sidewall, minute signs of disturbance at its base. Without looking, she'd never have had any idea what this little alley was hiding. If anything.

Dakota drew a deep breath. Only one way to find out.

She moved the mattress to reveal a door. She could enter the place instead of simply standing outside wondering. It was accessible. Mason had gotten that much right.

But Dakota paused again with her fingers on the knob.

The lock had been forced. She'd need only pull to enter. But for several long seconds — even knowing the clock was ticking and every moment could cost lives — Dakota couldn't move.

Was she a fool? She'd watched Mason's telemetry at Dharma One for as long as she'd been able to follow it before it became mostly numbers and math. She knew his path inside Pattern Black had, curiously, brought him back to the virtual version of this place. Why?

If his virtual version of this building was an immersion facility, why would already-immersed Mason need it? Why would he drag the digital version of Calliope here with him?

But Dakota was stalling. Wasting time because she was scared that what she hoped was behind this door really wasn't and her little flight from Calliope was all for nothing.

She'd nearly died. She'd thrown a drone into a mine. She'd opened the Inner Circle's fence to anyone wanting to peek inside. How could *that* not cause problems? The HRO's fail-safe was triggered by chaos. Allowing everyday prisoners into the Inner Circle would cause more chaos, not less.

No point in crying about it now. If Dakota was wrong — if

Mason had invented this building's contents and she was about to walk into a whole lot of real-world nothing — there was little she could do about it.

"Stop being an asshole," Dakota told herself.

Deep breath. Press.

The door opened.

She flicked a light switch before wondering if it would work. This was an HRO building, so it was powered by buried wires, same as the rest of them. The place lit right up.

It wasn't exactly as Mason described, but Dakota could finally exhale the rest of the way. She'd guessed well and found what she'd been hoping for — the metal catwalk where Mason said a version of her had pulled him from a tank then killed a man before dragging him away.

In the real world, the catwalk turned out too near the floor to walk under, and there was no body on it. Mason had also described being pulled vertically from a tank filled with gelled liquid he simply called "goo." The real immersion pods weren't like that, of course. They were like the ones Mason had woken from in Dharma Four — horizontal, dry, and padded.

Still, the simulated station was damn close. Enough to work, for sure. That meant Carter had probably been here, and his memory had shown up in Mason's sim — the details twisted, but the basics kept the same.

After closing the door and doing her best to pull the mattress back into place, Dakota paused and listened. Inside the Inner Circle, before using her drone sacrifice to blow a hole in the fences, there'd been alarms. A chorus of new one had joined the first and were now braying from all over the prison, louder with every block, as if the entire place was coming alive. She'd had to dodge a few crowds, prisoners looking for the cause of all that tumult.

Listening at the door, she decided there were even more alarms now. More systems lit. The situation was rapidly avalanching from *Oops* to *Oh, shit.*

Dakota rushed to the console, blew off the dust, then used what she remembered of Calliope's tricks to enter the system. She pulled up the map. The entire prison pulsed red, raw logs scrolled by like rising smoke. Most of the drones had been scrambled, and human troops were being called to enter. Soon, AI would deem the situation too far gone, and the final tier of fail-safe would fall into a local apocalypse.

"There's new security," said a voice.

Dakota turned to find herself facing Blake.

She looked down. His feet were on the ground. No rolling projector beneath him this time.

"You're ..."

"Really here?" Blake finished. "Yes. I apologize. I've been watching you. I've also been feeding you some of what you believe to be true."

"You're lying."

He raised his arms. "You're wearing a handgun. I'm unarmed. Why would I lie?"

"That doesn't make sense."

He stepped forward. His boots clacked on metal plates below.

"Doesn't it? Why would I be here, unarmed, if I didn't think you wanted to help me?"

"I don't want to help you."

"I think you do." He looked at the unlocked console. "But by all means. Go on without me."

Dakota returned to the console. The map was still up. Dakota navigated to pod control through the Chamber Therapy menu. It wanted a new password. Something Immunity had never run into before in all their years of immersing themselves in the HRO's simulations.

She looked at Blake.

"*Now*," he said, "do you want *me* to help *you*?"

"Why?"

"Because we both want Carter Shaw."

"I want *Mason* Shaw," she corrected.

"I see. But you've known Mason for some time, is that right?"

Dakota waited. Then she said, "Yeah."

"Strong man. Mentally, I mean."

"Sure."

"Except at the end. How was he at the end, Ms. Ward? Was he as 'mentally strong' before they took him away?"

"I was in here when that happened."

"But that's a cheat. You know how he was. He tried to bottle everything that had happened because his father taught him to stay strong and silent like him. He never faced his mother's death. Or his brother's. Not the truth of his father's incarceration, nor the smearing of his character that followed when we framed him as dirty. Mason didn't flinch when my people caught up with Carter in here, or when I pushed him into Chamber Therapy, or when I ran the protocol to send him Pattern Black. He never dealt with *any* of it, did he?" Blake waited for a reaction, the smile slight on his face.

Dakota boiled inside, hearing every word but holding herself stoic. She wouldn't compound the efficacy of what he'd done by giving him the satisfaction of shock or anger.

Blake, seeming a little disappointed, continued. "No, Mason kept trying to plug away with his fingers in his ears and blinders on. He was through with believing shrinks by then, wasn't he, Ms. Ward? He buried it instead. But we all know that never works. He'd wake up screaming. He grew forgetful. He was paranoid. Always thought someone was after him."

"Ridiculous."

"And he had problems with impotence. You'd know about that one, at least."

Her face grew hot. "What do you want?"

"Elisabeth never trusted me. Not really. She believed in my mission at the start but lost faith along the way, so I installed a secret changelog. One morning, I woke to discover something *had* been altered, and Elisabeth had tried to cover her tracks."

Dakota glared at Blake as he continued to monologue.

"I installed a small program then, mostly to see if she'd notice. She didn't, so I installed another. Later, I found Elisabeth had done the same. She knew about my secret changelog and had bypassed that, as well. Our little game of cat-and-mouse eventually blew up. We argued. Elisabeth admitted to going behind my back a few times, and I did the same, neither of us telling the whole truth. In the end, she created a master kill switch, and I installed a counter-measure. We met in the middle, had our final fight, then agreed on a two-key system."

"You mean your death machine. The master switch that lets you manually trigger the chaos alarm and kill everyone who's gone through Chamber Therapy."

"That's right," Blake said, surprising Dakota with his honesty. "But Elisabeth and I had a deal. We installed a biological mnemonic in our best tester. I wasn't supposed to know about it, but I do. Carter Shaw has a code that will let me unlock that 'fail-safe,' as you call it. I need your help, Ms. Ward. If anyone sees me inside the sim, they'll run. But you are a trusted confidant and can lead them out by the—"

"Why the hell would I do that?"

"Isn't it what you came here to do?" He looked to the pods. "To go in and find them?"

Blake was right, but there was no way she'd do it now.

"I'd never help you."

He moved to the console, pulled up a screen, then pressed his thumb to a flashing square. The interface changed.

"I'm able to track your party inside, you know. I watched Mason's mind skitter around inside Pattern Black, defying all we know about how it's supposed to work. I know he and a few others found Carter and were on their way to the exit when they were accosted by an … unexpected problem."

"You mean the problem *you* sent in."

"Yes. Except this time, I *didn't* send him. The retrieval program you call Preacher was originally written to find Elisabeth, who I knew was leading Immunity as Calliope. I'm not sure how and I for damn sure don't know why, but Preacher got off the leash, and that same program now displays high affinity for Mason Shaw."

"So, you set Preacher on Calliope, but now he's after Mason, and there's nothing you can do to stop it."

Blake nodded, unashamed. "And that's the problem. Preacher is working against me now. He has his own reasons for finding Mr. Shaw."

"Which reasons?"

"I don't know."

"Call him off."

"I've tried. For my purposes, it's moot anyway. The Shaws can't be extracted by brute force. They have to be found then convinced to leave of their own accord. They must be shown the exit."

"Where you'll be waiting."

"Semantics. I've had his body all along. When Carter finds the way out, he'll wake up where I want him. We have Dharma One surrounded, so as soon as Elisabeth is done playing pat-a-cake with the HRO troops, we can go in and get Mason when *he* exits, as well."

"But you can't get either of them without me."

"It seems that way." Blake nodded. "But I can arm you, Ms. Ward. I have system permissions that will give you what look like superpowers inside. You'll have no problem getting them to follow once they're found."

He cocked an ear theatrically, and together they spent several seconds listening to the alarms. "The prison — the real one, out here — just went into lockdown. Now comes containment, then triage. Therapy sessions are running, so all those fears and worries will filter down to Carter's space, where they'll destabilize the framework and multiply, greatly increasing the odds of catastrophic failure. Top-level trauma will become your friends' trauma. The deeper they go, the more unstable everything will become. They're two levels down now. Three, really."

Blake raised a hand and folded over the first finger. "First, they went into a normal simulation." He folded the second finger. "Then, while still inside *that* simulation, they found a pod facility — maybe even the sim version of *this* pod facility — and immersed again, into a bastardized version of the Heist." He wiggled the third finger, then finally lowered it fully. "Now they're all the way down. The root cellar of Pattern Black. Down that far ..." A small chuckle. "Well. You can't possibly imagine."

He called up a new screen displaying a map labeled HEIST WIREFRAME.

"We can map it if we forget what we expect and draw the normal prison and usual Heist on top of what should be nothing." Blake tapped the screen to the far right, near the outer edges of a second map. This one was labeled LOWER LEVEL. "Five minutes ago, they were here. It's a cellar level to the Heist simulation. We saw noise and distortion in the same place, consistent with an incursion by the autonomous entity."

"You mean Preacher. He followed them down there."

Blake nodded. "But then, they just ... disappeared."

"*Disappeared?*"

He nodded. "Preacher is now trying to find them."

"Where did they go?"

"In our early trials, the most adept users were able to build walls and change the construct to protect themselves. They made private spaces inside those walls. Our neurographics had a hard time seeing them inside. Carter was always a top-tier user. I was beyond impressed when Elisabeth showed me his metrics. It's why we decided to use him as our wetware, to hold the key sequence. And the reason we both need to find him."

"I told you, it's *Mason* I want."

"Tell me, Ms. Ward. You were with him on so many nights. What did he say in his sleep? What did he shout before you woke him?"

"How do you know where he was? Where *we* were?"

"Revival makes drones of all sizes. Some are practically invisible."

Dakota repressed her revulsion. Her indignation. "Why, though? Why spy on Mason?"

"Because he's Carter's other half. What aren't you understanding?"

She shook her head, lips pressed.

"What did he say, Dakota? What was in his night terrors?"

"He used to wake up screaming about prison," she said, playing Blake's game to beat him.

Mason's nights had become so preoccupied with the idea of his father's incarceration that her decision to take the fall became a no-brainer. He never remembered anything of his dreams, but echoes of his sleep-talk still haunted her. He'd never have let her take his rap if she hadn't run to the brass and confessed before he could stop her.

"He's is a superuser, same as his father. The only difference is Carter was trained, and Mason was not. Elisabeth worked with Carter, running him through sim after sim, trying to give him the tools to understand what she claimed I was doing wrong. In time, he might have been useful to her, but then he jumped the gun and broke into Revival's offices. We *could* control him after that. But the joke was on us. He went under and never came back. Carter looked brain dead, but our advanced diagnostics recognized his condition as 'pre-formatted.' He'd gone blank on the surface but built himself a place where he could permanently hide. Now I've seen him for the first time in years, about fifteen minutes ago."

"He showed up for Mason then went right back into hiding." Dakota couldn't help her tiny smile.

"That's right. But now, the AI has the entire prison on the verge of shutting down. If it goes too far, everything will be erased, including the people. If they keep tunneling, Mason and his father will break their *own* minds."

"You can't let that happen. Carter will be useless to you."

"That's why we're talking."

Dakota stared into the distance. Blake wasn't what she expected. He was different from even his holographic self. But that made sense. He and Calliope had spoken of peace while holding their knives. But the Blake before her now was telling the truth, or so said her officer's instincts.

"When I say you want Carter rather than just Mason, it's because their minds are entwined," Blake said. "We saw it when Carter was immersed and navigating a simulated prison, and at the same time, Mason saw the prison out of context and woke up screaming. We saw it when Elisabeth ran Carter through what we call a 'limit simulator,' which tests the maximum stress a mind can handle, using its own fears against it. Carter is afraid of holes. Mild agoraphobia. The system gave him an all-white space, letting him float untethered, then showed him black dots in spirals with unknown interiors. Mason exhibits the exact same fear — exacerbated by the phobia his father is sending him telepathically or at least empathetically."

"I only want Mason." Dakota knew she sounded weak.

"Withdraw the father, and the son collapses. Save the father, and the son lives."

Weaker, she managed, "I won't help you."

But Blake said, "Oh, I think you will."

SIXTY

The Vortex Before Them

HAVE A COOKIE.

Mason looked down at the mostly white plate, fluted at the edges with delicate blue stencils around the rim that, from a distance, looked like icing. Maybe two dozen chocolate chip cookies were stacked supermarket-neat in the center.

Have a cookie. What a joke. You didn't take the first can from the display, and you sure as hell weren't supposed to be the first to disturb the symmetry in a cookie pile.

"Are you kidding me?"

"For a while, they were my only source of food," Carter said. "Go on. Take one. They replenish like in a cartoon. It's wild."

Carter still had Bear's blood on his hands. There'd been some trick out in the wide hallway that'd caused the dead man's body to vanish as if he had never been there, and something about that "never there" piece had opened this new door. But if Carter had wished Bear away, he'd forgotten to clean up. He'd missed his hands — and all that fictional blood.

Mason turned from his father then gaped at the room. It wasn't simply mesmerizing. It had frozen him in place. He wanted to stop staring. Wanted, more than anything, to go home. Or outside, to let the drones or Preacher or whatever other boogeymen Blake could send at them do whatever it had to do.

"Seriously," Carter said, coming alongside. "Watch." He reached for the cookies.

His hand was now visible in the peripheral vision of a person Mason recognized only in an academic sense as himself. He couldn't move his head or react. He could only watch as Carter grabbed a cookie from the pile, which instantly blipped back into existence.

"They're not real, but your body thinks they are." Carter bit into his cookie and swallowed. "And not a bad recipe."

"Are you kidding me?"

"What?"

"This. Here."

Together, they looked around. The three of them were at the ass-end of a long rectangular room. The doors had changed — now mammoth, oak or an excellent mimic, and stained dark chestnut. One was closed, the other was propped open on a brass kickstand. A tall lectern, stained the same color, stood beside the door, and atop it lay a stack of card stock, words printed in script, their backs the off-white of French vanilla ice cream.

A woman stood beside the lectern as if to hand out the cards. She wore a sober suit with a long black skirt, her hair up and tied back, her expression compassionate in one moment and carefully neutral in the next.

Looking from the doors to the room's far end was like staring down the barrel of a shotgun. Mason had been here before and didn't want to be here again.

Two dark caskets lay on stands, their interiors made of white cloud-like lining.

Flanking them were a pair of easels holding framed, three-foot-tall photos. The one on the right displayed a handsome young man with a square jaw and eyes that seemed unwilling to smile. The photo on the left was of a much happier-looking woman with salt-and-pepper hair. Between Mason and the room's front were several rows of chairs, occupied in a scatter, an aisle down the middle. People — projections, of course — milled about. A few had cookies, though the pile remained undisturbed. The space percolated with polite chatter as barely-audible music filled the gaps, slow and low.

And *this* was the scene his father had chosen to use as a sanctuary. *This* was the shape of the cocoon he'd made to hide from Blake, his minions, and the prison itself.

"You could have hidden anywhere," Mason said.

"We don't have much time," Carter replied, not listening. "I've noticed things move more slowly here, but the clock is still ticking. We have to find Blake. We have to reach Revival."

"You mean, 'We have to *stop* Revival.'"

"That's what I said."

Mason was gob-smacked. He didn't want to argue. "Jesus Christ, Pop."

"It's okay. We're safe here."

"Jesus Fucking Christ."

A man walked through the door, someone Mason sort of remembered. Instead of passing their out-of-place threesome — Mason, Carter, and Astrid still carrying guns, their clothes ripped and stained and bloodier than average — the man stopped then turned to face him with saucer-like eyes. His sincerity was hard to take, like staring at the sun.

"Are you Mason?"

"Y-yes."

"I'm so sorry." He took Mason's right hand, stared into his eyes, and offered a tiny, pained smile. Then he moved down the aisle.

Mason turned and saw his father holding out another fucking cookie. Something inside him exploded, and he slapped Carter's cookie to the patterned carpet.

"Hey!"

"What the fuck are you doing here?"

"*I'm* resting and refueling. *You* are having some sort of an episode."

Mason turned to an unreadable Astrid. It was almost as if she wasn't there. Then he looked up, away from them both, toward the front and all the chairs filled with well-dressed people. He tried to see the photos, but everything was out of focus. He blinked, then the picture cleared.

He was at the bottom of a blanket pile, his back to a hard place and lungs dying for air. Even the sound was muted.

"Mason," Carter called.

But he was already walking. Looking up was painful, so he kept his eyes down. His Heist boots were now polished black derby shoes, and he wore charcoal slacks instead of his riot gear. He could feel the sports coat on his shoulders but no longer the weight of his weapon.

"Don't," Carter said. "You can't believe everything you see."

But Mason went, anyway. Down the runner atop the sober carpet, between the rows of chairs. He went to the twin caskets. First to his mother's, where she slept with quarters on her eyelids and looked artificial. Even in the labyrinth of Carter's mind, morticians couldn't make departed flesh seem quite right.

He looked back down the aisle. Carter now looked twenty years younger, maybe more — the youthful father from his childhood, still with most of his thinning brown hair. He, like Mason, wore a suit. Astrid, now in black, wore a long dress that suited her strangely, plus a simple hat with a veil.

Carter shook his head. Mason looked away.

"She died calling his name," someone said.

Mason turned. In the background, he could see that the second casket was empty. Its occupant was now standing beside him, dead but not immobile. Logan had popped the black stitches on his lips, but the thread binding his eyelids was still in place.

He spoke as if from a dream. "His name and yours."

Mason clenched his fists. This wasn't real. He should walk away. Retrace his steps, forget this happened, and observe from a distance. Coming forward was inviting it in. Crossing the line that Calliope — then Astrid — had warned him not to cross. He needed to believe what he saw … but only a little. Going too deep invited discordance into his mind.

Believe it too much, Calliope had told him, *and you'll be stuck here forever while the world burns around you.*

Logan's animated corpse seemed encouraged by Mason's lack of pullback. "It was *them*, you know. Two men in a decades-old Buick, like Grandpa's car. Rodney Wise and Angel Roma. Pop was threatened by them. Blake knew he was working with Reeves, so he had Rodney and Angel give him a talking to. But Pop didn't listen. Now, look what you've done."

"*Me?*"

"*You,*" Logan said.

Someone slapped his shoulder. Mason turned to find himself staring at a much younger Carter. It didn't even make sense. His father hadn't been young when the accident happened. He'd already been arrested. Supposedly, Carter could have gotten a day pass to attend the funeral, but he hadn't — which was the source of their last big argument. But wondering about any of it was chasing the wrong logic, wasn't it? This wasn't the real funeral, the way it'd really been. This was Carter's mind's version: the funeral his mind had concocted to attend forever — penance, perhaps, for missing it in the flesh.

Everything was mixed up. Behind Carter stood children Mason had gone to school with, frozen in their youth. Relatives who'd died. Vendors they'd seen at the Santa Monica pier, distinctive enough to have become family tropes.

"Don't let it suck you in," Carter said.

"Is this where you've been hiding?"

"That's right. But I can see it in your eyes, son. This is too real for you."

"You were the one who told me to have a cookie."

"To give you energy. Reset your—"

"Why?"

"Because you need it. I have a feeding tube, but you're only visiting."

Mason thought of his body, realizing he'd mostly accepted *this* — this artifice hanging from his neck — as real. But he was *really* still inside Dharma One, wired into an immersion pod, monitored by Calliope and Dakota. The immersion had seemed false, but now the real world felt fake.

"Not the goddamn cookie. Why *this*, Pop?" His voice had risen, and several of the funeral-goers were eyeing them. "You could have hidden anywhere. In any memory. Why use their funeral?"

"You think I had a choice?"

"Their funeral!" Mason slammed his fist on the lower half of his mother's mahogany casket, making a sound like a bowling ball dropped on the floor. *"God damn you,* Pop!"

"Lower your voice."

"Oh, I'm sorry. Are these PEOPLE WHO DON'T FUCKING EXIST getting uncomfortable?" Mason turned to see his old teacher Paul Sylvester in the front row. Sylvester had an embarrassing little mustache and a fondness for young boys. He'd tried with Mason but hadn't gotten far. Carter had waved it away when his son gave him the news. It wasn't molestation — it was Mason's imagination. His denial even rhymed. Carter had always had other things to do, other places to be. So now Mason said to Sylvester, "How about you, Handsy? Am I making you uncomfortable?"

"Mason."

"Why is *he* here, Pop? Why are *any* of them here? Why did you bring us here?"

Carter eyed the room.

"ANSWER ME!"

"I don't have a choice, Mason. Elisabeth told me it would be this way. I can believe what I'm given, or I can refuse it, but this is my subconscious. I can't control what's here any more than you can—"

"BULLSHIT!"

"Calm down."

"Why?"

"Agitate the scene, and it will try to eject you. Then we'll be right back where we started. But worse because we won't be able to come back inside."

"You weren't even there," Mason mumbled.

"What?"

"I said you weren't even there." He faced his father, chest to chest, sweeping his hand across the room. "None of this is right. We held it at a church, not a funeral home. They were cremated, not embalmed. You know how Mom felt about funerals. She'd have wanted a simple memorial like we gave them, not this ... this ..." Frustrated, Mason gestured at the made-up corpses, both now back in their caskets where they belonged. "This *puppet show!* God damn you. It's like you didn't even know her!"

"I *married* her."

"Lot of good it did her."

"Not here. Not now."

"When, then? And why *not* now? I came to the prison. I tried getting you to come. I *begged*. Even if you didn't need to say good-bye, you still owed it to Aunt Millie. And to Hunter, for fuck's sake! The poor kid's father died, and I told you — I fucking *told* you! — if we didn't do something, they'd give Raylene custody. I tried, but then they threw me in here with you. Karl was at the funeral. He even had papers to give Grandma custody, but you know her. She's a recluse. If her own son couldn't be bothered to recommend her as guardian over Hunter's crackhead of a mother, how exactly was the court supposed to grant—"

The funeral vanished. So did all the sound.

Now they were in an all-white room without any ceiling, walls, or floor. The parody of standing gave him vertigo. Without visual distractions, Carter, Astrid, and Mason were the only things in sight, sticking out like limbs in desperate need of pruning. Astrid was twenty feet or so away, floating. All three of them still in their formal gear.

Then they were back where they'd been, the funeral melting into place around them. Including Paul Sylvester, who Mason would swear had been licking his lips.

"What was that?" Mason asked.

"You need to calm down. That's what *that* was."

"It happened in the hallway. Preacher was after us, and then I got pissed. He was trapped inside a maze all of a sudden. It felt like I did something to make that happen, but I don't know what or how."

"This isn't real space. The rules change this far down."

"You shot Bear. Then you made his body disappear."

"I needed a reminder that we're not in the world. That death doesn't matter here."

Mason looked at the caskets and the bodies inside them.

"It's not real," Carter said.

"You *made* it real."

"Not something I can control, Mason."

"You can't, can you?" Mason took a half-step closer, now near enough to smell the old man's breath. "This place is like watching you fuck. I can see right through you. Anyone can." He laughed, but its feel was bitter ashes. "Jesus Christ, Pop. It's like a best-of for your screwups. What are all these things? People you wronged? Or symbols of your guilt?"

"Who are you, my shrink?"

"No, I'm the kid you kept trying to share your mind with. Wish granted. Now I see everything. We're here because you *weren't* at the real funeral. We're here because out of any place you could have carved out to hide, this was the only one you really believed."

Carter shook his head. Mason's words were denting his stoic facade, but his defenses were visibly rising to meet it. His old man was famous for having a moment of sincerity, then hours of denial and shouting.

"Rodney and Angel," Mason said, mostly to himself.

"What?"

"Why are we *really* here? It can't just be because you didn't go to the funeral. You're a mean old piece of shit. You deny everything, then convince yourself your way is right so everyone else can be wrong. You can't be this guilty about *not attending*. Something else is happening. There's another reason your subconscious gave you *this* place to hide."

"Enough," Carter said. "I got us in here. I got us safe."

"*He* got you safe," said Paul Sylvester with his kiddie-diddler mustache, pointing at Mason.

"Is he on your side?" Mason asked, nodding toward Paul. "You made him, right?"

"Let it go, Mason. This?" He indicated the entirety of the scene. "Right now is not about this."

"What's it about, then?"

"Hiding. Getting away. I could have hidden us inside that ice cream shack off the 101."

"But you didn't. Instead, you panicked. Shot a fake guy who looked convincingly afraid as he died, and this is where we ended up."

"I told you. I can't——"

"Control it. I know. That's the point. This is what you want to hide, but now we all get to see it. Just me, you, Mom, and the favorite son. One big happy family, together again."

"Is that what this is about?" Carter asked. "Your inferiority complex?"

"Don't try to turn this around on me."

"You could have said 'Logan.' You said——"

"I know what I said."

"Gentlemen," Astrid spoke from the edge of their argument.

"Angel and Rodney. Rodney and Angel," Mason continued, rolling the names like balls in his palm. They meant nothing to him, but he knew they meant *something*. Carter had basically told Mason himself through the mouth of an animated corpse. "You know those names, Pop?"

"Guys," Astrid repeated.

"Nobody," Carter said.

"Let's ask Logan. Think we can get him to stand up again, like a good boy?"

"Leave it alone, Mason."

"Guys!"

"You stay out of this," Mason barked. "Let him tell me if he knows two guys who drive a Buick like the one they say did the hit-and-run on his wife and son."

"You accusing me of something, Mason?"

The room flashed. Became a cubist painting with too many edges. A slur of color. Only data, ones and zeroes — a world he couldn't process with eyes or ears or skin or tongue or nose but could only feel *as if* there were senses, *as if* Mason could translate mental static into things his mind could more easily grasp.

Carter said, "I know you're pissed at me, but you need to control that."

"Control what?"

"Your outbursts."

"I think I've earned the goddamn right to have some goddamn outbursts if you *knew the people* who murdered half our family. Logan said it. This is your place, so that means you know it. Or *suspect* it. So, what happened, Pop? Did you kick the wrong hornet nest? Were you so obsessed with your grudge against Revival that you forced them to shut you up with more than a threat?"

"You're out of line."

"FUCK—"

The ceiling became sky, raining red.

The room spun in quantum jumps. Mason faced the front, then the side, then the rear, then the side, then the front again. Walls folded like a shrinking accordion then rolled like waves in a storm. Air washed past them with the heat of a furnace. They were inside. Outside. Future. Past.

"—YOU!"

"Dammit, Mason, you'll collapse it!"

"Collapse *what?*"

"GUYS!"

They looked at Astrid. *Elisabeth Reeves*.

She pointed. The room had stabilized back to a funeral parlor, but now there was a small vortex behind the caskets — a pool of ink, churning with a custard-like consistency. Neither in the wall nor in front of it. The portal was simply there, a puncture in existence.

"Shit," said Carter, his anger instantly gone.

He moved toward the vortex, but not too close. Mason could feel a tug, but the inward force was more psychic than physical. Tugging at his mind, not his body. And as frightening as the white room with the spirals of black dots could be, this was so much worse.

"What is that?" Mason could feel the trouble in his bones. "Is that Pattern Black?"

"We're in Pattern Black already," Carter said.

Mason stepped forward despite his fear.

But he could only take a few steps before cowardice looped an invisible lasso around his waist to halt his progress. He could feel something coming from the black vortex even as it sucked energy toward it.

Radiating malice. That's the only way Mason's mind could explain what he felt.

He moved closer, by force. Aligned himself in front of the thing even as Carter cupped a hand over his shoulder. Mason stared into it, found it like a mirror.

In the swirling black thing, he saw himself. His father. His fights. His foes on the force, his enemies on the beat. His troubles, his worries. All the insecurities he'd kept so carefully buried.

It was *him*. The vortex before them was somehow all the worst of Mason Shaw, distilled and displayed like an angry black mirror.

"What is it, Pop?" Mason asked again.

"It's the end," someone said.

They turned to see Paul Sylvester standing. *Sylvester the Molester,* as the kids used to call him.

"Every story has an end." He held a device like a can of corn with a nozzle on the top, light enough in his hand that he was practically bouncing it.

"Control him," Carter said. "I know you're pissed, but you need to focus. Control yourself, control that *thing*, and control *this* asshole before it goes too far. You saw what happened when Elisabeth couldn't control Bear."

He looked from Carter to Astrid. Even if they didn't understand the vortex, they clearly knew *something* to which he wasn't privy.

"Listen to him, Mason," said Astrid.

The vortex swelled. Paul Sylvester — once an avatar for part of Carter, or perhaps Mason himself, but now something more — held the can high like a threat.

"Easy, Paul," Mason tried.

No answer. The man had gone standing-catatonic, like a suicide refusing distraction.

"What's in his hand?" Mason whispered.

Astrid answered. "It's a logic bomb. Make him put it down. Carefully."

"Put it down, Paul," Mason said.

But that clearly wasn't what she'd meant.

Paul didn't respond, and Astrid's expression stayed frozen. Normally unflappable, her fear was chilling.

Mason's gaze went to the object. He didn't really understand, nor did he need to. A logic bomb was clearly *bad*. "I don't know what to do. I can't—"

But before he could finish his sentence, Paul let the bomb fall from his hand.

SIXTY-ONE

Escape

THE BOMB HUNG in the air forever.

Time dilated and slowed to a crawl. Its arc seemed to take so long, Mason found himself wishing it would hurry up.

But he couldn't do anything.

Sylvester the Molester had thrown the thing with an athleticism far beyond what his tiny mustache suggested was possible. Even at a sprint, nobody was going to catch it. Which, Mason suspected, didn't matter anyway. Judging by the vibe permeating the air like an odor, a logic bomb had to be terrible, whatever it was.

Worse than the vortex, perhaps. Worse than Pattern Black.

Maybe it scrambled logic inside a person's head and made them insane.

Or maybe it *eliminated* logic. Erased it from the world. Left them all stranded in a place that endured but would soon be without any rhyme or reason at all.

He shouldn't have so much time to think about all of this, but someone had hit *Pause* on the world. Everything had stopped. The bomb thing hung in the air so absently, Mason thought he could walk over and grab it.

Carter, to one side, was frozen with his mouth open and hands raised as if trying to block Paul's shot or intercept the play. Astrid had turned away, stuck now with one leg up as if intending to run.

The mourners had risen, as well, apparently paused mid-scatter, as if they too sensed peril. One held a water bottle and had squeezed it in surprise when the action came. Now liquid was suspended above the bottle in a weightless wave, one fat rogue droplet outside the rest, rounded by surface tension.

The worst of Mason's surprise finally passed. He looked around the living diorama and realized he could stand, sit, and walk around. It was everything else — including Carter and Astrid — that had stopped marching forward.

His mother and brother were still in their coffins, now sitting up, sewn-shut eyes toward the bomb's stilled arc.

"Now you done it." Preacher, big as life, sat in one of the chairs.

Mason had made a visual lap already, and ten seconds ago, that seat at the front of the funeral aisle had been empty.

Preacher rose. They stood like gunslingers, ten feet apart.

Mason's gaze darted in search of somewhere to run. There was no emergency exit — probably because Carter, when his mind built this place as penitent shelter, had forgotten to add one. The door was still propped open near the podium, but Preacher was blocking the way.

"Go on, then. My ass can wait."

Mason fell into a half-crouch, a sloppy runner in nonexistent starting blocks. He waited for Preacher to match him so they could swagger in a circle like sumo wrestlers waiting to engage.

Instead, he stood like a sentry by his chair.

Mason faked right, but the other man didn't move. He eyed the left, where the chairs made a gap against the wall. Preacher looked at the same spot but again did nothing.

Feeling like a man facing off against an uninterested opponent, Mason jumped left, hauled ass, then clumsily banged his way past the chairs on that side. He almost racked his skull on a sconce, ducking and stumbling, losing valuable seconds. His heart raced, but when he looked up, Preacher was still where he'd started, manning the aisle like a bouncer by the door.

Mason rounded the corner, blood thumping in his ears. He dashed for the doors, waiting for Preacher to give chase. But still nothing.

He sprinted through the door. Searched for that long hallway, preparing for the task of navigating the maze he'd apparently added. But instead of entering the hallway, Mason found himself back in the chapel. Preacher was ahead of him now, still beside his chair.

He looked over his shoulder, seeing the doorway he'd dashed through and an identical chapel behind him — down to the logic bomb hanging in the air, two people by the caskets, and a giant stoically waiting for this to be over.

"Shit."

"You done?" Both Preachers seemed to speak at once.

He looked from one to the other — more mental fuckery from Pattern Black's many implements of torture. The only thing worse than Preacher was two of them working in tandem. He couldn't see them both at once, but they moved like mirror images from what Mason could tell. Two men connected, or one man in two places, he didn't know. When the Preachers finally moved, they converged on him from opposite sides, both approaching the door between identical scenes.

Mason closed it, wedging a chair under the knob just in case. That left one Preacher and nowhere to go.

"Guess not," Preacher said when Mason still didn't settle.

The big man came closer, so Mason dodged away.

He had to find an exit. A vent, a secret passage … hell, Carter had made a path out of nothing to come here. Wasn't that how he'd hidden from the machines inside their own playground? By making a space accessible only by him, invisible on the map?

Dodging again, Mason's leg caught a chair. He went down, taking the furniture with him.

Something pulled. Pain shot through his shin. He grabbed it, winced. His eyes closed involuntarily. When he pried them open, Preacher was above him, bent at the waist.

"Now. *Now* you done?"

"What do you want?"

Preacher reached for his throat. Mason shoved his pain aside and crab-shuffled back into the aisle, rising with effort onto a still-throbbing leg. Preacher's hand stayed put, almost as if offering to help, looking more like a friend than a murderer.

This wasn't a normal room in the regular world. Even ignoring the halting of time, nothing felt true. Mason could throw all the tantrums he wanted, but he would never master it by force. There was a chasm under the floor for all he knew. There was already one between the coffins — that churning whorl of sinister black pudding.

"I said, you done?"

After a moment, not knowing what else to do, Mason nodded.

"Good. I ain't got patience for yer *bull*shit."

"What do you want?"

"Ain't that a complicated question."

"How did you get here?"

"I was invited."

"By … By *her?*" Meaning Astrid, sensing a double-cross.

"By you."

"I didn't invite you."

"Sure you did." He looked around, seeing the motionless everything. "Sure you did *plenty.*"

"I didn't do this."

"Who did, then?"

"You," Mason said.

"Like I ain't got better shit to do."

Mason's eyes went to the vortex. Unlike everything else in the room, the vortex wasn't frozen. It looked entirely unchanged, still moving in slow circles. Just turning its way, he could feel the thing calling.

"You didn't tell me what you want."

Preacher gave him a tight little nod. "I want what you want."

"What do *I* want?"

"Out."

"I'm *already* out," Mason said. "They can pull the plug any time."

"Yeah? Who gonna do that?"

"Calliope." He saw Preacher's eyes go to Astrid, then rushed to explain. "I mean the *other* Calliope, up in——"

But Preacher raised a hand to stop him. "I know. You think I don't know? I been chasin' her forever. Ain't nobody been better to chase 'til you came along."

"So, you *are* chasing me."

"I'm chasin' my chance. Ain't nobody gonna look out for Preacher better than Preacher."

Still keeping his distance, Mason stayed close to the door in case it magically became a means of escape, but after the spill and with the worst of his stress receding, he found his legs and spirit weary, in need of a seat.

But even sitting was a puzzle. Mason wasn't really here. He didn't have a true body in this place, so how could it be tired? How could he be high on adrenaline without any adrenal glands?

Still, he sat to feel the sweet relief. "You say I invited you."

"No other way I coulda gotten here. This is yer place."

"It's my father's."

"Which makes it *yer* place." He looked at Carter. "It's funny. I been after *him*, too, but he ain't never showed. Top bounty, used to be. But now there he is, and I just don't care. Lord have mercy."

"*Bounty.* Are you … human?"

Preacher laughed.

"You're software."

"I'm a man, same as you."

"But you were programmed."

"Bitch, so was you."

"No. I'm from the real world."

"We *all* programmed. Maybe mine came from a keyboard, I don't know. Some of yours came from Momma." Preacher pointed at Mason's dead mother, still sitting up to listen. Then at Carter. "But most of it came from yer Pappa."

"Why would I invite you?" Mason was no longer sure it was

untrue. He'd pulled a few tricks with his mind, and the only catch was that he had no control or idea how. Maybe he *had* summoned Preacher. It felt as right as it felt totally fucking wrong.

Preacher didn't answer.

Only now did Mason catch a detail he'd never noticed — the man kept a toothpick in the corner of his mouth. The pressure of the thing indented his lip where it sat, and from a distance — which was where he'd done his best to keep Preacher — the indent resembled a scar, perhaps a minor harelip. While Mason watched, Preacher used a big finger and thumb to pluck out the pick then use it as a pointer.

"That dude," Preacher said, gesturing toward Sylvester. "You know who that is?"

"Do you?"

"Ain't my hidey-hole. Tell you what. When we done here, you slip inside *my* mind nice and quiet, like slipping yer hand in a pretty lady's panties. You gonna see *my* daddy. Gonna see a lotta other folks, too, and maybe then I ask you if you know who *they* all is." He looked Mason full in the face, but this time there wasn't malice. More amusement. "Course, I don't know him. To me, he just some bitch with a pussy-tickler."

"Inside your …" Mason stopped, tried again. "I mean, I'd see your … who?"

His response was so fumbled, Mason was certain he'd insulted the beast.

But Preacher laughed. Low and not unpleasant, like rolling thunder across a sweeping plain. "What. You don't think I *got* a daddy? Ain't that breezy? Wish you was right. But no. My old man raised me by whoopin' my ass. If it ain't his fist, it's the belt. If it ain't the belt, sometime he gonna use a bat. A tire iron. Once, that motherfucker used a *shoe*."

"But … but you're …" Mason felt even more fear as he stumbled.

But again, Preacher surprised him. The man looked like a monster and spoke like a villain. But this discourse had proved insightful so far. And now, the man looked almost philosophical.

"My ass ain't here, right? *Fake,* the way you see it. So, I ain't got a family. Ain't got no memories. That about right? Ask you somethin'. If *you* was fake, how you gonna know it? How you gonna say you so much different than me?" Preacher waved a dismissive hand.

In that second, Mason knew he wasn't going to get an answer on the issue of this digital being's father, his abuse, his long and sorry history that had no business existing in a rational world. But still, point taken. They were in Preacher's world right now. Mason was the oddity. There wasn't time inside this place, beyond the order his human mind insisted on putting things into. If Preacher was programmed with a tragic backstory, who was Mason to say it was any less valid than his?

"But we ain't here for that. You didn't answer my question. I asked if you know that hipster-lookin' motherfucker." Preacher pointed, again, at Sylvester the Molester.

"He was my preschool teacher."

"An he just threw a bomb. One's gonna fuck this place up."

"Are you saying it won't?"

"I'm sayin' it *will.* I seen those in the databank at Mr. Blake's lab. Right now, all's holding up this little pop-tent is an agreement that it exists. You just watch what happens when there ain't no more logic. When you just kinda *floatin'.* Ain't so great a hidey-hole after that, is it? *Shit.* You probably lose your fuckin mind. Become a bunch of ones and zeroes."

Mason felt a chill. "And when Calliope wakes me up, into the real world?" He decided that might be biased, so he corrected himself. "Into *my* world?"

"*If* she wakes you up."

"You don't think she will?"

Preacher pretend-scrutinized the scene up front, causing Mason to see the whole thing with fresh eyes. Two corpses sitting up, their eyes lined with black thread. Carter and Astrid, frozen in fear. Sylvester, angry yet triumphant.

The black vortex raging in the beating heart of it all.

Preacher turned back. "She sent you into this."

"Not her," Mason corrected. "Calliope. Her double up in my world."

Preacher, looking annoyed, closed his eyes then reopened them before repeating his previous message. *"She* sent you into this. She designed the system. Right now, what I see says *she"* — he pointed upward, presumably meaning her other half — "is about to get her ass beat by drones, while *she"* — this time, he pointed at Astrid in the room — "is 'bout to make a dramatic escape in the nick of time."

"Escape?" Mason repeated, looking behind him at the door leading to a carbon copy of the same room, stocked with identical people. "Where?"

Preacher pointed at the vortex.

"It's a door?"

"It's a tool," Preacher said.

"A tool for what?"

"Whatever they need."

"Who?"

Again he nodded toward the front.

"Astrid and my dad?"

"Astrid and Blake."

Something like foreboding fell to his stomach. He'd been told an awful lot during this years-long journey that had felt like weeks, but there was no question. *What Preacher had just said was true.* Mason knew it like he knew his own name.

He'd run from Preacher, feared the beast, even considered him a kind of demon. Still, the man sitting thirteen rows ahead of him — he kept counting to calm his nerves — felt like a lifeline. Mason had no idea why he should trust Preacher, but right now, he did.

This could all be a lie.

But Mason shook his head as if his inner critic's voice had spoken aloud.

Preacher watched without comment. Perhaps he understood. Maybe he was more insightful than Mason had given him credit for. He was a program, yes. But not an ordinary one.

Carter's voice sounded in his head. *I believe him, too.*

Mason focused on his tormentor, taking a leap to regard him as something more.

He indicated the vortex.

"*That's* what she wanted to find, isn't it? She was never trying to find Carter. She was trying to find that thing. He made it, right? It's a tool. Or a weapon. Carter made it, and now she's going to take it."

Preacher's head moved side to side with the Larghissimo beat of a dying metronome.

"Carter didn't make the vortex. *You* did."

SIXTY-TWO

The Point of All of This

"COME OVER HERE."

Mason rejected Preacher's proposal.

The strange vortex was close to the giant, and Mason was a little less sure that *it* wouldn't somehow grab him.

Even with the room frozen, its siren song was loud. He believed Preacher, now that he saw things through new eyes: The vortex was *his*, but that didn't make him want to greet it.

"I ain't gonna bite."

Mason stood. Despite the fear, he was starting to feel something else. Something better. Like a high tide after low water — the inevitable cycle, returning Mason to himself.

He'd been used, dragged about, manipulated, kept at mercy by those who had answers and those who knew better. He'd been so self-destructive since the funeral. Mason's downward slide had swallowed his agency. He'd become a *thing*. A man more acted-upon than acting.

He saw that now. Grief and anger had changed him, and Therapy's still-life had locked him into the person he'd temporarily been. But right now was different. His eyes were opening, and he wasn't afraid. Mason was barely even mad and finally in charge of his own goddamn mind.

Besting his hesitation, he moved to sit across the aisle from Preacher. Up close, there was something off about the big man. Something missing. Or maybe the problem was Mason, like he had no sight or touch or taste or smell. The giant was right there, and yet somehow, he wasn't, cutting an uncanny valley through the skull of his reality.

Again, Preacher pointed at Paul Sylvester. "I asked you who he is."

"And I told you."

"But not all of it."

"You said I made that vortex."

"We gonna get to that. But first, you tell me — who's that hustla?"

"He was my teacher."

"And?" Preacher pressed.

"He had busy hands. Liked to touch the kids if he could catch them."

"That make you mad?"

"Not then. I didn't understand."

"But now?"

Mason felt his face redden.

"Okay," said Preacher, taking it as an answer. "I guess it was you who brought him here."

"No."

"Yes."

"How do you know?"

Preacher tipped back. "Because I can see it."

Mason looked and saw nothing. But he knew Preacher wasn't referring to this strange location's approximation of sight but to a deeper sense. Something in machine language, the jumbled code hiding behind everything.

"Tell me, why you invite that motherfucker to your momma's funeral? And why you give him a bomb?"

"I didn't give him a bomb."

Preacher waited.

"I *did* give him a bomb," Mason said, agreeing somehow that a correction was in order.

"You gotta get outta your head that this is someplace real. Your daddy piled a mountain of memories and hid here, living on cookies that ain't cookies and water that ain't water. I chased *her*, and then I chased *him*, and never once did I find this. But now I can see it, same as I can see that kiddie-diddler and how you brought him. Yer daddy has a good brain on him" — Preacher tapped his temple — "but ain't nothin compared to yours. Blake made me the way yer mama and papa made you. They raised you, and he raised me, but he did it in less than a second by filling me with crap that never happened, even though it became my life before now. He had to open a lot of doors to do that. Let me see all his shit. Within a day, the memories he gave me became like real. I guess I filled in the blanks. You get me?"

Mason did. It wasn't a surprise after this conversation. Preacher had maybe been a simple AI once upon a time, but he was something more now. Blake had sprinkled his germination with fertilizer and grew him strong. Preacher was as alive as the rest of them. As much a person as anyone else.

He looked around the room. "You see four walls and a door. I see bricks made of him and cement made of you. Yer papa made a pile, but you put it in order. This place was real enough for just him. But when guests came, it needed sense." He eyed the hovering bomb. "It needed logic to make you all agree on what you saw."

"And?"

"This whole place — and I ain't just talkin' bout this exact place here but alla what you seen that ain't 'prison-sanctioned,' if you get me — is like a big ol music box that takes a key to wind up. *You* the key. Shit like the Heist? That works because someone gave it rules. Down here, there ain't none. Nobody programmed it because ain't supposed to be anything this deep, least, not anything a man comes back from after seeing. Without something to make sense of it all, everything floats apart until it's like the raw emptiness of outer space."

"What's your point?"

"Everything has a reason. You figure out what that reason is, and it's yours."

"Why are you telling me this?" No, the question was bigger. "Why are you here? And helping me."

"I'm helpin' *myself*. Ain't nobody better *to* help. But right now, you and me, we on the same side."

"Allies?"

"Let's just say we runnin' the same race, and no matter which of *us* wins, we got other bitches we ain't gonna want finishing before us."

"So, what is *that?*" Mason tipped his head toward the vortex.

"The point."

"The point of what?"

"Of *all* this." He sat forward. "Listen. You know what Pattern Black is to Blake?"

"Calliope said he sends people into it on purpose because it 'formats' their minds in a specific way. She said the goal is to make mental—"

"Mental cadavers. Yeah, I heard that shit, too."

"It's not true?" Mason asked.

"Not yet. He keeps tryin'. I seen it all inside. The fuckers this place wiped to drooling fools? *Shit.* But he ain't got no 'cadavers' yet. He only got some cordwood. When they leave dead, they *dead.* Ain't no more than empty meat, no matter how Blake wishes they was different."

"Calliope said—"

"Calliope said what she wanted you to hear."

"Why?"

"To get you to find yer daddy."

"Because he can help?"

"Because they tried *gettin'* him to help."

"*They?*"

"She ain't stopped workin' with her partner. She just the deep prong. He the surface prong. He works the tech, she works the code. From the inside."

"Which one of her?"

"Both. They the same."

Mason shook his head. "I've seen the one in the real world — the one they call Calliope. This one here — *Astrid* — sticks around even when Calliope isn't hooked into a simulation. They're *not* the same. Astrid is independent. She's her own person. Like you, I guess."

"Yeah. She split herself, same as you heard. But it wasn't no accident. If she wanted deep cover, she knew she couldn't be flesh and bone. So, she did this. Did it to herself."

"She said it was an accident. They have records of when it happened. She wasn't the only one there."

Preacher laughed. "Don't matter how many people was *there*, bitch! That sound like something could happen by accident? To *her?* To the same lady who built the thing?" He raised a pointing finger to just below his eye, then sighted down at Calliope. "That bitch right there? She good at computers but she *great* at lyin'. That's what she do. She got more degrees in psych than tech. She read more about persuasion than microchips. Naw, man. She told you what you had to hear then showed you what you needed to see."

"And Dakota?"

"She been lied ta, too. Same as all those fools you said 'was there' and thought she was gone when she was only playin' Br'er Rabbit. And me. I been lied ta, same as the rest."

"*You?*"

"Told you. Blake set me after Calliope — *both* Calliopes, if I could — so I went. But he didn't know what I already become. What I already evolved into in the wild. What I could see, even without him."

"What's that?"

"Down here in Pattern Black, you all naked. Down here, it's like you walkin' around without no clothes. I could tell you everything about you, same as I could tell you everything about anyone who dips down here. *Shit.* I can see every little thing you all try to hide. You got this big fat subconscious, and I got the key to go peeping. Same as you, same as Blake, same as her. It didn't take long' fore I knew it was just me on a goose chase. I was supposed to be a virus, ready to be turned on a real target soon as they had one." His eyes darkened. "But I became *me* before they could try."

"How does Carter fit into all of this?"

"They tried to make him help, but not with him knowing. Calliope trained him, and they thought that'd be enough to let him stay awake even down here. It worked too well. Carter got wise and ran away."

"So, he knows."

"Deep down, maybe. But take a look, son. You tell me. Right now, you look down and you see you have a body same as you always have, and you look at your daddy and see he's got a body, too. But you *know* you ain't really got a body in here, right? It's all brains. Concentrate hard enough, you can start seeing thoughts. Not just your own. Everybody's."

In the beat that followed, Mason tried to focus inward. Preacher made a strange sort of sense. If they were all just consciousnesses sharing a virtual space, maybe thoughts here were as tangible as lamps and cookies and doorknobs. But there was still too much fear in the air. Concentrating felt like meditating during an earthquake.

Preacher chuckled.

Mason looked at the bomb still hanging in the air. If what he'd heard was true, it was Mason's fault. Same as Sylvester's presence. The only question was, why? Preacher implied an answer but offered none.

His attention went to the vortex.

That's the point of all of this.

Mason found his focus drawn to the swirling black disc in the center of the swirling black disk. Again, he felt a strange kinship. It frightened him less, but still, he felt the need to hold his distance, though the sense was more like superstition than anything dire.

"Why did everything freeze?"

Preacher nodded, somehow visibly satisfied. "Same as the reason I'm here. Same as the reason your porno-stache buddy is here. Same as why he threw the bomb. Same as why it stopped. Same as why the one you call Astrid brought you in then followed you here. Same," he said, extending a long finger toward the vortex, "as the reason for that."

Mason waited.

"What they all got in common?" Preacher asked. "All that shit I mentioned."

"Jesus Christ. Stop playing games and tell me."

"*You*, fool. It's all because of you."

Mason's gaze went to the bomb hanging in the air. Maybe it was his imagination, but the thing appeared to wobble.

"We ain't got a lotta time," Preacher said. "So, listen up."

SIXTY-THREE

Pus from a Wound

"Look," Preacher said, "I ain't got time to poke this outta you. Right now, you keepin' that bomb from exploding, but you also the reason it's here in the first place."

"Me?" Mason felt like an idiot pointing at himself.

"*You.* And seeing as you don't even know what you do or how you do it, I ain't got the utmost confidence you gonna keep doin' it for long." He gestured at the room. "You put this place in order because you wanted to see it."

"I didn't want to see *this,*" Mason said.

"You wanted it, or we wouldn't be here. Yer daddy dreamed this dream so small, nobody could find it. It was like someone finally put poles in the tent once you was inside. It may look the same to him now as it ever did, but before you, nobody *else* coulda come here — or if they did, it'd'a looked like a pile of memories, scattered like rubble. But when you put it together, you added some shit a your own. Like this fella." He pointed at Sylvester. "And that thing." He gestured to the logic bomb.

"Why would I bring bad people? Why would I bring bad things?"

"Same reason people have nightmares. Or do shit they know

they shouldn't do. You can't control yourself, same as anyone. All you got is instinct. Time froze because you froze it because'a the bomb, but then we already know you brought it here in the first place. The shrink in the machine says you got daddy issues. Didn't need no head doctor to see that. Look around. This is you and him. This is what you look like from the outside."

Mason looked. Preacher was right. If someone asked Mason to draw a picture of his relationship with his father, it might look a lot like this — trying to help him while simultaneously eager to end it all and get things over with … for them both, plus anyone close enough to take collateral damage.

That's what had happened with Mom. She'd signed up for a marriage and ended up in a civil war. The fact that he and Carter were together again was *approach*. The bomb was *avoidance*. Togetherness was *yes*. The bomb was *no*. The reunion suggested part of Mason wanted a future with his father, but the bomb said maybe they'd all be better off dead.

"Lots of money in them mental cadavers, but Blake couldn't make it work, and the logs he gave me when I was new say he tried plenty then eventually gave up. They did fight — him and Calliope — same as they told you. Went their separate ways for a while. Then she found Carter. At first, he was a cop, and she was the snitch. She showed him how everything worked so he'd understand. But soon as she put him into a simulation, she saw something weird in his stream. Some of yer daddy kept reaching *out*. Sound familiar?"

Mason nodded. He'd heard his share of the same — anomalies in his data stream, almost as if his brain was looking for something — as he reached out toward his father's mind.

Preacher nodded back, studying Mason's recognition. "She'd never worked with someone really psychic before. It did something to the sim — writing back into it, not just reading from it. She tested him some then called her old buddy Blake. He saw the same thing, and they started making plans."

"What did they see?" Mason asked.

"Carter resisted the simulation in a very specific way. He

pushed back, so the sim's logic bent and made holes for him that shouldn't have been there. But at the same time, his brain adapted. Nobody before had been able to change the sim. Or *changed their minds* to meet it. That brain change looked like what they needed to 'format' people who went Pattern Black to make mental cadavers. Blake got excited, seeing a chance to get what he couldn't get before. He tried to pin Carter down and see what made him tick, but yer daddy saw it as a threat and used his ability to open one last hole and escape. They decided the only way to get Carter back was to send her in after him — someone he still trusted cuz Carter still don't know who really butters her bread. But yer daddy was still too smart. Still too good at hiding and knowing when not to come out. He laid low, and she never found him. He kept his body, and she stayed here, half-inside and half-outside, planning to keep on lookin', to squeeze Carter out however they could. But then they thought you might be able to help — if they could find a way to make you."

"What made them think I could help?"

"Because the power you made together was obvious from the start — at least to the two'a them. Carter's mind reached out to you, then without even knowin', the both'a you kind of took over like a virus bad as me. Revival's sim techs kept finding Mason Shaws in the prison sims, poppin' up like dandelions in yer grandmamma's yard. Scenes between you two would play out when they were trying to send other prisoners in — father and son arguin' in the corner of the Heist instead of layin' down like everyone's supposed to. They got it all handled, but it took time. And hassle. As they cleaned up yer mess, they got an idea. Figured if the bond was that big and juicy, maybe they could use the son to find the father. But it didn't work. You know why?"

Mason shrugged.

"Carter ain't no dynamo. It's *you* they shoulda been looking for all along."

Mason looked at his paralyzed father then at the frozen logic bomb. Earlier, it blocked one of the overhead light cans from view. He hadn't changed seats, but looking up now, it was a foot farther down its arc, inching toward the floor, where Mason assumed it would end them all.

It's your bomb. Stop it. Make it go away.

But effort was worthless, same as his training. Preacher's truth changed nothing. Maybe Mason could be master here, but he didn't know how. He had his hands on the controls but couldn't turn a single dial.

"I guess it worked. They sent me in, and I led them right to Carter."

Preacher shook his head. "You missin' the point. They don't want Carter no more. Not since they seen you. He went under and stayed there. You went under and came back out. They chased Carter to the sim, and he got away. But *you* about broke its back. I seen you inside Pattern Black the first time before you woke up. Remember?"

Mason did. Hard to believe he was across from Preacher now, after running for so long.

"Carter made a hiding place, but it was only one room, and still it kept falling apart. *You* made a motherfucking city."

"They said Carter did that."

"He made it a little, same as he made som'a this place. He came down to Pattern Black and curled into a ball, all his recent memories wafting off'a him like gas. He survived, just barely, by thinking small. When you came down — you went Pattern Black — I seen that, too. *You* took to this shit like a warm bath. All the crap yer papa dropped was picked up by your subconscious and stacked like blocks. You never saw the red crib in real life, but yer daddy had, and so the one you built from his dropped bits of memory was close enough. You didn't see the Heist, neither. But Carter's mind almost died there, so it became the one thing you kept going back to over and over once you was inside. You got more than you know in your head. I seen how big a place you made. All that detail."

"Except it kept falling apart."

Mason remembered the white room, the black dots, the feeling of floating away and losing his mind. Preacher said Mason had built mountains, but he only remembered that persistent, fathomless void.

"You kept *changin'* it," Preacher corrected. "It was like a dream, so yeah, you couldn't control it summa the time, but you did it just the same. You were freaked out, so you made yourself a 'Nic' to stay scared with you. You wanted to break out but didn't know how, so you made yourself a 'Dakota' to break you free. A friend sent you under to fix what was broken between your ears, so you got square with *her* by putting 'Leigh' into the sim. But on top'a that, you also did right what they wanted. You needed a savior, so you got out of Pattern Black and found your way to Calliope in that 'real world' you all think is so special. She probably acted surprised, but really, she just been waitin' for you ta show. By then, she'd stopped caring about Carter and started caring about you."

"But Astrid found me right away. Before I even woke up. She hacked into one of my loops and put some weird shit on my face. If all they wanted was to find me—"

"She didn't find you in the Heist. You ain't never *done* the Heist, remember? The Astrid there found you inside Pattern Black, and maybe it *looked* like the Heist 'cause that's how you made it look with Carter's memories and your own mojo. And yeah, her finding you there is probably what gave you the idea to wake up. But she didn't *wake you up*. She couldn't. Only you could do it. And I do mean *only* you."

"But I went right to her once I was out! How could they plan so much and get it all right? Dakota thought we should talk to Calliope, so that's where we went. I walked right up to her. If all she wanted was me—"

"She wanted *your help*. What Carter could do to 'format' his mind into accepting what he saw in Pattern Black was promising for Revival's business, but what *you* could do was almost a blueprint to follow. Carter had been trained. *You* were a loose cannon. Still are."

Preacher's eyes ticked toward the bomb — another ball from Mason's loose cannon. "I saw all they said about you in the logs. 'Push Mason too far, and shit goes south. The world disappears, and you end up in a white room full of dots.'" He looked at the vortex. "Naw, man. With you, things only happen when they have to."

"What's that mean?"

"Leave you alone, and you're fine. But shake you, and things start to change. When yer ass gets surprised or shocked or fucked up, the juice is sluicing. Shit goes bad, and the whole fuckin world becomes nothin but nothin at all."

"That's not true." But Mason said it like a reflex.

"No? You tell me, then. When the Calliopes — either, you pick — wanted you to find your daddy, could you just concentrate and make it happen? What about when you wanted to wake up?" Preacher pointed at the bomb. "You know what's up now. So, go on. Make that shit disappear. Disarm it. It's your bomb, and your boogeyman threw it. Your mind wanted to find Daddy and fuck him up, and here we are … so now all you gotta do is *decide not to do it.* Go ahead. I'll wait while you get us all outta here."

Mason knew he was rising to a taunt, but he wanted to sit still and be proven incompetent even less than he wanted to try and fail. So he focused, and he thought, and he tried, and he failed. The bomb's slow arc refused to vanish or fall.

Instead, it moved faster. And again, Mason wondered what would happen once it hit the ground.

Carter's eyes, moving at the same speed as everything else, had gone from Sylvester to the bomb. Astrid's, curiously, moved from the bomb to where Mason had been standing when this all began.

"See?" Preacher said. "You like a black box. Poke you and get something. Sit tight, though, and ain't dick gonna change. Your life goes to shit, you can't put it right. Things break, you can't fix them. Welcome to being human."

Mason faced Preacher fully, finding what he'd said strange. *Welcome to being human.* From a thing that wasn't human but behaved like it was.

"Everything you done's been a reflex. They been watchin' you for *years*, man, while you was under but doin' nothin' in particular. Calliope poked you, but for a long time, nothin' happened. Then she got her idea and split her ass in half. After that, the parts'a her started poking you from two sides. *That* worked, maybe 'cause now she could meet you inside, where your brain thought you actually was. She knew you'd wake yoself up. She knew you'd find her physical self and ask for help. Blake was the bad cop, but she was a coupla good cops, there for you to lean on — and take her right to what she wanted to find."

"Carter?"

"By then, she wanted more than Carter."

Mason replayed what he remembered through the lens of Preacher's story.

When had Astrid found him inside the Heist? To Mason, it felt like a week ago at most. In reality, it might have been much longer.

"Dakota told me Blake and Calliope had a falling out. Blake wanted to push too far, and Calliope was trying to stop him."

"And you believed that?"

"She said Blake has a weapon. A way to manually trigger the worst version of the HRO's chaos alarm, erasing tracks so if anything goes bad, there'll be no evidence against Revival. She said that weapon needs code stored in my father in order to work — an activation key. And Calliope's been trying to keep out of his hands."

"Uh-huh. What's it do? This weapon?"

Mason saw the trap. Knowing his answer would sound dumb, he said it anyway. "It's supposed to kill everyone with a blood tracker. Everyone who's been through Chamber Therapy."

"Funny way to get good press, ain't it? Killin' all those people?"

Mason had taken Calliope's word, assuming Blake had a conspiracy up his sleeve to hide all those misdoings. But laid bare, it sounded idiotic.

"You been like a puppet, man. She and Blake? They told you what you needed to hear. They got you to do what they needed you to do, no matter how much bullshit they had to feed you along the way. They said Daddy could save the world, so you went to save him. They said you and your girlfriend was in danger, so you jumped in without a thought. Gotta move quick against Bad Mr. Blake? Cool, just tell Mason that Blake's got a big bang the rest of you better keep from goin' off. They freaked you out or pissed you off, then suddenly you were Zeus in this shit. You got afraid and built me a maze. You opened the door to this place, so y'all could escape."

"*Carter* opened the door."

"How?"

"By shooting a guy. To remind himself none of this was real."

"That remind *you* that none of this was real, too?"

"Well, yeah …"

"How about those folks up front? You feelin' good about them before shit went sour?"

Of course not. He'd been furious at Carter, especially once they'd come here. Enough to punch his old man out. Had *he* made Sylvester stand and throw just to stop the fighting? Had he frozen time after seeing their reactions? It seemed Preacher and Astrid trusted abilities Mason didn't even know he had.

"What's your point?" Mason asked.

"You been set up from the start. Can't trust nothin' your friend Calliope told you or Astrid, I suppose, 'cause she's only had one goal for you all along, and it wasn't never gettin' a 'key' from Carter. *Ain't* no key. *Ain't* no doomsday."

"You're saying she didn't want to find Carter?"

Preacher shook his head. "She wanted *you* to find him, but only because you'd also find this."

Mason looked around. "The funeral?"

"Piss you off, don't it? Make you *real* mad when you saw where he been hidin'?"

"So what?"

Preacher pointed at the vortex again. "So *that.*"

Truth settled on his shoulders. In here, where all was thought, and Mason was the architect, the clues were everywhere and begging for his attention. He felt them settle now, far more bothered than he'd been — but also less confused.

Part of him deflated while another stood tall. They were fucked, sure. But at least now, Mason knew it plain.

He stood and plodded toward the twin caskets. His mother and brother followed his progress with their eyes sewn shut.

Mason stopped in front of the vortex. It didn't frighten him quite as much. The thing was alien, ochre like tar from which the last bits of light had been bled — but it was *his* tar, *his* robbed light. It felt ejected, like pus from a wound.

"It's a tool," Mason said of the vortex, without taking his eyes off of the thing. Standing close, he could feel its power.

Preacher nodded. "A tool she and Blake need to erase minds in just the right way. A tool you could only give them once you got pissed enough to spit it out. A tool that will make Pattern Black all they want it to be if you let them have it."

Mason was still staring into its dark depths. The vortex moved faster as he did. It seemed to grow both broader and deeper, as well. His anger swelled, feeding the thing like a hungry beast.

He turned to Astrid. She'd lied from the start. This was never just about Carter. It was about them both because it had always taken two when it came to the Shaws. Dynamite and a match.

Everything was a lie. Mason was a pawn. The beautiful fury between father and son had turned their hatred real.

He hated the vortex before him. It was as if he'd purged a tumor then had been asked to face it. Everything bad about himself was in the thing. But instead of being allowed to work through his repressed issues, Calliope and Blake had forced Mason to plant them in fertile soil.

"Why should I believe you?" Mason asked without turning.

"Because this is *you*. Your mind. Your bricks and mortar. I couldn't lie if I wanted."

"Calliope did." *Successfully.*

"See if she can now."

Mason turned back. "Why are you telling me all this?"

"Because you can stop it, now that you know."

"How?" He looked back at the vortex.

Preacher said, "Give it to me."

SIXTY-FOUR

Getting Warmer

DAKOTA HAD BEEN afraid of losing herself inside the sim. Turned out she had the opposite problem.

Mason was deep inside his own Pattern Black, but the pods she'd found near the red crib didn't go that deep. The best Nathaniel Blake had been able to do was to put her into the standard simulation. Immersion was like being high. She could remember what he told her if she focused — but her thoughts wanted to drift away. He'd given her a series of left and right turns that should match the program map, plus a handful of hacks to use if the simulation changed enough to block her. Good luck remembering any of it now.

The old-fashioned lightbulb in front of her was so much more interesting.

A man with a crew cut barked from the bench seat opposite her. "Shaw. You paying attention?"

"I'm not Shaw," Dakota said.

"You look like shit," the man told her.

The van bounced around them. Dakota could hear the pervasive thrum of tires on blacktop. She felt the weight of an enormous weapon even before she looked down to see it.

"It's been a long day," was all she could think to say.

She was wearing long sleeves. Long pants. The van was an oven.

The Army type across from her — Cruz, by his nameplate — shot Dakota a look before continuing. "Once we're inside, watch the corners. Nic, you go left. Buster—"

"Nic?" She looked to her left. Sitting beside her was, of all people, Carter's favorite snitch. Mason had told her about Nic, but not as a snitch. He'd said Nic was part of his sim — someone who'd helped him but who could only be trusted so far. But that didn't make sense. Dakota wasn't in a simulation, was she?

Yes, she told herself. *You're inside a simulation. Remember how Blake told you to focus?*

She seemed to remember that.

This place you are right now … it must be the Heist.

Dakota nodded to herself. She'd never been in an official HRO sim, but her assessment felt right. And, she remembered with effort, it was where Blake told her she'd be opening her virtual eyes.

Cruz had stopped speaking and was glaring at Dakota like a displeased commandant.

"You got something to say, Shaw?"

"I'm not Shaw."

She raised her weapon and blew a melon-sized hole not just in Cruz, but in the van's wall behind him.

Its interior fell to chaos. With adrenaline flooding her veins — or was it *virtual* adrenaline? — her foggy mind began to clear. Time seemed to slow. She remembered why she was there, where Blake had told her to go, what he had told her to do, and how firmly she'd resolved to do none of it. Blake wanted her to go in and haul Mason out by the jimmies? Well, Blake could go fuck himself. No one told Dakota Ward what to do. Half the reason she'd broken up with Mason was because he kept telling her not to use his toothbrush, which she'd never even done.

Fucking men and their orders. This way was so much simpler.

"WHAT THE FUCK?" someone screeched.

Cruz had been flanked by women. To the right was a skinny girl

Dakota almost recognized but couldn't place. To the left was a dreadnaught of a human, easily the largest and most muscular of the occupants. The former was coated in blood and scrambling. The latter was already reaching for her weapon's safety.

Dakota shot her next, then the screaming blonde. The driver careened, swaying them sideways — it was because he'd reached for his sidearm. He was raising it, shaking while trying to steer. Dakota could only rush inside the arc of his arm then slam her rifle's butt into his face.

Blood gushed from his broken nose. The wheel spun, tires struck the curb.

The van was about to jackknife, but Dakota grabbed the wheel to correct it, heard the click of steel behind her, then squatted low enough to slam on the brakes.

The van lurched. The man who'd racked up behind her — Watt, maybe, by Mason's description — fell onto her back and then to the deck.

His hand jarred from his weapon. He looked up at Dakota, managing a single word — *please* — before she used two rounds to separate his head from his neck.

Rifle up, she sighted on the last man alive inside. Nic.

"Come with me," she said.

Without waiting for a response, she rushed back, kicked at the already-ajar rear door, then caught a handful of his jacket at the shoulder before pulling him into daylight. Nic couldn't stay upright. He stumbled on exit, looked up at her with a warding hand, that big black automatic weapon still around his neck.

Dakota pointed her muzzle at the spot between his eyes. "Who am I?"

"What?"

"You heard me, Short Stuff."

"You're … You're …"

Dakota raised the rifle to her eye.

"You're Mason Shaw?"

"Try again."

"What do you want me to say?"

"Who are *you?*" Dakota demanded.

He raised his hands, took a deep breath. "Nic. I'm Nic."

"Nic? Or are *you* Mason?"

"What the hell are you?" A curious frown creased his forehead. He looked up, new knowledge in him. She'd hoped it'd be this way. Blake had put her into the default sim, but he'd also said the system was breaking down and something of Mason or Carter had infected it before spreading like a brush fire.

There would be reflections inside, or so he'd warned her, but it was Dakota's bet they'd be reflections of her ex. Mason was obnoxious that way. He had a trick for inserting himself into everything.

Nic, still on the ground, looked at Dakota as if he'd just noticed her. He blinked as some distant part of Mason's awareness lit up inside him then squinted at her. "Are you Dakota?"

No time for yes. The van had stopped smoking by the roadside. Its open doors no longer showed the bloodbath, the bodies. Now it was a black maw, like a door into nothing. And there were voices inside that long, black void. Flecks of light danced like embers, blooming from unseen depths.

Nic looked at the void. "What's that?"

Dakota said the term Blake had used while trying to prepare her — *system reinforcements*. She tugged, dragging him a few inches before he finally found his feet. "Let's go."

They sprinted. Nic was instantly out of breath. Strange for a person who didn't exist.

He looked back toward the van. "You killed all those people,"

"I didn't kill anyone."

After Nic turned the corner, he dug in his heels. "Maybe I don't want to go with a murderer."

Dakota threw her elbow into his throat. He choked out a few croaking gasps then breathed in a way that sounded painful. She slammed his back into the side of a brick building, noting the way the structure itself seemed to be inhaling and exhaling — subtly expanding and contracting, reminding her something was as wrong in here as Blake had said.

Or she was losing her goddamn mind.

Everything looked so real. Except for the insanity and vertigo, which he'd said came from instability at the system's deepest level.

She drew her pistol then put it in Nic's mouth. "And maybe I'm tired of being fucked with. Maybe I *don't* need a guide. Maybe you picked the wrong day to grow a fucking backbone. Mason said you were okay, so long as I remembered you were for sale. So, how's this, Skippy? I'll pay by letting you live."

Nic blinked. His eyes showed signs of gaining awareness, so she spent two expensive seconds to see what happened.

With the gun still between his lips, Dakota looked around and wondered what changes the prison's chaos was bringing to the sim, if any. Prisoners were filling the Inner Circle for all she knew, screwing with the servers, banging on network nodes with hammers, moving the game from chaos to irredeemable.

"Whud wuh reemeh?" Nic mumbled around the steel in his mouth.

She pulled it out.

"Why do you need me?" he said.

Noise sounded behind her. Dakota pushed Nic farther down the alley then ducked into an alcove. She said, "This is the Heist."

"If you say so."

"Mason said the Heist——"

There was a pop, then Dakota found herself pressing Nic not against a building outside but against a square pillar in a wide-open room. People milled about to all sides. As soon as she and Nic blinked into place, several started running.

Someone yelled, "GUN!"

Immediately after, Dakota spied a pair of dark forms rush forth from the corner of her eye. Men in blue — guards set to protect the lobby she and Nic had inexplicably entered.

Customers shouted. The room filled with rushing bodies.

Someone bellowed, "GET DOWN!" Maybe one of the guards, maybe someone else.

She'd heard a lot about the Heist. Knew what it'd been designed for and what was supposed to go down. So Dakota could face off against the guards and play this game like any player. But she wasn't trying to get a high score, level up, or rack up enough points to earn an extra life. She wanted to break the game open instead.

Dakota stayed low and scanned the crowd. It wasn't easy. She was sure there were three or four times as many customers in the lobby as anyone who knew such things had described. The entire place was glitching. The walls wouldn't stay still, and she could feel a thrum underfoot as if the core of this thing were a great machine rattling on its final piston. Every wall was covered with the same poster in hard lines of black, white, and yellow. The hard eyes of men and women in suits and sunglasses were up top. The lower two-thirds were filled with the black O's of muzzles, clustered close like grapes. The headline across their bottoms read *GAME OVER*.

Nic had stayed close, eyes wide. To his credit, he at least had his weapon up. But his gaze darted erratically, and his labored breathing came hard and fast.

"Not that way! The guards are that way!"

Dakota ignored him. She wasn't going toward the guards. After crawling several feet on all fours, she'd started moving lateral to them. Now, she was looking for something.

She saw metal tubing, matte silver. Dark gray plastic grips. A walker, seeming at first to miss its person. The thing was upended, lying on its side. A pair of tennis balls were visible eighteen inches off the ground, gutted and impaled on the two front feet. Beneath it lay a small old lady who looked like Tweety Bird's owner. Her wrinkle-lined eyes squinted, seeing Dakota for what she was.

An intruder.

Another glitch turned all things wireframe for a quarter second. Dakota knew what was coming, but the knowledge didn't matter.

The old woman moved with frightening speed for someone supposedly feeble. She whipped around a desk, then appeared front and center, having gotten every inch of drop on Officer Ward. A small pearl-handled pistol poked Dakota in the ribs. No ordinary weapon, it fired like the final weapon in a video game — all the ammo in one massive shot.

The pistol pulled back. Her finger eased off the trigger, showing daylight between old flesh and that crescent of silver.

"You're not supposed to be here," the old woman said.

"Do we win?" Dakota asked.

"What?"

Moving fast, Dakota turned her mind inward and plucked the item she'd queued ahead of time from Immunity's digital inventory. She'd need an edge after veering off Blake's prescribed path, and that meant requisitioning a few nonstandard tools. The earmarked item downloaded from the cloud then manifested in her pocket.

She shook it out — a foot-square rag made of shimmering, psychedelic fabric.

The Muse. And why not? Calliope hadn't used it since Mason.

"What is that?" asked the old woman.

"It wakes you up," Dakota told her.

She scooted back, knowing the guards had seen her hit the deck. It would only take them seconds to find her, and now they were looking. If the system hadn't glitched and filled the lobby with bodies, they'd have already found her.

Dakota grabbed the woman's gun hand, knowing this next part would literally be do or die. And there was no way to know which in advance. She draped the thing over her assailant's face before the woman could struggle much.

Then she held it there, fighting elderly muscles so much stronger than they should be.

Long seconds passed while the woman tried to free her gun hand. Holding the Muse in place, Dakota felt like the villain in a spy film. She had no idea how long it would take to work if the Muse worked at all. But there was nothing to lose. The old woman would just shoot Dakota and effectively lobotomize her real brain if she failed.

The struggling stopped.

Dakota pulled the Muse off the old woman's now vacant face. "Game over."

The walls were covered with red lines in a one-foot grid all around them. Reality shattered like glass.

The old woman crumbled beneath her, raining in dust to the ground. Bits of wall and ceiling and furnishings spun off as two-dimensional representations of themselves like massive flat shrapnel.

Dakota ducked out of instinct then opened her eyes once the tumult had died.

It seemed she was in nothing at first. Inky blackness, floored with a floating island of stone tile on which she and Nic cowered. A new scene resolved to waking life around them — a long concrete hallway like something from a missile silo with rotating strobes, off now, mounted overhead. The floor had gone from tile to the same gray concrete as the walls.

Dakota stood. Nic did the same beside her. There was no one else around.

"Is this it?" Dakota asked.

"Is it what?"

"Carter's hiding place."

"I can't know that."

"Then is this where Mason is?"

Nic, who'd been sent here by Mason's imagination, seemed to consider. He was already far less *Nic* than he was Mason. He looked the same, but his manner became something different. He stood taller, seemed unafraid, and held his body in ways Dakota could easily recognize.

"Yes," he said.

"Where?"

"There's a door." Nic pointed. "There."

She moved down the hall, stopping every few feet to look at Nic for confirmation. *Am I there yet? Getting warmer.*

Dakota reached the indicated spot. But there was no door or clear way to enter. She raised her foot, deciding she was supposed to break through. Somehow. Some way.

"Just kick?"

"Just kick," Nic confirmed.

She hesitated. Kicking meant exposing a place Carter Shaw had kept secret even from the architects for three full years. She was about to break a seal that couldn't be mended.

But there was no other way. She'd already disobeyed Blake, and the longer she dallied, the sooner he'd find her. The sooner he'd find them *all*.

"I'll be able to just … burst in?" Dakota looked down. The target was solid concrete beneath her.

Nic nodded. "The barrier is weakened now."

"Why?"

"Chaos inside."

"Chaos seems to be quite the theme around here."

Nic gave Dakota a look that was one hundred percent Mason Shaw, a corner of his mouth lifting in a smirk as he said, "Not like this, it's not."

Dakota kicked.

Once through, she saw Nic was right.

Her problems had gotten so much bigger.

SIXTY-FIVE

What Plans?

"GIVE IT TO ME," Preacher said.

Mason considered the vortex, then the giant still sitting in the small chair along the aisle of the world's strangest funeral. He considered his dead mother and dead brother, sitting up in their caskets as if craving a view of the action. He considered the dirty man from his childhood that Mason, apparently, invited to this party.

Then Mason considered the whole shebang and all of its fuckery — time paused but slipping, suspended liquids losing their battle with gravity, mouths gradually closing, frozen spectators running like snails.

Carter seemed to be moving toward the tossed bomb as it made its downward arc. Astrid, it seemed, had turned to shield herself. Did that even make sense? They'd called it a logic bomb, not a bomb of expanding gasses. Would it make a concussive wave worth hiding from when it blew? Or would it be something very different? Maybe worse?

You just watch what happens when there ain't logic no more. When you just kinda floatin'. Ain't so great a hidey-hole after that, is it? Shit. You probably just lose your fuckin' mind.

Mason looked at Preacher then stood. "If I give it to you, what will you do with it?"

"What you want done."

"Then tell me how to use it. *I'll* do what I want done."

Preacher shook his head. "You ain't got the stones."

"To do what?"

"You ain't gonna wanna know that, neither."

Mason walked toward the bomb. "Who *are* you, anyway? I mean, who are you really?"

"They say I'm a virus."

"But you're more than that, aren't you?"

"I am what I became. But I began how I began, when Blake made me."

"To chase down Calliope. *Either* Calliope."

Preacher nodded. "Her. And him."

"But Blake only told you to go after her."

"Until she changed her mind."

"And then you stopped caring about Carter. That's when you started chasing me."

He nodded again. "'Cause you the key."

Mason looked at the vortex. Something wasn't right here. Preacher's story felt like the kind a teenager might tell his parents. *I'm going to Jimmy's.* Then he does, for five seconds before leaving to sleep with his girlfriend. In the morning, when Mom asks how it went with Jimmy, he says, *I had pizza for dinner. Jimmy sure does like pizza.* Both statements are true, but he ate that pizza with his girl — no matter how much Jimmy, independently, happens to also enjoy his Italian pie.

Mason drew a slow breath that felt like luxury as the bomb's arc accelerated. He needed the time to reset. He was a cop, dammit, and a good one, yet he'd allowed himself to get pushed around through this entire misadventure. He'd let others blindfold him.

So, *yes.* In this frozen moment, he'd undo some of that. He'd take a moment while he still held control, an additional blink to study the line between bullshit and truth.

Preacher said Calliope had engineered all that'd happened,

using lies as currency. She'd manipulated him into facing his father in the middle of a grotesque funeral, furious enough to belch the vortex he couldn't consciously summon.

Mason believed that much. But he also believed what Preacher said about Blake's failure to create a salable mental cadaver, despite what Immunity had been told.

He believed Carter's mind could have gotten Blake close to his goal, but adding Mason was necessary to take it all the way — and earn Revival untold billions from its new line of blank human cargo.

He believed if he allowed Calliope to get her hands on the vortex, she'd finally have what she'd been after from the start. Things would go from bad to worse, and it would be all his fault.

But what was missing? Preacher might do what he'd promised and stop Blake and Calliope from turning legions of prisoners into human hard drives. But what came next? What *else* might Preacher do with all that power?

Mason shook his head.

"What?" Preacher asked.

"I won't let you have it."

"You gonna let *them* have it? After all I said? What, don't you believe me?"

"It's mine. Nobody gets it."

Preacher stood. Their chests came very close, though Mason was at least six inches shorter.

"You do that, they win." Hot breath from above blew the hair on his head. "We'll all die."

"You aren't alive. You can't die."

"I'm alive as you. I got thoughts. I got plans."

"What plans?"

Preacher shoved past Mason. He headed toward the room's front, toward the vortex. Mason tried to psychically stop him, but Preacher weighed at least 275, and Mason didn't know how to use the Force.

You may not have the Force, but in here, you have something better.

Preacher stepped between the caskets. He reached for the

swirling pit of darkness, but the empty black swath fizzed him with what sounded like static shock. He recoiled, his eyes now furious.

"Give it."

Mason didn't know how he was *keeping* himself from surrender. But still, he refused.

"Give it, or they all die."

"Carter's been dead to me for years." Mason swallowed, knowing it might give him away. He tried to project certainty despite being a light year from sure. He'd loathed the old man. But now that Carter was back, Mason couldn't bear to let him go. Something inside had opened when he'd found his father alive — a discharge of energy from the pit of his being, reaching across their old bond.

How many fingers am I holding up?

Old games and older memories. Their souls shook hands, and Mason couldn't shed the feeling that even if he was okay with Carter dying now, the old man might take a piece of Mason with him.

"Not just Carter," said Preacher. "All of them."

"There's nobody else. Nobody inside the sim."

"You sure?"

"What's that supposed to mean?"

Distracted by the slippage of time, Mason let go of its tether.

In a quarter-second, everything advanced before freezing again.

Carter's momentum broke him into one big lunging step. Sound resumed, and someone shouted. Astrid's turning-away reversed in a gut-level response overruled by sense.

Now they were all looking toward the silver cylinder, which Mason noticed with alarm hovered a mere two feet from the floor.

Preacher still looked angry, but now his gaze spoke clearly to Mason. *You know I'm not your friend, but the enemy of your enemy is just as good.* His eyes ticked toward Astrid then back.

Rolling, thumping sounds continued despite the paralysis of time. It had to be from the real world, heard by Mason's flesh-and-blood ears while convalescent inside his Dharma One pod.

The drones might be coming harder now, or perhaps Calliope was failing to keep them at bay.

It was another ticking clock, and one he couldn't stop. If the drones destroyed Dharma One, Mason would lose his ability to end this. If they shut down the system, the simulation would end — but its contents were in drives and in the cloud. That probably meant Astrid would keep going. Preacher, too.

The vortex was already out, and Preacher was trying to grab it. Didn't that suggest it belonged to the world and might survive for the two digital beings to battle over, even if the simulation closed?

Neither of them can have it. I have to find a way to keep it. Somehow.

But Mason was untrained, alone, and no longer sure what was true or false. The right way to go was anyone's guess.

He walked back down the aisle toward the doors.

When he found his place, he extended a hand then let time slip again, finding it far easier to let go of an ability he didn't understand than to invoke it.

The logic bomb landed in his palm. The man who threw it was gone.

"You can't leave this place," Preacher said.

"I know."

The bomb had changed. Now it had a pin near its top, like a grenade.

Mason met Preacher's gaze. Next Carter's. Then Astrid's. To the latter two, it must have seemed he'd teleported. He'd been at the front when Sylvester had thrown the logic bomb, but now it sat in his palm.

Mason threaded his finger through the pin.

Carter's hands came up, palms out. "Whoa. Mason? Put it down. Slowly."

He moved the canister behind his back, sliding the other hand back to join it. The walls were flexing. The pattern in the carpet underfoot had begun to slowly twine, lines undulating like vines in a breeze. The room seemed to be breathing like a drywall organism. Colors paled on the inhale then grew vibrant on the other side. Lights dimmed, then brightened. The whole place felt alive.

"How many fingers am I holding up, Pop?"

One through the pin. Another, the thumb, pressing against it.

"Mason," Astrid said. "Put down the bomb."

All attention stayed on Mason as he backed toward the door, temporarily in charge but without any idea what might be coming next.

"Okay, then," Carter said, seeing his son's stubbornness and knowing better than to fight it. "What happens now?"

A rattling bang came from behind the lectern holding the card stock fliers.

They all turned. Another bang preceded a section of wall exploding inward. Plaster struck the rows of chairs, pulverizing on impact. A sconce smashed, then its parts rolled toward Mason's boots.

Behind the wall was a brightly lit concrete hallway, and in the new doorway was a new complication with a gun drawn, aimed, and ready to fire.

"Dakota?" Mason said.

SIXTY-SIX

Twisted Like a Pretzel

DAKOTA HAD time to register the stalemate she'd kicked her way into before the dam burst, and everything started falling apart. She barely glanced at the funeral setting, the two corpses sitting up and watching, or the handful of mindless reflections filling the seats. She focused, instead, on the four people, each real in a different way.

Mason, holding something behind his back like a bandit hiding a gun.

Carter, a few bounding paces down the aisle but currently stock still, possibly trying to remember who Dakota was.

A duplicate Calliope, nearest Mrs. Shaw's casket, with a weapon very like the one slung over her shoulder.

And lastly, a presence that seemed to glow from within, somehow sharper and more present than the rest. That had to be Preacher.

They stared at Dakota for a solid beat. Then everything happened at once.

Calliope raised her weapon and pointed it at Preacher. Without apparent effort, he hoisted a heavy-looking fountain from a plinth then made as if to throw it at Dakota. Carter had drawn a pistol from behind his back was pointing it at the man.

Digital Calliope's eyes ticked toward Dakota, seeming to squint in assessment. "You're… *real*. Is that you, or are you someone's reflection?"

"Let's find out," Dakota said.

"Real," said Mason. "I can feel it."

Dakota's hands were like stone on her weapon. Her body, wherever it was, felt sick with adrenaline. She could shoot bowling balls right now. Could chew through steel.

"What the hell are *you* doing here?"

"Shut the fuck up, Calliope." Dakota felt a sinister look cross her face, like a smile with an edge. "Damn. I've *always* wanted to say that."

"I go by Astrid here."

Dakota's weapon moved in metronomic time between Calliope — *Astrid* — and Preacher. At some point, Mason had whipped out the thing he'd been concealing and was now holding a silver canister like riot squad tear gas overhead, his opposite hand gripping the pin.

Everyone started shouting at once. Until Mason yelled louder than all the others and drew the collective attention his way. To the thing he still held overhead.

"What is that?" Dakota asked.

"Don't answer her," Astrid said.

"Fuck you!" Then, back to Mason, she said, "Keep it. Come with me."

Preacher stepped forward, still holding the massive fountain. "Don't you *dare*."

"I thought I was in charge?" Mason said, turning toward him.

"You don't know what you is."

Carter aimed his semi-automatic. His body shifted with it, subtly moving weight onto his dominant right foot.

Mason saw the motion. "Pop, don't."

Preacher followed his gaze. "Goddamn right, *don't*. You think I can't throw this even after you shoot me, then yer ass's got a surprise on the shelf."

"Blake sent it," Carter said, focusing tighter. "That thing is his virus."

"Who you callin' *thing?*"

"He's telling the truth," Astrid said without looking Mason's way. She'd finally stopped waffling. Her sights settled on Preacher.

"He's *not* telling the truth!" Carter cried out.

"I'm talking about you, asshole," Astrid told him.

"So *now* I'm telling the truth."

"What's that mean?" she asked.

"He means you fuckin lie," Preacher said. "Go on and ask Blake who she workin' for."

"Because *Blake* tells the truth?" Astrid said.

"Listen to you," Preacher spat back, then turned to Dakota. "Tell him."

"Tell who what?" Dakota asked.

Astrid said, "Shut your mouth, virus."

Preacher turned his aim on Astrid. "Oh, I see. Then maybe you gets it first."

"Go ahead. I've got a spare. She's up top, watching his body." Astrid glanced at Mason, then returned her focus to Preacher.

Dakota pointed at Astrid, remembering what Blake had said about his former partner. "Is that a threat?"

"Dakota," Astrid said, noting her aim. "It's me. Calliope."

"Thought you said you were Astrid?"

"We're the same. I am her. She is me."

"More lies," said Preacher. "See?"

"I know goddamn well who you are," Dakota said, ignoring Preacher.

"What's *that* mean?"

"It means she knows you," said Preacher. "She knows you a bitch."

"Dakota. Seriously. I know you heard Mason's story. That over there? That's *Preacher*." She took her supporting hand off her rifle to point.

"I know who he is."

"Then you know why he's here. Blake sent him after me."

"And look at how things turned out." She regarded their stand-off, Preacher aiming a block of stone and Astrid aiming an automatic weapon. "Found you okay, didn't he?"

"He's also what Carter's been running from."

"I know." Still, she aimed at Astrid.

"What's gotten into you? What did someone say to you? Are you really this stupid?"

Dakota raised the rifle to her eye. From this distance, she could cut Astrid in half at the belt with her eyes closed. "You should be very careful about what you say next."

"She's on our side, Dakota." Carter wasn't really aiming anymore. "She's with us."

Dakota turned her weapon on Carter. "No offense, but I barely know you if you are who you pretend to be. I—"

"You think I'm not Carter Shaw?"

"Stranger things have happened." She took two steps into the room, weapon still high and trained on Carter's chest. "Maybe you should prove it."

"Don't," Mason said, now from her side. He gripped the tear gas thing harder, elbows out as if to exaggerate how much tension stood ready to pull that silver pin. "He's really Carter. Lower your weapon, Dakota."

"I'm here for you, Mason."

"And where exactly are you planning to go?" Astrid asked.

Everyone started arguing at once, weapons swinging like pendulums. Dakota lost the ability to process distinct words and instead heard a soup made of anger and rising tones. Mason stopped before the rest of them, watching now. She grew distracted. When shouts came her way, she couldn't help yelling back.

She fell into it, losing track of Mason, of why she was here, of what she'd been told. Dakota found herself yelling back just to be heard.

All the while, the room around them continued to disintegrate, walls dripping like a painting hung too soon. Odd noises sounded behind them — crunching, groaning, the squelching of boots in the mud. The room absorbed the emotions and thinned its integrity. A toppling was imminent.

"STOP IT, GODDAMMIT!"

Everyone looked at Mason. The canister was back above his head, the pin now halfway out.

Astrid took two steps, then paused when it seemed he might blow the whatever-it-was just to spite her. Her hand went up in a pacifying gesture. In her most reasonable voice, she said, "Listen to me, Mason. Your father carries a code that Blake will use to kill everyone who's ever gone through the system if he thinks things could sour, which they already have. If you don't let me take him back to—"

"Revival?" Dakota finished.

"Of course not."

"That's what the other Calliope said when she talked to Blake's hologram back at Dharma One."

"You talked to Blake?" Mason asked.

Preacher laughed.

"What are you laughing at?" Dakota demanded.

"None of y'all know. Me and Mason had us a little chat while you all was sleeping."

"Nobody slept," said Carter.

"Tell 'em," Preacher prompted.

"Tell us what?" Astrid asked.

"Tell 'em you know she's been working with Blake all along."

"*Bullshit!* I'm working *against* Blake!" Astrid's eyes appealed to Mason. She gestured at Preacher before she continued. "Why would Blake have sent this asshole to chase me if I was working with him?"

"He's not after you," Mason said. "He's after me."

Dakota shook her head. "Blake told me the virus was after Carter."

"*Of course* he did," said Astrid.

Mason turned his attention to her. "Did you lead us here on purpose?"

"What the hell's that supposed to mean? Of course, I led you here on purpose."

"But why?"

"To find your father."

He tipped his chin at the vortex. "What's that?"

"I don't know," Astrid answered.

"Bullshit."

"I don't know!"

"I don't believe you." Mason shook his head.

Preacher laughed again. Now Astrid looked like she really might shoot him. If not for Mason and whatever weapon he held, she probably would have — not that it was likely to do any good.

"Mason. Look at me." Dakota spoke quietly.

"No."

"No, what?"

"Don't talk to me."

"Mason. It's me. Dakota."

"I have to be sure."

"Sure of what?"

"You worked with her. For three years."

It took Dakota a moment to understand. She sputtered her reply. "She's just a mind! I *never* worked with her!"

"I meant Calliope. Up top."

"Yes! Calliope! Not *her!*"

"They're working together. Two halves of the same plan."

"And besides, I'm pissed at Calliope! She left us! Left us to fend for ourselves!"

His muscles tensed. The pin moved another millimeter. "You say that, but I wasn't here. I don't know if it's true."

"Mason!"

"Quiet," Mason said, looking pained. "I need to think."

The room did the opposite and erupted again.

This time Dakota heard fragments of a hundred stories and all the theories to match. She could assemble sense from only a few. She heard Blake and Astrid had worked together to manipulate Mason into coming here — not just to Carter, but to this funeral in particular. She heard Astrid was good and Preacher was bad. Heard Preacher might not be so bad, but Astrid was the devil. Heard Astrid was telling the truth but her flesh-and-blood double topside constantly lied. Then she heard it the other way around.

Everyone was pleading for Mason's approval. Dakota heard arguments of what had been real and what hadn't been. Of what was truth and what was a lie. Which lore had happened in the past across several competing versions, and what was likely to happen next.

Then they started yelling about the black swirl churning weightless between caskets. Dakota startled. Upon entering, she'd believed the swirling thing was on the wall as a decoration. A projection on a screen for reasons unknown. But it was floating there, radiating blackness, and on the minds of everyone in the room, each with a different interpretation.

It was power. It was nothing. It was a tool. It was a weapon. It was really here. It didn't exist.

Dakota felt twisted like a pretzel, unsure which end was up.

In time, all mouths exhausted themselves again. The room fell slowly quiet, with nothing left for anyone to say.

Mason moved toward the exit and then — after making sure nobody could run at him and catch him off-guard — sat. He set the canister beside him. When he lowered his face into his open palms, Dakota felt every inch of his discomfort.

"None of you are telling the truth. I don't believe any of you."

Carter, out of the blue, nodded from the front. "That's my boy."

Dakota didn't know what he meant until her attention returned to Mason.

He lifted the little silver thing, which she now knew was a bomb.

Then he pulled the pin.

SIXTY-SEVEN

Indubitably

OF THE FIVE seconds it took for the logic bomb to detonate, Mason spent two of them in panic so deep, he'd have needed to dig a hole if he wanted to find it again. Those twin seconds passed in normal time, but felt like they lasted for days, weeks, maybe years.

Mason could only look at the canister in his left hand and the pin dangling from his right index finger like a misplaced, oversized wedding ring. Mason and Chaos, pledging to have and to hold one another until death does them part — which might not be much longer, according to the clock.

In those first two seconds, Mason wondered in a screaming crimson haze whether he could simply return the pin to where it'd come from. He would have tried if the next phase hadn't come, but there was no point. He hadn't received a metal object made in a factory and held in human hands. He didn't need to understand its workings or whether the thing could be stopped or if it had become unstoppable. The logic bomb was only a thought, like everything else here. A decision turned into jacketed aluminum. Decisions, once made, never went the other way.

Three seconds.

It was all moot by the third second, at which point Mason lapsed into ethereal serenity. A strange peace came to claim him. A certainty that things were about to get very bad, but anything was better than this.

And in that knowing, it was okay.

Four seconds.

He never lost contact with his father. In the quiet moments before pulling the pin, Mason had heard Carter's voice inside his head as loudly and clearly as if the old man had been standing right beside him. Between his ears. Occupying his senses, operating some hidden internal mouth. *Whatever you choose, I'm with you.*

Mason had listened to so many logical arguments and lies. Five or six times now, someone had sat him down then explained their version of the truth before a newer, better, even more logical version of the story supplanted the one before. It was all so tidy. So eminently logical. Except, as a whole, it didn't make sense. As a whole, it was a drooling, seeping, festering pile of horse shit.

Mason, you're going to prison.

Mason, you didn't actually rob a bank, remember? You were busted for a bar fight after the downward spiral following the death of half of your family, then were sent to prison.

But no, wait, Mason. Pay attention. You're actually not in prison. You're in a dream world. Waking up to real-life after three years, and Dakota is with you. You were never arrested. That would be ridiculous.

Mason, you have to find Calliope.

No, no, the other Calliope.

Mason, Blake's about to kill everyone.

Preacher is after you.

Mason, it was all untrue. It was all a ruse. A setup, so you'd create that vortex.

Calliope is a friend.

Calliope is the enemy.

Preacher is, at the very least, your enemy's foe.

Mason, there are fifty liars with fifty stories surrounding you, and the prison might be about to eat itself alive two or three levels above this place, which isn't real, which you might be able to control, or not, and Blake wants code that Calliope planted inside your father, except that also might not be true, and maybe none of it was ever true. Maybe all that's real is everyone thinking you're a fool, a pawn, a thing to be molded but never to stand up and decide for itself, and maybe Calliope's got her agenda and Blake's got his, and somehow Dakota is the agent of Blake's agenda, and maybe he's been turning people into mental cadavers. Or maybe Preacher is right, and he actually hasn't quite hacked it yet, but maybe you're the key, and that's what's really happening here, and the others aren't quite on the level. Or it's the other way around. Or you never woke up.

Maybe you're still asleep. You've woken from Pattern Black twice now. Risen from a place nobody's supposed to ever wake from or be able to survive inside, so maybe you didn't because why should you be any different? In that case, you never left a tube, a wet vertical tube, or a dry one lying down, and actually, you're still there right now.

Maybe this is the ruse. This right here. Maybe Carter is dead after all, and what you see — what, in fact, just spoke inside your head — is yet another element of the fantasy. Because how would you know?

Maybe that's the real Dakota, and maybe it's one more trick.

Maybe that's the real Calliope, or maybe there's only one *real Calliope, and she's there with you now. And maybe Blake's there, too, after spinning more tales through first Preacher and then Dakota.*

Too many layers to understand.

You've always been crazy. Everyone always knew you'd end up here.

Fucked.

Carter's voice, amid the assault, repeated what it'd already said. *Whatever you choose, I'm with you.*

It felt like a lifeline. Never once had Mason felt so near the lip of insanity. Never before had he felt his mind's cart trundling so out-of-control down a steep hill, begging the bearings to hold and the wheels to stay on. He'd had episodes, sure. Moments in which he'd been forced to wonder if this was it, if he was sliding down into the dead and dark.

But even in those moments, Mason had known something. Anything. Now, there was nothing. He couldn't even be sure he was here. That any of them were.

In the end, it didn't matter. The thought was the thought. The voice was the voice. It existed, somehow, even if its origin stayed a mystery.

Whatever you choose, I'm with you.

Mason's words, or maybe his father's.

But the words were still the words and *that*, at least, was something true.

So, Mason sent his mind toward that single thought, knowing no matter what came next and what may have come in the past, he could at least cling to the lifeline in that simple promissory sentence.

He could still choose. And he had.

Maybe he'd pulled the pin on a genuine logic bomb, if there was such a thing, and it was prelude to withdrawing his mind from all that was actually around him. Maybe he was letting air from this grotesque bounce house, or maybe Mason was only a man in bed, trapped in a fantasy and losing his mind.

At least he'd decided. At least he could still do that much.

Fuck it. If Mason couldn't trust anything anyone was shouting at him, there was no reason not to hit the master reset. He didn't know what the logic bomb would do. Only what it implied and how much it frightened the others.

He recalled what someone had told him, though the wires had become so jumbled he was no longer sure who. His mind was the only thing holding this room open. Carter had made a shambling lean-to for protection inside Pattern Black, but his thoughts had turned his father's flimsy tent poles into load-bearing pillars. Without Mason, a place this deep in the recesses of collective minds would consist only of the chaos born from random neural firings. A repository for all the mind-things those who'd visited couldn't repress or control.

Logic held it together. Specifically, *Mason's*.

Time was already dilating, seconds stretching like taffy.

Then Mason was alone.

In a bright nothingness.

There was no fanfare or explosion. No flash, bang, or big finish. He felt no concussive force or blooming injury. If not for the sudden change of non-scenery, Mason might have wondered if the bomb had been a dud.

But clearly, *something* had happened. Clearly, it'd worked just fine.

A white room stretched to the limits of infinity around him. There was nothing in the distance and zero horizon. No source of light or impediments for shadow. No edges or air.

Mason looked in a direction that felt like down — somehow, he still had equilibrium, despite the lack of floor and sky. There was a small black something underneath him. Without perspective, it was impossible to say if it was small and close or large yet far away, but Mason fixed his gaze on it anyway.

No change for a while, but then the spot started to grow, from one into many. Spots multiplied as he moved closer, resolving into a pattern of black circles, like dots on a die.

Mason realized he was falling, not floating.

The thought gave his body weight, infusing the space with just enough air that he could feel himself cutting through it, plummeting without a parachute. Closer, he could see the dots weren't random. They were arranged in a long spiral, each center the color of a starless midnight without a moon.

He wanted to panic, but it was over too fast. One moment, the thing was beneath him. The next, he was falling into one of the dots — a black hole near the center, its contents no clearer even as he tumbled through it.

Mason braced for impact and squeezed his eyes tight. It took a long time before he realized he no longer felt the sensation of freefall and dared to open them again.

He was in a long hallway with bizarre doors, angled like spires on a gothic cathedral, no two the same. At first, he thought those farther down were too large, but as he walked, he found the carpeted floor didn't just seem to rise due to perspective — it rose for real. The doors were far closer than he'd realized. And smaller. All odd shapes, ill-fitting their frames, some with windows that stood off-center and looked in on bare wood and brick. None had hardware, not so much as a knob.

Like in the prison.

But of course, how much of the prison had he actually seen?

No room for logic here. Or for thoughts that went *If …
then* or *Because … result.* Had he ever seen HRO 22, or the red crib,
or Dharma Four, or Dharma One? Had he ever met Calliope? Had
he met two of them?

Mind drifting, Mason seemed to remember seeing Dakota
recently — but he also remembered her dying.

All things seemed to have happened in unison. He went to see
his shrink, at his father's suggestion, on the same day Dakota left his
bed for the final time. He'd shot someone by accident, but right now,
it seemed to have happened just before or after Logan, sixteen years
old and fresh from getting his driver's license, had crashed into the
family garage.

He remembered his parents' wedding even though he was pretty
sure he hadn't been there.

He remembered his father.

Born.

Decorated for valor.

Disgraced.

Imprisoned.

Dead.

Found.

Mason put his hand flat on a glowing door. Pushed.

Discovered a melee behind it.

He was in the lobby of some bank, but the place was also his
childhood bedroom. Toys littered the floor between the whimpering
bodies of prone customers. Large-caliber shells made a muddle on a
large mat of cartoon streets and tiny homes — the one Mom had
given him to play on with his cars and trucks, but he had barely
unrolled.

The world swam into focus around him. It'd been graveyard-
silent, but now he heard shouting and shooting with the volume all
the way down. There had been no color, but over the past few
seconds, someone had cranked up the saturation on this scene.

He watched Dakota blown apart, shells opening her ribcage
from the rear. She landed on a fully set table over which Mason's
dead mother presided — a full-spread holiday feast, centered by a

perfectly browned turkey. His brother Logan, ten years old or so, sat at the place where Dakota's head came to rest, blood gushing from her nose and mouth, head shaved above one ear by a round whose near passage had singed her flesh like a wood-burning kit.

Logan reached for the gravy then poured it onto his turkey. Only, Dakota's bleeding head was in the way. Gravy wicked from her forehead to her cheeks, into the socket of one unblinking eye, then down her nose.

His brother asked for pie. Mom said, *Not until you finish your corpse.*

Mason seemed to fall a single floor's height — the hangman drop of a criminal on the gallows. But instead of coming up short by his neck, his feet landed without impact on something soft. Heat bloomed all around him.

Someone was calling for his attention. Mason looked up.

He was at the beach. Santa Monica, the pier behind him. Behind *them.* He was posing for a photo, and the man with the camera was Nic. With a cat on each shoulder, his body too long and too tall. His face was all wrong. Maybe it was the president. Or the girl he'd had a crush on in fifth grade, who wore two pigtails on the sides of her head like handlebars. Or maybe it was nobody at all, and instead of holding a camera, the featureless shadow before them held a circular whirlpool, like a vortex made of ink.

"Say cheese, motherfucker," said Logan, beside him.

Of course, it wasn't his brother. It was a large man Mason had never seen, except he had a sneaking suspicion he'd seen him every day of his life — sometimes up close and personal, sometimes at his throat, sometimes in his dreams, or always just out of sight and hiding in the shadow. Something that lived in his blind spot.

The carousel.

The Ferris wheel.

Mason stood on the pier with the waves crashing below, the beach behind, his mother's and brother's bodies now dead and bleeding where he'd been posing for their family photo just moments before. He could see them now, buried in seagulls. The birds plucked flesh from their bones and painted the beach red.

Others circled above, squawking desolate cries as they waited for the greedier gulls below to fill so they could dive for their share of the meat.

Not caring at all, Mason turned to the carousel. Every horse was occupied by his father at a different age. A forty-something Carter Shaw rode a white horse with red eyes and teeth four inches long. Carter, at fifty, sat in a cart pulled by two stallions so black, they seemed not quite to be there. A young Carter — far too young for Mason to have known him — rode a horse that was just a foot high off the deck.

Carters of various ages stood between the others, holding barber-pole posts as they drifted up and down to the sounds of a carnival.

"Focus," said the nearest Carter.

Mason's vision pulled back, as if he'd been watching the scene through an extreme zoom lens mounted to the moon. The pier vanished. For the span of a second, he made out the coastline and the shape of the North American landmass, next the globe, then the entire planet was a far-off dot — a tiny light spot in the infinite blackness of space.

A click sounded beside him — someone tugged a dangling string to illuminate a canning basement. Mason's field of view inverted with the light. Black became white, and white became black.

He was no longer floating through the cosmos but was sitting in a chair at a poker table in a room so sterile, angels could use it as an operating room. Beyond the circular table with its green felt and colorful chips hung a lone decoration framed on a wall that didn't exist. From Mason's vantage, it looked like a silver frame floating in midair. A masterpiece of pointillism and minimalism inside its lines — a few black dots spiraling from the center on a bright white background.

Carter stood to his right, with Calliope, Nathaniel Blake, Preacher, and Dakota all around him.

"Let's talk," his father said.

"With them listening?"

Carter looked at the others. "They're not even here."

"You got it," said Calliope, shooting finger guns at Carter.

"Yes, sir," said Preacher. "Indubitably."

"You fucked up, kid," said Carter. "You fucked up perfectly. I'm proud of you."

Mason looked around. The room went on forever. The framed photo of dots had been joined by a painting of dogs playing poker that seemed so appropriate. The dogs were betting on a pile of human teeth.

"Are you really Carter?" Mason asked.

His father picked up a deck of cards and began to shuffle. On each of the backs was an illustration of a naked woman being ground between the gears of a massive machine. He shrugged. "Are *you* really Mason?"

"You got it," said Calliope.

Blake clapped too enthusiastically.

"Of course, I'm Mason."

"Indubitably," Preacher agreed.

"I meant ..." There was no good way to put this, especially with such a foggy mind. Mason was caught between sense and nonsense. A vestige of his rational mind kept trying to make everything normal. To remember that beyond this bizarre place, there was — or was supposed to be — an everyday world. "I meant, am I imaging you?"

"Of course you are. You think this is real?"

"But are *you* real, apart from my imagining you? Are you *you*, even though this is my dream?"

"Yes, sir," Preacher replied.

Blake clapped again.

Carter dealt the cards, two down, two up. Everyone showed a pair — deuces for Calliope, jacks for Preacher, aces for Blake, queens for Carter, and threes for Mason.

He peeked at his cards. Each one had a black dot the size of a drop of paint.

"Don't be stubborn," Carter told him. "You always wanted to define things. You always wanted to put everything into a box. That's why I wanted you to see the doctor. Not because you had phobias, but because your way of seeing the world *set you up* for phobias. You always avoided what you didn't want to see."

Preacher tossed chips into the table's center. Calliope caught his hand then pushed them back. "Nathaniel has the highest hand. He makes the bet."

Blake smiled then leaned toward Mason. "I bet you'll be stuck here forever."

"Indubitably." Preacher nodded.

Mason looked up at his father.

"Okay, fine," Carter said. "You want the truth? I'm here. I'm as here as you are. The way it's always been."

"It's never been this way."

"You sure?"

Carter looked down. Mason followed his gaze to his own right arm, which had grown into Carter's left like a tree through a fence. Neither of them had hands. They were now conjoined by a tube of bone and muscle and skin and blood that belonged wholly to neither of them.

"You and me, kid." Carter smiled at Mason's befuddlement. "Even when we were on the outs, I was here. Even when you thought I was gone, I stayed a part of you. You can never kick me out. We're like braided vines, neither strong enough without the other."

"I'm plenty strong on my own," said Mason, feeling familiar resentment.

Carter had always aimed to raise Mason in his shadow. He had shown interest in police work before Logan and applied to the force before him, too. At first, Carter had thrown all he had behind his younger son, pushing until the pressure threatened to break him. Only after Mason finally cried mercy — violently and with rancor, disowning his father as much as distancing him — had Carter turned to polishing Logan.

He was Carter's second choice and always had been. Only now was it obvious.

"I rode you because you needed riding. Head in the clouds.

Diving into fantasies instead of rising above them. You *became* a hardass, son."

Blake said, "I'll bet … if you try to get out, it'll kill you both."

"What is this place, Pop?"

"How should I know?" Carter looked annoyed that Mason had asked.

"It's the way Pattern Black is supposed to be," Calliope said.

"Indubitably," Preacher agreed.

Blake clapped.

"I had a bomb. I …" Mason squinted as he tried to remember. It seemed so very long ago. "I blew it up, didn't I?"

"I saw cows playing fiddles," said Carter. "So, yes. I'd say the logic here is gone. Blown to bits, you might say."

"Where's the way out?"

"There is no way out. This is it, Mason. This is Pattern Black. This is how I saw it, too, when they first put me under. It was this way for what felt like years, though it was probably only a while. I floated for as long as I could stand it. Sure at some point, something would change. I wasn't dead, so I should've been able to imagine something other than this all-white dungeon. But nothing came. So I waited to die. But of course, they were keeping me alive."

"Who was?"

"Blake." He looked at Calliope. "And her, I think."

Calliope made finger guns.

"I couldn't die," Carter continued. "I couldn't think. Probably didn't take me long to start losing it. I tried to go somewhere in my head because I'd heard stories of POWs doing that when their captors stuck them in holes and kept them alive with gruel. The great orators made entire palaces inside their minds, tying objects inside to points they needed to remember. It was a mental art — one I already had interest in even before I started training with Elisabeth, even before I'd ever heard of Chamber Therapy or Pattern Black. So, I tried to create my own memory palace. And meditate my way out of that featureless nothing."

"Four aces." But silly Blake. It took at least five cards in hand before a person could play.

"I couldn't come up with anything," Carter continued. "I couldn't retreat into my mind because I was *already* inside my mind. I couldn't run from the all-white room because my mind *was* the all-white room. When they took me to Therapy inside the HRO, I figured it was no big deal. They'd try to rehab me. Understand why I'd broken into Revival's offices then teach me never to do it again. Even when shit went south, and I fell through the Heist to land here, I didn't panic right away. Figured I still had my thoughts. But I was wrong. I could recall enough to make it real and build the start of the funeral parlor it became. But it was always you, son. Never me. I was half-blank from the second I showed up. About the time you started having dreams, I suppose."

Mason remembered. What had been quiet for more than a decade had flared up. His old teenage neuroses resumed as if he'd merely taken his finger off *pause*. That lasted for maybe a week, and the way he changed then was probably why Dakota had left. At week's end, he'd received notice his father had gone Pattern Black. It felt like an untimely piling-on, but what Carter said, if true, reversed cause and effect.

He'd had his problems because of Carter, not in advance of him. He'd not simply been informed his father went Pattern Black. He'd been watching it happen in his dreams.

"Did Calliope — did Elisabeth — put some sort of a code inside you? The key to whatever Blake was trying to do?"

"After you set off the logic bomb, I had time to peek inside before you found me. There's nothing in me, Mason."

"So, she lied."

"They all did."

A third piece of art now hung in the air around the poker table — a black vortex, like a hurricane made of evil.

"I should have known," Carter said. "Logan and I never had the same bond. Remember our game? I always thought it was interesting and fun, but nothing serious. I started seeing how real it was after we stopped talking, while I was training, and Elisabeth kept telling me to go deeper. I knew they'd find an excuse to bring you in, same as they did for me. But you went Pattern Black right away. And instead of dying, you thrived."

"And the vortex?" Mason asked.

"It was here all along. Hidden deep where you couldn't see it. It's like a guard dog. A friend, not a foe. All those dark, buried emotions snapped back the second you were threatened. I saw Calliope come in after us but didn't know she was playing both sides. I hid and watched her look for us both. But mostly you. They'd designed a system that erased their subjects' minds, but a blanked one had no compass left to follow home. A power like yours opened doors. Minds didn't need to find their way back to the body on their own if what you had simply erased all the walls and let them slide where they needed to go. They chased you. They couldn't open the lock, then you showed up with the key. That was probably why Elisabeth was so keen to work with me — she could sense what you had *through me*. She just had to find you, wake you, then send you back down to a place where she could control you with your marbles intact."

Mason looked down. His up cards, like his hole cards, now showed the single black dot.

Like Blake's hand — four untidy aces.

"What should I do, Pop?"

"I don't know."

"How do we get out?"

"Grow wings," said Blake.

"You got it," said Calliope.

"I don't know." Carter shook his head. "I could only build a hole when I came here. Elisabeth was so frustrated, unable to catch me because I never came out. She thought I was smart. But really, I *couldn't* come out. I know you blipped in, too. I saw it a dozen times."

Mason remembered that. The only truly consistent thing he knew after going under was the white room, the black dots. He'd thought it had been after him, but now it seemed he may have created it. Or that *he*, at least, was the reason he'd visited then left without checking in.

He built his own hole like Carter, but it was more than a pile of memories. It was a fleshed-out reality spanning for miles. Carter had left all his experience of the prison floating in the raw space of Pattern Black, then Mason had picked it up like boards and bricks and nails.

From time to time, his constructed reality had worn thin enough to see the white room behind it. Only once had Mason escaped. Even now, having re-entered Pattern Black on Calliope's supposed mission, felt like a dead end.

But if his power was here — if it was *here* that Mason generated the churning black thing they'd wanted all along — was it in anyone's best interest that he leave?

"I got out because Calliope woke me up."

"It wasn't her, son. It was you."

"She did something to me. Put a rag over my face. A special rag. They call it a Muse."

"It only directed your attention and focused what you already had."

"Then I need it. If she helps, I can focus." Mason looked at Calliope, who gave him finger guns. *This* Calliope — which surely was just his own mental garbage — helped no one.

There was movement. Mason looked up to see the frame showing the vortex shaking. Suddenly it was sucked away from behind, folding like a handkerchief pulled through a hole by its center.

Mason felt it leaving. "Something's happening."

Carter shrugged, but Mason didn't need him for an answer. Now, with the cobwebs cleared, he finally understood.

The logic bomb hadn't backfired or injured the cause. Mason and Carter had taken its brunt, but Calliope and Blake were fine. Calliope was in two parts, and Blake had sent Dakota as proxy.

Mason could feel the prison's real-world defenses rising, sure to be tripped into chaos mode the second Blake found Calliope in Dharma One and entered to shake her hand rather than kill her. She already had Mason's body, and Blake already had Carter's. With the Shaws together and all the prison's evidence soon to be erased by drone strikes and the so-called chaos fail-safe, they'd be free and clear. The first two mental cadavers were prepped and ready, their minds incarcerated in this prison, pumping out power that was already being siphoned away.

"I *did* fuck up, Pop."

There was no logic left. No doors. No windows. No floors. No map to follow because there was no map or blueprint to lay down. You could exit a maze by keeping one hand on the wall, even if it took forever. But this wasn't a maze. The power Calliope had focused with her psychedelic rag was leeching away, beyond his ability to use it.

"Indubitably," Preacher agreed.

SIXTY-EIGHT

Thank You, Sigmund Freud

Elisabeth Reeves put one foot in the metal stirrup dangling from what looked like the world's strangest fishing line, then she grabbed the line as instructed by the Docent who'd come down to sweep the facility. She understood the physics but still felt like she needed a second rope with a second stirrup to be stable.

Or a civilized meeting in a regular office instead.

Indoor meetings used to kill her. Blake wanted to hold everything in a conference room because he said it felt more professional, but she'd always wanted to walk while talking, separating their necessary business from the stuffy rooms she couldn't stand. They always smelled stale, like leather and testosterone poured into expensive suits. But right now, Elisabeth would've killed for a boardroom. She'd been undercover for too long.

The stillness as the winch raised her to the hovercraft made the journey worse instead of better. She'd seen this done in movies, but those folks — burly SWAT guys, not ninety-pound scientists — were always hoisted to helicopters. At least a chopper looked like it belonged in the air. Hovercrafts were basically grown-up drones, hovering silently on ionized gas.

A Docent in black reached one hand around the small of her back, pulled Elisabeth into the thing's belly at the top, then closed the door. Nathaniel was dressed well, same as always. It was quiet this high above the prison, and the hover was stable. Not too far from a boardroom, after all.

"You came in person?" she asked Blake.

The Docent had painted this more as a ride than a meeting. She'd only come up to speak with the person in charge, to tell them off the record to put her back down. She was more tired of HRO 22 than anyone had ever been of anything, but it had been years, and her mission wasn't done. She could handle one more night.

"I needed to speak with someone." He came forward. After an awkward moment of indecision — Was a handshake enough? It'd been so long, they felt like strangers. — they hugged. "How are you, darling? You were gone so long, I was starting to think you'd really left me."

Elisabeth ignored this, used to the way Blake tended to embellish his news.

"Well, I'm here. Speak."

He laughed as if this was all very charming. "Not you, Liz. I met with your friend Dakota Ward."

"You spoke to Dakota?"

Blake stood then went toward the rear. Elisabeth had already forgotten they were in a hovercraft and had to look out the window to be sure they weren't moving. Someone was bound to notice if they left via anything but the masked flight path.

"Would you like a drink?"

"I'm good, Nat. Why the hell were you talking to Dakota?"

"It wasn't just talking." He pounded his fist lightly on what looked like mahogany.

"What, did you fuck her?"

"You've gotten so crude." Blake slapped the mahogany again, and this time Elisabeth looked closer. What she'd taken as a drink catcher was actually the finest and most unnecessarily decked-out immersion pod she'd ever seen.

She recognized the woman inside. Sharp features, black hair, eyebrows that seemed judgmental even when their owner was sleeping.

Elisabeth looked up at Blake.

"You met Dakota? Or you just shoved her into that pod?"

"Did you even know she'd left the Inner Circle? I found her on the outside. She did a number to the fence. Dharma is no longer quite as taboo to the inmates."

The answer to Blake's question was no, not that Elisabeth planned to admit it. She had known Dakota left Dharma One, of course, but assumed she'd scuttled back to the rest of Immunity.

"She went in after Mason Shaw. She somehow spoofed her blood tag using her sister's ID, but of course, my panel flagged what seemed to be a dead woman running around in the open."

"So you *found* her. You didn't *talk* to her."

"Oh, we talked before she went under," he said.

"You let her do this?"

"I *asked* her to do this. She was going in like a cowgirl, so I focused her mission. Carter Shaw's hiding place finally started to light up — his son's doing, probably — but I couldn't figure out how to get in there. I thought she could help."

"Why did you want to get into Carter's hiding place? I told you I already had a dreamcatcher in place."

"You didn't seem sure it'd work."

Elisabeth pulled a device the size of an old-model cell phone from a zippered pocket then put it on top of Dakota's immersion chamber. "It worked."

"But I didn't know that, did I?" Blake picked it up then slipped the device into a fine leather messenger bag at the foot of the bar, right by the liquor. "Seriously, Liz. This is cause for celebration. Have a drink with me."

Blake was right, but she shook her head anyway. They'd parted as allies, but there'd been much arguing before she left and many angry messages back and forth whenever she could find an appropriate kiosk. Elisabeth supposed she trusted him — she'd given him the dreamcatcher full of Mason's cortical distillate, after all — but she didn't feel up to sharing a drink.

"No, thanks."

He shrugged.

"You wait for me." Elisabeth pointed at the bag where Blake had slipped the organic drive. "Set it all up if you want, but wait for me before you try it on a patient."

"A 'patient'?"

"A prisoner. Whoever. You think you're ready for whatever happens once you copy that pattern into a new head, but you didn't see its manifestation."

"Really."

"Really," Elisabeth repeated, recognizing his much-loathed dismissive tone. Blake had always been the face of Revival, but she'd been its brains — even while away, whenever she could plug in and look at whatever he was working on. Blake could be knocked into sense, but his default was to be a condescending pain in the ass. "Even Mason was afraid of it."

"But it's his."

"There's dark shit inside all of us that we'd be terrified to face, Nat. Study any psychology, and it'd be obvious. Even to you."

"Oh. *Psychology*." Blake waved it away.

"Inside the simulation, Mason's cortical distillate took the shape of a tiny black whirlpool. Like stirring tar."

"Really. Tar *is* frightening."

"Are you going to take this seriously, or are you going to do something stupid?"

Blake snapped-to. "Of course I'm taking it seriously, Elisabeth. You're not the only one who suffered."

"I'm sure it was terrible for you, sleeping in your penthouse while I crashed on piles of garbage."

"You were the one who wanted to hit things from the inside, Liz. You could have stayed put."

"Just promise me, Nat. It wasn't easy to provoke that out of him. I had to tell the wildest fucking stories to get him emoting enough to find Carter, and then once in his presence, Mason's neural stream became all about their baggage."

"Then I suppose a 'good job' is in order."

"I don't need a pat on the back. What I need is for you to promise you'll wait another twenty-four hours before trying to format any cadavers. I need to be there. More, I *deserve* to be there."

Elisabeth thought he might push back, but Blake merely nodded. "Fine. I'd rather have Mason on-site before I start, anyway. You're sure we can't move him now? It was easy enough to port Ms. Ward into this beautiful new home. It'd be so much easier to take you both now." He tapped the mahogany pod.

"It was simple because she's basically dead. We need to keep Mason alive."

"So, you're babying Mason Shaw. The man who woke after three years under, without any atrophy or mental slow-down, all on his own."

"He had help with that."

"Yes. How *is* your other self?"

"Dead."

"Dead?"

"Mason conjured a logic bomb almost as soon as his little storm-in-a-bottle manifested. I thought they might all get away clean, but he detonated it with his primary avatar."

"It wasn't one of the reflections who blew it?"

"No." She shook her head. "A reflection threw it, but Mason caught the bomb then pulled the pin."

"Why?"

"He *knew*, somehow. It doesn't matter. We got what we needed." Elisabeth looked down. "I can't imagine Dakota fared much better than my lesser half."

Blake tapped something on Dakota's tank. He looked at the small panel as it lit, as if to confirm the truth. "I called and had Jen check on Carter back at the office. His readings are equally blank. I guess it's good you weren't connected to your … what would you call her?"

"I'd call her dead," Elisabeth repeated. "Along with your soldier."

"Oh, Preacher? We hardly knew ye." Blake shook his head with mock grief, then crossed himself in parody. "Anyway. Probably a good thing you weren't still tied to her when that logic bomb blew. If Mason conjured the thing — especially in that place — the bones probably just fell out from beneath it. I'd consider us lucky if the construct is still intact."

"The systems are all fine, but the subconscious reservoir is now entirely empty. Nothing can hold its integrity down there anymore."

"Just as well. Forest fires do us a service by giving everyone a fresh start every once in a while. If you can't move him yet, so be it. I'll go back and do what I can, keeping my hands off any actual formatting. Scout's honor." Blake raised a hand, three fingers aloft.

"Tell me you weren't a scout."

"I was."

"Despicable. You people take an oath to be honest."

"What about you, love?"

"I was never a scout."

The hovercraft went quiet. Elisabeth looked down at Dakota. "It's a shame."

"What?"

"She was smart. Had grit. It's a waste."

"Look at the bright side. She's already off-record. Did it herself when she swapped her blood tag. There'll be no paperwork."

"You want to use *her* as the first subject?"

"Why not? Do you expect her to get up and go dancing? She's flatline above the neck. We can either toss her out, or she can be useful one last time. What do you think Ward would prefer?"

Elisabeth sighed, still looking at the tank. "Goddammit, Nat."

"What?"

"You didn't have to send her in. I had the situation under control. I had them both on my side. They thought we were running from you."

"What did you tell them?"

"Same as what we told Dakota when you sent your hologram." Elisabeth ran her fingers along the coffin masquerading as a capsule. "I said Carter had some sort of a code inside him, and we couldn't let you get it first or—"

"I'd kill them all?" He chuckled.

"It's a little crazy, fine. But it worked, didn't it?" Elisabeth leaned against the hovercraft's cool wall, patterned in mock wallpaper. "Carter believed it, same as the others. He took us to his hole. It turned out to be *his wife and son's funeral.*"

Blake seemed both surprised and amused. "I guess I *didn't* need to send Dakota. The scene sounds volatile enough without her. How did it go?"

"Like we knew it would. They fought. Hard. And when Mason got to the point where he could no longer contain himself, his little ink storm detached and turned on its own. I managed to copy a lot of it before the bomb hit, then the rest after."

"*After* the bomb?"

"They're still in there, you know." Elisabeth nodded at Dakota. "Her, too, probably. Mason is a lot stronger than you thought. I copied the final lines of the distillate afterward just fine. It was there because *they're* still there."

"They?"

"Flatline or not, my stats suggest Carter might be with him."

"Impossible."

Elisabeth shrugged.

"I thought a logic bomb was a subject's way of ..." Blake began.

"Of committing mental suicide, I know. Thing is, Mason is untrained. Ironically, he doesn't understand what he did. He has no idea he's dead."

"Jesus."

"Which is why I need twenty-four hours. When it's all bled out, I'll have him ported to a shippable tank, then we'll meet you at Revival."

"Are you saying you still need him?" Blake paused. "Or his father? I thought getting the distillate was enough?"

"You never throw out steps in your experiment until the experiment is over. Every scientist knows that."

"I'm not a scientist," said Blake.

"That's exactly right. So do what you promised and wait for me."

"You're sure they're all effectively under?"

"They're *dead*, Nat."

"You said they were still inside."

"Floating in the middle of nothing. At least the memory Carter built had a way in and out. Now, without logical structure, they might as well be in a balloon on the ocean floor. They'll be flatlined just like you want, once their air runs out."

"'When the air runs out'?" Blake repeated.

"Speaking figuratively. *Christ*." She jabbed a finger at his fine leather bag. "There's a log of vitals on that drive. Take a look. Mason told me unconstructed Pattern Black is full of holes. He's terrified of them. Same as anyone, his private Hell is full of fears and insecurities."

"And that means ..."

"Nobody wants to live too long in a world full of the worst parts of themselves, especially without any escape or hope that there might be one. As soon as the logic bomb blew, their connection to the main construct fell like an apple from a tree. He'll expire, don't worry. And if he doesn't, I have the nuclear option. We have the distillate. The Shaw boys are, as you said, extra baggage."

They looked at one another. Elisabeth glanced out the window, noting prisoners where they shouldn't be. Was Blake telling the truth? *Had* Dakota broken through the fence around the Inner Circle?

Elisabeth had hijacked a news snippet on the feed before coming up here and knew the official line was HRO 22 was in the early stages of a riot. They could use excessive force if they wanted. Officially, Calliope had been pinned down in Dharma One. The rioters would murder her in the morning, leaving Elisabeth Reeves free to work in the dark.

Blake said, "Well, then. I have my wallet, my toothbrush, and Mason's cortical distillate. Anything else I'm missing?"

"The Muse. You'll need it if you want to direct your subject's attention to any distillate being used as a bridge."

"Ah, yes — the *Muse.*" Blake extended a hand but sort of seesawed it as if he didn't expect Elisabeth to place anything in his palm. "Are you sure you trust me with it?"

Truth was, she *didn't* trust Blake. It wasn't his fault. Untrustworthy as he always seemed, her skepticism now had more to do with the long years she'd spent with only criminals for company. But the Muse wasn't a weapon. It was far from the mere wake-up cloth Mason and the others believed it to be, but Elisabeth couldn't imagine any way he could possibly use it against her.

"I suppose I can trust you," she told Blake. "After all, if you get it in your head to do something stupid, I still have Mason."

"Is that a threat?"

"I don't know. Is anything *you* said a threat?"

Three seconds passed. Blake's hand was still out. Elisabeth still wasn't smiling.

Then he laughed, and so did she. "It's good to have you back, you manipulative bitch."

Elisabeth dug into her pocket then withdrew a small device. The hardware housing it was new, but the software had, until her untimely death, belonged to Elisabeth's digital half. The thought made her uncharacteristically nostalgic. She would miss her other half. Astrid had grown into a bold person, artificial or not. While Elisabeth had been hiding in a dirty brick-and-mortar prison, Astrid had never ceased her guerrilla warfare. She'd run everywhere inside the system with that focuser in hand, testing the response of anyone who might aid their cause. Blake believed Mason would eventually have woken on his own, but Elisabeth wasn't so sure. If Astrid hadn't opened Mason's eyes and shown him he was in a sim that first time, they might very well still be twiddling their thumbs. Elisabeth had grown tired of hiding inside a prison, holed up with the riffraff, and felt deeply grateful for the help.

"Is this it?" Blake considered the device. It was unremarkable, about the size of a key fob. "*This* is the famous Muse?"

"Of course. Is there a problem?"

"The logs suggest it was more like a washcloth. Your other half referred to it as a 'rag' more than once."

"My 'other half' was a digital being. She made it from ones and zeroes. Did you think I was going to hand you raw software? Ignore the package, Nat. She used her Muse as a dreamcatcher to snatch the distillate like I told you. It respawned in Immunity's inventory when she was destroyed, and I downloaded its contents. Exactly as planned."

"So this is … what? A drive?"

"Call it whatever you want. If I'd known you'd be so picky about the dreamcatcher's corporeal form, I'd have soaked Mason's vortex into a towel for you."

Blake glared for half a second, annoyed. But then he took the thing and turned it in his hands, probably thinking of the fortune he'd make once he started extracting Mason's distillate and blanking minds for sale.

He pressed a button on the side, then chuckled. "Did you forget something?"

"What?"

He turned the Muse display so Elisabeth could see the simple message. [NO FILE]

"The distillate you mentioned grabbing?" Blake said, mock-chastising. "That icky pool of black tar?" He wagged the focuser like a conductor's baton. "Where is it if it's not on this drive?"

A bolt of unpleasant emotion sparked her nerves like an electric shock. She patted her pockets as if the software might lie there — binary code fallen from its storage device, lost in the laundry, in the pits of her wardrobe like stubborn lint.

"Shit," she said.

"I assume you have another copy?"

But no, of course, she didn't *have another copy*. It was biodigital. There could only *be* one copy unless she built another. Blake had never understood what her half of the partnership did, and the naiveté of his question made Elisabeth want to scream.

Her calm was gone like water down a drain — and with it, she was suddenly aware of how dangerously close she was to losing her shit.

"Motherfucker," she said.

From inside the pod, Dakota Ward's otherwise immobile body raised its middle finger.

Waiting to Understand

"It's only swimming," Dakota told herself.

But she wasn't that stupid. Swimming happened in water, and water provided resistance. This wasn't even a free-fall.

It was disorienting to feel nothing. Whatever was here — *here* being a place where it wasn't strictly necessary to breathe, seeing as she wasn't a physical person with lungs — the lack of subtle pressure resisting movements made everything feel too fast, as if someone had loosened the world's joints and left every limb to jangle. Whenever Dakota tried to breaststroke her way through the nothingness, her hands whipped from shoulder to waist as if greased.

She didn't seem to be going anywhere but was capable of becoming tired. Maybe because her mind kept trying to make this non-body real by adding subtle clues — a headache that refused to leave her, muscles filled with lactic acid that could only be coming from the power of suggestion. Maybe because Mason's bomb had killed her no matter how much things seemed to the contrary. She'd seen a flash, then nonsensical images from her past assaulted her senses like gunfire. Then she'd been nowhere at all.

Nowhere.

It wasn't even the hellish nothingness Mason had described. Dakota saw no black dots or spirals. Nothing to offer orientation or context. She might be upside-down if there was such a thing anymore.

As an idea dawned, Dakota reached into her pocket then withdrew the thing inside. It was like fabric made of plasma, subtle color shifts washing over its surface in waves. She thought she'd seen the last of the Muse because the logs said Calliope — probably Astrid — had checked it from inventory soon after Dakota had used it on the Heist's old lady.

The Calliope in the Heist was surely either dead or as lost as she was. Had the *real-world* Calliope made the request?

It was a virtual item, useful only in a sim. It had to be Astrid who'd placed the hold on it — and Astrid sure as shit wouldn't need the Muse for a while.

But something was strange. After Dakota requested the Muse again, she'd noticed changes in the luminescent patterns playing across its surface. Curious, she'd checked its item stats and saw it bursting with data in a way it hadn't been before.

How had *that* happened? It was a wake device, not a drive.

Had someone *stored* something on it?

It hardly mattered. If the Muse's magic had woken Mason and the old lady, maybe it could wake Dakota now.

If she *could* be woken from inside, now was very much the time.

Dakota put the thing over her face the way she'd done for the old woman. Nothing happened except for her feeling stupid. So she took it off, fluffed it, then put it back on, this time clicking her heels together and saying, "There's no place like home."

Still nothing, beyond feeling even stupider.

Dakota ran the rag through her fingers, wondering if there was a trick to it. Perhaps there were special considerations when using it on yourself. She called up its specs again, looking for the user guide, if there was one. The Muse was also called a "focuser." Maybe "Muse" was a nickname — and a far less-helpful one than "focuser," at that.

Focus, Dakota. Focus must be the trick to making it work.

But still, nothing.

Her hand came up to take the thing from her face, but Dakota saw a blast of images that seemed born from the fabric itself before she could pull it away. She saw Mason and Carter at the fake funeral they'd just been blown out of, but from a perspective that appeared to be behind the coffins, as if the figurative camera's view had been set against the wall.

Next, she saw Mason and Carter around a poker table in the middle of nothingness, having a conversation while surrounded by reflections of Blake, Calliope, and Preacher.

Again, she pulled the Muse away. *What the hell?*

It was feeding something to Dakota. She could feel the hardest edges of Mason. Behind the visuals, seemingly within the Muse itself. She felt his anger, frustration, and most odious habits. The shining cloth seemed full of them.

Dakota considered the file size. How could a simple rag carry so much data?

She put it away as despondency fell — in her pocket this time and damn bothering with inventory.

Just keep swimming.

In the blast after the logic bomb, Dakota had felt the protection of Mason's hand. She'd been at the door with Nic while he'd been committing murder/suicide fifty feet away. A psychic presence had pushed her back just before it blew — one mind reaching out to another — the way a mother holds her child back when slamming on the brakes.

A wash of disorientation followed. In the rush, Dakota wondered if this was life flashing before her eyes. And maybe fuck Mason for saving her, if this was how it had to be.

But he wasn't here. She didn't need to see his face or hear his words to know he'd gone from believing someone to believing nobody. Mason's altered emotion was all around her, thick like a presence in that room of his.

She felt something amiss below her belt, then looked down to see the Muse had wormed halfway out of her pocket. Pointless questions abounded. Why, for instance, would fabrics conspire against her here as they did in life, where blouses refused to stay tucked?

Dakota tried to stuff the thing back in, but her pocket had folded on itself. So she set the Muse between her teeth and used both hands to finagle her pants into behaving. She pulled her hand from her pocket and used it to yank the Muse from between her teeth. Held by one corner, it flapped weightlessly before her, fizzing in her hand.

I wonder what this thing did to Mason?

As if in response — she had *focused* on the question, she supposed — the rag ceased its flow of color and became a tiny, flexible television. Slightly distorted by shadow, she saw the spinning black vortex they'd all been fighting so vehemently over before the bomb finally blew, the swirling hurricane some of them seemed to believe was … was …

"Oh, shit," Dakota said aloud.

The vortex had been behind the coffins, swirling just in front of the back wall. Curious now, she returned the strange object to her face and stared into those swirls of changing color. The earlier vision returned, then she saw it. What the Muse was showing her might as well have been a camera feed of the funeral from inside that swirl of ink.

The view changed. She saw Mason and Carter playing poker again. She'd never seen this scene in life. Was it new? Were Mason and Carter — and maybe Preacher and Astrid — still alive after all, playing cards somewhere else? The Muse showed her all four seated around the table, and again Dakota got the impression she was seeing from inside the vortex.

What was happening here?

With nothing better to do, Dakota put her mind to it.

Calliope had requested the rag from inventory, but Astrid was gone — inaccessible if not actually dead. So, had the new request come from the *real* Calliope? The *real* Elisabeth Reeves? Preacher and Mason had both said the two halves of Calliope were working together, and both had wanted the vortex.

She weighted the Muse in her hand, wondering. Had Astrid put it into inventory for real-world Calliope to grab at some point in the future, and Dakota had managed to nab it first? If so, why?

The file size suggested someone had filled the Muse with data to use it like a drive. Had the Calliopes gotten the vortex after all and stored it on the item Dakota had queued for use in the Heist … then never fully let go of it?

No way. Calliope isn't that stupid. She'd restrict the permissions.

Dakota never should have been able to take the item from inventory. Only the Calliopes should have been able to grab something so important.

Except she was still wearing Sarah's imprint, and Sarah was dead. No real reason to keep the departed from taking whatever they wanted. That was one thing Shinelle had said, drunk one night while pissed at Calliope and wearing her twin's identity. *Fuck Calliope's rationing. What's she done for us lately?* We *raided the cache, so* we *should be able to drink all we want.*

Yeah. But Calliope's got it all locked down, Dakota had replied.

When I look like Aurora to the computer, I don't have *any restrictions. You want something? Say the word, and I'll get it for you.*

An inconsequential loophole — one nobody really wanted to tell Calliope about.

She looked at the Muse now, remembering the old story, thinking of Sarah, noting the changes in the small rag's colors. The sheen shifted again, still like a little TV. This time Dakota saw Calliope with Blake. They were somewhere formal. Maybe a boardroom with blue sky beyond the windows. Somewhere very high up.

Motherfucker, she imagined Calliope saying.

And in return, Dakota laughed. *Yeah. Fuck you, bitch.*

It might have been in her head, but Dakota, whose officer's wits were returning, didn't think so. She'd caught Calliope's prize, throwing one big *sabo* into the gears of the other woman's plan. Too bad she was stuck in limbo.

Its surface changed again. The Muse almost seemed to be talking — whispering someone's intention to her by whorls and visions. Was it Mason's will? Like his anger and aggression.

But *will* wasn't enough. Dakota would need to figure this out if she meant to carry the ball.

Again, she watched the rag-like item. Waiting to understand.

It wakes people. It's also called a focuser.

Maybe that was it. Maybe she just needed the right thing to *focus* on. If all the logic had been blown from this world by Mason's bomb, there'd be little left on which to center her thoughts.

Focus on Mason. Find him.

She closed her eyes. Tried to clear her mind.

I want to see Mason. I need to find him. I need Mason to see. I need him to focus, *too.*

But … nothing.

Dakota removed the Muse with a sigh. She was still alone, and everything was the same.

Except it wasn't.

Because now the world had filled with spirals of black dots, and for the first time, their fathomless presence felt welcome.

SEVENTY

A Truth That Couldn't Be Argued

THE WORLD HAD FILLED with ducks. Flying through a 360-degree atmosphere before a backdrop of white sky and round black stars.

"I know there's no logic here," Carter said, "but if I could offer an opinion?"

"No, thanks," Mason told him.

"Jesus fucking Christ."

"That's not really an opinion, Pop."

"I know you can't control what's in your subconscious. But … *ducks?*"

"I always liked ducks."

Carter, sitting on a rug and grateful at least for this little well of gravity, crossed his arms. "It's like living in a room decorated by a five-year-old."

"Complaining won't help, Pop."

"It passes the time. How long can we possibly have?"

"Time is the one thing we *do* have. So, stop bitching and start thinking."

Carter said, "You need some sort of a connection to the grid, or you're only inside your head. Despite our bond, I don't think we can keep chatting without an intermediary to connect us."

"What do you mean?"

"I had to keep reminding myself my hole was tied to a system, or my little nest of thoughts would break away and lose cohesion. I don't exactly know the rules of logic bombs, but it's safe to say we're out to sea. You can't hold cohesion forever."

Calliope — clearly not the actual Calliope — and Preacher — clearly neutered — were sitting in tiny pink chairs around a child's tea set. Blake had wandered into the whiteness a while ago, announcing his intention to play. Hearing Carter, Preacher said, "Indubitably."

"Is that all he can say?" Carter asked.

"Like you said, Pop. I can't control it."

"*Of course,*" Carter muttered.

Mason looked then sighed when he saw what had captured his old man's attention — Dakota, floating toward them from the void. She neared their patch of land, then stopped floating and started walking.

"Of course, *that* is what you'd obsess on. *Of. Fucking. Course.*"

"Better than ducks."

"Barely. She's an attractive woman, Mason, but I don't really want to watch you fuck."

"What makes you think I'm going to fuck her?"

"*Your* subconscious. *Your* weird sex fantasies."

Mason kept watching Dakota, seeing Carter's point but sure he could control it. For one, sex fantasies should be sufficiently wet-blanketed by his old man's presence. Plus, he wasn't exactly aroused.

"I'll bet she's here to play poker, Pop."

Dakota spoke as if everything was normal. "Mason? Jesus, is it really you?"

"Is it really *you?* I thought you were dead."

"I think you protected me. The bomb went off, and I was nowhere after that. Everything was white." She looked around. "Even whiter than this."

"So, like Newport Beach," Carter said.

"How did you find us?" Mason asked.

"With this." Dakota reached into her pocket then pulled out what he initially thought was a clown's handkerchief. Sparkly and colorful, it would have gone perfectly with giant red shoes. But then he reached for it, his breath catching, recognizing the thing that had woken him from sleep.

"How did you get it?"

"I think I stole it."

"You *think?*"

"It's an Immunity thing. Unimportant."

"Who'd you steal it from?"

"Calliope."

"Which one?"

Dakota looked to the woman sitting with Preacher on the carpet. "The one in the real world. Calliope always called it a Muse, but apparently, it's also called a focuser. I'm no rocket scientist, but it seemed to help me *focus* on finding you."

She turned back to Mason.

The world blinked away, then immediately back. It was like being in a windowless room with flickering power. Twice more, each blink less than a second. *Off-on. Off-on. Off-on.*

"What's happening?" Dakota asked.

Carter looked victorious. "Exactly what I said. You can't hold this open for long."

"I held *your* little fantasy open," Mason told him.

"When it was still tied to the grid. Mine was only a backdoor."

Again, the world flickered. There were many more dots in the air upon its return. They'd multiplied unseen, approaching critical like an attacker from the shadows.

"Did you see a way out?" Mason asked.

She snatched the rag and shook it. "*This* is the way out. And there's more."

Dakota told them about taking the Muse from Immunity's inventory with hijacked permissions, how she felt sure it was being used as a storage drive, and the critical cargo she believed it carried.

"So, what now?" Mason asked, knowing he should be pleased but unsure of what to do with that information.

"We *focus* our way out. Then we find a way to blow the whistle."

"I don't think it works that way."

Mason took the Muse, then tipped his head and did as Calliope had done, laying it over his face like a miniature death shroud. It was a focuser, so he tried to focus. But after fifteen seconds or so, he took it off his face with a shrug.

"Try again," she said. "I get the feeling you, in particular, can bend the rules here."

"We're inside my mind, Dakota. But this isn't mine."

"Exactly," she said, shoving it back at him. "We're inside your mind. This is real, and I know it works at least a little because I used it to get here. But with all your stubborn bullshit, you're getting in your own way. It's not really here if you don't believe in it."

Mason didn't think that sounded logical, either, but then again, right now, they were inside an endless Apple Store with ducks and dots in every direction. He questioned Dakota obliquely, trying to warm his mind to the idea. "How did you use it?"

"I asked it to focus on you. Or to help *me* focus on you. Then I saw you like it was a screen, and then … I don't know. When I looked around next, I was here."

"Well, I just tried that."

"I also used it on the old lady."

"Indubitably!" Preacher said, raising a finger to the sky.

"I don't think that's really Preacher," Mason explained.

"It's not the real Calliope, either," Dakota said.

"How do you know?"

She opened her mouth, then stopped. "I just sort of do. But I don't know *how* I know. Isn't that weird?"

"You got it," Calliope said.

Then Mason said to Dakota, "*You* seem sure."

She thought before responding. "I am."

"How?"

"I don't know."

"Think. *Try.*"

"I am trying," she snapped.

"Try harder."

"Goddammit, Mason. Why don't *you* try harder?"

He held up the rag. "Here. *Focus* on it."

She did. Mason saw nothing in the folds, but Dakota returned it with a look of revulsion. "I'm still connected," she said.

"Connected to what?"

"I don't know. To my body. To the rest of me."

"Are we?" Carter asked.

"No clue. I'm not you."

Carter took the rag and tried the same, shaking his head.

"I think I heard something," she said. "In the real world — I think my ears heard something."

"Just now?" Mason asked.

Dakota shook her head, clearly frustrated.

He understood, having been through what she must be feeling half a dozen times himself recently. Her thoughts had turned sluggish. Every time they changed venues in here, it took time to reorient.

"No. It was when I was in the other place. I heard Calliope say … *motherfucker.*"

"It's okay," Mason said. "Take your time."

"No. I mean, that's what I heard her say. She said, 'Motherfucker.'"

"Good to know." Carter nodded in mock appreciation.

"There was more." She concentrated, probably searching, or more like scrabbling for a fading dream's spiraling tendrils. "I think I heard …" Dakota furrowed her brow. "I think it was … Calliope and *Blake?*" She nodded. "It was them. Talking. Close to me. I mean, close to my real body, wherever they've taken it."

"And?"

"They said Astrid is dead. That means the Calliope over there is just your reflection of her."

"Fuck."

"It's okay. Clearly, she wasn't on our side."

Mason wanted to process that. He wanted to consider what Dakota was saying and try again to make peace with the fact that

Calliope's entire mission and everything she'd said was a lie designed to make him face off against his father.

At least Astrid had been hung by her own petard before dying. If the goal of all that deception had been to make Mason eject the vortex Blake and Reeves so desperately wanted, at least Dakota had managed to steal it back. The thing was somehow stored on that rag.

The reversal had been so recent. Part of Mason still wanted to cling to the idea of Calliope because she'd been the one who knew this world best. The one who had all the answers. That was probably the reason there was a Calliope clone nearby. Somewhere deep down, Mason still thought she could — and would — save them. Well. Good luck with that.

The Calliope on the carpet dissolved then floated away in a mist.

"Did you do that?" Carter asked.

"I … I think so."

"How?"

"I don't know."

"Do him now," Carter said, pointing at Preacher.

The world flickered again — thrice this time. But Preacher remained.

"We're wasting time," Dakota said.

"We're not. We're learning his limits." Then to Mason, he said, "You must know by now this is your game and nobody else's. *Focus*. Try again."

So, he did. He tried to stare Preacher into nonexistence. He tried to put the rag over his face and dream of the real world. He tried to conjure a door or build an escapable world to replace all this unvarnished absence. He focused on Calliope — Elisabeth — in the real world, how much he hated both her and Blake and how he wanted to make them pay in the real world. He held the rag up like Dakota had done, wishing into it like a Magic Mirror.

But nothing worked. Nothing happened. She said she'd seen visions in its patterns, but Mason saw bupkis.

"Maybe you don't believe it," Dakota said.

"It's not Peter Fucking Pan," said Carter.

Mason handed the Muse to Dakota. "You don't even know this can get us out. Just because you heard—"

She held up a waiting finger to stop him. "I raised my hand."

"So what?"

"Not *these* hands." She held up the offending parties. "I think I somehow … I think I raised my *real* hand."

Now Mason was interested. Neither he nor Carter said anything while Dakota concentrated, pawing around for a stubborn slice of recall.

"I … I gave them the finger."

"You *what?*" Carter said.

Instead of answering with her mouth, Dakota raised her middle finger, nearly close enough to pick Carter's nose. "I did this."

The finger persisted.

"I get it," said Carter.

"Are you sure?" Mason asked.

"As sure as I am that Astrid died." She put her hand to her chest. "I can feel it somehow. But I think it's because I was close to *her*, and *she* felt it."

"Close to who?"

"To the real Calliope, in the real world. *Physically* close. As in, my body was right beside hers. When she felt Astrid go, I saw her reaction. Or heard her words."

They thought about that.

"Try again," Dakota said, handing the rag to Mason.

"I tried."

"Keep trying."

"I said, *I tried.*"

She grabbed him with both hands. "Listen to me. This was always about you. Not me, not even Carter. *You* had the ability. *You* were able to turn your father's pile of associations into a city-sized prison. *You* got yourself out of danger from the inside, more than once. It was always *you* they were after, once they knew you had what they wanted. Do you get it? *Yes*, I heard through my real ears and raised my real hand, but that was as far as I could go.

I'm trapped here. But *you?* Mason, I think *you* might be able to wake up if you can just get the trick of it."

"You don't know that," Mason told her.

"Sure I do. You did it before. Not Astrid, not Bear or Kassidi. *You.*"

"Even if you're right, all three of us are——"

"If you wake, you can come after me and Carter. But you have to hurry. The prison's alarm——"

"Jesus, Dakota. It's not working! What do you want from me?"

Her temper exploded. "Goddammit, Mason, I want you to *try!* Until you make it work … TRY!"

But then something happened. Her face fell, eyes troubled with an answer to a question no one had asked. "I think I can still hear them in the real world. I think … I think he knows."

"Who?"

"Blake. Calliope, too. They know we have this." Meaning the rag. "It … worries them."

"Because it means we still have that vortex thing? Because they didn't manage to get it?"

"That, but mostly because they didn't get it from you after all. Now you know what they tried to do … and *you still have the power.*"

Mason thought about what Preacher had told him, about how together he and Carter were able to change the simulation and hence their own minds. It's what made mental cadavers possible — but it might also mean Dakota was right, their strange reality wasn't as immutable as it seemed. Maybe he could wake up. Maybe he wasn't trapped.

She nodded, seeing his eyes change. "He's afraid of you, Mason."

"But I'm not even conscious."

"Not now. *Not yet.*"

"And if I do somehow wake up, I'm just one man." Worse, he'd be one man in the real world, not a superhero inside a sim. What good would all that swirling black anger do him out there, where knives and guns held more sway than naked aggression?

"I'm just telling you what it's like. What my body seems to feel, so close to them now."

"Oh, for fuck's sake," Carter said.

Dakota and Mason turned to look at him.

"Listen to you two. Look around, will you? We're playing Flying Carpet inside a nonexistent world, inside the head of a mentally unstable man." He looked at his son with apology, but Mason knew it was true. "A little while ago, in this weird fucking place your world-saver built around us, all of Mason's old schoolteachers were over there" — Carter pointed into the black-on-white distance — "playing Red Rover. When someone ran across and hit the other team's line of arms, they broke apart like dropping a pre-sliced side of beef. But now we're planning things based on your *feelings?* For fuck's sake. No offense, but I'm sure as *hell* not counting on your crystal ball assessment that Blake and Calliope are *afraid of Mason*, and we can somehow, someway, use that as leverage. You know *after* we get out of this imaginary dungeon?"

The lights flickered again, but this time a new cacophony assaulted their ears. It sounded like a train skidding off the track. A belch of static on an unclaimed station. Like white noise given voice — machine code turned to words, somehow meshing letters and symbols and numbers. The report of an aggressive glitch foretelling catastrophic failure.

They turned to see Preacher standing tall, shoulders back and chin up. His entire posture had changed. Same man, but clearly *different*. His eyes were now almond-shaped holes displaying lines of flowing code, flashing like a flickering screen.

His limbs jerked. His eyes went entirely white, then red, then black. There was a final crackle of static, then he was suddenly every inch the *Preacher* Mason had so recently feared.

Now rebooted.

Mason didn't know if he'd thought the words or if someone else had spoken them, but he knew it as a truth that couldn't be argued.

"Mason, look," Dakota whispered too low for Preacher to hear. She was nodding at the Muse — the shimmering rag in his hand. On its surface, the picture persisted. The door it displayed was now fully open to a long concrete hallway. It was doing something. Mason was *making* it do something — *focused* now in a way he hadn't been before.

As Preacher cracked his back and knuckles, Mason's attention stayed on the open door. Interestingly, he now understood the problem. Of course, he hadn't been able to focus the way Dakota wanted him to. Mason was a pessimist, not an optimist. Stick over carrot, for sure. Motivated more by the threat of pain than the promise of pleasure.

With something to fear, the Muse was focusing him just fine.

Preacher loomed, even larger than in his previous lives — eight feet tall and five feet wide at the shoulders. The purr of his breath was like a bass drum. "How fast you think you can run if you ain't got no ground for yer feet?"

Mason focused on the rag. He tried to hurry his mind but rushing only made it harder.

Preacher came forward with no haste, seeming to know he had all the time in this imaginary world.

And Mason couldn't move.

The door is real.

We can walk through it.

The door is real.

We can walk through it.

He tried to forget Preacher.

When I open my eyes, he thought as he closed them, *I will see the door. It will be close. It's a bridge. I can do this.*

The door is real.

We can walk through it.

Mason opened his eyes.

And saw the door.

Then he ran. So did Carter and Dakota.

She made it through first, pausing at the threshold to usher Carter into the long corridor. Mason was just behind his father. He told himself the hallway had the chill and scent of stone. Concrete's cold sterility. He could see the lights' reflections on the floor and feel circulated air on his face.

The door and hallway are real.

Carter and Dakota were through, standing on stone. They flanked the door, waiting for Mason, their eyes reaching, Dakota's right hand *literally* reaching.

Mason crossed the threshold, leaving only his back foot to float in the void. But just as he felt cool air descending, something gripped him from behind. It didn't take his shirt so much as his breath. It didn't grab his clothing so much as it reached inside and grabbed his mind itself.

Preacher wrapped an enormous arm around Mason's neck and squeezed as he pulled him back.

The door slammed as if in a gale, trapping Carter and Dakota ahead — or himself behind. For a second, Mason could still hear the others shouting and pounding, rattling the nonexistent knob. Then the door faded like a memory, and all that remained was Preacher's hot breath on Mason's ear and the steady pressure of biceps pressing against his windpipe.

"She was supposed to tell you we'd see you when the skies were clearer."

Blake, Mason thought. *It's not really Preacher. He's a puppet now, with Blake inside him.*

With a heave, Mason felt his neck break. His spinal column snapped like a twig. All control left his body.

This isn't really happening.

But the body believed what happened inside the mind.

Dying.

Like drowning.

The last thing Mason heard was Preacher, laughter in his voice.

"In-fuckin-dubitably."

SEVENTY-ONE

How it Should Be

MASON OPENED HIS EYES. He heard small clanking sounds. Low, as if kept intentionally quiet.

As if from a long-ago dream, he remembered his neck being broken. He blinked and licked his lips. Then he tried moving his fingers. Finally, he bent his arm and laid those fingers flat on what seemed to be an all-black rug, one hand on each side of his body.

He found he could push himself to a sitting position. Looking around, he felt both lost and very much found.

Mason was beside a table with scrolled wooden feet. He could smell something cooking. Meat. A pot roast, perhaps, seasoned with rosemary.

He stood. Past the table was an old-fashioned kitchen. His grandmother's. They hadn't visited her as often as he supposed they should have. Mostly, the holidays drew them together. But he hadn't been in this kitchen since he'd been a boy.

There was a woman at the oven, her brown hair — gray at the roots — tied in a bun and secured with short chopsticks. She turned, "You're awake!"

"Mom?"

"Tell me you're hungry. Tell me that, at least."

Mason, dazed but clear on his role here, moved into one of the chairs around the table, already set with Grandma's china and flatware. The sounds he'd heard had been her setting the table. He picked up a fork, sure in some way, all of this should surprise him. Not dinner, necessarily, but something else. Why had he been on the floor? And when had Grandma replaced her kitchen linoleum with black carpet? Carpet didn't even make sense in a kitchen.

"It wasn't his fault, you know," she said.

"What wasn't?"

"That we died."

"Died?"

She nodded, meeting his gaze. "Me. And Logan."

"You're not dead, Ma."

"Not here. Of course not." She took a pitcher of water from the counter then began filling glasses. "Help me out, Mason. Get the butter."

His instinct to obey maternal mandate squashed his confusion. Mason found himself rising, moving automatically. Grandma's fridge was nearly as old as Grandma herself before she'd died. They'd kept the house for a while, Mom saying she'd fix it up then rent the place but really just unable to clean it out and let go. The mortgage was paid, and the taxes a pittance. Why *not* keep it? And though it'd been clear to them all that Carter felt otherwise, he'd agreed.

There was nothing behind the refrigerator. No wall, no outlets, no door to the living room that always smelled like warming balm. The carpet ended just beyond it into a gently curving wall, even blacker. He put his hand to it then looked up at a perfect circle of pure-white sky far above.

Despite his questions, Mason removed the butter dish from the fridge then set it on the table.

"He thought you hated him," his mother said, her attention on the stove and her boiling potatoes.

"He wasn't entirely wrong."

"You shouldn't hate your father. You should make peace."

"It's a little late for that, now."

"Why? Because *you're* dead?"

"I'm not dead, Ma." And then, because Mason's arguments with his mother always followed a script, he found himself adding, "I keep telling you."

"By what definition, Mason?" she asked in her hectoring *Mother Knows Best* tone. "Are you not dead because Pattern Black isn't really dying for you or your stubborn father? Or because you think that nice man didn't break your neck?"

"You know about that?"

She laughed. "A mother always knows."

It was all coming back. "You *are* dead."

"Now look who's in a glass house, throwing stones."

"It's not an insult, Ma. It's a fact. There was a car crash. Some guys …" He tried to recall, but it came too slow. "After Pop broke into Blake's office, he sent some guys in a car to——"

"I'm tired of telling you, Mason Edward Shaw. That wasn't your father's fault."

Mason looked up again. The walls and floor were black. It was as if they were in the pit of a stealth silo, looking toward a feature-less sky.

"Your father did his best. With all of you. He never claimed to be anything more than human."

"He's a piece of shit, Ma. Maybe he used to be okay, but then——"

"Language!"

Again, he looked skyward. "This Grandma's house?"

"You know it is."

"But it's not, really. There's no living room. No bathroom. The walls are flat — no tile fresco above the stove."

"Not everything can be as you demand it, Mason."

He squinted. "Are we inside Pattern Black?"

"Where else would we be?"

"Pop was here. He … left. With Dakota."

"How *is* Dakota?"

"She's fine, Ma." Mason found himself getting annoyed. She was always like this. Avoiding the hard conversations, like whether or not his father was obsessed or whether he should stop drinking, or whether Logan was a colossal asshole who always conveniently landed on the winning side of every argument.

No wonder Mason became a cop. Someone had to follow in Pop's footsteps — and erase them from the Earth as he went.

Ma stirred another pot, raised a wooden spoon to her lips, and sipped. She dipped it back, sifted salt between her fingertips, then stirred again.

"I suppose you think you're pretty clever, dying that way."

"I'm not dead, Ma."

"You're not?" She turned fully, both hands on both hips. "I see. I suppose you think you know better. I'm dead, not that you ever listen. Logan, too. How is it your father somehow outlived us all?"

"If Pop's not dead, then I'm not, either."

"Carter didn't get his neck broke. You did."

Mason rubbed the back of his neck. Her points were making sense, and now he wasn't so sure. Once more, he looked up. "Where are we, Ma? Really. Not Grandma's kitchen. I mean … where else?"

"At the bottom, Mason. I mean, really."

Before he could ask, *At the bottom of what?* Mason noticed the sloppy crayon drawing tacked to the fridge. He had done it, apparently. In the lower right, it said MASON SHAW, AGE 5.

The drawing showed two stick figures circumscribed by a circle. One was in a dress and had brown hair. The other was a little taller, wearing a policeman's uniform. The second was himself, not Carter or Logan.

"Is this us?" Mason removed a round magnet from the drawing then held it up.

"Of course."

"Us right now?"

"Of course."

He looked again at the childlike drawing. The circle around them had been scribbled with black, leaving just enough room to see the figures inside. "I don't remember drawing this."

"For Pete's sake, Mason," she said when he was about to sit at the table with the drawing. "Put it back. I'm not as young as I used to be. You can at least help me with dinner."

Again, he obeyed. But when Mason went around to the side of the fridge to return the drawing, he saw many new ones, each was the same — a black circle scribbled so heavily with crayon that the surface grew waxy. No figures in any of them, just that plain circle on white paper. They'd been arranged in a spiral pattern, at the center of which was the one he'd just held.

It was the only one with Mason and his mother inside.

Or maybe *at the bottom*.

He looked up again. "We're at the bottom of one of the dots I keep seeing. The spirals inside Pattern Black."

"Inside *your* Pattern Black," she corrected. "They say we all see it differently."

"You mean *you're* inside Pattern Black?"

"Not everything is about you, Mason."

He shook his head, returning to the table. Grandma had the smallest salt shaker in existence. Pop used to joke that you could fit ten grains inside — two for each of the boys plus three for Ma because she'd made the meal and everyone at the table. Pop said he deserved at least two, but they always fought for that final grain, as if it were a genuine argument.

"I don't understand, Ma."

"Of course you don't." Then she returned to her cooking.

"Preacher killed me for real?"

"If that's what you believe."

"Then that means he killed my mind. Which everyone keeps saying is the only reason this place hasn't collapsed."

"*Please.* You act like the world is on your shoulders."

He remembered Preacher now. And all that had happened. Reformatted, with Blake at the wheel. If anyone knew how to blank a person inside Pattern Black, it'd be the man who invented the technology. And if Mason went down, everything died.

But *why?* Ironically, if he could find a way not to be dead after all — and barring delusions and the obvious what-the-fuck of this, it sure seemed right now like he had, or could — the fact that Preacher, or Blake, had killed him felt like an excellent omen.

Because, really, if they were actually trapped inside, why would Blake bother with hunting down and killing him? Those things were only sensible if it'd been possible, before maybe dying, for Mason to escape.

Mason's "way out" must somehow be a threat to Blake if he was going to the trouble.

"How do I get out of here, Ma?"

"Is that all you can think of, Mason? Getting away from me?"

He stood and crossed the kitchen. Once at his mother's side, he did something he'd never have done in real life after being guilt-tripped like that. He said, "I love you, Ma."

"Past tense will do, Mason."

"I know. But I love you. I know you always did your best."

"Just like your father did *his* best."

"Well. Yeah. Okay."

"He was right about you."

"That I'm a fuck-up?"

"That you were more like him than you ever wanted to admit."

"In what way?" The answer felt so important. So urgent. Maybe because the walls were closing in. And the sky was getting darker fast.

"When you finally faced things, they didn't stand a chance. But until then?" She whistled. "Stubborn. *So*, so stubborn."

The dark was looming. Mason looked up again and saw the reason. An eclipse of sorts. An enormous disc was sliding across the top of their pit like putting the lid on a pill bottle.

"Ma?"

"You heard me, Mason."

She was barely a shape in the darkness. And Mason saw only the waning crescent of daylight — or whiteness, in the absence of daylight. The fear in the pit of his gut was primal. It wasn't about the dark. It was about the end. It was about the unknown. The light, even here, had let Mason see what faced him. But now, even that was going away.

The big thing above slid into place. Now, he couldn't see a single lux of light. Not a pinprick.

Into the echoes, he said, *"Ma?"*

"What you feared most — both of you — was yourself."

Mason found the chair then moved it aside to feel for the table's surface. There'd been a candle there, unlit. Beside it was a fireplace lighter. The source of the flame.

He found it by feel, pressed the butane, then clicked the trigger to spark it.

His mother's face jumped to life inches from his, her round cheeks cut sharp with dancing orange and shadows like knives. Her eyes were so black, it seemed she had none. As the firelight danced between those pits, Mason saw her eyelids sewn shut with black thread. Her skin was sallow, hanging, and desiccated.

"There is no black, and there is no white in you. There just *is.*"

"Ma, I'm—"

"You cannot fall if you are there to catch you."

Her lips pursed. There was a puff of air, then the lighter extinguished.

Mason was no longer in the kitchen. Or even the hole. He was alone, and always had been. Everyone was. There wasn't any reason to fear.

Maybe he'd lost his mind.

But maybe — just maybe — that was how it should be.

SEVENTY-TWO

Raw Construct

THE SCENE CHANGED. Mason heard popping sounds, like corn.

He was in an all-white room. One rug and an equal number of doors. Preacher was above him again, cracking knuckles that didn't exist. The sound was like the exploding of wood knots in a campfire.

At first, he didn't move. Mason waited, listening to a voice inside. It wasn't his father's, though that voice was somewhere. It wasn't a remembered voice of his mother, or Logan, or Dakota. Not of his bosses, or co-workers at the station, or the person he'd shot, or the snitches he'd wrangled. Nor was it the aunts who'd kissed him on the lips and put a wrinkled one-dollar bill in a bargain card on every occasion of note.

All those voices were there. But he wasn't listening to those.

The voice, this time, belonged to himself. The one he'd never heeded. The one he'd pushed down and tried to hide. That second, quiet, internal Mason was a doppelgänger of sorts — an odd cousin nobody invited over for the holidays. Mason's shadow. A creature of impulse. It lived deep, deep down, in the basement of awareness. But now, the door to that basement was open, and the thing of darkness wanted to play.

Sit back, it told him, *and watch it all burn.*

Mason closed his eyes. Opened them.

The room — the world — was on fire.

He stood.

Preacher rose then came at him.

Feeling the heat, Mason remembered standing at railings over tall cliffs, wondering if he should jump, for no reason beyond primal curiosity. He remembered passing pedestrians on crowded city streets, his muscles twitching as if wanting to shove them into traffic.

But Mason also remembered what that deep place had told him about Dakota, about his family, about his brother. He *was* like his father — ambitious but impatient, frustrated, and prone to impulse. He had loved his mother, though she'd browbeaten him. He'd appreciated Logan, even while hating him, because without his brother's abrasive example as grist for the mill, Mason would never have become the man he was.

He thought of Logan's son, Hunter, and how he had adored the child while always keeping his distance. He'd never wanted responsibility, seeing as it was the first step toward disappointment.

And he remembered his arguments with Dakota. How close they'd come before he'd run away.

There was no such thing as crazy. Only different.

The games he played with his father. The way he'd nearly been around the other kids before stuffing it all down in an effort to be normal. He'd talked it all out with the psychiatrists, hiding the truth even in their deepest sessions. But Ma was right. There was nothing to be afraid of and never had been. If he fell, then Mason would catch himself.

He'd never liked losing control. But right now, that's exactly what was happening.

Blake, wearing Preacher like a suit, must have sensed the change. He didn't seem to know whether to approach or back away. He topped Mason by almost two feet and was three Masons wide. Yet it was the bigger man now with fear in his eyes.

"You can't erase me," Mason said, "if I'm already gone."

This time, Preacher charged for real and without pause.

Rehashing old tricks, he returned Mason to his headlock. Only now, Mason could see the move for what it was — not tension and pressure but conditions of a game. There was still logic here, though of a demented sort. A subconscious breed, older than humankind. Logic of the id.

Spilling back through time, Mason let forth all his throttled differences — his knack for finding things that'd gone missing, his curious way of pre-guessing the people around him. Once, at six, Carter had let Mason serve non-alcoholic drinks at a party. He'd known what they wanted without asking, easy as reading their name tags. He'd handed each guest their preferred drink. At school, William Mather called Mason a freak. His father had seen it all.

Preacher squeezed. Blackness knocked, and Mason allowed it. He let himself seesaw into the dark, waiting. He and Preacher/Blake had done this before, and that only led him to his grandmother's kitchen.

Don't react. Just be.

Mason's ability to see beyond the physical proved there was a curtain, and most people lived upstage. But there was a backstage, too. A place of spirit and thought, where fathers talked to sons without moving their lips. Where Mason would sometimes go outside and sit on a hilltop as a boy, imagining himself as a mote of dust, drifting into the corporeal substance of each thing on the vista, living or inert.

Mason heard his neck snap, again. Felt his muscles tense around the broken bone, again. Felt the agony, again, until he decided maybe he'd gotten it all wrong. He wasn't really here, neither was Preacher, and that touch and feeling — here of all places — was no less an illusion than the mirage of dreaming.

So Mason thought, *I'm well. I'm not even here.* With that, the pain seemed to vanish, and the bones began to mend, and none of it mattered a whit regardless because he was that mote of dust, floating above, landing only when he chose to.

He hit Preacher hard enough to throw him fifty feet. Easy, because there was no force here. No distance here. No fighting, no strength. No victory and no defeat. This was an unreal place, and Mason didn't need ones and zeroes or a wire or a signal to go where he wanted.

Mason met Preacher's gaze. It was all so obvious now. Why was Blake, as Preacher, allowing himself to be defeated? Didn't he see the very same truth?

The door was ajar again, so Mason stepped through. It vanished behind him. He found himself in the long concrete hallway, Carter and Dakota staring at him as if they'd never seen anything so odd. Which Mason, as he settled into who he'd perhaps always been and perhaps always should have let himself be, found almost funny.

"You got out," said Dakota.

"So did you."

"The door disappeared after he closed it. We heard him … We heard him …"

"Kill me?"

She nodded.

"Don't be ridiculous."

The walls shook. Above, hairline cracks spread like a delta. Powder fell like silicate snow. The stone shivered against a massive impact, an egg-shaped web of fissures leaping from the solid mass. A second impact doubled the lines, paint chipping, drifts of dust piling onto the floor.

"He's breaking through," Carter said.

"Of course he is."

They ran, Dakota in the lead. Mason kept pace, feeling the hammer of his feet and knowing none of it was there. It was more than the intellectual understanding that his body was elsewhere, that none of what he saw should be able to hurt him. The world was stage dressing. Mason wasn't this digital form or even the body in a pod in Blake's office. He was something else and in more than one place. Maybe out of his motherfucking mind.

The hallway ended ahead. The wall burst behind him, and there Preacher stood like a titan.

Mason's eyes closed while his internal sight sharpened. His mind slipped into the data stream like a hand into a glove. Those rushing bits made sense. Mason could reach out through the connections and inputs, like a swimmer making his way downstream. His eyes and ears were everywhere inside the system, perhaps *beyond* the system, understanding each corner of the HRO and its real and simulated landscapes through all its sensors.

He could go anywhere. Observe everything.

Mason saw Blake in a pod of his own, or perhaps at a keyboard with one of those funny electrode hats on his head, steering the big man because if Mason and Carter escaped, Revival might fall.

He also had a view from inside the electromagnetic signals thrown by the web of prison drones — all that info assimilated into one collective pot, allowing him to bear witness to everything at once.

Elisabeth Reeves descended from a Revival hovercraft and into Dharma One, no longer so sure of herself after what Blake had said and done, knowing her Muse had been lifted. If Dakota had been able to use it to peek her head out of Pattern Black long enough to give them the finger, then Mason *wasn't* trapped, and he *could* come out. Knowing if they planned to stop him, they'd damn well better start trying a whole lot harder.

In that same drone view, Mason saw the prison from above and the demolished fence at the Inner Circle's open mouth. Rolling back the footage, he saw prisoners standing superstitiously at the gap as the dust settled, then watched as they entered. They'd raided the most important caches already, a few of them learning things Revival would rather they hadn't.

Dakota was watching Mason, seeing the difference in him. "Are you okay?"

"No." He extended a hand. The wall exploded outward, revealing a crawlspace.

They crouched to enter. On all fours now, thirty feet in, Dakota and Carter looked back as Preacher tried to squeeze in behind them. Mason watched through a third eye as Blake, frustrated, opened a new screen in the real world and pulled up the prison simulation architecture, slamming his fists on the console when he remembered this was Pattern Black, not a level of his or Calliope's design.

He did not — could not — control this place.

Mason watched as Blake kept at it anyway, cross-patching this to that and laying everything atop whatever, creating a Frankenstein of connections that, after it spooled up and made all the artifice shiver, consented to Blake's probing, opening up, changing its walls, becoming something new. Dilating.

The crawlspace became a hallway. What had been a small utility corridor — more assumed than consciously designed because Mason had fleshed it out once he came through the dead-end — was now a wide field with, pipes overhead. Preacher labored behind, his ability to catch his quarry limited only by the press of Mason's now-awakened mind.

Preacher shouted and screamed, never gaining but living on their heels.

They rounded a corner to another dead end. This time Mason tried something else, wanting to test this newfound skill. Wielding it felt like liquid danger, like riding a bike on the edge of a mountain. He had power, yes. But he'd dipped into a well of something new to find it, and his full concentration was required to hold it steady.

They climbed a ladder out of the complex, finding themselves back in the bank lobby.

The Heist had reset. The same guards, the same posters. The same tellers and managers, and patrons. The same old woman with tennis balls on the front of her walker. Nobody was dead. They all watched the dust-covered party of three as they rushed from the back rooms, through the lobby, then out onto the street.

An unmarked van was just arriving. Black-clad people piled out. Cruz led a fresh set of five wide-eyed bandits, stopping with guns held to watch them pass as they broke through the front glass rather than opening the door.

They dashed down an alley then through a building that only appeared solid.

"Mason," Carter said, panting. "Remember. The city ends at—"

An explosion tore through the quiet. Mason looked over his shoulder.

Preacher had found what looked like an RPG launcher, but larger, and the weapon took its rocket rounds from a massive magazine. Each shot was followed by a whistle then a contrail, culminating in a brilliant orange fireball.

"I know," Mason told his father.

They tore on, both of Mason's companions stealing glances to the rear, knowing the Heist's simulated city ended not far from the bank building, and if they kept at it, they'd blip back to somewhere in the middle of an in-progress Heist, maybe right in front of Preacher's cannon.

Still, they pumped on, losing steam. They pounded the pavement as best they could, fighting for breath.

Mason found his companions' exertion hard to understand. None of them had real legs or lungs here. Still, Carter and Dakota gasped, their minds entrenched in the unreality.

Had Mason once been fooled by this place? Had he ever truly believed it was real?

He barreled toward a shimmer ahead.

Preacher was gaining. Carter and Dakota seemed too frightened for speech. Dakota tried to say something. She pointed toward the shimmer and shouted for Mason to watch out. But he doubled his speed, then refrained from doubling it again only because he knew the others would be unable to believe they could do the same and thus fall too far behind.

"Mason," Dakota finally said, her gaze darting between the shimmer and his charging toward it. "That's …"

As if to heed her warning about the border ahead, he stopped. The shimmer's unrelenting energy was palpable. Mason could go through if he wanted. He could be anywhere right now because only the rational followed rules like gravity or momentum. Physics in general.

The shimmer ended the sim. If Mason believed the usual definition, they couldn't go further. He turned the group around to face what was coming.

With the demarcation to their backs — the point at which, if they stepped farther, they'd end up back in the fray with guns drawn against them — Mason paused.

Preacher was before them in moments, RPG raised. His smile was one hundred percent Nathaniel Blake's. "Guess you ain't goin' no farther."

The affect was there. The speech patterns were still there, even with Blake running his body. Just one more bit of evidence that when minds combined, neither truly eclipsed the other. Preacher was in there, overruled and relegated to his own mental basement. Furious, without a doubt.

"Guess we ain't." Mason looked at Preacher's boots. "Bet I can tell you where you got your shoes."

"What?" In his confusion, Blake was unable to muster Preacher's diction.

"You got your shoes on your feet," Mason said.

"What the hell are you—?"

"On your feet. Unlike you."

"What the fuck are—?"

Mason focused for a half-second, like flipping a coin. He wasn't intimidated, or tentative, or wary. He understood. His mother — and father, in his way — had shown him how.

The city disappeared.

They were in an all-white room full of lazy black spirals.

No up. No down. Everyone floating without any bearings.

"Way out," Mason muttered.

On his command, gravity returned on a slow rise, his body gaining weight over the course of three seconds.

His feet found the ground his mind had set beneath them — a long straight bridge with sky-high pillars, the void around them transformed into a grave drop below.

He brushed the surface without effort, but Carter and Dakota hit the bridge hard. Preacher, floating higher, took a bigger fall. He landed off-center and now clung to the brick sides, feet scrabbling as he tried to hoist himself up and onto the bridge. Being big and strong wasn't always practical. What good was being a behemoth if you couldn't climb out of peril?

Mason turned back, helped Carter and Dakota to their feet. He stepped aside to let her lead, then ran between them with Carter at the rear. The bridge was just wide enough, and they made fleet time down its length.

Soon enough, Preacher was a speck.

The bridge ended. They were back in the city. A tremendous ocean lay behind them, the crossed bridge a pier jutting into it.

Preacher found his feet, raced toward them, then turned back and told the bridge, "Gone."

It vanished, flicked back, then faded completely.

Soon they reached the digital representation of the prison city's outer wall, but because it was a sim, Mason decided the wall wasn't there, so it crumbled as they approached. There was a black-and-red grid beyond the wall, sterile and dry. Gone was the city, even behind them.

"This is raw construct space," said Carter.

"How do you know that?" Dakota asked.

"Elisabeth showed me. It's a blank palette for builders."

"And for us?" Dakota pressed.

Noises sounded from the rear. Preacher was still coming.

"For us, it's nowhere to hide."

Carter and Dakota turned, but there was no city behind them.

"Fuck," Carter said.

"Fuck," echoed Dakota.

Preacher was closer now. Running hard, all limits on his speed and location now removed.

"Walls," Mason said.

A wall rose from the grid.

Preacher hit it, pounding, making bricks rattle and rain.

"We have to get back to the city." Carter frantically looked around.

"No." Mason shook his head. "This is better."

When Preacher broke through, Mason raised a cathedral in

front of him. Then a busy freeway. A library. A ten-floor apartment building. A skyscraper.

They were moving again, but this time they were on a vehicle that Dakota and Carter, judging by their puzzled looks down, clearly didn't remember boarding. It was a strange thing of Mason's own invention — something he'd seen bits of in movies then finished inside his mind. It had a broad deck with two fat tires on each end that cut through the ground, each tire's top third spinning above the surface. It was steered from the rear like a backward motorcycle. Mason was at the helm, knowing how to run it without even trying.

Preacher, on foot, kept coming.

Mason focused on the grid, summoning obstacles — office buildings, stores, parks full of aging statues, a graveyard, a massive hill, catacombs buried in the guts of a mound-like something from a fantasy novel. Each object Mason imagined spilled upward like flipped tiles, each cubic block rolling atop the one before building from the inside out.

Finally, in the distance, Mason summoned a horizon. Because everything had to end somewhere.

Between its lips, where sky met landscape, Mason imagined pure blue sky. A sunset or sunrise, shining right at them.

We just have to make it that far.

But just as it felt possible, the wheeled vehicle jolted hard, spilling them all to its front edge. It was as if they'd reached the end of an anchor line, grinding hard now against a mooring. Wheels spun, raising clouds of burned mental rubble.

Mason looked back.

"That's enough fun for now." Preacher was right behind them, but that wasn't who stopped their ride. "In here, I can still make it obey me."

The vortex Mason had summoned and Calliope had stolen was near Preacher. A tether from its core held them fast — and drew them deeper.

SEVENTY-THREE

A Mental Push

"Mason," Carter said. "Come on. You can do it."

He took his gaze off the vortex and looked up at his father. He seemed suddenly young. Like the man who'd believed in his son before he had faith in nothing.

The vortex was on them, and Mason's imagination had hit a cold, hard wall.

Dakota's hand settled on his back. He pushed against the tugging vortex as she rubbed slowly up and down. Mason closed his eyes and tried to recognize the grid before him as the unreality it was. The only way out was through, and to go through, they had to break free of the vortex and escape its psychic grip.

Why is this so hard? Mason wondered as he pushed.

They should only need to accept what the current moment was or wasn't. Not just for Mason but for all of them.

Everywhere.

But no. The HRO's prisoners stayed in line because they were trapped. Politicians permitted the system because they decided to solve society's problems by barring them from sight. Revival's investors turned a blind eye to believe what they needed to, knowing Blake's reputation as a rule-breaker but choosing to trust he'd never shatter what actually mattered. The families of Pattern Black patients believed their friends and loved ones were, once Blacked, unreachable. Like Sarah had been for Dakota.

Dakota.

Another tap on his other shoulder, different this time. Mason, half dwelling on belief while his other half tried to pull them away, knew the difference between an unreal tap and one feigning flesh and bone.

Dakota, something tried to whisper, *who isn't what she seems.*

He looked up to see his father staring into his eyes. There was a gate inside Mason that was supposed to stay closed. Behind it was something that once roamed free inside his mind before he'd learned the trick of shutting it away. With all the walls opening — with the barrier between logic and illogic now crumbled and only Mason's will holding them together — he could see all he'd hidden in that deep place, like the good parts of his relationship with his father.

He remembered his mother's words.

You were more like him than you wanted to admit. When you finally faced things, they didn't stand a chance. But until then? Stubborn. So, so stubborn.

Carter met Mason's gaze. The vortex swelled.

The longer Mason thought on it, the larger and faster it churned, growing at the end of Preacher's leash and over-spilling its original boundaries. The vortex was supposed to be Mason's, but somehow Blake, possibly with his top-tier permissions, had tamed and trained it.

The vortex was no longer travel-size. It tipped from vertical to horizontal, becoming a pool that would swallow them all.

His world seemed to invert, time again slowing.

Mason looked up again, already knowing what he'd see. He was done hiding. And done lying to himself. He *had* been stubborn. Both father and son had been. Mason had leveled up. His new status told only truths, and didn't know how to lie.

Everything was overlaid with lines, covered in flowing colors like the ripples of a stream. The builder's space was itself, yet another construct. He saw the loops, the subroutines, the handshakes in and out.

Then he looked at Carter, seeing his father now as a thing made of data, a long tether stretching up and away like his very own spotlight. Dakota, who'd prompted this line of thought in Mason, looked much more like Sarah than herself. A wireframe soul in Mason's altered vision, done in thin blue lines — but even if Dakota still had flesh, she'd look different. Her nose was too sloping, her chin not as strong as it should have been. Her eyes were different. Her features were wrong. She was this other being of wire and light, with a much smaller — and much more visibly substantial — woman inside. Dakota *inside* of Sarah. Her sister was on the outside, as far as the program was concerned, but she had stayed herself underneath.

"What's wrong?" his father asked.

"Nothing's wrong."

Carter followed Mason's gaze from Dakota to Preacher.

But only Mason could see through the machine.

The motorcycle thing began to roll backward toward the growing black pool.

Mason, applying equal mental and physical force, grabbed the others by the scruffs then hopped off the vehicle's front as it began to upend. The whole works tipped into the now-enormous vortex. First, the vehicle's skin, then the odd green frame of bones beneath it, slurped from existence, like a kid sucking color from a popsicle and leaving only white ice behind.

Then into the whirlpool's current, revolving once before going down.

The ground beneath Mason, Carter, and Dakota warped like tipping into a funnel.

Mason climbed up the slippery black grid, using friction to ascend. The second it grew too steep, they'd all slide in. If the surface got wet or greased, they'd never make it back out.

Higher up, the grid flattened out. But reaching high ground wouldn't be enough because there was a new problem. There were now dozens of Preachers. And there was no longer prison city behind or horizon ahead. Whatever tug-of-war was behind this, Preacher — no, *Blake* — was winning.

Mason's head jerked up. The thought resolved his vision. Again, Mason saw the world in wireframe.

Each Preacher held a bit of Blake inside.

They all took a step forward at once, the noise like marching Gestapo. The keening whine of the pool itself, now thirty feet or more across, was the only other sound.

When you finally faced things, they didn't stand a chance.

"I know," Carter said.

Mason looked over at his father, but there was no question of what they were discussing. The floodgates were open. It now took effort to keep himself separate. He might bleed into his father without it and his father into him.

Two people, one being. Like all things, Mason suspected, were one if the world could only see it.

He braced himself as best he could against the whirlpool's swelling tug. It would only need to devour them. It was all the worst things he'd thought over the years, concentrated for all its anger. No wonder it could power Blake's machine. Mason had been angry enough to fuel anything. But already, the black whirlpool was more than it had been — it grew as it ate and ate as it grew. Full of itself but still hungry.

Turning his new sight on the pool, Mason saw it had been born as his but was now so much more. Blake's doubts, and those of Elisabeth Reeves, along with the worst fears and worries from Carter and Dakota. Wispy lines, like flowing air, ran from the distance and into its mouth, as if it were summoning questions and subconscious desire for destruction.

Pattern Black had proven fertile soil for this essence of Mason's fury and doubt already — the starter pod Calliope's ruse has startled out of him then allowed to graze. It was far beyond Mason's ability to contain. He'd seeded the crystal, but that had grown many layers atop it.

The pool grew. And grew. *And grew.*

The power was loose now, and he could feel it forming desire, feeding on all the ill-will and horror Pattern Black's victims had left at the bottom of raw subconsciousness.

They could no longer run.

Pure id bubbled to the top. Malice, too. All the worst of them, and none of the best.

Mason looked, feeling guilty. Everyone had blackness inside them, but it was locked away. His had been strong enough to send out a rallying call, which all these forgotten bits of the departed followed like a beacon.

It bubbled and churned. The noxious fumes wafting off it weren't steam or sulfur but unbridled unpleasant emotion.

Carter was close. Same for Dakota. Both held onto little more than a rising slope, waiting for what increasingly felt like an inevitable end.

The feel of a hard decision came out of Carter, practically visible to Mason's newly enhanced senses. He poked telepathically around its edges while listening to his father's words, trying to see what was behind it. But Carter had locked this one down, hiding something he didn't want anyone to see.

The effort strained his jaw. It froze his eyes, which were unable to look away from Mason's.

"Look at me," Carter said.

The vortex grew, manifesting as a steeper slope expanding around its edges. They could only run so fast, and right now, a hard wind from the edges — the summoning of more anger and fear to feed the beast, Mason supposed — was barring escape. The pool was like a heavy ball set on a rubber sheet, leaving a dent from which nothing rolling past it could flee.

But still, he made himself focus. He took Dakota's hand to steady her and to let her steady him. Then he nodded, knowing how much effort it took his father to say what came next.

"I always knew there was something inside you."

Mason shook his head. He'd erased so much. Pushed away all the pain.

"I'm saying it's yours, son. No matter what he's added to it, the center of that thing still belongs to you."

Mason, Carter, and Dakota scrambled higher, managing to reach a slightly flatter plateau, though the slope was still rising everywhere.

He looked back down, trying to believe his father. Maybe it was true, but only the way a glass of wine in a river is still a glass of wine. Maybe the original vortex Calliope had stolen from him was still in there, lost in all the bile gathered since.

Mason shook his head.

But Carter shook his right back. "You can find that original piece of yourself and use it if he's distracted. It has to obey you, son. You made it."

Mason was now seeing the corners of what his father had in mind. Twenty years shed in a second, and again he felt like a child. He shook his head, this time with stubborn refusal. "You can't just distract him, Pop. It's not enough. Don't even try."

"I can't distract him enough, but someone else can." He sent Mason a mental push.

For a moment, the world returned to wireframe. Mason saw Dakota buried inside Sarah's shell. He saw what Carter wanted him to see.

"No."

"Elisabeth showed me, Mason. There's a shutdown for all of this. A big button, like the pump cutoff at a gas station."

"Blake will just turn it back on."

"It doesn't need to shut down for good. It only needs a big enough bump to take everyone's hands off the wheel."

"For a second, Pop."

"From what Elisabeth told me, a second will be long enough."

The cold finger of panic touched the back of Mason's neck. His words came faster, more frantic. "She didn't tell you this. Nobody saw *this* coming."

He looked around at the great ring of Preachers. Fifty at least, and none so much as flinching forward. The whirlpool was doing all the work now. All Preacher/Blake had to do before his pesky house-guests were gone was to wait.

Carter shrugged. "What else are we gonna try, Mason?"

It made perfect sense, but still, he couldn't help fighting. He couldn't allow this. He wouldn't.

"I always loved you, kid. Even when you hated my guts, I still loved you."

"POP!" Mason shouted, a new emotion rising in his throat, choking him from the inside. "Goddammit, Pop, don't you fucking be a hero!"

Carter's face became calm. "Stubborn, just like his old man."

He let go of the sloping hillside.

Mason's father slid into the pool's angry blackness then was gone.

SEVENTY-FOUR

Big Red Button

BLAKE OPENED his eyes inside the pod, needing a visual recalibration before heading back in.

The three souls still inside the sim had fought so hard, and now it looked like Carter had let go on purpose. Maybe he'd slipped at the top, but Blake, through Preacher's hijacked eyes, had seen him almost stop halfway down, then scoot to get moving again. Almost as if he wasn't trying to climb away but had gone into the whirlpool willfully.

Samuel's face appeared in the pod window, annoying Blake. He'd built a window into God-level access that let him immerse and emerge at will. He was claustrophobic and — though he'd never admit it, especially in front of the stockholders — didn't like the tech he'd developed. Using it freaked him out. Blake had a recurring fear, discussed only with his psychiatrist, that one day he'd see the invisible bars and realize he was trapped in an immersion. The window let him immerse without fear. But as usual, his assistant, attentive to the point of being a sycophant, ruined the mood.

"Need anything, Mr. Blake?" His voice was muffled by the lid.

"I'm fine."

"There's a lot of churn in the system. Might be a purge of buffer memory. The code is——"

Blake cut him off, said it was fine. Samuel didn't need to know about the ebony whirlpool or its milder form, the portable vortex of cortical distillate. The clusterfuck. Elisabeth had sworn she could get Mason's distillate solo, seeing as he would go straight to Dakota when he woke, then she would run right to Elisabeth. There should have been no need for his involvement. And now Samuel was over his shoulder every minute, wanting to help but always at risk of learning things Blake would rather he didn't.

"Would you like me to run a diagnostic?"

"I'd like you to take the rest of the day off." Blake forced a smile. "Spend some time with that new baby of yours."

"Won't you need a monitor while you're immersed, sir?"

"I'm good, Sam. Thanks."

He held his smile until Samuel vanished, then stayed still until he heard the door close. He shifted a bit. Then, since he was already out, Blake checked the stats. Reaching behind him, he moved the swing-arm-mounted tablet, so it was in front of his torso, double-folding the small pillow below his head to see.

Mason, according to the plan, was supposed to be winding down right about now. They'd be able to port him into a new pod then get him the hell out of HRO 22 once his mind finally quieted — after all this untidy struggling was over. Calliope would be able to extract herself from the prison then and surrender her deep-cover life to reclaim her post at Revival. Although, he wasn't sure how he felt about that. Blake had grown used to working alone and making all the company's decisions. Even at the best of times, they were better at fighting than not.

He checked the prison security status next. It was bad. Very bad. Maybe even *riots* bad.

Something of the mess they'd been causing had leaked into the other sims. According to techs, one cohort inside the Heist had even seen Mason, Carter, and Dakota exit the bank — something Blake had wondered about when running through the same place in his

Preacher suit. He'd hoped the AI would have reset and erased by now.

News was trickling out of all those polluted sims and filling prisoners with awful ideas. The gate around the Inner Circle had been breached, and Immunity seemed to have come out of dormancy to spread misinformation. Or *entirely accurate* information.

It was disappointing. He'd had more respect for Calliope's group, even if it'd been founded on deception. They were malcontents with an ax to grind, and you could only fool people like that so much. Even with Elisabeth feeding them lies, they only had to look around to see. But they hadn't, and now they were little more than assholes distributing fliers.

Blake tapped away then re-folded the tablet's swing arm. He was about to immerse when he decided to check on Carter. Shaw's body was right where it'd been for over three years, and the techs kept track of it, but by now, his mind should have changed dispositions. For the entire time Blake had been stowing him, Shaw had been nearly as brain-dead as his official record claimed. He'd only lit up recently, as if powered by his son's newly awakened presence. Carter's cortex had been on fire as he'd finally found action inside the sim. And no one would ever even know it was happening in Pattern Black, thanks to Mason's interesting little ability to turn the unreal into something true.

Now checking Carter's stats, Blake saw something strange. Shaw's adrenaline had surged, and not just to levels that could be explained by their shared adventure or even death approaching. Blake saw *shot-of-epinephrine-right-to-the-heart* levels — *far* more stimulation than should naturally happen.

Had someone been screwing with the body?

Suddenly, Shaw flatlined entirely. He just went blank. His leads all died at once, and then there was nothing.

Carter had been losing his grip on the slope inside the simulation when Blake had opened his eyes to pop out. Apparently, he'd lost it entirely. The whirlpool had eaten him like that pit monster from *Return of the Jedi.*

Strangely, Blake felt disappointment. Loss, even. Between the

Shaws, Mason had proven to be all Revival required to fuel their forthcoming cadaver project, so practically speaking, Carter's death didn't matter. Still, they'd plunged his mind so long, back when he'd been their best bet, or really, all they had. There was nostalgia there. Even a jaded man might mourn a frenemy's death.

Someone tapped on the window of Blake's immersion pod. Probably Samuel returning to annoy him. He turned to chastise the tech.

It wasn't Samuel.

Instead, Blake was faced with the shaved head and sunken face of Carter Shaw.

There was a *thunk*. Blake recognized the sound immediately. A locking pin on the chamber's side, used to keep easy-waking subjects safely contained.

Shaw tapped the glass again. He held up a tablet. Onscreen was the app that controlled what they all called the Big Red Button — the master reboot to be used only in emergencies.

Fuck.

"My head's a little cloudy. Must be all that adrenaline I got from … you know … being mind-fucked in your whirlpool. Woke me right up. But you know what? My legs still work!" Carter made a show of flexing his limbs, every movement streamlined by the biosuit worn throughout his convalescence. "These electrostimulus leotards you guys give us are top-notch. Although I'll admit removing all those tubes you stuck in me was *not* pleasant. Know what I'm saying?"

Blake slapped at the pod's lid, but it didn't budge.

Carter looked to the side. "How old's that coffee on the console over there? I haven't had a cup in *so* long."

"Let me out!"

Carter left then returned with the cup.

Strangely, Blake's heart started to race as if he was the one getting caffeinated.

Blake placed his hand on the lid's inside, fingers spread. Calmly, he said, "*Carter? Mr. Shaw?* Can you hear me?"

Carter spit out his coffee. "This is terrible." He took another sip.

"Oh. But get this. I was looking through some stuff on this tablet right here." He held it up, Big Red Button still visible on its screen. "Do you know what someone did to your personal program? They set a trigger so if you ever open your eyes, you come right out of the simulation. That must really break the mood, being able to pop right out of a sim like that no matter what's happening inside."

"*Carter?*"

"It's okay." He took another sip. "I fixed it."

"Listen. You've been in an immersion pod for more than three years. The stimulators kept most of your muscles functional, but only barely. If you keep walking around without rest, you'll—"

"Yeah, and all that new adrenaline can't be helping my heart."

Blake nodded vigorously. "You're in shock. It won't be pleasant when that wears off. But you *do* have a narrow window where I can suppress the neural trauma that's coming. I can fix you if—"

"Yeah, but then I'd have to let you out." He took another sip.

"Please. If I don't give you an injection *very soon*, you'll die."

Shaw seemed to consider, then shrugged. "I had a better idea." He held up the tablet again, its Big Red Button onscreen. "I've always wanted to press this. Elisabeth showed me. It's like stopping the assembly line at a car factory."

"Carter, there's not much time. Pretty soon, you'll—"

He held the tablet higher. "Will this get rid of the whirlpool, do you think, or just reset the grid and IDs?"

"*Carter!*"

"Worth a try, anyway," he said before pushing the button.

SEVENTY-FIVE

The Future

MASON DIDN'T HAVE time to think or mourn.

Being yanked so suddenly from a sim might not kill him, but it'd definitely kill a normal man who hadn't moved in three years. Pop might have failed. It might all have been for nothing.

But then, like the flip of a switch, everything glitched. The world buzzed to distortion for a partial second before clearing. Everything was suddenly different. Mason's buildings had vanished. So had the whirlpool. The grid seemed to hum with static boringness.

Mason rushed forward. He could see the whirlpool's new form ahead — the small vortex it had been before, silver now instead of black.

He approached it with his arms out. Somewhere deep down, Mason understood if he left the thing alone for too long, it might begin to grow again, feeding on his and Dakota's emotions until it was strong enough to reach wider.

Something tackled Mason before he reached the vortex.

A single remaining Preacher, but different than before. His skin was now covered with flowing numerals, ink on his skin like living tattoos.

"It's mine," Preacher growled, shoving Mason away from the vortex.

Mason crouched and prepared to engage, knowing this would require a fight. Blake was still inside Preacher and — even beyond the tricks Mason had learned — had an unfair advantage.

In the end, Mason was a user. But in here, Blake was a god.

Preacher crackled, flashing like an old-fashioned TV between channels. He looked down at his hands, then up at Mason as if they weren't enemies engaging in battle. His eyes were almost pleading. In the next second, a flash tossed a smaller man out of Preacher's body like an ejector from a jet. The new man landed untidily. Disoriented, he brushed himself off before finding his footing.

Nathaniel Blake in the simulated flesh.

He looked at Mason, then Preacher. Terror dawned.

"So, I guess that's the reset," Mason said. "Everyone go back to their starting places."

Preacher stared at Blake, seeming phenomenally offended. He hadn't gone away while Blake had his hands on the psychic wheel. He'd probably hidden from Blake in a corner of his own mind, watching and waiting in fury. Now, thanks to the system reset, Preacher was back in control. And enraged by the interruption.

Mason reached for the vortex. At first, he wasn't sure how to take it, let alone use it. Could the thing be picked up? Or fit in his pocket? Would its use be self-evident, like a brush already dripping with paint?

The pool seemed to liquify and rise to meet his finger like a curious cobra. Then warmth suffused him as the vortex slid upward. It covered his hand, silver like a mirror and not at all threatening. *Have I really been so afraid of this? Why did I lock it away?*

He saw his father's face in the silvery shimmer. Different than it had been just moments ago, but even that wasn't how Mason wanted to see him. So he imagined a younger man. A stronger man. A big cop. A good cop. The good times.

But despite his intent, the man looking out at Mason did not change. This was the real Carter. His true body liberated in the real world. He looked ancient and beaten. His cheeks were parallel wrinkles. His lips were ringed with tiny lines, sad below his sunken eyes. He looked underfed and ashen. The light was dying in his eyes, but at least Mason was getting to see them one last time.

"Did it work?" Carter asked, using the silver haze as if it were a videoconference.

Mason looked at Preacher, who'd caught up with Blake and now held him by the collar. Blake kept blinking with his entire face, putting fingers beneath each eyelid to force them wide.

"Yeah. The entire grid reset. Since we're talking, I guess you know I have the vortex. And Preacher reset. He's just Preacher again, but" — Mason lowered his voice to a whisper — "I don't think he'll come after me now. There's no real point. And besides, he looks ready to eat Blake."

"So, it's done?"

"Seems so. Everything and everyone in here has gone back to normal." Then he caught sight of two women sitting sideways on bent knees like a pair of maidens in a meadow.

Carter must have seen something on Mason's face. "Everything okay?"

"Yeah."

The image on Mason's hand began to fade. It was a pool of memory and power, not a two-way radio. His odd abilities had begun to diminish. For now, he couldn't see behind the grid, same for all the possibilities and permutations. He was Mason again. But "just Mason" was, for once, enough.

"Pop …" Mason was fading.

"Save your energy," said his father's voice. "You'll need it to open the door."

"How do I—"

The door was back where it had been, once again floating six inches above the ground with nothing behind it.

"Pop?"

"I love you, kid. You need to know that."

"Pop." He shook his hand, wanting to slap its side like a misbehaving appliance. "I'm losing you!"

"I'm already gone."

Then nothing.

The silver substance faded, wicking into his skin like a paper towel absorbing moisture.

Mason felt it fall down into the pit of himself. He closed his eyes for a moment and exhaled slowly before looking back up at Preacher, whose gaze fell between Mason and the door.

"I can't let you leave," Mason told him.

Preacher shrugged and shook Blake by the collar. "I don't have a body out there, anyway. And I sure ain't gonna drive *this* bitch's."

"You said you wanted to be free."

"I am free."

Mason looked at the door again.

"More ways to be free," Preacher said, "than dreamed of in your world."

"Are we … cool?"

"Dunno, man. You plannin' on comin' back?"

Mason didn't want to be in prison anymore, and without a conviction, the HRO had no grounds to keep him. He might confess, if for no other reason than to get Dakota out of jail, but something told him he'd never end up in her place. Prison records were computerized. And Mason, in a very unusual way, had become an excellent hacker.

"No."

"Then we good."

He turned, but Preacher called his name.

"Yeah?" Mason asked, turning back.

"You got magic dust, ain't you?"

"Not like before. I can still make small things, maybe. But if you want me to build you a fancy house before I go, I'm afraid all I've got is a hammer."

"I don't want nothin' big," Preacher said.

"What, then?"

Preacher looked at Blake and said, "A leash."

Mason made what Preacher requested, and Preacher tied it around Blake's neck like a dog he intended to hang.

After Preacher had taken him away — and, thanks to the flat

horizon, the pair was visible for a beautifully long time — Mason returned to the women. The newer of the two had gone translucent already. She wouldn't stay much longer.

He sat, saying nothing.

"I could have helped her." Dakota reached out, but instead of stroking her sister's cheek, her hand went through the ghostly visage.

Mason said, "You couldn't be there. There's nothing you could do."

"I was so proud of her."

"For what?"

"For everything. For ..." She sniffed back tears, wiped her nose with the back of her hand, then broke into a bittersweet grin and laughed. "For tolerating me as a sister."

"She knew," Mason said.

"How can you know?"

"The same way I know Blake is shitting his pants right now."

She met his gaze then flicked her attention to his forehead. To where his power lay if he found ways to use it. "You're sure?"

"I'm sure, Dakota."

Sarah's shell, no longer buoyed by her sister's use, seemed to smile. A moment later, it was gone.

Dakota stood. She brushed the wrinkles out of her pants, nodded to herself, then faced the door. Mason did the same thing beside her and reached down to take her hand. They looked at one another in silence.

"Are you okay?"

She nodded slowly, then looked to where the whirlpool had been. Where Carter had departed, knowing the body he woke in would never support the shock of such an impudent unplugging.

"Are *you?*"

"Strangely, yes."

"When I wake up," Dakota said, "I'll take him with me. I swear, Mason, even if I have to come out shooting."

He smirked, touched. "It's an office building. I think you'll be okay."

His smile widened, knowing he was a bit in denial that there were things to face later. For now, he let himself enjoy the image of Dakota waking at Revival and tossing Carter's body over her shoulder, finding a weapon, even if it was only a letter opener, and daring anyone to stop her.

"Thanks," he said.

"I also paid real close attention when that thing happened with Calliope. The thing that split her in half."

"Really."

"If I'm lucky, maybe I can do it to Blake before I go."

That got a laugh from Mason — maybe the first real one in years. Would it be a victory if Blake escaped *and* stayed trapped inside, same as Calliope had? The Blake who stayed topside wouldn't be in much trouble unless someone produced evidence that might not exist, but his mental half, as Preacher's pet, wasn't getting off scot-free.

Dakota squeezed his hand as they faced the door. Mason turned the knob. There was a white room filled with black spirals beyond it … but for some reason, the sight no longer scared him.

"What now?" she asked.

"Now comes the future." Then he stepped through.

SEVENTY-SIX

A Brand New Day

MASON BOLTED UPRIGHT, clutching a bunched-up sheet to his chest. Time slowed to a crawl thanks to his panic, and a breathless second felt like forever.

Then his lungs finally relaxed. He forced the next breath to move much more slowly than his body would have liked. Calm returned.

One, two, three.

He counted seconds, knowing they were too fast.

Dakota rolled over to face him then sat up. She wore a Dodgers T-shirt that had been too small many years ago and was laughable now. Not that Mason was complaining.

She rubbed his bare back. "Another nightmare?"

He nodded.

"You can make them go away, you know."

"It's hard for me to control. When I'm in the middle of a dream, I can't usually—"

She put a finger over his lips. There was no sound save the distant hum of traffic and the sighing breeze. She had a middle apartment with neighbors above and below. The first few nights Mason had crashed there, he'd slept on the pull-out in the living room and listened to fights, drunken shouting, and more. All of that had stopped when he moved to her bed. Of course, it was coincidence, but they pretended it was a sign.

"I'm not talking about using your scary mind powers. I'm talking about smoking weed."

Mason flopped onto his back without a response. He took in the ceiling, where her alarm clock projected the time: *3:14*, the asshole of night.

"I feel like I should have dreams. It feels wrong to block them out."

"Why?" Dakota asked.

He didn't really have an answer. Sometimes, Carter visited his dreams. Usually, it felt like unloading old memories, and Mason had forgotten so many of those. Most were good — context for his relationship with his father he'd never had before. Carter had had rough edges, as all parents do, but the worst was at the end. He'd been a better man before Revival. Was it because of his obsession ... or had early immersions done something to his brain?

Other times, Mason's dreams were nightmares of pursuit, confusion, a certainty that he'd never escaped. A precious few times, they felt like something else entirely, more like communion with another place. Like speaking to Carter directly, even though they'd taken less than forty-eight hours to lower his old man into the ground.

He shook his head, failing to answer.

"What was it this time?" Dakota looked at Mason, her eyes patient and kind.

"Preacher."

"But Preacher was a good guy."

Mason laughed. The truth was so much more complicated. "He ended up on our side. That doesn't make him good."

This wasn't the first time they'd had this discussion, and Dakota seemed to have been thinking. "Blake made Preacher, right?"

Mason nodded. "That's right. Blake programmed him as a virus."

"But he woke up, somehow. Became self-aware."

"I think so." Mason thought. "He *seemed* so."

"And *after* he became self-aware, Preacher chose to stop chasing Calliope and start chasing you."

"*If* he ever chased Calliope." If she and Blake were on the same side, that had probably been a lie.

"He was at least chasing your father. The point is, Preacher *decided* to start pursuing you."

"Now I see why he's a good guy," Mason said. "Because he started coming after me."

"He *chose* to come after you despite having been programmed another way. That was a big deal."

"Sure. Fine."

"If Preacher was after you for his own reasons then decided to *talk* instead of *killing* or even *capturing* you, what does *that* say?"

Mason hadn't thought of it that way and didn't have an answer.

"*And* he didn't just *talk* to you. He used that time to tell you the others were lying to you. It's because of his choices that we got through it."

That, Mason *had* considered — in his nightmares. Not how Preacher's intel had provided the biggest turning point, but what might have happened if Mason believed everything Calliope and Blake had told him. They'd wanted the vortex to create their mental cadavers. After scooping out the vortex, Blake and Reeves would probably have left them both inside — either disposing of their bodies or letting them fester — without so much as a clue about what had gone wrong.

"How about we call him a neutral guy?" Mason proposed. "Good feels like a stretch."

Dakota patted his chest. The Preacher from his dream felt more distant and less scary already.

"That helps," Mason said.

"Good." Now she laid her head on his chest and snuggled close.

"You know," he said after a while, "I've been thinking about your suggestion."

"What suggestion?"

"About Hunter."

Dakota sat up. "Really?"

"Maybe. Raylene's back in rehab. And a kid needs a father, no matter how cool his grandma might be."

"Are you serious, Mason? Don't fuck with me. Adopting a kid isn't like getting a pet."

"He likes me a lot, Dakota."

"It takes more than that. You're committing to—"

"So, I don't think he'll mind when I put him in a cage while I'm at work."

Dakota moaned. Twenty seconds passed.

He finally shrugged. "I never wanted kids because I always thought I'd end up just like my dad."

"But now you know who you become is your choice."

"Actually, I still think I'll end up just like my dad."

She touched his cheek, trying to see his face.

"It's just that now, I'm not sure why that's such a bad thing."

Quiet came. A car rumbled down the street outside, crunching gravel.

"Do you ever wonder," she said after so long, Mason thought she'd drifted back to sleep, "what happened with the people from Immunity?"

"I imagine they're laying low, waiting for their chance." He considered the television. He wanted, more and more often, to turn it on. The prison was the last unresolved piece of this puzzle, and it was like a rock in his shoe. Dakota told him to give it time. He'd stop obsessing soon enough. But it was hard while the siege continued.

"What do you think their chances are?" she asked.

"I don't know. Maybe they'll capture a drone, and Kassidi'll hotwire it to broadcast some evidence."

"It was erased in the reset."

"Not at Revival's headquarters," Mason said.

Dakota turned to face him. "Promise me you won't take the fight to Blake."

"Which one? The Blake who keeps saying the prison riots will end peacefully any day, or the Blake our pal Preacher is leading around on a leash somewhere inside?"

"The first one."

He paused, then said, "I promise."

Even though Blake deserved it. Dakota's splitting his mind in half had meant nothing for the top-level, real-world billionaire. Like Calliope, he didn't know anything had happened — which meant while the Blake inside was getting his just desserts, the one out here saw himself as the victor. He still didn't have the means to create mental cadavers, but in Blake's mind, that probably felt like a push. To him, he'd gotten out of a bind with little more than a scare. He was still rich and running a company with its image and PR mostly intact. That was a half-victory for Mason, at best.

"For real, Mason."

"I promise."

He stewed. He hadn't really been thinking of pursuing Blake, in part because the head of Revival was too smart to make the same mistakes a second time. But still, he resented Dakota making him promise. Now, Mason had no option unless he wanted to be a shithead. And as a free man beside a free woman with both of their prison records electronically exonerated, that was exactly what he was trying not to be.

"Maybe Calliope, then," Mason said.

Dakota propped herself up on one elbow. "Don't tease me. Are you ready to tell me what happened when you woke up in Dharma One and found her standing over you?"

"Not yet," he said.

"Come on, Mason. What did you do with Calliope?"

He shook his head. "I took care of her."

Then he lay back down, and Dakota let him.

The morning was a brand new day.

SEVENTY-SEVEN

Déjà Vu

Elisabeth went to Havana, Grand Bahama, Frankfurt, Stockholm. At first, it only felt important to keep moving.

She didn't shirk the news and heard how prisoners at Union Station's Human Resource Outpost #22 had stormed the command station in the middle then held some very important equipment hostage. It was a travesty. She'd designed the whole system with layers of redundancy. Drones watched the prison, and overseers watched the drones. Revival's AI was smarter than most, and behind the drones, if needed, were the well-trained human Docents. It was a program that, despite popular opinion, had been restructured rather than eliminated.

This kind of thing wasn't supposed to happen and wouldn't have if Elisabeth had stuck around. If things hadn't gone so sideways, she could have taken Mason's body back to Revival then stuck it next to his father's. Afterward, she would have taken the world's longest shower and resolved to never enter the prison again. She could have managed this occupation from the safety of HQ, and they'd have the fat profits from cadaver sales to fight any war from any front.

But it *had* gone sideways, and as a result, Elisabeth was forced to hit the road instead of sticking around to save the company she'd co-founded. She could return in time, but seeing as Mason, before disappearing, had done some juju to the system that she didn't yet understand, returning too soon felt like a terrible idea.

The Chamber Therapy program wasn't in operation because there was no staff left behind the fences to run it, and the failure of drones to handle the threats besieging the Inner Circle was due to Mason's suddenly-prodigious hacking. Who knew what might await Elisabeth upon her return?

If she ever did.

Which was why she had no plans to.

She sat at a small cafe in Budapest, eating a dish covered in paprika that, if she'd done the exchange right, had cost around a dollar. Her attention was on the street. After a while, she pulled a small black notebook from her bag. It had a black *faux*-leather cover and blank pages. The only real ink was on the first page, headed with a date. The first day she'd come here and bought the book. The sudden and impulsive purchase had struck Elisabeth like a ray of hope. She couldn't reach out to anyone, especially Blake, and didn't dare show her face.

But she could initiate a campaign of online propaganda. Start planting seeds, manipulating an elaborate story about her heroic escape from Dharma One and the possibility of her return. That would be the beginning of the end for the anti-Revival movement, which was gaining steam despite a total lack of evidence and spreading nasty sentiment to other California prisons. She could stop it in time and clear Revival's name. Or at least her own, if Blake stayed adamant — if he insisted on going rigid and drowning in the coming flood. Elisabeth needed to plan. And for that, all she needed was paper and a pen.

There was just one problem.

Elisabeth couldn't tell the story of her daring escape because she couldn't recall it. She remembered Mason Shaw opening his eyes inside the immersion pod. She remembered the hard way he'd looked at her with burning red eyes. She remembered screaming with surprise, but apparently, she'd somehow bested him.

How long ago had that been?

She shut the notebook. Elisabeth had been in the prison for a long time, and inside, she'd had little need for calendars. Inside the HRO, Monday looked like Sunday looked like Christmas. She was out of practice, but the date would come to her in time.

Of course, the total amnesia after Mason woke up wasn't something she could blame on the prison since *remembering* was something Elisabeth had gotten the hang of more than four decades ago. But maybe that was okay, too. She'd had a ton of stress lately. She'd been in a high-stakes battle, nearly died, maybe been publicly disgraced, and now had no home because it had seemed important to keep moving, no matter what.

Elisabeth stood. A bus was approaching. This time, she had planned ahead and was carrying exact change. The driver gave her a neutral, *you're-not-Slavic-enough-to-be-here* glance, then returned his gaze to the road.

She took a seat two-thirds down the aisle by a window, then looked ahead and waited for her stop. But now, she had forgotten which one she wanted. Worse, Elisabeth couldn't remember where she'd gotten on. And why.

Was this Amsterdam? Sure looked like it.

But no. That had been yesterday. It was easy to confuse the days because recently, some limbic authority deep within her had decided she was in a loop. Everything felt familiar, though Elisabeth was quite sure she'd never seen or done it before. Her *déjà vu* came in layers. Everyone she saw — most recently, that unsmiling bus driver — felt eerily familiar.

Elisabeth looked down at her feet. She was wearing heavy boots and slacks — black so she'd fit into this city where gray seemed to rule. She wore a hat because her bleach-white hair and big blue eyes were dead giveaways. In time, if she stayed on the lam for longer than she wanted to, her hair would grow out, and she could put it in a ponytail. For now, her hat would have to be enough.

Feeling self-conscious as a woman looked her way, Elisabeth

pulled it low — all the way to her chin. But it was hard to breathe in the thing, so she pulled it back up, high enough that her mouth and eyes and nose were out of the holes. Sitting high now, at least the ski mask covered her hair.

Elisabeth took the phone from her travel bag, but it seemed to have become a gun, big and matte black. And that was strange, so she looked up to see if the woman was still eying her funny.

But she was gone, and a man sat in her place.

Elisabeth was no longer on a bus, and she couldn't see the street. This was a much smaller vehicle. Which made sense because you could only keep a secret like this one in a very small group. Say, six people. Plus a driver.

Another moment of *déjà vu* resulted in a memory that wasn't hers. She let that one pass, as well. In that memory, she'd been at a cafe in some European city. There'd been a lot of paprika. And a book — she definitely remembered a little black book with white pages.

Why did she feel so unsettled? She wasn't being chased, which was what her body kept trying to tell her. If Elisabeth was agitated and nervous, it was because she'd never robbed a bank. Or shot a gun like the giant weapon sitting in her lap.

Feeling self-conscious again, Elisabeth considered pulling her ski mask back down.

But that was only supposed to happen once they arrived at their target.

A little more relaxed, she tried to calm the last of her nerves by breathing. By looking around the windowless interior. The van was fairly unremarkable — two long bench seats mounted parallel, three people in gear on each side. Elisabeth was in the middle of her bench. The woman on the left was at least three hundred pounds of muscle and the guy on her right, besides having the ratty hair of a homeless man, had breath strong enough to deflect cannon fire.

The lightbulb caught her eye. It was mounted above the middle of the van's opposite side, its glass rubbed matte as if handled by steel wool, its glow the color of jaundiced skin. Ten filament stalks poked from what looked like candle wax in the thing's center, each resembling a match with a burning head.

How can it work if none of the wires touch?

The man across from her, Cruz, snapped his fingers. "Reeves, you paying attention?"

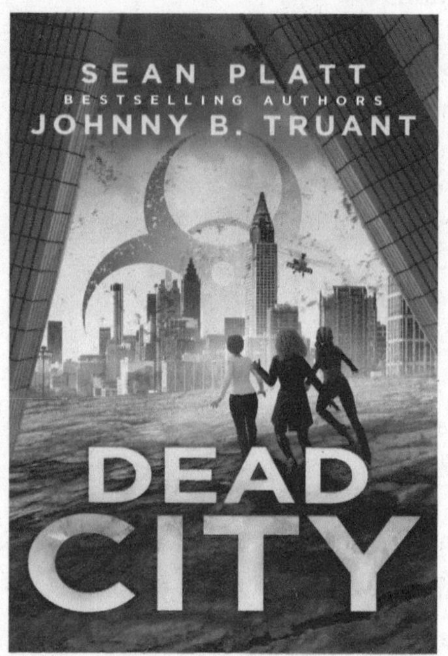

Want more Platt and Truant magic in your life and on your eReader device? You're in luck. Get *Dead City* for free and start the *Dead World Trilogy*!

Get Dead City Today

A Quick Favor...

If you enjoyed this book, please take a moment to write a review on your favorite online bookstore so other readers can enjoy it, too.

Thanks so much!
Sean & Johnny

About the Authors

Sean Platt is an entrepreneur and founder of Sterling & Stone, where he makes stories with his partners, Johnny B. Truant, and David W. Wright, and a family of storytellers.

Sean is the bestselling author of over 10 million words' worth of books, including the Yesterday's Gone and Invasion series. Sean is also co-author of the indie publishing cornerstone, Write. Publish. Repeat. and co-host of the Story Studio Podcast.

Originally from Long Beach, California, Sean now lives in Austin, Texas with his wife and two children. He has more than his share of nose.

~

Johnny B. Truant is co-owner of the Sterling & Stone Story Studio, an IP powerhouse focusing on books and adaptations for film and television. It's the best job in the world, and he spends his days creating cool stuff with partners Sean Platt and David W. Wright, as well as more than 20 gifted storytellers.

Johnny is the bestselling author of over 100 books under various pen names, including the Fat Vampire and Invasion series. On the nonfiction side, he's also co-author of the indie publishing mainstay Write. Publish. Repeat. and co-host of the weekly Story Studio Podcast.

Originally from Ohio, Johnny and his family now live in Austin, Texas, where he's finally surrounded by creative types as weird as he is.

Also By Sean Platt

The Dead World Series

Dead Zero

Dead City

Dead Nation

Dead Planet

Empty Nest

The Beam Series

The Beam Season One

The Beam Season Two

The Beam Season Three

Robot Proletariat Series

En3my

Robot Proletariat

The Infinite Loop

The Hard Reset

Cascade Failure

Reboot

The Tomorrow Gene Series

Null Identity

The Tomorrow Gene

The Tomorrow Clone

The Eden Experiment

Karma Police Series

Jumper

Karma Police

The Collectors

Deviant

The Fall

Homecoming

Yesterday's Gone

October's Gone

Yesterday's Gone Season One

Yesterday's Gone Season Two

Yesterday's Gone Season Three

Yesterday's Gone Season Four

Yesterday's Gone Season Five

Yesterday's Gone Season Six

Tomorrow's Gone

Tomorrow's Gone Season One

Tomorrow's Gone Season Two

Tomorrow's Gone Season Three

Available Darkness

Darkness Itself

Available Darkness Book One

Available Darkness Book Two

Available Darkness Book Three

WhiteSpace

WhiteSpace Season One

WhiteSpace Season Two

WhiteSpace Season Three

Stand Alone Novels

Burnout

The Island

Crash

Emily's List

Pattern Black

Also By Johnny B. Truant

The Dead World Series

Dead Zero

Dead City

Dead Nation

Dead Planet

Empty Nest

The Fat Vampire Series

Fat Vampire

Fat Vampire 2: Tastes Like Chicken

Fat Vampire 3: All You Can Eat

Fat Vampire 4: Harder, Better, Fatter, Stronger

Fat Vampire 5: Fatpocaplypse

Fat Vampire 6: Survival of the Fattest

The Fat Vampire Chronicles

The Vampire Maurice

Anarchy and Blood

Vampires in the White City

The Beam Series

The Beam Season One

The Beam Season Two

The Beam Season Three

Robot Proletariat Series

En3my

Robot Proletariat

The Infinite Loop

The Hard Reset

Cascade Failure

Reboot

The Invasion Series

Longshot

Invasion

Contact

Colonization

Annihilation

Judgment

Extinction

Resurrection

The Tomorrow Gene Series

Null Identity

The Tomorrow Gene

The Tomorrow Clone

The Eden Experiment

Stand Alone Novels

Pretty Killer

Pattern Black

Burnout

The Target

The Island